Memories of a Dinosaur Hunter

By: Douglas Lebeck

To my very good friend Barb,

Best wishes and thanks so much for your support and continued friendship.

2002

This book is a work of fiction. Places, events, and situations in this story are purely fictional. Any resemblance to actual persons, living or dead, is coincidental.

ISBN: 1-4033-4223-7 (electronic)
ISBN: 1-4033-4224-5 (soft cover)
ISBN: 1-4033-4225-3 (hardcover)

This book is printed on acid free paper.

1st Books - rev. 08/06/02

This book is dedicated to my wife Lynn Lebeck and my sister Debra Luesse.
Their love and support inspired me
to do things that I never knew I could.

Dreams really do come true!

TABLE OF CONTENTS

PROLOGUE

I was sent here many years ago to retrieve data that could not be gathered in any other way. I did it willingly, despite the hardships, the loneliness, and the danger. And I have accomplished what I was sent here to do. I have seen wonders that no other human has ever witnessed. I have had adventures that even the most acclaimed writers of fiction could scarcely imagine. I have proven some long-standing theories, and made a mockery of others, including many of my own. I've been surprised by some things and awed by others. I've laughed and cried, experienced unimagined terrors, and seen things more beautiful than I ever thought possible. I have reveled in the joys of discovery, and experienced the agony of total isolation. I have been near death on more than one occasion, yet having been through it, I would make the same decision again. No man has ever taken a greater journey.

Ten years have come and gone, and yet everyday there is something new and exciting to see, old mysteries to unravel, new questions to ponder, and always data - more and more data. But it is time to retire the scientist, to cease the never-ending analysis - a time to live, and not just survive. As yet another winter approaches, this chronology becomes more tiresome and less important. Winter is a difficult time - the chore of staying alive is hard enough in the best of weather. I wish to spend my remaining days enjoying the wonders of this world and to leave some things unexplained. Let the future scientists have theories to prove and puzzles to solve. After all, what is life without a little mystery? My work is done!

*However, unless the right people find this book, in the right time, my work will have been for nothing. No one will believe it. They will think it some elaborate hoax, or the work of a madman. Sometimes I hardly believe it myself. I can only imagine what a stir will be caused should my remains be discovered in some distant cave or buried under tons of earth during the excavation for yet another mini-mall. It will cause a scientific riddle such as the world has never seen. For this reason, I must go to the beginning, long before I came to this strange land, years before the great journey began. I must take you back 70 million years into the future. Only then will you understand how this came to pass. This is my story_*

D.E.W.

CHAPTER 1

The single drop slid slowly down the aluminum pole, occasionally stopping to join with others before starting off again on a new path downward. The drop, starting and stopping, but gaining speed as it grows in size, reaches the end of its journey and adds to the ever-growing pool in the dirt. I stare at the murky water, watching the ripples spread outward, symmetrical around the pole, until they reach the outer edge of the pool, just a few inches from where I stand. I'm oblivious to everything else, totally fixated on the pool, seeing my own distorted reflection in the dark, muddy water. I'm not sure how long I stand there watching as the pool continues to grow, but I begin to fantasize about what might happen when the puddle reaches my shoes.

There is something frightening about this tiny pool of water. Perhaps it is deeper than it appears—much deeper—an entrance to some horrible place filled with hideous creatures. Perhaps it is a shortcut to hell and the devil lurks just beneath the filmy surface, ready to reach out and grab me, dragging me down to share the company of his legions of demons. Or perhaps I will simply drown, sliding silently down into the murky pool, increasing the size of it by that of my own.

Then again, perhaps it is not just a pool of rainwater, but rather something much more sinister—maybe acid or some other corrosive fluid. I imagine it touching my shoe, instantly dissolving the leather, going to work on my feet, working ever upwards, like flesh-eating bacteria. As if I'm in some third-rate horror movie, I see the pool bubbling and boiling, a stench rising in the air that is only in part the acrid smell of the fluid itself. Added to the stink is that of rotting flesh—a sour smell that brings the bile up from the belly. It begins to take my legs, my trousers smoking as the acid is drawn up the material.

The image is disturbing. Why should the sight of this simple pool of water evoke such horrible images, and why don't they frighten me? I should turn and run, and yet I'm equally tempted to stick my toe into the little pool to see what happens. Either way, it doesn't seem to matter and I know that that is wrong—terribly wrong.

Staring at the pool, I try to think of something that I *do* care about—anything at all—but my mind is a blank. That realization disturbs me more than anything, more than the idea of stepping into the pool to face whatever merciless fate awaits me. Gazing at my shattered image in the dark water before me I wonder how I ever got to the point where living ceased to have any meaning.

The pool continues to grow, and when it finally reaches the tip of my shoe, I'm surprised that nothing happens—surprised—but not relieved. In a dark recess of my mind I know that anything is preferable to what I have yet to confront. It's here, just beyond the surface, lurking like a ghost, faintly visible, but not quite tangible. I can't quite grasp it, and I'm happy with the fact that it remains in shadows. Bringing it into the light will cause only pain. I know that whatever it is can't be hidden away forever—the respite can only be temporary. Ignorance is bliss, but I doubt that it's permanent.

The wind shifts and drives the rain directly into the pool, shattering my already distorted reflection and causing the pool to lose all sense of shape and form. My shoes are immersed in the pool and I can feel the rain pelting the back of my legs, soaking them, numbing them, yet I continue to stand there. The rain comes down harder and my stupor is at last broken by the sound the downpour makes as it strikes the green canvas tarp overhead. I raise my head, surprised at the stiffness in my neck. How long had I been standing here? Just where the hell was I?

I look through the rain and fog, seeing only a forest of trees, the leaves a kaleidoscope of colors—each of them clinging on to its branch for dear life—each about to die. I try to figure out what I am doing here, on the fringe of a forest, alone in the pouring rain.

I have no idea where I am or how I got here. It is autumn. The trees are changing color—reds, oranges, and yellows—beautiful, but of no help to me. Between here and there is nothing but well-manicured lawn, the once emerald carpet turned to the brown-yellow of a summer that is long past its time. Beyond the trees, although barely discernable through the pouring rain, I can just make out the hazy tops of skyscrapers—a city—a big one. Chicago stands tall just a few miles away. I know that it is Chicago, but not sure why I know it and offers no clue in helping to solve the riddle.

The answer is here and I have to find it. I have to face it.

I shift my gaze slowly to the left, stopping again at the aluminum pole. The beginnings of recognition and I swing my gaze quickly to the right to seek out its mate, the one that I know is there. I stand under some kind of temporary structure—an ominous structure—and I am beginning to remember its purpose. The structure with its green canvas top and aluminum poles is here to keep the rain off the assembly, even though I am the only one here.

My gaze shifts back and forth between the two poles, but I refuse to lower my eyes, knowing that there is a terrible sight there, one so horrible that it will force the events of the past few days to come flooding back.

But I can't hold off the inevitable. My eyes take that terrible journey downward, and as I knew it would be, the gleaming silver casket stands before me, my hands just inches from the polished steel surface. On the top of the casket lay two-dozen yellow roses—my wife's favorite.

*****

Seven days before is when it began.

It all started with the phone call from Chicago PD. I was at the museum working, *expecting* the phone to ring—*waiting* for it to ring. It was getting late, and I hadn't been able to get a hold of Liz all day. I was worried because it was Wednesday, and on Wednesdays, she had no late classes—she should have been home cooking dinner—it was her turn.

My calls became more frequent and more frantic the later it became. The only answer was that of our machine—my wife's cheerful voice with the typical message—"*We're not at home, leave a message at the beep.*" I tried her pager as well, but my messages went unanswered. God, how I hated technology! I despised the impersonality of it.

The later it got, the more concerned I became. I thought about the weather. An early snow squall had hit Chicago that morning—the season's first. It wasn't a serious snowfall, but it was a surprise. We had been in the middle of a beautiful Indian summer, and we were still getting used to the idea that Thanksgiving was little more than two weeks away. That morning we had woken up to an inch of snow, not unusual for Chicago, but it had caught us by surprise and the salt trucks hadn't been around when we headed out to work.

The later it got, the more frequent the horrifying image flashed through my mind; the car sliding into a ditch, overturning, gas dripping from a ruptured tank, people driving by but not stopping—too afraid to get involved.

Liz was an excellent driver, but the first snow always seemed to bring out the worst in drivers—especially *other* drivers.

I'm the kind of person who imagines the worst, always anticipating the most terrible and illogical outcome every time I'm faced with a potential catastrophe. I'm a worrier, but that's not always such a bad thing. The worry makes it so much sweeter when things turn out okay, despite my fretting and hand wringing. But on that day, when the phone rang, I didn't think I was going to be let off the hook.

It was the sound of his voice, and not the words themselves that made me know that it was the worst possible news, that Elizabeth was dead. He had trouble actually saying the words, speaking in barely more than a whisper, hesitating several times as if he was trying to find how to deliver them—trying to find some way to lessen the blow.

He introduced himself as Lieutenant Jakes, and after confirming that I indeed was the husband of Elizabeth Allison Williams, apologized repeatedly for contacting me by phone—rather than in person. He had been trying to reach me all afternoon, but only had my home number. Eventually he tracked me down—after all he was a policeman—that's what they do.

He had trouble getting to the point, but I knew what he was about to say, even though I didn't want him to say it. Even having formed the words in my head, it was still a shock when he finally got around to saying it. In a voice that was shaky and barely audible, he confirmed my worst fears. Liz was dead.

As my eyes welled up with tears, a million images flashed through my mind. It is said that just before you die your life passes before you, from your earliest memories to the present. I now know that it also happens when a loved one dies, unexpectedly, and tragically, because our whole life together came at me in an infinite series of images bursting forth at amazing speed like the grand finale of a Fourth of July fireworks display.

I remembered the first day we met, me making a fool of myself, her giggling uncontrollably. Images of us helping each other put our robes on for graduation, the excitement in telling each other about our first real jobs. The day that we were married, the long talks into the early morning hours, the countless times we made love, images of her beautiful body and smiling face. The visions flashed before my eyes at increasing speed, turning quickly into a blur of color behind tear-filled eyes. The room began to spin, and my guts turned liquid, threatening to spill out across the floor.

The voice on the other end of the telephone continued to drone on, as if the lieutenant had no idea the impact his news had on me, no idea that my mind was elsewhere. He was rattling on as if I'd been following the conversation right along, as if we'd been discussing something as trivial as the weather. I didn't hear much of what he said, but I heard him ask that I come to the eighteenth district station, and then he hung up. I stared down at my hand holding the phone and saw that it was trembling, and suddenly I realized that I didn't even know how she died.

The shadows stretched across the desk in front of me telling me that the sun was setting, and I had been staring at the picture of Liz for far too long. An overwhelming feeling of being lost and now alone slowly gave way to anger—more anger than I had ever experienced in my life...but at whom? Was it God who took my Liz away? Is God, if there *is* a God, that cruel that

He would take away the only person that I ever loved? So heartless that He would kill one of the kindest, gentlest people that He had ever created?

Or was it just chance? I took no comfort from the idea that it was just some random event, like winning the lottery or finding a four-leaf clover. Thinking that she wasn't singled out didn't make it any easier.

Perhaps it was fate—that all things are pre-destined. Maybe everything that happens to us is already set. We're all just following some big, sadistic plan with no warning as to the direction that our lives are to take.

I searched for answers, but found none. I only knew that whoever took my wife from me was one sick son of a bitch.

I heard that annoying sound the phone makes when it's off the hook and I looked down to see that the receiver was still in my hand. I placed it back in its cradle, knowing that I had to get up and start moving, but not wanting to, having trouble getting the muscles to respond. I had neither the strength nor the inclination to get out of my chair.

I stared out the window for a few more minutes, seeing only darkness beyond the intermittent headlights speeding along Lake Shore Drive, dreading the trips that I had to make—first to the station—then to the morgue. I was terrorized at the prospect of having to identify the body, seeing my beautiful wife lying motionless on some cold slab of marble, watching as they slid the drawer open from a whole wall of such drawers.

I didn't want to get out of the chair, but I guess that what I really feared was closure. I was still holding on to the unrealistic hope that it was just some sick prank, or an awful nightmare—that I would awaken to find everything was just as it was before the terrible phone call.

*****

I had had these times before, I guess everybody has, where I suddenly find myself pulling into my usual parking spot at work, not remembering a thing about the drive—marveling at the fact that somehow I successfully navigated the trip without killing myself or someone else. And on a few occasions, I actually had to sit in my car for several seconds to figure out just where the hell I was.

This time, I realized just exactly where I was, but nothing about the drive to get there. It was a short trip and I knew the area well, but I didn't remember driving down Lake Shore Drive, or the quick turns onto Jackson Drive, Michigan Avenue, Ontario or La Salle. Shit, I didn't even remember getting into my car. The last thing that I *did* remember was sitting at my desk in my office staring at the phone in my hand.

I turned into the narrow driveway beside the non-descript, two-story, tan-brick building, into the parking lot behind the West Chicago Street police station. I drove my car through the short, narrow alley, past a building on my right whose back wall was charcoaled, a man exiting its back door with a barrel on a dolly. He was masked to keep some kind of noxious fume from invading his lungs. Two men clad in white grease-stained aprons, stood in the shadows of the building next door, arguing in some Chinese dialect that might as well have been Martian to me.

There was no visitor's parking that I could find, so I pulled into a long unmarked area flanked by two aged white meter-maid motorcycles. I parked next to them, probably illegally, but I didn't much care. I sat there, not quite ready to get out, looking around seeing that the ground was littered with scraps of paper and bits of trash. The lot was free of snow and I vaguely remembered the sun shining earlier in the day.

My stomach was doing flip-flops as I pushed my way through the glass doors and up the five faded tan steps of the police building. I paused for a moment before passing through the second set of doors that led to the lobby. What was the lieutenant going to tell me, and how was I going to react? A million possibilities went through my mind—most of them pretty far out. I thought about a heart attack, an auto accident, even a drive-by shooting. Maybe she was struck by a bus crossing the street, or maybe drowned in Lake Michigan. Hell, maybe the earth just opened up and swallowed her. Because the police wanted to talk to me I didn't think it was anything ordinary.

As I reached for the door handle, I realized that my hand was still trembling. I paused once again, squeezing the handle—trying to stop the shaking, to regain some composure—some control. I steeled my mind to handle whatever it was that I learned inside.

I finally entered the lobby, a long, well-worn Formica counter stretching across the right side. Behind it sat the night-shift sergeant—the largest woman I had ever seen. It was easy to see why she was behind a desk, although I'm not sure how she *fit* behind it. I wondered how someone so grossly overweight could be kept on the force. I thought better than to ask her.

She was in the middle of an argument with a woman who was bleeding heavily from a head wound. She held a filthy scarf to the gash—a scarf that may have once been pale yellow but was now soaked crimson. She was screaming at the sergeant, telling her that someone better arrest the pimp boyfriend of hers before she gets killed. She may have once been an attractive woman, but you don't stay that way for very long in her line of work.

Spit flew from the hooker's mouth as she spewed out every obscenity I'd ever heard—and a few that I hadn't. The sergeant took it all in stride, more bored than angry.

I kept my distance and my mouth shut as I waited for the sergeant to finish with the hooker. I looked about the room, really seeing it for what it was. It was a battle zone. There were more than twenty people crammed into the small area between the wall and the front desk—a diverse mixture of cops, criminals, and victims. They were all shouting or bleeding and wandering around aimlessly, and, as I did, they all wanted to be somewhere else. But I was there for a purpose, and I was determined to see it through.

I waited at the desk for what seemed like hours, taking in the madhouse around me, before the desk sergeant finished with the hooker and rudely asked what the hell I wanted. I thought about responding in the same crude fashion, but then thought better of it. She wasn't the kind of person I wanted mad at me—besides—I wanted to get this over with.

I asked for Lieutenant Jakes, not really expecting him to still be there. To my surprise she pointed over my right shoulder to a tall, thin black man in a gray business suit. He was standing next to the soda machine calmly talking with a sergeant in uniform.

Trying hard not to get anything on me, I shouldered my way past a couple of drunks to where the lieutenant stood. When I interrupted and introduced myself, he didn't seem to know who I was and turned back towards the other officer. I interrupted again, "Excuse me, Lieutenant Jakes?" A stranger knowing his name must have startled him because he spun around to face me and asked for my name again. "I'm Doctor Williams—David Williams. We spoke earlier, my wife..."

His eyes registered surprise and quickly turned to sadness, surprising me, stopping me in mid sentence. I could see that it had been a very long day for the lieutenant, as it had been for me, and it wasn't about to get better for either of us.

I followed him into his office, which was little more than an oversized closet cluttered with mountains of folders that covered most of the desk and floor. The dingy walls were badly in need of paint, but were covered with photographs. Jakes was in most of them, standing next to, or shaking hands with, other cops and what I assumed were local dignitaries and VIPs. I didn't recognize any of them, just as I was sure that I wouldn't have recognized anyone at that point.

Jakes lowered himself into the chair behind his desk with an audible sigh and motioned with a nod of the head to have a seat in the only other chair in the room. As I pulled the chair up to the desk, Lieutenant Jakes began apologizing again for the way he had contacted me and again expressed his sympathy for my loss. He had yet to look me in the eye and I sensed that he was stalling. Several seconds passed with neither of us saying a word, as he struggled with what he was about to say. "Where were you at one o'clock this afternoon?" he finally got around to asking.

What the hell was this? I was there for answers, not questions. Did he think that I had something to do with my wife's death? "I was at work, like I am every day at one o'clock," I said angrily. "What are you trying to say?"

He ignored my question. "Where is your wife normally on a Wednesday afternoon?"

I put my questions and rising anger aside and explained that she was a college professor and only had morning classes on Wednesdays. Normally she would have been home by one. I had no idea why she wasn't or where she was today.

He continued to stare at me, and it occurred to me that there was something on the policeman's mind other than just my wife's death. "Doctor Williams, your wife was murdered this afternoon downtown."

I was stunned. Murdered. It was not something I had even considered. Who the hell would want to kill Liz? For the second time that day the tears start—tears of anger and frustration. Someone had killed Liz, intentionally, but what could she have possibly done to make someone want to kill her? She didn't have an enemy in the world. The idea of being caught in the crossfire of some gang rivalry popped into my mind.

I asked, no demanded, to know who had done it, and if he was behind bars. Better yet, maybe he was dead, killed in the same gang fight that took my Liz. Gang wars were not uncommon in Chicago. The papers were filled with senseless violence, of innocent people killed for being in the wrong place at the wrong time.

I hoped that they were all dead, the last member of one gang finishing off the last of the rival gang, just as he himself lie dying. I hoped that living or dead, that they were suffering horribly. But it wasn't a gang war, or a drive-by shooting, and it wasn't any of the other crazy things that my wild imagination had conjured up.

Jakes flipped open his little black notebook. "According to the video surveillance cameras, at twelve fifty-three, two men armed with hand guns entered the Bank One on Wells Street. They took all the money the tellers had in their respective tills—about fifteen thousand. No one in the bank was injured, but in the commotion that followed, a shot was heard coming from outside the bank. Liz was nothing but an innocent bystander. She just happened to be walking by the bank as the two were making their getaway—the wrong place at the wrong time.

Liz was murdered for a lousy fifteen grand.

"We got there fast—three or four minutes, tops. But it was too late." Jakes said that they found Liz on the sidewalk amid an ever-growing pool of blood. She was unresponsive and the officers detected no pulse. A deputy coroner arrived minutes later and confirmed death by a single bullet wound to the chest. While the autopsy was pending, the assumption was that the bullet hit her heart directly, and death was nearly instantaneous.

The robbery was captured on film, but because the thieves wore ski masks and gloves, their identity was unknown and they were still at large. I was frustrated at not having identified a face to direct my anger towards. I asked what the police were doing to capture these murderers and was told that the investigation was ongoing, but there were no strong leads at the time. This is why the lieutenant had asked of my whereabouts. He was fishing. He was trying to piece together the events, and needed to know where I was and why my wife was in the vicinity of the bank at that particular time. She was one small piece of the puzzle, a puzzle that was a long way from coming together. He didn't think that she was involved, and he told me that, but as a cop he had to question everything. I had no clues to give him, but I intended to find out.

I was at the station for hours, or what seemed like hours, when my business there was finally concluded. I had but one terrifying thing left to do. Lieutenant Jakes put me in contact with the coroner's office before I left. To my relief, they explained that it was not necessary for me to identify the body. They had her purse, plenty of positive identification. However, because Liz was killed during the commission of a felony, an autopsy had to be performed before they would release the body to the funeral home.

Before leaving, Jakes told me that the police were doing everything that they could to find the killers, and that I would be contacted should there be any breakthroughs. For the third time he told me how sorry he was. He was sincere ... I could see it in his eyes.

*****

I didn't drive straight home. Instead, I found myself headed to the scene of the murder. I had no idea what I was looking for, but I needed some answers and I wouldn't find them at home. Besides, a dark and lonely house wasn't what I needed just then. I had to keep my mind occupied, and this was how I was going to do it.

I drove the short distance into the heart of Old Town. The area in front of the bank was still cordoned off with yellow police tape stating CRIME SCENE - DO NOT CROSS. The police had nothing to worry about—I had no intention of getting that close. I wasn't trying to solve the murder. I was only trying to figure out why Liz was there. I had no desire to see the chalk outline of my wife's body drawn on the blood-soaked pavement.

I had never been a customer of that particular bank, but the area was familiar to me. It was a popular shopping district with many small businesses and specialty stores. Liz shopped here often. Even at the late hour, quite a number of people were on the street, entering and leaving the many restaurants and coffeehouses. I looked up and down the street for something that would give me an idea of what Liz was doing there, some explanation that would help me come to grips with what happened. It didn't take me very long to get the answer. Maria's Bakery was but a few doors down from the bank. It was a place that Liz visited often. I loved their Black Forest cherry cake, and she liked to surprise me with one from time to time. Then it dawned on me—the following day was my birthday.

*****

During the next two days, while waiting for the coroner to release the body, my home and office were flooded with phone calls—people expressing their condolences and to get the details of the funeral arrangements. They were being polite, doing what was expected of them, but their conversations were tentative and much too formal, as if by discussing it casually would show disrespect—would somehow transfer my sorrow onto them. Each of them tried their best to console me in their own way, but with little effect. I shared the responsibility for her death.

I had been foolish enough to call the bakery. Apparently the young clerk didn't watch the news or read the papers. He asked why Mrs. Williams hadn't been in to pick up her cake.

*****

The following Monday Liz's body was released to the funeral home. I had spent the days before filling out page after page of legal-looking documents, first at the bank, then at our lawyer's office. Saturday afternoon I spent at the funeral home, selecting the music and the Bible passages that I thought appropriate, helping to put together the obituary ... and selecting the casket. And that's when it hit home. As I wandered around the spacious showroom, looking at caskets made of polished wood and metal, it struck me that Liz was dead and one of these boxes would hold her remains from now on. I chose one of metal, one that would last.

That evening, I drank—and I cried. I wept like I hadn't since I was a child, sobbing uncontrollably, tears streaming down my face, my nose running nearly as steadily. I cried for her. She was so young and beautiful, with so much still in front of her, so many things that she talked about doing, but would now never get the chance. I cried because it was so damn unfair.

And I cried for me. How was I going to spend the rest of my life without her? How could I go to work each morning knowing that she would not be home when I got there and how could I sleep at night without her beside me?

During that long, long night I pulled myself together long enough to call Lieutenant Jakes. It was late at night, but Jakes was there—I had a feeling that he would be. He had received the results of the autopsy, and, to no one's surprise it confirmed that Liz had died from massive trauma to her heart's aortic valve caused by a single .38 caliber bullet, which exited through the back. She was dead before she hit the ground—she never felt a thing. At least that's what *they* said. The killers still hadn't been caught, and there was no news from the police regarding any progress in solving the case. Jakes reminded me that it had only been a couple of days—I had to be patient.

Time, I had. Patience, I didn't.

Liz and I had no other family, so I opted against the traditional family viewing session, limiting visitation to a single day. I had always looked forward to our times alone. Now I had this one last chance, just Liz and I, but I couldn't do it. Not this time, and not this way. This time I needed other people around.

*****

The funeral home was packed. The director of the home said that it was one of the largest crowds he had ever experienced. Her casket was placed in the largest of the viewing areas. Still, it was standing room only for the entire day, and the continuous line of people waiting to pay their respects surprised me. But towards the end of the day, as I sat in the first row of chairs and watched the mourners file past, it occurred to me that there were very few close friends among them.

For ten years my life had revolved around my wife and my job, the two things so intertwined that they were hardly separable. Liz and I met at the University of California in Berkeley, both doing graduate work, me pursuing a Doctorate in Paleobiology and Liz completing her Ph.D. in Anthropology. Sharing similar pursuits, and having matching personalities, we fell in love almost immediately and married shortly after graduation. As our careers grew, so did our love for each other. Neither of us were "party-people". We preferred quiet nights together having dinner or taking in the theater.

Our educational and vocational pursuits resulted in many opportunities to travel extensively. We knew thousands of teachers, professors, students, and coworkers around the world, yet few could be considered close friends. We weren't standoffish or anti-social we just preferred each other's company to that of others.

I looked around the large crowded room seeing that there were two groups of people, separated roughly down the middle by a barely perceptible line that meandered like a drunken sailor from the casket to the opposite end of the room. They were in small groups of two and three—husbands and wives speaking quietly, small groups of students huddled together weeping softly into tissues, and groups of co-workers and associates who knew one another. But the two large groups were separate and different. Other than a nod or shared look of sorrow, there was no interaction between the two. And I knew why this was—one group was my friends, and one was hers—and the groups didn't know one another.

*****

The morning of the funeral was damp and dreary. It began cold and gray, and was a perfect match for the despair that consumed me. The service was conducted at the funeral home, which was overflowing. Every one of the chairs was occupied, while I sat alone on the huge sofa that stood lonely before the casket. Every available spot was filled, the latecomers having to stand in the lobby. Everyone wanted a last chance to say goodbye.

Only a few chose to join the procession to the cemetery. I blamed the weather, which had worsened continuously throughout the morning. But I was sure that there was more to it than that. Few wanted to see the final resting-place, knowing that it is a reminder of the final trip that each of us must take.

*****

The rain continued during the short service at her grave. It fell so hard that it seemed as if I was standing within a solid structure—shimmering walls of water surrounding the small space defined by the four aluminum poles. Trapped within, the noise it made as it struck the green tarp overhead drowned out everything else. The sound reverberated off the water-walls across the interior of the small, lonely space. The puddle, the edge of which only moments ago was at my feet, now covered the entire area. I could hear the sound of the water pouring into the grave.

The few who joined the tiny assembly at the graveside had long since gone home. For them, the ordeal was over. They would wake up the next morning and go about their day as they had on all the days before, their lives no different save for an occasional fond remembrance of someone they once knew. Those moments would become less frequent, the memories fading, being erased by time as all such things are.

For me, it was just beginning. I had a life too, but it would no longer be the same—not tomorrow—and not in a thousand tomorrows. A part of me, perhaps the biggest and best part, was gone, and no matter how much I prayed, it would never return. It was if someone had opened me up and scooped out a whole bunch of what was inside—what made me who I was—and then just closed me back up. What was left was incomplete, a jumble of unanswered questions and unfulfilled promises. It was gone forever and I didn't know if I could survive without it.

I tried to look beyond the wall of rain, barely able to see the lone vehicle idling fifty yards away. The other cars were gone, leaving only the funeral director and the minister waiting in the long black limousine, considerately giving me a last few moments of privacy with my wife. I stood alone with my grief for a long time, my hand resting gently on the top of the casket. I looked down at the roses, knowing that they were the last ones that I would ever buy for her, knowing that this was as close to her as I would ever be again. I did not say a final prayer, nor did I say good-bye, but I asked God to explain all this to me, and I demanded vengeance from Him.

CHAPTER 2

Mid-August in central Utah could be brutal, and that one had been unusually hot—cloudless, rainless days, with temperatures hovering at the century mark. The heat radiated off rock and sand giving everything a shimmering quality that made it difficult to see straight. Salt pills, washed down with tepid water from our canteens were of little help, and only made the inside of our mouths crave water all the more. There was precious little shade from the blazing sun, the heat having already caused two diggers to fall from our thin ranks, forcing us to cut back on our digging when the sun was at its peak.

It was late in the day, but the sun remained high in the sky, beating down upon us, wearing us down. We were into the fifth week in the field and the relentless heat and frustration of finding nothing significant was taking its toll on my small team of ten. I had nearly exhausted the sponsor's meager funds and the expedition was scheduled to end in just a few days. I sensed that a few on the team were starting to lose confidence in me. Patience was wearing thin. Arguments had become commonplace and I'd already had to step in more than once to keep disagreements from becoming fistfights. I was as hot and tired as anyone, but not yet discouraged. I knew that there was something out there. I just needed more time to prove it.

I had a reputation for knowing where to search for the really big finds. Experience, a wild imagination, and maybe something just a bit more, had given me a strange ability to see things as they had been, long before man and nature altered the landscape. This unique talent had paid off before, having discovered some of the museum's finest pieces in this very area.

I needed it to pay off again. The museum relied on significant finds periodically in order to insure continued sponsors for research such as this, and a really good specimen could boost museum attendance substantially for several years. But expeditions were expensive. I didn't have much time left before the museum pulled the plug. I needed to give them a reason not to.

We were in the southeastern portion of the Wasatch Mountains, in an area known as the North Horn Formation. It was a region that I was familiar with, having been there before. The location was remote and was untouched by civilization—a place where I had to be reminded from time to time was deep in the heart of the US, and the time was the very end of the twentieth century. Things changed very slowly around there, and not at all since my first visit.

*****

I was still a student at Berkeley, working as a digger, trying to earn my tuition for the last year of graduate school. And to get some much needed, hands-on research for my dissertation.

As a digger, the work was grueling, but fascinating. I had been excited to be working with Doctor Eugene Fairbanks, a brilliant researcher and scholar, but as I was to discover was an egotistical prick that took great pleasure in abusing his crews. Nothing was ever good enough for him. You could work your ass off for him fourteen, sixteen hours a day, but at the end of it, if you didn't come up with something useful, you were worthless—less than worthless.

Fairbanks hogged all the credit when an important discovery was made, but refused to get his own hands dirty. He may have been something special in his younger days, but all I ever saw was a fat, lazy bastard who sat on his little folding chair, with his little umbrella, issuing orders like some third-world dictator, while everyone else busted their asses.

Fairbanks took credit for anything discovered on one of his digs—the actual discoverer getting nothing, discredited actually, if there was a chance that it would lessen the glory for the old professor. I learned this simple fact the hard and painful way by becoming the target of his ire just a few days into the dig. It angered him when I roamed off on my own, choosing to search an area other than where he had directed. It really pissed him off when an inexperienced kid found what *he* was looking for.

I had never even been in Utah before, in any of the states between California and Illinois for that matter, yet it all seemed so familiar, like I *had* been there before. It was an impossible memory, as if I had been reincarnated and was seeing things from a former life. But of course that was impossible, because what I was seeing was a landscape that no one had ever seen—millions of years before man's earliest ancestor. It wasn't exactly a vision, and yet I saw the mountains differently, how they looked when they were first formed. They were gone now, but I could tell where the great rivers and forests had once been. Somehow it just seemed to all fit together, and I knew that it was right.

When we arrived at the dig site I could see clearly that there once had been a vast river, where now existed only a barren, dusty plain. I saw that the surrounding mountains once had tall, sharp peaks, although now they were worn by time. I pictured a time long ago when a game trail existed between the river and the mountains, an area surrounded by plants and animals long since extinct. For the first time in my life everything seemed right, as if each of the puzzle pieces were jumping into place all by themselves. I had only to stand back and watch as the entire picture was revealed to me.

Fairbanks had the crew working the game trail, about two miles north of the ancient trackways that had made this area famous. They were working in ten-meter square grids, scraping off the top layer of dirt, looking for more tracks. Fairbanks figured that if he could further identify the boundaries of the game trail, he would eventually find the remains of the animals that perished there.

I disagreed. Not about this area being a game trail—to me, that part was obvious. But I knew that the trail itself would be an illogical place to actually find animal remains—their tracks yes, but not their remains.

Game trails were hunting grounds for carnivores. Plant eaters traveled in packs, and I believed that because they had nothing to fear from one another, they tended to travel in large herds containing many types of species, as well. The meat eaters had but to hide along the fringes of the trail to pick their meal from the huge, traveling smorgasbord.

But competition was fierce among the fearsome carnivores. If an animal were wounded on the trail, and if it was lucky enough to escape, it would seek refuge elsewhere, understanding that it was an easy target if it stayed on the trail. And when a meat eater was victorious, it would feed someplace else, away from the trail, protecting its kill.

I also didn't buy the professor's theory that many animals would die of natural causes while on the game trail—that the remains would be there—waiting for us to find. I didn't buy it because, first, as I already mentioned, no carnivore is going to leave a meal somewhere where it can be taken away from it. And secondly, I liked to believe that dinosaurs were like any other living creature, when dying, they were going to head for home, or at least some place they could die on their own terms, much like the fabled elephant graveyards. No, we were not going to find what we were looking for on the game trail.

Between the trail and the foot of the mountain range there had once been a dense conifer forest. It would have been an ideal nesting spot for the smaller herbivorous animals that relied on running and hiding to stay alive, or for a wounded animal that was trying to escape further harm. It was also an ideal place for a meat eater to feed without worrying about having his lunch taken away by a larger, more aggressive predator.

I made my way in that direction, toward the base of the mountains, and away from the rest of Fairbanks' crew. I wasn't paying much attention to the old windbag, and he must not have been watching me either because he didn't say anything. And I knew that he didn't like anyone to just wander off on his own. Even had he seen me and tried to stop me, I doubt that I would have complied. I was on to something, and I wasn't going to let him deter me. So I continued on, brushing away the small rocks and pebbles, pushing aside the little bit of scrub so that I could see under and behind—searching—looking for something.

I *was* looking for something, but not really sure what. This was all new to me, being my first dig. So, even though I wasn't sure *what* I was looking for, I continued to inspect the ground closely as I walked, making my way past the sparse, wild vegetation to a rise, barren of any kind of life, swept raw by the strong Utah winds. Working my way outward from the center, on all fours, I passed the palm of my hand back and forth across the hard packed soil, feeling beneath the thin layer of dust, working in a spiral outward toward the outer edge of the circular clearing.

Before I felt it, I saw it out of the corner of my eye. With growing excitement, I scurried a few feet to a slight ridge that seemed out of place on the relatively flat surface. I pressed my hand over it, feeling a solid object, not moving under my touch. It was only a few inches long and rose from the surface no more than an inch or so, but it looked like it didn't belong there.

At first I thought it to be a small rock that was imbedded in the hard-packed soil, refusing to budge after years of wind and rain. Using my brush, I cleared away the dust and small bits of debris that had collected at its edges. It was more than just a small rock—more like the tip of something much larger that was just beginning to be uncovered after years of constant erosion of the earth above. With a small spade, I began carefully removing thin slices of earth surrounding the object. When I had uncovered several inches of it, I pushed hard against the exposed surface with the edge of my hand, but it didn't budge. I laid flat on my stomach, my face no more that an inch from it and blew across its surface revealing the tiny pits and pores that characterize fossilized bone.

I screamed for the other diggers to come running, I had found something. I wasn't sure if I startled them with my screaming, or if they were just surprised to discover that I was no longer with them, but each of them stopped and turned in my direction with their mouths open wide. With only a moment's hesitation, as one, they dropped whatever equipment they had and headed toward me. But before they took more than a few strides, Fairbanks ordered them to stop where they were IMMEDIATELY!

It was really pretty comical. Everyone stopped instantly and for several seconds froze in whatever position they were in when the issue was ordered. I was surprised that those in mid-stride didn't fall on their faces.

"Get back to work!" ordered Fairbanks as he started after me. "Williams, what the hell do you thing you're doing? Who the hell told you to dig over there? Goddamit, I run this show, you dig where I tell you to dig. Got it?"

He was panting and sweating, and swearing like a sailor. He was nose to nose with me, screaming at the top of his lungs like I was on the other side of the planet. He wouldn't let me get a word in edgewise, so I decided to wait him out. I said nothing, but simply pointed at the partially uncovered fossil.

It surprised me, but with some effort, old Fairbanks actually got right down in the dirt to examine the bit of bone protruding through the ground. He was quiet. I had never known him to go more than a few seconds without making some profound statement, trying to impress us with his all-knowing wisdom. Eventually he began stuttering and sputtering—looking for something to say. He was trying hard to find a reason to dismiss the discovery and start in on me again. But despite being an asshole, he wasn't stupid. That wasn't to say that he was going to give me any of the credit, but he knew he was standing on something that could turn out to be important. As it turned out, he was right.

*****

Utah and its neighboring states were famous for the tracks and fossils left behind by creatures of the Jurassic and Cretaceous periods. Some of the world's most spectacular skeletons had been unearthed in this area, including the nearly complete skeleton of a rare duck-billed hadrosaur that I had found on that first trip many years ago. Fossil records show that this particular location had been inhabited by dinosaurs of the late Cretaceous period—the last of their kind. Some sixty five million years ago when that period came to an end, the dinosaurs, the largest creatures to ever inhabit the earth, disappeared.

A hundred and fifty million years of evolution was halted, some believed in a single, cosmic event. Countless theories have been proposed—some dismissed and some not, but no matter how it happened, some of the most magnificent creatures that ever inhabited this planet ceased to exist. Among those that were living when the great cataclysm occurred, perhaps the king of them all and arguably the most ferocious creature of all time, is what we were there for—the *Tyrannosaurus rex*.

Liz had been dead for less than a year. Since her death I had thrown myself into my work with a vengeance, working twelve-hour days, weekends, holidays ... whatever. Sometimes I hadn't gone home at all, instead pulling all-niters like in my old college days. I busied myself cataloging relics, reviewing the work of my staff, and writing inane articles for journals that nobody ever read or heard of. I did it for no other reason than to keep myself occupied.

It had been four months since I completed the reconstruction of one of the largest *Tyrannosaurs* ever found—one that had been bought at auction, funded by a fast food chain no less. It was a magnificent specimen, but to the director of one of the great dinosaur exhibits in the word, and a respected field man, *buying* a skeleton was an embarrassment. No paleontologist worth his spit wanted to work on someone else's discovery.

I needed to reestablish my position amongst my colleagues and to find something that I felt passionate about once more. It took four months of pleading, groveling, and outright begging, not to mention some surprise sponsorship, before the museum let me go out to find my own *Tyrannosaur*.

*****

As I stood on a spot where no human had every stood before, looking down at my crew, I felt that same sense of excitement returning, just like on that first dig so very many years before. My team was inching their way toward my position and their progress was slow and uneventful, with no sign of pending discovery, yet as I watched them, I knew that we were headed for something—it just felt right. I wish that I could explain the sensation, and, more importantly, I wish that I could determine the cause, because then the long, tedious, expensive, process of discovery could be more direct, the results not determined by blind luck. Nevertheless, the feeling was real—I *had* been here before.

I was perched on a large bolder atop the rock pile at the foot of a long cliff that traveled to the south as far as I could see. My friend and colleague, Susan Ansbach, my project assistant, was supervising the work of the nine graduate students as they carefully removed the smaller stones in the debris field, working in towards the base of the mountain. It was tedious and exhausting work and the group had to be careful not to dislodge the wrong stone and end up with a ton of rock on their heads. I was hoping that from where I sat, high up the slope, I could pick out the safest route that would get us a bit closer to the mountain's base.

Above my position the rock rose more than two hundred feet straight up—the face, flat and true, climbed into the sky like a New York skyscraper. The rubble at the foot of the cliff had once been the eastern-most edge of the original slope, no doubt the result of some kind of seismic event that shook the earth and sent the eastern side of the mountain down below, burying whatever was beneath. It is what I was there to find out—what was buried beneath the rock.

It had always been a theory of mine that dinosaurs were more than just dumb brutes, lumbering their way through time, from continent to continent, with no idea where they were going or what they were doing. I couldn't come to grips with the common belief that millions of years of evolution resulted in life forms that were without significant intelligence. Man had been around for only a few million years, yet had progressed to the point where we had surpassed all other forms of life—intelligent enough to split the atom, to travel to other worlds, to begin to unravel the mysteries of the universe. Dinosaurs were one of the most successful groups of animals of all time. They had roamed the earth for a hundred and fifty million years. I believed that they had come further along the evolutionary ladder than most of my colleagues thought—more than just dumb, lumbering beasts.

I theorized that dinosaurs, especially those of the late Cretaceous period, likely the most evolved intellectually, would have nested in areas that offered at least some fundamental protection from the elements. Moreover, the larger, carnivorous animals would have populated areas that smaller animals were incapable of defending. Because of their size and strength, these animals would not have been concerned with finding areas that were hidden, but instead would have looked for larger, more permanent areas to nest in. I had been successful before searching in areas along the base of mountain ranges where caves and overhangs would have kept the animals out of the worst of the icy northern blasts in winter.

I intended to find out if the base of this particular range was such a place. I had my sights on this spot for years, but as many of my colleagues disagreed with my theory, the museum didn't offer much support and I had problems finding a sponsor to fund the expedition. It was really Susan Ansbach who made it possible. She had agreed with many of my theories, including this one, and through her affiliations with the Smithsonian, she had many more connections than I did. Dinosaurs had become big money, and Susan knew *where* that big money was. She had found a group of investors willing to put up a substantial part of the money with the stipulation that I lead the team. I was honored, and more than a little surprised when Susan asked to be my assistant. She was more than capable of leading the expedition herself.

Susan and I made a pretty good team. I had the instincts, and she had the brains. Together, we were a pretty unstoppable duo. Collectively, our talents put us at the base of the mountain in a position that had become all too familiar. Me, staring off into space, trying to form a picture in my mind of just how the landscape all fit together, and Susan, tearing into the mountain, stone by stone, and pebble by pebble, never missing anything. It was an unfair arrangement, but it worked, and as the tension and excitement built, we knew that it was going to work again.

But it was getting tougher and tougher to get any closer to the mountain. From where I kneeled, I could see a slight curvature to the debris field, the midpoint of the arc curving inward toward the mountain, as if there had originally been less mass in that area of the cliff. A cave or at least a depression in the face of the rock would result in such a pattern. Susan and her group had picked away all that could be moved away by hand, weaving a convoluted path around the larger stones toward the center. But the closer they got to the mountain the larger the rocks became and they were going to be at a standstill in another couple of days. I needed to bring in the big earth-moving equipment, but this was beyond our budget and I wasn't going to get it unless I found something to justify the added cost.

I had been watching Susan and one of the smaller kids wrestle with a large rock. Each had a pry bar underneath and they were straining to knock it over, out of the way, but it wasn't cooperating. I decided to help, but as I began to rise pain hit me like a shot, my leg in agony. I had been so intent on watching the team working that my leg had cramped up from kneeling too long on the rock. Not being on a very flat surface, I stumbled backward, latching onto another boulder to keep from tumbling down the fifty feet to the ground below. I clung to it while my feet scrambled to regain some purchase, kicking up a cloud of dust and a shower of small stones.

As I lay flat on the rocks calming myself from the near catastrophe, my head pressed against the hot stone, I listened to the sound the pebbles made as they bounced down the pile. The sound had a soothing quality not unlike the sound that the rain makes on the roof during a summer shower, but there was an underlying resonance that was out of place. It was a hollow, echoing kind of sound, something like that of tiny footsteps, hurrying down a long empty corridor. I tracked the sound to a point just a few feet below my position where I could see that a portion of the tiny pebbles moving past was being absorbed into the mountain.

The rocks were disappearing behind a large boulder that was sitting just inches from the edge of the cliff. I crouched down alongside the rock and tried to peer into the small space, but there wasn't enough room to get close enough to see beyond the shadows. I pressed my fingers into it, feeling a narrow, jagged fissure that seemed to follow the curvature of the boulder. I scooped up a handful of loose stones and pushed them into the ragged slit, listening to the sound as they hit bottom. Getting as close as I could with my ear pressed hard against the boulder, I listened as the stones hit a solid surface close by and then bounce off and away. They struck the unseen surface with a resonant sound, indicating a large area that extended inward toward the center of the mountain. I tried to move the boulder, but only managed to kick a few more of the small stones through the opening. Afraid of losing sight of the boulder's position, I tied my red bandanna around my spade and jammed it underneath.

The pain in my leg was forgotten as I raced down the slope as fast as the uneven terrain would allow, ignoring the surprised look on Susan's face as I ran past, heading toward the supply van. I threw open the doors of the van and cringed at the sight. We were not a tidy crew. With the exception of a narrow isle down the middle of the van, equipment was piled to the top on either side. Shovels, picks, spades, bags of plaster, clothing, foodstuffs, and a thousand other things were stacked, piled, crammed, heaped, and jammed into every available space with no thought to any kind of organization whatsoever. Digging through the pile, throwing things left and right, I eventually found what we affectionately called the *Big Mamas*—two pry bars, each ten-foot long and an inch and a half thick, made of hardened hexagonal steel, and weighing in at about ninety pounds apiece. They were buried under a ton of equipment and supplies, but, being that they *were* pry bars, all I had to do was lift at one end and they slid right out. They looked as if they could move a mountain if you had the right leverage. Well, I was about to see if they could move a small piece of one.

I slid the massive bars out the back end of the van and they landed on the ground with a resounding thud. Susan was still staring at me as I called out to James, who at six foot four, and two hundred fifty pounds, was the only other that could handle the *Big Mamas*. I told him to grab the other bar and follow me. I answered Susan's questioning look by telling her to stay put and keep the rest of the diggers moving forward, I'd be right back.

Reaching the boulder, I pushed some of the small pebbles into the fissure, both of us listening intently as they fell through the opening and rattled around inside the space. A smile spread across James' face, and I knew that he understood immediately. The man-sized rock that blocked our way looked to weigh six or seven hundred pounds. Without having to tell him what to do, James began working his bar under the rock on his side while I worked it from mine. He managed to work his bar several inches under the rock, but I was having trouble getting at it from my side.

The boulder had really settled in, like a fat man in an old comfortable chair. It had probably been here, in this spot, for millions of years, gravity causing it to settle in deep. The years of wind and rain, washing the dirt and dust into its base, had locked it into position. But James loved a challenge, and was young enough to believe that his determination alone could overcome anything. Without my help, he was able to get the rock to wiggle. And by applying force and then releasing, he started it rocking back and forth ever so slightly until I was able to jam my bar underneath. Using every ounce of strength we had, muscles bulging and sweat pouring from our bodies, the rock gave way.

I had intended to push the rock off to the side, along the right edge of the slope and away from the gang digging. But the mass and the shape of the rock caused it to pitch forward away from the side of the mountain. Bumping against another boulder, the angle of its descent changed further, heading straight down the center of the pile ... directly towards my team.

James and I began screaming out a warning as the rock began to pick up speed as it hurled itself down the rubble. Behind the boulder, a small avalanche began to form, spreading out like a fan, some of the smaller rocks racing ahead of the original, bouncing from one boulder to the next, causing them, in turn, to be ripped free and start downward. James and I watched in horror, helpless to do anything but yell. The whole pile had become unstable, the two of us frozen in place, afraid to take a single step out onto the shaky terrain. It was moving forward at such a rate of speed that there was nothing that we could have done on even the flattest of surfaces.

The rockslide became so wide that there was only one route to safety for the gang at the bottom, and that was in a straight line directly away from the mountain. And that was exactly where they headed, just as fast as their feet would carry them.

They must have been watching James and I work the boulder, because they started running even before our words of warning reached them. They must have seen the danger in what we were doing, even if we didn't, and instinctively headed in the opposite direction.

The whole event was over in less than a minute, but it seemed to stretch on forever, thousands of tons of rock chasing my team, gaining on them with each passing second.

The outcome was in doubt until the last rock came to a halt and the dust settled. It took several minutes before we could see clearly through the cloud of dust, and it appeared that everyone was still in one piece. They were badly shaken, and more than one needed a change of shorts, but no one was hurt. I can't say the same for the equipment truck, which was right in the path of the slide. One big boulder hit it broadside, crumpling it, and popped the rear doors open, half the contents spilling out onto the ground. Well, things would probably be easier to find with them so nicely spread out across the ground.

I looked down at Susan and she returned my look with a furious gaze that said, *what are you, fucking crazy*? I held up my arms, palms up, in a gesture of apology, but without saying a word, I made my way back up the pile, returning to the hole that was left by the displaced rock. It was more than just a hole, more of an entranceway eighteen inches wide, large enough to get my head and shoulders through. There was just enough light to see the pile of rubble on the inside of the opening, mirroring that which was on the outside. But this pile only extended a few feet. Even in shadow, I could tell that there was a flat floor only five or six feet below.

I sent James to fetch a lantern while I squeezed through the opening, backing in feet first and being very careful of where I stepped. The light extended just a few feet beyond the base of the pile. Beyond, it was only blackness. Afraid to go any farther without better light, I stretched across the rocks, peering out through the opening, waiting for James to return. Despite the uncomfortable position, it was wonderful to get out of the blazing sun and I laid there, enjoying the temporary relief, concentrating on other sensations. In addition to the relative coolness, there was a surprising feeling of dampness and a bit of a musty smell. I tried to glance around the space, but could make out nothing of the interior. For all I knew, I might have been on the edge of a deep crevasse, one wrong move sending me to a quick death. Or maybe there were some priceless artifacts just beyond the light, one bad step damaging them irreversibly. Not willing to take a chance, I held on tightly to the rock, the only movement that of my rising and falling chest as I struggled to control my growing excitement.

James returned with two lanterns and made as if to enter the hole above me, but I told him to stay on the outside. I wasn't too sure how stable this place was and I wanted someone outside to alert the others if problems developed.

With the flashlight I looked beneath me to see that the floor was indeed only a few feet away. I stepped carefully down over the last few rocks onto a very flat surface that was surprisingly spongy. Out of curiosity, I reached down and scooped up a handful of earth. It was very dark, almost black, with a fine, uniform consistency, as if it had been run through a sieve of some kind.

With the light probing farther into the darkness across the floor, I could estimate the dimensions of the room. At the point where I had entered, the ceiling was only four feet above the floor, but sloped upward another ten to twelve feet before curving back downward, meeting at a point about sixty feet away. The width was about half of that, but was continuously arching outward as it disappeared into the floor on either side. The floor was very flat throughout the space and looked like a calm body of water on a moonless night. It was obvious that I was in the upper portion of what once had been a much larger space.

I had found my cave.

Returning to the entrance, I stuck my head out and shouted. "Susan, come here, you've got to see this!" To my surprise, she refused.

"You come down here, she shouted back. Now!" I was onto something here that might just rescue this expedition, but she didn't seem the least bit curious. I asked James if he had any idea what was going on down below, but he was as much in the dark as I was.

Grudgingly, I squeezed back through the hole and began climbing down the rocks to see what the hell Susan was up to. I had to be careful. The rocks had been redistributed by the slide and were no longer resting in stable positions. It was like walking a tightrope with one end tied to a spring. Every step was shaky, a wrong move might result in a broken ankle—or worse. Carefully picking what looked to be the most stable path, I worked my way down the slope, and I nearly made it. Just a few feet from the bottom I stepped out onto a large rock and it gave way. I ended up on my can, after first bouncing a few times for good measure.

Although momentarily stunned, there didn't seem to be any real damage other than a few bumps and bruises that I would feel more the next day than I did just then. At the bottom of the rock pile, once again on firm ground, I rose to my feet and dusted myself off. At first I was embarrassed until I realized that no one had seen my acrobatic show, even though the whole group was no more than thirty feet away, off to my left. They were all on their hands and knees, forming a ragged circle, working over something in its center. My short-lived embarrassment gave way to curiosity, and I limped over to the group. I had to put my hand on Susan's shoulder to get her attention, which startled her, being so fixated on whatever it was before her. When she recognized me, she threw her arms around me in an unexpected bear hug. Looking over her shoulder, I saw the workers uncovering the last of the debris from the track of a *T-rex*.

*****

That evening, after preserving the print by making a plaster cast of it, Susan filled me in on what had happened. While James and I were exploring the cave, the rest of the crew began sizing up the affects of the rockslide, seeing if they had a newly exposed route that would take them closer to the mountain. As they were exploring, they noted that the slide had shifted enough of the debris around so we now had a lot of previously unexplored territory. When the dust settled, a brief examination of the field revealed a portion of what looked to be a very large footprint. By the time I made my dramatic, but unseen, entrance, the group had completely uncovered the print.

My near disaster had turned into triumph, and we weren't done yet.

Over the next three days, we uncovered several more prints and partial prints, some made from the *Tyrannosaur*, others from another species—different sizes—several different animals. The closer we got to the mountain, the more we found.

By the fourth day, the progress began to slow, because, once again, we were into territory covered with rock that could not be moved by hand. With the work slowing down, I finally had a chance to show Susan the cave.

We spent most of one afternoon exploring the vault, but except for the unusual composition of the soil and the surprisingly smooth surface of the floor, we found nothing of significance. However, we knew that there was something of great importance directly beneath our feet. Because of the presence of so many prints and their relative position to what had once surely been a cave entrance, we were sure beyond a doubt. More importantly, we now had all the proof we needed to insure sufficient funding from the sponsors and extend the dig.

CHAPTER 3

When the phone rang, it was a welcome interruption from the long hours sitting in front of the computer. My head was pounding and my eyes were tired and unfocused from staring at the CRT for too long. Computers really aren't my thing and I hated sitting in front of them for days at a time. Computer geeks must have some kind of built-in resistance to this shit or else they have a masochistic streak a mile wide. Thank God I wasn't one of them, although you'd have never known it by the way I'd been spending my time.

I had been practically living in my office during those weeks, eating take-out at my desk, and even sleeping on the cot in the corner on occasion. I was working with a new computer program developed jointly by a paleontologist friend of mine from Berkeley and one of the leading software companies. I knew it was going to be a great tool for those in my field and specifically for the task that lay ahead for me, if I could only get the damn thing to work.

It was Lieutenant Jakes on the phone. I hadn't spoken with him since before I left for Utah, but we had formed the beginnings of a real friendship in the months following my wife's death. During those first weeks I had nagged him endlessly, wanting to know how the case was going, constantly demanding results. The incessant calls angered Jakes—I was probably keeping him from doing other important work.

After six weeks of nearly constant harassment, Jakes agreed to meet me at a bar after work. I wanted to confront him face to face, thinking I might get more answers that way than I had by going the phone route. I found out later that the only reason that he'd agreed to meet was so that he could tell me to leave him the hell alone. As it turned out he was as frustrated as I over the lack of progress.

After the initial whining, complaining, and not-so-veiled threats (all on my part), we actually came to an understanding—police work sucked and husbands of dead victims were a pain in the ass. I could live with that.

We closed the bar that night, getting so sloppy drunk that we had to call a cab to get home. During the course of the night, while we were still coherent, we agreed that I would cease the frequent calls to his office. Instead, we would meet occasionally after work for dinner or drinks, and during those times he would fill me in on any developments in the case … should there ever be any.

The arrangement had worked well, but just as I had agreed not to call him at his office, it was unusual for him to call me at mine. He might have been calling to invite me to dinner, but I didn't think so. He had something else on his mind, but, nevertheless, we began the conversation with the regular chitchat. His wife and kids were fine, the weather was crappy, and he was overworked and underpaid—in other words—the usual. I filled him in on the success of our expedition out west and what I was up to now. After a few more minutes of meaningless chatter, he got to the point.

There had been a break in my wife's case.

His name was Julius Green. According to Jakes, he was a low-life, penny-ante crack head, who would do anything for a buck. He had a lengthy and impressive rap sheet, and although the cops knew that he was into all kinds of illegal activities, he had never been convicted of a major crime. Among other things, Green ran a string of low-cost, aging prostitutes. One of them, who just happened to be his most current live-in, ratted on him after receiving a severe beating for allegedly holding back some of the money from her tricks.

Apparently, besides the dope, Green liked to drink, and not only was he a violent drunk, he was a talkative one, as well. On more than one occasion, when drunk, between kicks and punches, he bragged to her about how easy it had been to rob that bank and what a bunch of saps the cops were. It had been easy. Walk in and walk back out, and nobody knew a thing. He never said anything about the murder, but the girlfriend was pretty sure which bank it was … and Green carried a gun. She was sure of that. He had just recently pistol-whipped her with it.

According to the woman, Green had a partner named Sid, a goofy-looking little shit who was not altogether right in the head. She didn't know if Sid was involved in the robbery, but they were always together. Sid wasn't smart enough to do anything on his own. Green pushed him around and treated him like shit, but Sid hung to him like they were brothers. The woman was sure that if Green were into something, Sid would be right alongside, buried in it up to his nose.

It was the woman's house that Green was staying at, so the cops knew just where to find him, but Green had flown the coop before the cops got there. He must have known that he went too far in administering his brand of justice on a woman the last time. His clothes were gone too, but now the cops had a solid clue. There was an all-points bulletin out for Green's capture.

After agreeing to meet the next night for drinks, Jakes and I ended our conversation and I tried to return my attention to the computer, but I was a bundle of mixed emotions. There was no real proof that Green was the killer, and that based solely on the word of a known prostitute—with a grudge—no court in the land would have convicted him, yet I was sure that Green had done it. Maybe I just *needed* him to be the one. I needed *someone* to hate, and a worthless piece of shit like Green made a pretty good target. In my mind he was the one and I was monumentally pissed off that he was still on the loose.

Along with the anger, the sadness and loneliness came back, too, as if the past thirteen months hadn't existed and it was just moments before that I had found out about Liz's murder. It was like I was reliving that first phone call from Lieutenant Jakes all over again. The pain and the frustration jumped out at me, renewed, bringing fresh tears to my eyes.

I hadn't forgotten what had happened to Liz, nor had her loss become any less painful over the weeks and months since her death. But recently I had begun to find moments, more and more often, where my sorrow was tucked away in some recess of my mind and replaced by the excitement of what we had found in the cave, and the terror of the dual disasters that led up to it.

*****

Despite the urgency of the situation, and our own anxious energy, it had taken nearly a week to bring the heavy earth moving equipment to the site. The delay had taken us beyond our original date to end the dig. Fall was quickly approaching and weather in this area was unpredictable. It would be difficult to work in frozen conditions, and after the first winter storm hit it would be impossible to preserve the conditions of the site. I figured we had maybe six weeks to wrap this thing up.

The equipment was all we needed to clear away the rubble in front of the cave in a manner of days, but progress was extremely slow. We had to walk a fine line between getting the area cleared out before the weather changed and destroying the artifacts. *Tyrannosaur* tracks were not so common that we could afford to lose any and the state of Utah had a representative there to insure that we did not. Just as we in the museum were counting on the relics to boost museum attendance, so was the state counting on the preservation of the tracks to increase tourism.

I was concerned with disturbing the rock at the cave's entrance and possibly destroying whatever happened to be inside, under the tons of dirt. Based on the size and shape of the top of the space that I had explored, it was evident that most of the cave was buried under the rock, close to the face of the mountain. The rock covered a large portion of the fragile soil that I had discovered during my first trip to the cave. Moving the soil would be a risky proposition, even if what we wanted was directly beneath it.

I decided to remove the rock from the top down following the curvature of the side walls of the cave's entrance, so that the path widened as we proceeded downward. The rock pile spread out for well over two hundred feet from the mountain, so we had to use a crane to reach out over the rock as far as possible. But even with the crane, we had to remove about half of the rock in order to get the crane in close enough. We hoped that we could get this done without causing a major rockslide.

Once at the bottom, we would work back outward, away from the cliff, clearing a path wide enough to maneuver the equipment, all the while trying to preserve new tracks as they were discovered. We would then continue working our way from side to side, always increasing the width of the path until all of the debris was moved. It was important to uncover the entire area so that we could see every print that was left.

Our sponsors must have been impressed with our progress and the possibility of seeing their investment pay off in a big way because they sent a well-known geologist. It was perfect timing. He showed up two days before the earth moving equipment arrived. Although we had never met, I knew Brian Huntsville by reputation. He had worked often with other paleontologists in unraveling many of the mysteries of prehistoric times, helping them discover sites rich in prints and skeletal remains by identifying the rocks and mineral deposits common to the era of the animals being sought.

It was common knowledge, especially among scientists, that since the mid-twentieth century, the age of igneous rocks could be estimated pretty accurately through radiometric dating. As rock of this type cools from its liquid to solid state, its crystalline structure, which contains radioactive particles, decays by throwing off atoms and thus becoming non-radioactive. By measuring the ratio between radioactive material and non-radioactive material, and comparing to the known half-life of the element, the date can be derived. By dating samples of igneous material found in the area, the age of other mineral samples found within the same strata could be determined.

The same thing worked with fossilized bone, which is really not bone at all. Fossils are actually rock, made up of whatever elements surrounded the animal when it died. In a relatively short time the organs, skin, and muscles of the animal would decompose, and very gradually be covered with sand and mud, brought forth by winds and rain. The bone itself would slowly decompose as well, and over a long period of time, the space left over would be filled with nearby elements carried to the location by ground water.

So, I could understand what Brian did in a technical sense, but he was known for far more than just his technical expertise. Brian knew things that he had no business knowing. He *saw* things. He was famous for it. Many people thought that he was a crackpot—a storyteller—someone who could spin a convincing yarn for the sake of book sales. And it sure as hell worked. His books read, and sold, like novels, the reader being drawn into a world that he could scarcely believe, or even imagine. Brian never theorized, and he never used words like perhaps, or maybe. Brian wrote as if he'd *been* there, and a lot of scientists took exception to that. They thought that he was full of shit. But few ever said it to his face. He got results, time and time again.

For me, I hadn't quite decided if he was full of shit or not. Even knowing of his success rate and how well he knew his field, no matter how many articles and books I read detailing Brian's research, I just couldn't quite understand it. I loved his work, but I too was skeptical. How could he possibly know so *much* about what it was like millions of years ago? His descriptions were so vivid and so colorful it was as if he actually *were* there, as if he was describing the sights that his own two eyes had seen. Maybe he could tell how and when a mountain was formed, maybe he could tell where the shores of a now nonexistent sea were, but how could he possibly see it in such detail? How could he have the audacity to say this is how it *was*? Not how it might have been, but how it actually *was*.

I guess he really wasn't that different from myself. After all, didn't I tend to form pictures in my own mind about how things were before man had taken his first step on the evolutionary trail? Wasn't it I who created theories from those pictures and tried to force them down the throats of nonbelievers and skeptics? And didn't I get results despite my detractors? I *know* that it was me who profited from the reputation that was created. I had come a long way in my career, and I sure hadn't done it because I was the smartest kid on the block. I didn't pick up the nickname Dinosaur Hunter because of superior intellect. It was because I got results—just like Brian. No, Brian and I really weren't very different at all—maybe we were *both* nuts.

I was surprised by Brian's appearance though—the pictures on the backs of book's dust covers never quite capture the real person. He was incredibly young looking for someone of such notoriety and accomplishment, and very small, both in height and build. He looked more like someone you'd run into (or knock over) in the halls of junior high school. He had a high-pitched voice as if still waiting for puberty to strike, and had a bit of a stutter. But, he walked like a man full of confidence, and, as I was soon to find out, he knew his stuff.

He brought with him a portable material analysis laboratory in the guise of a full-sized van. It contained a scanning electron microscope, an x-ray spectrometer, and a lot of other stuff I had never heard of. I had no idea what he was going to do with them, but I would have bet a year's salary that he knew exactly how to use them.

He gave me a quick tour of his lab, jabbering excitedly about what each piece was for and how much it had cost. He was really in his element, but little of it made any sense to me. At first I mistook his childlike glee as an excessive amount of pride in his knowledge of his tools, like a toddler shows off some newfound ability or possession. Or maybe he was just showing off, easily impressing me with knowledge that I could scarcely begin to grasp. But the smile on his face told me that it was something else altogether. His exuberance was due entirely to the excitement of being in the field again—being part of what may be another major discovery. Like me, he loved his work. To confirm that fact he promptly escorted me out of the van, stopping just long enough to grab a small cardboard box, and asked to be taken to the cave.

As we approached the edge of the rock pile, I pointed out the cave's entrance which James and I had expanded somewhat by removing a few more boulders. Brian's eyes lit up like a child's at Christmas and I had to grab him by the arm to keep him from racing ahead of me up the pile. The footing was still precarious from the earlier slide and made worse by the frequent trips that James, Susan, and I made to the cave. I didn't want to be responsible for killing Brian off before he even had a chance to examine the contents of the cave.

From our previous treks I had established a safe route to the top, so I instructed Brian to walk behind me and to step on only those stones that I did first. I began making my way to the top slowly, thinking that Brian was right behind me, but about half way up I turned to see that he was still at the bottom, his back to me, crouched down on one knee. He was holding a rock in his hand and staring off into space. I called his name, with no response. I called out to him again, and there was still no acknowledgment. Exasperated, I started back down again.

I approached him from behind. In my rubber-soled boots, I was quiet, sure that he was completely unaware of my presence. But before I could reach out to him, he began speaking as if from a trance, all the while staring into space. I tried to see what he was seeing, but there was nothing but Utah's dusty plain, stretching on for miles. Above that, nothing but clear blue skies for as far as the eye could see. Whatever he was looking at, it wasn't there now.

It was if he was talking to himself, but loudly, each word clear and distinct. "This was once a rich fertile land covered with ferns and flowering plants, deciduous trees just beginning to take root. To the east was an inland sea, but its shores were beginning to recede, leaving behind billions of shells and the remains of tiny aquatic creatures. The abundance and diversity of animals were amazing, some species soon to disappear, others just beginning. The west was mountainous, but they looked very different than they do now. The great, floating continents that crashed together a hundred million years ago hadn't yet finished their work. The climate was changing from one that was consistently hot and moist, to one more seasonal, with winter storms beginning to impact the environment, endangering the life."

He continued to talk and I listened with fascination as I began to form my own picture in my mind, one much more colorful and detailed than I had conjured up on my first visit there. I lost myself in his words and in his world. He brought each object to life in my mind as we began to turn, taking in a single, shared, panoramic view of the ancient world that now surrounded us. As if through *his* eyes, I saw the incredibly blue skies, clearer and bluer than anything that I could imagine. In fact, all the colors were more intense and vibrant than those of this world—more alive. The sun was bigger and brighter than I had ever experienced, and I could feel the increased warmth on my face, bringing a smile to my lips.

His words began to float away like he was distancing himself from me, yet I knew that he hadn't moved, and his images never wavered. Our plateau remained, but many of the surrounding mountains had disappeared. The rock pile too was gone and the cave was now visible, huge and inviting, the promise of untold treasures within. The blackness of the cave's mouth stood in sharp contrast to the surface of the surrounding rock, which shown nearly white in the sun's reflected brilliance.

I had the feeling that something was lurking in the cave and I strained to make it out, but the unformed image evaporated instantly when something struck me from behind. It was a football thrown by one of the kids. I ignored the pleas of the errant thrower to pass him the ball and returned my sights to the cave. But the magic was gone—it was once again nothing more than a pile of rock. I turned to see Brian, who had finished speaking, but was continuing to stare at the cave's entrance. Not wanting to ruin his fantasy as mine had been, I remained quietly at his side, waiting.

It was several more minutes before Brian's gaze shifted from the cave. Without a word, he began climbing the mountain as if nothing had happened. The event was an epiphany for me—for him it was nothing more than the blink of an eye, as if time and space were momentarily suspended while another part of his being, a part not quite belonging to this world, took over. I had to run to catch up with him and once again lead the way.

Once inside the cave, Brian spent the first hour wandering the perimeter, carefully examining the walls while making notes in a small book that he carried, but never uttering a sound. Once he had circumnavigated the interior, he pulled a tape measure from his belt and proceeded to measure the distance from the entrance to the wall directly opposite. He then removed several glass vials from the box, and after measuring and noting the exact position, filled them with five samples of soil, one at each end, one at the center, and one mid-point between the center and the ends. He then measured the distance across the cave from the left and right side walls through the center point. He took four more samples on this line. He labeled each of the vials as he went. Without a word he took the box of now filled vials and left the cave.

He exited the cave so abruptly that I didn't have a chance to get in front of him so that I could lead him back down the treacherous path to safety. I called out, but he didn't respond or even acknowledge me, and it didn't look like he was paying attention to where he was going. Like my car, he must have had some kind of built-in guidance system or maybe a guardian angel, because somehow he made his way down uneventfully. Once at the bottom, he headed directly for his van.

From the time he came out of his trance or whatever the hell it was, all through his examination of the cave's interior, and during his descent of the rock pile, he had never uttered a single word. Frustrated at being ignored, I grabbed his arm just as he was stepping up into the van, which startled him. I think he had completely forgotten that I had been with him. "Well, Brian ... what do you think?"

He seemed surprised by the question. He held up one of the vials, looking down at me as if I was a stupid child. "It's silt. What did you *think* it was?"

I didn't know a lot about geology, but I was pretty sure that silt was what was leftover when floodwaters receded, and Brian did state that this area had been completely covered with water periodically throughout the Cretaceous period. But I wasn't sure whether that was a good sign or a bad sign with respect to the chances of finding something at the bottom of it. Did the waters advance slowly, the animals vacating the cave long before it flooded? Did the waters carry away anything and everything that may have been left in the cave? The existence of large numbers of tracks made it pretty obvious that the *Rex* lived here, but when, and was anything still there? I was going to have to wait to get the answers to these questions.

*****

It wasn't until the next afternoon, just hours after the earth-moving equipment began showing up, when Brian called me into his lab. He confirmed that the cave, at least its top layer, was filled with residue from a flood. He described the composition and make up of the samples, using a lot of technical jargon that was way over my head. I did pick up, however, that the silt contained a large percentage of coal, which was formed by millions of years of decomposition of microscopic sea organisms. The composition was very consistent throughout the floor of the cave, probably due to a single flooding event occurring very late in the Cretaceous period. He also stated that the rocks filtering the floodwaters as it entered the cave caused the fine, uniform consistency. The seismic event that sheared off the front edge of the cliff undoubtedly occurred prior to the flood.

I found that last fact to be the most significant one—the avalanche occurred *prior* to the flood, meaning that there was a good chance that the rising waters of an impending flood may have happened much later and would not have driven the animals away. If the rockslide occurred while the dinosaurs were still alive, and if they weren't out hunting at the time, they may have been trapped inside the cave.

Experts believed that, like other large land-based animals, most dinosaurs slept at night and hunted for food during the daylight hours. If the slide occurred during the sleep period, they would still be inside and we could learn a lot about their social organization. The number of animals, their age, and sex might tell us if they lived as family units, if they were segregated by years or by gender, if they were monogamous, if they traveled in packs. So much could be learned, if only something was there.

With the heavy equipment on-site, it wouldn't take long to find out. We proceeded slowly, removing the rock from the leading edge of the pile, slowly working in towards the cave's entrance. It took nearly a week to remove enough rock to position the crane where we could begin working from the top. We worked in small areas using two bulldozers situated about fifty feet apart, working in parallel to one another. As each of the bigger stones was cleared from the area, the diggers would go in to remove the smaller debris, sweeping the area clean, looking for more tracks. They found several more, each time causing a further delay of two or three hours.

With the crane in position, the dangerous work began. We couldn't just push the rocks from the top for fear of damaging what was underneath or ruining the cleared area below, which was scattered with valuable tracks. We had to actually be at the top of the pile to help position the boulders. Two of us, positioned on either side of the rock being picked up, used pry-bars to move the stone enough for the crane's claw to grasp it. Moving the largest rocks in this manner, we would then have the bucket attached to the crane and proceed with manually loading it with the smaller stones. The system worked well, but was tedious and exhausting, and we were constantly fighting to maintain our balance on the unstable terrain.

Because I was the leader of the expedition, I felt responsible for taking a regular shift at the top, and Susan insisted that she work by my side. We had been at it for more than a week and had moved probably thirty percent of the stone when disaster struck.

Susan and I were up top and had just positioned a large boulder between the claws of the crane. It appeared that the claw had a good grip on the stone, but when the crane tried to pull it away, the claw sprung free—without the rock. Susan didn't expect the sudden shift of the claw, which she was steadying herself against, and immediately lost her balance, reaching out for something to grab hold of but coming up empty handed. Panicked, trying desperately to regain her footing, she didn't see the huge claw coming towards her on the back swing. I dove towards her to push her out of the way, the claw crashing into my side. I managed to deflect it, but not enough. The claw glanced off the side of Susan's head with a sickening sound and she pitched backwards into the pile of rock.

I must have lost consciousness for just a moment, because I found myself lying ten feet away from her, about thirty feet down the pile, unsure of how I got there. I was lying flat on my back, stunned and disoriented. I could tell that Susan was out cold and bleeding badly from a deep cut just above her left eye. I tried rolling over onto my side and the pain hit me like an explosion. It sucked the breath from my lungs, white spots danced before my eyes. Everything seemed to hurt at once, but nothing compared to the pain in my side. Somehow I managed to crawl over to Susan. She was breathing, long, slow breaths that seemed to rattle around in her chest, as if each were her last. The eye beneath the horribly ragged cut was half opened, but revealed only the white. You didn't need to have a medical degree to see that she was in trouble.

I wasn't going to let Susan die on that goddamned pile of rock, but I was realistic enough to know that I was in no shape to carry her down. Even if I weren't injured, I couldn't risk carrying her down across the uneven and unstable pile. One wrong step and we'd both go down, and I knew she would not survive another fall. I pushed the rising panic from my mind and tried to force myself to concentrate.

Gradually, I became aware of the sounds around me. I could hear Brian shouting, his voice getting closer, telling me that he was on the way up the heap. Beyond that, I could hear a rhythmic creaking sound directly overhead. I looked up to see the hook dangling just above us. I had an idea, but as I tried to call out to Brian, I found that I couldn't seem to get enough air into my lungs to make much of a sound, the pain doubling and tripling with the attempt. I laid on my back, taking little, short, shallow breaths, waiting for what seemed like hours for Brian to reach me. When he did, I explained my plan.

While the switch was made I used the time to tie my bandanna across Susan's head, slowing the flow of blood. Her face was deathly pale and she was still unconscious. Her breathing was a desperate sounding hiss, and was now irregular, the pauses becoming terrifyingly long.

In a matter of minutes, the hook was replaced by the bucket and was being lowered down to our position. Brian proved to be much stronger that his fragile appearance indicated. He wasted no time in carefully lifting Susan into the bucket. He was incredibly gentle, knowing that he might be harming her further. Neither of us knew the extent of her injuries and we knew that it was wrong to move someone without medical assistance, but we also knew that she would die if we didn't act fast. I tried hanging on from the outside, but hadn't the strength to do it. I was alert and my legs still worked, so I slowly walked down the rest of the way while Brian guided the bucket down to the bottom.

Someone must have been smart enough to have grabbed the cell phone and called 911, because I could hear the sound of approaching sirens as I stepped to the bottom of the pile.

*****

It had been four days and I was just beginning to feel human again. It still hurt like hell when I moved in the wrong way, but at least now, if I was careful, I could breathe without the fear of seeing the dancing fairies before my eyes from the agony in my chest. The x-rays revealed three fractured ribs on my left side, but no punctures, which was real hard to believe during those first couple of days. Every breath I took was torture. It was a sharp pain, and no matter how hard I tried, the air just wasn't there. I thought for sure that I had sprung a leak—the air had to be going somewhere. But the doctor said that in six weeks I'd be as good as new, although he insisted that I didn't leave the bed for a week. After that, if I was a good boy, I could go back to work … if I promised to take it easy and stay off the rock pile.

Susan was not so lucky. She suffered a fractured skull and a laceration that required thirty stitches to close—and she was still unconscious. Until all the tests were done I worried constantly that we had made matters worse by taking her off of the mountain, that maybe she had an injury to her neck or back, and by us moving her we had left her paralyzed. But, according to the doctors, Brian and I had saved her life by acting quickly. Susan had not suffered any injury to her spinal chord, but she had suffered brain damage, the extent of which was not yet certain. That should have made me feel better, but it didn't.

I stared down at her, wondering what, if anything was going on inside. The top portion of her head was totally encased in bandages. They had already performed two operations—the first to remove the splinters of bone from her brain—and the second the following day to reduce the pressure that fluid buildup was causing. The wrappings extended to, and partially covered, her left eye, but you could still see the massive swelling there. It was strange, but despite the swelling, the discoloration, and the bandages that hid so much of her face, there was incredible beauty there. The right portion of her face, the exposed and undamaged side, seemed so natural, so relaxed, so at peace. I couldn't help but think of *Sleeping Beauty*.

At that point, the doctors didn't have any answers. A lot depended on how long she stayed in a coma. As a biologist, I know something about the complexity of the brain, and about how little we really knew about how it works. Although Susan was unconscious, there was still a lot of brain activity. She was breathing and her heart was still beating strongly. No one could tell why those functions continued to work while others ceased, and none of the so called experts knew very much about what else was going on in there. The doctors encouraged me to speak to her—that perhaps my words would somehow penetrate that portion of the brain that we knew so little about—that just maybe she would recognize the sound of my voice and show some sign of life.

I sat in a rickety wooden chair pulled up to the edge of Susan's bed, leaning close to her, whispering into her ear. I had been talking to her almost continuously for two days, nearly every minute that the nurses would allow. I was supposed to be in bed, too, but the staff could at least keep an eye on me as long as I was in the hospital, so they didn't protest too much. And I was sure that the nurses were tired of seeing me, but they tolerated it. Susan had no one else.

It was easy talking to Susan, even if she couldn't talk back. Hell, I wasn't even sure she could hear me. Sitting there thinking about it, I realized that I had had a continual relationship with her longer than anyone I had ever known. We had been friends for more than fifteen years, and although sometimes separated by hundreds, and even thousands of miles, we had stayed in touch on a regular basis. There was so much that we shared and so much to talk about.

I started at the beginning—when she, Liz, and I had been a threesome. I had actually known Susan first. We had dated a couple of times, and although we really liked each other, it was a very casual relationship—we were buddies. We met in advanced microbiology class as sophomores, and we both hated it. There was too much studying, too much memorization, and way too many terms, most of them unpronounceable. We tolerated it because we didn't have any choice. It was a required class for our major.

The professor of micro-B, Doctor Swynner, was tall and incredibly skinny, with a huge honker. He looked more like Ichabod Crane from *The*

Legend of Sleepy Hollow, than he did a respected college professor. Worse, he was unimaginative and unyielding. Following our first test, I had the audacity to question his intelligence regarding one of the exam questions. It became a bitter argument, and even though everyone in the class got it wrong, Susan was the only other one to stand up to him. We didn't win the argument, but I had made a new friend.

I stopped Susan after class to thank her for siding with me against that pig, Swynner. Instead of simply responding with a simple "you're welcome," or "don't mention it," she began giggling. The giggling quickly turned to uncontrollable, sidesplitting laughter. At first I thought she was laughing at me, maybe my fly was down, or I had something stuck between my teeth. With tears running down her cheeks, she finally got it out. I had called him a pig—what an appropriate term for a guy named Swynner. I hadn't intended the play on words, but after Susan pointed it out, and after then thinking about the *snout* on the guy, I couldn't help but laugh myself.

From that day on, any time Swynner said something outrageous, or we were just plain bored with his monotonous lecture, we had but to point at our nose to lighten the mood. By the time the semester had ended, everyone in the class had caught on to our act and they were all doing it, although several of the class clowns mistook pointing *at* the nose to a finger *up* the nose. At least once a day, someone would do the nose-pointing gag and the whole class would crack up. Swynner was pissed, but never had a clue what we were all laughing about.

Because we both had a break after that class, we began having coffee together in the cafeteria every day. It was very natural for us to begin seeing each other after school and on weekends. An occasional movie or a burger and fries, but I didn't think you could actually call it dating. At least it didn't feel that way to me. We were buddies, and we did the things that buddies do together.

Liz was Susan's roommate and we met about a month after Susan and I began seeing each other outside of school. Susan was cramming for a final and really didn't have time to go out, but I kidded and harassed her until she gave in. She agreed only if I came by her place to pick her up, and was only going to go out long enough to grab something quick to eat.

When I arrived at Susan's house, I was surprised when someone else opened the door. It was the first time that I ever saw Liz, and I made quite an impression. I became so tongue-tied that she must of thought that I was a complete idiot. To make matters worse, I tripped over the threshold, knocked over a lamp, and ended up sprawled across the entranceway with the knee torn out of my best jeans. I felt like a total doofus, but Susan was smart enough to see what was happening. This time I let myself be convinced that she really was too busy to go out, and suggested that Liz go instead. I was always surprised that Liz agreed—I think I was drooling at the time.

From the moment Liz and I met, I knew that there was no one else for me, and within a few weeks I knew that Liz felt the same way. Susan didn't seem to mind, although maybe I just assumed that she felt the same way about me that I felt about her. We were friends, and continued to be friends throughout my marriage to Liz, and even after her death.

But as I sat there staring at her, so beautiful, yet so helpless in that damn hospital bed, I wondered if her feelings for me were more than just that of friendship. It would sure explain a lot—our continued friendship, even though frequently she must have felt like a third wheel—finding the funds for this project and insisting that I be named its leader—wanting to work by my side at the top of the rock pile, despite its dangers. And thinking of it, I didn't recall Susan ever having a serious relationship with anyone in all the time I'd known her. She dated, and often doubled with Liz and I, but none of her suitors ever seemed to make the cut beyond the first or second date.

It took the accident for me to realize what a dumb shit I was.

Susan was in love with me, and had been for fifteen years. All that time I had been so in love with Liz that I failed to see what was going on right in front of me. It never even occurred to me that someone else could love *me*. I figured Liz had used it all up.

The realization had forced me to look at Susan in an entirely new light. I guess that I had always loved her, but I had always thought of her as more like the sister that I never had, rather than in a romantic way. Had Liz not entered the picture would something have developed eventually between Susan and I? Had the accident not happened, would our relationship have grown and changed into something more than just friendship? I had all these questions and no way to get at the answers.

The doctors were noncommittal, but for every day that went by without some improvement, the less likely it was that she'd return to me.

I couldn't help but feel responsible for the situation that Susan was in. She was on the project because of me, and she was on the mountain when the accident occurred because of me. Had I not been so blind, would I have made different decisions? Would I have tried harder to keep Susan off of the mountain, knowing the potential for danger there?

I needed Susan to get better. Not only because I felt responsible for what happened, but I also had to discover what my true feelings were for her and whether or not we had some kind of a future together.

*****

First Liz's death, then Susan's near fatal accident, then learning that the two killers were still on the loose was just too much for me to take. I sat in my office shaking from frustration and anger. I looked down at the phone and saw it as the enemy. Why does it seem that so much bad news is delivered by telephone? I didn't see the person at the other end as being the bearer of bad tidings. It was the phone itself. It was no mere inanimate object, a useful tool, which simply improved human communication. No, it had a life and an evil mind of its own and constantly rained terror down on its unsuspecting victims.

Like everything else that had happened to me in my adult life, both good and bad, my first reaction was to grab the phone and call Susan. When it was good news, she made me feel even better about it. When it was bad news, she always had a way to find some good in it and she never failed to pick up my spirits.

I wanted to call her. She, and no other, would be able to quell my anger before I lost control, before I did something that later I'd regret. She alone could get me past the rage over the police's ineptitude.

But I couldn't call Susan. She had not come out of her coma. Irrationally, I blamed the phone for this too, and I picked it up and hurled it against the wall, smashing it to bits, and knocking down a dozen pictures from the wall.

CHAPTER 4

Things had finally started to come together. It had taken two weeks to figure out the computer program, and there were times when I damn near gave up. It was like trying to speak a new language without having any lessons or a translator around. Every time I hit a snag, I was at a complete standstill. I'd have to get on the phone to my pal at Berkeley to learn the next step. More times than not, he'd laugh because it was so simple. It may have been simple for him, but it sure as hell wasn't simple for me. Usually, it was just a matter of hitting the right key, or combination of keys, but if you didn't know which key to hit, you were shit outta luck. That's what I hated about computers. The keys always meant more than just what was printed on them. But I had finally gotten the hang of it, and I was having a ball.

The program was written to aid in the assembly of animal skeletons. Although originally written for modern-day animals and humans, it was quite easily adapted for other creatures. It was simple, yet elegant. By inputting the type of animal, the software called up a list of every bone that made up the entire skeletal structure for that particular animal. By selecting just a single bone from the list, and typing in its size—length and thickness—the computer created a three-dimensional model of the completed skeleton. There was even a three-axis scale that gave the size of the animal, and rotated along with the image itself. The software allowed the user to look at it from every angle, pose it in any position, and to even add skin and hair—color, texture, and style of your choice.

The system was based on studies, referred to as systematics, of similarities and differences between animal species in an attempt to track evolutionary patterns. The study had resulted in the theory of cladistics, which allows for the grouping of animals into those that share common inherited traits. The groups, or clades, could be arranged to form a diagram, which, if complete, would trace an animal's descendents back to the originating species.

To make it easy to understand, consider the family tree. Genealogical studies allow people to reach back through time to find their early ancestors and the family relationship of each. Cladistics works in much the same way, but instead of dealing with hundreds of years, and family names that change over generations, we're dealing with millions of years and animals that change in dramatic ways through the evolutionary process.

The previous year, the college at Berkeley had been adapting the program for use with extinct animals—chief among them, the dinosaurs. The program had evolved to the point where the software could make some pretty good educated guesses. Where extinct animals were involved, there were many in which the fossil records were incomplete. Sometimes, only a handful of bones, or even fragments of bones, were all that remained. By making comparisons to known species, taking into account the dimensions and uniqueness of the specimens, the program filled in the blanks and created a model of what the complete animal *might* look like. Of course the more complete the remains, the more chance of an accurate picture of the whole thing.

Months of experimenting led the paleontologists to believe that the system worked pretty well, but until more complete skeletons were unearthed, they would never be sure that some of the computer's creations were even close. Some of them were pretty outrageous and caused quite a stir among academia. It had quickly become a very expensive play-toy for many researchers, who would *invent* new data to input to the computer just to see who could come up with the most unusual concoction—the most bizarre, or terrifying looking creature.

A number of museums were beginning to use the program to help in reconstructing dinosaurs for their exhibits, and mine was no exception. I had spent nearly three weeks entering the bone data, and late on that last night I got to see the fruits of my labor. It was so fascinating that I stayed at my desk until the wee hours of the morning, playing with the program, trying different poses, and looking at the results from all different angles. I had been rather pleased with myself. Without a single phone call, I managed to figure out a way to get more than one figure on the screen at the same time.

Using the computer, I had been trying to determine the best means to portray my find to the public. I intended to keep trying different poses on the computer until I found just the right one before beginning the reconstruction process. The new program was a godsend. It was incredibly fast and it took out all of the guesswork. Before we could actually begin assembling the bones, the framework had to be constructed to support the weight of the skeleton. With the turn-of-the-century technology, the framework, referred to as an armature, could be fabricated from space-age metals, light in weight and very thin, thus was much less conspicuous than the frames used years ago. But the cost had increased proportionately, so we needed to get it right the first time. Before any of the work started, we would know exactly what the finished product was going to look like.

Not sure where I wanted to go with it, I decided to start at the beginning. I recreated the scene exactly as I saw it for the first time. Besides my memory, I had pictures to work from, and it took only a few hours to get the computer to arrange the bones exactly as they were in the picture. The computer even allowed me to design a custom background. By the end of the day I was finished and it was hard to tell the difference between what was on the CRT and what was in the picture.

I had worked late into the night and I had left my desk long enough to turn off the lights. The custodian had come in earlier and closed the blinds so the only light remaining was the faint glow of the illuminated exit sign in the hallway outside of my office and that which emanated from the glow of my computer's monitor. Using this little bit of light I carefully threaded my way back to my desk. I sat and stared at the image the program had created, and soon everything around me began to fade away. All that remained was the image on the screen. Everything else was hidden in darkness. I became a part of the scene before me. The here and now seemed to get all tangled up with the there and then, and I was again back at the cave in Utah.

*****

I had driven them all crazy at the hospital, forcing them to let me out a day earlier than they wanted to. My side still hurt like hell any time I moved too quickly and a deep breath still made me feel like my chest was going to explode. Of course they had me so taped up that it was hard to get a deep breath even if I wanted to. I made the mistake of sneezing once. It was a mistake that I didn't intend to repeat. I didn't care if I blew out my eyeballs from the backpressure—I was keeping all future sneezes contained.

Brian Huntsville picked me up at the hospital, after I first stopped in to check on Susan. I didn't stay with her long because there had been no change in her condition and I was both embarrassed and sad that I was getting out and she was not. Susan's doctor was just coming in to check on her as I was leaving, but he didn't say anything. He just wore the same sad expression that I saw whenever talking about Susan. I think that he was one of those "the glass is half empty" kinds of guys.

Brian seemed nearly as glad that I was out of the hospital as I was. Things had not progressed very far in my absence, and Brian was hoping that my presence would speed things up. With Susan and I both out of commission, the kids were unsure of how to proceed, afraid of making a mistake and somehow screwing up the site. The machine operators, on the other hand, refused to take any more risks until some additional safety precautions were put into place. So after six days, not a whole hell of a lot got done, and time was getting away from us. The days were getting shorter and the nights colder. We had to get our asses in gear.

As we drove up to the site, things looked pretty much as they did when the accident occurred, but Brian assured me that now that I was here, we were ready to proceed full-speed ahead. And, although the team hadn't made much progress on the mountain, Brian had been busy. He turned out to be talented in more than just the field of geology, and a better leader than one would suspect by his physical presence. He had ordered in a second crane, and with the help of the machine operators, had constructed a safety cage for the kids to work in. The cage was enclosed from the front and back to protect the workers from the swinging hook and falling rock, yet the upper portions of the sides were left open so to allow the workers access for their pry bars to reach the rocks. Additionally, Brian had installed a safety harness to keep the workers from accidentally stepping out of, or falling from the cage. I wished like hell that I had thought of it a few weeks earlier.

The kids were up on the pile as we drove up, and despite the aggravation of having to work around the cage, things looked like they were going pretty smoothly. I could hear the sounds of the pry bars clanging off the sides of the cage as they worked on a rather large rock. The design of the cage was really pretty ingenious. It was a double cage, with an opening in the middle, spanning maybe five feet. I watched as the cage was lowered so that the boulder was situated in the middle, between the two cages, and the kids began attacking it with the pry bars.

The cage offered an additional feature—the rails on the lower portion of the sides worked as a fulcrum, giving the pry bars some leverage over the rock. And they used it often—there was a considerable bend in the middle of the topmost rail. But it worked. I watched as the two of them put their bars under the rock from either side and in less than a minute, the rock was in the grips of the claw.

I got out of the car and headed for the base of the rock pile, when Brian asked where the hell I thought I was going. I tried to explain that I was going up and spell one of the kids, but Brian wasn't having any of that. He must have spoken with my doctor, because he wasn't about to let me back on the rocks again. But unless Brian was prepared to fight me, he wasn't going to stop me. I had been out of the action too long and I had way too much on my mind to just sit around and do nothing.

I started climbing, and I hadn't gone more than fifty feet, when I realized something—I was never going to make it to the top.

Climbing boulders was nothing like walking across a flat surface. I never realized before how much twisting and turning was involved in going over a rough surface. The last few days I had wandered the corridors of the hospital just getting used to walking again, but that hadn't prepared me for anything really physical. Nevertheless, I tried climbing a few more rocks when I felt myself getting dizzy, so very slowly I headed back down.

When I reached level ground again, Brian was standing there waiting for me with his arms folded and a great big smile on his face. Boy, I hated a smart ass! He knew that I'd be right back down and was ready for me. He handed me a walkie-talkie and pointed to a tent set up at the edge of the rock pile. The tent had an awning extending out toward the mountain, and beneath it sat a director's chair. I looked at Brian and he just stood there with that big stupid grin on his face and pointed to the chair, which was to become my home for the next few days.

Besides the walky-talky, I had a pair of binoculars and an ice chest filled with soft drinks. All the comforts of home, but I was antsy. It was damn hard for me to just sit there when the action was right in front of me. And I felt guilty, too. I was supposed to be in charge, yet here I was sitting in the shade, cold drink in hand, doing nothing constructive. My kids were taking all the risks, while I sat there comfortable and safe.

I kept thinking about Susan's accident, fearing a repeat performance, so I watched the kids like a hawk, cringing at the slightest misstep, holding my breath every time one of them leaned outside of the cage, every time the hook swung in their direction.

I couldn't stand just sitting there. After the first hour I got out of the chair and paced back and forth on flat ground just outside the leading edge of the rock pile. I did this for about fifteen minutes, until the pain in my side flared up and I was out of breath. To the delight of Brian, I returned grudgingly to my chair by the tent. But it didn't take long for my breathing to return to normal, and within a few hours, the pain subsided as well.

By the third day, I could pace my route for hours at a time without much pain, and I began to venture out carefully and slowly on to the larger boulders at the bottom of the pile. From my perch, I took to directing traffic between the two cranes. Using hand gestures to tell the operators which rocks to move out next and where to put them, I felt like a traffic cop, but without the whistle, which was just as well because the operators were already getting pissed off from the hand signals. I'm sure that they would have loved to give me a few hand gestures, as well, and I know where the whistle would have ended up.

Since my return I had watched the work go more smoothly from one day to the next, and the amount of rock moved from the pile increased almost exponentially each day. The kids were paired up in teams, working in two-hour shifts, moving from one rock to the next, with little wasted effort. They had gotten used to working within the cage and I rarely heard the hard metallic clang of metal on metal. It was very systematic. Only the really stubborn rocks required the pry bar from both sides, so they alternated. First one kid, working from the right side of one rock, would push the pry bar under, giving it one good push, using the guard rail for leverage, the claw latching on to the now loosened rock. Then, no sooner was the first rock on its way down, when the next kid had his pry bar under the next rock from the left side.

I had given the second walky-talky to the operator of the crane handling the claw, and from my perch on the rock, gave him his next target before he had even released the one he had. I felt useful again, but I suspect the work would have gone just as well without me. What I really wanted to do was to get back on top with one of the pry bars—to get closer to the opening of the cave—to be there when the discovery was made. But, I had to admit that this way was working too well to screw it up by interfering with the process.

We had finally cleared a narrow path all the way to the cave's entrance, but had not yet penetrated its opening, which was still solidly blocked. The path had to be widened further before it was safe enough to approach the entrance, so the cranes continued to move rock at the leading edge of the pile, continuously increasing the width at the point farthest from the mountain and gradually working forward. At the rate we were going, it wouldn't be more than a few more days before we were ready to attack the cave's entrance.

The weather had been perfect all day with clear blue skies and just an occasional white, fluffy cloud passing overhead. As the day was nearing its end, I turned away from the activity at the foot of the rock pile to see the sun disappear behind the mountains beyond the ridge. I was greeted by one of the most spectacular sights that I had ever witnessed. The sun was perfectly positioned behind the mountain's tip so that it looked like the mountain was wearing a crown of blazing fire, an impossibly bright light that faded into a sky made up of the most unbelievable colors of pinks, reds, and purples. The mountain itself seemed to burn from within, taking on the illusion of a shimmering mountain of gold.

Brian saw it too. He approached me from behind, lightly touching my arm, and we both stared silently at the magnificent sight until the colors began to fade back into their natural state. There's an old sailor's tale about a red sky at night, and I don't know much about that, but I took this magnificent gift as a portent of good things to come. It was still too soon to get a glimpse of what lay inside the cave, yet I knew that the next day's dawn was going to bring something special.

Anticipation kept me from sleeping well that night, and I arose early, at the first sign of daylight. Everyone else was still asleep, so I made the coffee, and with a fresh cup in hand, I wandered down the cleared area towards the cave's entrance. The scientist in me came out as I scoured the area, my head down, looking for more clues as to what we might find when we at last got to the bottom of the cave.

Other than the scrapings made by the shovel of the bulldozer, there was little of interest, although I still experienced wonder. Thanks to Brian's hypnotic episode upon his arrival to the site, I had little trouble picturing what this area looked like a hundred million years ago. I felt that if I closed my eyes, and turned away from the cave, I would be able to see the dense foliage with the sea just beyond. And if I returned my sights to the mountain, I would see the cave, unblocked by the tons of rubble. But, I lacked Brian's gift, and I wasn't able to enter the mystical cave without him to guide me.

I managed to force myself back to the present, continuing to stare at the ground in the half-light of the new day, trying to find something—anything. As I got closer and closer to the cave, the path narrowed and the debris on either side of me rose higher and higher into the air. It reminded me of the scene from the *Ten Commandments*, with the tribes of Israel walking through the parted waters of the Red Sea. I only hoped that the walls of this gallery didn't collapse on me as they did on the Egyptian charioteers.

The end of the path was still in shadow, the sun not yet high enough in the sky for its rays to reach the foot of the mountain. I restricted my search to the forward portion of the cleared area, where the sun was already heating up the rock. The kids who cleared it had already inspected most of the area closely, so I concentrated on the ground just at the edge of the path where the excavation would take place that day. I paced back and forth along both edges, each time getting a little bit closer to the mountain as the shadows continued to recede.

After about twenty minutes, I had pretty much explored all the area that was not in shadow, so I decided to have a seat on one of the boulders piled closest to the cave's mouth and wait for the sun to come to me. The last of the shadows cleaved the pathway into two distinct areas of nearly black and white, so sharp was the contrast. The line separating the two was like a razor's edge and was advancing towards me, speeding along the scraped ground. I watched it approach, closer and closer, all the while unconsciously kicking at the pebbles alongside my stone seat.

The sunlight reached the tip of my boots, changing its color from chocolate brown to brilliant yellow as it moved quickly past and started up my leg. Its radiant rays warmed me as they continued up my body, relaxing me, clearing my mind of all problems and concerns. Had the earth quit spinning around the sun just at the moment that its rays hit my chin, I suppose that I just would have sat there forever, warm and comfortable—at peace. But the earth kept moving, as did the sunshine, making the brief trip past my nose and directly into my eyes.

My pupils must have contracted to mere pinpoints and for several seconds I was nearly blind. There were no clouds in the sky, and the sun, sitting low on the horizon, seemed twice its normal size and brilliance. I turned my back on it, waiting for my eyesight to return to normal. After a few moments, I turned, shielding my eyes from the sun by looking down at the ground, and returned to my search of the unexplored territory.

I didn't spot anything of particular interest until I returned to the spot where I had started—my granite throne. Still using the toe of my boot to shove aside the smallest of the rocks piled up against that particular boulder, I noticed that one refused to move. Trying again, I found that the rock was lying in a depression of some kind, and I had to exert a little upward pressure from the side of my boot's sole before it sprang free. Squatting down on one knee, I brushed the area clean of all the dust and dirt to discover two cup-shaped depressions, side by side, like two half moons almost touching at the corners. They were perhaps half an inch deep, and grew wider as they disappeared under the rock. It looked like the impression left by the heel of a dinosaur—a good-sized one—a *rex* perhaps.

Being that we had already discovered more than a dozen *Tyrannosaur* tracks during the excavation, the new find wasn't much to get really excited about, although I was happy to find another one *there*. We had made steady progress towards the cave's entrance, but hadn't found a new print in days. I was afraid that maybe we were looking at the outer edge of a game trail, or perhaps just some random tracks, rather than the entrance to an animal's dwelling. If it was indeed another print beneath the rock, another *Tyrannosaur* print, we could be sure that at least one *rex* had an interest in this particular spot, although not necessarily the cave itself.

I was still brushing dirt away from the area surrounding the small depression, when a shadow fell over me. "What are you doing here, Doc? We're ready to get to work." I looked up to see one of the crane operators standing by.

The guy spoke in the most arrogant way, which really pissed me off. The last time that I had checked I was still the boss. "Your vehicle's way over there. Fire it up. I'll let you know when I'm done here, I yelled back in a no-nonsense tone." Well, at least he wasn't stupid. He skulked back to his machine without uttering a word—at least not out loud.

During the next twenty minutes, the kids began staggering out of their tents, grabbing coffee, and milling about aimlessly, waiting for things to get organized. James, who was not only the biggest, but apparently the most curious, wandered over to me, asking where I wanted to begin today. When

I showed him the partially exposed print, he was less than impressed, but agreed it was as good a place as any to begin the day's work.

As James went off to fetch the rest of my team, I saw Brian emerge from his lab, which was also where he slept. Brian was a bit of a health nut, so he bypassed the coffeepot and headed straight for me. When he saw where we were about to begin work, he immediately got down on all fours, putting his face against the rock that hid the footprint. But he wasn't looking at the print. Rather, he had his eyes tightly shut and a look of rapture on his face. He remained that way for several minutes, unaware of the gathering crowd around him. The kids had no idea what was going on, but I did—I had seen it once before.

His eyes still closed, Brian began talking in a whisper, but speaking to no one. I approached him from behind, cautiously, not wanting to break his concentration or interfere with his monologue. I missed the first several words, and what I did hear didn't make much sense. "... is why we came here. Here is where we'll find what we're looking for." He wasn't in the same trance that I had witnessed several weeks ago on the day of his arrival. This time he was aware of where he was, and *when* he was, and he knew that I was there with him. "Move this rock David. Beyond it you will find what you've been looking for your entire life."

It was crazy talk. "Brian, there's nothing under this rock but another print ... maybe. I've seen a hundred prints—a thousand prints—what's one more? I sure as hell haven't waited my whole life for it."

Brian wasn't looking at me, but I knew that he heard me because he kept shaking his head from side to side, saying, "No, no, no, no!" He had a warm smile on his face, as if someone had just shared the most extraordinary secret with him. "Not under the rock, beyond it. In the cave—that's where you'll find it. That's where you'll find what you've been looking for all your life."

Call me crazy, but I believed him. I had no idea what he was talking about, but I believed him nonetheless.

The problem was we weren't quite ready to excavate the cave. "What do you see Brian?" I asked. "Is it dinosaurs? Are there dinosaurs buried in the cave?"

"Yes," he answered. "But David, there's more ... so much more."

There were tons and tons of debris on top of and piled up alongside the entrance. We were going to have to back off to a safe distance and approach it methodically from all angles, working slowly so as not to damage whatever it was that we found.

I ordered the operators of the bulldozers to begin cutting into the pile beginning from the path made down the center and parallel to the face of the mountain, about a hundred feet out, and then to start working their way in towards the cave. Meanwhile, I had the crane operators and the kids concentrate their efforts on only those rocks directly in front of the cave's entrance, only venturing beyond those boundaries to keep the slope from caving in and recovering the area.

*****

It was three weeks later and I was sitting at my usual spot at Susan's bedside. I had been coming here each evening after leaving the site, and, as hard as it was to see her so unresponsive after all this time, it had become one of the highlights of my day. The excitement at the dig continued to build, and knowing that Susan would have been as excited about the impending discovery as I was, I thought that in telling her what happened I would somehow get through to her. I started that day's talk, as I did every day, by recapping the most recent events.

It had taken nearly the whole three weeks leading up to that day to clear out all of the rock in front of the cave, but it had been an incredible and exciting three weeks. The work had gone well at first, the pace quick and efficient. Progress was sure and steady, the distance to the cave shrinking rapidly. At first there was nothing to impede our march towards the cave's entrance, and aside from Brian's prediction, nothing to make the kids feel that we were onto something. Yet, the excitement was maintained at a fever's pitch by Brian's constant motivation. He was all over the place, spelling the kids in the cage, getting them sandwiches and drinks, directing traffic between the cranes and bulldozers, anything to keep them going. He even tried to take a turn operating one of the bulldozers, but the operator told him NO WAY—something about union rules—or some silly nonsense like that.

By the end of the first week, my health had pretty much returned to normal. I could climb around on the rocks, work the pry bars, and about anything else that was required, with only an occasional twinge of pain in my side. I bounced around from place to place, issuing directions, talking on the walky-talky—trying to be useful. But I really didn't have much to do because Brian had everything under control. So it became my job to scout each new area as it was uncovered, knowing that if we missed something as we went speeding along recklessly, the damage could be irreparable. The team had to be ready to stop at a moment's notice when, and if, we found the beginnings of any new evidence. It was my job to find that evidence. It had taken more than a week before I found it, but from that point on things happened very quickly.

We had cleared more than half the distance to the base of the mountain, and on a few occasions were forced to slow down because we *thought* that we had found something of interest. But every time it turned out to be nothing: an imperfection in the rock, an unusually shaped stone, a strange coloration of the soil—nothing of significance. All of that changed very quickly six days after I first spotted the partial print under the bolder at the foot of the mountain.

We had been working in two crews—the first moving directly toward the cave's opening, and the second working the periphery of the clearing. The second crew's bulldozer had just cleared a stretch of ground about two hundred feet from the cave's opening, a hundred feet west of where the first print was found. As the equipment backed out of the area, I moved in to search the ground, as I had become accustomed to doing several times a day. I paced back and forth atop the newly cleared territory using my feet to brush away the small stones and pebbles missed by the bulldozer. I was searching for the smallest of traces—trying to isolate them from the normal imperfections of the ground and the markings left by the bulldozer. I must have passed over the same ground a half dozen times without seeing it. At the risk of using a worn out old cliché, I guess I just couldn't see the forest for the trees.

It wasn't some small portion of a print hiding under a rock, or small piece of fossilized bone protruding through the soil. This was an area of at least two hundred square yards that was *covered* with footprints. Nearly the entire area exposed in the most recent pass of the bulldozer was covered with them, and what was most unusual was the direction of the prints. We were hoping for a clear trackway, leading either directly into or away from the cave—one print following another, the distance between them matching the length of the animal's stride. But these prints were everywhere and pointing in all directions—print on top of print. Something had happened here, but it was too soon to figure out what it was.

I had missed it at first because it was the last thing that I expected. I was looking for something unique, something that stood out from the surrounding area. But, like looking for a ketchup spot on a very loud tie—I'm so intent in finding the spot that I never even notice the pattern on the tie. Only by standing back, looking at the entire area, rather than just that of a few square feet, could I discern something different and special.

Standing on my old perch at the top of the pile, it was as clear as could be and I was astounded that I didn't pick up on it earlier. Yet at the same time, amazed that I was able to spot it at all, there was so much of it.

Once we knew what to look for we were able to narrow the search, and stop wasting time clearing out areas in which we were unlikely to find anything of interest. In the future perhaps some other paleontologist would clear the rest of the area, looking for any scraps that we left behind.

Someday, I would return, tying up any loose ends that might come to light in the weeks and months to come—but not just then. We were heading on a straight path—from the prints to the entrance of the cave.

The search was narrowed, but progress was slow because we didn't dare run the risk of ruining the tracks that we were uncovering. We kept the bulldozers on the edge of the track field, always working in towards the cave. We used the cranes to pick up the rock in the middle of the field, lifting them straight up and over without damaging the area. Brian helped the kids carry off the smaller rocks and brush away the dirt and sand from the prints. I stayed busy with my notepad, making rough sketches of some of the more interesting or unusual tracks and markings. I had one of the crane operators take me up in the basket so that I could get some aerial photographs of the entire area as it was cleared.

We worked from sun up to sun down for the next two weeks, the length of day getting shorter from one to the next. Each afternoon, when the sun passed behind the mountain the temperature plummeted, forcing us into our sweatshirts and jackets so that we could keep working. Nights were colder yet, and we took to passing the time sitting in front of a bonfire each evening. The last few mornings before we reached the cave's entrance, we saw some early morning frost. Winter weather was only a few weeks away.

At the end of two weeks, we had reached the cave, and uncovered all the tracks in the area immediately in front of it. Although it wasn't easy to see at ground level, the view from above, as captured in the photos, was remarkable, and revealed an amazing story. The majority of the footprints belonged to a *Tyrannosaur*, and judging from the size and shape, I was betting a single, adult male—a big one. To everyone's surprise, interspersed within the melee of prints were those of another creature, clearly not those of another *Tyrannosaur*. Many of the prints, especially in the center of the area, were smeared and twisted out of shape, almost beyond recognition. Some of them were obliterated by scrapings and deep gouges cut into the earth.

By moving away from the main area, we were able to isolate the prints of the second animal. There were a series of other trackways that emerged out of nowhere, about sixty feet to the left of the entrance of the cave and merged with the others in front of it. These were at least two distinct sets of prints, and possibly a third—at least one adult and one adolescent—without a doubt those of the *Triceratops horridus,* long believed to be a chief prey of the *Tyrannosaur*. I didn't need Brian's visions to see for myself what had happened here. I wandered over to where the first *T-top* footprint emerged, staring at it, letting my mind drift back some seventy million years ago.

It was morning. Dense fog, still heavy with moisture from the thunderstorm the night before, hugged the ground, hiding all but the tallest trees. The mountains, rising from it like a chain of volcanic peaks from a primordial ocean, reached into a gray sky that was just beginning to allow the first shafts of sunlight through. Raindrops still clung to the flowering plants, dropping occasionally, soundlessly, as they hit the saturated earth below, running down the gentle slope to the pool forming at the front of the cave.

The forest was just coming to life, the sound of birds singing, occasionally interrupted by the voice of a bullfrog seeking its mate. A single splash from the river beyond could be heard as a fish jumped out of the water in search of its morning meal. The flapping of great leathery wings resonated off the walls of the cliff as a flying mammal searched for its morning perch. Periodically, the roar of one of the larger animals, proclaiming to the world that it was now awake, broke the peaceful setting. And beneath it all, a constant low-level buzzing could be heard as the insects and smaller forest creatures began their never-ending daily activity of finding food and shelter.

Suddenly, the quiet is shattered by the noise of a thousand birds flying from their nests, their cries of alarm echoing through the valley, darting as one away from the mountain, scattering in all directions. What is left when their calls fade away is an eerie silence that is but a clue of impending danger. It can be felt, even before there is a sound. There is just the slightest of vibration coming up from the ground, and it continues to build until it reaches a frequency and intensity that is audible. Heavy footsteps are moving quickly towards the cave, crashing through the dense brush that surrounds the base of the mountain. Now, breathing can be heard above the din—short, explosive breaths that are labored, difficult—sounds of frightened and tired animals. And they're getting closer.

The head of the lead Triceratops, its massive seven-foot frill held low, the two curved horns pointed menacingly straight ahead, enters the clearing in front of the cave. The small family had become separated from the herd somehow and in a confused frenzy had charged blindly through the forest, guided only by the cliffs on their left flank. The sudden change in scenery as they emerged from the dense growth brought the one in the lead to a sudden stop, its head lifted high into the air, sniffing for a familiar scent. The big animal gasps for air—nostrils flaring—breath visible in the cool, damp air. It proceeds slowly, cautiously now, catching the scent of something familiar, but not at all pleasant. It comes within a few feet of the cave's entrance when the smell became recognizable. The beast's eyes go wide with terror, as it tries to reverse its direction and head away from the cave—away from the source of the terrible smell. But an animal of that size and weight can't change direction instantly, and it is caught as it turns away from the gaping mouth of the cave.

The Tyrannosaur comes out of the cave and strikes at the Triceratops with near blinding speed. The six-inch long razor sharp teeth of the rex sink into the back of its prey, just below the base of the thick tail. At that instant, the Triceratops turns to face its enemy, huge chunks of meat pulling away from its hindquarters as the Tyrannosaur loses its purchase. Blood spurts from the ruined backside of the wounded animal, spraying into the nose and eyes of the attacker, enraging it. The Tyrannosaur raises its head and emits a deafening roar that echoes throughout the valley as the Triceratops lowers his head, preparing to defend itself.

The Triceratops understands intuitively that it is no match for the larger, quicker predator and it begins to back away, its head low to the ground, its eyes searching for a way out. The Tyrannosaur, ever wary of the lethal twin horns of the Triceratops, pauses, lowering its head, staring directly into the eyes of its foe. Saliva, tinged pink with the three-horned animal's blood drips to the ground in front of the cowering beast, and the Tyrannosaur snorts its contempt for it. It takes two huge strides along side the Triceratops, casually, as if it were moving away, when suddenly, at unbelievable speed, it swings around, lunging at the animal's neck, just behind its bony frill. But the Triceratops is a savvy veteran of such encounters, knowing full well the tactics of the ferocious carnivore. As the Tyrannosaur moves to the side, the Triceratops pivots towards the attacker, keeping its head low, its pointed chin digging a deep curved gash into the mud. Instinctively, it raises his head just as the Tyrannosaur attacks, burying one of its three-foot long horns into the soft abdomen of the rex. At the same instant the Tyrannosaur's powerful jaws clamped down on the neck of the Triceratops, its teeth severing an artery.

Each animal has suffered a severe wound, but each refuses to yield. Blood is pouring down the sides of both, mixing together in the mud. The Tyrannosaur is impaled on the horn of the Triceratops, unable to extricate itself without first letting go. It is killing itself by not doing so. The Triceratops is dying, and no longer has the strength to raise its head on its own. By releasing the Triceratops, its horn will slip free, but instead, the rex holds tight, throwing his massive head from side to side, trying to inflict still more damage. And with each movement the horn tears deeper and wider into the belly of the Tyrannosaur.

The Triceratops is dead—its neck broken in the mighty jaws of the fierce Tyrannosaur. Even knowing it has won, the Tyrannosaur refuses to release its grip, instead using the last of its strength to drag its massive prize the few yards into the cave to feed. In the exhilaration of victory, and in the anticipation of the well-deserved reward, the rex momentarily forgets the painful wound. But the blood continued to flow from the animal in huge and life-threatening quantities, and as it drags its meal into the cave, the horn continues to dig deeper into its stomach.

Inside the cave, safe from other carnivores that would try to commandeer the kill, the Tyrannosaur finally releases the Triceratops from its jaws. As the dead animal crashes to the ground, the horn slides from the belly of the Tyrannosaur, releasing a stream of deep red blood—too much blood. The Tyrannosaur, now understanding its own mortality, raises its head and makes one last earth-shattering roar before staggering and falling to the ground alongside the Triceratops, their blood mingling one last time as it soaks into the ground.

I smiled down at Susan, knowing that she loved a good story, especially if it included dinosaurs. Of course, I don't know how much of it was true. What we had found in front of the cave—the *Triceratops* trackways, the riot of prints from at least two different animals, and the long furrows leading into the entrance of the cave—were significant clues to a battle between the two animals—and probably the inevitable victory of the *Tyrannosaur*, as well. Everything else was pure fantasy.

Had Susan been able to talk, the scientist in her would have questioned every one of my statements, forcing me to use facts and evidence to support every part of my story. But I had no evidence that the *Tyrannosaur* died in the cave, or was even injured in the fight. I couldn't even be certain that there *was* a fight, although I could not have explained the mix and quantity of footprints in any other way. Hell, the *rex* may have lived for another fifty years, and maybe it didn't even live in the cave. Maybe it just used the cave to feast on the *Triceratops*—if *that* actually happened—because the cave just happened to be there—it was convenient. But I liked my story better, and Susan was in no position to argue.

In another few weeks we would know the truth. There was nothing left but the contents of the cave, and the first thing the next day we would begin the task of digging it out. Although what we had found so far insured the success of the expedition, I wasn't yet satisfied. I knew that the best was yet to come.

I was awakened by one of the janitors working the early shift. He came into my office to empty the trash, turning the lights on, putting an abrupt end to my dream of the cave. I had fallen asleep while staring at the scene on the computer screen and subsequently dreamed of the cave. I remembered clearly my conversation with Susan, and my fantasy battle between the *Tyrannosaur* and *Triceratops*, but I wasn't sure which part were my memories and which part was a dream. As I wakened fully, the part that was a dream was sure to fade, as dreams always seem to do. But none of it did. Which meant that either it was a most unusual dream, or it wasn't a dream at all, a thought that did little to excite me. The dream, like the discovery of the cave, should have left me breathless with excitement and anticipation. Instead I was left with feelings of frustration and emptiness, because I had no one to share it with. Well, technically I did share it with Susan, but if she wasn't able to hear it, did it matter that I said it? I hoped so, but I doubted it. I wasn't getting anywhere at all with her, and even *my* hopes were beginning to crumble. In despair, I tried to hide from the thoughts of Susan by thinking of something else, but only managed to wander into an equally depressing memory. It had been well over a year that Liz had been gone, and the agony of her death had been replaced by an emptiness that begged to be filled. So I filled the emptiness with rage. Liz's killers were still on the loose, and although Jakes assured me that they would be caught, I wasn't convinced, and my anger had become a sickness, eating at me like some super-aggressive form of cancer. Each time it got a hold of me, I became despondent, unable to function like a normal human being. I found myself coming out of it as if from a trance, staring off into space, oblivious to everything—my heart racing, sweat running down my face, and my body trembling uncontrollably. The spells sometimes lasted for hours and seemed to be getting longer each time. If I wasn't able to find an outlet for my anger, I was afraid that one day I wouldn't come back at all.

CHAPTER 5

On legs of rubber, I stepped out from under the bar and out of the power rack. Blood rushed from every part of my body to oxygenate my quadriceps as I struggled to eke out one last rep, leaving me dizzy and gasping for air. As I tried to massage some feeling back into my legs, I glanced up to see some of the other regulars watching me, a couple of them giving me the thumbs up as they dispersed to go back to their own routines. I had been doing squats—an impressive exercise because of the weight involved, and had just done a personal best—ten reps at 465 pounds—not too bad for a scientist.

With only a few seconds of rest, I moved over to the leg extension table and began pumping out repetitions at my warm-up weight. I held the weight at full extension for one second, squeezing the muscles, watching the striations become more defined with each successive rep, feeling the muscles heat up until the burn was nearly unbearable. Pausing between sets for only seconds at a time, I continued to increase the weight until I was using the entire stack. I didn't count the reps—I just kept going until the muscles failed. The last rep I held for as long as I could bear it, feeling as if the muscles were about to explode through the skin. I could feel the blood pulsing in the vein at my temple, and I screamed, expelling oxygen into my bloodstream, holding on for one more second.

The scream brought the gym to a momentary standstill. Some of the newcomers and part-timers stared at me with wide eyes and mouths gaping, wondering if I was nuts. The instructors and the regulars just looked at me and smiled. They were used to me and my assortment of grunts, groans, whimpers, and shouts. They also knew to keep their distance. I wasn't nuts, but I was a loner, and I preferred to workout by myself. Besides, no one could keep up with me. When I was at the gym, I was an animal.

As I set up the weights for my final exercise, the leg curl, I thought about why that was. Why did I punish myself night after night, pushing myself harder and harder, past the point of exhaustion? I had worked with weights since high school. I was never really into team sports, and didn't run around with a crowd in school. Lifting weights was one thing that I could do on my own, and it was the one thing in sports where I could actually see the results as I slowly molded my physique, changing my appearance.

I curled the weight with my legs, pulling my feet back towards my hips, feeling the familiar cramping of my leg biceps, counting the reps, finishing my first set. I added more weight, lying flat on my stomach, pulling my toes forward to stretch out the muscle, preparing for the next set. I stared straight ahead, not focusing on anything, but thinking only about the next set.

I started again, concentrating hard on the first few reps until the body started to take control and the mind began to drift back to the question—what was I doing here?

Throughout high school and college I continued to work out every day, but it was never little more than a hobby. School never came easy for me and by the end of each school day I felt drained mentally, the day's lessons confusing and the homework daunting. The gym was a refuge, a place where I could go after school and work my body rather than my mind. By the end of each workout, I felt refreshed—my mind cleared, ready, if not eager, to hit the books once again.

I was straining to complete my last set and I still hadn't answered the question that had been haunting this day's workout. I thought about why I started this hobby and why I continued it through all those years of school, why I was still at it. At some point it had become more than just a hobby. Why had I taken it to nearly a maniacal state—beyond that of passion, almost an addiction?

I knew the answer to the question even if I didn't like to think about it. I stood in front of the wall of mirrors as I always did at the completion of my workout, thinking about the answer. I flexed each muscle, one at a time, checking my progress, looking for imperfections that I could work on the next day.

I stood with my hands on my hips, shoulders pulled forward to spread my lats—my right leg slightly forward and turned to expose the calf. I squeezed every muscle with everything that I had, trying to control the trembling caused by such exertion.

Finishing my routine, I relaxed my body, staring into the eyes of my own reflection, ready to finally answer the question. It really wasn't much different now than it was when I was in school, except for the intensity. It was escape, plain and simple—escape from the sadness caused by the death of my wife—escape from the anger for the people who took her from me—escape from the frustration of watching Susan lay there day after day, unable to speak, to move, to think—unable to fill the void that had become such a big part of my life. And it was escape from the blame that I placed on myself for what happened that last terrible night in the cave.

For at least a couple of hours a day, I could clear my mind of all the emotions. I could escape into the blissful pain of tortured muscle and heaving lungs. For those two hours, I could tune everything else out, hearing nothing but the clanking of iron and the sound of my own labored breathing. I saw nothing but the machine in front of me, and my own reflection staring back at me from a hundred mirrors. My thoughts were only of the next rep, the next set—one more time, five more pounds. It was but a small part of each day when I was free of the memories that haunted my days and tormented my nights.

The nightmares had become more regular and more real each night since Susan's accident. In them, I relived that terrible scene on the rock pile, but in the dream, everything was in slow motion. I saw the huge iron claw coming toward her while her arms reached out for something that wasn't there. The claw was moving so slowly, yet my mind seemed to move at regular speed, and each night I knew that I had all the time in the world to rescue her. But as I tried to react, I found that I could move no faster than the speed at which the hook was moving. In the dream, I was reaching out to her, shouting out a warning as I did so. But my warning and my reactions were always too slow to stop it from happening … over and over again.

The daylight hours were not any better. My work, which I had always been able to throw myself into when I needed to escape other problems in my life, was so interwoven with Susan's that focusing on mine alone was impossible. Every move that I made, every thought that I had, made me think of Susan. Each time that I wasn't quite sure how to proceed, I'd wonder how she would have done it. Every time I saw the pictures of the cave and its contents, I remembered that Susan should have been there with me. And with each step that I took in the reconstruction, I knew that she would have been a part of it—guiding me—challenging me.

I was still staring at my reflection. How had I gotten so old so quickly? Oh, the years weren't all that obvious—the average person on the street wouldn't see them. Years of exercise and good diet had left a youthful appearance. And at well over six feet, and a physique that many consider freakish, people tend to see my size—the thickness of my arms, the width of my shoulders, the girth of my neck. They wouldn't even see it in my face unless they looked really closely. They *would* be able to see it in my eyes. The truth can always be found in the eyes, and mine looked very old indeed.

I usually ended my workouts feeling better than at any time of the day. The fifteen minutes of posing usually made me feel good about myself, and the troubles that I had to face later, forgotten ... but not on that day. On that day I looked a little too closely in the mirror—a little too closely at my own reflection. My eyes reminded me that all was not right in my little world. I turned away from the mirrors, seeing that there were several others watching me. It wasn't unusual. A small crowd often gathered to watch me pose. Some of the regulars watched because they were into it, and others were just curious. On that day it was different. The look was more one of concern. I guess that I had been looking at my reflection too long after the posing was done.

I had just one thing left to do to complete my workout, and even though on that day I hadn't found the peace that I usually did, I wasn't going to give in. With a good sweat going, I liked to extend it for another twenty minutes in the sauna. After a great workout, it was a wonderful sensation to sweat without having to work for it. I was hopeful that on that day, the warmth and quiet would calm me and help me forget what the weights had not.

I sat alone on the wooden bench, gazing though the glass wall across from the pool, watching the remaining few people finishing their routines. I turned up the heat a couple of extra degrees, and the sweat ran down my face, dripping from my chin, forming a pool on the bench between my feet. I felt the temperature increase, forcing more sweat from my pores, relaxing my tired muscles. It was hotter than was deemed healthy by the manufacturer of the sauna, and it was more than most of the other members could take, but I was alone in the room. I could feel the heat pressing on my flesh, as if wrapped in a hot blanket, and I loved the sensation.

I loved the heat. The cold, on the other hand, was something different. To me, cold was a painful thing, a tangible thing that went right to the bone like a knife. It sapped my strength, and made it hard to think, as if every muscle and brain cell shifted to a lower setting to conserve energy.

While sitting in the sauna, I liked to think about some of the times when it was really cold—not a difficult thing when you lived in Chicago, where the winters could be as bitter as any in the country. It gave me a sense of power over nature to sit in that warm cocoon, and think back to some situation where I was so cold that I thought I'd never be warm again. I was thinking of such a time then. I was back at the cave in Utah ... we had not been able to beat the coming of winter.

*****

The wind blew hard against the mountain, causing the air inside the cave to resonate with a high-pitched whistle. I shivered inwardly, thinking of the temperature drop that was sure to occur in the hours to follow. Walking over to the cave's entrance, I pulled the sweatshirt hood over my head before peering outside. The wind brought tears to my eyes, making it hard to focus on the activity around the tents, some two hundred feet away. As I wiped my eyes, I could hear fragmented shouts carried over the distance by the howling wind. When my vision cleared, I saw several of my team struggling to keep the tents from blowing away. I tried yelling to them, but the sound of my voice wouldn't carry in that direction.

I told the others in the cave to stay put, and headed out into the gale. Arriving at the campsite, I had to yell to be heard over the wind and the shouting of the others. I grabbed the first kid that I saw and told him to get the others, grab their gear, and take shelter in Brian's mobile lab. I found James and told him I was going back to the cave to wait out the storm. I would have liked for all of us to go to the lab where there was some warmth, but there just wasn't enough room for everyone. Before heading back to the cave myself, I went over to check on Brian in the lab, and to tell him he was about to have some visitors.

Despite its mass, the lab was swaying noticeably from the wind, which was striking it broadside. Brian was running all over the place trying to keep his precious equipment from tumbling onto the floor. He was on the verge of panic, and I had to grab him by both arms to get him to stop. At first he struggled, forcing me to tighten my grip until I saw the pain in his eyes. Backing off slightly, I continued to hold on, looking directly into his eyes I said, "The kids are on the way over. They're scared shitless. They need someone to calm them down. You're up for that, right?"

I took Brian's keys, yelling loudly over the sound of the wind, "Get everything tied down. What you can't, pile under the benches." While Brian went to work, I went forward and jumped into the driver's seat. Firing the engine up, I slammed it into gear, and drove it directly into the wind. Immediately, the violent swaying from side to side stopped, leaving only a mild rolling sensation from front to back. I looked back at Brian who was staring down at his shoes in embarrassment for not thinking of moving the lab and for losing his cool. I touched his shoulder gently and he nodded a reply. It was a silent thanks for settling things down. I returned the nod and left the lab just as the kids were tumbling in.

It was nearly dark as I reentered the cave, arriving just seconds before the first of the freezing rain began. The wind blew the needle-like slivers of ice directly into the cave, forcing us to move off to the sides of the entrance for protection. I could hear the icy shards die on the mountain as they crashed against the granite surface, sliding down, leaving behind a glistening coat. A couple of the kids had grabbed whatever spare blankets they could find as they fled the tents, but there wasn't enough to go around. There were six of us, so we split into two groups, half on one side of the entrance, and half on the other. We huddled together as best we could, sharing the blankets and each other's warmth.

We were cold, but at least we had light. With the days getting shorter and the temperature dropping day after day, we had begun to work into the night in an attempt to get the excavation completed before the really bad weather started. The lab was powered by a gas generator, which we had connected to portable floodlights positioned throughout the cave. Unfortunately I hadn't thought to bring in heaters. I made a mental note to order them the very next day.

I watched the ice blast into the cave, driven by seventy mile per hour winds, forming a slick skin on the floor of the cave that extended nearly to the wall at the opposite end, and bringing the temperature to near freezing. If I hadn't been so damn cold, I would have enjoyed the sight. The bright light from the floods bounced off the ice particles, reflecting and refracting this way and that, like a giant kaleidoscope. Like a billion tiny prisms, light of every color of the spectrum filled the interior of the cave, and created huge rainbows around each of the light sources.

Like precious jewels, the tiny weapons struck the floor with such intensity that the sound was nearly deafening, as if a ton of pebbles were dropped upon a tin roof over our heads.

I tried to shout across the entrance of the cave to check on the others huddled there, but if they heard me they didn't respond, the sound of my voice no doubt absorbed by the roar that separated us. I looked around at the two kids next to me. They looked cold and afraid, but no more than I. I got out from under the blankets and stood looking down at them. "Stay warm," I ordered. "This will pass in a couple of hours." The look in their eyes told me that they doubted it. I didn't say so, but I doubted it, too.

The storm was intensifying, and the only way around its path was to stay close to the interior walls of the cave and go all the way to the back. But even the wall opposite the cave's entrance was slick with ice. The winds were getting even stronger now, forcing the ice farther into the cave. I could see it striking the wall a foot or two up from the floor, part of it bouncing back, and part of it running down to the floor, freezing as it went.

I put my hand out, into the ice, and pulled it back instantly. Like I had just placed it onto a hot stove, it felt as if my hand had been shot with a thousand tiny arrows, and I thought that I would pull back a bloody stump. But to my relief, it still looked like a hand, a very white hand. As I watched, the ice was already melting, leaving the skin beneath red and raw. I knew that if I was going to make it safely to the other side, I was going to have to move fast, and keep any exposed skin out of the path of the ice.

I tried kind of a sideways jump with my back facing the incoming ice, which proved to be a mistake. My leap had not taken me much more than half way across, and when my leading foot touched down, there was nothing but ice to land on. As my feet went out from under me I seemed to defy the law of gravity. I went up in the air higher than I would have thought possible and landed directly on my shoulders and the back of my head. Momentarily stunned, I made a greater mistake by turning my face directly into the path of the driving ice, which blinded me instantly, the pain turning to numbness almost as quickly. Lying on my side, turning away from the ice, I tried as best I could to cover my head with my arms, all the while trying to use my feet to push my body across the floor.

I made little progress, as my feet found no friction to push against. The freezing rain struck my back and legs, running down to the ice beneath, refreezing almost at once, causing my clothing to stick fast to the ice. One hand struck the ground, and that too froze, a layer of skin remaining behind as I ripped it free. I spun a quarter turn, tearing my clothing free of the ice, and lying on my back with my head nearly up against the back wall of the cave, I began to roll.

Rolling, slipping, and sliding, making slow but steady progress—bits of clothing and skin being left behind—I eventually made it across to dry ground. I lay there for several seconds, curled up in a tight ball, taking stock of my assortment of aches and pains. There were raw patches on both hands where the skin had been torn off and my knuckles were sore and discolored, yet there was very little blood, undoubtedly due to the intense cold. I could feel another raw patch on my right cheek, and the back of my head throbbed where it had struck the ice. My eyes burned, but I was relieved to see bright light, even though I couldn't get anything to focus.

Over the din, I could hear the three kids, now on my side of the cave, crying out to me, their fear of the storm momentarily replaced by concern for me. I raised one arm high into the air to let them know that I was okay, but it was still another minute or so before I tried to get up. When I did, it was very slowly, feeling new pains with each movement, my already damaged ribs alive with fresh pain caused by the fall. I looked down to see my clothes in tatters, but I felt generally in one piece.

As I limped over to the kids, I looked at them, realizing that all three were among the newest of my team. When school started back in September, I lost most of the diggers to college commitments, and had to replace them with others who were taking a semester off for fieldwork. They were good kids and hard workers, but they sure as hell hadn't signed up for *this*. I looked them over carefully as I spoke to them, reassuring them, noting that Christine, the youngest and smallest of the group, looked paler than the others, and hardly spoke. She was trembling, and I could see that she had been crying, pale trails burned into her already white cheeks.

There were two blankets to share between the three of them. To their surprise, I pulled both from around their shoulders. I rearranged the trio so that Christine was between the other two, pushed them tight against one another, and put the blankets back around them. "Don't worry guys, I've seen much worse than this," I lied. "Storms don't get too bad around here and they never seem to last very long, especially this time of year. It'll be over before you know it."

But the temperature continued to drop. The rain had turned to snow, and was still blowing into the cave at the same velocity, covering the ice with a fresh blanket of white. I was concerned about Christine, and felt that I had a duty to stay with her, to protect her, but there wasn't much that I could do for her. If I hunkered down against the wall with the other three, I would just deprive someone of their share of blanket. And I was freezing. The trip over had left me soaked to the bone, and if I didn't get some warmth, I was going to be in serious trouble. I decided to return to the other side.

There were already several inches of fresh snow on the floor, and, even though still blowing hard, was not nearly as slippery—or as painful—as the ice. Getting wetter in the process, I made it back across uneventfully. The two kids huddled there seemed no worse than when I left them, but were obviously glad to see me. I slid in alongside them, taking an outside position, and they wrapped me in a portion of blanket. I pulled my feet in as close to my body as I could, pulled tight the cord on my hood so that I just had a slot to see through, and put my hands inside my jacket. I tried to make myself as small as possible, as if there would be less of me to be cold.

The time passed excruciatingly slowly as I sat there waiting for the storm to die. The snow continued to pile up in the cave, and with each passing minute, crept closer to where we sat. Knowing that one of the first signs of hypothermia was becoming sleepy, I tried to keep the kids talking, but it was becoming more difficult. My words stopped making any sense some time before and all I got from the other two was an occasional, unintelligible grunt. Besides the cold, the snow being driven into the cave was a blinding white against the floodlights and had a hypnotic effect. I had to struggle to keep my eyes open. I tried to concentrate on the snow, watching the pile grow before my very eyes, when suddenly—the lights went out.

The two kids at my side let out a sharp yelp, and I probably did as well, we were so surprised by the sudden change. The lights had gone out instantly, like flipping off a switch, leaving the cave in total blackness, our eyes unaccustomed to the low-level light coming from outside the cave's entrance. Without light it seemed even colder and more terrifying and I knew that we were going to have to wait out the storm in the dark.

Our eyes slowly became accustomed to the darkness, but the snow fell so heavily that it was still difficult to see anything but the faintest outline of the cave's entrance. We could still hear the howling of the wind, and occasionally feel it, as well, as the wind swirled around the cave. The best protection from the wind and snow was just inside the mouth of the cave, so I nudged the other two to scoot over a few more feet. It was a little better, but not much. It would have to do until the storm was over.

I sat shoulder to shoulder with one of the kids, and yet I had never felt so alone. I was in charge. I was responsible for putting us in this untenable position. I had put my team in danger—and for what? I wasn't feeling any pressure from the sponsors to finish the dig. They had all they needed to insure a huge return on their money. But I was determined to clear out every last pebble, look under every last rock, sweep out every last speck of dust because I thought there was still a lot to be learned from that cave.

*****

Once all the rock had been moved away from the entrance of the cave, things developed very quickly. We had established two teams, one working inside the cave and one outside. One team removed the dirt—the other ran it through the screens to separate any possible tiny fossils or other artifacts. The work went smoothly, the coarse, dark soil easily removed and carted away. We were taking slices from the top, working our way down in six-inch increments. Little impeded our progress. We found remnants of small marine life, which we collected and categorized, but nothing that was really significant or surprising. That is, until we were a mere few feet from the cave's floor.

James was the first to hit pay dirt. We were approaching ground level and had begun working from the walls inward using the small spades and brushes. James was working towards the center from the left of the entrance, when he began to whisper something. I was the closest and apparently the only one that could hear him. I couldn't tell what he was saying—I thought that he was praying, which seemed pretty damn strange. I watched him for a few seconds, realizing he wasn't praying, and he was pointing down at the ground. I stayed close to the wall and made my way over to him. As I got closer I could see that James was shaking, and his whispers were no more than short gasps for air—he was hyperventilating. Holding him gently by the shoulders I turned him so that we were facing each other. "What is it James, what's wrong?" I asked in barely a whisper.

Within a few minutes, he had calmed down and his breathing had returned to normal, and in a shaky voice and tears in his eyes, he said, "I've found it ... right here." He continued to point at the floor, at a spot equal distance between us. I knelt down before him, the strange object now in plain sight. Protruding about six inches above James' little excavation was one of the outer tips of a *Triceratops*' frill.

Fossilized bone, especially such a small portion of one, is usually very difficult to identify at first glance, but I knew in an instant what it was because it was such an extraordinary specimen. The little bit that was exposed was free of imperfections and the distortion usually apparent from the compression that tons of earth and millions of years causes. Its most astounding feature was its color. It wasn't the typical tan or gray, or even brown—it was black—as black as night. And it had a gloss to it, as if it were wet or freshly varnished. I had never seen anything quite like it.

We were a team, and each of us played a part in the discovery, but James felt very special. He made the initial find, uncovering the first piece of what was to become a historic discovery. He felt like a proud father showing off his first born as the others began to gather around, staring in fascination at the small bit of bone protruding from the dark soil. "You did it James—it's your find. Lead your team, get this sucker out of the ground." His smile stretched from ear to ear as he got to work.

It went swiftly, the matrix being relatively soft as compared to the fossilized bone, making it easy to separate the two. Besides the *Tyrannosaur*, which was nearly a perfect specimen, there were two fully-grown and one adolescent *Triceratops*, each in equally remarkable shape. All four specimens were nearly complete, and the individual bones had been removed from the cave, incased in plaster, labeled, and shipped of to the Chicago Museum of Paleontology where they would eventually be reassembled.

But I had a feeling that there was still more to be found in the cave so I held half of the crew back and sent the rest home. That had been a week before, and in all that time, we had found little else of note other than an unusual outcropping of rock toward the rear of the cave in what turned out to be an alcove, almost like a separate room within the cave.

While clearing out the little room, I noticed that there was a depression in the floor, filled with the same silt deposit as the rest of the interior of the cave. Thinking that it may be the *rex's* nest with the possibility of fossilized eggs lying beneath the soil, I began digging through it, searching for an end to the depression. After several hours of digging and cleaning out the edges as I went down, it became obvious that it was not just a depression, an irregularity in the floor's surface. It was a fissure of some kind—a crack in the rock that seemed to spread out as I went deeper.

By the end of the day, I had gone down nearly four feet and there was no end in sight. I really hadn't found a thing of value, only more of the fine black soil, but I *needed* to know where this thing led. It was my curiosity that kept us there days after the job should have been done.

*****

If Susan were with me in the snow-filled cave, would she have done things differently? I answered that question with a resounding YES! As I said,

Susan was the smart one. Despite her natural curiosity, she would never have done anything to put those kids in danger. She would have wanted to know what was down the hole as much as me, but she would have waited until the next season, or, at least, she would have gotten the kids out of the way first. She and I could have done it on our own. There wasn't room for more than one at a time in the pit anyway.

I wished that she had been there then to get me through this. Hell, I wished that she were just *there*—period. I nodded off with thoughts of Susan filling my troubled mind.

I dreamt of Susan. It was the first of a long series of nightmares that would continue to haunt me for months to come—the hook coming right after her ever so slowly—me unable to do a goddamn thing about it. Maybe the dream was more a manifestation of my current predicament—cold and alone and in need of her help—than it was of the accident itself. Perhaps if I had been able to save her on the mountain, maybe she'd have been here to save my ass in the cave.

I awoke with a start, the tiniest fraction of a second before the hook made contact with Susan's head. I could feel the fear-induced sweat running down my sides despite the cold. It took a few moments to realize why I was cold and where I was. Before I even dared to open my eyes, I tried to move—first my fingers, then my toes. I had a problem there—I couldn't feel my feet—they were numb. I was relieved to find that my legs worked, as did my arms. I tried moving my shoulders and then my head, and even with my eyes still closed tightly, I could tell it was daytime, light filtering through my eyelids as I turned my head to the right, toward the entrance to the cave. I tried opening my eyes, but the lids wouldn't separate—moisture had frozen the lashes together. I gently pressed the warm palms of my hands against my cold eyelids. It didn't take long for the ice to melt, and my eyes opened to reveal an amazing, but terrifying sight.

Snow had piled up in the center of the cave nearly to the ceiling, some forty feet high, trailing off as it moved toward the exterior, much like the slope of one of the surrounding ski mountains. It had made it all the way over to our position, to a depth of two feet, covering our legs and most of our bodies, almost burying us. Only the very top of the cave's entrance was visible above the snow, daylight flooding in, reflecting off the impossibly white snow, in stark contrast to the small patch of brilliant blue sky that could be seen beyond.

The scene was incredibly beautiful, and the shock of waking to it numbed my senses for several moments, but as I became more familiar with my surroundings, I began to feel the cold, and realized the danger we were in. I turned my attention to the two kids on my right where there was no movement and I began nudging them, shouting out their names.

There was no response.

I pulled the blankets from around them, pushing piles of snow off to the side in the process. At that, each one muttered a groan of protest, having been pulled from the little bit of warmth that the blanket had offered. Thank God, they were alive, but I had to get them warm immediately!

My feet were still without feeling, so I couldn't stand up, but I could move. I grabbed the kid next to me by the shoulders, and shook him while I massaged his arms, up and down, from shoulders to hands. He let out a moan as feeling reentered his arms, and as he began to awaken, he started fighting me, confused and afraid. We faced each other, both in a sitting position, and wrestled for several moments until he began to come around. As I tried to calm him, I told him to keep his eyes closed, and if he still had feeling in his hands, press them lightly against his eyes until the ice melted from their lashes as mine had done. He did so, and a minute later, his eyes opened, and I could see the same sense of awe in them that mine had experienced only minutes before.

By this time the third member of our little group began to come around and in a short time we were all alert, moving around as best we could, trying to get some feeling back into our lower extremities. With considerable difficulty, I managed to stand, and very carefully and clumsily, took a few steps, shuffling through the small area where the snow was only knee-deep. As the blood flowing through my feet began to warm and pick up speed I felt a warming sensation, which turned quickly into pain as if I were walking through hot coals rather than snow. I knew this was a good sign—feeling was returning to my feet despite the burning sensation.

Stomping my feet, while brushing the snow from my clothing, I began urging the other two to their feet. It took a few minutes and a lot of yelling on my part and even more bitching on theirs, but they managed to get up and moving. I told them to *keep* moving and stay warm (as if that was possible). We were still stuck in the goddamn cave, and we weren't getting out on our own—we were going to need some help from the outside. I hadn't the slightest idea how well Brian and his crew survived the night. *If* they were okay, they may be snowed in as well.

With all the yelling and stomping of feet, we had created quite a din, but I realized that we hadn't heard anything from the other three on the far side of the snow mountain that had appeared during the night. "Shut up," I told the others. "Listen." But not a sound could be heard from the other side. I began shouting their names, and my two young partners did the same. I could hear the beginnings of panic in their voices. Friends, fellow students and classmates, were on the other side, and we were suddenly struck with the awful realization that something was terribly wrong.

We continued to yell at the top of our lungs for several minutes, our throats becoming raspy and horse, when I thought I heard a foreign sound, faint, as if coming from a long distance. "Shut up!" I yelled, as I raised my hand up to get the attention of the other two, placing a finger to my lips to silence them. Although muffled by the snow, I could tell that it was Brian—help was on the way. We were cold, but knowing that we were to be rescued drove out any concern for our personal safety. We still hadn't heard a word from the other side. The two kids looked at one another and then at me, their eyes glistening with the tears of grave uncertainty, and I had to look away to hide my own.

It took the rescue crew the better part of the morning to dig us out, and a few more hours to reach the three on the other side. They had taken the brunt of the storm. The snow, preceded by the freezing rain, must have entered the cave at a slight angle towards their side. They had been buried to a height of about ten feet. Miraculously, in what must have been a last grasp at survival, the three had managed to carve out a pocket of snow around them that contained just enough oxygen to keep them alive—to keep *two* of them alive. Christine didn't make it. She had died during the long, cold night.

*****

The pounding on the glass door brought me back to the present. One of the instructors was standing outside of the sauna, pointing at his watch, telling me that it was time to go. I held up an open hand with fingers spread, indicating that I needed five more minutes. He nodded his head and walked away, knowing that I would probably stretch it to ten. I stared across at the pool, empty then, the water still and dark, and thought about Christine.

The autopsy had revealed that she had had a congenital heart disorder that had gone undetected. The cold and the terror that she undoubtedly suffered during that last night were just too much for her damaged heart to take. But these factors were not listed as contributors in the cause of death. She was a walking time bomb—anything could have caused it to go off. In an attempt to avert any possible legal implications, the museum conducted an official inquiry into the incident and consequently shut down the dig until the findings were reported, meaning at least until the following spring.

Based primarily on the findings of the coroner's report, the inquiry found that the death was accidental, and that Christine's medical condition should have prohibited her from participating in the dig in the first place. Regardless of the weather conditions or the predicament that we ended up in on that last night, she should not have been there. Furthermore, I was not found to be negligent, that the storm had been a fluke, a mysterious and unprecedented phenomenon that occurred without warning.

Despite the official report, the museum thought fit to reprimand me for showing poor judgment, and I was suspended for thirty days without pay and prohibited from taking part in any field work for one year. The museum was far too lenient. I knew better and I should have had to pay the consequences.

CHAPTER 6

The bandages were all gone, the scar nothing more than a thin white line across her brow. If it weren't for the tube running into her arm and the rack of medical equipment near her bed, one would have thought she was but sleeping. The sun came through the window, softly filtered by the sheer cotton curtains, landing on her face in such a way as to make it appear as if there was a radiant source from within. Someone on the staff had seen it too and had thoughtfully applied some light makeup, and had even brushed her hair. It lay fanned out against the pillow, and she looked beautiful, like she was about to waken from a peaceful nap, full of beautiful dreams. And I hoped that she *was* peaceful, and *was* having beautiful dreams ... but I doubted it.

As I stared into her face, peaceful as it appeared, I imagined the battle raging between Susan's subconscious mind and whatever malevolent forces were trying to keep her in her physical purgatory, halfway between life and death. The doctors said that hope was dwindling for any chance of recovery, but they didn't know Susan. As long as there was a heartbeat, she was alive, and if she was alive, she would be scratching and clawing her way back.

It wouldn't have made sense to most, but I figured that I could help her in the battle, so I talked to her—even if she couldn't answer. If she could only hear my voice, then maybe she could follow it to the source, finding her way through the maze, making the connection that would bring her all the way back.

I talked in hushed tones, telling her how wonderful she was, how important she was to me, and how I needed her back in my life. I spoke harshly to her, hoping to shock her back to reality, to make her mad—fighting mad. I tried begging, pleading, cajoling. I joked with her, yelled at her, and even swore at her. I tried everything that I could think of to elicit a response. But other than an occasional twitch or moan—probably involuntary—there was nothing indicating that anything that I said got through. But I wasn't about to give up.

So I talked. I talked non-stop the whole week before. Following my little phone-throwing incident, I had received a week's vacation at the insistence of my boss. He said that I needed some time away from the office, to get away from the pressures of my job. Actually I think he was just afraid that I'd break something *important* next time. However, I didn't argue with him. I knew that I wouldn't be giving my job the attention that it needed at that critical stage.

Of course, with a week off, I had a problem with what to do with my time. What my boss didn't seem to understand was that it wasn't my job that was pressuring me, even though I may have taken it out on the office furniture—it was my personal life, or what was left of it. I had become obsessed with the notion that I was responsible for Susan's accident and for Christine's death, and little else seemed to matter around then. My job was a needed distraction in my life, and for another week, I didn't even have that.

But I still had Susan, so I had spent that week at her side in what had quickly become a much too familiar place.

Although Susan lived in a remote section of Maryland, she had been moved to a long-term care facility just outside of Chicago. I had made the arrangements for the transfer. There was no one else to do it, besides I wanted her nearby so that I could continue to talk with her every day.

Thankfully it wasn't a hospital, at least not in a conventional sense. Yes, there were lots of doctors and nurses and the faint, but omnipresent, smell of antiseptics and disinfectants. And, oh yeah, the rooms were filled with the sick and the dying. But the place had a different *feel* to it. Hospital whites were gone, in favor of casual, colorful dress. Soft pastels and cheerful, but modest, wallpaper replaced white tiled walls. No gurneys or crash carts were visible in the hallways. Framed pictures, rather than health-care posters, filled the walls of the hallways and patient rooms. And the pace was noticeably less frantic—no hysterical shouts, no running through the corridors, no intercom constantly blaring away.

Not that Susan was able to enjoy it, but even the view had been pretty good. There was a small park with a nice wooded area just across the road from her room. The night before, there had been a fresh snowfall, but with the dawn had come bright sunshine and blue skies. All the trees were decked out in brand new sparkling jackets of white, the sun twinkling off them to the rhythm of the soft breeze.

I was at the window, staring out at the picture postcard scene. There was a young couple, holding hands, walking across the cobblestone path that bisected the park. They had the smiles of young lovers, perhaps newlyweds. I remembered what that feeling was like, although it seemed like a lifetime before. I wondered if they knew how precarious their happiness was—how quickly it could just disappear. Did they know that disaster lurked around every corner—was hiding in every shadow?

Probably, they didn't. They were in love and love tends to skew reality, tends to push it behind a rose-colored fog that lacks substance. The realist knows that it can be blown away by the slightest breeze. And I had become a realist, or maybe even a cynic. Or was I just jealous?

Sadness forced me to turn away from the window, returning my gaze to Susan, lying helpless on the bed. I imagined that it was she and I walking through the park, holding hands. The image in my mind formed easily, as if it was meant to be—it was right—and it was wonderful. Even with Susan incapable of speaking, of expressing her emotions, the events of the previous few weeks clarified Susan's feelings for me. I knew that she loved me, and I knew that I was falling in love with her. I sat in the chair alongside her bed, gently holding her hand, staring at her lovely face, wondering if we would ever actually be those two people in the park—or anywhere else.

By then, Susan had become an integral part of my life. It was a one sided affair to that point, but I found myself thinking about her constantly. And I was spending more and more time with her. Of course I didn't have a whole lot to do with my time about then, but the fact of the matter was, I enjoyed being with her, even though I doubted that she knew I was there. I looked forward to getting to the hospital every day, hoping that I would see just the slightest sign of improvement. I was less discouraged by her lack of progress than perhaps I should have been, but the truth was, I just enjoyed sitting there holding her hand. It had become the best time of the day for me. And with Susan being in Chicago, a mere few miles from where I worked, I could be with her often. It was on that day that I decided to share with her the story of how we ended up there together in Chicago.

*****

It was eight weeks after the accident when the hospital in Salt Lake City informed me that there was nothing more that they could do for Susan there, and that a long-term care facility was best suited to deal with her condition. That really pissed me off. How could they so simply dismiss her? It was as if they were throwing up their hands in defeat, that they weren't smart enough to figure out a way to help her, so they were just going to get rid of her. What a bunch of heartless bastards! Didn't they understand how important she was to me?

Despite my anger, the doctor was very patient with me, explaining that Susan needed care—not treatment. There were other places better suited for that care ... and at much less cost. So, *that* was the real reason. It was all about money. No doubt Susan's insurance company was putting the squeeze on the hospital to move her out and reduce their losses, and the unfeeling administration was no doubt squeezing the doctor. This only enraged me further, and I took it out on the doctor, questioning his integrity, and his skill. I ended up storming out of the hospital, leaving the doctor bewildered and confused by my outburst.

It took most of that evening to calm down. I sat in the armchair in my darkened hotel room, drinking scotch with just a splash of water, rerunning the day's events in my mind. By the second drink I began to unwind, my emotions in check. By the fourth I began to see the light—the doctor was right—Susan needed to be in a place that could best care for her special needs. She didn't need surgery, or around-the-clock attention. She didn't even need much in the way of medication. She didn't need the hospital.

By the sixth drink, I began to feel like an ass. I had taken my frustrations out unfairly on the doctor.

I had been no help to Susan at all. To my way of thinking, the hospital was her only chance, the only thing that was taking active steps toward her recovery. I saw the move from the hospital as a step backwards, another patch of ice on an already slippery slope leading to oblivion. I had accused the doctor of being too impersonal, but the fact of the matter was—I was too personally involved to see things for what they were.

However, I could see *much* better with half a dozen drinks in me.

The next morning I awoke feeling like I'd been on the wrong side of a cattle stampede. But the alcohol had apparently not clouded my ability to reason the night before. I was still embarrassed by the way that I talked to the doctor, and I still knew that deep down he was right. I made up my mind to see the doctor first thing and apologize for my behavior, and then to begin the process of finding the best possible place for Susan, and *that* place was definitely not Utah.

I lived in Chicago, Susan in Maryland. Nobody we knew lived anywhere near Utah. Ever since the dig had wrapped up, I had been commuting from my home to the hospital on the weekends in order to be with her. It occurred to me that the long trips were unnecessary, nor would they serve any purpose. I would never have asked that she be moved from one hospital to another while there were still things that the hospital staff could have done for her in Utah. But she was going to be moved anyway, so why not move her to a more convenient locale? Surely there were excellent care facilities in the Chicago area.

Of course there was a minor technicality. Who had the responsibility and authority to make such a decision? The doctors were willing to transfer her anywhere in the world as long as they knew that someone was going to pick up the tab. And Susan's insurance company was paying, so they were the only authority the hospital would recognize.

Susan had no living relatives, and like me, she had damn few close friends. During her two months in the hospital, other than myself, there was but one visitor—a member of the board of directors at the institute.

He was an elderly gentleman, not more than a year or two away from being in such a facility himself. He was terribly emaciated, his expensive suit hanging off old bones that creaked and groaned with each movement. Leaning heavily into a cane, he made his way slowly into the room. I couldn't help but be reminded of Ebenezer Scrooge, and I thought that perhaps he was there to raise hell about the health-care costs that Susan was rolling up.

But his actions, if not his words, told me that he wasn't there for that reason. He glanced at me as he shuffled over to Susan's bedside, a look of sadness on his face. He hung his cane on the rail of the bed, taking Susan's hand in his as he slowly lowered his head to hers, his lips an inch from her ear. He whispered something to her that I couldn't quite hear. As he raised his head, I saw a single tear roll over the deep crevices in his leathery face.

He introduced himself in a voice that was barely above a whisper, a voice choked with emotion. As I was about to introduce myself, he raised his hand in a gesture that said, *no need, I know who you are*. He then placed his hand on my shoulder, mouthed a silent thank you, and left the room.

As a member of the board at the Smithsonian, it was obvious that he and Susan must have had some kind of working relationship, but I didn't know the nature of that relationship. What could cause this frail old man to travel a thousand miles to visit someone for no more than a minute? Why would he have made such a difficult trip to see someone who probably didn't even know he was there? And what could he have possibly whispered into her ear?

There were no other visitors. The phone calls to the hospital stopped after the first few days, as did the tons of cards and flowers from other coworkers in Washington. There were even a few from former classmates and professors, but there were no others that came to see her. There was only me, and it would be up to me to find a way to have her transferred to Chicago. And I was happy to do it. There was just one problem—I wasn't sure *how* to do it.

Thus I began the investigation. I started off by making the trip to the Smithsonian Institute, where Susan was the resident paleontologist, to discuss with them my wish to have her transferred to Chicago. I had no trouble convincing anyone there. They all thought the world of Susan, but hadn't a clue what to do about the situation—they didn't really have the authority either. They were still paying her salary, but the insurance company was paying her medical costs. So I went there next. That's when the real problems began.

The insurance company didn't take issue with her being cared for in Chicago, versus Salt Lake City; however, they would not pay the expense to transfer her there. And, *they* would select the care facility. They assured me that Susan had very good coverage, and that, if I were lucky, there may even be a selection to choose from. That wasn't good enough for me. I intended to pick the facility, and I intended to pick the best.

Between my salary and Liz's life insurance, I was in good shape financially, so I offered to pick up any expenses that the insurance company didn't cover. The insurance company agreed, but we had to get past some legal hurdles first. My good intentions were not enough. Whatever actions were taken had to be in the best interest of Susan, and only her next of kin, or a person having her *power of attorney* could determine and authorize that. My only hope was her will. If she had one, it was anybody's guess as to where it was.

I needed to find her lawyer, if she had one, and trying to find one particular lawyer in the District of Columbia was like looking for a particular rat in a junkyard. I had little to go on, other than knowing where she worked and where she lived.

Her coworkers and bosses were of little help. Susan was a very private person, who didn't socialize with others on the staff. She rarely discussed her personal life, and only a few even knew where she lived. Everyone thought that all she cared about was her work, and after a while they stopped asking about anything beyond the job.

That left her house.

*****

It was a huge old Victorian place just south of Annapolis, Maryland. It had a spectacular view of the Atlantic and no neighbors within shouting distance. Its location alone would have put its price at close to a million dollars, but anyone with that kind of money to spend would have first torn the house down and then start over.

It was the kind of place that you didn't see very often—over a hundred and fifty years old, slate roof, lots of gables and dormers, and an old fashioned pillared and spindled porch that wrapped nearly around three sides. The inside and outside of the house were covered with old gingerbread, and there was more carved wood than you'd find in Geppetto's workshop. There were three stories, each filled with rooms of every size and shape, crooked hallways, and dimly lit nooks and crannies everywhere.

When the house was built, it would have been one of the most fashionable houses in New England—surely owed by one of the area's most prominent citizens. It was probably the home of a large family with lots of kids, and more likely than not, some grandparents, other relatives, dogs, cats, maybe even some livestock thrown in for good measure. It *was* an incredibly beautiful house. Was—not any more.

Time and neglect had taken their toll.

What paint remained was chipped and cracked, tiles were missing from the roof, the eaves sagged, and several windows were boarded over. Every third spindle was missing from what had once been a magnificent porch and one whole section of railing was gone, that which remained sagged and drooped. The house had become half-hidden by shrubbery that looked like they had gone without pruning for the better part of a decade.

Susan had only been gone four months, but it looked like the house had been without care for as many years. I had been here once before—ten years before. Susan had just bought the house from a retired professor who had had moved south after having had enough of the cold, damp New England weather. Even then, I had wondered why she would want such an old relic, in such dire need of maintenance. The price was right, downright cheap actually, but who would want to take care of such a big place, and who would want to live out here in the middle of nowhere?

A decade latter, I questioned her motives even more. She certainly didn't care anything about the house. By the looks of it, I doubted if anything had been done to it since the last time I was here.

I left my rental car off the side of old gravel road at the edge of the woods and was staring at the house from just outside the ancient wrought-iron gate. I would have preferred to drive my car through the gate and around the far side of the house to keep it out of sight, but the gate was locked. Along with my flashlight, I had a crowbar, but I didn't plan on using it unless I absolutely had to. I wasn't here to rob the place.

I hopped the fence and headed towards the house.

I was beginning to think that what I was about to do was a bad idea. It was nearly dark and the house looked black, foreboding against the gray autumn sky. Beneath the old house, at the base of the cliff, the surf could be heard pounding against the rocks. Thunder and lightning crashed and flashed from above.

I had no key—that's what the crowbar was for. As it turned out, I didn't need it. In the back of the house I found a window with a broken latch. Like the rest of the house, it was old and in need of repair. Moisture had swollen the wood, making it stick, but a few heavy hits on the frame loosened it enough to slide the lower sash up far enough to squeeze through.

I ended up in a sink. Thankfully, it was empty and dry. I wanted to try the lights, but as an uninvited guest, I thought better of it. I switched on the flashlight instead. I was in a tiny laundry room containing only a small washer and dryer, in addition to the old tub. The plastered-walls were chipped and cracked, pieces of the old lath showed through in places.

There was a single closed door at the opposite end of the room. It caught my eye, not only because it was the only door in the room and I couldn't have missed it, but because it was new. The door and the casing surrounding it looked heavy, solid, like red oak with an intricately carved leaf pattern. They were heavily lacquered and had antique brass hardware.

The door opened noiselessly.

It opened onto the kitchen, which to my surprise was very modern, and with the exception of several months of accumulated dust, was in excellent shape. Where I had expected an old pump and a wood burning stove, I found modern equipment: microwave oven, food processor, large side-by-side refrigerator, and ceramic top stove. It was a huge kitchen with a central counter and overhead racks of copper pots and pans. The cabinets and woodwork matched the carved oak pattern of the laundry room door. Everything looked new and state-of-the-art, and totally out of place as compared to what I had seen of the house to that point.

The kitchen was a surprise, but I wouldn't find what I was after there, so I moved through a wide, elaborate archway into the dining room. This room was much more in keeping with the outside of the house. Everything was old, with even more dust than what had built up in the kitchen. The dark walnut paneling that started at the floor and went halfway up the wall was cracked with age and dull from inattention. Likewise the table, which would easily accommodate twelve people comfortably, had not cast a reflection in many years. I doubted that Susan had ever used this room for its intended purpose—if ever at all.

The dining room also contained a massive china cabinet and two buffets, each matching the style and sad state of repair of the table. I looked through its drawers, but as I expected, each was empty. There were no longer pictures of any kind hanging on the walls, but I could see the shadows of where they once hung, the peeling wallpaper darker there than elsewhere. The carpet was worn and faded, the color no longer discernable. Overhead was a massive chandelier, cobwebs stretching from one sconce to the next. Moving through the room, I had disturbed the air, making the cobs sway gracefully to and fro, bisecting the rays from my flashlight, casting macabre shadows on the plastered ceiling. A chill ran up my spine as I made my way into the next room.

I was in the living room, probably called the parlor back in the time that the house was built. Like the dining room, it was large, and unused. It was furnished, in a general sense. There were chairs and sofas, end tables and bookshelves. There was even a grandfather clock in one corner, its pendulum still, and its hands frozen at twenty minutes past two. I wondered what day it had stopped, or what decade. There was nothing that you would expect to find in a living room that was actually *lived* in. There were no family photos, no knickknacks, no books or magazines, no television or radio. There were no drapes or shades over the windows. The floors were wood, oak I thought, and were probably once beautiful when cleaned and polished. On that night they were scarred and dirty with a well-worn path between the front door and the grand staircase leading to the second floor.

There was one other room on the first floor—the library. I didn't waste much time there. Except for the floor to ceiling bookcases, the room was empty. Not a single book, nor a solitary piece of furniture. There was nothing there to search through. I turned from the room, gazing again across the parlor to the staircase. I felt like I was in a grade-B horror movie. This place had the look of a hundred different haunted mansions that I saw at the Saturday matinees of my childhood. I half expected Vincent Price to step out of the shadows.

I approached the set of double doors under the massive staircase with more than a little trepidation. It seemed like an obvious place to hide something ... or someone. I slowly twisted the knob on the right, pulling it gently at first, then, more forcefully when it refused to budge. I had no better luck than with the first tug. I was sweating, but not from the exertion. Next to beneath the bed, I knew that under the stairs was the second most popular place for monsters, murderers, and demons. But I had to get in there. If I left the house without finding the will, the unknown space under the stairs would haunt me from that day forward.

I grabbed the doorknobs, one in each hand, took a deep breath, and pulled as hard as I could. For just an instant there was nothing ... then there was a loud shriek and the doors sprung open, something in black lunging out at me, striking me fully across the chest.

I hit the floor, letting out an involuntary shout as I fell. On my ass, I scooted across the worn oak as fast as I could until the wall on the opposite side of the room stopped my progress and any hope of escape. During the fall I had dropped the flashlight, and it sat there in front of the open doors, spinning wildly, casting eerie shadows across all four walls. I was too frightened to move as I watched the turning flashlight slow to a stop. The dark object now stood in the now open doorway. It swayed back and forth, as if waiting momentarily to decide when to strike. But it refused to move, except for its rhythmic swaying, which seemed to be slowing. I was terrified, but the longer I sat there the more the fear was displaced by curiosity. The black thing stopped, but still it refused to strike. The rapid beating of my heart also slowed to normal as I approached the thing that had nearly caused it to stop altogether.

I arose and crept slowly toward the stairs, hugging the wall as I went, afraid of making a noise that would cause it to move once more. I was just a few feet away, standing above the flashlight, but not close enough to make out the exact shape of the black creature. I slid down the wall, and carefully, slowly, reached for the light. I sat there for several seconds, afraid that any sudden movement would arouse it—anger it. In my mind, I counted to three, before shining the light directly at the thing, thinking that I might surprise it, or blind it momentarily, so that I could make my escape. But I missed my target by a foot or so, aiming the light directly into the interior of the closet, seeing nothing but a clothes pole and a few stray hangers swaying silently from the sudden pull of air caused when I yanked open the doors a few moments before. I moved the light hesitantly to the right, landing directly on the black thing.

It was nothing but a heavy dark topcoat. Jesus Christ! It was hanging on a hook on the inside of the right door. Apparently, it had caught between the two doors, holding back until I had separated the doors enough for it to spring free, swinging forward with the momentum of the door that it was hanging from.

Nothing but a goddamn topcoat! Then why the hell was I still shaking? What else did this house have in store for me? At that moment I didn't really want to find out, but the thought of having to return in the future frightened me even more.

I was committed to finishing this. I scanned the beam of the flashlight around the first floor, and saw nothing more. This house was big enough for fifteen or twenty people, yet, not only did Susan choose to live in this house alone, she wasn't even using much of it. Other than the kitchen, the entire first floor of the house had an abandoned feel to it, the way a useless appendage will wither and die. It radiated an unpleasant smell, more than just the musty odor of a room kept closed for too long. This had the smell of rot, of wood and carpet too long without sunlight and fresh air. Why did Susan choose to live like this? Perhaps the answer lay on the second floor.

There was a multitude of doorways leading from the main hallway. Guessing by the way that they were situated and the space between each, there were six bedrooms, three baths, and several closets on the second floor, each of a unique size and shape. All that I entered were furnished, but none were lived in, and that was yet another surprise. Susan had to sleep somewhere, but it wasn't on the second floor, and it sure as hell wasn't on the first. I tried looking in the closets and in the dressers, and there were no clothes in any of them. The smell of rot was more pronounced in each of the rooms. The doors had not been opened in years. Some of them wouldn't open, and I didn't try to force them. Neither Susan, nor anyone else had been in them for some time.

At the end of the hall was a door that *did* open—it led to yet another floor—the top floor. The enclosed stairway was up against the back outside wall of the house and I could hear the wind whistling through the old boards. The narrow stairs creaked and groaned under my weight, my heart raced, as I made my way upward. The blood in my veins had grown cold, and my mouth was as dry as dust as I reached for the knob on the door at the top of the stairs. I didn't know what lay behind that door, but by that time my imagination was running wild. Nothing good ever happened behind closed doors in the attics of old, spooky houses.

I turned the knob and pushed the door open slowly, just a few inches. I had turned the flashlight off, and I pressed my back against the drafty wall, waiting to see if something was going to happen. I waited a minute ... then two, trying to muster up the courage to cross the threshold.

I switched on the flashlight, shined it into the interior of the room, and peered around the doorjamb. The tension had built as I searched the house, increasing from room to room and from floor to floor. The top floor was the end of my search and the tension had reached a crescendo. I expected something incredible, but I hadn't expected this.

I didn't trust what I was seeing with the poor light from my flashlight, so I reached for the light switch just inside the door. I flipped it on—no longer caring if anyone could see the lights from the outside, not sure if the electricity was even on.

Instantly, bright lights illuminated every part of the room. With my mouth hanging open I entered, looking from one end to the other on the most beautiful space I'd ever seen. It was like something from a fairy tale. It was one gigantic room, taking up the entire width and depth of the house. The ceilings were multifaceted, some disappearing into the floor, as the roofline met the exterior walls, while others soared twenty feet high, no horizontal surfaces anywhere. All the gables and dormers visible from the outside of the house were also evident from the inside, but now an inside-out image. Nothing was in shadow. Recessed lighting was strategically placed so that every detail was exposed and gave the entire room a surreal quality.

The interior of the room was entirely finished in knotty pine and was framed in massive twelve-inch pine beams, using wooden dowels, rather than nails or screws. The windows were leaded glass, with brass frames, the central pair stained glass, a scene from what looked like prehistoric times. It was somehow familiar to me, but with nothing behind it but darkness, it was hard to see it clearly. I saw flashes of its brilliance as the sporadic lightning illuminated it from behind.

The floor was wood as well. Plush red and white rugs were scattered throughout. There was a huge fieldstone fireplace with an elaborate carved mantle. One wall was completely covered with floor to ceiling glass-fronted cabinets, most of which were filled with books of every kind.

I began browsing through them, hoping that I would spot something that would lead me to Susan's will, or the name of her lawyer—maybe a personal ledger, or even a diary. I had no luck, but her collection was impressive. There were hundreds of leather-bound, first editions, some even autographed. I was surprised to find an entire section of cheap romance novels—quite a few by the same author—someone by the name of Lacy Wanderlust. Now there was an alias if ever I heard one. It was probably some old lady who relieved her sexual frustration by writing crap for other, equally love-starved old ladies. I never had any idea that Susan was into that kind of trash, although by then I should have been getting used to surprises from her.

On the far side of the room there was a short alcove with doors on either side. Within this area was a dressing area, with the better part of three walls covered with mirrors, their edges webbed in red. Bright lights surrounded the central mirror, and sat upon a large bureau, which was capped with pink marble. In it were every kind of makeup and grooming devise imaginable. Looking at Susan's personal articles made me feel that I'd invaded her privacy, but curiosity got the better of me, and I continued on.

The door to the left of the alcove led to a huge bathroom, complete with Jacuzzi, steam room, skylight, and double vanity. Walls and floor were covered in blue and white Italian tile, with custom borders around all the fixtures. The room was filled with plants—dead plants—the shrunken brown stems lying flat against the black, dry soil.

It was a bathroom fit for a king—or a queen—and was altogether proper considering what the rest of the third floor was like.

The other door off the alcove was a walk-in closet, but not your every day, run of the mill, walk-in closet. This one was the size of most people's bedrooms, and was completely built in cedar, with individual shelves and racks for everything from shoes to coats. All of them were on bearings or concealed hinges that opened silently with the simplest touch. Besides the size and grandeur of this closet, it differed in one significant way from every other closet in the house. This one was not empty. Skirts, blouses, pants, coats, and shoes were all neatly hung or arranged in a nice, neat orderly fashion. That's not to say that the closet was full. There was enough space there for an entire family—a large family. But clearly, this is where Susan had kept all of her clothes, and without question the third floor is where Susan had lived.

Armed with this new insight into Susan's life, I reentered the main room. Although there were no walls separating the various living spaces, it was evident that this was a space for living, and someone was living there … at least until four months ago. No interior walls, but clearly there were distinct areas dedicated to specific functions of life.

One corner was a bedroom, more accurately called a sleeping area. A four-poster, king-size bed, complete with canopy and heavy red drapes tied back against the posts, centered it. Sheer curtains enclosed the bed, revealing only shadowy images from anyone peering in from beyond. Matching dressers of carved pine flanked either side of the bed, and an eight-foot hope chest stood at its foot.

Directly in front of the double stained-glass windows was what would be considered a combination living/family room. It was directly below the highest ceiling in the room, making the area look enormous. Red leather chairs and a black leather sofa surrounded a heavily lacquered table made from a gigantic tree stump. There were a couple of end tables made in similar fashion, each holding unusual, but interesting wrought iron lamps. On one side of the windows was an expensive stereo system, on the other, a big-screen television.

There was one more distinctive area in the room—a study. Two very large desks, on which sat two powerful personal computers, were the focal point. Attached to one of the PCs was a laser jet printer—to the other was a plotter. I went to the desk with the plotter, which was covered with computerized architectural drawings, most of them for what appeared to be bedrooms. There were also several artists' renderings in color of the same spaces. I knew that if I took the time and compared dimensions, I could match each of them up with the bedrooms on the second floor.

Susan did care about this house. She cared about it one hell of a lot. She was systematically refinishing and refurbishing one room at a time starting with the third floor. The new kitchen on the first floor must have been completed first. Hell, we all have to eat. All this work must have given her a huge appetite, so that's where she began.

What Susan had accomplished was nothing short of miraculous, and it had to have cost a fortune. As a paleontologist I knew what she earned and it wasn't enough for this—not nearly enough. So, as well as finding her will—I had hoped to find some other answers.

I opened each of the desk drawers, as interested now in learning more about this mystery house as finding what I had come there for. One drawer was filled with photographs of the house, hundreds of them, of both the inside and the outside. Each had the date written on the back, and most had notations as well. They had been taken over a period of several years, the changing seasons evident in the exterior shots. There were panoramic photographs of the whole house and entire rooms, and there was shot after shot, and angle upon angle of the smallest detail of every wall, window, molding, and door. Even the furniture had been photographed. Written on the back was the room that it occupied and its specific location.

The second drawer, the larger of the two on the right side of the desk, held several very large photo albums, each filled with similar pictures. However, unlike the hodge-podge collection of pictures in the top drawer, this one had a flow to it, some rhyme and reason to it all. It began with the outside shots from every angle, each picture getting tighter, showing more detail than the one before. As the pictures went from outdoors to indoors, the pattern continued. The first shots revealed as much of the room as possible, followed by pictures of each wall, and then the detail of the baseboards, crown molding, window casings, and everything else in the room. There were crystal clear close-ups of the cracked and faded wallpaper.

With wonder, I slowly made my way through the album, stopping about ten pages from the end. It was where the pictures of the attic, or what once could have been called an attic, began. The dimensions, and the general shape of the space were the same, but nothing else. Even with the bright lights provided by the flash and whatever other artificial light Susan had used, you could tell that this was once a dark and gloomy place. There was insulation between the joists on the floor, but little else. Between the rafters and studs, there was nothing but the exterior wood boards, nails showing through in random patterns. The dominant feature of the huge, empty space was cobwebs. They were everywhere, some as thick as curtains, patterns intricate and beautiful, yet strangely haunting at the same time.

I peered over the top edge of the album, taking in the beautiful room once more, scarcely believing that this was once the space in the pictures. I looked at each snapshot, trying to pick out its real, although much improved, counterpart. The placements of the windows, if not the windows themselves, and the position of the peaks and valleys of the roofline, were the only clues. The change was that great. It was nothing short of miraculous.

The second album was filled with pictures of the kitchen, the earliest pictures being that of what it must have looked like before the renovations began. Like most of the rest of the house, it was a wreck. There was no water pump, or wood-burning stove, as I had expected when I first climbed through the window, but things were pretty bad. The appliances looked like they were from the fifties, the white enameled finish worn and yellowed.

The cheap laminate on the countertops was peeling away, with the wood beneath looking water damaged. None of the cabinet doors hung true, tilting this way and that.

The first few pages were more of the same, and then they began to change. There were a dozen or so shots of the room stripped down to the studs, an empty shell, a dead space. Thumbing through the pages, the room began to take on life as a new floor was installed, followed by new windows, moldings, and all new light fixtures. I saw the step-by-step construction of the central workstation, and watched as the gleaming pots and pans magically appeared overhead. Each new appliance was photographed as it was installed. The last pictures were of the kitchen as I saw it on that night.

The final album began the way the first one did, with pictures of the *old* attic. I went quickly to the end of the book, knowing that I would find pictures of what stood before me then. They were magnificent, but they didn't do justice to the real thing. The pictures were flat and lifeless, but the room was warm and alive. Many of the photographs were in full color, yet they couldn't match the rich golden glow of the pine, nor the wonderful contrasting color scheme of the reds and blacks. No picture could do justice to this room.

I closed the book, disappointed in the knowledge that there were no others of its kind. I had been through the entire house, there was nothing more to see, and the renovation had proceeded only as far as the top floor and the kitchen. There was nothing more to photograph, everything was right up to date. If the doctors were right, there would never be another album, no more reconstruction. If Susan didn't recover, the house would forever be an unfinished piece of art, and no one would ever know the life that she had returned to it.

The drawers on the left side of the desk contained little of interest and nothing that would help to answer my questions. All three were crammed with art and photographic supplies. Drawing paper, colored inks, chalk, charcoal sticks, pencils of every kind, and watercolors filled the top two. The third contained a Minolta thirty-five millimeter camera and several lenses of varying focal lengths. There was a box of a dozen rolls of film, half black and white, half color—all unopened.

Unless there was a false bottom in one of the drawers, I had seen everything that the desk had to offer. But it had taken me on a fascinating journey through time and space. It was like taking a peek at someone's family album. The house had been reborn. Through the photos, I watched it take its first steps, saw it grow, becoming more mature and beautiful with each passing day. The house had taken on life, developed its own personality, shaped and guided by Susan. This was more than a hobby for her. This was life for her—her child.

But I still hadn't found what I had gone there for. The second desk was my last chance. If desk number one was where Susan worked on the house reconstruction, then what did she do from desk number two, and why did she need an entirely different desk, complete with its own computer, to do it? Aside from the PC and printer, there was only one other item on the desk's surface. It was a manila folder, about an inch thick. I opened it to reveal the first of what looked to be about two hundred typewritten pages. Centered on page one was simply *The Devil's Desire*, by Lacy Wanderlust.

I stared at the page for several seconds, my brain overloaded, trying to put this new information into the right compartment so that it made some sense. I scanned through the first several pages when the connection was made, the data finally dropping into the right niche, things coming into hazy focus. A slight smile was on my lips as I hopped over to the bookcases, opening the glass doors to look at the dozen novels written by Lacy Wanderlust.

Holy shit! Susan was a romance novelist.

I picked one out at random, turning it over to look for the author's picture. Sure enough, it was there, but you had to look really closely to tell that it was Susan. Her hair was pulled up severely into a tight bun, and she had on black horn-rimed glasses with impossibly thick lenses. I knew for a fact that Susan had twenty-twenty vision with no corrective lenses, and I had never seen her hair worn that way. Under the picture was her alias, and a brief autobiographical sketch stating that the best-selling author, Ms. Wanderlust, was a high school English teacher in a suburb of Seattle, where she lived with her husband, two children, and a dog named Max.

Well, one mystery solved. I knew how Susan was paying for the restoration of the house, but I didn't know which came first. Did Susan begin writing strictly to finance the house, or was she already an established writer before she started this incredible project, maybe before she even owned the place? I guess it really didn't matter. She was obviously a talented writer who used the proceeds to fund her passion. I only hoped the world hadn't heard the last from Lacy Wanderlust.

I returned to the folder, rifling through the pages to the back. In reading the last page, it was evident that it was unfinished. This must have been the book that Susan was working on when she left for Utah. I began looking through the desk drawers. One was filled with several boxes of floppy discs, some new, and some not. One box was labeled *The Devil's Desire*—her unfinished manuscript. Others had the names of her other books, all finished, I assumed. There were eleven in total, not counting the yet to be completed one.

Most of the other drawers contained little of importance, mostly writing supplies and little bits of junk that desk drawers tend to accumulate. There was but one drawer left and it was locked. There's an old saying that things are always found in the last place that you look. Of course they are. Why continue to look if you've found what you're looking for? However, in this case, it was the last place that I *could* look. I had scoured the rest of the house, and not found what I was looking for. This was my last chance. I took it as a good sign that it was the one secured place in the whole house.

I was prepared to pick the lock, well, try to, but that turned out to be unnecessary. In one of the junk drawers I found a small ring with two small keys attached. The first one slid easily into the lock.

Inside the drawer I found a fireproof box, which was also locked, but the second key fit this one nicely, as well. I opened the lid of the box, and right on top was a folded legal looking document tied with a gold braided string. On the top of the front was a single word—*Will.*

Once again I felt as if I was invading Susan's privacy, but I had come too far by then to turn back. I untied the string and unfolded the paper. I began reading the document, looking for the name of her lawyer, knowing that it had to be there somewhere. On the third page, I stopped, hardly believing what I was seeing.

It was *my* name.

Susan had named me as the only beneficiary. In the event of her death, I inherited everything that she owned, including this house. The words began to blur as my eyes filled with tears.

It took several minutes for me to regain enough composure to finish reading the will. Sure enough, the lawyer's name and address were on the last page. I jotted the information down on a note pad and returned the will to its hiding place. As I was about to replace the box, I noticed one other thing in the drawer—an envelope. I had found what I had come for, and shouldn't have touched it, but I was pretty numb by then, and my brain was still in search mode. So, I removed the envelope and opened it. It was filled with about three-dozen pictures—pictures of *me.* There were other people as well, including some with Susan, but I was in every one of them.

It was a huge room, yet I felt that the walls were closing in on me. I had to get out of there. I headed for the stairs, and raced down them in the pitch darkness. I had forgotten my flashlight, and ended up falling down the last several steps, twisting my ankle and crashing into the wall at the bottom of the stairs. I rolled through the open door, and aided by the tiniest bit of light coming from the windows, made my way back through the kitchen. I climbed onto the old tub in the laundry and literally fell through the open window—through the window and into the hands of one of Maryland's finest.

*****

I watched Susan's face carefully as I told her of my encounter with the local constabulary. She would have loved the story—you know—local boy makes good—that kind of shit. She would've busted a gut over that. She'd have got an even bigger bang over the part with the coat hanging in the closet scaring the bejeebers out of me. The very notion that an old house would have intimidated a big strong guy like me would have left her rolling in the aisles. But there was nothing—not a twitch, not a moan—not the slightest sign of the corner of her lip turning upward in the beginning of a smile—not anything.

My heart was no longer into it, but I finished the story anyway. I told her about the old, overweight sergeant that clearly was pulling easy duty watching the homes of the rich and famous living on the coast, waiting for retirement—how he reached down with his left hand to help me up from the ground while the right hand held his service revolver. It was the right hand that shook so bad that I thought he was going to shoot himself in the foot, or worse, me. I would have been surprised if he had ever drawn his weapon outside the firing range, let alone actually firing it at someone. Falling out of the window as I did, I couldn't say that I blamed him for pulling his gun, but it sure scared the hell out of me, and I think it scared him even more. I produced some ID for him and he looked it over while I tried to explain what I was doing there so late at night. He didn't cuff me for the ride back to the station. He did however, pat me down and put me into the back of the squad car, which more resembled a cage than the back seat of an automobile. Maybe I deserved to be treated like an animal.

He must have believed my story. Maybe I sounded more intelligent than your average, run-of-the-mill cat burglar, or more possibly, because I wasn't carrying anything when I emerged from the house of my own free will, without a weapon of any kind. I was a pretty lousy burglar coming out of a place that I robbed empty handed and unarmed. It was a good thing that I had accidentally left the crowbar behind. That might not have looked so good.

It must have been a pretty boring and thankless job that the old sergeant had, because, once he had me in the car, he talked as if I were the first person in years that was willing to listen. He made a stab at interrogating me, but no sooner had he asked me a question than he was off on a tangent, before I got an answer halfway out of my mouth. He was more like a tour guide than a cop. He pointed out each and every house that we passed, telling me about the current inhabitants, their social position, and how they ranked on the hierarchy of local celebrity. He acted like he knew them all personally, which, of course, I doubted.

He seemed genuinely happy to have me in his car, even if I was under arrest. In the movies, cops always complain about the administrative aspect of their jobs, and I was sure that the good sergeant was facing plenty of it as a result of my arrest. But I was also pretty sure that he was looking forward to that part of the arrest, too. He probably didn't have much cause to do the paperwork very often either. I bet it had been years since he had made an arrest—an actual single-handed apprehension of a desperate criminal.

Chicago could learn a thing or two about their accommodations from the Annapolis police department. It was a modern facility, clean and orderly. Everybody was polite and efficient. No bedlam in the lobby, no bleeding, no yelling, no near fistfights, and no big fat sergeant manning the desk. But in fairness to Chicago, they don't have a population made up of rich politicians and affluent professors. Annapolis had neither the crime nor the slums to deal with that Chicago did.

I had to thank Jakes for the fact that I didn't spend the night in the slammer. After about an hour of questioning, I got to make a phone call. They didn't tell me that I could only make one, but that's all it took. It was still the middle of the night, so I called his home and he was actually there—with Jakes you could never be sure. I told him where I was and what had happened and he told me to give the phone to the sergeant.

I didn't know exactly what Jakes told the sergeant, but there was a glint in the old guy's eye and a smile on his lips. He showed Jakes the utmost respect, yes sir this, and yes sir that. He was obviously impressed to be talking to a big city lieutenant. I was seeing the famous brotherhood of policemen in action—I do you a favor, you do one for me—and I intended to take full advantage of it. After a few moments the sergeant told Jakes, "No problem, I'll take care of it," and handed the phone back to me.

"You dumbass," he said, and then began to laugh. He thought something was pretty damn funny, which surprised the shit out of me being that I had probably just woken up his whole family from a sound sleep. When he finally finished laughing he said, "Get your ass back to Chicago. Be in my office first thing in the morning. I've got news."

After I hung up the phone the sergeant made a pretty good stab at dressing me down. He pointed out that although my intentions may have been honorable, I was still breaking the law by entering the house without permission. I argued that, as I had her power of attorney and was the executor of her estate, I did have her permission … well, sort of—I didn't really know that until *after* I had broken in. I also tried to point out that I really didn't break in, as the window was unlocked. I just opened it. These were both mere technicalities, but pretty good ones I thought. The sergeant was not amused by my poor attempt at playing Perry Mason, and he had a point, not to mention the power. I knew damn well that I wasn't supposed to be there. I should have gone to the police first. With perfect twenty-twenty hindsight, I realized that Jakes could have greased the skids for me, avoiding this whole mess had I just called him in the first place.

The sergeant rambled on and on about how the police were there to help me. If I had confided in them, they could have worked something out—that as a citizen I had to respect the law, even if I thought that I was within my rights, or trying to do a good deed. He had raised his voice with me, obviously trying to prove a point, to let me know that he meant business, but the more he tried to shout, the more it came out as a high-pitched squeal—not very intimidating.

I decided not to argue. He wasn't a bad guy, probably a pretty decent guy in fact, just not a very good cop, and not a very scary one. I sat there quietly, putting on my contrite act, hoping that he would recognize my repentance and stop yelling, to make the whining stop—to get on with business. After a minute or two, he kind of ran out of gas, or so it seemed, and he buried his head in his hands. Oh shit! What did I do? Did I make the old guy cry?

I felt like such a heel. He reminded me of the grandfather that I never had, and here I made him feel so bad that he was crying right in the middle of his own police station. "Hey," I whispered. "It wasn't your fault, it was me—I screwed up. I'm sorry about this. You were just doing your job."

At that, he opened one eye, peeking just above his hands, which were resting on the desk in front of him. He looked at me with that one red-rimmed eye, clearly clogged with tears, and made kind of a choking sound. I didn't only feel guilty, and sorry for his sad display of emotions in front of his fellow officers, but just about then I was figuring that he was having some kind of fit, or maybe a heart attack. He stared at me with that one eye before he began to raise his head, slowly at first, and then quickly, throwing his head back to the point where I thought his neck would break, and let out a scream of laughter.

I was more than just a little confused as he howled in glee for several minutes, tears streaming down his face, unable to control himself. Most of the others in the large office area emerged from their cubicles, or at least stood up so that their heads were above the partitions so that they could see. All had smiles on their faces, apparently knowing something that I didn't. The more that everybody stared in our direction, the redder my face became. I could feel it getting hotter as the group joined in on the laughter. When the good sergeant finally got control of himself he said, "That lieutenant of yours is some character. You just been set up, compliments of the Chicago and Annapolis police departments."

CHAPTER 7

Jakes was pretty high up in the chain of command because he had his own office, not like the string of tiny cubicles and open office areas that dominated the twelfth district building. It was small, but an office nonetheless, with real walls that went all the way to the ceiling and an actual door that opened and closed. It was closed just then, but I could see him through the glass, his head down, his shoulders stooped over some document that he was studying. I rapped on the glass, startling him, not the least bit sorry that I did. He waved me in but went right back to studying the paper in front of him.

I pulled the chair up to the desk and sat down, not waiting for permission. We were well past that point. We were friends, and friends didn't need to ask if such things were okay. Matter of fact, I guess he was about my best friend, maybe my only friend. Not that I ever had many, certainly not that I'd call close, but the few that I used to have, I hadn't seen or thought much about during the past year. That was fine by me. Those friendships were superficial—business associates, bosses, subordinates—not people that I spent a lot of time with—not people that I trusted. Jakes was different. I liked him ... and I trusted him.

Jakes always did things on his own time schedule, so I sat and waited, knowing he'd get around to me sooner or later. And sure enough, after two or three minutes, he closed the file, pushed his chair back from the desk, and stretched out with his big old size thirteens, nicely crossed atop of his blotter. I thought that I was in for an ass chewing for my little stunt at Susan's, but instead I saw a smile spread across Jakes' face.

Then I thought that I was going to get a little more sarcasm, a few words of wisdom to further humiliate me, more of what I got from Annapolis police the night before. Jakes was a pretty serious guy, but with a mischievous side that I seemed to bring out in him. Maybe it was because I was always so serious, almost to the point of being morose. I was never a jokester, never into pranks or practical jokes. Never the class clown or cutup at parties, but I used to think that I was pretty normal, and had a decent sense of humor. But that was before the events of the past year. Before I lost all that I cared about.

Even though Jakes didn't know me before Liz's death, I think that he sensed that there was a change in me because of it. From time to time he tormented me in order to recapture a little of what I had lost.

However, Jakes wasn't trying to get cute with me, wasn't trying to make me feel worse than I already did. But the smile didn't leave his face, and it was infectious, causing me to smile, as well. The smile could only mean one thing—a break in my wife's case. He tapped the folder twice with his index finger, looking directly into my eyes, the smile on his face getting bigger.

My hands trembled with anticipation as I reached across the desk for the manila folder. I spun it around as I pulled it towards me, noticing the writing on the tab—WILLIAMS, ELIZABETH. I had seen the file before, even if it was unofficial, technically not supposed to exist. Jakes was not a homicide detective, not assigned to find Liz's killer. He was supposed to solve the bank robbery, which wasn't exactly the same thing, even though the same person committed both crimes. It wasn't his file, and he sure as hell wasn't supposed to show it to me. He could get into trouble for it.

I had seen it before and I knew what was in it—a lot of nothing: the coroner's report, depositions from eyewitnesses, anonymous leads that led to nowhere, ballistic reports, police records for both Julius Green and his partner, like I said, a lot of nothing. A year had come and gone, and they were no closer to finding Liz's killer than they were the day after it happened.

I looked down at the folder and then back at Jakes. The smile on his face told me that something new had been added. He returned my gaze and arched one eyebrow as if asking if I were going to look at it or not. I hesitated for another minute, knowing that I was going to open it—just not quite ready for it.

What was I afraid of? Was there something in there that was going to surprise me, to anger me even more than I already was, something that would forever change me in some unforeseen way? I touched the folder, rubbing the tip of my finger lightly across the tab with my wife's name neatly typed, as if there were something magical in her typed name, as if it were actually her that I was touching.

I opened the folder. The top page was a fax. Neatly typed across the top of the page was the name and address of the sender, someone from the Detroit Police Department. It was sent to Sergeant Damian of the Chicago P.D., the officer heading up Liz's homicide. Green had been caught. He was being held under police custody at Henry Ford Hospital. In the lower right hand corner of the fax was a small picture of Green—a mug shot.

I couldn't stop staring at the picture. I had never seen Green before. He had a long history of arrests, and his face was well known to the Chicago police. Surely they had his picture, but I never thought to ask to see it. Now, here it was right in front of me and I couldn't take my eyes off of it.

The picture shocked me, but not because I didn't know what he looked like before. I was surprised because he looked exactly as I imagined he would. I had never actually seen him, not even a picture, but my mind had begun to put together his image from the first day that I heard his name. It began as a blurred, undefined image, shadowy, like looking through shattered glass at an old, worn black and white photograph. Over the past year the picture became clear, gradually, time causing each broken line to mend itself, each hazy shape to solidify. Perhaps more than just time, it was my anger that forced the picture into sharp focus. I needed to put a face to my anger. I needed something solid to hate.

In the picture, Green had close cropped hair, almost a buzz job, but it was obvious that he wasn't *styling*, he was going bald, his hairline receding several inches in the front. I knew that he was a fairly young man, in his late thirties, yet he had heavy lines across his brow and dark circles under eyes that were half closed, like he was about to fall asleep or, more likely, under the influence of some chemical. He had a pimp-looking, pencil-thin mustache that wrapped around a cruel looking mouth into an equally thin goatee. He was an evil looking son of a bitch.

Jakes explained that it was a picture taken following a prior arrest in Chicago, about two years old. There was no current photo taken in Detroit because Green was in no shape to stand up for one.

Green had moved from banks to liquor stores. Apparently, he decided that one of the corner bars in the half-burned out area of Detroit's inner city would be easy-pickings. What he didn't figure on was the fact that shop owners in that particular area of the city are better armed than the police.

The fact that the bar, like most of them in the inner city, had iron bars over all the doors and windows, should have given him a clue. But then Green wasn't exactly the brightest bulb in the string. He made the mistake of turning his back on the owner after grabbing the cash. Before he could flee the store, the owner pulled a handgun from under the counter and shot Green twice in the back. One bullet passed through a lung and lodged against a rib. The other passed clean through, taking out one of his kidneys as it went. Green was in critical condition and the doctors gave him a fifty-fifty chance of surviving.

Green had been alone when he entered the bank, no sign of his dim-witted partner. I couldn't care less about Sid. Everyone knew that it was Green who masterminded the bank job, and it was Green who fired the gun that ended Liz's life. I actually felt kind of sorry for Sid. He didn't have the brains to go it alone, and it was probably just poor damn luck that teamed him up with Green. Maybe Sid would pick a better partner now that Green was out of the picture. One thing for sure, he wasn't going to be getting back together with his former partner. Green was either going to spend the rest of his life in jail, or his life was going to be real, real short.

I wasn't at all sure how I felt about that. I was thrilled that he was caught. Thrilled nothing! I was fucking ecstatic. I wanted to shout it from the rooftops, but, at the same time, part of me hoped that he'd die from his wounds, very slowly and very painfully. Another part of me wanted him to pull through. If he lived, he would have to face trial for murder, and with the evidence against him, he would spend the rest of his life behind bars. He didn't deserve to live, and it would be a shame for the public to have to pay for his upkeep. But the idea of him locked away for the next forty or fifty years, sharing his cell, not to mention certain parts of his anatomy, with a bunkmate named Bubba, had a certain appeal to me.

Jakes had to bring me back to reality. It was going to be a long and involved process. *If* Green survived, and that was a pretty big if, he would be tried for the liquor store holdup, a long and drawn out process in itself. Only when that trial was over, which would take months, maybe even years with the backlog in the Detroit judicial system, could he be extradited to Chicago. Once in Chicago, he would most certainly be convicted of the bank robbery and the murder of my wife, but with a good lawyer, and the appeal process, it would be years before this thing was wrapped up.

Jakes saw the smile fade from my face, followed quickly by his own, only to be replaced with a look of concern. This had been a difficult year for him too, what with the perpetrator evading capture, only to be caught by someone in another city, made even more frustrating because of our developing friendship and his perceived failure to help. But his concern was over *my* reaction to the news.

He had witnessed my periods of deep depression and my fits of anger, and wasn't sure how I was going to react to what he had to tell me. I was not a violent man by nature, but events can change a person. I had never killed, or even harmed another human being intentionally, but I think I could have murdered Green. Even after his capture, no longer a threat to anyone, I could imagine sneaking into his hospital room and putting a pillow over his face, holding it there until he quit struggling. If he had suddenly appeared in this office, I know that I would have made a grab for Jakes' gun and used it.

But Jakes wasn't afraid of me doing harm to Green. He was afraid of me harming myself. I had to think on that one for a minute before I answered. I could see how Jakes could get that idea. I hadn't exactly been a rational man that year, what with Liz's death and the double tragedies on the mountain. I had no friends besides Jakes, no social life outside of the gym, and even my job was on tenuous grounds. And now faced with the possibility of having to wait years to see justice done to the man that started the whole goddamn nightmare, *may* have sent me to seek an end to it all in that way.

I was still pondering the question when Jakes' phone rang. The thought of ending my own life really hadn't occurred to me up until that point, but Jakes' question made me think about it then. It would certainly be easy enough. I had taken a class during my undergraduate studies called *Death and Dying*. It was about the legal, religious, and emotional aspects of dying—really a pretty depressing class. One of the required textbooks was about suicide. It was actually a how-to book, detailing many of the more popular ways of doing one's self in, including a section dedicated to Detroit's Doctor Death, Jack Kervorkian, and his death machine.

The author's method of choice involved taking an overdose of sleeping pills with alcohol and tying a plastic bag loosely around one's head so that as one fell asleep, the lack of oxygen would gradually cease life, painlessly, and with no mess. Seemed simple enough, but also kind of slow. I thought faster was better. Perhaps a bullet between the eyes, or maybe, jumping out in front of a bus, or dropping off the top of a really high building—messy, but quick. And, for me, messy would be okay. I didn't have anyone else to worry about. There was no one to identify the mess, no one to live with the shame and the horror of what I'd done.

But even after I had a chance to think about it, I knew that I wouldn't be taking my own life. It wasn't that I thought that it was morally wrong, and I didn't have any religious hang-ups like worrying about going to hell for it. I just thought it was stupid. Oh, it was okay for those suffering from a painful, terminal illness. It was an intelligent, courageous choice that only hastened the inevitable, and lessened the suffering for all involved. But I thought that it was stupid to kill one's self because of other reasons—not wrong—just stupid.

And I wasn't stupid. Besides, I still had something to live for, someone who needed me. I was about to tell Jakes that he didn't have to worry about that, but he was still on the phone, thoroughly engrossed in some conversation, probably forgetting that I was sitting right in front of him. That's the way Jakes was—very single-minded—able to block out everything around him when he's concentrating on something. It was a quality that I admired, even if sometimes, like at that moment, I was the one being ignored.

So I sat quietly in my chair, feeling only slightly ignored, and waited for him to finish. I thought again about suicide and why it wasn't an option for me. Like I said, it was stupid, and completely unfair—unfair to Susan. I might have been the only one, but I hadn't given up on her. She was a fighter—always had been and always would be. She had to be—life had always been tough for her.

*****

Susan's parents were killed in an auto accident when she was just a baby. For some reason, Susan believed that it had been her parent's first night out since her birth—a celebration of sorts—having survived the long months of anticipation, the long hours of labor, the weeks of sleepless nights and smelly diapers. Irrationally, Susan blamed herself. Maybe if it hadn't been such a difficult birth—maybe if she had been a better baby. As if she had any control over such matters. I was never quite sure whether or not someone had actually told her that it was indeed her parent's first night out, or she just convinced herself over time that it was. Regardless, right or wrong, irrational or not, she believed it and she carried it around on her back all of her life—a big bag-full of guilt.

Her grandmother took her in following the death of her parents, but she was old and in frail health and, for the good of the baby, had to give her up after just a few years. Susan wound up in foster care and went from one temporary family to another. The problem was, her grandmother had had her too long. She was no longer the cute little baby that childless couples want so desperately. She was a toddler, extremely intelligent, but fiercely independent and insolent. To Susan's point of view, nobody wanted her—and she didn't want them right back.

Susan never managed to last with any one family for more than a year, and usually not more than a couple of months. She wasn't a bad kid and didn't get into any kind of serious trouble. She just simply refused to conform to what the adults wanted her to be, frequently leading her foster bothers and sisters in acts of rebellion and childish pranks. As she herself put it, " I was a real pain in the ass."

The foster care system didn't know how to deal with the likes of Susan. Every time that there was a call to come and fetch Susan back from her current home, she just acted innocent and confused, unaware that there was any kind of problem. She never had anything bad to say about any of the families that she was left with, never gave the foster care workers a hard time. She completely confused the system. But it was all an act. Even at an early age, Susan was much smarter than the foster care people, smarter than most of her foster parents. So, they just kept passing her along from one family to the next, always hoping that one would be able to deal with what they could not.

Susan hated the orphanage, hated the rules and regulations, and hated being told what to do and how to do it. It was a controlled environment that completely stifled her inquisitive nature, stunted her desire to discover new things. At the orphanage she had no freedom, no chance to express herself. Yet she was smart enough to know that if she became a problem, the system would only punish her, enforcing more rules and regulations. So she continued with the act and every time a new home became available, Susan was offered up as a well-behaved, ideal little girl.

The foster homes varied from one family to the next, but nearly all of them allowed for more freedom than what she had at the orphanage. Some of them were only in it for the money that the government doled out for each child taken in. Those homes worked out the best for Susan because those families tended to care less what Susan did—as long as she stayed out of trouble. But with a kid as inquisitive as Susan was, trouble was never far away, and, money or no money, there was only so much that the families were willing to put up with.

The most difficult thing for Susan in going from one home to another was the disruption in school. She loved to learn and she could hardly believe that there was somewhere that she could go where she was actually supposed to ask questions, supposed to learn about new things. She excelled in school. She couldn't get enough of it, but she couldn't just turn it off, like a light switch, when the school day ended and she was back in the house of her foster parents. There, she would continue to question everything, continue to dig into things that were none of her business.

So, Susan went from one home to another, one school to the next.

She was a brilliant student who got nothing but perfect grades, no matter what school she was in, no matter what teachers or subjects she had. Teachers loved her, despite her incessant questioning and pushing to go faster and faster. It was never enough. When homework was assigned, she had it done before school was even out. When projects were due, she did twice what she was asked to do. When tests were completed and she got an infrequent question wrong, she questioned it endlessly, so that she would never make that particular mistake again.

As she got older, into junior high school, Susan got worse—or better—depending on your point of view. The questions never ceased, and the teachers became frustrated because they couldn't always answer them to her satisfaction. Intelligence is something one is born with, and Susan's was higher than most—much higher. By high school her knowledge had surpassed many of her teachers, intimidating them, sometimes making them feel insecure and insufficient.

During her junior year there was a history teacher, Elliot Thames, who was *not* intimidated by Susan's intelligence. Just the opposite, he was captivated by her eagerness to learn, her willingness to challenge that which she did not know, to push herself and others beyond what was expected, beyond what was understood.

Like many teachers, Doctor Thames was frustrated with the whole educational system. Schools had become like factories—just push the students through—get them from one grade to the next with as little fuss as possible. And the kids just didn't seem to want to learn. They did just enough to get by—get by, and get out. And who could blame them? Schools were under funded, teachers were underpaid, and the classroom had become a war zone, filled with drugs and violence.

The professor was well past retirement age and he wondered why he stuck with it. He didn't need the money and on more days than not, he left his classroom downhearted and bewildered. But he loved to teach, and he loved reaching those dwindling few that responded to his sharing of knowledge. In Susan, the teacher had found a willing student. She never tired of learning, and he never tired of teaching. They became more than just teacher–student, they became fast friends.

Elliot Thames just happened to be an archeology buff, and had traveled all over the world, being in on a number of significant discoveries. He even wrote a book on the subject, *In Search of Yesterday*, required reading at many major universities. I was amazed years later when Susan told me that—I had a copy on my own bookshelf.

Elliot loved archaeology, but he never taught it. It was a hobby, not a vocation, and by the time he met Susan he was too old to go traipsing around the world, but that didn't stop him from sharing his passion with her.

It didn't take Susan long to get on board. The very idea of digging into the earth and finding something that had been lost for years, maybe hundreds and thousands of years, excited her like nothing had before. Trying to answer all of its mysteries was the ultimate challenge to her. The idea of digging and finding something unsuspected was the biggest thrill of all. The earth was a never-ending treasure trove, and digging it up a never-ending source of surprise.

So, Susan took to digging. Unfortunately, she didn't always give a lot of thought to where she dug. About two months into living with her last set of foster parents, she decided that there was unquestionably something of value beneath the soil of their front yard. She had no idea what was down there, if anything—she only knew that she had to check it out. By the time her foster father came home, some five hours later, it looked like the Battle of the Bulge had been fought there. A perfectly good sod job had been destroyed, holes and matching piles of dirt everywhere. It was the last straw as far as the most recent set of foster parents were concerned. Susan was out of there by the next day. It was funny, but Susan actually did find something of value—an old tin can filled with nineteenth century coins. She had never told anyone, but she still had the coins. She never considered selling them—they were the first things of value that she had ever unearthed.

Being that Susan was only a year away from graduation and her eighteenth birthday, the kindly old professor and his wife took her in. The foster care system was only too glad to find someone who was actually *willing* to take her off its hands. It turned out to be a match made in heaven. Despite their advanced age, the professor and his wife were free spirits, letting Susan voice her opinion freely and even challenging her with new ideas. It was the one thing that had truly been missing in her life—intellectual challenges. All of her earlier rebellion and anger were simple frustrations at not having an outlet for her ambition and natural curiosity.

Susan became fascinated with discovery and she loved all things old—the older the better. There was mystery to them all. Old coins, books, pictures, letters, buildings, works of art ... and people, were incredibly interesting. Especially people—people long since dead—had a special fascination to the young woman. They all had a story to tell. They had a life, each unique, with a beginning and an end and infinite surprises and adventures in between. Susan liked to learn about those lives, and she did it through research. She was a natural at it. When there was an object or a person that she was interested in, she'd dig and dig until she knew everything that there was to know about it. She was like a dog with a bone. She wouldn't let go until there wasn't even the smell of meat left on it.

Through Elliot's influence, she became infatuated with American history. She was interested in all the events that shaped the nation's history—the wars, the discoveries, the important people. She pieced it together like a giant puzzle, always working backwards in time. By the time she was through her senior year she knew more about our country's past than most of the experts. But there was something missing. The history of America is very well documented—there's not much guesswork—it just took research. Susan wasn't satisfied in learning things from books—she wanted to figure things out on her own.

So Susan continued to go back, back to a time when things weren't quite so well documented. With Elliot's guidance, she began intensive research into ancient civilizations and cultures, constantly working backwards in time. She learned of the great Indian and Aztec civilizations of the Americas. She studied the cultures of the Roman Empires, of China, and of Egypt. She did extensive research on the world's first civilization that developed in the Middle East's Fertile Crescent, between the mighty Tigris and Euphrates Rivers. But she still wanted more. She wanted to go back further. Thousands of years just weren't enough. She wanted to go back long before humans existed, long before there was sufficient evidence to figure out what really happened. She wanted to discover things that no one else had discovered before, things that no one even thought of before.

Susan graduated summa cum laude from Boston College with a degree in ancient history. On a whim, she decided to spend the following summer, before beginning on her graduate studies, on a dig in Colorado. Unlike my first experience, Susan was teamed up with a remarkable paleontologist, Jerome Froilage, a researcher known as much for his warmth and sense of humor as for his breathtaking finds.

Professor Froilage's specialty was the Jurassic period, a time when North America and Africa were still connected and most of Europe was under water—when the largest animals that ever lived roamed the earth—more than a hundred and fifty million years ago. And Susan's team found one of the biggest, an *Ultrasaurus*, well over one hundred feet long and nearly complete. A relative of the *Brachiosaurus*, the *Ultrasaurus*, an herbivore, weighed in at one hundred and fifty tons, about twenty times that of a full-grown African elephant.

Susan was hooked. Not just by the enormous size or condition of the find, but by the mystery of it all. All her life, she had been digging, searching for this and that, looking for the reasons why, and trying to answer the questions that inevitably popped up. If she dug up an old coin in the dirt, she would wonder how it got there, who owned it, and how many things it had bought. When she had first learned the name of some historical character, she wouldn't rest until she knew everything about that person, where and when he was born, how he grew up, how he achieved his notoriety, and how he died. She loved solving a puzzle, or maybe she just loved *trying* to solve a puzzle. She loved the hunt—the search for things unknown.

For Susan, dinosaurs proved to be the ultimate mystery. So little was known about these magnificent creatures. Although dinosaur fossils had undoubtedly been unearthed for thousands of years, they were not recognized for what they were—the ancient remains of living creatures—until the early nineteenth century. Little is known about how they lived ... or how they died. Susan saw in dinosaur research a never-ending series of riddles, puzzles, and questions. She could live for a thousand years and not find the answers to more than a tiny fraction of them. But she was going to try.

That fall, Susan switched her major to paleontology, and was accepted readily at California Berkeley. She had the grades to get a scholarship had she applied, but money wasn't a problem. During her junior year of college, her mentor and adopted father, the kindly Doc Elliot, as she called him, had died peacefully in his sleep from heart failure. The professor's wife followed him within a year. Susan's adopted parents were not wealthy, but they left most of what they had to Susan, knowing that she would use it wisely in her relentless pursuit of knowledge.

During her undergraduate years, Susan was pretty much just a regular student, albeit very driven and single-minded. She was relatively friendly and outgoing, yet didn't have a lot of friends because she just wasn't into socializing. She preferred evenings at the library, with her nose buried deep in a book, to seeing a movie. She favored wandering through the woods with her metal detector to going to a party. Because of her intelligence she got her share of teasing and a few of her fellow students made the occasional smart-ass remark about her ambition, but mostly college life was pretty routine.

But grad school was another matter. Back then, paleontology was still a male-dominated profession, and women taking it as a major were still outnumbered ten to one in the classroom. To make matters worse, the better jobs with the major museums and universities were few and far between, making competition amongst students severe. So Susan had two strikes against her—she was female, and she was the smartest in her class.

She didn't try to show up the others in the class and never felt superior to any of them, but her unquenchable desire to learn and her extreme intelligence made her a dominating presence in the classroom. She just couldn't stop asking questions and wasn't above arguing with her professors when she thought they were wrong. She consistently got the highest grades in class and was constantly singled out when the rest of the class was unable to answer a question. A few students took exception to the attention she received, so they decided to get even.

During mid-terms of her second semester, Bobby Overmann, former high school and college jock, a guy just barely hanging in there grade wise, decided to hatch a plot to get her into trouble with professor Wrigley, one of the tougher professors in the program—a professor that Susan had had more than a few arguments with and was probably not on his best side. The day of the mid-term exam, Bobby and a couple conspirators, jimmied the lock on the professor's door. They didn't take anything, but just left the lock busted so that there was no doubt that someone had broken in. They then started a rumor that somehow Susan had come into possession of the test questions.

It didn't take long for word to reach the professor, and being that Susan had received a perfect score on the test, not to mention an already shaky relationship between the two, he confronted her. Susan wasn't just defensive—she was pissed! She got a perfect grade because she worked her ass off for it. How dare he assume she was a common thief, how dare he think that she would need to stoop to that level to do well on a test. Didn't he know how hard she worked, how long she had been getting top marks?

She really let Wrigley have it. The combination of yelling and swearing stopped the teacher dead in his tracks. With a beet-red face he had to pause to take stock of the situation. Susan *had* done well on every quiz, every test, and every assignment for as long as he'd known her. It was preposterous to think that she had stolen the answers to *all* of them. Someone had set her up, and in the process, set him up as well. But Wrigley wanted to save face, afraid to just admit he was wrong and to apologize.

He decided that the most appropriate thing to do was to administer a retest for Susan, a different, more difficult test. Susan could have objected, it was unfair as hell and there was absolutely no proof that she had stolen the test questions, but she was eager to prove to Wrigley, beyond a shadow of a doubt, that she earned every grade she ever received.

So Susan took the test ... and got another perfect score. To Wrigley's credit, he apologized to Susan in front of the whole class and announced that he would make it his mission to find the culprit.

Wrigley never did find out who was responsible for the break in, but that didn't stop Susan from extracting her revenge. Susan knew who did it and could make a pretty good guess as to whom his accomplices were. Bobby and his little group had been a royal pain in the ass the entire semester, always looking for ways to harass or embarrass her, covering up their own shortcomings by trying to elicit laughs at her expense.

Susan didn't date much during her college years, although it wasn't because of a lack of interest on the men's part. She could have had her pick of the guys, and they kept asking. But she kept turning them down. Dating just wasn't an important part of her life. A few of the guys that had been turned down, including Bobby Overmann, made up their minds that Susan was a lesbian. Why else would she turn down the likes of Bobby Overmann? Bobby took to making snide little remarks about Susan's sexuality, under his breath at first, louder as he failed to get a rise out of her.

It was about two weeks after the break-in of Wrigley's office when Susan and I were sitting at one of the school's favorite hangouts, a little pub with the unimaginative name of *The Berkeley Bar*. We were sitting at the first booth by the door when they walked in. Bobby and two of his pals sauntered in like they owned the place. They spotted Susan immediately and as they passed by, Bobby bent down low and whispered—just loud enough for both of us to hear—a few off color comments about her sexual orientation. They saw me, as well, and they knew that I could kick the shit out of any one of them individually, but they were together, and together cowards can put up a pretty brave front.

I started to rise from my seat when Susan gave me a little smile and a barely perceptible shake of the head. Instead, Susan swiveled in her seat so that her long legs were dangling out the side of the booth and in her most sexy voice said, "It's too bad you're such a peckerhead, Bobby. I've been giving it away to half the campus. And it's good, too. Ask just about anyone. But you'll never even get a smell of it, you limp-dick cocksucker."

Bobby halted immediately, the other two nearly climbing up his ass. With his fists clenched, Bobby turned, taking a step forward as he did.

It was one step too many.

It put him directly in front of Susan, and she wasted no time swinging her leg just as hard as she could, her foot connecting with the guy's testicles. His scream rose in pitch to a height that I would have thought impossible for a man to make, or any human being, but not at all surprising considering the young man's nuts must have been somewhere stuck in his throat. The sound continued despite the laughter of nearly everyone else in the bar as he crumbled to the floor, his hands wrapped around the scrotum that used to hold his balls.

*****

I was still thinking about Bobby lying on the floor, rolled up into a tight little ball with his hands stuck between his legs, when I heard Jakes slam the phone into its cradle, making the windows in his office rattle. He was mad as hell at something or someone, but I had no idea at what or at whom. It must have had something to do with the phone call, but I hadn't paid any attention to the one side of the conversation that I could have heard because I was lost in my little trip to the past.

Jakes sat there with his arms crossed, jaws tight, the little vein in his forehead jumping up and down. He stared at the ceiling, breathing hard through his nose. He refused to talk, but every once in a while made a little hissing sound through clenched teeth and muttered a curse under his breath. He wasn't looking at me but he knew that I was still there. As I said, he was single minded. When he was ready, he'd talk to me. No way was I going to interrupt him in that state ... he had a gun.

He finally looked me right in the eyes and let out an angry growl. Still not speaking, he got up from the chair and paced back and forth across the tiny office. He reached from behind me and picked up the file, taking out the top page before tossing the folder back down on the desk in front of me. He continued pacing the office, back and forth, back and forth, never taking his eyes from the single page. After what seemed like an eternity, he laid the fax on the table and placed one long finger on the picture of Green.

"Green's gone!" he said through clenched teeth.

At first I wasn't sure that I heard him right. "What do you mean, Green's gone? How the hell can he be gone? You just said the son of a bitch was fighting for his life in some hospital in Detroit. How could a guy with two bullet holes in him be gone?" I was beginning to get angry when I thought—maybe Green was dead. Yeah, that must have been what Jakes meant. Green was dead *and* gone.

I still hadn't made up my mind whether dead was better than in prison, but I sure as hell knew that dead was better than gone. My temper started to ease up a bit when I realized that if Green really was dead, Jakes was taking it way too hard.

"That was Detroit P.D.," Jakes said. "Despite Green's wounds, and the presence of a Detroit cop positioned just outside his door, he escaped out a second story window. Nobody saw it, but when the nurse came in on routine rounds, he was gone, and the window was wide open, the curtains flapping in the breeze."

"Come on Jakes. How in the hell can a man that has been shot, not once, but twice, climb out a second story window?"

Jakes let out a sigh, saying, "Things don't always move quickly in the land of law enforcement. Just because I heard the news a few minutes ago, don't mean that it *just* happened."

The liquor store holdup had happened more than a month ago, but it was some ten days later that, just by pure luck, an officer involved in the investigation happened to stumble upon the all-points bulletin out of Chicago. Computers are great, but you have to know what you're looking for. When the Detroit P.D. realized that Green was wanted for murder in Chicago, they made a call to officer Damian, who then, just in passing, mentioned it to Jakes. Jakes tried desperately to get in touch with me, but of course I was off on an investigation of my own, trying to find out who was going to handle Susan's problems.

Green was in intensive care, in a coma, teetering between life and death for nearly two weeks. The damage caused by the bullets had been repaired and the wounds were healing, but the loss of blood that had brought on the coma continued to threaten his life. There may also have been brain damage, just how extensive could not be determined until he came around.

During the third week he regained consciousness and all of his vital signs were strong, but they still couldn't fully ascertain the extent of any damage to the brain. Green was alert and responded to sensory stimuli, but couldn't, or wouldn't, talk. His eyes worked though—they followed anyone in the room with an intensity that bordered on the spooky. He watched, but he never made a sound.

Within a few days the doctors said that Green was out of danger and could be questioned by the police. The police got nowhere. Green looked the sergeant right in the eye during the questioning, but never uttered a sound, never made the slightest facial expression. Just that stare, that seemed to say, "*I hear you, I just ain't talking.*" They tried for the next several days, never for more than an hour at a time, and never got a response from Green other than that continuous, mocking stare.

The police were frustrated. They thought for sure that Green was just conning them—that he could both hear and understand every word that was said to him. The doctors weren't quite so sure. With an injury of this kind there was just no way of knowing for sure what was going on in Green's mind. He might very well have heard every word spoken to him, but might not have known how to respond, or maybe, heard, but didn't understand. To Green's brain the words may have sounded like just so much noise, or a foreign language.

The police gave up after a couple of days. Perhaps they let down their guard.

Perhaps everybody did.

It was the third day after the questions stopped that Green disappeared. There was no longer any doubt in the police's mind that Green had been acting all the time, at least since coming out of the coma. He had been looking for a pattern. The cops came in about the same time every day for questioning, then one day they stopped. One day was not a pattern.

Two days were, and when the second day came and went, Green was ready to take action. On the third day there were no cops, and even fewer hospital staff. It was hours between visits, no poking and probing every fifteen minutes. No one knew for sure how he did it, but he sure didn't do it alone. He might have been acting, but there was no faking his injuries, the two bullet holes that were not yet healed. He was in no position to escape on his own. I couldn't help but think of Sid, his half-wit accomplice, but I found it equally as hard to think that an idiot like Sid would be of much help in figuring out something like this.

How the whole scheme was planned was another mystery. Green was allowed no visitors and no phone calls. No one from the outside could have just strolled up to his second floor window and struck up a conversation with him. He may have been able to talk, but the doctors didn't think he was able to get out of the bed and make his way over to the window. I guess it really didn't matter to me how he did it. The fact was—he was gone.

That certainly explained why Jakes was so pissed. He had a lot invested in this case, both personally and professionally. It took a year to catch up with Green, only to lose him again. Even if it wasn't his fault, it was frustrating as hell to be so close, and then nothing. The friendship that had developed between Jakes and I during the past year made it that much harder for him to swallow.

I made a feeble attempt to make him feel better. "You guys caught him once, you'll catch him again. There's no place for him to hide."

He looked up at me slowly, deliberately. "That ain't exactly how things work around here, David. Before he was caught and interrogated, Green had no idea how badly we wanted him. As far as he knew, no one had tied him to the robbery and murder in Chicago. He left the city because he had beaten the shit out of his girlfriend. He didn't know that she told us about the robbery, or about the murder of your wife. And no one in Detroit cared about him beating up some cheap, back-alley whore, nearly three hundred miles away.

"But now, Green knows everything. He figured it all out while he was in the hospital. He'd have to do something really stupid to get caught again. Everyone's looking for him and he'll go so far underground that nobody will ever find him. Whoever helped him escape the hospital will make damn sure of that."

Now I *was* pissed! As pissed as Jakes was. And not just at Green. The cops had let Green get away, and it was a cop telling me then that the chances were slim that he'd be caught again. I realized later that it wasn't Jakes' fault, but that's not how I felt about it at that time. I blamed the police. It didn't matter whether it was in Detroit or Chicago. They were all cops, and they had all screwed up.

I got up from my chair and stood nose to nose with Jakes. He had a look about him that made it clear that it was the wrong time to mess with him. I knew that look. I'm sure that it was on me as well, so I said nothing. We stared into each other's eyes, sharing a common thought. As I turned to leave his office, I looked him in the eye and said, "Just find him, Jakes—just fucking find him."

CHAPTER 8

The arms were still the problem. They looked so damn useless, so disproportionate, like somebody just stuck them there as an afterthought. The leg bones were huge, twelve feet long when straightened, and a girth capable of supporting seven tons. They were legs built for speed, the legs of a predator, covered with huge slabs of muscle, capable of covering vast distances in a short time—able to chase down and destroy slower animals even when outweighed by three to one. Pound for pound, they were the legs of the most fearsome creature that ever walked the face of the earth.

But the arms were tiny. Even outstretched, the ulna and humerus combined barely measured two feet. Even with the two, clawed fingers extended, they were smaller than those of an adult human. They looked absurd on this huge body, not only out of place, but seemingly without function as well.

A few paleontologists believed that the arms and claws were used when feeding, that, indeed, they were necessary for eating. I thought the idea was ridiculous. The tiny appendages didn't even come close to reaching the massive head of the beast. Besides, there were thousands of species of animals that fed just fine with no arms at all, no legs either, for that matter. With its rows of sharp serrated teeth and powerful neck and jaws, the *Tyrannosaur* had everything it needed for killing and consuming its prey.

Others thought that they were used in battle, either for defending itself or attacking its enemy, that the long double claws on each hand made formidable weapons. I didn't like this theory either. Had the claws been on the ends of long, powerful arms, then, maybe they would have been serious weapons. But, as small as they were, an animal would have to have been practically on top of the *Tyrannosaur* before the claws would have been of any value as a weapon. The animal's three-foot long jaws extended far beyond the reach of the short arms, making them completely unnecessary in battle.

The other popular theory was that the arms were used to help the dinosaur rise from a prone position. But the bones of the arms were spindly and fragile compared to the rest of the skeletal structure, very unlikely that they could support much of the weight of an animal twice the mass of a full-grown elephant. And they were so short that the only way that they could have been any use whatsoever in helping a *rex* right itself was if the body was so precisely balanced that it only needed the tiniest push. Admittedly a possibility, but so little was known of the musculature or internal structure of a *Tyrannosaurus rex*, that its center of gravity was impossible to predict with any accuracy.

No, I didn't care for any of the popular theories, but I really didn't have a good one of my own. I didn't think the arms had any useful function at all, but were nothing more than an obvious result of evolution. *Allosaurus*, an ancestor of the *Tyrannosaur* from the late Jurassic period, some seventy million years earlier, had arms that were comparatively, two to three times the size of those of the *rex*. It had three distinctive curved claws on each and it was commonly believed that they were used for killing and holding its victim while it fed. Over time, other anatomical changes made the function unnecessary and the arms obsolete. Very slowly the arms began to shrink, both in purpose and physical presence. If the *Tyrannosaur* survived a few more million years, I believed that the arms would have disappeared altogether.

Of course, it was just a theory.

As they hadn't survived long enough for that to happen, I was stuck with what to do with mine. Oh I knew where they went, which bone was connected to which, but beyond that, I was lost. The few skeletons that existed, and in every drawing that I had ever seen of a *Tyrannosaur*, the arms looked out of place. If the restorer or artist went for a menacing look with arms reaching out as if to attack, the effect seemed unrealistic, even humorous—like a malformed *Frankenstein*. On the other hand, if the arms were left just to hang there, which may have been the more accurate depiction, the effect was worse, even stupid. It made the king of the dinosaurs look like it was begging—like some pathetic dog.

I tried moving them every which way, had been at it all day, but couldn't find a position in which I was satisfied. Of course there really wasn't much to work with, or many options to choose from. Arms out, or arms down, one out and one down, arms bent or unbent, maybe one of each. Those were the limited choices. If, perhaps, I could figure out a real purpose, a reason for the damn things, maybe I could put them in a position that had some meaning. But of course, I couldn't. They were bound to stay one of many unsolved mysteries surrounding the *Tyrannosaur*.

It was too bad though, because the rest of the picture on the computer terminal was pretty damn impressive, if I did say so myself. I positioned the creatures as I had imagined them on the day that we had uncovered all of the prints in front of the cave. It was the moment just as the *Tyrannosaur* turned to attack the *Triceratops*, the carnivore's body twisting toward its prey, its mouth open wide, just beginning to lunge toward the exposed neck of the *Triceratops*.

As it would have been in life, the predator's tail was lifted off the ground, curled slightly at the tip, and just beginning to swing away from its prey, a movement designed to reverse the *Tyrannosaur's* direction and accelerate its attack. The right leg was raised slightly, the three-toed foot pointed down, the claws just inches above the earth, moving up and forward, about to slam against the body of the *Triceratops* at the instant that the eight inch teeth sank into the soft, unprotected area behind the frill. The dual strikes were meant to be the death blows, the teeth cutting through the thick hide and muscle of the *Triceratops*, to the bone, while simultaneously pushing against the huge body, causing the neck to snap, killing it almost instantly.

The *Triceratops*, being much slower than the predator, had not yet fully turned its lumbering body to confront the *rex* as it moved past, but its head had turned to face it's foe, lowered, its pointed chin just touching the ground. It was an instinctive move, inherited from millions of years of fighting for its survival. It was a move developed to keep its primary defense, that of the twin horns and hardened frill, in front of the attacker. Its body twisted slightly toward the *Tyrannosaur*, as it tried to keep up with the much quicker animal, its left leg bent slightly, in an attempt to reverse its direction. The back portion of its anatomy was held high, ready to follow the lead of its forelegs. It was a last ditch effort to save itself.

Poised in the background, not as I saw it inside the cave, but just to the left of the entrance, was the female *Triceratops*, not cowering, but bent slightly over the infant, protecting it, shielding it from the possibility of a wild charge of the *rex*. The baby was sitting back on its tail, its head held high, as if trying to understand just what was happening, sniffing at the air, as if that could put some meaning into the situation. The female, knowing all too well what was about to transpire, understood that the *Tyrannosaur* was a killer that was likely to turn on them if it was victorious with its current foe.

It was a moment frozen in time. A moment, just one small fraction of a second before everything significant occurred, a moment that was to decide the end of one life and the continuity of another, a moment that was to tell which one lived and which one died. It was how I pictured it, standing before the mountain all those months ago, a snapshot taken a heartbeat before the *Tyrannosaur* snapped the neck of the *Triceratops*, a moment before the *Triceratops* impaled the *Tyrannosaur* with its deadly horn.

That was how I saw it. I had agonized over the placement of all four animals, over every position, over every bone. I spent hours looking at every angle, every possibility, making the image on the computer monitor match perfectly the image formed in my mind of that final moment. They were only skeletons, bones that had been buried under thousands of tons of rock and dirt for millions of years, the flesh and organs long since rotted away. And yet, I had made them come back to life.

When completed, they would become the crown jewel of the museum's collection. They would stand in the atrium of the Chicago Museum of Paleontology, just inside the entrance where everyone would see them as they first entered, where they would be seen from anywhere on the balcony of the second floor. No others were as complete, or instilled such emotion. Just bones, but no other display captured the intensity of the moment. Even though the *rex* stood motionless, it was positioned in such a way as to emote the blinding speed and savagery of its strike. And there was no facial expression on the *T-tops*, but his stance caught the fierce determination to defend itself. The other two figures, those of the female and infant *Triceratops*, although in the background, portrayed a strong sense of family, the love between a mother and her child.

It was a Monday, nearly two weeks after I completed the computer model, with the exception of the position of the arms, of course. I had spent the entire day fooling with the hands without coming up with anything that I was happy with. But to be truthful, I really wasn't giving it my full attention. I had been preoccupied with other things. Preoccupied thinking about the amazing conversation that I had in a dimly lit booth of the local tavern the previous Friday night—a most remarkable conversation with the most bizarre little man that I had ever met.

*****

I had just finished my Friday night workout, disappointed that I didn't get the kind of satisfaction from it that I usually did. It was a good workout. I did all the exercises, got up a good sweat, went through my posing routine, but I couldn't quite free my mind of my troubles. I pushed myself even harder than usual, trying to get that separation between mind and body. I went at it frantically, reducing the time between sets, minimizing the time when my mind was free to roam, until I was going from one machine to the next with almost no rest at all.

Like always, I finished my workout with a trip to the sauna, and as good as the heat felt on my tired muscles, there was just nothing there to block out the memories of the past. I couldn't stop thinking about the events of the past eighteen months: Liz's murder, Susan's accident, Christine's death, Green's arrest and subsequent escape. Haunting images kept flashing through my mind, crystal clear and always in chronological order. Yellow roses on a gleaming silver casket, Susan lying broken across the rocks, Christine's pale, frozen tear-stained face looking up at me that last time in the cave, Green's pimp-looking face staring back at me from the fax. Those same four pictures, over and over again, like a video that keeps playing, rewinding, only to begin playing again—over and over again.

It was getting harder and harder to block them out. Workouts hadn't been doing it very well the last few weeks and not at all on that day. My job wasn't going as well as it should have either. Working with the computer program, figuring out how we were going to put my skeletons together should have engrossed me totally, should have had my undivided attention. It was what I had been waiting for my whole career—maybe my whole life.

But the joy just wasn't there.

And I had a weekend staring me right in the face. I dreaded the thought of sitting around the house by myself, nothing to occupy my mind, nothing to block out the images—two whole days with nothing to do but watch with frustration the same four mind-numbing pictures flash through my mind one after another ... endlessly.

I left the gym and headed for my car, dreading the thought of going home. Pulling out of the parking lot a flashing neon light caught my eye—Leon's Bar and Grill—a place where a lot of the gym rats hung out. I figured what the hell, I needed to eat, and the thought of a couple of beers sounded pretty good to me right about then—maybe more than a couple of beers. If I got a good enough buzz that night then maybe the images would drown, at least for the night. Even the thought of the next day's hangover was preferable to a morning full of flashbacks.

The tables were full, so I took a seat at the bar and ordered a double cheeseburger, an order of onion rings, and a draft. Cholesterol-city, but I loved a good burger and Leon's had the best. I didn't splurge often, but I deserved it that night. Maybe I needed it more that I deserved it. I intended to indulge myself in whatever ways possible.

The bartender brought the first beer right away, telling me that the food would be up shortly. The place was jammed so I figured I'd be well into my second or third beer by the time that the food actually got there. As I suspected, there were a bunch of the regulars from the gym there, and several of them stopped by to say hi. I didn't hang out at bars very often, so it was unusual for them to see me there, and they wanted to buy me a round. But I didn't want to socialize—I needed to be alone that night, so I politely declined, telling them that I'd catch them another time.

I was working on my second beer, still waiting for the food, when someone took the stool next to me. Not wanting to appear rude, I checked him out from the corner of my eye in the mirror over the bar. I tried not to stare, but he was such an unusual looking man. With him sitting, it was hard to tell, but I'd have bet he was no taller than five foot, probably a couple of inches shorter—not a dwarf, just someone really short, or should I say severely vertically challenged. He wore incredibly thick, horned rim glasses, and was nearly bald—just sparse, wild tufts of thin blond hair scattered around the fringe of his scalp.

He was wearing a single-breasted, threadbare suit that was probably forty years out of date. Very narrow lapels from the sixties, and a knit tie to match, its color gray, or an extremely faded black. It hung askew from a neck nearly as thick as his head, under a multi-layer chin. The suit coat was unbuttoned, and the way that it was stretched tightly over his arms and shoulders, I doubted that he could button it.

This was a man who wasn't used to dressing up. The outfit was probably the closest thing he had to formal. Either that or he didn't give much of a damn how he looked. And considering his physical stature, maybe clothes really weren't that important. He was short-changed by nature, but it didn't seem to bother him any. He had rosy red cheeks and a glint in his eye. The corners of his lips turned up in a permanent half-smile, as if he were about to break into a laugh at any minute.

He had his elbows on the bar, which was a real stretch for him, being that the tip of his chin barely cleared it. Actually it was more than the elbows—his arms were stretched out across the bar, its padded edge snug up against his armpits. He was so short that the bartender didn't see him for several minutes, but it didn't appear to bother the strange little guy. He just sat there with that silly look on his face staring into the mirror.

It must have been his hands dangling over the far side of the bar that got the attention of the bartender because he appeared very suddenly. The bartender was experienced enough to not say anything stupid like he didn't see him sitting there, but he was overly gracious and polite, like he knew that he screwed up. The little guy refused the menu that was offered, but ordered a scotch straight up instead. When the bartender poured it, the rumpled little man said in a deep, resonant voice, "Leave the bottle, please." This guy was a serious drinker!

But the man didn't immediately pick up the shot glass and down the scotch as I thought he would. Instead he just sat there staring into the mirror, spinning the glass around and around on the bar, creating a little slick of scotch beneath the glass as it dribbled over the sides. I tried not to stare, but it was almost impossible with the huge mirror right in front of us, and with him setting next to me. I only had to shift my eyes the tiniest bit to the right, and there he was. There wasn't anyone to talk to, so there wasn't much for me to do but to just stare straight ahead.

I couldn't help but to take a peek every now and then, and every time I did, he was still in exactly the same position, looking straight ahead, slowly spinning the glass, making the little wet spot bigger and bigger. This went on all throughout my *gourmet* dinner and through my third beer. He still hadn't touched his drink as I polished off the last of mine. I thought about having another, and figured, what the hell, I had no place else to go. The little man must have been waiting for that exact moment because, as I began to lift the mug to let the bartender know that I wanted another, the man to my right spoke up.

"Let me buy one for you." When I heard the first sounds come from him, I wasn't sure whom he was speaking to. I glanced over at the bartender, thinking that the little man was talking to him, but he was way over at the other end of the bar. I returned my gaze to the mirror to see that the little guy never so much as turned his head. He just kept staring at his own reflection as he said very quietly but very clearly, "How about letting me buy the next drink, Doctor Williams?"

He must have thought that I was deaf, or maybe just stupid. I sat there staring at his reflection with my mouth hanging open, not sure that I actually heard what I thought I heard. I wasn't what you'd call a regular drinker. Maybe the three beers had got to me and I was hearing things. But after a few moments, he asked a third time. "Doctor Williams, will you share a drink with me?"

At that point, if he didn't already think I was stupid, I put that question to rest. I turned to look at him, my mouth still hanging open, and simply nodded my head in the affirmative. He had a big fat smile on his face, and suggested that perhaps we'd be more comfortable in a booth, that perhaps it would be more private. Still struck dumb, I rose from my stool and let him guide me to a small, secluded booth in the back of the pub.

As we left, he motioned to the bartender to bring over another shot glass. He was there before we were even seated. The little guy poured as I continued to stare at him open-mouthed. It was probably about that time that I realized I was drooling, and probably looked like a world-class doofus. I fought to get it together, finding just a touch of dignity and a sense of reality. Who was this strange little man, and how in the hell did he know who I was?

"The name is Dermot, Anson Dermot," he said as a way of introduction.

The name meant nothing to me, which should have came as no surprise on that night. Nothing was making a hell of a lot of sense to me.

"I teach astrophysics at Cal Berkeley, or, at least I used to before I retired," and he reached out to shake my hand. He still had that big smile on his cherubic face while mine continued to register nothing but stupidity. Nonetheless, I took his hand, which he shook vigorously.

We sat down and I continued to stare at him for several minutes, confused and spooked at the same time, before I finally asked, "How do you know my name, Mr. Dermot?"

He chuckled at that and said, "Oh, I know much more about you than just your name Dr. Williams. I'm very interested in your work, have been for quite some time."

I thought that perhaps he had actually been one of the two or three people who had read some of my journal articles. I asked, "Oh, are you interested in dinosaurs?"

He laughed even harder at that and declared, "Oh, my good man, to be sure, to be sure."

But as quickly as the laugh came on, it disappeared, along with his smile. He abruptly changed the subject. "I was so very sorry to hear about the loss of your wife. And Susan, how's she doing? Has there been any change in her condition? I think it's marvelous what you're doing for her, talking to her every day, trying to bring her out of the coma."

This was getting spooky. The hairs on the back of my neck were standing at attention and I had goose bumps up and down my arms. Was this guy spying on me? Was he a stalker? He sure didn't seem threatening in any way, and he didn't act threatening, but how did he know so much about me, and why should he care? Lots of people knew about Liz and about Susan, it was a matter of public record, but damn few knew about my daily visits to the hospital.

If he *was* spying on me, maybe he was a private detective, although he couldn't have looked less the part. It was certainly one fine disguise. But why would a private eye be after me? I didn't owe anybody any money. I hadn't been hanging around anyone else's wife or girlfriend. And other than my little indiscretion in Maryland, I wasn't in any trouble with the law. I couldn't think of anyone that I had pissed off recently except for Jakes, and I really didn't think that he would have sent someone to keep an eye on me. Hell, he could have done that himself. If someone suspected me of something underhanded or illegal, I had no clue as to what it could have been.

I had been on a pretty short fuse in recent months, and ordinarily I would have gotten upset over the idea of someone delving into my private life, but I just couldn't get mad at this guy. He was so unassuming and exuded such an air of humor and good will that all I could muster was curiosity, and a good measure of amazement. As the night went on I didn't change my opinion of him. He was indeed one of the most friendly, outgoing people that I had ever met, and whatever surprise I had felt initially became downright astonishment.

I didn't know what to say to him, so I picked up the shot glass, drinking the scotch down in one quick swallow hoping that it would loosen up my vocal chords. It burned going down and made my eyes water. While the warmth spread through my abdomen, my newfound acquaintance solved the dilemma for me.

"When are you going to begin the reconstruction of the four skeletons?" he asked.

This was another piece of common knowledge—it was in most of the papers. But it still wasn't the kind of thing that the average Joe on the street knew, and there weren't more than a handful of people that knew that I was the one doing it.

I was beginning to get used to his surprises when he asked about the hands. "Have you figured out what to do with them?"

I didn't see that one coming. Apparently, my life was just one big open book to him.

I wasn't aware of the passage of time. Maybe it had been an hour, maybe three. We had gone through more than half the bottle of scotch and he had told me nothing of himself. Between drinks we discussed nothing but me, or really, my problems. He wanted to know all about the expedition to Utah, specifically the details of Susan's accident. He was especially interested in what the doctor had to say about her condition and prognosis. He was a very intelligent and educated man. He knew all the right questions to ask—all the ones that I had been asking—all the ones that he knew would piss me off. I had the feeling that he already knew all the answers. He appeared to know more about Susan's case than I did.

Working well into the second half of the bottle, we got around to discussing Christine. With my thoughts preoccupied with Susan, I really hadn't thought too much about her in recent months, or maybe I just pushed it to the back of my mind because it was just too much to deal with. In some ways, Christine's death affected me in more profound ways than the other things did. Liz and Susan were adults, capable of making their own decisions, their own choices in life. I did feel some sense of responsibility for them both. They were both people I cared about and I couldn't help but feel that I had let them down in some way—didn't do enough to prevent the tragedies.

But Christine was just a kid. Her parents had trusted that I would take care of her, that I would protect her from harm. Kids don't always make good decisions. I was supposed to do that for her, but I let her down. I had let my whole team down. The other four kids had recovered physically, but who knew what kinds of scars I had left on their young souls.

I stared into the flame of the candle that was centered on the table before us, seeing Christine's small, pale body as they pulled her from the snow. Her face glistened from the ice formed by the tears that she shed the night before. She looked like a fragile china doll as they brushed the last of the snow from her. The others on the team wept openly, hugging one another, comforting each other, holding on to a piece of reality in the middle of a nightmare. I had cried on that day, too.

Sitting in the dark corner of the bar, reliving the experience, brought the tears again. The light of the candle blurred; yellows, reds, and a touch of blue, mixing into an orange haze that obscured everything else in sight. I wept unashamed, the tears striking the table in front of me, forgetting for the moment the professor sitting across from me.

The hard liquor wasn't helping my emotional state, but I was beyond the point of caring. I took another long swallow of the bitter, amber fluid. I dabbed at my eyes, wiping away the tears, clearing my vision. Seeing Mister Dermot once again, I felt a twinge of embarrassment. The look of sorrow on his face told me that I shouldn't feel that way.

"Is Lieutenant Jakes making any progress in the recovery of Julius Green?" he asked.

I went to the bar that night to try to get away from my problems, but the strange little man sitting across from me wasn't making it easy. The mere mention of Green's name pushed the sadness of Christine's death back into some far away recess of my mind, and displaced it with white-hot rage. I felt the heat rise to my cheeks, more from the anger than from the booze. I glared at Dermot, but he only stared back with that same silly expression plastered on his face. Now *he* was making *me* mad. Was he goading me, *trying* to get a rise out of me?

First he brought up Susan, reminding me that her situation was nearly hopeless, that the doctors could do nothing more for her. Then he brought up the subject of Christine's death, forcing me to deal with a memory so painful that I had hidden it away rather than deal with it. And just when he's got me blubbering like a baby, he zapped me with Green's escape. How the hell could he know that? Did he have Jakes' office bugged?

I lost my temper and lunged for Dermot, grabbing him by his skinny lapels, knocking over the bottle of scotch in the process, spilling out the bit remaining on the table and onto his pants. It got very quiet, very quickly in the bar. Everyone turned in our direction, but Dermot never moved, never tried to defend himself. His expression never changed, which only infuriated me further. The bartender started toward me, so I let go of Dermot and held my hands up, indicating that I wasn't going to cause any more trouble. Dermot never said a word, but righted the bottle, and, using a napkin, wiped the scotch from his pants.

I was still standing, gripping the edge of the table to keep my balance. I had drunk too much and the room was beginning to tilt, first one way, and then the other. Dermot was coming in and out of focus and the room began to spin. I fell, more than sat back down in the chair, a death-grip on the table, trying in vain to make the room stand still. I closed my eyes tightly, but the dizziness only intensified until I felt my stomach begin to turn inside out. I ran for the toilet as fast as my inebriated condition would allow.

And I almost made it, too. But all three stalls were occupied. I turned for the sink and made it half way there before I erupted, the greasy contents of my stomach spewing forth with a velocity that was startling, bits of hamburger and onion reaching the opposite wall, covering the sink, and dribbling down on my shoes. The whole disgusting mess was held together and propelled by the best part of a fifth of scotch, its once golden yellow color transformed to a revolting shit-brown.

I hated throwing up, which is probably why I didn't drink very much. Besides the stench and vile taste, the gagging left me choking and coughing, unable to catch my breath. My nose ran like a faucet, the same awful bile running from those orifices as well. My eyes burned and filled with tears such that I couldn't see where I was aiming the second round.

Basically, I felt like I was dying.

By the third or forth round I was choking up nothing but spittle, which ran down my chin, staining the front of my shirt. It left me panting and clutching my aching stomach, sweat pouring down my face, kneeling on the dirty tile floor, my pants soaked by the filthy mess. My three toilet buddies had long since fled the premises as I staggered to my feet, reaching out to the one sink that I hadn't soiled. I stared at my reflection, hardly believing that it was me staring back. My eyes were red, my face still wet with perspiration, my hair a matted mess, sticking up every which way.

After washing my face and gargling some of the lukewarm water from the sink's faucet, I headed for the door, embarrassed with the mess that I had made of somebody else's bathroom. I was dizzy when I straightened up and had to grab the handle of the door for a moment before I opened it. But I was more or less sober again, the agony of the event having worked better than a gallon of strong coffee and an hour long soaking in an icy-cold river.

I opened the door to find Dermot waiting patiently for me in the darkly lit hallway. The end of the hall, opposite the main bar, led to a back door. Grabbing me by the arm, he led me outside to the parking lot. By then, I was past the point of being angry, long beyond the inquisitive state, and not quite in shape to launch into the thousands of questions that I had been eager to ask only minutes earlier. I didn't argue as I let him take me to his car, although I was just the least bit afraid of where he would take me.

He navigated the trip without the slightest problem—and why not? He had very little to drink that night. I drank enough for the both of us.

He drove me home, and I wasn't at all surprised that he knew the way. Once there, he guided me up the walk, took the keys from my hand, and unlocked the door. I didn't know what to expect when we crossed the threshold of my home, but, to my surprise, he didn't come in. He just stood there, handed me a business card, and said, "Call me, I can help."

I was too screwed up to look at the card that night. I just threw it on the nightstand and fell into bed without even changing from my puke-stained clothes. I was asleep instantly, but my slumber was tormented by nightmares of Christine. In them I was lying in the cave, having just attempted the leap across the icy path that separated the two groups of kids. I couldn't feel the pain caused by my misguided jump, and yet I couldn't rise, couldn't move my legs or arms.

I turned my head to see Christine's half-frozen face, icy-blue in color, her lips frozen shut, icicles dripping from her chin and ear lobes. She forced her lips apart, tearing ragged chunks of flesh in the process, the blood not flowing, but exploding in all directions, crystallized pink projectiles that fell like hell-hail from the sky. She was pleading with me. "*Don't let me die, don't let me die*." I tried to scream to her, to the other two sitting beside her, but nothing came out. It was like my continuous dreams of Susan. I saw it happening, but was powerless to prevent it.

I awoke with a start—sweat pouring from every pore—the image of Christine still clear behind closed eyes. I lay there for several minutes, willing my heart to slow down as the disturbing visage began to dim. As it did, the memory of last night began to materialize. Just bits and pieces at first—the bar, the funny little man in the rumpled suit, drinking scotch with him—too much scotch. I remembered getting angry. He was digging too deep into my personal business, bringing up things that I didn't want to discuss. But I couldn't remember much after that—couldn't think of the little guy's name.

I opened one eye to see the clock at my bedside. The glowing red digits said 3:07. My throat was raw, and the inside of my mouth tasted like raw sewage. I rolled over onto by back, pain exploding in my head, forcing an involuntary groan. I tried lying motionless, as if I could hide from the throbbing headache by not moving. But this was a hangover, not a head wound. Lying motionless only intensified the pain.

Then the smell hit me, a nasty combination of sweat, onions, beer, scotch, and vomit, realizing then that I was still dressed in the clothes I wore the night before, a smelly reminder of a night that I would sooner forget. Disgusted with myself in about every way that I could think of, I got out of bed, my first few steps shaky—still half in the bag—dehydrated from the copious barfing just a few hours before. I peeled off my filthy clothes as I crossed into the bathroom and turned on the shower faucet.

I let the water beat down on my back and shoulders, just as hot as I could stand it, and began piecing together the events of the past evening. It came back to me slowly, as if the intense heat was somehow dissolving the goo that was keeping oxygen from getting to my brain.

Eventually, everything came back to me in humiliating clarity, except for the car ride home, which was still pretty much a blur. I was no longer mad at Dermot, but I was still astonished at how he knew such intimate details about my life. And as surprised as I was, I was even more curious about why he felt the *need* to know. Unquestionably, he went to a great deal of trouble to research my past and present, but for what possible reason? Blackmail? I couldn't think of a thing that anybody could possibly want from me, and besides, I had nothing of value left for him to take from me that hadn't already been taken.

As I vigorously brushed the awful tasting film from my teeth, I tried to concentrate on the drive home. Maybe he had said something to clear up the mystery. I remembered walking out of the bar holding on to his arm, and I remembered him unlocking the door to my house, but nothing in between, except for the glow of street lamps as they passed overhead. Everything else was shrouded in blackness. I scrubbed my teeth and gums, trying to remove the stink of the night before, straining to remember the drive home, but there was nothing. Perhaps there was nothing *to* remember—no words exchanged.

I was making coffee, still hours from the morning's first light, when I remembered the card. I remembered it very clearly, and what he said—*call me—I can help*. I remembered *taking* his card, but no idea where I'd put it. In a moment of panic, I charged into the laundry room, where I had tossed my clothing in the tub, and had then filled it with water. I dug through the pant's pockets, then into the one in the shirt ... nothing. Where the hell did I leave it?

I rechecked my steps, as best I could remember them. It was a short trip actually. I was too drunk to wander about the house. I went outside, thinking that perhaps the transition from his hand to mine never quite made the connection. Perhaps his card was lying there on the porch.

It wasn't there, and it wasn't on the nearby lawn or stuck in the surrounding shrubs, perhaps taken by the wind. Nor was it anywhere on the floor between the front door and the entranceway to my bedroom. I crossed the threshold and sat on the edge of the bed, sweating from overexerting myself in the middle of a monumental hangover. I sat there, my head in my hands, thinking about how badly I needed a handful of aspirin when I glanced up at the clock. It read 4:11. I watched it as it went to 4:12 and then 4:13, still puzzling over where the card could have ended up.

I closed my eyes and rubbed my temples, trying to dispel the ache there so that I could concentrate on what I had done with the card. I was obsessed with finding it. I had to get in touch with Dermot. I was determined to know what it was that he wanted from me. I *needed* to know how he could help me.

I raised my pounding head from my hands, looking once again at the clock beside the bed. Out of the corner of my eye I caught the fuzzy image of something white against the contrasting dark wood of the nightstand.

It was the card.

Elated, my headache forgotten for the moment, I grabbed the card. It had the size and shape of a standard business card, but about as plain as you could get. There were no colors, only black and white, no logo of any kind, and very few words. Just his name and title—he was a Ph.D. by the way, not just a mister—and a fax number.

I turned the card over. There was a hand-written phone number there—nothing more. I was tempted to call him right then, but it was the middle of the night, and I needed some time to think things through. I needed time to recover from my hangover. I didn't know how he could help me, and not even sure whether I wanted help. I put the card back on the table, secure in the fact that I knew where it was, and headed for the kitchen for aspirin and coffee.

*****

Three days had passed and I still hadn't called Dermot. I stared at the card, soiled and worn from handling it. Constantly, I thought about calling him, even began dialing it a few times, but I just couldn't quite muster up the courage to go through with it. I didn't know what he had in mind, but I didn't need any more complications in my life. I was trying hard to be content, working on my fossils, hitting the gym, an occasional beer or two to help me sleep. I was trying to get my act together.

Dermot *was* a doctor. Perhaps he wanted to put me into some kind of therapy. I could understand why he thought that I needed it. My life pretty much sucked. I lived for the moment, spending my days in a dusty old office fooling around with something that had been dead for seventy million years, and my nights consumed with sitting with a girl who was more dead than alive. But therapy of any kind wasn't something that I wanted to go through. I didn't need someone to tell me that I was okay, that it was all right to feel cheated, like I was forgotten by whatever powers controlled the universe. I was pissed, but still functioning. It had been a rough time, but I was capable of dealing with it.

I was sitting at my desk, eyeing the computer monitor in front of me, turning the card over and over between my fingers, the problem with the *Tyrannosaur* hands forgotten for the moment. Most of the weekend I had thought about the possibility of emotional therapy—I probably needed it. The thought left me depressed. Even if I did need it, I didn't want it. Therapy was for wimps, for people who couldn't control their emotions, couldn't control their lives. I had always been in control, always on top of things.

I was just about to turn off my computer and call it quits for the day, head over to see Susan for an hour or so, when the question of whether or not I should call Dr. Dermot was taken out of my hands. *He* called *me*. I wasn't surprised that he had my office number—he knew everything else about me. He didn't ask, but told me that we were going out to dinner, said he'd pick me up in an hour at the front entrance of Susan's care facility, and then hung up without my reply.

By the time I got to Susan's room, I had less than half an hour before my meeting with Dermot, but that was okay. It was more than enough time. I had spent most of the day before sitting with her, telling her all about my encounter with Dermot. There wasn't much left to tell her, and I was so preoccupied with my pending dinner with the retired professor, that I couldn't think of a single thing to say. I just sat with her, holding her hand, watching the clock.

Dermot was right on time. He was standing patiently under the front awning when I exited the building. His greeting was less formal this time, calling me David, extending his hand, clasping mine and giving it a single, firm, two-handed shake. He politely insisted that we take his car, which was idling in the parking isle, just off the main walk under a sign that read NO STANDING. It was a new Lincoln Town Car, black on black—ominous—but very classy. Well, the man had style, not to mention some money.

Of course he picked the restaurant, as well. The ride over was uneventful, the conversation polite and way too formal considering what we went through together a few nights before. He asked me how Susan was doing, if she showed any response from that day's visit. He asked whether I had any ill effects from our night out, and did I have any trouble recovering my car from the bar's parking lot the next day. If he had any revelation to share with me, he was taking his good, sweet time getting to it.

We drove for another ten minutes in complete silence. He wasn't ready to tell me, and I didn't feel like pushing him. I wasn't even sure what to ask. We drove all the way across the city to an expensive steak house, and I couldn't help but think that I was being set up. I loved a good steak. Undoubtedly, Dermot knew that about me, too.

As he finished parking the car, he turned to me and asked if I had any luck with the *Tyrannosaur's* hands. With that, I instantly switched back to idiot mode. I just turned and stared at him. I probably had my mouth agape … again. There was just no possible way that he could know that I had been struggling with that very problem that very day. Nobody knew. Just when I thought that there was nothing he could say to surprise me, he surprised me. But I didn't say a word, couldn't think of anything quite appropriate, nothing that would voice my amazement. I silently followed him into the restaurant.

The maitre d' appeared to know Dermot. He greeted him by name and showed us to a table despite a long line of others waiting to be seated. Like the night in the bar, the table was dark, secluded, tucked away in an isolated alcove in the back corner of the restaurant.

Dermot motioned for me to choose a chair, still being the perfect gentleman, but he had a much more serious air about him on that night: polite, friendly, but no funny little grin, no laughter. Unlike Friday night, he didn't look as if there was something tickling his funny bone. He was dressed very differently, too: a colorful knit sweater and a pair of Dockers, neatly pressed. Both looked new, or at least well cared for, and fitted him just right. This was definitely a man more comfortable in casual clothes, and the effect was startling. With his unusual size and shape, and round little face surrounded by those wild tufts of curly blond hair, he was never going to be called handsome, but he no longer looked like a joke, not someone to be laughed at or trifled with.

After we were seated, a waiter approached, calling Dermot by name and handing me the wine list, which I quickly passed over to Dermot, shaking my head. It would be a while before I regained my taste for alcohol—well, at least another day or so. Dermot declined as well, handing the leather covered folder back to the waiter, and asked for the menu. I wasn't drinking, so he didn't either. Damn, I felt like I was on a date.

I knew what I was going to order, but I went through the motions of perusing the menu, unsure of what to say to this strange little man. At least the menu gave me something to do while I waited for him to get on with it. I was silent, and so was Dermot. He made a show of turning the pages of the menu, although I would wager that he knew it backwards and forwards. This restaurant was obviously a special place for him. He was known here. He was comfortable here.

There was no small talk, no questions. We just sat there, our noses buried in our respective menus, waiting for the waiter to return. When he did, we ordered—me first, then him. He requested exactly the same as I, maybe out of coincidence, but probably because it was more expeditious. When the waiter turned to leave, Dermot placed his hands on the table before him and looked deeply into my eyes—a haunting look, full of compassion and sorrow.

I returned the look, knowing that this was it. This was the moment that he had been building up to, not just the night in the bar, but for however long he had been studying me, researching my life. It had all come down to this moment—this place and this time.

With his hands still resting in front of him, fingers intertwined, his eyes never leaving mine, he asked a second time, "Have you solved the riddle with the *Tyrannosaur's* arms?" This time the question didn't shock me, and unlike so many of the questions he had asked me that night at the bar, I didn't think that he was trying to. Nor was he trying to stir up my emotions by reminding me of things I didn't want to think about.

And I didn't think he was just beating around the bush, making small talk, wasting time. He truly wanted to know about my dinosaurs. I didn't have any idea where we were going with this, but by then I knew that we weren't going to be discussing therapy, and I was only too happy to answer his question now that we were on a familiar and cheerful subject.

So I told Dermot all about my dinosaurs. I felt some of the old excitement return as I explained how I had positioned them to capture both the excitement and terror of the battle between the two fearsome giants. I told him all about my vision at the foot of the mountain all those months ago, and how I had attempted to capture that moment, a mere second before the decisive end for them both. I talked of how I positioned the *Tyrannosaur* and the *Triceratops*, one on the offensive, one on the defensive, each about to strike in their own way.

I was in my element then. I covered a lot of detail—how I positioned each body part, what each one meant, and what action and emotion I was trying to portray with each decision that I had made. It was like I was teaching a class, or once again out in the field with a bunch of new, eager students. And it seemed like I had an interested pupil in Dermot. He remained silent during my lesson, occasionally nodding his head, an appropriately timed smile at the best parts, a look of keen interest on his face.

The one-sided discussion went on throughout an exceptional meal. Waiters came and went, plates set before us, and eventually removed, dessert declined, and coffee cups refilled. I told Dermot that sometime within the next week, I would be presenting my final recommendations for the museum exhibit, and that I had no doubt it would be overwhelmingly approved. There would be no other like it in the world.

The waiter was just presenting the bill when Dermot said, "You still haven't answered my question about the hands, David. What are you going to do with them?" It was the third time that he had asked me that particular question. When he asked me the previous times I had assumed he was just making a general inquiry about how I was coming with the project. Now I realized that he had something much more specific in mind. He had sat through the entire dinner and for quite a period of time after, listening to me drone on and on, all the time waiting patiently for me to get to the hands.

So I explained to him the difficulty with the hands, the mystery surrounding them. I told him about my theory, how I felt the arms were gradually disappearing through the evolutionary process. I told him that my specimen had been dated at very late in the Cretaceous period, right at the Cretaceous-Tertiary boundary, and because, the arms on my *rex* were comparatively so much smaller than others, my theory had merit.

The arms were so small as compared to the rest of the skeleton, and I had captured exactly the right pose that I was after, that in the greater scheme of things, the arms probably weren't that important. The average visitor to the museum would be so overwhelmed with the rest of the scene, that he probably wouldn't even give them a thought. Only an expert would notice them and there were damn few of them around.

"To tell you the truth," I said, "I'm not sure what I'm going to do with them."

Dermot asked, "If the arms are relatively insignificant as compared to the whole, why are you so concerned with them?"

"It's just that the arms represent all the things that we don't know about the *Tyrannosaurus rex*," I answered. "The worst part is, we will probably never know. Dinosaur fossil records are too incomplete, and despite what we all saw in *Jurassic Park* we were not going to be bringing any of them back to life."

The last comment brought a mysterious smile to Dermot's lips. By then I had learned to respect those little signals. Now something *was* tickling his funny bone. With the smile spreading, he said, "No, you probably won't be bringing any of *them* back, but what if I could send *you* back?"

CHAPTER 9

Spring had been a tease that year—sixty-degree afternoons popping up randomly, surprisingly, only to be followed by longer periods of sub-freezing days, confused patches of green appearing prematurely on lawns, turning quickly brown again with the next morning's frost, people rotating between heavy winter coats and lighter spring jackets, not quite keeping up with the change, always either too hot, or too cold.

It had been an especially rough winter in Chicago, twice the average snowfall and long stretches of bone-numbing temperatures, made worse by the winds that lent credence to its famous nickname. When those first few warm days hit, they gave people hope, and when the snow fell the following day, hope was quickly snatched away. On the warm days, the sun shown brightly and lifted the spirits of the city in a way that the warm temperatures alone could not. But this too was short lived as the sun was quickly chased away by day after day of dull Midwestern gray.

But that morning, for the third day in a row, the sun had risen into a clear blue sky. The days had become noticeably longer, the sun still high in the sky, even though it was nearing five o'clock. The outside temperature-gauge in my car read a pleasant seventy-one degrees, as I sped along Lake Shore Drive. The driver's side window was rolled all the way down and it felt good to feel the wind again without the accompanying chill. The air smelled clean—the last of the winter winds having blown away the smell of stagnation off the big-city streets.

Spring was here. Hot weather was on its way, and I should have been excited by the prospect. Others were. I saw it on their faces, in their walk. People ambled along the shore of Lake Michigan, hand in hand, at last free from the confines of their homes and offices. There were bicycles and skateboards racing along the concrete walkway, children in strollers being pushed by young mothers in spring dresses. They were happy people—hopeful people. Spring does that.

And I should have been happy, too—a long winter filled with frustration and sadness finally at an end. It was the time of year when I could flee the dark laboratories and corridors of the museum and begin to think about the next excursion—to get outside into the fresh air and do what I did best—dig. I should have been reviewing resumes and applications from the college kids, selecting the brightest and the best to take with me on the next expedition.

I had double reason to be happy on that particular day. I had finished with the computer model of my dinosaurs. It had taken me three more weeks to figure out what to do with the *Tyrannosaur's* hands. Actually, it was three weeks before I finished them, but I really couldn't say that I worked on them for most of that time. To be honest, it probably wasn't much more than two or three hours of actual work.

I ended up with both arms reaching out, the left one bent at approximately ninety degrees, and the right one at an angle between that and fully outstretched, and about twelve inches higher. The two claws on each of the hands were slightly separated, turned upward—one elevated a few inches above the other. The outcome worked pretty well. It added to the overall effect of the predator ready to strike at the lesser-capable foe.

They looked to be offensive weapons, ready to strike, eight-inch killer-claws poised to rip holes into flesh and sinew. And that's the way the public would see it—wanted to see it. One more weapon for the fierce meat-eater, one more way to kill. Everything about it had to be fierce, had to be about domination, about total destruction. Only a handful of my compatriots, and, of course, me, would see the sham in it. But I had no better ideas, and certainly nothing that looked quite so impressive.

The reason that I had not actually spent three weeks *working* on the skeletons was because I had been in my office no more than a couple of hours a day. Even then I wasn't giving it my undivided attention. I had spent countless hours with Susan, talking to her, listening to her. Yes, she was still in a coma, and while she couldn't actually talk to me, I still believed that she heard me and I knew what she expected of me, what she would say to me.

But the day before, as I was leaving her room, her doctor asked if he could speak with me. He led me into the office of the facilities administrator, who was there, already waiting for us. We took seats around a small coffee table in the large, well-decorated office, and the administrator got right to the point. He was concerned about the amount of time I was spending with Susan.

"We're worried about you, David, about the amount of time you're spending with Susan. Sometimes an illness like Susan's is harder on the friends and family than it is on the patient. You've become so preoccupied with her that your own health will suffer."

"But you don't understand," I pleaded. "Without me, who is going to help her?"

"David, you have to be realistic. It's been too long, and there's been no improvement whatsoever, no sign that she's going to come out of it."

The doctor had seen it more than a few times. Patients who were in coma for that long almost never came out of it. Their systems would continue to atrophy from inactivity, becoming more and more difficult to fight infection, harder and harder for the heart to continue to do its job. Eventually the kidneys failed, or the lungs filled with fluid, or the heart just stopped beating. A thousand things could happen, and none of them were good.

In barely more than a whisper, the doctor said, "We'll be here for her, David, for whatever she needs, for as long as it takes. Don't do this to yourself." I knew that he spoke the truth and it was like a knife in my heart.

Driving along Lake Shore Drive, I thought about those last talks with Susan, realizing that at some point the visits had stopped being about Susan and started being about me. I was confused and alone, unable to sort reality from fantasy. I was using Susan as a sounding board, hoping that if I said the things that were troubling me out loud, bounce the questions off another human being, maybe I could get it all figured out. But Susan wasn't answering, and by then I didn't think that she was listening either. Somehow I had to get some answers. I couldn't deal alone with what I had discovered during the past weeks.

*****

I had been dividing my time between work, Susan, and Anson Dermot. As the days went by, I spent fewer hours with Susan and even less time at work. By the third week, Dermot pretty much had my undivided attention. He and I had spent a lot of time together following that night at the restaurant.

The first days that followed that dinner were filled with serious doubts of this man's sanity, but as the days went by, I began to question my own. At first I found his story to be utterly impossible, laughable, completely unbelievable. But hour after hour, day after day, after seeing what he had to show me, I began to believe. And I was both fascinated and terrified at the same time.

And I had kept it all bottled up inside, partly because I had promised Dermot, but mostly because no one was likely to believe me. I could shout it from the rooftops, and no one would listen, and if I shouted it loud enough, I was likely to be hauled away by the men in white coats brandishing rather large nets. But I couldn't keep it stashed away, it was too important, too big a decision for one person to make, so I was going to have to share it with Jakes.

I was headed to his house, having finagled an invitation to watch a ballgame through the guise of being bored and needing something to do. We had patched things up after the little disagreement that we had in his office the day after it occurred. We were both mad at the same thing—it was stupid to be mad at each other, as well. We were friends again, and that's just what I needed on that day.

It had taken nearly three weeks to make up my mind to tell Jakes about it, and I had been struggling with how to go about doing it. It took a couple of weeks for me to decide that Dermot wasn't insane. I didn't want it to take that long with Jakes. But Jakes was as skeptical a man as I had ever known. He didn't take anything at face value, and rarely believed in anything that he couldn't feel, taste, or see. I wasn't sure how I was going to convince him that Dermot was sincere. Of that I was sure—Dermot *was* sincere. He believed every word he told me. Of course that didn't mean he wasn't crazy or that his plan would work. I tended not to believe the former, but was unsure as hell of the latter.

I still hadn't figured out how to begin the conversation with Jakes as I pulled into his driveway. He lived in a pretty upscale neighborhood for a cop. It took most of his wife's salary as a grade-school teacher, not to mention a good chunk of his, to handle the mortgage payments, taxes and upkeep, but he was willing to do almost anything to keep his kids away from the influences of the inner city. The city had nearly killed him as a teenager. He was determined to give his family a better life than he had had.

As I got out of the car the front door of Jakes' house popped opened and out he strode. He put his arm around me in greeting—Jakes was a touchy-feeling kind of guy if you were someone close, and he escorted me around the back of the house. He had set up the portable TV on the deck and was already tuned in to the pre game show. I had a beer in my hand even before I sat down in one of the two lounge chairs positioned before the set.

He had the grill fired up, but nothing on it. He looked in no hurry to cook, instead taking the other chair with a noisy sigh. I was preoccupied, trying to figure out a way to broach the subject of Dermot. I was lost in my own thoughts so that I really didn't even notice that Jakes was as equally quiet. He was a White Sox fanatic and I figured that he was following the game closely.

When he finally spoke up, it startled me, having been so quiet for so long. He said he had something to tell me, and he didn't want me to lose my temper again. I couldn't imagine what he could say to make me angry, but I was happy that he started the conversation because I still didn't know how to begin. He got out of his chair and went into the house, coming back out just seconds later with two more beers. He handed me one, but remained standing at a distance of several paces.

"David, do you remember what I told you in my office about Green going underground? How we'd never find him?"

I don't know how he thought that I could have forgotten, but he felt the need to reiterate because he had something to add. "What you didn't know then was that we had a line on his partner, Sid. He wasn't hard to find, you know? They found him hanging around a run down pool hall in Detroit just days after Green disappeared. We figured that if Sid was in Detroit, then Green must be around, too."

"So did the cops pick Sid up?" I asked.

"No, they decided to tail him to see if he would lead them to Green. For three days they followed him. Each day he hung around the pool hall and each night he returned to the same boarded up, condemned house on Detroit's East Side."

On the fourth day, Sid stopped at a pharmacy before going home. He came out with a white plastic bag filled with who knows what. The tail called for assistance, and while they followed Sid back to his hideout, another detective went to the pharmacy to question the guy behind the counter. They discovered that Sid had bought several roles of gauze, some antiseptic cream, a large bottle of extra strength Tylenol, and two bottles of cheap whiskey. Just the stuff he would need to treat a wound.

They developed a plan to take Sid, and hopefully Green, that night while they slept.

At two the next morning, a four-man swat team broke into the house, two from the front and two from the rear. But they hadn't considered that Sid might still be awake. The element of surprise was gone. Sid had been sitting in a back corner of the house working his way through one of the bottles of whiskey when they went in the rear. We never knew Sid to carry a gun, but he had one that night. He started shooting as fast as he could pull the trigger.

The shots were wild—most struck the floor and ceiling twenty feet from the door, but one random shot caught one of the swat team in the leg. His screams brought an immediate response from the two coming in the front door. In the gunfight that followed, Sid was blown away by at least half a dozen shots.

He was dead before he hit the floor.

They searched the house, found the bag from the pharmacy—intact—nothing had been opened, but there was no sign of Green. If the first-aid supplies were for Green, he must have been going to deliver them someplace else, at another time.

"With Sid dead," Jakes went on, "we've got no leads—no idea where he is. We're not even sure the supplies were for Green. We acted too quickly. We blew it."

It surprised the hell out of Jakes that there was no reaction from me. After he finished telling me the story of Sid's demise he sat there waiting anxiously for the eruption that he felt was sure to come. The fraternity of police, for which Jakes was a member, had perhaps ruined the best, maybe the only, chance they had at capturing Green and making him pay for the murder of my wife. He expected a repeat of the scene that played out in his office nearly a month ago. But I just sat there quietly finishing my beer.

I was quiet, but my mind was churning, processing this new information, and judging its impact on the choice that I had yet to make. I looked at the TV, not seeing the game, thinking about the most monumental decision of my life.

I had been on the edge of a cliff, half the way up, a hundred feet above a river of unknown depth, just barely holding on. I could stay where I was, trapped, unable to move, afraid to make a decision one way or the other. Or, I could step off, knowing that I would probably break my neck or drown in the water below, but with just the most miniscule chance that I would land unhurt in an unexplored river that would take me to some new, fantastic land—a land where all my troubles would be left behind—a whole new world before me.

The final loss of Green could have been the last straw—the one remaining question that might have forced an answer—yes or no. But it didn't. Nor would Jakes' reaction to my story help me decide to do it … or not. I only then realized that I had already made my decision. I turned to Jakes, ready at last to tell him about Dermot, about the conversation at the restaurant, and about what happened during the next three weeks.

*****

I stared at him for several seconds, unsure what he meant by that. "You can send me back where—back to Utah?" I didn't need Dermot to get back to Utah—I knew the way. Besides, what good would that do? Had I missed something in the cave? Were there additional clues that I had overlooked that would solve the riddle of the *Tyrannosaur's* hands?

I asked Dermot these questions, but he just sat there shaking his head from side to side, his eyes sparkling, a wry smile plastered across his face.

"No," he said, "nothing like that—something a bit more dramatic."

He knew that he had my attention, but he refused to discuss it any further that night. Instead he paid the check and drove me back home, despite the fact that my car was back at Susan's care facility. As if reading my mind he said, "Don't worry about the car—you won't need it tomorrow. I'll pick you up at your house at seven A.M. sharp."

He drove off without saying another word, leaving me standing at the end of my driveway. I stood there for some time, watching the taillights of his Lincoln get smaller and smaller until the tiny red dots blinked out entirely. I had to admit, he piqued my curiosity, but I had no idea what he was talking about.

I tossed and turned throughout the night, unable to shut my mind down. I thought about Susan and the discussion with her doctor. Should I give up hope just because everyone else did? Was I being unrealistic in believing that she could beat this thing? Was I fooling myself thinking that I was helping in any way?

Maybe I could back off without really giving up—perhaps a couple of extended visits a week, instead of every day. Maybe I could do that—but what next—*once* a week, once a *month*, once every couple of months ... until I wasn't going at all. I just didn't know.

And there was Green. With the one solid lead that the police had now gone, would they give up? With the passage of time, the case would become less important. Other things would get in the way, resources pulled, other priorities taking precedence, until Green was nothing but a dusty folder on the bottom of a stack of similar folders on some overworked detective's desk. I could hold on to the possibility that he died of his wounds, hiding out somewhere in an old abandoned house, as his partner had. But I would probably never know for sure.

But most of the time I thought about Dermot. Everything led back to him. It wasn't just the problem with the dinosaur. Everything in my life was going to be impacted by this little man, everything resolved, or at least changed in some significant manner. I didn't know how, but I knew that it was true.

At five o'clock, I finally gave up the idea of sleep, got out of bed, and started the coffee going. Surprisingly, I didn't feel at all tired, but rather excited, full of great expectations, much like the first morning of a new expedition.

That was it exactly.

It was just like the anticipation that I felt when starting a new dig, not knowing what was to come, what discoveries we were going to make. It was the first time that I had felt excited about anything in months and the thrill blew away any fatigue I might have felt from a sleepless night.

I showered, shaved, and dressed. Dermot had said casual, so jeans and a sweatshirt were the dress of the day. I was on my fourth cup of coffee, tense and excited at the same time. I was pacing back and forth across the living room when I spotted Dermot's Town Car pull into the driveway. I glanced at my watch. It was seven on the nose, not one minute sooner, not one minute later. He had this thing about *time*.

He declined my offer for coffee and led the way back to his car. The sun was just coming over the horizon, the shadows stretching long over the frosted grass, our breath a frozen fog as we hurried down the walk. As he slid inside and closed the door behind him I asked, 'Where are we going?"

He responded simply, "You'll see."

He was talkative that morning, in a delightful mood, but he gave no clue where we were going or what he had to show me. As he drove though the streets of Chicago, he chattered on endlessly about the weather, how he was so tired of the cold, how he was so looking forward to summer. "I don't know why we stay here in this damn cold city. It seems that the older I get, the colder winter feels. I really envy you, David."

Why? I wondered. *I live in Chicago, too.*

He drove south along the lake, past the old stockyards, deep into the slums of south Chicago. It was early in the morning, not much going on along the deserted streets. It was too early and too cold for the gang-bangers to be out, but there were signs of their presence. Colorful graffiti proclaimed the dominant gang every few blocks—gang colors—misspelled obscenities.

We drove through neighborhoods of houses crammed together, postage stamp-size yards, chain-link fences brown with rust. Many of the houses were abandoned. Nearly all had plywood where glass used to be, long-dead weeds coming up through the cracks in walks and driveways. Sometimes we passed a house with toys in the yard, but more often than not there were rotted-out hulks of automobiles, old milk crates under their axles lifting them off their tireless rims.

It was a neighborhood of crack houses and welfare mothers. It was a neighborhood that was once middle-class, but was now filled with adults with no hope, and children with no future. It was a neighborhood that you didn't want to be in if you where white and driving a new Lincoln.

We passed through the residential area into one zoned for commercial use, filled with abandoned offices and empty warehouses. The few still viable were heavily padlocked, with bars and gates on every opening. Dozens of homeless people huddled in doorways, sleeping along the curbs, trying to gather warmth from heat coming up from the sewers, trying to hold it in with blankets of cardboard and newspaper.

Guessing by the car he drove, and the restaurants he frequented, Dermot was a man of some wealth, yet there we were in the worst section of Chicago, and we weren't just driving through it to get to something on the other side. We could have stayed on the Dan Ryan expressway for that. No, we had been zigzagging through the side streets with a specific destination in mind, one that was nearby.

I was proven right as we turned the next corner and approached a large, fenced-off complex with, what looked like a huge warehouse, situated in the center. The fence itself offered little security as the gate was missing, but there were no windows in the structure and only a single huge door on one of the two sides that were visible.

As we approached the gate, it opened as if by magic, the huge warehouse door rising just as mysteriously. We drove into darkness, the only apparent light coming in from beneath the rapidly closing door.

As it closed, there was but a single, dim patch of light coming from the lone window of a small, enclosed area in the far corner. Dermot pulled the car forward and parked along the exterior wall of the enclosure, directly under the window. As I exited the car, I peered through the darkness into the interior of the huge space to see that it was completely empty. There were no windows and just a single, small door directly opposite the enclosed room.

I followed Dermot around to the side of the enclosure to another door that led us inside. He stepped inside and flipped a switch, which flooded the room with high intensity light. It was an office area, filled with computers, drafting tables, storage files, and an assortment of hardware in various levels of assembly. There were several desks against the wall beneath the window—each covered with blueprints and schematics.

Instead of inviting me to have a seat and explain to me what we were doing there, Dermot handed me a white lab coat, a white cap with an elastic band, and some paper foot covers to slip over my shoes and said, "Put these on, but not the booties". He then reached over to a control panel mounted on the wall alongside the window and threw a circuit breaker, at which time absolutely nothing happened—at least as best as I could tell.

I knew what the garb was for. I had used it a few times when working in some laboratory environments. It was for working in a clean room, but it didn't seem to apply to anything here. The office was anything but dust free, and judging by the oil spills in the main warehouse, clean was not a word that applied there very often either. But I put them on, hurrying to catch up with Dermot who had already left the office.

He strode across the main floor as fast as his chubby little legs would carry him. I had to run to catch up, afraid that he would lose me somehow, although there didn't seem to be anywhere that he could lose me to. We went to about the only place that we could, which was the other door at the opposite end of the warehouse.

He entered a series of numbers into the small keypad located just to the right of the door and pulled the handle. It opened with a whoosh and I could feel cool dry air spring forward as the pressurized air sought equilibrium. It

was a room designed to keep any air-born contaminants from entering from the outside—a clean room.
We were in a room within a room—a tiny five by five space with a second door that led to a much larger area. The floor was a mat of some unknown sticky rubber substance intended to remove particles from the bottom of our shoes. Before entering the final door, Dermot began putting on his booties. I followed suit.

He opened the last door, which made another whooshing sound—even higher pressure—and entered. It was an immense room, at least two-thirds the overall size of the warehouse as it appeared from the outside: brightly lighted, immaculate, the interior of the room covered in white ceramic tile, a place where serious work was being conducted.

The far end of the warehouse was sectioned off by glass that ran from floor to ceiling. Behind the glass were several rows of consoles filled with switches and lighted indicators. Against the wall opposite the glass was a huge display panel, but I had no idea what it was for as it was dark, the surface black and glossy. The walls on either side were filled with television screens, monitors of some kind, dozens of them, but like the display panel, were switched off, nothing on them but black. I had seen enough movies to know that this was the control center. It looked like a slightly scaled down version of NASA's Mission Control. But what Dermot intended to launch, I had no idea.

The opposite end of the room, the one closest to the airlock that we had just emerged from, was almost entirely taken up by huge doors, much like those on an aircraft hangar. They were without a doubt large enough to bring in or take out a rocket, maybe even the space shuttle, although I had never been close enough to the actual spacecraft to know. And the doors were big enough to pass the incredibly strange object that sat in the middle of the floor.

It was at least fifty feet long, with portholes, each perhaps six inches in diameter, evenly spaced along its length, eight in all. The base was approximately twenty feet wide, but the sides were slanted inward such that the top was only about twelve feet across. Its height was sufficient for a tall man to stand fully upright within, at least seven feet. It was a structure that was designed for stability, able to withstand tornadoes and earthquakes.

The object appeared to be made of metal, anodized with some type of matte-black finish. It reminded me of a Stealth aircraft, minus the wings, of course. Enclosing the thing was a series of rings, fifteen or twenty of them, four inches in diameter each, not smooth, they looked as if they were made from miles of thin, flat metal, wound about itself, lengthening it by an inch with each successive wrap.

Each ring disappeared into a polished metal base that was flush with the floor, isolated from the ceramic tiles by a one-inch gap that was filled with a dull black substance, perhaps rubber, or a plastic compound of some kind. Attached to the object itself were hundreds, perhaps thousands, of thin rods, tipped with a small spherical device, smaller than the size of a golf ball. Each was of the same dull black finish, but varied in length, such that each tip was just a fraction of an inch from touching the inside edge of the surrounding rings.

The thing looked like an inbred porcupine.

Ten feet away from one end of the object, between it and the control room, were two more structures, much less massive, but complex and fascinating in their own right. They were almost identical, back to front, like mirror images. Like the rings surrounding the main object, they were circular—more rings—but with a larger circumference. And they were heavier, much more complex than the series of smaller rings. The upper two thirds of each was as smooth and shiny as a platinum bracelet, but the bottom portions were elaborate, complicated, full of electronics: buttons, dials, lights, and fittings of every kind. Their bases rested on the floor and connected to metal rails on either side. The rails ran the length of the thing, and were parallel to it, just inches from the polished base.

Dermot approached the main object and touched a small depression on its side. A door, hinged from the top like an exotic sports car, popped open. I hadn't even noticed the door—its fit was so precise—the seams barely discernable. Dermot effortlessly raised the door the rest of the way and stepped into the object. I followed, wondering if the door was going to automatically slam shut behind me.

It didn't.

Any thoughts that I might have had about the object being a space ship or vehicle of any kind quickly vanished as I looked about the interior of the thing. There was no pilot's seat, no controls of any kind, no way to tell the front from the back. And with no wings and no wheels, this thing, whatever it was, was not moving from this spot.

There were no artificial lights in the thing, but there was enough coming through the portholes to see clearly. There wasn't a lot to see. Two thirds of the space was filled with empty storage racks, separated by three aisles running their length. At the open end of the object, centered on the end wall, was the only other item. I could only describe it as a space age, pot-bellied stove, a wide base with a door in front, a flat surface with an iron grate on top, and a wide cylinder that extended to the ceiling.

There wasn't much else to see and I couldn't imagine what the whole setup was for. It was both mysterious and eerie. The light coming in from the portholes and the quiet isolation made me feel as if I was in a submarine. But if this thing were placed in the ocean, it would drop like a brick to the bottom. No, it wasn't meant for the water any more than it was meant for the wild blue yonder.

I had absolutely no idea what it was for and why I was involved, or why Dermot would even think that I'd be interested. So I finally asked, "What the hell is it?" It was the first time either of us spoke since we had entered the contraption, and the sound of my voice surprised me. It sounded loud and hollow, as if I was talking from the bottom of a deep well.

It was a ghostly sound, but it was Dermot's response that sent chills up my spine. "It's your home, if you want it to be."

He said that and nothing more. He turned and walked out, leaving me alone in the *house*. By that time I shouldn't have been surprised by anything that Dermot said. It seemed like every time he opened his mouth something surprising came out, but this time he really shocked me.

Why the hell would I want to live here? Hell, I wasn't even enjoying visiting here. It gave me the creeps. I just stood there for the longest time trying to figure one what the strange little man was up to this time.

Then I had it—at least I thought I did. Dermot was going to make me the guinea pig in some wacky experiment. He probably figured that because my life was such a disaster, I'd jump at the chance to do something really different—something to take my mind off my problems. I remembered the first time that I met him, thinking that he reminded me of the prototypical mad scientist.

But what was he trying to involve me in? What kind of experiment did he have up his sleeve? It had something to do with me living in this contraption, but I was at a loss as to what that would accomplish. Perhaps it was one of those sensory deprivation chambers, although the windows seemed inappropriate. Maybe he was going to blast me with gamma rays, see if I grew a second head. I believed I would have had to take a pass on that one.

I stood alone in the strange silence trying to think of a single reason why I would want to live in this thing—why I would be willing to subject myself to some kind of experiment. Did Dermot really think that submitting to this experiment, or whatever the hell it was, would make me forget about my problems? It certainly wouldn't solve the riddle of the *Tyrannosaur's* hands.

True, Liz was gone, Susan's condition was hopeless—my life was a mess, but I still had my job, and I still had my dinosaurs to look after. There would be months of work reconstructing the skeletons to look forward to—something to occupy my mind and my time. Here, I would have nothing—except more time to think—something I didn't need ... or want.

Realizing that there was but one person to tell me why I should want to live here, I chased after him.

He had already returned to his office, sipping on a cup of coffee. I didn't remember seeing a vending machine, so he must have brewed it while I was lost in thought inside his less than seaworthy submarine. He seemed to always be one step ahead of me, asking would I like a cup as he opened a cabinet holding a coffee maker. I must have been in the contraption longer than I thought.

Dermot had an incredible sense of timing, and was a master of the one-liner. He waited several minutes while we drank our coffee. He said nothing as we finished the first cup. To break the monotony, or maybe the tension, I got up to refill them. I filled mine first as I walked over to where he sat.

As I began to pour his, he looked up at me and said as calmly as you please, "It's a time machine."

It was a good thing that the pot contained little more than a cup's worth because most of it ended up on Dermot's desk and the floor. He anticipated my shock, taking the pot from my trembling fingers before I could do more damage. He returned it to the cabinet and put a stack of white paper towels on top of the mess on his desk. After cleaning the outside of his cup, he sat back down, wrapped both hands around the steaming mug, and pushed himself back from the dripping desk.

He sat there, cool and calm, not saying a word. He stared at me and I stared right back. And then I laughed. What else could I do? At first it was but a snicker, and watching Dermot's face, which refused to register any kind of reaction, I laughed harder, uncontrollably.

He was baiting me—had to be.

I threw back my head and roared, tears forming in my eyes. All the tension in my body, all the pent up anxiety and concern for this man's sanity gone in a flash. It was all a ruse, something to make me forget my troubles.

I didn't know why he pulled this stunt, but I was grateful as hell. I hadn't felt so good in months—hadn't laughed like that in even longer. In time I regained some sense of control and began to think about the situation. I began to question why Dermot would do such a thing. Prior to a month ago, I had no idea who this guy was. Why would a complete stranger go to all that trouble to make me feel better about myself? Why would he set up such an elaborate hoax for someone he barely knew?

The answer of course was, he wouldn't. This was no hoax, and as I began to understand that, realization set in. Dermot was planning to send me in that contraption to somewhere in another time.

I could feel myself shaking, getting light headed. It was a terrifying thought, even though I found it absurd. Time travel was impossible. Newton's laws of physics proved that.

I tried to make that argument to Dermot, but he only scoffed. "Newton's laws were severely flawed," he replied. "Newton thought only in terms of three dimensional space. He left out the all-important fourth dimension, that of time. Einstein knew about time. It was the cornerstone of his theory of relativity. He knew that time travel was possible."

*****

An amazing three weeks followed that first visit to Dermot's lab. I hadn't agreed to become his guinea pig, but as the days went by I became less skeptical with the idea that he could actually pull it off. I spent more and more time at the lab, my friendship with Dermot growing day by day. He was no longer the mysterious stranger, confusing me with riddles and surprising me with little-known details of my private life. He was straight forward, answering all my questions, hiding nothing.

I had asked why, out of all the people in the world, he chose me for this journey. And he told me that I was but one of several candidates. It had begun with the newspaper story of my wife's murder. I was a young widow with no children, and a well-known paleontologist—someone who had a special interest in the past. I was the kind of person Dermot was looking for: not a lot of family ties or close personal connections, unhappy with life, someone who had plenty of reasons to want to escape his current situation. Along with a couple of other people in similar circumstances, he began digging into my background and he kept a close eye on my future.

Dermot had contacts, some of which he was not free to discuss, whose job was to keep track of us and update our files. He knew all about the expedition to Utah, Susan's accident and Christine's death. He had daily reports on Susan's progress and knew about my regular visits to the hospital. He had a mole on the inside, either the doctor or administrator—he knew about that last discussion.

As things continued to go wrong in my life, the other potential candidates began dropping off Dermot's short list. Their lives were apparently moving forward much smoother than my own. He continued to keep an active file on them, but I was his clear choice to lead the experiment. I guess that he felt that I should have considered it a great honor, but all I felt was scared to death.

In those first days I learned about the project, although most of the technology was way over my head. It was all I could do to get through the two required semesters of physics during my undergraduate years. But Dermot was patient with me. He put things in their simplest terms, although I even had trouble digesting those. Everything had to do with fourth and fifth and sixth dimensional space—I had trouble thinking beyond three.

He talked about hyperspace, time dilation, antimatter, and singularities—a hundred different terms that I had never heard before, and don't understand them even now. He said that it was important to him that I understood the basics, but it was all Greek to me.

I had seen way too many movies about time travel, most of them requiring a spaceship or superhero to travel faster than the speed of light. Dermot corrected me on that fallacy. Einstein proved that exceeding the speed of light was impossible, but time did indeed change with speed, increasing asymptotically toward infinity as an object *approached* the speed of light.

The scriptwriters got one thing right. Time travel required motion through both time *and* space. The key, however, was that motion, like time, was a relative phenomenon. Conventional thinking assumed traveling through space meant that a moving object traverses distance through a fixed space. But thinking unconventionally allowed for the idea that the object could remain stationary while space moved across it—the theory behind time travel, without spatial differentiation.

It was how Dermot's machine worked. He had found a way to create an artificial wormhole, and to stabilize it, a feat thought improbable, if not impossible. The two giant rings between the machine and the control room that I saw that first morning was where the wormhole was born. Exactly how Dermot did it I would never understand. After establishing the wormhole, the first ring moved forward enclosing the machine as it went, beginning the journey through time. The second ring, which followed the first by some period of time, determined, by an astounding mathematical equation, the duration of the trip—the final destination in time. Thus, space moved past the stationary object.

The smaller rings that surrounded the machine, and the porcupine projectiles that emitted from its skin, had something to do with establishing a magnetic field—something essential for the object that time was passing across. According to Dermot, it mimicked the field established by a moving particle, but, of course, ours was stationary.

I found it extraordinary that I'd come to consider the machine as ours. When did that happen? I was intrigued, but not committed. I admit that at the time I was caught up in the excitement of being the first. I thought myself a modern day Christopher Columbus, or more appropriately a futuristic Neil Armstrong. The first to do it—the first to seek a new world, but I hadn't decided that I *would* do it. A part of me wanted to do it, to be the first to see, firsthand, what really happened all those millions of years ago, to solve the riddle of the *Tyrannosaur*, perhaps even discover what happened to all of the dinosaurs. But I wasn't a hero. I wasn't ready to give my life for the sake of science.

Another missed notion, according to Dermot, was that of time being a linear function. Time did not exist in a straight line, as did the three normal-space dimensions. It was helical, like a spring, coiled, one ring upon another, existing from the beginning of time to the present, from bottom to top. Near-time travel to the past could be attained by traveling down the spiral, around the circumference of the coil. But that was time consuming—traveling backwards around the coil required as much time as traveling up the coil—the normal passage of time. Simply put, to travel twenty years in the past took twenty years of the future. Not a very efficient way to revisit past history, unless one was looking to see what happened yesterday.

But, on the other hand, if one could drop from one coil to the next, without traversing the circumference to get there, the process could be expedited considerably. As an example, Dermot suggested that in normal-space, the shortest distance between two points was a straight line, however, if one could fold space so the two points occupied the same space, then the distance and time to get from one to the other approached zero.

Of course there was one obvious drawback in traveling back through time by dropping from one coil to the next—one could only visit discrete periods in time, separated by the duration represented by the length of a single wrap—about a thousand years, according to Dermot. He intended to send me back to the time of the dinosaurs—a thousand years one way or the other didn't make a damn bit of difference.

There was another advantage to traveling back through time in millennium-size chunks. One avoided the problems of paradox. If a time traveler could go back in time and kill his own grandfather, would he (the time traveler) suddenly cease to exist, blink out like a light because he could not have been born? Or would he be even able to kill his own grandfather, could he change the future by altering the past? According to Dermot, the grandfather example was but one form of paradox that had puzzled scientists since the earliest discussions of time travel. In traveling back in time in thousand-year intervals, there was little chance of running into one's own grandfather.

I learned that this experiment was not just a one-man show. Dermot was in charge, but he had a lot of help. After that first day, technicians began showing up, around the clock, ten to twelve at a time, all dressed in immaculate white jump suits, replete with booties and hair covers. There were guards there at all times, one at either end of the facility. They wore side arms and serious expressions. Security was tight.

I watched the technicians day after day, while Dermot filled my head with facts and theories, most of which went in one ear and shot out the other at a speed that would have challenged Einstein's theory about the speed of light. I tried to stay on Dermot's coattails, but I felt that I was constantly getting in the way of the workers. They tolerated it, never treating me with anything but the utmost courtesy. They knew better than to fuck with me—I was their meal ticket.

By the third week I had pretty much absorbed everything that I was going to, which wasn't very much. It was late in the afternoon. Dermot and I had been in the interior of the machine, discussing supplies, what I would need for the journey ... and beyond. The question just jumped into my head. "How long was it that we needed to plan for—how long will I be gone?"

Dermot was quiet for a long time before he answered. "Forever," he said, and walked away.

My mouth dried up, I had to sit down, but there was no place to do so. Instead, I simply sagged against the cold, metallic inner skin of the machine, by breaths coming in short little gasps, the world before me spinning faster and faster, my vision growing dim. Not coming back was something that I never considered.

*****

I had finished my story, except for the part about not coming back. Like I said before, Jakes was skeptical. He was going to give me grief over the entire idea. The part about being stranded in the past was definitely going to be a showstopper for him. He sat there chewing on it, sipping his beer, quiet as a mime. I didn't dare tell him the rest of the story.

Dermot had told me that it was impossible to travel into the future. When I asked why, he said that because the future didn't yet exist, one couldn't travel to it. I tried to argue—if I was traveling into the past, then the future *did* exist, I had come from it. He said no ... emphatically. From my perspective, which was in the past, I was on a parallel time-line, and the future did not exist from that parallel time. It was why I couldn't return.

I couldn't tell that to Jakes. He was a pretty powerful person—someone who could get things done—someone who could prevent things from happening. As strong as our friendship had become, I didn't hesitate for a second thinking that he would go to whatever lengths he had to, to prevent me from taking the irreversible leap.

We had another beer, the ballgame long since over. It was dark, yet still warm for so early in the season. The ten o'clock news was on, something about the President's latest attempt at quelling the violence in the Middle East. I was pensive, waiting for the outburst from Jakes. I had seen it before. I was expecting it then.

But it didn't come and he still hadn't spoken a word. When he finally did, he had the look of sorrow on his face—not at all what I expected.

"Has it really gotten so bad, David? Are things so terrible that you're willing to just chuck it all, to submit to a crazy experiment that no one has ever attempted? How do you know it will even work?"

It was a question that I'd been asking myself for three weeks. Dermot had no guarantees. In his gut, he knew that it would work, all his precise calculations, all the research, every experiment said that it would, but he had no absolute proof. I had asked him if he had sent anyone back in time and he had answered, "yes … and no."

They *had* run a series of experiments, beginning a few years back, early in the program, using scaled-down versions of the machine. The first attempts were disastrous: equipment destroyed, millions of dollars lost, researchers discouraged. Thank God they had not used *live* subjects. But they learned from their mistakes, each successive attempt getting closer to getting it right. At one point, some six months after their first attempt, the time machine simply disappeared after passing through the artificial wormhole. It could only be assumed that it had disappeared somewhere in time. It was the result they had been looking for.

It was a big step for them, but it didn't instill me with a lot of confidence. I asked what he meant by the time machine disappearing. Where did it go? Dermot then said the strangest thing. "I don't know, somewhere in outer space I assume."

If Dermot was trying to win me over, he was failing historically. He then went on to explain that because the solar system is constantly expanding as a result of the *Big Bang* some five billion years ago, the relative position of the earth changes from one moment to the next. Furthermore, the earth is continuously rotating around the sun and revolving on its own axis. In other words, a body's position in free-space is constantly changing. Gravity keeps our positions relative to the earth's surface fixed over time, but in traveling *through* time, the laws of gravity do not apply.

Like I said, his words didn't exactly instill confidence. But he assured me that this minor problem was corrected. He said that the time machine had to be firmly attached to the earth's bedrock—a mechanical connection would do what the earth's gravity could not. The machine would remain in a fixed position relative to the earth, rather than to free-space.

They constructed one final experimental machine, this time firmly connected to a remote stretch of land just outside of Manitoba, Canada, where some three thousand-year old Mastodon tracks were found. They sent the machine, with passenger, back in time a thousand years. The time traveler, a single white mouse, was given no supplies for the trip: no food, no water. As the wormhole moved past the magnetic field surrounding the machine, it disappeared just like the one before.

And, again, nothing happened. Nothing happened for three days, when the machine suddenly reappeared without warning. Inside was the tiny Plexiglas case that had entrapped the rodent. And there was nothing in the case except a small pile of dust. Analysis revealed it was the remains of the long-dead mouse—dead for a thousand years.

Dermot tried to explain that it took three days for the mouse to die from lack of water. The three days occurred a thousand years ago on a parallel time line. The death of the mouse, in turn, caused a secondary rift in the time continuum, bringing it back to the present—three days later. It made my head hurt to try to see the logic in it. I didn't understand a word he said, and I wasn't so sure that Dermot fully understood it either. But I *did* believe it.

I asked Dermot why he thought that the south side of Chicago was a good, solid place to launch the latest machine from. It seemed pretty unlikely to me. He agreed. The machine and all of its controls would have to me moved. The entire control room was modular. It, along with the time machine, could be disassembled, moved, and reassembled in a new location just like a prefabricated house.

But it wasn't as simple as picking a flat spot of ground and just anchoring it. They weren't planning on sending me back just a couple of years, but millions of years. The earth had changed dramatically over that stretch of time—volcanic eruptions and earthquakes had changed the landscape, continents changed positions, water had covered a much greater percentage of the globe's surface. They had to pick a place that was relatively unchanged since the time of the dinosaurs. Even before Dermot said it, I knew where that place was …

The cave in Utah!

Other than the rockslide that sealed the fate of the four animals, the cave had existed at least seventy million years—unchanged. But what if they didn't send me back in time quite far enough? I would be trapped inside that goddamned contraption with several millions tons of rock piled on top.

I would die like the mouse, but probably much quicker, my air supply running out before a day was gone.

Or, what if they sent me back too far? What was I in store for then? Was the cave underwater a million years earlier? Did the cave even exist much before the time of the dinosaurs' deaths? I could wind up drowned or entombed in solid rock. It seemed that my odds of surviving the trip—if I decided to actually go—were dropping by the minute.

That's when Dermot threw another monkey wrench into the works. His time machine wasn't like the one in the movies. One couldn't just dial in a date and a time, and presto, change-o, you hit right smack on the dot. There was a margin of error with Dermot's machine. The math was precise, the machine built to exact specifications, but the circumference of the coil was not. It was somewhat in a state of constant flux, expanding and contracting by a few percentages. Dropping from one ring to the next was a thousand years, give or take twenty or thirty. Dropping through sixty or seventy thousand rings gave an error of two million years or so.

Of course I didn't tell Jakes any of this, and, I was surprised when he didn't ask me a lot of questions. He asked me just one.

"Are you really considering this?" He sat there, his head hanging low, his long arms dangling between his legs, twirling his empty beer bottle, his sixth or seventh, atop the deck.

I told him, "Of course not, I just found the whole thing fascinating, as if I were stuck smack dab in the middle of a science fiction novel, and I wanted to get as close to the climax as I could without actually becoming part of a sad ending."

I felt guilty. For the first time since I'd known him, I'd lied to Jakes. It was true, before going to his house that afternoon I didn't think that I had made up my mind. I hadn't entirely ruled it out, either. During the past three weeks, as each day went by, I had become caught up in the project, confident that the thing would actually work. I started thinking of it as *our* machine … and then *my* machine. After all, if I actually did it, the machine would become mine for a lot longer than it had been Dermot's.

I had misled Dermot, just as I was misleading Jakes. I hadn't told him that I would participate in his experiment, but I hadn't exactly told him that I wouldn't, either. I even became involved in the planning, leading him on, making him think that I was on board, constantly asking questions, making suggestions.

A week before, I was worried about how to tell Dermot that he had picked the wrong guy. As I sat there with Jakes, just seven days later, I wasn't so sure that he made a mistake. A part of me wanted to go—a big part—the part of me that longed for my wife, the part of me that was filled with remorse over Christine's death, the part that worried over Susan's condition, and the part that was tormented by Green's escape from justice.

It was a lot of parts—the biggest parts of me. If the trip to the past were successful, I would be up to my ears in adventure and wonder, and, yes, even danger. I would be far removed from the pain of the present, too busy to feel the longing, the remorse, and the anger. It could be a new beginning for me.

And I thought about what might happen should the experiment not work. There was no question that something would happen. I knew that the wormhole would pass over the machine and it would simply disappear, as it had twice before. What I didn't know, and what Dermot couldn't tell me, was exactly *when* I would end up ... *if* I ended up.

No one knew how long the trip would take, and what would happen to me during the journey. Dermot said that traveling to the past would not be instantaneous like in the movies, and he couldn't guarantee that I wouldn't feel it one way or another. But he did estimate that the duration of the trip could be measured in hours, possibly days, not weeks or months ... or longer. And he didn't think that there would be an unacceptable measure of pain or discomfort during the trip. The machine that was recovered following the prior trip showed no signs of damage or change in any way, except for a millennium's worth of dust and dirt.

I didn't take a lot of comfort from that. What the hell did an *unacceptable measure of pain* mean? The machine's hull was made from six inches of solid titanium, and the shape was as stable as one could possibly make it.

I was not.

I was made of flesh and blood, pretty damn easy to damage, and I was anything but stable, in whatever way you wanted to measure it. Nobody knew what time travel would do to the human body.

I also thought about the dangers. I would be alone, seventy million years in the past, in a world filled with animals that no one had ever seen first hand, animals that could devour me in a single gulp and think nothing more of me than just a tiny snack between meals. I had no idea how to protect myself from these predators. They had never seen the likes of me—they would think me no more than a strange bug.

What about the atmosphere, and the climate? Was the oxygen/carbon dioxide content suitable for my puny human lungs? Were the climatic conditions such that my frail body would survive for any length of time? The experts thought that they were, but no one was all that sure. And how would I eat? Surely the vessel that I was to travel in and live in would not accommodate a lifetime of rations. Was I expected to fend for myself, to kill my supper? I was not a predator, I had never hunted, never intentionally killed another living creature.

All these questions that I had no answer for, and yet, I knew that I was going to do it.

I left Jakes sitting on his deck, sipping at yet another beer, thinking that it was all just someone's wild fantasy, and that I was an unwilling participant. He was satisfied and probably not going to push me any further. The problem was, I was caught up in the fantasy. I *was* a part of it, like being trapped beneath an approaching avalanche, knowing what was in store, but unable to stop it.

CHAPTER 10

I stepped down from the trailer, looking off to the left where I was greeted by a familiar scene. It looked the same as it had a year ago, with the exception of the twelve-foot high fence that extended nearly as far as the eye could see. It was shiny, reflecting the light of the sun—double rows of razor wire ran along the top. It was still early, yet the sun was already high in the sky, heating up the plain that stretched on for miles in front of me. The sky was a dazzling blue, not a cloud to be seen. It was probably hot as hell, but I couldn't tell.

I wasn't accustomed to the bright sun and had to squint in order to raise my eyes above the level of the far-off horizon. I lowered the sunshield on my helmet, the scene before me coming into sharper focus, although darker, as if a huge cloud had mysteriously appeared from nowhere and settled in overhead.

I was stiff from inactivity, the bulk of the suit and the weight of the pack across my chest added to my discomfort. The wide, heavy boots made my short trip down the two steps awkward and unsure. I was surprised to make it down to the good earth in one piece, without tripping, going head over heels, sprawling across the hard-packed Utah soil.

I stared at the horizon, the faint outline of the city of Price in the background, trying to steady my breathing. It was a little like using an aqualung, not quite natural, having to think about the acts of inhaling and exhaling. The air was artificial, emitted from a miniature battery driven compressor tucked within the sealed polymer receptacle that was form-fitted to my chest. And it was filtered, having no detectable odor, but not the same as breathing fresh air.

I forced myself to exhale, pushing the unnatural air from my lungs, turning to the left as I did. They were all there waiting for me: twenty technicians, all dressed in immaculate white, sparkling in the not yet noonday sun … and Dermot standing right in the middle, a radiant smile splitting his face in two. As I faced them, they burst into applause, Dermot clapping the hardest as he stepped forward to take my arm.

As I let him lead me towards the group, I twisted by neck to look behind me, seeing one last time the prison that had kept me captive for the past ten days. It wasn't the sensory deprivation chamber that I thought Dermot was going to stick me in a few months back, but I had sure felt deprived. It was a sterile environment, literally and figuratively. It was antiseptic, pressurized like the lab where I first saw the machine. There was nothing in it that didn't absolutely have to be there.

I had lived under strict rules, a Spartan lifestyle for the ten days. No one was allowed to enter—no one was allowed to open a window—not that they could, they were sealed. The door, which could only be opened from the inside, had an elaborate lock that only I knew the combination to. Despite my belief to the contrary, I was not a prisoner—I could leave any time I wanted. But it felt like a prison, and I couldn't get past the thought that I was being punished for something—perhaps for Susan's accident—perhaps for Liz's or Christine's death. Shit, there were plenty of reasons to choose from.

Furniture was minimum—one chair, a futon to sleep on, and a small metal table. There was no refrigerator—food could spoil—but there was a freezer and a microwave, and there were canned goods—fruits and vegetables. There was a television and radio built into the wall, and Dermot supplied me with a small selection of books, and a deck of playing cards. I had a chemical toilet and a trash compactor, both cleaned after every use via an entry panel from the outside that could only be accessed after being closed and sealed from the inside.

The trailer was designed to keep germs out, to insure that I had no bugs with me on the journey. I had yet to determine whether I actually had the ability to change the future, but Dermot was taking no chances.

The viruses of the twentieth century didn't exist millions of years ago, so there were no tolerances built up to combat them. Wouldn't it be ironic if I carried a simple cold virus back with me that caused the extinction of the dinosaurs? Hell, who knows, maybe that's what actually happened to them.

Although, if I understood even a small part of what Dermot told me, that wasn't possible because I hadn't yet made the trip back through time, and the dinosaurs had indeed become extinct without my help. A hundred years of research said that it was true. But in going back in time, actually living in a period millions of years before evolutionary forces created man, wasn't I then changing the future, even setting in motion a chain of events that could have killed off the dinosaurs?

My head spun trying to untangle the logic, or illogic, of it.

The ten days had been miserable. The first few crept by in slow motion, spent mostly pacing the floor, doing pushups and sit ups, bored, missing my daily gym routine, feeling penned up. But as the days passed, knowing that I might be trading one kind of captivity for another, or maybe worse, I thought less about the tedium of my daily routine, and more about the unknown that I was about to enter. And the unknown was terrifying, causing the last days to pass much quicker than I wanted.

During the last few days I had forgone my exercise routine and I had quit pacing—stopped doing almost anything else. I sat in front of the television, hour after hour, but not watching anything, my mind in turmoil. Dermot could sense my anxiety and spoke to me often through the intercom. I kept telling him that everything was okay—I was just relaxing. He didn't believe me. He was afraid I was going to chicken out at the last minute.

I wasn't at all sure that he was wrong.

That last night, I stayed up nearly all night, sitting in front of the tube. I knew that I wouldn't be getting much sleep, but maybe I stayed up because I knew that I'd never see a television again. I was grasping for one last bit of the modern world.

But eventually I did sleep, fitfully, in little bits and snatches, dreaming—nightmares mostly. For a change, I didn't dream of Liz or Susan or even Christine. I dreamt of monsters, huge flesh-eating machines that were chasing me. And I could never outrun them. Each time I woke up just as they were about to pounce, their mouths wide, saliva dripping from a serpent's tongue.

I was fully awake when one of Dermot's technicians came to get me that morning. As I opened the door to let him in I saw that he was dressed in a space suit, just like an astronaut's. He had a second, similar suit for me, and he spent more than an hour helping me put it on. Just before putting my helmet on, the technician gave me a little white pill. It was the tranquilizer.

Dermot and I had argued about using the drug for the trip. I had no desire to be stoned during the journey. I was nervous, but my ego prevented me from saying that I was. Dermot had to remind me that he had no idea what effects time travel had on the human body. No human had attempted it, and the mouse that did wasn't talking.

The truth was—I wasn't nervous—I was scared out of my mind. And Dermot was right. What scared me more than anything else was the trip itself. I had little doubt about the machine surviving it, but I was much less sure of myself. I thought about a lot of possible scenarios, but the one that I thought about the most was of myself growing younger as we began the backward travel through time.

The machine was anchored to Utah's bedrock, but what anchored me? If I went back in time one year, was I not one year younger. What about ten years ... twenty years ... thirty? What kept me from regressing with the years? Dropping through time in thousand year plops, I was going to disappear pretty damn quickly.

I took the pill.

As Dermot and I approached the group, they separated to let us pass. The technicians were still applauding, shouting out words of encouragement, a few stepping forward to pat me on the back, to touch my arm. I had become more than an experiment to them. I had become a member of the team, part of a select few that shared a common dream, a very special secret. They had become even more than that to me—they had become my family.

Over the months I had worked with each of them individually, and in groups. Save for Jakes, I hadn't felt a close bond to anyone in a very long time. They were good people, not just good technicians. Dermot had picked his people well.

As my little group of supporters parted, the mouth of the cave became visible, the gate of the iron fence stretching across the entrance now open. The gate was not for security. The razor wire topped fence was for that. The gate had an entirely different function.

The time machine had to be connected directly and firmly to the earth, but that was easier said than done. The bulk of the machine had to be free-floating such that the moving rings that controlled the wormhole could pass over its entire length unimpeded. The rails running its length made that possible by transmitting the flux energy through the metallic base beneath the machine as the rings traveled forward. The one end of the machine, opposite the end from which the rings were positioned, was where the ground connection took place. There was a series of three titanium bars, three inches square that were inserted into the base of the machine, running its entire length. The other end came up from the base and spread in opposite directions—three bars going up into the roof of the cave and three into the bedrock of the floor, some twenty feet. It looked damn stable, but Dermot was taking no chances. The gate was an added precaution. Should all else fail, the gate would insure that the machine stayed in the cave, while the planet itself went racing, and turning, and tumbling out into the cosmos.

I didn't like the thought of the massive time machine rattling around inside the cave, banging off the walls, tumbling, spinning, with me inside, being tossed and turned like a rag doll. And I wasn't so sure of the gate keeping me inside the cave. It had only been constructed a few short weeks ago. Wouldn't it just disappear during the initial part of my trip? I held my tongue, trusting that Dermot knew what he was doing. Besides, I was pretty much past the point of questions.

We passed through the heavy gate into the cave, glad that I had put down the visor on my helmet. The artificial lighting was even more intense than the bright Utah sun, illuminating the time machine so that there wasn't a hint of shadow anywhere. The dual rings that would pass over the machine reflected the light, penetrating the sunscreen of my visor so that I had to lower my eyes.

Coming out of the base of the rings were bundles of wire harnesses, some as thick as my thigh, snaking out of the cave, entering the control room that had been reassembled just outside of the cave's entrance.

Even with my suit on, I could hear the hum of the generators that pressurized the time machine. I knew that once I was sealed up inside the thing, they would disconnect the air hoses and all other external connections. The air trapped inside would have to last the duration of the trip. I had my own air supply strapped to my chest, but it was only intended to get me from the trailer to the machine.

As we reached it, Dermot stopped and turned. He stretched out to embrace me, hugging me tightly even though his short arms would not come close to reaching around my waist with the bulky suit on. He had to shout for me to hear. He said just one thing, "I wish it were me." He had tears streaming down his face as he turned away.

I watched him pass through the gate, closing it as he went, and then he was gone, having passed out of my sight into the control room. I hesitated for just a moment, knowing that that might have been the last time that I saw another human being. I took in the scene, looking out from the interior of the cave. I had seen it a hundred times before, and I wondered how it would look the next time I saw it.

I turned back towards the machine in time to see the door silently open, having been unlatched by someone manning the appropriate switch in the control room. I entered my new home, closing the door behind me. I could feel the tranquilizer kicking in, my shakes subsiding, the fear along with it. It was as if I were a bystander watching the events unfolding in front of me, but not actually participating in them.

The inside of the machine had changed considerably since I last saw it ten days before. The three rows of shelves that comprised two thirds of the interior, in what I had come to think of as the back of the vehicle, were now filled to overflowing. I had helped make the decisions regarding what to take. The process took weeks. There was limited space and we argued and debated over every single item, selecting one, discarding another. I wasn't packing for comfort—I was packing for survival.

There was box after box of clothing—rugged outdoor stuff—things that would last, things that would protect me from a hostile, unknown environment. The shoes, work boots mostly, a dozen pair, were of heavy leather, thick rubber soles, high-tops, half way to the knee. They were clothes one would wear in the jungle, or climbing an ice-capped mountain. They were explorer's clothes—they were hunter's clothes.

Several boxes contained medical supplies—bandages and gauze pads of every size and shape, salves and ointments for burns, bites, scrapes and cuts, and pills for headaches, muscle cramps, diarrhea, and constipation. There were vitamins and nutritional supplements galore and powders for athlete's feet and jock itch. We packed a dental kit and a small surgical one as well and the necessary drugs to anesthetize myself should either one of them be needed. One box, marked in red, had drugs normally attained only by prescription. Dermot had connections—he could get whatever he wanted. I had everything for anything that might ail me—a lifetime's worth.

Of course I didn't know what half the drugs were for and I didn't know how to perform even the most routine surgical procedure. That's what the books were for, an entire set of medical procedures, from the simplest to the most complex. There were other books, as well—ones on gardening, sewing, carpentry, hunting, cooking, and thirty or forty other subjects—how-to books, all. Dermot made sure that there was room for pleasure reading too—fifty books in all. I chose my favorites; Stephen King, Clive Cussler, Robert Ludlum, Leon Uris—books I had read before, and looked forward to reading again. I had little choice—I would never see a newly published one again.

One row of supplies was taken up with hardware. Everything from woodworking tools to ones for gardening. Axes, files, and chisels, spades, shovels, and hoes—were all mixed in with about every kind of tool imaginable—hand tools, of course. And in with the cartons of tools, were weapons. Dermot and I had no disagreement about that whatsoever.

I was going in packin'.

I had a number of hunting knives, several of which were combat style like those carried by soldiers and mercenaries. There was an assortment of handguns, with lightweight shoulder holsters and a number of long barrel guns, including two fine shotguns. There was enough ammunition to start a small war, but that was not my intent. I wasn't there to take trophies and I didn't give a damn for the sport of hunting. However, I did intend to protect myself with whatever it took, including unloading the biggest gun I had into the belly of whatever animal fancied me as an appetizer. But the main reason I wanted firepower was because I had to eat.

That left one of three storage racks to account for, enough space for a hundred good-sized boxes. They were filled with foodstuffs, enough for perhaps twelve months, maybe eighteen if I rationed. They were, of course, all non-perishable: canned fruits and vegetables, powdered milk and soft drinks, boxes of dried pasta and bottled sauces, cases of beans, chili, and soup—and several hundred bottles of mountain-spring water. There was no way of telling whether the water of seventy million years ago was drinkable, although we thought it was—we hoped it was.

There was no way that we were able to store a lifetime of rations. We packed enough to get accustomed to my surroundings—enough for the time that it took to plant a crop and see it harvested. We packed enough for me to learn the manly arts of trapping and shooting. After that, I'd be on my own. If I couldn't grow or kill my dinner, I would go without any.

There were tons of supplies, maybe even hundreds of tons of supplies, enough to fill the twenty foot width of the machine and at least thirty feet of its length, clear up to the ceiling. It looked like one huge package, all tied down with heavy canvas straps. I couldn't even guess how much it all weighed. It's a good thing we weren't flying or sailing this thing.

The other end of the time machine, the front end, had changed considerably, as well. Dermot's team had done their best to make a home for me. There was a decent size bed that would fold up tight against the wall to give me more space. A commode sat in one corner. Not one of those fancy chemical types, like in an RV, just a plain looking toilet with one added feature—the inner bowl was removable. I would have a comfortable place to do my business, but I wouldn't have to live with the results. It sat there in plain view—there would be little need for privacy.

In the opposite corner was a big, overstuffed recliner, *my* recliner. Without my knowledge, Dermot had taken it from my home. I smiled. Dermot didn't have a key to my place, but a little thing like a key wasn't going to stop someone like him. There probably wouldn't be much time for sitting, but it was a nice touch, and I appreciated the fact that Dermot thought of it. The recliner was bolted to the floor, but, of course, I could change that when the trip was over—I had the tools.

The stove was still there, and in a shelf next to it was a supply of firewood, not a lot, but enough to get me through the first few days until I could obtain more. I would need it for both cooking and for warmth. If I wound up in summertime, the meager supply would last much longer, needing it only for cooking. Winter was another story.

I didn't know what to expect. The late Cretaceous period began with only minor seasonal variations, but by its end, they were much more severe. Some believed that the drastic shift in climate hastened, if not caused, the end of the dinosaurs. Maybe it did, and maybe it didn't, but either way, if I ended up in winter, I would need to find a source of wood quickly.

The rest of the space was taken up with cupboards, each having a door that was securely fastened for the trip. I had watched the technicians install the cabinets, but I had no idea what they contained—except for one. I walked over to it and unlatched the door. The built-in table unfolded easily, the stool in a recess beneath it. Above it, on a shelf, was the powerful laptop computer that I was to use to record my journey. It was solar powered. There was an access panel in the roof of the time machine so that I could easily charge the cells. It was stored in a titanium case, along with several boxes of discs. I was to keep it stored there anytime that I wasn't using it or charging it.

There was only one thing remaining in the space, something that was only temporary. It was a chair—another chair. But this one was not soft and comfortable like my recliner. This one was rigid and unyielding, thin pads over hard steel. It reminded me of a fighter pilot's seat with some special modifications. Connected to the bottom of the chair were foot rests, clamps actually, that were activated by a lever on the side of the seat. The headrest was sculptured so that my helmet sucked deeply into it, and there was a wide strap to hold my head motionless against it. Lying draped against the back of the chair, the other half dangling from the seat cushion was the three-point harness. Like my recliner, this chair was firmly bolted to the floor.

It looked like an electric chair.

As I approached it, Dermot's voice came over the speaker, "It's time, Doctor Williams." He hadn't called me that since the first time that I met him, that night in the bar.

He must have begun recording the events. I looked up at the camera mounted in the upper corner to my right and gave him a thumb's up.

Things were quiet in the machine, but I knew that it was otherwise in the control room, the activity fast and furious. I began to strap myself into the seat under the watchful eye of the camera. The whole process only took a minute. I connected the three-point harness that came together at my waist, cinching it up as tight as I could. I placed my feet in the stirrups and pulled the lever to clamp them in position. I pushed my helmet into the headrest, pulled the strap tight, and I was ready.

Dermot's voice came across the speaker one last time. He said, "Initiating wormhole simulation. Godspeed Doctor Williams." With that, there was about three seconds of static, followed by a loud popping sound from the speaker, and I knew that the connection was gone.

There was a single six-inch porthole in the front of the machine that was not covered by closed cabinets. It didn't offer much of a view, but I could make out one section of the gleaming transport ring as they began powering up the system. Within a few seconds, the ring began to shimmer, glowing with a pulsating energy, becoming at times almost transparent, as if losing its solidity. Within the ring's core, colors began to appear—all the colors—sliding across an oily surface, one color merging into another. It reminded me of the little wire hoop that kids use to make bubbles, the soapy water making colorful patterns as it slides around the confines of the little wire loop.

I focused on the colors. Everything else just sort of went away. The tranquilizer was in full effect. I couldn't feel the hard seat beneath me, or the pressure of the harness across my chest. I felt as if I was floating, rising like a cloud above the seat. My body had become numb from the powerful sedative, and the colors of the ring began to fade as the drug began to take control of my mind, as well.

The fear was gone. I don't know how much was the drug and how much was the total sense of awe that engulfed me, but for the first time I felt sure of my decision. I had actually made my choice following the last meeting with my boss, but until that moment when I was about to pass through the wormhole, I was never sure that I had made the right one. As I drifted off, I thought about that choice and why I made it—why I felt *compelled* to make it.

*****

A week had passed since I had seen the time machine for the first time. I had been back to Dermot's lab twice since then and had my first introduction into the theory of time travel. I was still at the point were I didn't believe him, and filling my head with facts that I couldn't comprehend didn't help. I was both skeptical *and* confused.

My time was less often spent with Susan, visiting her every second or third day, instead of daily. There had been no change in her condition, one way or another. When I was there her doctor made a point to see me. Not to give me an update on her condition, I could see that for myself. He did it because he was compassionate. He knew that the situation with Susan was tearing me apart and he felt responsible, and guilty, for suggesting that I back off.

I had only been there a couple of times since meeting Dermot, and I hoped that my wild tale would ignite a spark in Susan. I still had not lost all hope that somehow, in some way, she was picking up bits and pieces of my endless monologues. If there was anything in the world that would get her attention, anything that could pierce the darkness that entombed her, it would be the idea that one could go back through time and actually see the dinosaurs, live among them, study them up close and personal.

The only one that I had ever met who loved dinosaurs more than me was Susan. She was fascinated with them, couldn't get enough of them. She used to fantasize about somehow bringing one back to life. So many questions could be answered by studying a single living dinosaur. She never even considered the possibility of studying them all at the same time, in the same place, and all of them alive. She never gave time travel a thought. I didn't need to ask Susan what she would do. I knew the answer. She would do it in a *New York minute* and never look back.

The time that I wasn't spending with Susan, I was spending at work. The computer simulation was complete and I had made my formal report to my boss, making my recommendations. I had expected immediate approval and authorization to proceed full-speed ahead. This was a moneymaker and I knew that Doctor Trenton would jump on it like ugly on an ape. But I still hadn't heard from him, not a word in two weeks. I assumed that he was just too busy to look at the proposal. He might have been my boss, but he was a tight-ass bastard. We didn't see much of each other.

Getting a formal approval didn't slow me down much. There was so much to do that didn't cost money—didn't need his approval for. Assembling the skeleton was time consuming, expensive, tedious work. It took a hell of a lot of planning. But there was a lot that I could do to prepare for that eventuality. And that's what I was doing. I was getting back into the routine, spending longer hours at work, once again finding something that I really cared about.

I would be the one to figure out where the animals would end up being displayed, which could end up taking as much time as the actual assembly of the skeleton, and could cost even more. I was the curator of the dinosaur exhibit, and I had the authority to do pretty much anything that I wanted within the walls of my exhibit. But I wasn't willing to sacrifice any of my current space, which left me two choices: either I stole space from another exhibit, or I added space by adding on to the existing building—both were problematic. Very few curators were going to be willing to give up space to me. Space was at a premium—everyone was fighting for territory, and putting an addition on the building was big bucks.

I started to think about putting together an annex to the Hall of Dinosaurs. It was an expensive proposition—one that I knew would pay for itself within three years—maybe sooner. Money was something that Trenton understood. He was tight fisted, as well as tight-assed. I really felt that my exhibit deserved center-stage, right in the heart of the atrium, where everyone entering the museum would see it right from the start. My find was significantly more impressive that the fast-food-sponsored *rex* that stood there at that time. So I prepared an elegant economic justification profile: initial cash outlay, cash flows—in and out—factored in the present cost of money, calculated the payback period, all the things that Trenton understood. How could he say no?

And while I was preparing my financial argument, I was busy making plans for the actual assembly of the thousands of bones. The skeletons were of such a unique color and in such an amazing state of condition and completeness that I had decided long before to use the actual bones in the reconstruction, and not plaster casts, which were more common. Many dinosaur fossils are found in such poor condition—broken, misshapen, or incomplete—that they can only be assembled into a complete animal by making casts and replicas of individual bones using plaster. There's an advantage in doing it this way, as no external armature is necessary. The *fake* bones can be drilled and thin metal rods inserted, strengthening them and making it possible for connecting one to another unobtrusively. It appears more realistic and the public seemed to favor this method. I looked at it a bit differently—fake bones—fake dinosaur.

My specimens were not fake and would require an armature—an external support system, to hold the bones in place. But I would use the most modern techniques and materials to make it nearly invisible to the average observer. The skull alone weighed more than six hundred pounds. A very special armature would have to be constructed in order to support that much weight. With the support of a metallurgist, I would design it myself. The design of the armature and its construction would be done under a veil of secrecy.

The unveiling would be spectacular.

So I was working on both things at once. I was nearing the completion of the business plan and just beginning to start on the armature when I got a call from Trenton. It was a summons actually—Trenton was like that—he never called you in for a casual conversation. He was above all that. He was the boss, and he wanted everyone to know it.

I was one of the few curators who were not afraid of him. I knew that he was full of shit, and he knew that I knew that he was full of shit. So, he pretty much stayed out of my way and let me do my job. He was smart enough to know that my exhibit brought in the majority of visitors, and made the most money for the museum. Besides, I think that he was a little bit afraid of me. He was really quite a wimp.

Calling me to his office was unusual. He summoned others, but rarely me. I called him by his first name, Edgar, which he really hated, but he had given up trying to change me years before. I treated him with all the respect that he treated others, which worked out pretty well from my point of view. He treated me a lot better than I treated him.

That time, I expected the call—surprised actually—that he hadn't called earlier. My dinosaurs were going to make a lot of money for the museum, and Trenton would be pushing me to get on with it. Of course he would be friendly, full of smiles, so that he would get my complete cooperation. When someone came up with an idea that was going to make money, he was a different person—happy—full of good cheer. That's what I expected on that day as I approached his office.

I should have knocked on the door. It's what he expected—it's what everybody else did. I startled him when I just walked right in, but he didn't seem angry. No, he wouldn't be angry—not with me—not then. But, in truth, he didn't seem all that happy either. If anything, I'd have said that he looked embarrassed, like I had caught him with his hands in the cookie jar. Fumbling with a folder on his desk and staring off to the side, he asked me to sit down. He refused to look me in the eye as I took a seat. He was still fooling with the folder, turning it over, sliding his fingers along one edge, then another. It was *my* folder, the one with the proposal.

He made a quarter turn in his swivel chair so that he could look to his left out the window at Lake Michigan. The folder was still in his hands, held out in front of him as if it would burn him if he held it too close. He refused to look in my direction as he said softly, "Damn fine piece of work, Doctor Williams."

With that he looked away from the window, but sat staring at the folder, refusing to look directly at me. I moved forward in my chair so that I could get a better look at his eyes, even if he wasn't looking at mine. I replied with a simple, "Thanks," nothing more. I waited. Seconds turned into minutes—nothing from him other than a deep exhale. I could see that small twitch in his eye that all of us knew developed when he was nervous. His fingers trembled, as well. I could see the corners of the folder rustle.

After an interminable length, he began to speak. He rambled, sometimes incoherently. The museum was in serious financial pressure, tourism was down, the board was putting the pressure on, there was talk of cutbacks.

He got up and began pacing, changing gears on me. He started rattling on and on about what a great job I had done in Utah—it was an incredible find, one of a lifetime. It was too bad what happened to Susan, and I shouldn't be worried about what happened to that little worker that got killed.

I stopped him right there. "Her name was Christine Chamberlain. She was a *real* person, with a *real* life, and she died too young. She was working for this museum when she died. You could at least remember her name."

Trenton's face went beet-red and the eye twitch kicked up a couple of notches. He finally turned to face me, blurting out, "Yes, of c-c-c-course, I meant to say, C-C-C-Christine." The stutter was something I hadn't heard before. He was a nervous wreck, and I was beginning to smell a rat.

"Edgar! What the hell did you call me in here for?" I was getting fed up with this crap. I didn't like the little jerk, and he knew it. At first I thought that his hesitation was just a reflection of that dislike, but this was something much more. I had never seen him quite like this. He was a guy that took some kind of perverse pleasure in giving bad news—it made him feel powerful, in charge. But on that day, he wasn't in charge of shit.

I started to get out of my chair, which, thinking back, was probably the wrong thing to do. He was already frightened enough. He probably thought that I was getting up to kick his ass.

He panicked, running toward the open door, shouting as he did, "I sold the dinosaurs!"

I was too stunned to kick his ass, or do much of anything else except drop back into the chair. For just a few seconds I wondered *what dinosaurs*? Moments later, I understood what dinosaurs—my dinosaurs. He had sold *my* dinosaurs.

I wished that I *had* kicked his ass.

He fled the office that day and didn't return until the next. I called his office every hour on the hour the day he returned, but he refused to answer. I knew that he was there, his secretary was taking all of his calls, and, according to her, he was tied up in conferences.

I knew that he was doing nothing of the sort. He was cowering in his office, afraid to confront me. I considered just busting in, but I was afraid of what might happen if I did.

As it turned out, that was the last time that I ever saw Trenton. Two days after our confrontation in his office, he sent me a memo. Actually, he sent my department a memo—I just happened to be in charge of the department, so, naturally, I was copied on it. I was surprised that he didn't have his secretary delete my name from the distribution. In short, it stated that, due to difficult financial circumstances, the Chicago Museum of Paleontology was compelled to agree to terms with Toronto's Museum of Science for the sale of the four Cretaceous specimens from the recent Utah expedition.

It was a couple of days later when I learned that my dinosaurs were sold for a record forty million dollars. A staggering amount, but that didn't make me feel even the slightest bit better. Trenton had pulled the rug out from under me. They were my discovery, and even though I was under salary to the museum, meaning that anything that I discovered actually belonged to them, it was still a cheesy thing to do. He never discussed it with me—he went on letting me believe that I was in charge, that what we did with the animals was entirely up to me.

As I said before, Trenton was a businessman. He knew that forty million dollars, when invested now, was worth a hell of a lot more than forty million that trickled in over ten or twenty years. But he was shortchanging the exhibit. There would be none other like it in all the world—money would have poured in, and that money would have financed countless other expeditions. Who knew what marvelous discoveries could have been made? I left my office that day feeling completely empty—nothing left inside. I went to the gym because I didn't know what else to do. I found no relief from it, and ended up doing only half of my normal lifts, not bothering with my posing routine or trip to the sauna. But the workout served two purposes. It gave me time to think—time to make a decision, and it gave me the opportunity to say some good-byes.

The next day, I turned in my resignation. I gave Trenton the usual two week's notice, but he never so much as acknowledged it. After three days, I simply turned my back and just walked away. I cleaned out my desk, took all the pictures, diplomas, and acknowledgements from my walls, thanked my stunned staff, and left the building once and for all.

That night I called Dermot. He arrived at my home twenty minutes later. He must have had the Lincoln floored the whole way. I told him what had happened to me that day, all about my boss, the asshole.

I said just one thing, "Anson, I'm ready. Let's do this thing."

I fully expected him to be excited, giddy actually. He finally had his guinea pig. It was the moment that he'd been working towards for years, probably most of his adult life. But he was unusually quiet, somber, as if he were about to lose his best friend. And maybe that's how he thought of it. We had become extremely close over the months, not like best friends, but like father and son. I *did* see him as a father figure—after all, mine had been dead for twenty years. Dermot had no children, had never been married, as a matter of fact. I was probably as close to a son as he would ever have.

It might have been that he felt that any excessive exuberance on his part might have put me off, might have made me second-guess my decision, and he didn't want to jinx it. I didn't think so. He was like Jakes, as honest as they come. Dermot knew that I was putting my life on the line, and he put me there. Maybe *he* was second-guessing himself.

We talked through the night. He had brought a bottle of scotch. And we drank it, but neither of us got drunk. It wasn't a night for getting drunk. I think that there are certain times in your life where you can't drink enough to get drunk. That was one of those times.

We talked a little about what I needed to do to tie up loose ends from my current life. We talked a little more about the technical aspects of my trip, about what would occur during those first few minutes. But most of all, we talked about the dangers that lay in front of me. If I survived the trip, which was still up for serious debate, how would I get by day to day, by myself, in a land where only the best writers of fiction could imagine, where even the scientific experts weren't at all sure what the conditions were?

Dermot left that night with the promise that he would be there bright and early three days from then, seven A.M. sharp. I had that long to get my affairs in order.

We were into it then.

In three days, I would have no further contact with anyone outside the project. There would be no more trips to the hospital, no contact with Jakes, no discussions with my former coworkers. I had three days to change my mind ...

But I didn't.

*****

It might have been the high-pitched whine that brought me from my drug-induced slumber. It was increasing in both intensity and volume, loud and piercing, annoying, but not yet painful. I concentrated on the sound, not quite sure if I was actually hearing it, or just feeling it. My entire body was abuzz with it. It was inside my head.

But perhaps it was the vibration that woke me. Like the noise, it was building in strength, my hands tingling from the resonating grips on the chair's armrest. I could feel it through my feet, transmitted through the clamps from the base of my chair. And the vibrations traveled into my neck and down through my torso, the strap around my helmet sending the signal.

I couldn't have been out for very long. Dermot told me that I would feel an increasing vibration before I entered the wormhole. This would be accompanied by an auditory sensation that built in proportion to the shaking. But he didn't know when they would stop—if they *would* stop. He said that several minutes from initiation of the system, the machine would disappear from their view, the vibration and sound still building. As it did, all evidence of its existence would disappear, as well. From their perspective, the vibrations would stop instantly, and the only remaining sound would be a few seconds of echo as the last of the sound waves dissipated as they rebounded back and forth across the interior walls of the cave. I wasn't sure why, but I could sense that the machine was still within view of Dermot and his team.

I was awake then, but in a completely relaxed state, not the least bit frightened, the drug still enforcing its will upon me. I even remembered smiling, thinking to myself, *is this really happening?* I desperately wanted someone to talk to, to tell them to check this out, look what's happening to me. But of course, there was no one else there. I was all by myself.

I looked towards the tiny window, but I could see nothing but an incredibly intense white light. There was no way to tell if the rings were still present—the light was so blinding. I wondered if Dermot could still see me. I glanced away from the light, up towards the camera. I doubted that it was still working. It probably stopped at the same time as the speaker. Maybe the cameras inside the cave were still sending back images of the machine. Or, perhaps, it was already gone.

The vibration continued to increase steadily. I had to clamp my jaws tightly to keep my teeth from rattling, and I held on to the armrests for dear life, pressing my elbows into the thin pads to keep them from tearing themselves to pieces on the sides of the cold, hard chair. Even with the airtight helmet on, I could hear the groans of the canvas straps as the hundreds of packing crates tried to break free. The dozen cabinet doors were firmly latched and in no danger of popping open, but they were banging against their mechanical constraints, articles behind their closed doors jumping around to the rhythm of the frenzied beat.

The intensity of the sound continued to increase, as did the frequency, and I wondered at what point it would be beyond that of human hearing. Hopefully before the sound level broke my eardrums. But I didn't feel any pain, not the slightest bit. And I found it amazing that I could still hear the equipment and supplies ratting around above the constant shrieking in my ears.

It was then that I knew that the sound was in me, but not transmitted through my ears, the way sound normally is. It was in my mind, in every part of me, as if the very molecules that made up my form and structure were vibrating, faster and faster, separating farther apart with each octave that it climbed. It was an indescribable sensation, like my body was expanding in all directions at once. But there was still no pain … thankfully.

At some level I was aware of the passage of time, but had no idea of how much of it had actually gone by as I sat there contemplating the strange physical sensations. It might have been seconds—or hours. Surely not days or weeks, but I couldn't have sworn it. I was neither tired nor hungry, so I doubted that more than a few hours had passed, and besides, the effects of the drug had not yet dissipated. I looked up at the wall clock. It was stopped, and somehow that didn't surprise me. Something that measured the passage of time in nice, evenly measured segments was somehow incongruous with the very idea of time travel.

Suddenly, abruptly, the violent vibration ceased, leaving only a residual hum, complementing the buzz that I was feeling from the tranquilizer. In its place, I began feeling a sense of acceleration, pressing me forward against the shoulder straps, as if the machine was beginning to pick up speed in the reverse direction. Of course, I knew that the machine was not going anywhere, at least not any *place*.

I worried about the straps giving way as the acceleration continued to increase. Dermot could not have known about this phenomenon, or he surely would have positioned the chair in the opposite direction. The idea of freeing myself from the chair and crawling towards the front wall of the machine popped into my head for just an instant, before realizing it was too late for such a move. There was no mechanism for releasing all three straps at the same time.

Had I released the head strap first, before releasing the shoulder harness, my head would have been thrown forward with such force that I would have instantly broken my neck. Unbuckling the three-point shoulder harness, with both my head and feet held fast would have folded me in two, shattering my spine like a toothpick. I may have gotten away with releasing the foot clamps first, but where would that have left me? I would still be left with the other two. Even if I had the ability to release them all at once, I would have ended up as a permanent part of the pot-bellied stove. Instead, I did nothing. There was nothing that I *could* do.

I was no longer able to grip the armrest at my sides. My arms were being pulled forward, stretching to an unnatural length, afraid that they were going to be torn from their sockets. My lungs were squeezed up against my ribs, making it increasingly difficult to breathe. I could feel my cheeks and lips being stretched like rubber, saliva being propelled forward by the unbelievable speed. My eyes felt like they were about to pop from their orbits, yet I was unable to force the lids shut to keep them trapped inside.

I was forced to watch as things continued to happen. I didn't think that I could have looked away, even if it was physically possible. An amazing scene was developing right before my eyes. The wall where the stove sat was directly in front of me, no more than five or six feet away, but as I watched, it took on life, moving away from me, slowly at first, but accelerating quickly. My peripheral vision was pretty much shot to hell, but I could still see portions of the adjacent walls. Those sections of wall that were closest to me seemed to be moving forward as well, but not at the same speed.

The time machine had become elastic. The wall in front of me was stationary and I was moving at incredible speed within the machine, forcing the opposite end to stretch as if accommodating my fixed position. Within moments, I was looking into a tunnel that seemed to stretch to infinity, the stove long out of sight as the far end of the tunnel disappeared into nothing more than a single point in space.

The sound was still intensifying. It drowned out my screams. My brain felt as it were being liquefied, as the rest of me felt about to burst, like an overripe melon. The tunnel that stretched before me twisted and squirmed like a snake, and I was peering into its open mouth. I waited to be consumed by it. I *wanted* to be swallowed up by it—anything to stop the madness.

At the time that I felt I could take no more, a split second before I was about to explode, scattered about the machine in a billion microscopic molecules, it stopped. Like a giant rubber band, the tunnel reversed its direction, the front of my time machine racing towards me at blinding speed. I saw the stove hurtling towards me, at the last moment reflexes taking over, my eyes slamming shut and my muscles tightening up, expecting the stove to overshoot its original place and pass through me to the back of the machine.

But it didn't happen. My entire body was clenched like a fist, my mouth hanging open, the last echo of my screams fading as they bounced off the metal interior of the machine. Despite the air-conditioning of my suit, I was soaked with sweat. I could feel it running down my sides and down my cheeks. Every muscle and joint in my body ached from the strain of fighting the acceleration. I was breathing heavily, the inside of my visor fogged over.

My vision was hazy, yet I could tell that the machine had returned to its original solid structure. The stove was back where it belonged, a few feet from where I sat. As best I could with my head held firmly in place by the strap, I glanced to either side. Nothing looked out of place. All the cabinet doors remained closed and latched. There was no sign of damage whatsoever. Perhaps what happened never happened in a real, physical sense. Perhaps, it was only in my mind.

Even though the feeling of acceleration had ended, there was still a vague sense of motion. I could still feel a very low-level vibration coming up from my chair and an occasional slight bump or twisting motion. I felt like I was in the back of a big tractor-trailer traveling at a constant speed down a relatively smooth, straight stretch of highway, with only an infrequent shallow pothole or slight curve in the road.

I was just beginning to relax, my breathing returning to normal, sweat cooling on my skin. I was thinking about removing the constraints, anxious to flex my stiffening joints, to ease the pressure of the compressor digging into my chest. My mouth was dry as dust—my throat raw from the constant screaming. The thought of the bottled water packed within the supplies behind me was too much to ignore.

I unfastened the harnesses, the head strap and foot clamps first, followed by the main shoulder harness. I immediately felt a sense of freedom as I extended my legs, the joints popping, my feet tingling as fresh blood began to flow freely. I rose shakily from the chair, the feeling of movement more pronounced now that I was no longer firmly planted. I walked like a drunken sailor between two of the racks of supplies, gripping the end of the steel frame to maintain balance.

I was searching the labels for the crate holding the water when the machine was rocked by a sudden jolt, nearly knocking me to my feet. The bright light coming from the lone porthole up front went out a second later, leaving me in total darkness. There was a terrifying sound, tortured steel being twisted or torn by some superhuman force, and I could feel the front end of the time machine rising into the air.

It continued to rise, and I could feel it beginning to twist, as well, some of the straps beginning to give way under the weight of all the equipment. And the high-pitched wail of steel being mangled increased, became deafening—ear piercing—like amplified fingernails on a chalkboard.

There was a loud popping sound, like a small explosion, and the machine began to twist more rapidly, the rear end dropping in an arc, like hanging from the end of a swinging pendulum. An instant later, there was a second explosion, louder, more violent. I felt the time machine rip free from its constraints, and then …

Nothing.

CHAPTER 11

The first thing that I became aware of was that I was upside down, or nearly so. The blood rushing to my head told me that it was an inverted position. It made my head pound like someone was taking a two by four to it, but I was too disoriented to do anything about it. Disoriented, and confused. How in the hell did I end up in such a position?

I wasn't aware of any other sensation. Very slowly I opened my eyes, as if awakening from a long sleep. There was only darkness, so complete that I questioned whether I was actually awake or not. It added to my confusion. I didn't know where I was. I could never remember waking to such a total lack of light. No moonlight filtering in through the window—no faint shadows stretching across the room, no reflections to catch the eye—just nothing.

I feared that I had gone blind. I tried to speak, to ask for help, thinking that there was someone nearby sharing whatever bewildering fate had befallen me. The sound that came out was foreign to my ears—raspy and ringing, as if I had my head stuck in a box. Little bits of something fell into my mouth as my lips parted. They were hard and sharp, cutting my tongue and the inside of my mouth as I tried to spit them out.

I laid there, trying to sort out the confusion, the pain in my head getting worse with each passing minute. I tried to raise my head, succeeding only a few inches. I could turn it from side to side, but again, only a few degrees. Although my neck seemed to function, the range of motion was limited by my inability to move my shoulders. Panic crept in as the notion popped into my head that I had been in some terrible accident that had left me both blind and paralyzed from the neck down.

I tried to calm myself, knowing that panic was the thing that I could least afford. I remembered a lesson from one of my undergraduate classes—don't jump to conclusions—use scientific evidence to form a hypothesis. I couldn't see, but that didn't mean that I was blind. It could just be that there was no light for which to see with. And I couldn't move my shoulders, but I shouldn't assume that I was paralyzed. Perhaps there were external forces that prevented it. I needed to fully examine my situation … then I'd panic.

I took a lesson from all the years of exercise. Breathing was the key. Long, deep, steady breaths, getting oxygen into the body, all of its parts taking it in, maximizing their ability to function. I inhaled powerfully through my nose, exhaling through my mouth. I repeated a second time. Something was terribly wrong. The air was thin, not enough to fill my lungs by half, and it was stale, the taste of moldy cardboard filling my mouth, irritating the delicate lining of my nose. I fought off a second wave of panic and began taking shorter, shallower breaths.

I needed to take stock of the rest of my body to see if anything below my neck was still functioning. I began to concentrate on each part, beginning with my toes. There was feeling there. I could wriggle them, although I couldn't move my foot more than an inch or two—first the left foot, then the right. All the toes seemed to work just fine, but neither foot, nor the legs. I couldn't move them, but it was still a huge relief. If I could wriggle my toes, my spine was not damaged, at least not irreparably so.

I worked on my other extremities next. The fingers—they were stiff and sore—but they moved. Not much, but I exercised each one, and each one responded on cue. But that was as far as I could go. Like my feet and legs, there was very little movement. They didn't move, yet there was sensation. Like in the gym, I could feel each muscle respond to command—expansion, contraction, like doing isometric exercises. Something was holding them back, and it wasn't a lack of feeling. The brain was sending the message to the right places. There was just something keeping them from responding significantly to the message.

As I flexed each muscle, attempting to create movement, I began to notice sensations other than just a limited amount of motion. There was pain. As my body began to come back to life, each muscle screamed out in protest. My legs and arms were bent in uncomfortable, if not, unnatural positions. The pain crept up on me like the tortoise on the hare. It came slowly out of nowhere, and landed everywhere—unexpected and frightening. Not a single body part was exempt, not one muscle, didn't feel like it had been through a meat grinder. I still couldn't figure out what exactly happened to me, but I knew that I was in trouble. I couldn't see, couldn't move, and there wasn't enough air.

I had been buried alive.

There just wasn't any other explanation for it. The mere thought of it scared me beyond belief, yet at the same time, my mind continued to think of other possibilities. I wasn't dead. And I hadn't been buried by mistake. In the very end of the twentieth century, that was pretty damn unlikely, if not impossible.

I wasn't in a casket, or a box. I would have had more movement. I'd be able to move my arms and legs—everything—not very far, but farther than I could now. And I wasn't buried in the earth. I could feel hard, angular objects sticking and poking me in just about every spot. No, I wasn't under the ground, but I was buried under *something*.

Using all my strength, I tried moving my left arm, pivoting at the elbow, pulling my hand toward my head. It moved but a few inches before it struck something hard and unyielding. I forced the arm back in the opposite direction, getting no farther than its original position. I tried the same with my right arm and made no better progress, but the object that my hand struck was cylindrical, a rod of some kind. I was able to twist my hand around enough to grasp it. It was then that I became aware that I had gloves on—at least on the right hand.

I gripped the bar as tightly as I could and pulled with all my might. I felt the right side of my upper body move forward, my shoulder sliding along a wide, flat object. But it didn't move very far, the object sliding back in place as my strength gave out. I tried the left hand again, seeking out the hard object that I had struck during my first little foray. It was another bar, like the one on the other side—how convenient.

I grabbed on to both and pulled with everything that I had. I started to move, ever so slowly, and I could feel the objects around me begin to move, as well. As my upper body moved upward, it created a path for my legs to follow. But for every few inches that I progressed, I was battered and bruised by objects falling as things shifted position.

There was pressure on my neck and shoulders, and yet there seemed to be nothing touching my head. It was being protected in some manner, but without sight and the freedom to move my hands, I couldn't tell what it was.

I continued to worm my way forward, inches at a time, running into immovable roadblocks every few minutes, forcing me to alter my course constantly. And every time that I did, it caused even more objects to be dislodged from their resting place, each one slamming into my body. It was like the most intense workout that I had ever had. Every muscle was strained and tired, every joint stiff and sore. Pain was everywhere, some areas worse than others. I couldn't tell how much of the pain was due to injury and how much was from the weight of the objects piled on top of me. Either way, I had to get out of there.

It was getting more and more difficult to breathe. The extreme effort that I was exerting was using up the precious air more quickly. I hoped that if I got out from under this pile, there would be fresh air at the top.

Holding tightly to the two bars, I had pulled, and then pushed up through the pile as far as my arms would reach. The hole I created in the process gave me room to maneuver my arms. Squirming and shoving, I managed to snake one up alongside my body and up past my head. It struck something solid. I pushed with everything that I had, but it wouldn't budge. I was going to have to find another route.

I managed to get the other arm up in front of my chest, and using both of them, pushed outward with all the strength that I could muster. The years of bench-pressing paid off—something gave way. The object moved, not an inch, but a foot, and I heard other items falling behind it, bouncing and rattling as they fell away from whatever made up the pile. Other objects fell into the void that I had created, but others tumbled down to take their place. They were easily pushed aside.

Five more minutes of pushing and I had freed myself from everything above my chest. My head was out from the pile, yet the air was still too thin... and I still couldn't see a thing.

I reached to my head, finding that I had some kind of helmet on. I tried desperately to understand what I was doing wearing a helmet. Had I been on a motorcycle and gotten in some kind of horrible accident? That would have been pretty amazing, seeing that I had only been on one a single, solitary time in my life. I had crashed it, and vowed that I'd never get on another.

I still wasn't convinced that this was not some bizarre dream. How else could I possibly explain this extreme situation?

I could tell that it was a helmet through the bulky gloves, but I couldn't feel any detail with them on. I tried pulling them off, to no avail. They were attached in some way. I fumbled with the wrist, finding a protrusion there that slid in a circular fashion when I pushed on it. It was a locking mechanism. I pulled the glove off and repeated the process with the other one. My hands were free, but, curiously, I felt no new sensation, neither hot nor cold. There was no air passing across them.

I reached again for the helmet. It was smooth and slick. My fingertips made their way toward the front. If the face shield was intended to protect my face, it had failed miserably. It was shattered, as if someone had pitched a brick through the middle of it. The edges were sharp and ragged, the section before my eyes gone. Yet, I still could not see.

With the gloves off, I could feel that the helmet was more complex than one designed for motorcycles or racecars. It wouldn't just pull straight off—the visor didn't simply flip forward. The helmet was firmly attached at the bottom.

The mechanism was easy to find. It was a larger version of what held the gloves to my sleeves. I found the little knob and slid it in a circular fashion around the circumference of my neck. It was sticky, difficult to move, like it had been damaged, no longer a true circle. But with enough force, I got the knob to slide the four or five inches it needed to click into a detent, and the helmet was pulled free.

I grasped it in both hands and gave it a gentle toss in the direction that I was facing. I heard it bounce, two or three times, the sound moving away from me and downward. It struck something solid, perhaps ten or fifteen feet in front of me, and I could hear it roll a few more feet. The sound told me that there was an end to this pile. It didn't tell me what the hell the pile was, and I still had no idea where I was, or how I got there.

With my hands free, and the gloves off, I could begin to explore, to gather information that might shed some light on my predicament. I was still firmly stuck, up to my armpits in whatever made up the pile, but I had a small area directly in front of me and to either side, as far as my arms would reach, that I could explore.

The first thing that I touched was cardboard, a box, or crate of some kind. I could feel the corner of it, but couldn't stretch far enough to find an opposite end. It was a good-sized box. I pushed against it. It was heavy, but it moved. I twisted as best as I could to my left, reaching behind the first box, to discover another. I found a cardboard edge that was ragged, as if the box had burst open. I reached inside, touching a familiar object. It was a book. I pulled it out and fingered through the pages. I tossed it aside and reached back into the open box. It was filled with books, at least as far as I could reach. They were of all sizes and shapes.

I twisted to my right. There was one more carton that was within my reach. I slid my hand along one edge of it, finding the top corner. It seemed intact—I could feel no opening. I slid my hand back down along its edge, having to force my way past a few loose items, searching for a bottom corner. It was there, and it was wet. I could feel something liquid dripping through the soaked cardboard.

I brought my hand to my lips. There was no taste, but it was cool and wet—it felt wonderful on my dry tongue. I dug back through the rubble, finding the soaked corner of the box. With my fingers, I tore away the disintegrating cardboard so that I could reach my hand inside. More liquid poured out as I penetrated the box. I reached in and pulled out some kind of bottle. It felt like hard plastic, and it had one of those little pull out spouts on the top. It was a bottle of water. With trembling fingers, I tore off the cellophane wrap around the nozzle, pulled out the spout and raised it to my lips. I squeezed the bottle, sending the soothing liquid down my parched gullet.

I drank nearly the whole bottle down in one long squeeze. The rest, I squirted across my face. The water revived me to a point, but I could feel the exhaustion set in. I leaned back into the pile as best I could and let my arms relax atop the objects before me. I still had the empty water bottle in my hands, and I was toying with it, squeezing it, pushing the spout in, pulling it out again.

There was something special about the bottle. There was significance to it that I couldn't quite comprehend. My mind flashed with the image of the bottle, hundreds of them, all packed away nice and neat in big cardboard boxes. I had been searching for them, looking amongst hundreds of identical boxes, reading the labels trying to find them—needing to find them.

I couldn't see, and yet images kept bursting forth in my mind: a long tunnel, men dressed in spacesuits, an entrance to a cave. Like flash bulbs going off in a dark room, pictures burned into my retina, only to disappear a second later. The image of the cave kept returning, staying longer each time. The entrance to the cave grew more distinct with each successive fire burst. It was as if I was walking towards it in the blackest of nights while a strobe light provided the only source of light.

The strobe continued to flash, its frequency increasing the closer I got to the cave's entrance, until it was constant—brightly lit like the brightest of days. The entrance loomed before me, an iron gate across it. I could see through the gate into the interior of the cave. It was as brightly lit as the outside. Inside the cave was a long, black metallic structure, bundles of electrical cables running to and from it. It was a machine of some kind … the time machine.

It all came flooding back: closing the door to the time machine, strapping myself into the chair, hearing Dermot's voice one last time, giving him a thumb's up in reply. I remembered the vibration and terrible noise that continued to build as the rings powered up, the terrifying acceleration that nearly ripped me from the chair, and the way the machine seemed to change its very form. The last thing that I could recall was one end rising into the air and the squealing sound of metal tearing.

Now I knew what the pile was. I had been buried alive in my own supplies. I remembered just before the end, hearing some of the straps that held the boxes in place break away, boxes tumbling forward. I had fallen in amongst them, others falling in behind. Along with my spacesuit, they probably saved my life. But the pile still had a hold of me—I was still buried up to my armpits in it.

And I remembered that the time machine was sealed. The mini-compressor strapped to my chest was only designed to run for an hour, give or take a couple of minutes. It was only intended to supply my needs for the time it took to get from the trailer to the machine. The compressor was no longer working, not that it would have been much good with half my face shield gone. The time machine was my air supply for the trip, but I had been using it up for who knows how long. I had to get out of there before it ran out altogether.

I was still pinned too deeply to simply crawl out. I didn't need the portable air supply, so I removed the straps and ripped it from my chest. I felt lighter and free, able to work faster, less encumbered. I started pushing the boxes in the front forward. Many were busted open, their contents filling in the gaps between them. I began throwing the loose items forward as fast as I could, not caring what they were or where they landed. The air was getting thinner by the minute and my strength was almost gone.

I was in a race against time. I had to get out of the pile and out of the machine quickly, but the faster I worked, the faster I used up the little oxygen that remained. Every time I inhaled, I used up a little more of it, and each time that I breathed back out again, I replaced it with carbon dioxide. If I didn't die from lack of air, I'd die from carbon dioxide poisoning. I said to myself, *fuck it*, and tore into the pile with every ounce of strength that remained.

I could hear boxes tumbling down the pile and objects clanging off the walls and one another as I flung them every which way. I had cleared the area in front of me to my waist and found that I could move my legs. I forced my right knee upward, pushing a large, heavy box away. I reached down with both hands, the right one striking an unknown object in the way. I grabbed it and started to fling it on ahead. I put on the breaks, nearly throwing my shoulder out of its socket. At the last possible moment, I realized what the object was. It was a flashlight.

Flashlights were among a hundred things that Dermot and I argued over. I didn't see the point. The batteries would be dead within the first few weeks, and I sure as hell wouldn't be running to the nearest convenience store for replacements. Dermot was insistent though.

The first weeks were going to be the most crucial. I would be in a whole new world. We couldn't possibly comprehend all of the kinds of challenges that I would be facing. I would need time to adjust. Everything that he could provide during those first difficult days to give me a chance of survival, he was going to do.

I wasted precious moments doing nothing other than just holding the flashlight. Ever since I had come to, beneath tons of my own supplies, I hadn't seen a thing. I had half convinced myself that I was blind. In the modern-day world, that may have been only an inconvenience, but in whatever world I was in on that day, it was an absolute necessity. I was disoriented, but I wanted to survive. I couldn't do it without my eyesight.

I was scared shitless. I held the flashlight in one hand—my fingers wrapped around the shaft, my thumb touching the button that would switch it on. What would I do if the light didn't come on when I flipped the switch? What if I couldn't see it when I did, and how would I know the difference? For the moment I forgot just how tired I was. Forgotten was the lack of oxygen. I thought of just one thing.

Please God, let me see.

I acted cowardly. I shut my eyes as I pushed the switch forward. I was terrified of the outcome, so I squeezed them tightly—so tightly that tears ran out from their corners. I thought about all the weapons on board. If I couldn't see the light, would I be better off finding one of them and ending my life right there in the time machine? I wouldn't last a day without my sight. I would be defenseless.

Even with my eyes shut tight, I saw a change from the blackness behind my eyelids when the switch moved forward. The feeling was indescribable. The tears turned to those of joy as I realized that when I opened them I would be alive again.

I opened my eyes.

The light wasn't bright, yet it was the brightest thing that I had ever seen. It had been hours, maybe longer, since I looked upon anything but darkness. A darkness that was absolute, palpable, a substance that lacked the reality that only light could bring to bear.

The light hurt my eyes, but it was exquisite. I knew that the pain would go away in moments and I would be able to see things clearly. With my eyesight, I could survive in this place, wherever, and whenever I was.

But first I had to get out from under this pile, out of the time machine with its stale, used up air—out into the light.

I looked at the interior of the time machine—my home. It was a wreck. The supplies that we had spent weeks assembling and neatly packing and storing were in shambles. They were strewn about the length of the machine from front to back—more at the back end from where I was at the time trying to extricate myself.

I pushed forward, throwing the loose items left and right, carving out an aisle. I made my way towards the front of the time machine, past the rows of shelves. As I worked frantically, it occurred to me that the racks themselves had helped to save my life. It was the metal rungs of the racks, one on either side of the pile that I had first wrapped my fingers around, had used them to first pull, and then push, myself through the pile.

The debris was knee-high, the height of just a single packing crate. There was little between the door and me, but it was like moving through quicksand. I was getting dizzy from the rarified oxygen, my movements slow and uncoordinated. I dropped to my knees, intent on pushing things aside with my shoulders—using my own weight rather than my strength, which was almost gone. I had never felt so tired. I had to fight the impulse to just lie down and go to sleep. My brain was full of soggy cotton candy, but I knew that if I lie down, I would never get up again.

It was no more than a minute before I reached the door. It just seemed like hours. I fell at the threshold, the flashlight falling from my hand. I laid there, my cheek pressed against the cold metallic floor of the machine, sliding in and out of consciousness. During a momentary lucid moment, I opened my eyes. The flashlight's beam struck me right in the face. I stared directly into the light, afraid to close my eyes, terrified of the darkness.

I struggled to my knees and fell face first against the door. With my left hand I pulled the door's release handle. I heard the metallic click that was supposed to release the door, but it didn't open. The top of the door was hinged and connected to a series of springs so that when the latch was released from either the inside or outside, it would open by itself, swinging upward.

But it failed to do so. Either the door's mechanism had been damaged in the trip, or something was holding it from the outside.

I pushed the door with my shoulder. I felt it move just slightly—not enough to overcome the rubber seals—not enough to allow fresh air to enter. I pushed harder. More movement and I thought that I heard something outside the door, a scraping sound. I rolled over onto my back, pressing both feet against the door, close to the floor. I pushed with both legs and all the strength that I had left. I heard a popping sound and could feel warm damp air rush into the machine. But when I released the pressure, the door slammed shut, more scraping and the sound of heavy objects striking the machine's titanium skin.

The air was better. Some had gotten in and I could feel some strength returning. I knew that it wouldn't last long. I grabbed the flashlight and began searching for something that would help. Digging through the objects and boxes I found a hatchet, about fourteen inches long—it would do. I crawled back over to the door and resumed my position, on my back with my feet planted firmly on the door. I scooted my ass up to it as close as I could to give myself some leverage. I laid the flashlight by one hand and the hatchet by the other.

I pushed, finding more strength than on my last attempt. Having nothing to hold on to, I could feel my back begin to slide away from the door just as the seal broke. I reached forward, grabbing the inside edge of the door's threshold, enabling me to push with far greater force. The door began to move. Something was on the other side pushing back—hard. My thighs were trembling from the effort, but the door kept rising slowly.

I let go with the left hand, reaching for the hatchet. Continuing to push with my legs, I shoved the hatchet into the opening, wedging it between the threshold and bottom edge of the door. I slowly released pressure with my legs.

The hatchet was holding.

I shoved the flashlight through the opening and followed it out, headfirst. I proceeded slowly, afraid to disturb the hatchet. There was a tremendous force on the outside trying to keep the door closed. One wrong move and it would slam shut, cutting me in half.

I pushed with my legs, the bottom edge of the door scraping my chest as I passed under. It was only a drop of two or three inches onto the ground. I wiggled my shoulders back and forth, snaking across the ground, my feet following, clearing the threshold. They no sooner did when I head a loud cracking sound and the door slammed shut. A second later I was showered with rocks, one striking my head, knocking me unconscious.

*****

It was the pain in my legs that woke me, yet it was the sound of running water that I was focused on. It wasn't loud, but it was unexpected. I raised my upper body, resting on my elbows, listening closely, trying to identify the origin of the sound. The movement sent new agony through my legs, and crashing through my head. I reached up, found a big wet spot over my right eye, stinging pain when I touched it.

The flashlight was still working. It was just out of my reach, shining its light on the opposite wall. It was a familiar sight. I had seen it only hours ago. Well, in my frame of reference it was only hours ago. But how long had it actually been? For all I knew Dermot and his crew were just on the outside of the cave, unaware of what had just happened, for some reason unable to rescue me. That seemed pretty unlikely—too much time had passed ... in *whatever* way you cared to measure it.

And I was struck with another thought. Before I found the flashlight, I was blind. Things were not just dark, like nighttime, they were black, no light whatsoever. Yet all the supplies had been redistributed across the floor of the machine, meaning that most of the twenty portholes were unblocked. There should have been some kind of light. Even on the darkest night, there is light. Light enough to see something, but I hadn't been able to see anything. Even inside the cave, I should have been able to see something.

I needed that flashlight. I spread out across the dirt, but it was a good foot from my outstretched fingers. I sat upright again and reached for my legs, which were covered with rock—where they came from, and why they ended up on me was anybody's guess.

My legs hurt even more as I pushed the rock away, my left one more than the right. It was a stabbing pain, like a knife being twisted every time that the weight shifted across it. I cleared most of it away, enough so that I could pull my legs out from under the rest. There was an excruciating pain from my left ankle as my foot slid free from the last rock. It continued to throb as I sat there panting and perspiring.

On my butt, I scooted over to the flashlight, delighted with my tiny victory, despite the pain in my leg. I shone the light around the room. It looked much like it did the last time I saw it ... but newer ... if that made any sense. The walls had the same sense of proportion, the same dimensions, the same striations and color. But, it reflected the light differently than it did the summer of the dig. There was a shine to it, as if the walls were liquid, sending the light back at me like the reflection in a pond. When I had seen it before it was an old space, locked away from seeing eyes for millions of years. On the day of my journey it was new, not yet having been exposed to the ravages of time.

The light carried full circle, landing on the time machine. Fully, two thirds of it reflected back at me, the black metal surface still shining by the light of the flashlight despite its long trip. The remaining portion was obliterated, covered by rock and stone and dirt. Protruding from its rear end were the remnants of the three titanium bars that had anchored it to the floor of the cave. They were twisted, with jagged edges where they had been ripped apart.

I passed the light across the floor of the cave, seeing the bedrock torn up in long furrows, the opposite ends of the bars sticking up at odd angles. The same for the roof of the cave—three rods curving inward from the ceiling like a huge metallic claw, its fingers wickedly sharp. It took an incredible force to tear the machine from its anchor. It was nothing short of a miracle that the machine survived—that I survived. I gave Dermot my silent thanks.

I returned the beam of the light to the machine, looking closer at the rubble surrounding the front end. The entrance to the cave was completely sealed, partially by the time machine, which was protruding through the entrance at a slight angle, and partially by the rock covering it. Even before I thought of the predicament that I was in, I wondered how the hell the cave got sealed.

It was sealed the first time that I saw it. We had spent months unsealing it. Brian Huntsville had estimated that it had been sealed since the very end of the late Cretaceous period, roughly sixty five million years ago, probably by some seismic event, perhaps during the formation of much of the

Wasatch Range, which was still taking place during that era. Or maybe, the six-mile-wide meteor that struck Mexico, believed by many to be the cataclysmic event that ended the reign of the dinosaurs, caused the rockslide that sealed the cave.

Most experts agreed that the mass extinction of the dinosaurs occurred sixty five million years ago, about the same time as the rockslide—possibly as recently as sixty three million years. Dermot's calculations intended to send me back seventy million years. Even with a margin for error of two million years, I should have landed safely on the other side of the landslide.

But what had happened at the conclusion of my trip? I had experienced an acceleration that almost killed me. I concluded that traveling through time caused the sensation. After all, my understanding was that I was traveling through space as well as time. In seventy million years, the earth traveled one hell of a long way in space. In order to get up to the speed necessary to traverse that distance, incredible velocity was required. Although the time machine never actually moved relative to the cave, it did move relative to free-space, and the feeling of acceleration should have been no surprise. Through that period, when the acceleration was increasing, almost to the point of human endurance, and then the decrease in speed, followed by the idea that perhaps I might even survive the trip, I thought that everything was going as planned.

But what happened when the time machine ripped free of its moorings? My senses said that we were still moving—translated—we were still progressing backwards in time. Did we not quite hit the target? Did we not actually go seventy million years into the past? Was the duration of the trip cut short when the machine ceased being anchored to the interior of the cave? When it did, I sensed that it was no longer under the influence of the rings, beyond the protective confinement of the wormhole, out of Dermot's control.

Maybe we only went sixty million years into the past, maybe only fifty … or less. If it were less, I knew that the age of the dinosaurs was over, and there was another fifty or sixty million years before the first human ancestor inhabited the earth. If so, what the hell was I doing here?

Other creatures had survived the purge: other mammals, insects, amphibians, but they were not my specialty—I wasn't interested in them. I hadn't given up everything that I knew, everything that I had studied all my adult life, to live among a bunch of animals that anybody else could study, those that were still around in the twentieth century. I didn't have to leave my home, my *time*, to study them.

I didn't want to even think of the possibility that I had wasted what was left of my life.

If I landed in a time following whatever event took the front of the cliff down, I was in serious trouble. It had taken us months, and some serious, heavy-duty equipment to remove the thousands of tons of rock from the front of the cave. I wasn't exactly equipped to do it again. And if that were the case, how was I to get out of the cave?

If the landslide had occurred before I had arrived on the scene, then I had somehow plunged into the middle of it and about two hundred feet of rock was in front of me. But if that were the case, where were my dinosaurs? They should have been exactly where I found them the first time, but with a whole lot less dirt piled upon them.

I scanned the floor of the cave. There were the ragged ends of the titanium bars, hundreds of scattered boulders, but not much of anything else.

The sound of rushing water was still all around me. I searched everywhere with my flashlight for the source, but I saw nothing that looked like it, no other entrances or exits from the cave. I continued to probe with the light ... then I saw it, the outcropping of rock, the little alcove that I had been searching on the night of the terrible ice storm.

I tried to stand, my leg buckling as soon as I put a little weight on it. I reached down, touching my ankle. I winced in pain at the slightest touch. I was not a medical doctor, but I didn't think that it broken. There were no protrusions through the skin, no raised surface below it. Despite the pain, I could turn my foot freely. Keeping my weight on the good leg, I managed to stand awkwardly.

Holding the flashlight in front of me, pointed down at the ground so that I didn't trip over the rocks strewn about, I limped and hopped my way over to the outcropping. The noise intensified as I approached the partial wall, but I still couldn't identify the source. The sound bounced endlessly off the hard rock of the cave, trapped within, sounding as if it came from everywhere at once.

I noticed an odor in the air, at first indistinct, but growing stronger and more familiar as I got closer. As I approached the edge of the wall I reached out, touching the cold stone. It was damp with moisture, slick despite its rough, ragged appearance. I peered around the edge, looking in with the flashlight. The alcove was much as I had seen it originally, fifteen feet long and half as wide, the walls jagged, as if ripping a chunk out of the side of the cave had created the space.

The floor was very different however—there wasn't one. The hole that I had been excavating on that last day of the dig was no mere depression, it was a tunnel in the rock, cutting through it at an angle down and away from the entrance to the cave. The sound of running water was louder yet and the smell more pronounced. I closed my eyes and inhaled deeply through my nose, the odor now recognizable.

It was seawater.

There was water running beneath my feet, by the sound of it, a lot of water, moving in a hurry. It was loud now, made more so by the resonant effect of small alcove, but I could tell that it was quite a distance away. I picked up a fist-size rock from the ground and pitched it into the crevasse. Even over the din, I heard it bounce several times, the sound growing dimmer with each successive bounce. The sound faded into the background noise long before it came to rest.

The fact that the crack in the rock wasn't filled with seventy million years of built-up silt was incredible. It meant that I had reached my destination—at least somewhat. The experiment worked. I had traveled back in time—a long way back in time. Perhaps not seventy million years, but a long way back. It had been millions of years, tens of millions of years since the tunnel was free of debris, since there was water running below. I became excited at the prospect, but I had bigger worries to be concerned with.

I still had no way to the outside. The time machine was buried by who knew how many tons of rock. I had a bum leg, and a knot on my head the size of a walnut. I needed to step back, catch my breath, and think about my next move.

First, I needed to get back into the machine, to assess the damage, to check on my supplies—I would need them to get out of this cave.

I hobbled back over to it. The hatch was visible, free and clear, but there was a good-sized boulder trapped between it and the pile that had settled in around it. It was level with my chest and was maybe two or three hundred pounds. I got underneath it, positioning it on my right shoulder, my legs bent, ready to take the strain. On one good leg I pushed from underneath with all the might that I could muster and the rock went up. At first it seemed like I accomplished nothing but to wedge it more firmly between the door and the other rock, but it suddenly shifted direction and began falling. With it came a shower of smaller rock and choking dust. I managed to pivot away at the last moment, missing the bigger part of the mass, taking a few small stones across my back and shoulders.

The door was accessible, but it was scarred and dented from the collision with the rocks piled at the cave's entrance and the secondary avalanche caused by the impact. I reached around to the far side of it, searching for the recessed button that would release the door. It had taken a direct hit, the small fold of metal that kept it hidden had been bent inward, making it a struggle to get to the button. I reached a single finger in from the top, managing to snake it around the bend, finding the button. I pressed it, but even before I realized that the door wasn't opening, I knew something was wrong. The button pushed in, but did not immediately pop back out the way that I knew that it should.

The latch worked from the inside but could no longer be activated from the outside.

I slid my fingers along the seam of the hatch, searching for a gap, any gap. But there was hardly room to slide a single piece of paper between the two metal surfaces, let alone the width of my finger. On the far side, where the modest damage occurred, adjacent to the door's release button, there was enough room to slip three fingers in, just up to the first joint. I pulled as best I could with the poor grip, but there was no movement whatsoever. I might as well have been trying to open the solid titanium hull with a can opener.

There was no way that I was getting back into the time machine from this side. And even if I could, it wouldn't have solved my long-term problem. I had to get out of the cave and my wide assortment of hand tools inside the machine was not going to be of much help. I couldn't survive for any length of time sealed inside of the cave.

But I had a more immediate problem—food and water. I wouldn't last more than a day or two without them—and they were in the time machine. I had to find a means to get inside and there was but one other way. Dermot had put an access panel in the roof so that I had easy access to the light for recharging the cells of the computer. I wasn't at all sure that it was big enough to get through, but it was my only hope.

Holding tightly to the flashlight, I used the porcupine-like quills to climb to the top. The sore ankle and the clumsy boots made it a difficult chore. It was only about eight feet to the top, but the climb left me exhausted. I lay spread-eagled across the roof, shining the light down its length, to where it disappeared under the rocks. The access panel was nowhere to be seen.

I thought back to the day Dermot showed me the roof panel. It was situated roughly in the middle of the forward section of the machine, which should have put it somewhere about forty feet from the back edge. With the poor light, it wasn't easy to estimate the distance between the back of the machine and the beginning of the rock pile, but I had to guess that it was at least thirty feet, probably thirty five. The access panel had to be within a few feet of where the rock began.

Smaller stones were scattered across the length of the roof. I began pushing them off with my foot, working from back to front. The closer I got to the front of the machine, the bigger the rocks got. It didn't take long before they were too large to sweep away with my foot, especially while on just one good leg. I sat down and started pushing with my shoulder. The flashlight was getting in the way, so I placed it on the roof, carefully, so that it didn't roll away. I aimed it as best I could directly forward, and, fighting my own shadow, went back to work.

I had been at it for perhaps thirty minutes. Most of the smaller rocks were gone, even the mid-sized ones had been rolled aside. What was left was a solid mass of stone that went straight up to where the ceiling curved down toward the floor. It was solid, but not one piece. There were mostly larger rocks, bigger than I could handle, packed tightly together by smaller stones, pebbles and dust. And I still hadn't uncovered the vent ... but, almost.

I could see part of it, perhaps half. The panel was damaged, dented inward. I could probably smash it open simply by jumping on it. However, that would have done absolutely squat. After seeing my potential escape hatch one more time, I was even more concerned that I might not actually fit through it. With half of it obscured by a wall of granite, I knew that I wouldn't. I had to remove more of the stone.

I had no other choice but to start pawing away at the little stuff that was tucked away among the larger rocks, knowing that any wrong move could send it all down on top of me. I had hardly begun when I heard a low rumble, and I could feel the time machine below me begin to shudder. The smaller rocks began to shake loose from the pile, dropping down around my feet, bouncing off the metal skin of the machine. Dust filled the air, filtering the already dim light.

Suddenly, what little light I had, changed. It was pointing in another direction ... and it was moving. I turned to see the flashlight rolling away from me, towards the edge, dropping off the side, winking out with a last bright flash of light as it struck the ground below. I was left once again in complete blackness as I heard the rumble of rock all around me, the contrasting higher notes as smaller rocks continued to rain down upon the top of the machine.

And the rocks did not discriminate against me. I was pelted right along with my machine. I had to get away from the front of the cave, away from the source of the rock shower. I got down on all fours and scrambled toward the back of the machine, sliding down the angled side, grimacing as my bad leg struck the earth.

Dragging one leg, I crawled away from the machine to the opposite side of the cave. I huddled there, my back against the partial wall that separated the hole from the rest of the cave. I was tired and hungry and confused. I didn't know what to do next and too exhausted to think about it. As the sound of the falling rock faded away, I fell asleep to the sound of running water.

*****

I had no idea how long I'd slept, no way to tell if it were day or night—no concept of *time*. Wasn't that a joke?

I hurt everywhere, but more importantly, I was thirsty. I didn't know how long I had been without water, but the dust that filled the stale air in the cave only made my thirst worse. I could feel the grit in my nostrils, taste it on my tongue. My throat was raspy with it.

In total darkness I sat up, my back against the wall and tried to assess my situation. I had been without food or water for God knew how long. I was injured, not seriously, but the number of places that I hurt made it feel worse than it was. Every muscle in my body ached, my head throbbed, and it felt like someone had driven a ten-penny nail into my ankle. All of it made it hard to think straight.

The total absence of light told me that the cave was still sealed, despite the rockslide that occurred. But, just maybe, it had cleared the hatch on the top.

I made my way blindly to the time machine. It was easy—it took up a very large part of the cave.

I managed to climb up to the top, feeling my way up and over the boulders. It was no use. There was no more than ten feet of the back end of the time machine exposed. At least forty feet of it was buried beneath the rock.

If I had some tools, if I had a couple of days to work on it, maybe, just maybe, I could have removed enough of the rock to either get inside of the machine or, working around it, get to the outside of the cave.

But I had neither the time nor the tools. The few short minutes that I had spent exploring the area had left me winded, used up, wishing I could just lie down and go to sleep, not really caring if I woke up or not.

I slid back down the machine, coming to rest in a seated position on the hard rock that made up the floor of the cave. I sat quietly, thinking about Dermot, about Susan, and about Elizabeth. Dermot had given a lifetime of research to this project. I owed it to him to see it through. Susan wouldn't have quit. On the other side of the cave were wonders beyond her wildest imagination. She would never have given up the chance to fulfill her dream. And Elizabeth, Elizabeth had faith in me. I had never let her down when she was alive. I couldn't conceive of the possibility of letting her down now that she was gone.

I sat there for the longest time. It may have been twenty minutes, it may have been an hour, all the while the sound of running water in my ears. I knew from the first time that I heard it, from the first time that I saw the tunnel, that there was a way out. I knew, but I pushed it from my mind.

It was a terrifying thought. I wasn't an explorer of caves—I was not someone who liked tight places. I was a borderline claustrophobic, not afraid of being in a small room, or locked up in a tiny cell, but I was absolutely horrified at the prospect of being wedged into something that I couldn't get out of, trapped where I couldn't move, couldn't raise my arms.

I remembered back to a story years ago when I was just a kid. Some little boy had gotten himself trapped in a drainage pipe in some podunk town in the deep South somewhere. I remembered the nearly nonstop television coverage. The National Guard was there and so was the media from all over the country. It was a circus atmosphere with thousands of out-of-towners swelling the tiny population of the rural community. I could still picture the dirty, scared-shitless face of the boy as they hauled him out of the hole.

I was only a boy myself, but I had glued myself to the six o'clock news show every one of those three days. The story fascinated me ... and terrified me, all at the same time. For years I had nightmares about it. Even as an adult, the mere thought of something pinning me down where I couldn't move my arms sent a cold shiver down my spine.

The slit in the earth behind the partial wall of the alcove was large enough to slip into. I could crawl into it without a problem, certainly not standing, but I could slither into it like a snake and still have room to move about, to move my arms back and forth. It sliced through the earth diagonally, rough-hewn, plenty of handholds, lots of places to put my feet.

I knew that it was true. I had seen it with the light of my flashlight. The opening, for the first ten or twelve feet, wasn't a problem. And I knew that it went all the way through. My ears confirmed that—the sound of the water moving past the opening proved that. But how big was the opening, and how far away was it? Would I get half the way down and get trapped, unable to get back out, unable to move my arms? If so, I couldn't expect the National Guard to help. No, there would be no media and no circus atmosphere for little David Williams.

I followed the sound of the running water back to the opening in the earth. My heart was beating way too fast, and my throat had closed to the size of a pinhead. Not that it mattered much as I had nothing to swallow. My hands were stiff—the skin stretched tight over swollen fingers—a sure sign of dehydration. My stomach turned and twisted, and rumbled over the sound of the water, partly due to hunger, but mostly due to fear.

I didn't have any other options. I either took my chances down the chute, or I stayed where I was and died. I might last another day in the cave, not much longer than that. And when I died, what would happen then? Would the sealed cave suddenly appear in the future, right in front of Dermot's eyes, before he even had a chance to clear out his gear? If they uncovered all the rock, would the time machine still be there ... would I? Would there be even a hint of me left, a pile of dust left from my long-rotted body?

Dermot would have proven nothing, would have had no data, no computer files. He would have found nothing in the time machine but a mess—nothing missing—nothing added. If I remained in the cave to die, all that Dermot had done would have been for nothing.

He would have found the hatch to the time machine still sealed. And if he dug out the cave, Dermot would have discovered the solid titanium bars intended on holding the machine in place twisted and torn. No doubt he would have assumed that I died during the trip—that I had perished from a spectacular collision as the machine tore loose and slammed into the wall of the cave. He may have concluded that traveling into the future was far too dangerous for humans. It may have all stopped right there.

But even beyond the experiment itself, I wanted to live. I wanted to see what was beyond the cave. I wanted to see what the source of the water was running beneath my feet. I wanted to see blue skies and brown earth once again. I wanted to see *anything* once again. I didn't want to die in the dark.

With the exception of the helmet and the gloves, I was still wearing the spacesuit. It was bulky and heavy. It would be a problem squeezing through the narrow crevasse, especially the boots, which were nearly twice the width of my feet. But, it was about the only protection that I had. Underneath, I had on nothing but underwear. The suit would give me some minimal protection from whatever I was to come in contact with. The boots would not only protect my feet, but would give me some grip against the slippery surface of the rocks.

I felt like a condemned man, facing the electric chair or the hangman's noose, sure that I was about to die, but holding on to that one slim chance that the chair would short-circuit, or the rope would break, or the Governor would intervene. But things like that generally took human intervention of some kind. The electrician fucked up, the rope was defective because someone didn't braid or store it properly, or a really good lawyer convinced the Governor of my innocence. If humans were indeed still sixty or seventy million years in the future, I couldn't count on their help.

About the only thing that I could hope for was another landslide of some kind—one that would free the time machine, or open up the entrance to the cave. On the other hand, any shift in the mountain above me, any change in the bedrock beneath me, may have shut off my only route of escape. The more that I thought about it, the more nervous I became. Not only because my escape route could be cut off, but also because it could happen while I was inside—buried alive ... again.

I had never been a procrastinator. I wasn't going to become one then. I had too much at stake. I scooted over to the hole until I felt the edge with my boots. I tuned over, on all fours, and stepped down into the hole.

Instantly, the sound of running water intensified, as did the smell of the sea. As my head cleared the floor of the cave, I could feel the increase in humidity, feel the dampness on my hands and face. The rocks were slippery with moisture, but the walls were jagged, plenty of solid surfaces for my boots to grip, for my hands to grasp. The tunnel sloped downward at about a forty-five degree angle. Even without the good footing, the early part of the descent was easy.

Five or ten minutes into my descent the shaft leveled out, almost on the horizontal. The floor was flat, the opening enlarged to the point where I couldn't reach the ceiling for long stretches. The walls were far enough apart that I could no longer reach both at the same time. I hugged one wall, moving slowly, afraid that I'd lose my sense of direction if I didn't stay in constant contact.

I faced the one wall, both hands pressed against it, shuffling my feet along the ground, inches at a time. First I tested the floor with my left, then the right, feeling the ground with my bulky boots, skirting obstacles, searching for a drop off. The darkness remained absolute. For all I knew I had wandered into an immense cavern. Perhaps I was in one of several tunnels branching off from the main. Maybe all but one led to a dead end.

I didn't trust the sound of the water. It was all around me, bouncing off the hard walls, reflecting in all directions, no detectable source. I couldn't follow the sound to its origin. I might well have ended up back in the cave. So, I was afraid to let go of the wall.

I traveled on—for an hour, maybe two, lengthening my crab-like steps as I gained more confidence from the sheer monotony of the sure-footing and smooth walls. I was getting careless, less from inattention than from thirst and anxiety. If I had the strength, I would have run to the end—wherever, and whatever it was.

But, of course, I didn't have the strength, and I didn't run anywhere. I kept on feeling my way along, slowly, but not slowly enough. Suddenly, there was an outcropping of rock. I jammed my left knee into it almost at the same time that my head struck something unforgiving from above. I refused to let go of the wall as I grabbed both my head and my knee, leaning my backside up against the wall as I did.

I was stunned but momentarily, simply adding the new pains to the wide assortment I had accumulated in the last day. Within minutes the pain blurred into the rest and I began to feel my way around my new surroundings. I reached above, easily locating the rock that struck my forehead. I searched around its circumference, finding the structure that held it in place. The ceiling had lowered significantly. I found that I couldn't stand up fully without striking it. I stooped, reaching my left hand out, touching the opposite wall long before it was fully outstretched.

In front of me, where my knee landed, was a ridge, more of a shelf really, carved into the rock, the bottom portion a full eighteen inches closer than the part above it and probably two feet above the floor. The tunnel was narrowing, drastically, and until that moment, I hadn't noticed a thing.

I reached forward, trying to figure out exactly what was in front of me. The corridor had narrowed to three feet, but that was only an approximate measurement taken at waist high. Below that was a narrower path, twelve inches, perhaps fourteen. I could feel the ceiling sloping downward, five feet and decreasing rapidly. The feeling of being trapped—claustrophobic—crept in, as I took my first step into the confined space.

I had to slip into it edgewise, one foot next to the other, my head bent low in a squat position, my ass resting on the ledge as I crept forward. The dimensions continued to shrink as I pushed forward. After a few more scoots, the slot in which my feet rested had grown too small for my boots. Rather than risk getting them wedged where I couldn't get them out, I lifted my feet up on the shelf opposite the one that my rear end resided. I was crunched up in a ball, my legs bent painfully, my knees jammed into my chest on either side of my head, which was shoved forward, making it difficult to breath.

I had the feeling that I was forcing my body into a place that I could not possibly extricate myself. My body no longer felt that it was my own. I had lost all feeling, all sensation. I was part of the rock, part of the solidity that was all around me. As the tunnel narrowed, I was being absorbed into the rock, becoming an integral part of it. I couldn't tell where I stopped and the rock began. I was stuck.

I wriggled and squirmed, backing out of the tight space until I had room to maneuver. I slid the little ring around my ankle, releasing the boots. I threw them behind me, risking cutting my feet to shreds rather than getting stuck. I changed positions, now able to get on all fours, one hand and one knee on either side of the shelf. I continued forward, fifty feet—a hundred feet. My knees were bruised and sent a sharp pain up through my thigh each time I set one down on the hard, uneven surface. The top of the tunnel continued to slope downward, my head beginning to skim across the continuous protrusions. And the walls continued to grow closer together with each tentative step.

I stretched my body out, down on my elbows, my shoulders scrunched down, pulling my head in like a turtle. But at least I was off of my knees. There was no longer enough clearance for my backside in a kneeling position, so I pulled my body forward using nothing but my elbows. Within a few more yards, I was completely prone across the shelf, my arms underneath me, bent at the elbows. My progress was now marked in inches, rolling my hips and shoulders forward, crawling like an earthworm.

I had to fight off the panic that threatened to consume me. It was my worst nightmare coming true—worse than my worst nightmare—in my dreams I could see. In the nightmare that was real, I couldn't see a thing, but I could still move. Not very much, and unless the shape of the tunnel suddenly changed, within minutes I was going to be as stuck as the little boy in the pipe.

The sound of running water had become louder, filling every little space that my body wasn't occupying. And there was wind. I had noticed it shortly after descending into the tunnel hours before, or was it days? It began as a mild breeze, barely perceptible on my bare skin, carrying with it the smell of the sea. But throughout the long trek, it had grown, become a force, a howl that threatened to overtake that of the rushing water. But it was a welcome distraction. I could feel the wind, and I could hear the roar, even if I couldn't see. It kept the approaching panic at bay.

I reached an obstruction a few minutes later. Not a complete blockage, but enough to stop my progress. I felt it first with my head, chewing up a patch of scalp despite the slow speed that I was traveling. My hands were still trapped beneath my chest. I couldn't raise my shoulders enough to bring my hand forward to explore the impediment.

I backed out of the tube several feet until I could get my arms out in front of me, and then proceeded forward once again. Progress was even more difficult stretched out as I was from hands to toes. Basically, I did it with my hips, rolling my torso back and forth, pulling up one hip with each turn, alternating them on every other roll, moving a quarter of an inch at a time.

It seemed to take forever before my hands found the obstacle. I was worn out, pain everywhere, and thirsty beyond belief. Before I began exploring the obstruction, I took a minute to just lay there, catching my breath, thinking about what I would do if I couldn't clear the roadblock. I knew that I wouldn't just stay there to die. I couldn't bear the thought of dying like that—trapped, unable to move more than an inch in any direction.

On the other hand, I was sure that I hadn't the strength for the return trip to the cave.

I reached out, probing the rock, tracing its contours with my trembling fingers. It wasn't anything as simple as a loose rock that could be pushed aside, or rolled forward with me following close behind. It was a ridge of solid rock, extending from the top of the shaft to the bottom, blocking at least a third of the opening. I squirmed in closer, reaching my left hand in behind the ridge, feeling nothing but space. I extended farther, as far as my arm would reach. Whatever space was behind the ridge was larger than what I was squeezed into then. And the unknown was the best chance that I had. I was going to get past the ridge, or die trying.

But the wide circle of steel around my neck, the thing that locked my helmet in place, was never going to pass through the small opening. I had no choice but to back out of the tight space and strip down to my underwear.

Nearly naked now, I returned to the obstruction. Using my hips and digging in with only my toes, I managed to twist sideways, reaching both hands through the hole, pushing onward until my face was pressed against the ridge. I was stuck there, the widest part of my body mere inches from passing through. I brought my forearms together, elbows pointed outward in opposite directions, and began pressing them into the backside of the ridge. At the same time I rolled my hips and pushed with my toes with all the strength that I had left.

The rough surfaces of the ridge cut deeply into the underside of my arms and chest, but I moved forward, perhaps an inch. There was no give to the rock, and I still hadn't gotten the largest part of me through. I exhaled, blowing all the air from my lungs, deflating my chest, making it smaller. I pressed and scrambled one last time, popping free, the rocks tearing chunks of skin from my sides.

I was lying half in, and half out of the shaft, bent at the waist, my upper half resting on the diagonal against the damp rock. Despite the darkness, bursts of light flashed before my eyes as I fought to remain conscious. I struggled to suck in the heavy, damp air, willing myself back into the world. I couldn't get enough of it. The rock was pushing my abdomen into my chest, collapsing my lungs. I could hear a whistling sound above the sound of the wind and water as I exhaled.

I pushed against the rock with my forearms, lifting my hips up and through the hole. Gravity took over as the bulk of my mass moved from the horizontal to the steep slope of the new space. I began sliding down the slope—head first—flailing with both arms, trying to find something to slow my descent. But I was moving too fast. One arm struck an outcropping of some kind, painfully, sending me into a spin, doing nothing to slow me down. I was tumbling in all directions, head over heels and turning in a clockwise direction.

I had no control as I sped down the slope—my speed increased as the grade grew even steeper. I tucked my head into my chest, burying it in my forearms as my hands locked behind my neck. I managed to stop the summersaults, but continued to roll along the long axis of my body, like a log down a hill.

It seemed to go on for miles, my knees and elbows being struck repeatedly as I bounced from one uneven surface to another. I was moving so rapidly that I might as well have been in a free fall, when, suddenly, I felt myself slowing down, the slope beginning to level out.

My roll turned into a slide, one leg out in front of me and one bent underneath, like a ballplayer sliding into second base as he stretches a single into a double. I was still moving at a good rate of speed when my leading leg struck a solid object, flipping me up and over it. I reached out with both hands, searching for something to hold on to.

Miraculously, my arms found the ledge, but my feet found no purchase. My legs swung back and forth, my toes reaching out, trying to find something solid. I hung on to the edge of the precipice—not knowing whether there was solid ground an inch beneath my feet, or a mile.

I tried using my arms to raise my body up, trying to gain enough height to swing one leg over the ledge, but as I pressed down, the fragile ledge gave way and I tumbled into space.

CHAPTER 12

I hit the water like a brick, sinking to an unknown depth, my body wracked with pain as if I had been struck broadside by a hundred hammers. My lungs weren't prepared for the plunge, no chance to suck them full of life-giving oxygen, and yet I sprung to the surface like a dried cork. Even then, I had sucked in a mouthful of water, swallowing it, instantly regretting the fact that I did. I came to the surface, retching, my stomach rejecting the foul water that I had just taken in.

The taste of it dried out my mouth even more that the day's lack of water had done. It left a heavy aftertaste of salt, like I had poured half a container of good old Morten's down my throat. It burned, from my lips down to the pit of my belly: hot, acrid, sending rippling waves of nausea, from bottom to top. My stomach went spastic, tying to purge the burning sensation from my very core. I choked and coughed, but still nothing came up but dribbles of the awful water that just seconds before had gone down. It left my throat hot and raspy, like I had been chug-a-lugging sand.

I flipped over onto my back, the buoyant force of the salt water easily keeping me afloat. The water was cool, but not cold. The feeling was incredibly refreshing on my tormented, moisture starved body, but within seconds, the pleasure turned to pain—indescribable pain. The water, laden with salt, hit my assortment of wounds and made me forget everything else. It was a thousand tiny flesh-eating fish nipping at every part of my body, their tiny little teeth digging in, taking a thousand little bitsy chunks from my flesh. I gritted my teeth, and waited for the pain to subside. There was nothing else that I *could* do.

The darkness was absolute. The roar was reduced to the dull sound of water lapping upon itself as the waves rolled over one another, an occasional slap as one flattened atop the next. The water ran swift, and a warm breeze accompanied it, both flowing in the same direction. I was weightless, drifting along with the current, deeply satisfied to be out of the cave.

As the pain subsided, I became relaxed, as relaxed as I could ever remember being. With the salt content, the viscosity of the water was such that I doubted that I could have sunk if I tried to. I actually relaxed to the point where I clasped my hands beneath my head, like I was sitting back on a chaise lounge, vacationing at the beach on one of the Keys, nothing to worry about except the evenness of my tan.

I tilted my head back, keeping my lips as far above the water as I could, all the while breathing through my mouth. In and out, each intake feeling cold on my parched throat—the sensitive membrane tight, drying out a little more with each breath. Each exhale rattled in my chest, whistling on the way out, extracting just a bit more of the precious moisture. I didn't even attempt to swallow, the last one feeling like I was gulping down razorblades.

I became accustomed to the temperature of the water, and the salt had dried my cuts and scrapes, preventing any further penetration of the pain that it had caused initially. The sound of the water was soothing, monotonous, adding to the overall sense of peace. I was weightless, floating in space—my senses numb. I had to concentrate to feel anything at all, and when I did, I quickly shut out the conflicting emotions, satisfied to drift along free of all sensation.

I wondered if this was how Susan felt. Was there a small part of her brain that was still functioning? Was she able to think, just unable to feel, unable to express herself? It was how I felt. Yes, I could express myself, I could speak—I could move. But if no one was there to hear me, to see my movements, what good where they? I was like the tree in the forest. If I fell, and no one was there to hear me, did I make a sound?

I couldn't help but feel that Susan was still alive. Not just in the clinical sense—her heart beating, a sign of brain activity—but *really* alive, somehow understanding where she was and what was going on around her. I had never felt more strongly about it than I did the day before I left for Utah, the last time that I saw her—the last time that I would *ever* see her.

*****

I had been sitting at her bedside, my chair pushed in as close as I could get it, my knees rammed into the hard steel of the bed rails. I was holding on to her hand, stroking her hair, leaning down close to her ear, whispering to her. Over the weeks I had told her everything about Dermot, about the time machine, and about my decision to take the journey.

On that day, I was telling her goodbye.

With tears running down my cheeks, I kissed her on the forehead one last time, and told her that I loved her. As I did, I felt her squeeze my hand. It sent an electric charge up my arm and a chill down my spine. I jumped from the chair, knocking it over, nearly tripping over it as I went for the door. I charged down the corridor towards her doctor's office.

I barged in on him without knocking. He was sitting at his desk, reading something in a brown folder. I tried to tell him what had just happened, but I was so excited, it didn't come out right. It sounded like just so much gibberish. He looked up at me like I was nuts. I paused a second, and tried again. "Susan moved, she squeezed my hand."

"Stay here!" the doctor demanded, and he left the room, closing the door behind him, leaving me alone to ponder my situation. I don't know why I didn't follow him. What could he have done to me? Thrown me out? Have arrested me? I don't think so. But I didn't go after him. The fact is, I think that I was just plain scared.

Hell, I wasn't even sure what I was scared of. Maybe it was the commitment that I had made minutes before. I told Susan that I loved her. It was the first time that I had ever told her, and only the second person that I had ever told it to. Perhaps I only told Susan that I loved her because I knew that she couldn't acknowledge it, couldn't force me to show love in return.

I wouldn't have to betray the memory of Liz.

I didn't follow the doctor. Instead, I just stood with my back to the door, staring out the window, anxiously waiting his return.

He didn't keep me waiting long. I could tell by the look on his face, by his demeanor, that no miracle had occurred. He closed the door behind him and as he sat down at his desk, he motioned me to the other chair.

"Doctor Williams ... David. I know that this is going to be hard for you to understand, hard for you to accept, but what you felt was just an involuntary response. You had hold of Susan's hand. You may have even squeezed it. She responded to that, but only on a subconscious level. She didn't hear you, wasn't aware of your presence. It's not at all unusual for a comatose patient to respond in some physical manner to some physical stimuli. I've seen it many times before, and I've seen it with Susan. I know how hard this has been for you, but I'm sorry to say that there is no change in her condition."

For just a few moments, I thought about arguing with him, but I knew that he was right. I guess that I knew it all along. It was nothing more than a squeeze of the hand. Shit, I wasn't even sure that she really squeezed it. I had been holding on hard, probably squeezing like crazy. I was searching for any kind of response—wishing for it, praying for it. I thought that I had felt something. According to the doctor, I may well have. But it wasn't the response that I was looking for.

I wasn't just looking for it. I needed it. The next day I was leaving for the adventure of a lifetime, perhaps the adventure of *all* lifetimes. Or more likely, I was racing to my death. I might not even survive the trip. And if I did, what were my chances for surviving more than a few days or a few weeks in such an alien environment? I could think of a thousand things that could kill me: flesh-eating animals, poisonous vegetation, unstable geography, the lack of food and water. Even the weather or the very air that I breathed might kill me. But most of all, I was afraid of what I couldn't think of.

I was going to a place far different than anything that I could even imagine. There were times that I thought I was crazy for even considering it.

I needed for Susan to know what I was doing. I needed her to tell me that it was okay, that I wasn't crazy to do this thing. But most of all, I needed her to tell me that she didn't need me. Despite what the doctor said, in my mind, the squeeze of the hand was real, was meaningful. Not an involuntary response, but a conscious reply to my request.

She was giving me my leave.

I had convinced myself that she understood what I was telling her, at least the important part. In my heart I knew that she would have wanted me to go—she would have gone herself if she could have. I forced myself to believe that when she squeezed my hand, she was telling me to go.

*****

Two weeks later, drifting along with the current of an underground river, some seventy millions years in the past, I hadn't changed my mind. I was still convinced that Susan knew exactly what I was doing. I wasn't naïve enough to think that everything that I had said to her in all those months had gotten through, but I thought that the important things did. And on that last day, I didn't imagine that she squeezed my hand. She *did* squeeze it, and it was her acceptance and blessing to make the journey.

I felt a closeness to Susan at that moment, like we were sharing the same experience. Just kind of floating along, weightless, no physical sensation, our minds functioning—sharp—aware—but no way to express our thoughts, our emotions. For some inexplicable reason, it seemed that Susan and I were of one mind, sharing the same sensations, the same thoughts. Thinking that she was with me gave me a sense of peace and whatever fear I had of the future simply faded away.

Thirst and hunger were momentarily forgotten as I drifted in and out of sleep, or perhaps, unconsciousness. Either way, it didn't really matter. I was content to float along with the current, satisfied to let it take me where it would. I thought that maybe I would just continue to drift along in the dark forever, feeling comfortable, thinking of Susan. And the thought didn't bother me a bit.

I was dozing to the rhythmic sounds of the waves, not sure how much time I had been in the water, hours at least, when I was startled by a tremendous splash off to my right. The sound bounced between the walls of the cave like a pool ball, for the first time giving me some sense of dimension to the space. I heard it ricochet off the wall to my left, close, maybe fifty or sixty feet. The second splash was even louder, closer yet, and I could feel the water begin to churn around me.

I rolled over onto my stomach, letting my legs drop beneath the waves, treading water with my arms—fully awake—alert. The water continued to boil around me and something brushed against my leg, something large, pushing me sideways in the water several feet. The waves that formed crashed against a solid surface, closer now. I began swimming toward the sound, pulling the water past me with all my might.

I was a good swimmer, thousands of laps in the gym pool made me one, but fear had taken away any kind of form. I flailed at the water, close to panic. I could hear something behind me move in the water, changing direction. The movement created a mini-tidal wave, pushing me toward the surface that reflected the sound, more than making up for the lack of speed that my poor technique had caused.

Within seconds I crashed into the wall, catching a sharp edge across my chest. I choked on the salt water as I began to sink below the surface. I reached up, grabbing hold of the smooth rock, hauling myself up and over. It was a ledge of some kind, and as I rolled myself onto it, I could hear something rise above me, water dropping down on top of me in sheets. I kept rolling, slamming into a wall just a few feet away.

I could hear breathing from above me, and a strange high-pitched clicking sound that seemed to move from side to side—moving back and forth across a considerable distance. Whatever it was, was big, and it was searching for me.

The thing making the sound moved closer, closing in on my position as I scrambled along the floor, feeling my way along the wall. I hadn't gone more than ten feet along the uneven surface when I came upon a depression in the rock. I followed its contours, wedging myself into a small recess, perhaps four feet deep, two feet wide, with just enough headroom to duck underneath. I pushed up against the back of it, forming my body along the curvature of the far wall, distancing myself as best I could from whatever the hell was coming for me.

The breathing grew closer, the odd clicking sound more pronounced.

It had found me.

The smell of fish and seaweed was overpowering, adding to the acrid taste of salt already in my mouth. It made me gag. It could hear the sound of my dry vomiting and snorted in response, blowing a foul mucus across my face. A wet, rough textured surface that I could only equate to double-0 sandpaper stroked across my body, taking the skin from my cheeks and bloodying my lips. The smell that accompanied it was even more powerful, but I was too terrified to make any additional sound. I sucked in my breath, and held my body rigid against another assault by what I could only assume was the monster's tongue. I had just been licked by something that could only be an *Elasmosaurus*.

There were other animals of the sea during the Cretaceous period, if I was indeed in the Cretaceous period, but nothing that I could think of that could stretch so far above me and needed to breath air. The *Elasmosaurus*, from the family of Plesiosaurs, was not a dinosaur. It was a marine reptile. They had been around since the beginning of the Jurassic period, the species becoming more diverse and growing larger over the millions of years of its existence. Fossils from the late Cretaceous period stretched to nearly fifty feet.

Elasmosaurs had four long flippers, diamond-shaped, much like those of giant sea turtles, and they used them to propel themselves through the water at great speed. They had extremely long necks, more than half their total length, and short, pointed tails. They had long powerful jaws filled with razor sharp teeth. They were flesh eaters. Fish mainly, and other marine creatures, but I doubted that it would see me as anything other than its next meal. After all, I was in *its* territory.

Its tongue was on me again as I struck with my foot. I lashed out as hard as I could, kicking upward, connecting with its lower jaw. Warm sticky fluid spattered my face as the strange clicking sound turned into a deafening, high-pitched shriek. The source of the sound immediately moved up and away from me, followed by a thunderous splash. The fluid stung my eyes and it left the dull copper taste of blood on my lips. My kick must have driven its teeth through its tongue. I only hoped that I had injured it enough to make it wary of me, avoid my scent.

I waited hunched over in the little cubbyhole, drifting in and out of sleep, listening to the lapping of the waves, alert to any new sounds, making sure that the beast was gone for good. Eventually, I was going to have to get back into the water, and even on my best day, I was no match for the *Elasmosaurus*.

I awoke with a start, my body stiff from the unnatural position that I had endured for too long. This time I came to knowing exactly where I was, for once, not disoriented, or confused. But there was something new—something unexpected. I could see. Not clearly, but there were vague shades of gray, rather than total blackness. The light came from the right, the opposite end from which I first entered the water. It was an extraordinary moment. It had seemed like … well, forever, since I had been able to see anything at all.

Silently I crept from the hole in the wall, feeling my way along the shelf carved in the rock. Both the floor and the wall were incredibly uneven, yet smooth at the same time. Some force had ripped through this mountain thousands of years ago, and left it ragged, with outcroppings everywhere. And, in all the years that followed, the rushing water had worn away the roughest surfaces, made it slick and smooth.

The shelf ran for a long way. I followed it in the darkness, my hands firmly planted along the surface of the wall, my feet on internal shock absorbers, moving up and over the irregular floor. At a point several hours into my journey the shelf narrowed, my feet barely finding the space to set. At almost the same time, I could feel the walls curving inward, the ceiling lowering.

I couldn't see well enough to navigate, so I continued to feel my way along, following the fuzzy gray haze in the distance. The ledge continued to narrow, and the slope of the walls began to push me towards the water. It wasn't long before I had to ease back down into the briny river, silently, trying not to attract the attention of another hungry creature.

For several minutes I just hugged the ledge, listening, making sure that I was alone. Convinced that I was, I started out, slowly, silently, keeping within touching distance of the wall. I went on like that for an hour or more, the underground river bending and twisting through the solid rock. I was no longer shrouded in blackness. Everything around me was now a dark gray and I began to see vague shapes close up. I could see my hands, not in detail, but I could at least make out the shape.

As more light became apparent, I knew that I was nearing the end of the long journey, but I was growing more concerned about the shrinking of the cave. The sound of the water changed, imperceptibly at first, but more so the farther I went. It seemed to be coming from above my head, very close, rather than from the side, and every now and then I could feel water dripping down from above.

I reached my hand upward and could feel the ceiling of the cave, not more than a foot from the top of my head. I wasn't sure how long the ceiling had been lowering, or even how high it was at the beginning. I knew that it was a hell of a drop from the precipice, maybe forty or fifty feet, but I didn't know how far the ceiling was above that. I had been in the water for many hours and had surely traveled several miles. Had the ceiling been dropping steadily the whole time, and would it continue to do so?

I kept moving, pulling myself forward with one hand on the wall and one hand on the ceiling. It was a gradual change, but discernible—the ceiling was definitely getting closer. I had perhaps gone a hundred yards and the ceiling had dropped three or four inches. At some point, four or five hundred yards downstream, the ceiling was going to meet the water.

Within just a few minutes the rough-hewn ceiling began scraping the top of my head. I rolled over onto my back so that only my face was above water. The light continued to get better and I could begin to see the outcropping of rock that hung suspended above my upturned face. Moving away from the wall, I used my renewed, but limited, sight to steer a path around the obstacles.

I was going from one concavity to the next, my lips pressed against the rock, sucking in oxygen each time. But, for more and more of the time, I was holding my breath, under water. And each time, I was sucking in more of the salt water, choking on it, making it more difficult to take in what little air was available.

I kept working toward the light. It was more beneath me now than in front of me. It was too dark to make out detail under the water, but looking down, I could see the shape of my feet, moving back and forth, helping to keep me afloat. I was so close to the ceiling that in order to look down, I had to submerge myself so that only the top of my head was out of the water.

I didn't get more than a few yards when a solid mass of rock stopped my progress. The dim glow of the light was now directly beneath me and I pushed off from the ceiling toward it. I slipped downward along the smooth face of the stone. About twenty feet down, I found the entrance to a tunnel, ten feet high and perhaps twice as wide. A brighter light was coming from the other end, but no way to tell how far away it was.

I rose slowly back to the surface, feeling my way along the sheer face of the rock, my arms outstretched above me, searching for the ceiling. My lungs were bursting as I reached the top, but I had to hold out for several precious seconds as I searched for an air pocket. Finding one at last, I sucked at the warm, moist air, swallowing more of the salty water. I had to fight off another round of retching, my strength nearly gone.

It was decision time. Either I risked everything and made one final dive into the tunnel, swimming until I reached an end, one way or the other. Or, I swam back, against the current, to where I fell from the cliff. There was no way to get back to the cave, but there was always a chance that I could find another way out by following the river beyond the cliff. But I hadn't the strength, and I knew that I would not survive another encounter with the *Elasmosaurus*.

It wasn't much of a choice. As slim as it was, there was only one chance to get out, and that was through the tunnel. I couldn't afford to waste another minute thinking it over. I took three deep breaths, flipped over in the water, and with my feet, pushed off the ceiling, propelling myself through the water.

I reached the tunnel in a matter of seconds and entered it headfirst, immediately starting to breaststroke. I started with long, slow, steady strokes, looking about from side to side, skirting obstacles. Within the first minute, my lungs began to ache from the dwindling supply of oxygen. I started stroking faster and faster, my muscles becoming like rubber, my coordination gone.

All the while, the light was becoming brighter, the water clearer. I could see tiny sea animals, fish, bits of sea kelp, and small particles of stone swirl past my face. The current was growing stronger, pushing me through the tunnel making it hard to avoid the outcropping of rock. I was literally being hurled through the tunnel, bouncing and scraping along the hard stone corridor.

I was moments away from passing out, my lungs screaming for air, my vision beginning to fade when I popped from the tunnel and shot to the surface like a balloon. I gasped for air even before I was sure that I had cleared the foam. My whole body arched backwards from the effort, crashing down into the surface, a sense of elation like nothing I had ever felt before.

In my whole life, nothing had ever felt quite as good as that first lungful of fresh air. It seemed like I had never tasted anything so sweet or so satisfying.

And the sun had never seemed to shine so brightly. It was a wonderful blindness that struck me, forced tears from my eyes. Perhaps it was the brightness of the sun. Perhaps it was just being able to *see* the sun once again.

The sky was a dazzling blue, the blazing sun about two-thirds across the sky, either two or three hours from rising or setting. I searched for the horizon, able to see nothing but water. I had to be facing east, the sun closer to rising than to setting. I was staring across at the great salt sea that separated eastern and western North America some seventy million years ago.

I had made it.

I turned in the water, back in the direction from which I came. Behind me were the mountains of Wasatch, but nothing about them was familiar. They were jagged towers of granite, the sun reflecting from the sharp angular surfaces like glass. Everything was sharp angles and flat surfaces, knife-like projections extending miles into the sky. The colors were intense, vivid, not at all like the dull grays and browns that I saw before. What I remembered was old, tired. What I saw before me on that day was new and full of energy. It was being born.

The cliff rose directly in front of me, two, three hundred feet, straight up, its face, flat and smooth. To the north, it stretched on for as far as the eye could see, disappearing into the far off horizon. To the south, the cliff began sloping downward toward the sea turning to the east, out of sight, perhaps a half mile to my left.

The face of the mountain dropped straight into the water. No slope, no rocks, no stretch of land to step up on to. I was stuck in the water for at least another hour—maybe longer—much longer. I had no choice but to follow the water south, hoping that around the bend I could find a way out of the sea and back to the cave. I started out—short, slow strokes—ever watchful for things in the water.

Fatigue reentered my body as the exhilaration of being out of the cave and into the sunlight faded away. I had been physically and emotionally beaten to a pulp. I had been without food for a couple of days at least, depending upon how long I was actually in the time machine. But worse, I had been without water, the kind without salt, for at least twenty-four hours.

My lips were swollen and split, blood dried at the corners, in part due to the lack of moisture, but mostly from the literal tongue-lashing I had received from the *Elasmosaurus*. My entire body was wracked with shakes, and my arms trembled with every stroke as I made my way slowly along the edge of the great sea.

I had sustained no permanent damage: no broken bones, no serious lacerations, but I felt that I was bruised from head to toe. I had been ripped from my chair in the time machine during the initial journey and buried in a pile of my own supplies. Rocks in the cave pummeled me—not once—but twice, and I had been knocked on the head, scraped and gouged from my trip through the tunnel. I had survived the fall into the sea from the precipice, and been nearly eaten by a prehistoric sea monster. And I had tumbled head over heels through the final water-filled passage, only to be dumped into the sea, with no idea where the hell I was. Generally, I felt like shit.

As I rounded the bend, my arms gave out. I had little strength left, and nothing in my upper body. I turned on to my back and without much will, did a rough approximation of a frog kick, moving myself forward in the water at a snail's pace.

I pushed myself on with no conscious thought of doing it, my eyes staring at the clear blue sky, my knees pulling up, pushing out again, my feet pressing against the warm water, propelling me forward a few feet at a time. Not really realizing I was doing it, my right hand flirted with the rocky rise of the mountain, afraid to lose contact with the land.

I didn't even notice the change in the geography as I made the turn to the east. I just kept following the curve of the rock, my fingers tracing the intricate surfaces of the granite as I drifted along.

I completed the wide, slow turn, not aware that I had lost touch with the rock, when my shoulders bumped into something. It startled me and I tried to roll over onto my stomach, discovering that I could touch the bottom. I looked over to my left, finding the sheer face of the cliff gone, replaced by a long stretch of deserted beach. I rose to my knees and crawled on all fours out of the water.

I tried to stand, but my legs wouldn't support my weight. I collapsed—half in—and half out of the surf. I struggled to roll over on to my stomach, and managed to drag myself another twenty feet onto the hot sand before passing out.

*****

A feeling of something pulling at my foot woke me up. I opened the one eye that was not buried in the sand to see that it was still light out. I was looking out over the sea, the sun behind me, sending long ribbons of red and gold shimmering across the water. The tug on my foot repeated and I became aware of a shadow moving across the sand around me. I raised my head slowly, just enough to see what was blocking the sunlight.

I was too stunned to move—not afraid, just frozen in place—awestruck. Standing at my feet, its long beak tugging at my foot was a six-foot tall *Pteranodon*. I jerked my foot from its mouth, and it stepped back on short spindly legs. Like me, it seemed more curious than frightened.

It was a beautiful red-brown, almost the color of dark mahogany, that spread into a brilliant crimson through its neck and head. The red transfused into dazzling yellow at the tip of its two foot-long crest, a matching color scheme on its beak, mirror images of each other. Its thin body was covered with short, fine hair, like that of mouse. I knew what it was at first glance. Aside from the beautiful and distinctive coloring, it was just as I imagined it, like the hundreds of drawings I had seen over the years. The *Pteranodon* was a flying reptile, and not a dinosaur, although a close relative. A member of the pterosaur family, it was distinctive because of its long slender crest and lack of teeth. It had a tremendous wingspan, although not the largest of the pterosaurs.

Its wings were folded back just then, pointing behind it, the three short claws clearly visible at the hinged midpoint of its thin, hollow wing bones. They were the same color as its body, but hairless, shiny, like fine leather.

Its head bobbed back and forth like a modern day bird, as I turned over onto my back and sat up. The *Pteranodon* was known to be a fish-eater and probably skimmed the surface of the sea, scooping up marine life as a pelican does. There was a theory that it was a scavenger, as well, feeding off dead animals like a vulture. It must have thought that I was some unidentifiable, dead creature that washed up on shore. That's why it was tugging at my foot.

I hadn't made any threatening moves, so it approached me again. I was fascinated—not afraid. Despite its size, I knew that it didn't weigh more than twenty-five or thirty pounds. Its bones were hollow, as was most of its skull. Its wings were paper-thin. Even in my weakened condition, I could crush it with a single, well-placed blow. I let it grasp my foot a second time, pulling back against the little force that it exerted.

I toyed with it because I didn't want it to leave. But after several more unsuccessful attempts at grabbing, it began to peck with its beak, which was pointed, sharp, and instantly started a little trickle of blood flowing along the edge of my foot. Not wanting to hurt the beautiful creature, I simply threw up my hands and let out a scream. It was then that it realized that I was indeed not dead—perhaps smart enough to know that it was no match for me. It stumbled backwards several steps and let out a cry—a low-pitched moan that rose in pitch to a sharp staccato finish.

The startled *Pteranodon* spread its magnificent wings, perhaps twenty-five feet from tip to tip, and turned into the wind. It lifted off gracefully, effortlessly, its wings curved to catch the mild breeze, shifting slightly from side to side to keep it level. It didn't flap its wings like a bird, but just wrapped them around the air currents, which sent it out over the sea.

I stared at it until it was nothing more than a tiny black dot against the failing daylight. My whole body quivered with excitement. I had just had an encounter with an extinct animal. It wasn't a dinosaur, but it was a creature that existed at the time of the dinosaurs, and I had been the only human being to have ever seen one. For the first time since entering the time machine, I felt that I had made the right decision. If I had died right there on the beach, I would have felt that it was all worth it.

But I didn't die, and I was determined not to—not there—and not then. I looked down and was surprised to find a fish not more than three feet from where I sat. I wasn't a fisherman—I had no idea whether it was a pike or a mackerel, or even if it was a species that existed in modern-times. All I knew was that it was food. It was probably the *Pteranodon's* dinner, and it had traded it in for what it thought was a whole feast.

On hands and knees I crawled over to the fish, picking it up and bringing it to my face. I smelled it. It was fresh, the brisk aroma of the sea the only detectable odor. I bit into its flesh, the precious liquid squirting into my throat. I had never been much of a fish fancier, but it was about the best thing that I had ever tasted. I sucked on it, squeezing every last drop from it. I swallowed. The first time it hurt like hell, but as the moisture began to lubricate my parched esophagus, it loosened up, the fish sliding down easily. I devoured its flesh, scraping every last piece from its bones—meat, organs—the whole thing. I began to understand people's fondness for sushi.

It was a meager meal, one that would probably have barely met my expectations for an appetizer ... in my former life. But after having been without any kind of subsistence for days—it revived me—it was lifesaving. Perhaps the revival was only temporary, but I was prepared to go forward, to find the time machine—to go home.

I scanned the beach. It was semicircular, extending from the ledge that I had followed along the western edge of the sea, five hundred yards out, until curving back to the sea, a half-mile farther west. It was a half-moon stretch of pure-white sand, completely surrounded by mountains, inaccessible to anything that walked.

I checked out the area from a wide perspective, trying to get the general idea of what I was faced with. The situation was bleak, but not hopeless. I was out of the cave, not endangered by an impossible environment or air not fit for human lungs. I had an entire sea right in front of me—a smorgasbord of delectable morsels, if I could but learn how to catch them. I wouldn't starve, nor die of thirst, but that wasn't enough. I wanted to live, not just to exist. I had to find a way out of this remote cove.

I began to look around once again—this time, going slowly, checking out every detail, hoping to find the slightest fissure in the rock, the smallest hole in the mountain that might lead the way out. As I scanned from left to right, the shadows working against me in the now-setting sun, I saw nothing of interest until I made it two-thirds of the way around the arc.

I almost missed in, despite my intense scrutiny. There was a reflection. The meager light reflecting off of the calm sea bounced off an object with a white-hot glint that passed with the movement of my head as fast as it had appeared. I shifted my vision back to the left just a fraction of one degree, picking up the sparkling reflection once again. It was different from the mirror-like quality that I had seen when first witnessing the sharp contours of the newborn mountains of Wasatch a few hours before. This was a metallic glint, maybe silver or gold—definitely larger that just a pebble or streak in the rock.

I moved towards it, my strength renewed by the small meal of fish, restored more fully by anxiety and curiosity. I shuffled forward, heading toward the source of the reflection. When I had crossed half the distance, I realized that something was out of place. Surrounding the flickering reflection of light there was rubble. The light came from the center of a pile of debris—rocks and dirt, some fifty feet high and nearly as wide. It was unlike the surrounding stone, which was smooth-faced, precisely cut as if by the hand of a jeweler.

I came closer, within fifty feet, when it came into focus. It was protruding through the rock, rectangular, of precise dimension—man-made. Even before I reached it, I knew that it was made of steel. It was the remnants of the gate that had once stretched across the opening of the cave.

My journey of several days had led me back to within a few hundred yards of where I started. Under the pile of rock was my time machine.

When I first entered the tunnel I was headed west, away from the cave's entrance. Between the long tunnel, and even longer underground river, I must have doubled back, past the cave and into the sea.

I stood in front of the cave, looking at the sharp ragged ends of the twisted steel bars. It was half in, and half out of the pile, bent and distorted, folded nearly in half, ripped into several pieces. Immediately to the left of the mangled pile of steel, a corner of the machine was exposed, its dull black finish coated with fine dust. I brushed it away to find the surface scratched and scraped, but in remarkable shape considering how the trip had ended.

There was several tons of debris on top of the machine, far more than was atop the other end of it. However, on this side, I had light to work from and a possible source of food—I had time. I used that time for the first decent rest that I had had in days. I sat back against the warm rock and fell asleep as the last light of day slipped beyond the mountains.

*****

I awoke refreshed, glad to be alive, ready to begin my new life. I walked down to the shore to find that the tide had provided my breakfast. There was an assortment of clams and crabs washed up on the sand. Something that I would have looked at as garbage a week ago now looked like a delicious all-you-can-eat seafood buffet.

As I sat in the sand, finishing off my delicious meal of seafood I stared into the bright Utah sky, a *Pteranodon*, perhaps my friend from the afternoon before, plucked its morning meal from the sea, swooping down in a graceful arc, scooping up a big fat fish. He did it not once, but twice, flying off somewhere behind the mountain each time—perhaps providing for its family. And I got my first *look* at an *Elasmosaurus*, albeit at quite a distance. It was difficult to see its color, nor could I see any detail of its appearance, but its long neck was a giveaway. It looked like the tabloid photographs of Scotland's "Nessie".

It was just incredibly peaceful. The only sound was that of the gentle waves of the sea and an occasional cry of a gull. I stretched my legs out across the sand and leaned back on both elbows, wondering what Dermot and his team was doing about now. How long had I been gone in their frame of time—two days, three, a week? Were they still on site, working from the control room? At some point, the staff would be reduced to a security team and one of Dermot's technicians. They would stay there for as long as it took.

My death would bring the machine back to their time. Dermot must have been ecstatic that there was nothing to see after several days. It meant that I had survived, that his experiment had worked, at least in part. He would know that I went back in time, but until the machine returned, until he unloaded the contents of the computer, he wouldn't know just how *far* back I went.

I got up and brushed the white sand from my underwear and strolled over to the machine. I looked off to the right where the control room had been. In my frame of time, it had been there just a few days ago. In real-time, it would be another seventy million years until it appeared. Now, there was just sand.

I looked back at the machine, much clearer now in the direct light of the rising sun. The crumbled mass of the gate lay to its right. One bar had broken free from an end. It stuck out from the pile six or seven feet like a flagpole. I grabbed the end and pulled. It moved, but wouldn't come free. I began pushing aside the rocks at its base until I had cleared the area. The bar was still connected to what was left of the gate at one end. I pulled and pushed on the bar, rocking it back and forth—the free end swinging in a greater arc with each pull. In just a few minutes the weld gave and the bar was free. It was ten feet long and weighed close to a hundred pounds. I had myself a pry-bar.

Using the bar as a staff and the rocks as stepping-stones I climbed onto the exposed corner of the machine. I slid the bar in between the first and second stone and pushed. The rock lifted and rolled off the side of the machine with a minimum of effort. With the bar, I had the strength of ten.

I removed a half dozen more in quick succession feeling like I had done this before. But this time it wasn't just a feeling, one of those things that you can't quite explain—a sensation with no real substance. I rested the end of the bar on the top of the machine and looked up at the mountain before me. I had been here before—right here, and I was doing the same thing—exactly the same thing. I was excavating rock from the front of the very same cave in order to get back inside, to get at what was buried underneath. I had been in this exact same spot doing exactly the same thing two years ago … or seventy million years *from* now, depending on one's perspective.

I worked until mid-day, happy to be using my strength, feeling the muscles burn and the sweat form, dripping down my body. I thought of my previous life, my daily trips to the gym, the systematic routine. I would never see a *Nautilus* or *Universal* machine again, never a polished chromium bar with pair of precision matched Olympic plates, but I had the feeling that I would not be lacking for physical activity—a more natural form of exercise—maybe that's the way it should be.

There was a lot less rock than there was the first time I was here and I had the top of the machine uncovered, access to the cave regained in a matter of hours. But I refused to enter it. No way was I going to end up trapped inside a second time. In my peak, I could make the trip through the tunnel again, especially knowing ahead of time what I would face—but I was not in tip-top shape. Instead, I worked my way back to the front of the machine without ever having had to step down from its roof.

I had cleared the dented access panel on top of the machine, but I wasn't yet prepared to try entering it. I still wasn't convinced that I could squeeze my way through, but even if I could, I had to be sure that I had another means of egress—I had to clear away the path to the door. I wasn't able to open it from the outside, but I thought that I could from within. I just didn't want to squeeze back through the top panel again, especially from beneath where gravity was working against me.

I slid down the side of the machine, still on the outside of the cave, and began attacking the pile on the left side—the side with the door. It was well past mid-day and I could feel my stomach rumbling from hunger. I didn't stop for lunch though. I didn't want to put back any of the nine or ten pounds I had lost since my journey began until I had managed to squeeze back into the time machine. There would be time enough for food when I got back inside.

Clearing the side of the machine was more difficult. The rocks didn't simply fall out of the way as they did from the top of the machine. Plus, I had to push away those that had fallen from the top. Even after having dislodged a rock from the pile, I had to work my bar underneath it and roll it, or flip it over and over until it was out of the way. I needed a clear path, the ground free of any obstacles.

It was nearly dark when the area around the door was clear. I tried once again to open it and was actually relieved when the button failed to work. I would have hated to think that I made the arduous trip through the cave and the underground river for nothing.

I was incredibly thirsty, but I had the momentum going, so I decided to forge ahead and clear out the remaining rock that blocked the entrance to the cave. It was late, but there was a full moon, plenty of light until it dropped behind the mountain.

I entered the cave a few hours later with just enough light to avoid stumbling on the debris strewn across the floor. Like before, the air was filled with the sound of rushing water. I walked over to where the sound was coming from, behind the small alcove. I got down on my hands and knees and crawled toward the sound, running my hand along the edge of the tunnel. Thinking about crawling down into the crevasse again, even having done it and survived, sent a chill down my spine. I wasn't sure if I could have done it again or not. But I was thankful for its existence—it had saved my life.

The rocks were slick and wet. I brought my fingers to my lips, tasting the salty residue. It reminded me of how long I had been without water—since early that morning. I had to get some fluid in me, and I had a source not twenty feet away. I had to get back into the time machine. The time was now.

I climbed back on top of the machine and walked down to the access port. Like I thought, one good stomp, and the panel gave way. In my underwear, which I left on in the hopes of keeping my nether regions from protruding beyond the edge of the small opening in the roof, I went down through the hole. I didn't make it beyond my waist before my bare feet came in contact with the top layer of crates that were jammed against the front half of the machine. I tried pushing them aside with my feet, but they were too firmly wedged into position and I was pretty well drained of strength.

I just went with the flow, pulling my legs up into a sitting position and letting myself drop down through the hatch up to my chest. I didn't hesitate for even a moment—I had been through something similar before. I just raised my arms, let the air out of my lungs, and dropped through the hole with no problem at all.

The sharp corners of the boxes and cartons scraped and poked at my nearly naked body, but I ignored them all, unbelievably happy to make it back home—happier yet to make it through the hatch so easily. If I failed to get the door open, I could always escape back out through the roof. I'd just have to stay thin.

The light coming though the portholes was dim, but infinitely better than when I was in here the last time. It was a clean room when I started out, but the collision with the inside of the cave and the subsequent rockslide while I was trying to uncover the door, stirred up the contents of my machine. The cardboard and wood boxes that had been bounced around the interior of the machine had left millions of particles and fibers that floated around, dancing to the currents of air that I had stirred up during my intrusion.

I was sitting in almost the same spot that I was in when I awoke from the crash. I could feel the damp spot where the water bottles had burst open. It was soaking my bottom. I reached down, digging through the boxes and found the same open corner. It was easy to find another bottle—intact. I opened the cellophane wrapper, pulled out the spout, and downed the whole thing in one long, satisfying chug.

CHAPTER 13

It took two full days to organize my new home, despite the fact that the collision with the cave's wall had unpacked half of the boxes for me. They had ended up in the forward half of the machine, leaving the back portion of the shelves relatively free. I began unpacking the boxes and crates at the front of the pile, neatly storing things on the far ends of the racks—the left one for food, the center for clothing, and the right one for tools and assorted hardware.

I was surprised to find things relatively undamaged. Miraculously, most of the boxes of clothing had hit the front wall of the machine first, splitting open, scattering the soft material across the front end of the machine, cushioning the impact of everything else that followed—me included. It was another miracle that the heavier boxes of tools and equipment didn't do some serious damage to my person as they piled on afterward.

Unfortunately, the clothes being stuck under all the heavy equipment meant that I had to toil all of that first day mostly naked. Being barefoot was the worst problem. Even during the daylight hours, the light coming through the tiny portholes on but one end and one side of the machine left much of the inside in shadow. I was constantly stepping on something sharp, or stubbing my toes on something blunt. It was a huge relief when I found the box of shoes.

In the afternoon of that first full day back inside the machine, I had found most of my tools. With the exception of a few broken wooden handles and an assortment of nicks and dents, they had made the trip pretty much unscathed. I used them to disable the latch on the main hatch and remove the spring mechanism. It no longer rose on its own, but was balanced well enough to open with a minimum of effort. I wasn't worried about not having the ability to lock it from the outside. There didn't seem to be any way for a wild animal to open it even if one managed to find its way over the mountains that protected this tiny isolated beach.

Most importantly, I found the cache of food—a hundred boxes—some split wide open—some relatively intact except for a split seam here or there. Some of the cans were dented and creased, but, not only did I have a can opener, I had found one of my hatchets. A silly thing like a bent lid was not going to keep me from feasting on the canned delights. That first afternoon

I dined on a can of chili and a bottle of natural spring water. It was a meal fit for a king. I ate it cold, right from the can, dented though it was, and it tasted like I had gotten it from a four-star Mexican restaurant.

I thought that maybe I deserved a break or two, and I got them. As I uncovered the mess in what was to become my living area at the front of the machine, I found that my pilot's chair, the one in which I was seated during the frightening trip through time, had been ripped from its moorings. It was a chair meant for function, not comfort. I took a great deal of pleasure in throwing it out the door of my home. If I thought that it would fit through the tunnel behind the alcove, I would have gladly pitched it in.

The second break involved a chair as well. My big, old recliner made the trip without a scratch. I'll never know if Dermot did an especially good job of bolting it down or if it was just pure luck, but, either way, I was grateful as hell. That first evening, I ate my dinner sitting in it and immediately fell fast asleep wrapped in its soft cushions, not waking until the morning light peeked through the front porthole of the machine.

The second day, I got yet another break—a surprise actually. I had made my way to the very front of the machine, slowly, purposely, picking up and organizing everything as I went. It was the end of a very long day when I shelved the last of the crated items and was anxious to sit down to dinner—my first *hot* meal in perhaps a week.

I had stacked all the wooden slates from the crates alongside the meager supply of firewood and cut the cardboard from the boxes into smaller pieces that would easily fit into the stove. But when I opened the door of the stove, there was no place to put the cardboard. Stuffed inside, carefully wrapped in a blanket was a wooden barrel. I carefully pulled it from the center of its padding, smiling in anticipation. It was a five-gallon oak cask filled with twenty-year-old scotch.

Dermot really did think of everything.

Five gallons seems like a lot, but not when it has to last a lifetime, so I'd use it just on special occasions. Special occasions like that night. It had been a most remarkable week, and I had survived it, ready to start my new life. I celebrated with a plate of piping hot beef stew and a cup of coffee. I enjoyed it alfresco, sitting on a folding chair outside the cave, alongside my new home. I watched as the shadows crept out over the sea as I sipped a big glass of scotch.

I had one thing left to check on the next morning. Everything else had been recovered, inspected, and stored away—ready to be used. But I had yet to check on the computer, hadn't even opened the cupboard door. When I had finished unpacking the night before, it was getting dark, and I needed the sunlight for the photocells to run it. Yet the real reason was that I was afraid of what I might find. Had it been damaged during the trip, no longer capable of functioning? Dermot showed me how to operate the thing but I sure as hell didn't know to fix it. I wanted to give it every chance to work, so I waited for daylight.

If it were broken, how would I record my findings? Sure, I had paper, pens, drawing supplies, all kinds of office supplies, but even locked away in the titanium case, I questioned whether they would survive the millions of years to reach Dermot's hands. The experts said that the computer would survive as long as I kept it in the case. I was skeptical, but no expert. I hoped for Dermot's sake that it did, and I hoped that it had survived the trip.

The next morning I unlatched the cupboard door. The gleaming metal case looked snug, nestled in its little niche, surrounded by soft, anti static foam padding. I unfolded the built-in table, but the morning sun had not yet moved sufficiently high in the sky to shed daylight into the interior of the machine. The top of the desk remained in shadows. I pulled the case out and opened it atop the desk. I removed the computer and one diskette and went outdoors.

Out in the sunlight, I pushed the on button and the little green light came on and I could hear the laptop begin booting up. As it did I thought about how I would begin. So much had already happened, and yet my journey had hardly begun. And where *should* I begin? So many things occurred *before* the actual trip through time.

As the computer finished booting up, the main menu appearing on the screen, I used the built-in mouse to center the cursor over the word-processing icon and pressed the button. As the program came up I thought back to all the events that led me to make the decision to come to this place. It started long before the museum took away my dinosaurs, and even before Christine's death and Susan's injury. I went all the way back to that rainy autumn day in Chicago—the rain soaking my shoes as I stood before the gleaming silver casket.

I began to type. *The single drop slid down the aluminum pole …*

*****

For two weeks I wrote, all the while my strength returning, my cuts and bruises healing. From the first light of morning till the sun dropped below the horizon beyond the mountains, I sat at the laptop, my two index fingers flying across the keys. I had never fancied myself a writer, not much of a typist either, for that matter, but the words came easily, each paragraph coming faster than the one before, twenty and thirty pages a day.

I wrote quickly, and yet it was difficult. Bringing back all the painful details of the events of the past two years, the reasons for deciding to take the trip that landed me on this lonely patch of sand, was excruciating at times. It was like reliving them all over again. Each evening I was drinking more and more of the scotch, more often than not, falling asleep in the folding chair at the edge of the cave. At the rate that I was drinking it, I would be out within a month. But it helped me sleep at night, and helped me get through the first part of my story.

By the time my story was right up to the present, perhaps three weeks had passed since I had stepped down from the isolation chamber that had been my home for more than a week. It had been well over a month since I had any contact with anyone other than Dermot and his staff. I wondered what had changed in my old life.

I wondered how Jakes was doing, whether he had made any progress in finding Green, whether anyone was even following the case after all this time. I would never know, and to be honest with myself, I wasn't sure that I cared any more. His cohort, Sid, was dead, and it had brought me no satisfaction. If anything, I had felt sorry for the little shit. Life had short-changed him and he didn't deserve to die simply because he got paired up with a loser like Green.

Green, on the other hand, probably did deserve to die, and I wouldn't have shed a tear to learn that he did. But I seemed to have an entirely different perspective of things since making the trip through time. Things just didn't look quite the same from seventy million years in the past.

Liz and Christine's death, Susan's accident, Green's escape, and the loss of my dinosaurs, hadn't happened ... at least not yet. Everything in my life—my former life—was still a million lifetime's away. None of it had happened, and the thing that kept jumping into my mind was the fact that perhaps they never would. My mere presence in this ancient time proved that the past could be changed. Prior to my trip here, no human had lived during this time. No one had ever seen an *Elasmosaurus* swimming in the sea. No one had viewed the majesty of the beautiful *Pteranodon*, or one had witnessed, firsthand, the great sea that had extended clear across the North American continent. But I had, and that was proof enough for me that I had the power to make a difference.

Whether or not I could change things so far in the future was immaterial. Maybe the fact that I lived now, and would surely die within a few years—more than just a few—if I was extremely lucky, meant that I couldn't possibly be born again in the future. And wasn't I an integral part of all those unfortunate things that were to happen all those years in the future?

Wasn't Liz in front of that bank on that particular day because it was *my* birthday? And wasn't Susan, and then Christine, at the dig because *I* had set it up? And surely it was me who found the dinosaurs that my boss sold out from under me? Without *me*, how could any of these events have taken place? If I weren't there to be a part of it, could it really have happened at all?

And if I couldn't be born again in the future, how would Dermot be able to send me back into time? If he couldn't, then how did I get here? Could a person die before he was born? These were all rhetorical questions of course. I couldn't answer them, and there was no one else around who could. Rather than drive myself crazy, I decided to just accept the fact that I was here, now, and whatever happened in the future would just have to sort itself out.

And I would have another drink.

*****

My thoughts returned to Jakes. I hadn't been honest with him. I didn't have the courage to tell him that I had quit my job, and was going to be Dermot's guinea pig. I was afraid that he'd talk some sense into me. He was one persuasive guy, and I didn't want to be persuaded. Instead I simply told him that I had taken a leave of absence and was going on an extended vacation. Knowing my deep despair, my overwhelming sense of loss and frustration, he bought it. In a matter of days after I had left, he would learn the truth. Maybe when he found out that I had left him everything, he would forgive me.

It wasn't an easy thing, leaving Jakes all my worldly possessions—I wasn't dead, and I wasn't missing—although I was going to be. My lawyer had a little trouble with the idea that I was going to just disappear. Of course it didn't help any when I refused to tell him where I was going. I just told him I was going away and wasn't coming back, and, oh by the way—I wouldn't need any of my things. I really kind of enjoyed toying with him. I didn't like lawyers very much, even though I had known mine for quite a few years.

Despite his protests, I refused to budge, partly because I promised Dermot that I wouldn't tell anybody, partly because I knew that he wouldn't believe me, but mostly because I just liked fucking with him. In the end, my only option was to have myself declared missing and *presumed* dead. The problem was, it took seven years for the powers that be to make that ruling … and I couldn't very well have myself declared missing.

So, I did the next best thing. I put it in a letter to Jakes, and gave it to my attorney with instructions to mail it on a certain date—one-week after I was scheduled to make the journey. I made it a week rather than just the next day, because I knew that a thousand things could go wrong that would delay my trip. My lawyer simply shook his head when he took the sealed and notarized letter, and said, "You know something David, you're one crazy son of a bitch."

In the letter, I told Jakes everything—well, almost everything. He already knew about Dermot and his crazy experiment. He knew that I was Dermot's choice of subjects, and he knew about the cave in Utah. By now, he would have read the letter, and he would be after Dermot. Jakes was tenacious, like a dog with a bone. He would find Dermot in a matter of days, probably still at the cave. Jakes would demand answers. He would probably call Dermot a charlatan, a fraud, a dreamer, everything in the book. But Dermot had the upper hand. He had the tapes. On them, Jakes would see me leave the shelter of the sterile trailer, walk across the barren stretch of land before the cave, and enter the time machine. Twenty minutes later, he would witness the rings begin to shimmer and to move forward over the machine. A few moments later, he would see the time machine just disappear.

Some would have questioned what they saw with their own eyes, thinking it but an elaborate hoax. But Jakes was too smart for that, and he knew me. He knew that there was no point in trickery, and he knew me well enough to know that I was not into playing games—it wasn't my style. No, once he saw the tapes, he would know that it was real. He would know that I was really gone for good. What he didn't know, couldn't know, was whether I was alive or not.

Dermot would try to explain that, because the machine had not reappeared, I wasn't dead, but he would not be able to say with any real confidence exactly where, or *when*, I was. Dermot would be honest with Jakes. He would tell him where he tried to send me, but time travel wasn't an exact science. He only knew that I went back somewhere. And one thing was for sure—I wouldn't be returning.

I knew that Jakes would be angry—angry with Dermot—angry with me. He would be mad at Dermot because he had orchestrated the whole thing. He was the one who sought me out and convinced me do to this crazy thing. He was the one who sent me away—for good.

He would be madder at me because he would think me a quitter. I had given in to the little setbacks in my life rather than facing them head on and beating them. It's what he would have done. Mostly, he would be mad at me because I was his friend—his best friend—and now I was gone.

But Jakes wouldn't be mad at me for long, and not just because I was his friend, and not only because he wasn't the kind of person to stay mad. Once he thought about it, the anger would melt away like the frost on a spring morning. He would see that making this trip was the only thing that I could have done. It was the chance of a lifetime. For a paleontologist, it was a-dream-come-true. And there was nothing to keep me there in his time.

Yes, by now, Jakes would have gotten over it. He probably had a great big smile on his face from my letter, which he would have read by now. In it, I told Jakes the truth about almost everything—where I was going, and when I hoped to end up. I told him not to worry about me. I had a safe place to live, and I was packing heat—just like him. And I wasn't going to be lonely. I was going to get a pet just like he had always nagged me to do... can one train a dinosaur?

I told Jakes things that I could never quite tell him face to face. Like how he saved me after Susan's murder by just being there for me—by understanding my grief. How he talked ... and drank ... me through the blame that I placed on myself following the dual tragedies at the cave. How he let me into his little family, making me feel that they were my own, like I always had some place to go. Mostly, I told him that he was my friend, my best friend—perhaps my only true friend

But I didn't quite tell Jakes everything. I didn't tell him about the money. He wouldn't have cared about it, probably would have been embarrassed to be the beneficiary of my entire monetary worth, me not being a blood relative. But, it would be a nice surprise seven years from now, I mean, seven years from then. I hoped it would accelerate his retirement—get him into a safer line of work—pay for his kid's education. With investments and the equity in my home, it should have added up to well over half a million dollars. If my lawyer invested it right, by the time it was Jakes' it should be worth twice as much.

There was a provision to my generosity, even though it would take seven years before Jakes understood that it was a condition of my gift. I actually had two letters delivered to Jakes, one for him, one for Susan. In my letter to him, I had asked that he look in on Susan from time to time—not to incur any financial responsibility—I had already taken care of that by transferring her power of attorney and inheritance to my lawyer. No, I just wanted him to visit her once in a while and talk to her, to let her know that I hadn't forgotten her, and that someone was still there for her ... and to give her the letter.

The letter to Susan was much like the one I had written to Jakes, but longer, much longer. She knew nothing about what we had found in the cave in Utah, nothing about Christine's death. For that matter, she didn't even know who Christine was. She hadn't learned of the discovery of Liz's murderer, and his subsequent escape from justice. In her mind, just learning about what my boss had done with our discovery would have justified my risky trip into the past.

In my letter, I told her of my visit to her house and finding her will. I chastised her for not telling me about the massive remodeling ... and about the books. I wrote at length of the fascinating discovery in the cave and how I posed the skeletons. She already knew about Jakes, and I filled her in on how great our friendship had become. I told her about all the bad stuff as well—Julius Green and his partner Sid, the little girl, Christine, who died because of my stupidity, and the selling of my dinosaurs.

And I told her that I loved her.

In the hospital I had said all those things hundreds of times, but I didn't know how much, if any, had actually gotten through to her. It was important to me that she know everything—the reasons why I left her—why I was willing to just walk away from everything. But, most important, I wanted her to know that she was loved. If she ever recovered, I wanted her to know everything, and everything was in the letter.

I knew that Jakes would deliver the letter if that time should ever come, and I was sure that he would visit her regularly, for as long as it took. I continued to hope the day would come that she would awaken and resume her life, but I would never know. It was the most painful part of my decision to make the journey, and the thing that had haunted it ever since the day it began

I had hired a caretaker for Susan's home, giving him the key and strict instructions as to how to maintain it. He was to make sure the furnace was working in the winter, the roof was kept free of leaks, and the faucets free of drips. He was to hire groundskeepers to trim the grass and shrubs, and a cleaning person to come in once a month to remove the accumulation of dust. Under no circumstance was he to make any unnecessary changes to the house, no improvements, and no resumption of Susan's reconstruction. It was Susan's home, and it would remain unchanged until she returned to it.

I had been to the house one last time to make sure that everything was buttoned up tight. When I was there before I left in such a hurry that I wasn't sure how I had left it. I was confused and terrified when I plummeted down the steps, stumbled though the kitchen, and out through the window, into the hands of the local constabulary. I had just discovered some pretty incredible things. The magnificence of the top floor, would in itself, have left me pretty amazed, but the contents of Susan's desk, her last will and testament, had left me dumbfounded.

When I returned, I was a different person. I had learned so much about Susan since that last trip, and so much more about myself. I entered her home with the understanding that she was so much more that I had known before. My love for her had grown immeasurably between visits.

As I had the previous time, I entered her house as a thief. I was stupid to do it the first time—more stupid to do it a second. I had a right to be there—Susan's last will, and my lawyer said I did. I could have easily taken the paperwork to the police, and avoided any problems, but that last time was a very private moment—I didn't want to discuss it with anyone, didn't want to get anyone's permission.

I had been with Susan earlier that day. I had spent several hours with her without saying a word. There was nothing more *to* say. To speak then would have only made me second-guess myself. She couldn't talk, at least not in the physical sense. But I knew her so well, had spent so many hundreds of hours in a kind of one-way conversation with her, I had begun to believe that she was talking back, sort of a telepathic link between the two of us. I would speak out loud, and she would answer, just a whisper of a voice that went directly to my mind, bypassing the normal auditory canals.

When I talked with her, I knew her responses even before the words left my lips. If I asked her a question, she answered to my mind before the sound of my voice faded from the room. But during that last day, I feared her answers, afraid that the phantom voice that spoke to me would suddenly turn on me, change, because of my own fear and confusion. I didn't want her to talk me out of it.

And I was afraid of an emotional scene as well. I was leaving for Utah in the morning. Where I would end up was all theory. If I survived the trip was mere conjecture. Whether the experiment was successful or not, I knew that this was the last time that I would ever see her. So I just sat at her bedside, staring at her beautiful face. It was the day before leaving for Utah—it was the last time that I would ever see her. Before I walked out of her room, I bent down and kissed her warm lips, without saying goodbye—walking away, without looking back.

I had saved my good-byes for the house. The house was no mere inanimate object. It had a life of its own—Susan's life. There was more of the real Susan there, in that house, than there was in the fragile, unconscious body lying in the cold Chicago nursing home. This is where she lived, what she lived *for*. It's where her heart was.

I had a key, but I didn't use it. I entered through the laundry room, just as I had before. I told myself that I needed to check to see if the window was still unlatched, accessible to anyone who happened to wander by. Really though, I needed to come into the house the same way that I did the last time. The eeriness of it, the sense of wonder, as I explored the house, the magnificent discoveries that I had made on that night was, one of my most vivid memories, one of the things that I would marvel at until the day that I died. I wanted it to be the same on that last night before my world was turned upside down. It would be my last trip to the house that was so important to Susan. I wanted it to be special to me, also.

This time, I wasn't terrified by the unknown, not spooked by every dark recess and wandering shadow, not anticipating horrors behind every closed door. But I didn't race through the lower-floor rooms, knowing what I would find, or wouldn't find, in them. I took my time, not searching, but just soaking it all in. It was an amazing house, even though incomplete. It showed so much promise. I wanted to capture every image. I wanted to memorize every detail of the house, both the completed portions, and the undone parts. I wanted to plan for its completion.

As a tribute to Susan, and as a way of linking the two of us through our separation, beyond the millennia that kept us apart, I was going to finish her home ... and not just in my imagination. It's why I had Dermot fill one container with all kinds of art supplies. I was going to finish Susan's home for her ... at least on paper. I owed it to her.

So on that night, I took my time, storing away all that I could in my mind, getting the feel of each room, memorizing the layout. That night I studied the pattern of the carpet throughout the first floor, rather than just looking at the worn threads between the front door and the grand staircase. I looked closely at the detail of the carved wood paneling and trim, instead of just noting its dull, dusty finish. I looked beyond the delicate cobwebs stretched across the elaborate chandelier to see the beauty of the brass fixtures and cut-glass sconces. I counted the stairs to the second floor, rather than simply sneaking up them.

And on that night, I refused to let a few stuck doors keep me from seeing each room on the second floor. There were no surprises there, no monsters hiding behind the door, no cache of treasures or new surprises from Susan. They were just more rooms—bedrooms and closets—the odd piece of furniture, and plenty of dust, mold and mildew. As I suspected, the rooms had been locked away behind the stuck doors for many years. Perhaps even Susan had not entered them before.

I still hadn't turned on the lights, relying on the beam of my flashlight—just as I had the year before. I had already seen most of the rooms, but it was different somehow—this time. I wasn't racing through each room, afraid of being caught, afraid of being somewhere where I wasn't supposed to be. I didn't simply shine the light into each room—quickly—afraid of being discovered. I took a long, leisurely tour through each room, checking out the detail, measuring each space by the number of steps that I took.

It was obvious that Susan hadn't put forth any effort to reconstruct these rooms. None of them showed any improvement, or cleaning for that manner, for maybe fifty years. I thought that perhaps I would find at least one room where the work had started. The upper floor seemed complete. I wondered where she was moving her efforts. But there was no clue. She must have left for the dig in Utah before she had a chance to begin on the next floor.

I started up the last flight of steps, the light of the flashlight leading the way up the narrow passage. As I approached the door to the attic, I was surprised to find myself sweating, the hand holding the light shaking. I knew what lay behind the door, and yet I felt the same sense of dread, the same nervousness that I felt the first time. Maybe I was afraid that it would be gone, like it had been nothing but a fairy tale dream. Perhaps I had imagined it all.

Like before, I slipped my hand through the partially opened door and found the light switch. I flipped it on and simultaneously pushed the door open.

Nothing had changed—it had not been a dream.

If anything, it was even more breathtaking than I remembered. The bright lights reflected off the honey-colored woodwork in an infinite, dazzling display. The reds and blacks that Susan had decorated with seemed even brighter, more intense, and more beautiful than I remembered.

I looked up at the stained-glass window, seeing once again the prehistoric scene captured there. It was a volcanic mountain range, the sky red with fire, likewise, the molten rock running down its side. The foreground was a forest scene, replete with ferns and flowering plants—some of them seemed familiar, others not. A single pair of winged animals was flying away from the glowing mountain peak. They were too small, and the reflection bouncing from the intricate panes of glass made it impossible to tell for sure, but I bet if the sun had been shining, light streaming through the hundreds of pieces of leaded glass, I would know that they were *Pteranodons*.

I stared at the scene, wondering why it seemed so familiar to me. It was yet another shock when it finally came to me. Susan hadn't designed it—I had. It was a drawing I had done years ago to accompany an article that I had written about life in the Cretaceous. She had asked me for it, never stating a reason other than she liked it. And this was it—exactly—right down to the pair of *Pteranodons*.

The two figures in the stained glass were dark, nothing but an indistinct dark blur, but I knew they were supposed to be *Pteranodon*— they looked just as I had drawn them. At the time I didn't know exactly what the winged creatures looked like—now I did.

I had spent a long time standing in rapt attention in front of Susan's magnificent window. Anyone would have—it was absolutely beautiful, and yet haunting at the same time. It was a scene from hell—the end of the world. It was exactly what I was trying to portray—the day, sixty five million years ago (five million years from now, if Dermot's calculations were precise) when the great comet struck. The blast sent out shock waves across the globe, created worldwide volcanic eruptions that would, in the months to come, blanket the earth with thick ash, choking the atmosphere, blocking the sun, killing off entire species—the dinosaurs included.

As *I* did, Susan believed in the comet theory of the mass extinction at the KT boundary. She believed it and it pissed her off. She had even named the comet—*That Fucking Rock*. She blamed it for depriving the world of some of nature's most beautiful creatures, for abruptly ceasing millions of years of evolution before its conclusion. Who knew if other factors would have resulted in their eventual extinction? Perhaps the climatic change that began to occur later in the Cretaceous period, perhaps disease, or a food shortage. Perhaps their eggs were destroyed or consumed by the growing population of smaller mammals before they had a chance to hatch and grow to adulthood. Even had they survived, would man's earliest ancestors hunt them to extinction as they did the mammoth and the mastodon? No one would ever know for sure, but Susan blamed it on the comet—*That Fucking Rock*.

It was what I was trying to depict in my drawing, and what Susan had captured so beautifully in the glass—the lush green foliage in the foreground, the beautiful flying animals fleeing the terrible scene on the top of the mountain. It was the beginning of the end—the end of paradise.

I found it beautiful, but I stood there for another reason. During the next few days I hoped to find out whether it was accurate or not.

But on that night, I was on a mission. I wanted to see Susan's house, to be close to her one last time, to fix the imprint and the feeling of the house in my mind and in my soul. And, oh yeah, I was there to steal something.

I took one last look around, circling the room, glancing in on the elegant bathroom, stepping into the massive closet. I held a silk blouse to my face and took a deep breath, inhaling the fragrance that was distinctly Susan's. My eyes clouded and I wept into the soft, expensive fabric. I couldn't take it any more. I crossed to the library wall, pulled the twelve Lacy Wanderlust novels from the bookshelf and fled the house nearly as fast and as panicked as I was the last time.

*****

All of this had happened just a few, short weeks ago, yet it seemed like a lifetime ago—someone else's lifetime. It seemed like it had happened to someone else. So much had separated me from what I once was. Nearly everything that I had once cared about—had once loved—was gone. I was no longer someone's husband—someone's best friend ... someone's experiment. It was all behind me—not by days, or months, or even years. I was separated from it all by millions of years—a million lifetimes. It couldn't have been me who had lived all those generations ago. It had to have been someone else.

I couldn't get over the feeling that I was separated by distance and not just by time. It felt as if I was on the other side of the world—on some remote deserted island, isolated from everyone else by thousands of miles ... not millions of years. If I could but cross the vast sea that stretched eastward from the cave, I would again find civilization.

It seemed that way because I didn't feel any different that I had before. From my sheltered view of things, everything *looked* the same. The sky was the same radiant blue, the sun rose into it the same blazing ball of white-yellow. The air smelled the same and tasted the same. It expanded my lungs in the same way that it always had. And it felt the same—cool in the evenings—warming through the day, hot enough when the sun was high in the sky to make me break a sweat. Other than the sea, which wasn't there before, it seemed like every other late spring at the cave in Utah.

Based on the temperature and the length of daylight hours, I was guessing that I had landed sometime in late spring, about the same time of year as when I left. It got pretty hot when the sun was directly overhead, in the lower to mid-eighties according to my thermometer, but the nights cooled off considerably, enough where I needed one of my blankets when I went to bed.

I had found the wind-up clock that Dermot had given me. Somehow, miraculously, it had survived the trip. The glass face was cracked, but the mechanism still worked. I wound it and the pendulum kept moving back and forth on its own. I had nothing to compare it to so I couldn't be sure that it was keeping good time, but by checking it each day against the rising and setting of the sun, I could adjust it pretty closely. It's how I knew that it was late spring and not early fall—the days were getting longer.

I was determined to track the passage of time as accurately as possible. Of course I would never be able to know the year more closely that a couple million, and I was a long way from being able to do that. I hadn't seen enough of my new world to even venture a guess. The couple of extinct animals that I had encountered to that point led me to believe that I was indeed in the late Cretaceous period, but that extended over a pretty lengthy period—some thirty million years.

Nevertheless, I could still note the number of days as they passed, marking each event, each discovery, as day number such and such, noting each season as they came and went, each year that I survived. And at some point I would *guestimate* the date as well—not the year, but the month and day. I figured that I could come pretty close based on the climatic change from day to day—from month to month.

In the larger scheme of things, did it really matter? Of course not! But there were certain days that were important to me—Liz's birthday, our anniversary, the day of Susan's accident, the day that Christine died, the holidays, the day that I left my world. Not all happy days, but important days ... to me. I intended to recognize them, to celebrate or honor them, in one way or another. I just had to figure out when they were.

I had defined the day that I made the trip into the past as day one, in the year one. At some point in time I would define the month and the day, but not yet. I had guessed that it was late spring, but that was only based on my experiences of the late twentieth century when certain temperatures at specific times of the year were typical, and expected. But geographic evidence said that the late Cretaceous period had moderate seasons—not too hot, not too cold. The polar caps didn't exist during most of the period, thus winters were thought to be mild. However, much had changed from the beginning of the epoch to the end. And I had no idea just *when* the hell I was.

Perhaps at the beginning of the Cretaceous period there was no discernable change in seasons—one day, one month, year after year—was the same as the next. But as the ages passed, there were changes. Ice began to form in the north and in the south, changing the conditions, colder in the north, hotter in the south. By the end of the period, the difference in seasons may have been as severe as those experienced in the time of modern history ...perhaps more severe.

But for now, the climate was moderate. Whether or not it would stay that way was something that only time would tell. I would record the temperatures throughout the day, comparing them from one day to the next, noting any discernable change, any trends one way or the other. If winter lay ahead, I would know it.

So here I was in day nineteen, in the year one. Nineteen days was yet another guess. I wasn't really too sure how long it had been between the day of the journey and the one in which I landed on the beach—at least a day—perhaps as many as three. I split the difference at two. Seventeen days had passed since then. Of that I was sure—seventeen sunsets—seventeen sunrises. And seventeen was too many.

I had done nothing in all that time to prepare for the future. I had accomplished little beyond sitting at the computer, eating, drinking and sleeping. I had not gone beyond the mountainous boundaries imposed upon this small stretch of beach, had done nothing to see what lay beyond. Sooner or later I was going to run out of food, run out of drinkable water, run out of things to write in my computer … run out of things to do.

I had a year's worth of supplies, but at the rate that I was consuming them, I wouldn't make a full year. My foodstuffs were designed to get me started, a mere supplement as I became accustomed to my new environment, to carry me through the rough times during the first few months, to last until I had planted and harvested my first crop, until I learned how to trap and kill.

I had a sea filled with fish at my disposal, just a few hundred paces from the mouth of the cave, but I was going to get pretty damn sick of fish after a while. And there were no dinosaurs in the sea, and wasn't that what I was here for? It was time to begin to explore my new world.

I had two options: One, I could scale the slope of the cliff that wrapped around the water's edge to the north, back in the direction that I emerged from the underground river some two weeks ago. Or, two, I could inflate the rubber dingy, and head south along the cliffs on that side, and see what was around the bend.

But I already knew at least a few hundred yards of the northern trek—sheer rock cliff that went on for who knew how long. Besides, I wasn't in the mood to go back in the direction of the water-filled cavern that damn near took my life. To the south, on the other hand, was uncharted territory. Perhaps just around the bend I would find what I was searching for.

In the early part of the Cretaceous period, some one hundred and forty five million years ago, there were no polar caps, thus the global water levels were several hundred feet above where they were in modern times. Much of what became North America was covered with water, including the great Epicontinental Sea that divided the continent in half, extending halfway across what many years later became the state of Utah. The sea extended for more than six hundred miles to the east, covering nearly half of what was to become the western United States.

By the end of the period the ice caps at both poles had begun to form, and, as they did, water levels began to drop. The immense body of water separating the two halves of North America gradually receded, leaving the Great Salt Lake as a singular reminder of what once was. Most of what became California surfaced, and what was left was thousands of square miles of mud, sand, and gravel.

The trouble was, there were a couple of million years for error. The water levels dropped over a period of millions of years, but couldn't be pinpointed closer than that. And, to make matters worse, I was sent back into time with a margin of error of a couple of million years. The point being—where was the water level in the era that I ended up in? That's why I had insisted on the rubber dinghy.

The raft was packed into a box smaller than I would have thought possible—not more than one cubic foot. Along with it were a couple of cans of compressed air with which to inflate it. If I had to inflate it beyond that, I was on my own—I would see if all those years of exercise gave me the required lung capacity. There were also a couple of oars, three actually. I guess that Dermot thought that I might need a spare. I couldn't help but wonder, why just one spare? If I was to lose one, chances are I would lose them both. Perhaps he thought one would be broken during the trip—they *were* made of wood.

But all three had survived the trip, as most everything else had. It took no more than a few minutes to inflate the dinghy and attach the oars to the pivots molded in the sidewalls of the raft. I dragged it out to the shoreline and walked back to the machine—there were a few items that I still needed.

I hadn't planned to be gone very long, no more than twelve hours—at most. I would be back before nightfall. So I needed some water and a bit of food, at least enough for one light meal. But more than anything else I needed some firepower. I had no idea what to expect as I ventured from my protected cove. I selected a rifle, one with a wide range of fire, a shotgun.

I felt like a child. I had never owned a gun in my life, never even fired one. Dermot had taken a couple of hours to show each one to me, how to load, how to fire, muzzle velocities, range—everything. I think that there were even manuals for each one. The problem was, there just wasn't enough time to actually fire one. Hell, I'd probably shoot myself in the foot—or worse. Maybe I'd shoot a hole in my foot *and* in the raft and have to tread water all the way back to the cove.

CHAPTER 14

It was daylight when I pushed the dinghy from the white sand into the slow-rolling surf, but it was early, the sun a huge radiant ball just clearing the razor-sharp line formed by the waters of the Western Interior Sea. Its rays reflected off the water in shimmering tones of gold and silver, but even with the fierce glare, once I passed the white foam along the shore, I could see through the crystal clear water to the bottom. There was an abundance of small fish of all colors, even though their images were distorted by the reflections of the indirect sunlight. Not being an expert in the field, I didn't know one from another, but some looked familiar, others did not. I thought that there were some that probably wouldn't look familiar even to the best of experts.

There were also a number of shellfish, many of which I was familiar with, having already plucked them from the beach during my morning forages. They were all very tasty, but, once again, I didn't know what half of them were. What was most amazing was their size. Some were no bigger than what I was used to, but some were gigantic, two and three times the size of anything that I had seen in the seafood shops and restaurants. I wondered if they simply grew larger during this time, or if the centuries of man's hunting them had somehow shortened their life span, or interfered with their normal growth in some way. Or perhaps it was the pollution of the earth's waters that had stunted their growth. Either way, they were bigger now than they were then, or is it that they were bigger *then* than were *now*. I was still trying to get the hang of being in the past and thinking of the future.

Because of the clarity of the water, it was hard to judge the depth, although I suspected it was deeper than it looked. I had rowed about two hundred yards out, still under the illusion that the bottom was only a few feet beneath me. I was overcome with the temptation to jump in and do a little bit of wading in the clear water. I sprung over the side, coiling my legs, anticipating hitting the bottom immediately and shooting back to the top without having to let go of the edge of my little raft.

But the bottom wasn't where I thought it was and I plunged down farther than I anticipated, way over my head. Thinking that it would only be waist deep, I hadn't taken much of a breath before I jumped in, and inadvertently, I sucked in a mouthful of salt water in surprise when my feet refused to touch solid ground. I panicked, struggling in the water, the sudden pain in my lungs forcing out what I had just sucked in.

I hit bottom, perhaps eight or ten feet down, my legs still bent at the knees so that my ass bounced against the hard-packed sand. By sheer instinct, I pushed with my legs, straightening them, propelling me back toward the surface. I came up underneath the raft, causing a secondary bout of panic, unsure for just a moment, where I was and what I had struck. I thrashed with my arms, easily pushing aside the lightweight dinghy. I pushed my face into the light, breaking the surface of the water, choking and spitting up water. Thankfully, I had decided to skip breakfast that morning.

As I struggled to climb back into the dinghy I was struck by the fact that I had been in this prehistoric sea just twice—both times I ended up nearly drowning.

I was beginning to think that my seaside home was not the ideal setting for me. Funny—an isolated place like this in the twentieth century would be worth millions: beautiful white sands, a spectacular view, and neighbors not within—well, anything. However, so far, it wasn't proving to be an ideal spot for me. All I could think about was a way to move to solid ground—as far as I could get away from this goddamned water.

I lay in the bottom of the raft, now filled with several inches of water, and thought about what the hell I was doing there. Here I was, the only human being in the world, a nice warm day, nothing chasing me, no place that I had to get to in a hurry, not much of a care in the world. Yet, I had to get out of the damn boat … and damn near kill myself in the process. The scientist in me, the need to explore, to check out every situation, was going to get me killed.

I continued to lie there in a pool of water that was growing ever warmer by the approaching sun. I began to laugh, just a giggle, but with a broad smile across my face. It had occurred to me that no matter what happened to me, I couldn't go back. I had made my bed. Now I had nothing to do but lie in it. And I *was* lying in it—three or four inches of it.

It felt good to laugh. It was cathartic—healing. I was approaching this thing as a scientist—making observations, recording data, analyzing that data, drawing conclusions, and developing theories. But the fact of the matter was—I was on my own. All in all, it was all bullshit. There was no one to tell me if my theories were right or wrong, no one to argue with, no one to provide contradictory proof. No one had ever been in my position—I *was* the expert.

I had felt a moment of embarrassment as I surfaced alongside the raft, before I remembered where I was. One would have thought that I had never been in the water before. For just a moment I thought what if somebody saw me? They would think that I didn't know how to swim—when in reality I was a pretty damn good swimmer. The embarrassment only lasted for a few seconds as I realized that there were no other people ... anywhere. And I doubted that the fish and crabs noticed a thing.

Basically, I needed to lighten up.

So I took a dip in the drink. I had a scare—no more than that. I just needed to think before I acted—not like a scientist—just a normal, semi-intelligent human being. The depth of the water had surprised me. I wasn't used to seeing water so clean, able to see the bottom so clearly from ten feet. I needed to be prepared for more surprises. I suspected that when I found a way around these mountains, I was in for a lot more of them.

I was intact, as was my little boat. The oars were just as I had placed them in their divots. My gun was right where I left it, propped up against the side of the raft with the barrel out of the water. Nothing was lost other that just a bit of pride, and no one would ever know about that. I grasped both ends of my oars and started paddling farther along to the south.

I continued to move parallel to the cliffs on my right, ever aware of the sandy sea bottom, watching for the signs of marine life below me. Constantly I scanned the horizon to my left, knowing that there were creatures that might come at me from the surface, not just from underneath. I stayed about two hundred yards out, the cliffs seeming to go on forever, rising from the sea, at first as a gentle slope, but increasing in angle the farther I went.

The sun was approaching the mountains and was directly overhead, reflecting off the nearly still waters, making me squint as I stared at the face of the cliff. It had been probably three hours since I had left the beach. The mountain now rose straight up from beneath deep waters. I could no longer see the bottom even when I paddled in close to the smooth surface of the rock.

I reached out, touching the sheer edge of the mountain, steadying the boat as it rose and fell with the shallow waves, rubbing up against the vertical granite. Looking straight up from my position caused a moment of vertigo. With my head spinning, I nearly fell from the boat once again. Instead I eased down into the dinghy, flat on my back and continued to gaze at the spot where the top of the cliff met the clear blue skies.

Two *Pteranodons* circled overhead, chasing one another—an avian game of tag. They glided along silently, effortlessly, trimming their wings one way, then the other, catching the gentle breezes as they deflected upward from the side of the mountain.

With the sun behind them, they were nothing but remote black shapes, distinguishable only by the odd shape of their heads, which were huge—all beak and crest—very little intelligence. Or so their relatively small brain pans indicated. And why not? Nature tended to more fully develop the intellect of those that needed the smarts to protect themselves from deadly predators. Watching the pair soaring high in the Utah sky lent credence to the theory. There were not many things, even in this time of fierce, flesh-eating animals, for them to fear.

I was envious as I watched them disappear behind the cliff, and reappear moments later, able to see what I could not. At four or five hundred feet, they could see both sides of the mountains—I couldn't see beyond the wall of rock bumping against the right side of my little boat. What sights were they seeing? What wonders were just beneath their wings? What dramas were unfolding on the other side of this mountain?

But Dermot had packed a rubber dinghy, not an airplane, or even a helicopter. One of those little one passenger jobs would have been just fine, despite the fact that I wasn't a great fan of flying, and I always thought those guys in the ultra-lights just a few bricks short of a load. I would have risked it for just one quick peek over the mountain.

I continued to watch and fantasize as the *Pteranodons* glided back and forth, in and out of view until, on one trip, they didn't return. I wondered where they went, what they did when they weren't soaring through the skies, weren't swooping down to catch their lunch from the surface of the crystal sea. Where did they live? *How* did they live? Did they build a nest like the birds, high above the earth on an outcropping of rock? Were there eggs in the nest, or did they produce live young like other mammals? It was one of a million questions I would answer when I got around this mountain. With a sigh, I returned back to my paddles and pushed off from the rock.

I paddled on for another two hours, and other than the sun continuing farther along its westward arc, an-ever growing shadow that stretched inch by inch across the sea, the scenery didn't change at all. The sun was behind the mountain, well past its highest point, telling me that it was time to head back. Disappointed at not finding a southern way out of the range, I decided to travel away from the cliff to gain a wider perspective, hoping that I would see a sign that there was indeed an end to the hundreds of feet of towering rock.

I traveled out several hundred yards, perhaps half a mile, but the view didn't change very much. A few of the higher peaks became visible behind the cliffs at the water's edge. The cliffs themselves, however, seemed to stretch on forever, mile after mile of monotonous run until they merged with the far off horizon—no stretches of beach, no interior passageways, no vegetation – just more rock coming straight out of the water.

Stroking with only one oar, I turned the little boat so that my back was to the cliffs. As I began to pull on the two paddles, beginning the journey back to the mountain and then northward back to my beach, I glanced across the vast sea.

A hundred yards away the head of an *Elasmosaurus* broke the surface of the still water. I watched as it rose twenty feet above the surface, perched upon an impossibly long gray neck that thickened as it emerged from the water like a gigantic snake. Behind the neck, the top portion of its body rose out of the water several feet, the same steely-gray covering that area as well. Around it, I could see the water boiling as its flippers brought it to the surface.

It came out of the water, facing south, out to sea, and away from my position. I let go of the oars and held my breath, thinking that if it were unaware of my presence, it would simply swim off without seeing me. But it circled in the water, scanning its surroundings, searching for its next meal.

I remained still, unsure of its visual acuity, hoping that it relied on movement to see. It kept turning, full circle, until it was facing me. Immediately the strange high-pitched clicking that I had heard in the underground river started, and I knew that it had spotted me.

It started after me, slowly at first, unsure of what it had found. As I reached for the oars I wondered if it was the same one that I encountered in the cave. If it was, was it more angry—or wary? Either way, it was coming in my direction, and I wasn't sticking around to find out.

I began pulling on the oars, slowly, matching the creature's speed. I knew that I couldn't outrun it, and I had nowhere to go that I'd be safe. I could only hope that it would lose interest. It had spotted me, but seemed only curious, hopefully indifferent.

I had closed half the distance to the cliffs, and it had lessened the gap between us only slightly. I picked up my pace, trying to reach land, even if there was no way onto it. Suddenly it stopped and began bobbing its head, up and down, and side to side. I stopped rowing at the same instant that the strange clicking sound came to an abrupt halt. Slowly, afraid that any sudden movement would startle the huge animal into action, I reached for the shotgun. Almost as if it anticipated my next move it dove into the sea, its small pointed tail flipped high into the air for an instant before following its large body down below.

I clicked the safety off on my weapon and sat there cradling it in my lap, my heart pounding in my chest, cold sweat trickling down the small of my back. There was an eerie stillness, the extreme kind of quietness that speaks of impending doom—the calm before the storm. The sea had gone dead, and the muted sounds of waves lapping at the cliff had died away.

Several minutes passed—agonizingly slow, but nothing happened, not a sound—not a movement. It was as if the world had just stopped in its tracks, suspending all movement, swallowing up all sound. I peered into the sky hoping to see the *Pteranodons* ... or anything else. But, with the exception of the sun, the sky was as empty as the feeling within me.

I lowered my gaze to the clear water, seeing a dark shape circling below. As I leaned over the side to get a better look, the creature burst from the water on the opposite side of the boat. Startled, I fell overboard, catching the side with one arm, keeping me from going completely under the water.

The *Elasmosaurus* rose high above me, water cascading down, threatening to swamp my little boat. I held on tightly as the creature shot to the surface, tossing the boat across the water. Its neck was bowed, the head lowered, pointed directly towards me. Its head was surprisingly small, yet its mouth was huge, filled with dozens of small, sharp, deadly teeth. It approached closer, the mouth open wide, water continuing to fall upon the raft in waves. It reached out a dark purple-black tongue, bisected with half-healed scars, and licked the opposite side of the raft.

The monster then threw its head back and let out a familiar screech before lunging downward. I froze, terrified, and closed my eyes—sure that it was the end. But instead of feeling pain or the nothingness of sudden death, I heard a popping sound and the hiss of air escaping, as the rubber dinghy jumped backward several feet, me holding on for dear life.

My eyes flew opened as I realized what had happened. The *Elasmosaurus*, not having ever seen the likes of the raft or of me, struck at the closest object, luckily for me, the wrong one. It punctured the side of the rubber wall, and the dinghy was rapidly deflating. The animal, despite not being one of the more intelligent of the prehistoric creatures, was smart enough to know that it had made a mistake. It raised its head one more time, the clicking sound starting again, increasing in frequency as it readied itself for another strike.

Knowing that I wouldn't get a third chance, I reached for my gun before it went down with the boat. Pushing away from it, churning my legs to stay as high in the water as I could, I raised the gun to my shoulder. I looked up to see the monster's face three feet from my own. It snorted, mucus flying from its nostrils, nearly blinding me. It seemed to waver for a moment, trying to decide whether I was more delectable than its last taste of something unfamiliar.

Its head wandered from left to right, and from right to left, never taking its eyes from me, when, suddenly, the ear-piercing shriek started again and its neck ached backward. Surprisingly, I saw with incredible clarity the event that was about to be played out. I raised the shotgun with blurred vision as the monster began to attack.

It wasn't a lightening move. At least that's how I saw it. But, rather, it seemed to move almost in slow motion. I tracked the movement of its head as it towered above me, slowing lowering itself to meet me: water, or maybe saliva dripping down on top of me. I was nearly prone in the water, my legs still frog kicking, not trying to escape, just trying to keep my aim true, aligned with its gaping jaws. It seemed to drop right into the barrel of my weapon, just inches away, when I squeezed the trigger.

I watched its head explode, sending out a cloud of red and silver—blood, brain, and skin—that dissipated as it went the way of the soft afternoon breeze. For a split second, I saw the long neck straighten, and then, coil upon itself and drop into the sea with a resounding *plop*.

The bubbling water before me was crimson with the creature's blood, and I felt the warm fluid flow over my face as I struggled to remain upright in the water. My ship, as well, was covered with the carnage as I watched it slowly sink into the briny foam.

I dropped below the surface of the water to rinse myself of the gore, my eyes open, seeing the creature begin to sink to the depths. As I popped to the surface I suddenly realized that the gun was still tightly in my grip. I was angry with myself for having gotten it soaked. I had no idea whether it would still fire, and then it occurred to me—the extra shells had gone down with the raft. The rifle was useless without shells, and although I had several more boxes back at the machine, I had five or six miles of sea to swim to get to them. The gun would only weigh me down. I let it drop into the sea.

With my legs, I pushed away from the bloody scene, out towards the open water. When I had cleared the area, I pressed my hands against the water, pushing it to one side, causing my body to rotate. My eyes took in the vast expanse of the sea.

Not twenty yards away were three huge dorsal fins, brilliant blue, almost metallic in the bright afternoon sunlight, and they were headed right for me. There was no escape, absolutely no way out. I did nothing other than turn my back to them, wrap my arms around my body, and close my eyes.

Forcing my legs to stop flailing, I began to drop below the surface, my heart racing—the rest of me as still as could be—my eyes tightly closed. My heart seized up and my blood turned to ice as one of the sharks brushed against me, its skin rubbing against my own, causing me to spin in the water, sinking farther.

Several seconds passed when, suddenly, the water began to churn in front of me. I dared open my eyes, and all I could see was turmoil. The water was boiling and bubbling, white-water, that tumbled me end over end. I swam to get away from the commotion, and shot to the surface.

An incredible, but horrifying, sight met me as I broke the skin of the water. Sixty feet away was a vision from a nightmare. A circular area, whose circumference nearly reached where I was treading water, was bubbling like a witch's cauldron—huge bubbles that burst when they hit the surface, sending out bright red gore in all directions. It rained down upon me, grisly pieces of *Elasmosaurus* mixed with the pink-tinged water. The sharks had found their next meal—one that I had so graciously provided.

I watched in stunned fascination as the four rose to the surface. I should have swum for my life, but I just sat there, treading water as the carnage continued. The *Elasmosaurus* was already dead, so I didn't feel any compassion for it as it was ripped to shreds, but the efficient way in which it was devoured was mesmerizing. There was no methodology to it, no taking turns, no taking their time. The animal was already dead. There was no reason to hurry, and at forty feet in length and well over three tons of meat, there was plenty for everyone. But the sharks were in a feeding frenzy, and nothing was going to slow them down. Just like their modern-day counterparts, they would eat the entire animal, regurgitating the indigestible parts later on.

I watched as they devoured the beast, lunging at anything that was red, everything that smelled of meat. They were adult sharks, each between fifteen and twenty feet in length. They were a dazzling cobalt blue at the tips of their dorsal fins and across their backs, fading to a medium gray through its midsection, to a pure white on its underbelly. They were thicker through the midsection, and perhaps a bit more colorful, and reminded me of a twentieth century mako shark. They were *Cretoxyrhina mantelli*.

The *mantelli* was a late Cretaceous shark that was believed to have become extinct about eighty million years ago, fifteen million years before the K-T boundary, and several million years before the time that I was supposed to be in. Almost everything known about the *mantelli* came from fossil teeth and a few bits of vertebrae. Sharks, like most species of fish, have a skeletal structure that is more similar to cartilage than to calcified bone, thus few remnants exist in the modern world. But the teeth, which have been found in abundance in the Upper Cretaceous sediments of the Western Interior Seaway, particularly in an area around what was to become Kansas, had been dated at eighty-two to eighty-seven million years. Either the experts were wrong about the demise of the mako shark's ancestors, or I wasn't quite where I was supposed to be.

Other than the physical similarities to the mako shark, there was another reason why I thought that they were *mantellis*. Based on fossil records and some expert theories, some of which were mere wild speculation, the *Cretoxyrhina mantelli* was thought to be a scavenger, a species that relied on something else to do its killing, and they would clean up the mess—by consuming it. The fact that they brushed me aside to get at the dead carcass of the *Elasmosaurus* lent some pretty damn good support to the theory.

Scavenger or not, I wasn't staying around to prove a theory. Very slowly and deliberately, I backstroked away from the terrible scene, never taking my eyes from the sharks, making sure that I kept all three dorsal fins in view. But I was swimming in the opposite direction of land, so after separating myself from the pack of hungry predators by several hundred feet, I started working my way back towards the cliff, but at a wide angle that would keep a significant distance between us.

By the time I made it back to the face of the rock, the drama had ended and the sharks had headed east, out to open water. The sea was again calm and clear, the sun shining down, creating a gently rolling blanket of sparkles. It was once again just another quiet, peaceful summer day on the sea. It was if the horrifying event had never taken place.

As I made it back to the cliff, I found a small outcropping in the rock and I grabbed hold of it long enough to catch my breath. As I rested, I wondered how many times each day a similar drama unfolded without warning, only to be over with just as quickly. On the sea, death came swift and unexpected. The death of one meant the survival of another. It wasn't cruel or unfair—it was just how it was supposed to be. Surely I would find it to be the same on land—if I ever found land.

But just then I needed to find my little patch of beach once again. I was hungry, tired, and frightened—and I was miles away from a hot meal, a soft bed—and safety. I let go of the rock and began breast stroking northward.

*****

I slept the sleep of the dead. I read that somewhere. I don't remember where, but it seemed appropriate. I had been asleep for eighteen hours. No dreams, no tossing and turning, just the sleep born of total exhaustion. I barely remembered climbing into bed.

I had crawled onto my beach just as the first rays of sun became apparent in the east. I had been swimming the whole night, and part of the afternoon before. It was the longest, loneliest night of my life. The encounter with the *Elasmosaurus*, and then the sharks, had left me shaken, spooked at the slightest noise, startled by the smallest thing that happened to brush against me in the night.

I had hugged the cliff during my swim, making sure that my fingers brushed the smooth, water-worn rock with every stroke. The remaining daylight hours went smoothly enough, my eyes constantly searching the horizon to my right, looking for more fins, or outstretched necks, or anything else protruding from the surface of the water. I was startled several times by fish jumping out of the water, but other than that it was uneventful.

The panic came with the darkness. It wasn't a total absence of light, nothing like what I had experienced in the cave and the underground river. It was a bright, cloudless, full moon kind of night. The black sky lit up by a million stars, each seeming close enough to touch. They reflected in the water, the gentle waves causing them to move one way then the next, like a sea full of lightning bugs. They made it impossible to distinguish anything in or above the water.

The waves were gentle, but in the stillness of the night, and the closeness of the cliff, they slapped the hard rock surface like a continuous cannonade. I couldn't hear anything else. If I were a hundred yards out, even fifty, I probably wouldn't have even heard them, but with my ear less than three feet away, I could hear nothing else. But moving farther away meant losing the safety of the land ... even though it was really of no help at all.

Even at the water's edge there were marine creatures everywhere. Some just happened to be there—others were curious. I had to remind myself that they had never seen the likes of me. A large pale body with long, thin appendages flailing away in all directions must have looked pretty strange to them. They didn't see me as a threat so they came in closer to get a better look. Nothing bit me, nothing hindered my progress, but every touch, every brush against my body, caused me to jump, to reach for something on the rocks that wasn't there.

During the journey south in the rubber dinghy I really hadn't paid much attention to the detail of the cliffs. I was more concerned with finding an end to them, rather than looking at the actual surface of the rock itself. But heading northward, I looked much more carefully, hoping to find a simple ledge or a seam in the stone, anything to get out of the water for a rest, perhaps to spend the night. But the simple fact was—there was nothing to grab hold of, not one thing to cling to. It had been polished by a couple million years of running water, worn down to a slick, hard surface.

So I kept going, despite my fears, ignoring the possibility of more sharks and other prehistoric carnivores. I realized that whatever happened—happened. I was in no position to change things. If something was going to finish me off, right then and right there—there wasn't a hell of a lot I could do about it. I was without a weapon, without a fast route to safety. All I could do was keep on stroking. It reminded me of when I was a kid in the early seventies. I remembered the dude with the bell-bottom pants, stepping out under the glow of a street lamp, a watch fob spinning at his hip, the logo, *Keep on Truckin'*, under the figure. That was me. I just shut everything down and kept on strokin'.

The night seemed endless. I thought more about the returning daylight than I did about returning to my own beach. I kept my head turned to the right as I swam, watching the east, hoping to see the first faint glow of the new day's sun.

Hour after hour I watched, and I stroked. The water, which had seemed warm when I first entered it, had grown cold. I was shivering, despite the grueling exercise.

It felt as if I had been in the water for days, not hours, and that I had covered much more than just five or six miles. Had I ventured farther to the south than I had thought, or had the cave with my machine somehow, magically been transported farther to the north? Had it disappeared altogether, swallowed up by the sea, or displaced by a new mountain rising from the deep?

I had just about succumbed to the outrageous fantasies when I realized that there was a bluish tinge to the eastern horizon. I breathed a huge sigh of relief as my toes brushed the sandy bottom of the sea. I stood up, the water at chest level. I looked to the north to see the gentle waves lapping the white shore of my beach. I half walked and half crawled my way back to the machine.

*****

It had taken four days for the ache in my chest and shoulders to go away, and my legs to stop shaking when I took more than just a couple of steps.

The first day, I did next to nothing. I couldn't even gather the energy to wander down to the shoreline to scavenge for food. Instead, I ate right out of the can, not even bothering to light a fire to warm the food. For an hour afterwards, I worked at the computer, entering the most recent account. Immediately afterward, I went back to bed where I slept until daybreak.

On the second day, I managed to stay out of bed, but I was moving very slowly, as the rubber-like feeling in my shoulders gave way to pain.

By the third day, my muscles were screaming, but I was recovering. Rested and well nourished, I had survived the worst of it. I knew that the pain would pass.

The day had begun with unusual circumstances. Instead of waking to bright sunlight shining through the eastern porthole, there was nothing but a dim gray, filtered luminance greeting my day, an hour later than I usually awoke. I stumbled slowly out the door, my muscles screaming in protest, to find the morning sky dead. That's how I saw it. I was used to blue skies, an occasional white, fluffy cloud, and a bright yellow sun dominating the scenery. It was life—the ideal setting for plants to grow, for animals to go about their daily routines, for a man to survive. But on that day, the sun was gone, the skies the dullness of once-polished metal that had been too long subjected to the elements.

At midday, the sky began to flash from behind the mountains, and the stillness of the day was shattered by the sounds of thunder. At first, just a low moan sounding in the distance, a long, drawn-out rumble that seemed to build with each passing minute. But as the storm approached from the west, the noise became sharper, louder, until each blast seemed right on top of me, making me jump as if stricken.

It was strange, because, up to that point, I hadn't seen any change in the weather, not a single black cloud, not the slightest tinge of gray sky. Every day was blue skies and bright sunshine. I had begun to feel that the weather was different in this time. Perhaps rain didn't fall here at all. But of course that was impossible. I had probably just landed in the middle of a drought.

The dry spell was definitely over. The rain came in sheets, blowing nearly horizontally to the east. I was able to stand several yards outside the entrance to the cave and watch it come down without getting the slightest bit wet. It came down with such ferocity that it seemed to push the shoreline backward as wave after wave of rain rolled across the churning waters, making the surface foamy-white. The sky was dark, nearly nighttime dark, lit up every few seconds by flashes that were now directly overhead.

I backed into the cave, away from the time machine with its titanium skin. With the original structure, with the long metallic rods stuck deeply into the earth, there was probably a pretty good ground. Any lightning strikes to the exterior of the time machine should have been discharged directly into the earth. But now, with the rods reduced to a pile of rubble, I wasn't too sure. Would the metal machine sitting on top of the ground do the trick? I thought it best to keep my distance.

The lightning and the thunder were terrifying and the rain was coming down harder than I had ever seen, and yet, I saw it as life saving. I had used up a sizable portion of my water supply. If I could find a way to capture the rain, I could replenish it.

I tried timing the flashes of lightning, dashing into the machine when it appeared that I had enough time to get in and out between strikes. Inside, I grabbed the two largest cooking pots from the shelf. As I grabbed for my camouflage rain slicker, lightning struck the hull of the machine. There was a deafening roar, accompanied by a blinding blue-white flash that seemed to make all the interior surfaces of the machine glow as if ignited by some internal fuel. It knocked me to the floor, but I felt no pain. I was stunned, my nerve-endings tingling, my skin crawling like a billion ants were scrambling across it. I lay there for a few seconds making sure that I was still me, still the same lunatic that decided to make this incredible trip … yep, it was still me. I could tell because my head was wedged between the metal racks and a wooden box … and it hurt like hell.

The luminescent glow was fading as I struggled in the nearly black interior to get back on my feet. Heat, or perhaps something else shimmered from the thousands of objects in the machine, and the smell of ozone permeated the space. There was a thick haze all around, like being in the middle of an intense fog. I looked down to make sure that the rubber soles of my boots weren't fused to the floor. They weren't, and the rest of me seemed okay, as well, except for the renewed ache in just about every muscle in my body.

Well, I guess I had my answer—the time machine was indeed grounded. The lightning strike hit the machine, sending its energy around the exterior of it, throughout its metallic skeleton, directly into the earth below. It only comforted me to a point as I righted myself—it wasn't a fun experience. I didn't plan on being inside during any future thunderstorms.

When I finally regained my senses, no worse the wear, I grabbed the rain slicker that had been just beyond my reach when the lightning struck, and headed back out the door. As I stepped down from my machine, I threw it over my shoulders, sticking my arms through the holes, and marched towards the exit to the cave.

I walked nearly twenty yards toward where the rain was pushing back the shoreline before I felt it pelting the back of my head, like tiny pebbles blasting into my scalp. I raised the poncho, covering the back of my head, wishing that I had put on the matching headgear. I continued to walk toward the sea, feeling the bullet-like rain moving slowly down my back until it reached my feet, the feeling softened by the thick leather of my hiking boots.

I threw the pots to the ground, hearing the rain beat against their sides in a continuous drum roll, amplified by the open ends of the metal containers. But most of the rain was striking the front sides and washing uselessly down, soaking into the already soaked ground. Squatting behind them, I reached down, tilted the backs of the pots, easily filling them half way until water poured in a torrent from the lower rim. I released the pots, stood between them, facing out to sea, and spread my arms. The rain hit the stretched-out parka, ran down its back, and filled the pots to overflowing in seconds.

I stood there with my arms outstretched in a howling gale, the force of the wind nearly lifting me from my feet. My head was painfully bent forward, trying to keep the stinging drops from shredding the backs of my ears and digging into my scalp. I must have been quite a sight and, for just a moment, I forgot where I was and had another brief period of embarrassment. I wondered how long it would be until such ridiculous emotions would disappear—probably the first time that they caused me real trouble. The way things had gone up to that point, that day ought to be right around the corner.

By the time the rain stopped, I had refilled every water bottle and still had two full pots of fresh rainwater. I used it to bath in. It was the first time I had washed in anything other than cool salt water since I had been here. I heated it on the stove and sponged the layer of brine from my skin with water so hot I could hardy stand it ... it felt wonderful. And I shaved with it. My first time in weeks that my chin was free of the constant itching caused by newly grown beard.

The other steaming pot of water I used to soak my feet. For no other reason than it felt so damn good. I sat there in the fading light, the sky swept clean by the downpour, a most amazing rainbow forming a brilliant half circle of color above the flat, shiny surface of the great sea, its reflection forming a perfect circle of color.

I stared at the gradually sloping mountain ridge, coming out of the earth from the left side of the beach, rising as it headed north and then winding west as it passed some three hundred feet above my head. I sipped on a glass of scotch, the numbing affects accentuated by the hot, steaming water enclosing my feet. In my mind, I picked a path through the rubble lying at the foot of the ridge, knowing that tomorrow I would begin to make the climb that was my last chance of getting off of this beach.

*****

I had completed what I hoped would be the most difficult part of my climb. It had taken more than two hours and I had only made fifty feet. But it was fifty feet nearly straight up.

There was a slowly rising ridge that went around and above the cave's entrance, and looked to be extremely navigable. But to get to it, I had to climb up fifty feet—fifty feet of large, odd-shaped boulders.

The rocks were solid. They had rested in the same position for thousands, perhaps millions of years. They had plenty of time to settle. But it wasn't a pile of rubble like what I had climbed when I had first visited the cave—not a huge pile of small, pulverized stone that I easily ascended. No, these were huge blocks of stone—stone that time hadn't worn down—rock that was new, at least comparatively speaking.

The first rock—the main one—was at least twelve feet in circumference, a third of it sliced off smoothly, lying flat side up against the larger part.

From a distance, it looked easy to climb. Up close, the ridge of the upper portion, even standing on the fallen part, looked accessible, perhaps eight feet high. Just a small hop placed my fingertips upon the smooth top of the boulder, but I could not pull myself up. Three times I tried—three times I failed, my shoulders and arms refusing to find the strength to pull my body up and over. It wasn't like doing pull-ups at the gym. There was nothing to grip, no bar to wrap my fingers around. I could have done it a month ago—in my former life—not now. I was still in great shape, but a month without the weights, the food supplements, the strict diet, left me fifteen pounds lighter—fifteen pounds of muscle—lighter.

I ended up building a pile of smaller rocks, pushed up against the flat surface of the big one. It brought me three feet closer to the top, about chin-level. With my hands flat on the top of the stone, I jumped straight up, as high as I could, pushing with my arms, throwing my hips up and over the top.

For ten minutes I just sat there, my legs dangling over the edge, trying to catch my breath. I had made it all of eight feet, and already I was pooped.

The first boulder was the biggest, but not the only one that I had to climb before I reached the main ridge. I worked my way up the remainder of the pile moving on a diagonal, using the gaps between the rocks, working one against another for leverage, the thick rubber soles of my boots providing the grip to propel myself surely, if not quickly, to the top.

As I stood at the lowest part of the winding ridge, I looked down at the half-buried time machine, the front end sticking through the opening of the cave at a slight angle, the mass of twisted and broken titanium bars laying off to the side like shimmering pick-up sticks. It looked like anything but someone's home, and yet in the short time that I had been here, I had come to think of it in exactly that way. And as I prepared to make the long, possibly dangerous trek along the ridge that would hopefully take me to the other side of the mountain, I was already missing it. The machine represented warmth, shelter, and safety, and even some level of comfort.

I wasn't planning to be gone long. I had packed light, only enough provisions for three days, four, if I stretched it. But anything could happen in a couple of days. I could think of hundreds of dangers, and, even more, I feared what I couldn't think of. I couldn't help but wonder if I would ever see my home again.

In less time that it took to climb the initial fifty feet, I had reached a point on the ridge directly over the machine, perhaps some three hundred feet above the ground. It was mostly walking, not climbing, and yet I could feel each step burn deep into my thighs as I walked off each steeply inclined pace.

I knew that my machine was directly below me now, but I was too chicken to venture out to the ledge to peer over. Instead I took a few moments to just sit there and stare out to sea. It took on an entirely different perspective from three hundred feet up. Records, and fossil artifacts said that this was a shallow inland-sea, but that hardly did it justice. This was an ocean. From where I sat, it looked as deep and vast as any ocean in the modern world. It extended in three directions for as far as the eye could see. Except for the absence of a deep, rolling surf upon the beach, it looked like the Atlantic Ocean off the coast of the northeastern seaboard.

Despite the calmness of the water, it was hard to imagine that the sea was shallow. It just didn't seem right that a body of water covering several hundred miles from east to west and more that a thousand miles from north to south, could be anything but proportionately deep. Although hard to believe, it was true. The relative flatness of the American mid-west said that it was so. The average depth of the Western Interior Sea was only three hundred feet at its peak, and if I was indeed in the latter period of the Upper Cretaceous, it was considerably less than that.

I remembered sitting on top of the rock pile the day I discovered the cave, looking out upon the flat plains of central Utah. Other than a slight change in elevation, I was in the same spot, taking in the same view. And in some ways it was the same—still, quiet, a monotonous lack of topography—in other ways it was not the same ... not the same at all.

The ridge continued to rise more than four hundred feet, heading in a southern direction for several miles. The sun was beginning its descent by the time I reached the pinnacle, my progress slowed only by a deep crevasse across the ridge that I had to skirt around.

The view from the top was even more spectacular. At this height, the sea had not lost any of its ocean-like quality—its vastness only more apparent, the shadows of the mountains now beginning to creep across its still surface.

To the west stood the mountains of the Wasatch, twin-peaks towering more than two thousand feet into the sky directly ahead. They were ten or twelve miles away, separated from me by a ragged valley of desolation: dull grays and tans, rock, and more rock—nothing else. If there was life down there I couldn't see it—no color, no movement, nothing—just a barren, ugly valley.

I rested there, sitting on the edge of the ridge, my legs stretched out across the fine gravel that led down the western slope into the valley, and ate a simple lunch of dried jerky and bottled rainwater.

I couldn't see anything beyond the mountains, although the valley wandered off in the direction between the two. If I were another hundred or so feet higher perhaps I could see through the gap into what was beyond, but I was at the top of the ridge. To go farther would only lower my line of sight. And to travel farther to the south was out of the question. The ridge died out some few hundred yards out, turning into a steep, sheer slope that was impossible to climb but for all but a few professional mountain climbers. I had but one goal, and that was to aim between the two peaks. If I made steady progress, and got off my dead ass right there and then, I could make it by nightfall.

The slope was steep, made up of pea-size gravel created when the mountains, grinding and sliding against one another, rose from the ancient ocean during the formation of the Rocky Mountains.

I slid rather than walked down it, the tiny pieces of stone more like ball-bearings than rocks, each one rolling over on top of the next, making it as if I was wearing roller blades instead of boots—each pace taking me twice as far as just the length of my step. Each step sent miniature landslides in long ovals in front of each foot. The angle was too steep to stay upright without pitching forward. Instead I went down on the seat of my pants, digging in with my heels to slow my progress, to keep me flipping end over end.

I was out of control the whole way down. I'd take a few steps, started running, my feet taking strides much too long to control, my arms flailing away to keep my balance until, just when I was about to lose control completely, I would launch myself forward, legs out, butt down. It was soft enough but the seat of my pants took a severe beating.

The gravel was surprisingly dry considering the terrible storm just the day before, attesting to the depth of the absorbent material. I stopped half way down to look around. There was no sign of water anywhere, even at the base of the valley that looked to be solid rock and should have held water like a trough. The sun was bright and hot on that day. Perhaps the water simply boiled off the surface of the hot rocks like a summer shower on the hot pavement, turning into vapor as quick as it hit. But I didn't think so. Not as hard and as long as it rained a day before. No, the water went somewhere, and I'll bet it managed to snake its way into the underground river that was somewhere beneath my feet.

I wasn't sure whether the floor of the valley was above or below sea level, higher or lower than where I started on my beach. I only knew that I got to the end of the slope a hell of a lot quicker than I climbed the rise.

I had made it down a difficult slope, but I still had a long way to go. It was a long plain, strewn with thousands of rocks and boulders, most of them easy enough to dodge. The biggest problem was the threat of turning an ankle on the uneven surface. So I moved cautiously across the valley floor.

I wound my way toward the area between the two mountain peaks that loomed high above the valley floor. As I got closer I could see that one of the peaks was set back slightly from the other, their slopes, as they merged into ground level, offset by a couple of miles. The area between was a puzzle of twists and turns, strangely shaped formations and escarpments, clogging up the gap, making it look impassable from a distance.

As I approached it, things became clearer, alleys and corridors that might permit a man to pass. But the shadows were growing long against the valley floor, making it more difficult to see clearly with each passing moment. Long before I made it through the gap, it would be night. And whatever lay before me at the other side would require all my senses, my full attention.

At the rise of the first peak I came upon a strange outcropping of rock, almost umbrella shaped with an abbreviated tunnel through the center. Along the inside edge of the opening was a series of ridges, ripples really, that traversed from side to side at uneven intervals of a few, to several inches. Like the rings of a tree, they were marks of age, identifying the passage of a river or stream cutting through the valley thousands of years ago.

I passed through its center, running the fingers of both hands across the rough, uneven surface, pausing midway, wondering what things had passed through this portal before me. My fingers traced each indentation, each ridge, thinking about how many years had passed between each, how many *things* had passed through its center. Perhaps, many years ago, this was the one and only pass through the mountain peaks. Water rushing between the mountain pass millions of years ago when the Western Interior Sea was at its highest level, carrying with it any number of sea creatures. But not land animals. Only water had passed this way before, flooding through from west to east as the mighty Rocky Mountains rose from the sea with volcanic might.

No, I doubted that dinosaurs had ever roamed this stretch of land between the mountain's edge and the great ancient sea to the east. Birds, insects, snakes, and perhaps even a few of the smaller mammals that were early in their existence, had scurried and crawled across this barren valley of rocks and gravel, but no dinosaurs. But maybe, just maybe, they were just beyond the base of the second mountain.

The detail of the ridges and ripples of the tunnel faded into shadows as I reached its exit. The sun had dropped behind the mountains, slipped beneath whatever was on the western horizon well beyond my field of vision. I would go no farther on that day, so I found a comfortable spot to spread out at the edge of the hollow rock and watched as the stars came out and began their slow dance across the sky.

CHAPTER 15

The earth was born from fire four and a half billion years ago, the surface of the planet covered with molten rock ten miles deep. Over millions of years, the liquid rock found its way to the center of the earth to form a liquid core a hundred miles in diameter.

For more than a billion years the surface of the earth cooled, despite tremendous volcanic activity that spewed water vapor into the atmosphere, forming rain, filling the depressions of the globe, creating the oceans. Beneath the surface, the heated waters formed a "primordial soup" containing biomolecular material that produced amino acids, proteins common to all living things, when bombarded by the sun's ultraviolet light. That life first began to form more than three billion years ago. Life, single-celled, living in the waters of the world, moved about it freely, wherever the currents took it. Perhaps three hundred million years ago, animals first crept out of the water and onto the shores for the first time. They were no longer forced to live within the boundaries of the water. They were free to venture out onto the land, but they didn't venture far. It took hundreds of thousands of years before they adapted to dry land, could move about it freely, their bodies evolving slowly, eventually able to travel long distances, moving from one end of the land to the other.

Three hundred million years ago there was but one dominant land-mass, a single continent known as *Pangea*, a huge landmass that incorporated most of the individual continents of the modern world. A single body of water known as the *Panthalassa Ocean* surrounded *Pangea*. The earliest dinosaurs inhabited and spread across this singular body of land, and roamed the continent from north to south and east to west, evolving along a single path, a shared environment two hundred and thirty million years ago.

Thirty million years later, the landmass split into two super continents—*Gundwanaland*, consisting of Antarctica, South America, Africa, India, and Australia—and *Laurasia*, made up of North America, Europe, and Asia. The evolution of life began to diverge, two independent paths, each taking its own course, changing, based on two different environments, two distinct sets of climate and geography.

Over the next hundred million years, new species developed, unique from one landmass to the other. But the two great continents didn't remain stationary. The nine major tectonic plates supporting them continued to drift, dividing the land into yet smaller areas, colliding with others to form all new ones. North and South America joined forces, Europe and Asia broke away and the globe began to take the general shape of what we call the modern world. And all during that time, animals wandered the face of the earth, some contributing to the gene pool of the newly formed lands, others becoming more diverse as new, natural boundaries limited their travel, forcing each to develop and evolve under more isolated conditions.

Towards the end of the Cretaceous period, the relative positions of the individual landmasses were much as they are today, although much different in appearance. Antarctica and Australia were still a single continent, most of Western Europe was under water, and, of course, there was the great Inner Continental Sea that cut North America in two, east from west.

Animals shared a common ancestry, many similarities in species traceable back to the super continents *Gundwanaland* and *Laurasia*, and before that—*Pangea*. But the diversity in species of the land animals continued to increase as one group became isolated from another by natural barriers. The effects of the tectonic plates ramming together continued to wreck havoc upon the continents. Mountain ranges were formed, and, as they rose from the depths, new lakes, rivers, and seas were born.

And as the great Rocky Mountains formed, stretching from north to south across most of North America, following the western shores of the inner continental sea, fertile valleys were created within their confines. It was in these valleys, along the shores of rivers, lakes, and even seas, that life flourished, evolved—lived—and died.

It was in just such a valley that I found my dinosaurs.

*****

That was two weeks ago. Since then, I had been planning my return, to begin the life that Dermot and I had begun to plan all those months ago. I couldn't live my life from the isolated beach at the foot of the eastern cliffs of the mountain range. I was going to have to build a new home—in the lush valley on the other side of the mountains—among the dinosaurs.

I would have two homes. Perhaps one for summer and one for winter, or a different house for whatever passed as seasons in this time. Except for a few necessities, I was going to have to transfer the contents of the time machine across the mountains and build a new home.

But I would have to return to the machine from time to time. The computer was there in its protected environment. And it would have to remain there. The titanium hull of the time machine would serve as double protection for the computer, but, more importantly, it was the only place where Dermot would be able to find it seventy million years in the future.

I would record my story the old fashioned way—using pen and paper. Periodically, perhaps every few months, or perhaps seasonally, just once a year, I would return to the cave and transfer my story into the computer. It's what I was doing on this day—bringing my story up to date.

*****

I had woken stiff and sore from the long trek the day before and from sleeping on a bed of rock. I had a crick in my neck from using my lumpy backpack as a pillow. The long walk had worked off the last of the soreness from my long swim, but by elbows and knees, shoulders and back were sore from the hard, uneven surface of the rocky tunnel.

All was still in shadow as the morning's sun was yet hours away from clearing the cliffs behind me. As I waited for the light, I stretched the stiffness from my joints, shaking out the last remnants of sleep from my half-functioning brain. I would have killed for a hot cup of coffee, but I had to settle for a few swigs of warm rainwater from my bottle—the first of which I used to rinse out the dry, stale taste from my mouth, wishing that I had packed a toothbrush.

The water was the last of my second bottle, leaving just one left. My food supplies had to be running low as well, so I unpacked my knapsack to take inventory.

I leaned back against the curvature of the tunnel, spread my legs, and dumped my pack between them. I agreed with Hizenberg's uncertainty principal—" Those that we study, we also change", so I had packed all of my refuse. I was determined to leave as little impact on the land as possible. Along with the two empty water bottles, there were three wrappings from beef jerky, one empty can of pork and beans, one full bottle of rain water, one package of jerky, and one more can of beans, a can opener and one slightly used spoon. In addition, I had a short length of nylon rope, a compass, a small first aid kit, a hunting knife, and one of two Glock 32, .357 caliber pistols with holster and two full extra clips.

I had worn the gun under my arm like a detective when I started off, but even with the lightweight holster, I wasn't used to carrying it. It was wearing a sore spot along the inside of my upper arm as I hiked up the long, winding ridge. I was rather terrified of the gun and afraid that I'd shoot myself with the constant rubbing up against it, so I took it off in order to put it in my knapsack.

I picked the gun up with both hands, dangling it between my legs, as I examined my pitiful stash of food. The Glock was a compact model, but it still felt heavy in my hands. I had never fired it, or anything like it, and it was hard to imagine using it for either defending myself or for hunting. But I knew that I would use it for both. I would have to.

I let the gun twirl back and forth with my index finger caught in the trigger guard, thinking about my next step. I had enough water and food to make it back to the cave. I could restock with more provisions than I carried this time and head back out again, or I could carry on for a bit longer—and run the risk of not being able to get back at all. I couldn't help but think that there was something just beyond the next ridge.

I weighed my options. I was rested, and having just woke up, not all that hungry or thirsty. I was ready and anxious to go on. My curiosity still had the best of me—I had to know what lay ahead.

On the other hand, I just barely had enough provisions to make it back. I had been gone just one full day and I had used up more than half of my food and water. For every hour that I continued on, away from the cave, an hour of thirst and hunger would be suffered on the return trip.

I knew that I could take it. I could get through the next several hours without touching my supplies, leaving them for the return trip. The food wasn't much of a problem, and I knew that I could make one bottle of water last a full day.

I decided to give it another few hours, until the sun was high in the sky. At noon, when the sun was directly overhead, I'd turn back, regardless of what I'd found, or where I was. I had a feeling that a few hours were all that I needed.

The dull grayness continued to dissipate, replaced by a golden hue as the sun entered the far edge of the valley. Details began to come into focus, the black shadows stretching long against the lunar-like landscape.

From where I sat, the floor of the valley angled off to the right, sloping up gradually, merging into the rise of the next mountain, an easy climb, free of any major obstacles. I checked the compass to see that the easy route led off to the northwest. But I knew that I had a better chance of finding life beyond the mountains, to the west—due west.

Checking my compass again, setting a course in that direction, I started up the rocky slopes of the first mountain. It was a difficult, if not impossible climb, littered with more boulders than I could count, many of which were of the multiple-ton variety, several times my own height, some seemingly insurmountable.

I shook my head in amazement. Why did I never take the easy route, the one clear of obstacles and wrong turns ... and bad outcomes? I could probably travel six or seven miles before mid-day by taking the easy route. The path I was about to choose might lead nowhere and it was going to be damn painful to get there. Perhaps I'd wear myself out to gain a couple of hundred yards, and get nowhere at all. But I was working on gut instinct. I was going to take the path less traveled—so to speak.

I repacked what there were of my supplies and stepped out from the opening of the short tunnel. As I walked across a small clearing toward the rise of rock I emerged from the long shadows. I could feel the heat of the sun on the back of my neck, sending little stinging hints of a long, hot day to follow.

I approached the first of the boulders, big, but not too big. I easily leaped to the top of it, perhaps four feet, amazed at the spring in my legs borne of the recent loss of weight. I stood there, staring up, over, and around the maze of rocks, trying to map out a route that would advance my progress in a westward direction.

The slope of the mountain rose steeply, one huge rock piled against the next, ascending as quickly as it did unevenly. It looked precarious, so precisely balanced that the slightest breeze might topple the whole thing, from top to bottom, and me standing at its base.

I stepped up onto the next, higher rock, tentatively, testing its stability, moving slowly, afraid to even breathe for fear that the slightest breeze would set things in motion. But the rock held fast, not a hint of movement. I pushed against the next, lightly at first and then with more force, feeling for the slightest movement. Like the one before it, it was solid, as if it were but a part of the one beneath.

I climbed another, then another. Each was held firmly in place, but each became more difficult then the next as the angle grew steeper. I was sweating freely even though the full heat of day was not yet upon me. My muscles began to heat up with the all too familiar feel of heavy exercise. My knees and elbows were already tender from the bruising caused by the hard, rough stone. I was getting winded, and I had hardly begun my climb.

I continued to check the compass for a western heading, its floating pointer leading me on a path away from the base of the mountain, forcing me to pick my way between the rocks instead of just around the periphery. I sighted in on an irregular-shaped obelisk of stone about half the way up the slope, which was at true west. I wondered what incredible forces could have created such a bizarre formation. Unlike most of the rocks surrounding it, this strangely shaped needle of stone was twisted, its tip pointed at an unnatural angle away from me, tortured by some unknown and unimaginable force. It was a rock that stood out on its own, different than everything else. It was a sign—a marker. I could put the compass away if I kept climbing towards it. Perhaps it pointed the way to my own personal pot of gold.

I had progressed perhaps two hundred feet up the slope, two hundred feet up, maybe three hundred feet in actual linear distance—the slope being more up than across—feeling more like miles. As much as climbing was a problem, squeezing between the rocks was even worse. Even in my slimmer state, I was having problems navigating the shrinking distance between one boulder and the next. My backpack was becoming an increasing nuisance.

Another rock, another bruise on the knee, another blister on my fingertips, and I reached what appeared to be an impassible overhang. A huge block of stone, oblong, resting on its side, overhanging the one below by ten feet, jutted out from the side of the mountain, blocking my progress. To one side was a sheer wall of stone extending up fifteen feet, well beyond my reach. To the other side was a sheer drop, thirty feet or more.

I would have to go around the boulder by going back the way I came, down to the rocky ledge thirty feet below. I would have to work my way around the massive rock, and then across it, hoping that there was a way on the other side to get to the top of it.

As I stepped down from the rock, I turned to take a final look at it, noticing a strange patch of lighter colored stone standing out from the shadow beneath the overhang that I hadn't noticed during my ascent. Now perched on the rock below, the space was just at eye level and I could see a gap, perhaps fourteen inches between the overhang and the rock that I had just stepped down from.

I climbed back onto the rock, sliding into the crawlspace as far as my backpack would allow. Reaching my hand forward toward the golden hued rock, I realized that the shadows didn't seem to change as my body blocked out the early-morning light that penetrated the small space from behind. The light had to be coming from another source.

Before my hand actually came in contact with the rock I was reaching for, my fingers took on a glow as if lit up from the inside. I could feel the warmth of the sun on my fingers as I moved my hand back and forth, in and out of shadow. The light was coming from somewhere up above.

I pushed my way back out of the space, struggling out of my pack as I emerged. I laid it against a rock and scrambled back under the ledge, head first, on my back. Without the pack, I was able to squirm all the way into the tight space, easily reaching the far end, directly under the opening in the stone.

There was a gap between the huge boulder and the ones adjacent to it, angling upward and to the west, perhaps forty feet in length. I could see blue skies through the end, but nothing else.

The opening was large enough to get through and the climb was easy. Unlike my previous experience with tunnels, this one was not formed by eons of water eroding the stone as it passed through. This one was created by pure luck. As the mountains rose from the sea during the collision of two great tectonic plates, the rock cracked and crumbled, and cascaded down the rising sides of the newly born peak, settling in whatever way gravity dictated. By some miraculous twist of fate, these thousands of rocks were of just such a size and shape, and bounced in just such a way, and landed in just such a position as to form this natural pass through.

I made it quickly to the top, but not through the opening. There was a rock, a large one, blocking part of the exit. The opening was not even big enough to push my head through.

I had a decision to make. I could put my shoulder to the task, perhaps with enough strength to push the stone away from the opening, enlarging the space enough for me to crawl free. Of course, in the process, I might just send the rest of the rocks down on top of me. Or, I could sneak back down the tunnel, and cower my way down the ledge, skirt around the rock, and maybe, just maybe, find a way beyond the mountain.

Stupid decisions had become my specialty, so I climbed closer to the opening, stepped up on the next higher stone, my body doubled over into a crouched position, my face pressed painfully up against the seemingly immovable rock, and pushed.

The rock began to move.

My shoulders trembled from the strain as the huge stone moved upward. But the tremendous force that I was applying to the stone above me was equal and opposite to that being applied through my back onto the rock that rested beneath me. I pushed even harder. As the rock above continued to move upward, the one below it, the one pressed up against my back, gave way.

As I arched backward, my hands separated from the stone, and it crashed down onto my chest. It pushed me half way down the tunnel, turning end over end, colliding with one hard, rocky surface after another.

I ended up sprawled across the inside of the rocky passage on my back, upside down, as the rock continued to skip downward from one stone to the next, lodging itself between the base of the tunnel and the rock below, blocking the way back down. I lay there quietly, listening, waiting for the next rock to fall, for the rest of the surrounding stones to come crashing down on top of me, too afraid to move.

But nothing happened, all was silent, nothing else fell from the walls of the tunnel, I only *felt* as if the whole of the pile fell on top of me.

I looked up, seeing a much larger patch of clear, blue sky. I sighed, taking in a huge relieving breath, nearly passing out from the pain in the center of my chest. The falling rock had struck me right smack in center of the sternum. It felt as if it were shattered, pain exploding with every movement. A deep breath caused me to see stars, little dancing bursts of fire exploding before my eyes.

I took little short breaths, inhaling through my nostrils, trying to minimize the rise of my chest. Gradually, and slowly, I began to flex my arms and legs, testing them, making sure that everything was still attached and in one piece. I tried to sit up, and the pain forced me back down again.

In time, remaining still, the pain eased up—as long as I kept taking shallow breaths and didn't move too quickly. Eventually, I rolled over, very slowly, and lifted my chest from the hard ground by using my elbows. I looked up at the end of the tunnel to see the expanded opening, and began climbing.

It was only twenty feet or so, but it seemed to take forever, each move sending fresh waves of pain through my chest—my knees and elbows so sore that it felt like I was scaling a wall of broken glass. Each step that I took felt like another hammer blow to my chest, each foot of progress deepening the bruises on my joints.

I emerged from the exit in shadow. It stretched across the opening and half the way down the slope in front of me. I turned ... slowly ... to see the stone obelisk before me. It looked even more bizarre from up close. Its edges were sharp and twisted like a corkscrew, like a clay sculpture from the wheel of a psychotic potter, the tip hovering thirty feet above me, bent downward, pointing to the west.

I had come up from underneath, emerging just behind it. I wondered why the incredible mass of the three or four ton block hadn't caused the tunnel to collapse entirely thousands of years ago. Surprised that it didn't come down with me inside. Momentarily forgetting the pain, I struggled up and over the lip of the tunnel, rolling ten feet down the slope away from the formation.

I rose up into a sitting position, slowly, feeling my heartbeat through my damaged sternum. Gazing down the slope just to my left, I saw the shadow of the obelisk pointing the way across the crumbled remains of the mountain. My eyes followed its direction, beyond the base of the mountain, and across a long hard stretch of barren rock that gently rose until abruptly ending several miles in the distance.

It stopped abruptly, a straight edge, segregating the tan color of the earth from the dazzling blue of the sky. A precise line, as if drawn by a ruler, denoting a ridge, or a ledge, something caused by nature. Perhaps it was a river that over millions of years carved through the rock, leaving a fine line of demarcation between where the rock left off and where the water began. Or, perhaps, it was the remnant of an ancient landslide, the eastern part of some new mountain peak separating, and sliding into some valley beyond my range of vision.

Whatever it was, the shadow compass formed by the still rising sun behind the pinnacle was pointing right into the heart of it. I could almost see a dotted line emanating from the bent tip of the obelisk's shadow to the center of the horizon, a path for me to follow, like a comic book, saying follow this path to buried treasure. But if X marked the spot, I couldn't see it.

I had nothing to lose, and nowhere else to go, so I followed the imaginary path up the slope. It was clear, but it was long and uphill all the way. My heart pounded, pain rippling through my chest with every beat. My thighs burned from the exertion, quivering a little more with each successive step. My head throbbed—too much heat for too long. I was regretting leaving my last bottle of water back at the base of the tunnel. My mouth was dry, my throat raspy, but I knew that I would need the water later if I were to make it back to the machine.

I looked up at the sun. It was directly overhead, blazing hot, the temperature easily in the high nineties. I began praying for rain, but there wasn't a cloud in the sky. Not a cloud, but an interesting darkening of the sky just over the horizon. Perhaps a storm was brewing far off to the west.

As I trudged up the long rise, perhaps two hours since I left the foot of the obelisk, and perhaps three miles from it, I could see the sky over the ridge darkening further. It wasn't a storm. It looked like smoke, huge black clouds of it, rolling upward, dissipating into the clear sky. Something was on fire.

The closer I got to the rim, the blacker the horizon got. I was only a mile from the edge when I discovered the source. The peak of a mountaintop appeared, sliding upward into the sky as I got closer to the end of my trail. The mountain was in the far-off distance, as many as fifty or sixty miles, yet even at that distance I could see that the tip of the mountain was gone. Replacing it was a plume of black smoke that jetted into the sky, widening as it went, spreading out in all directions for several miles. There was the hazy, red glow of fire at the perimeter between the mountain and the smoke. It was a volcano ... an active one.

I kept marching up the rise as more of the mountain came into view. I was within a quarter mile of the ridge when the valley revealed itself, as well. It took several moments for my brain to recognize what was spreading out before me. It wasn't a barren valley of rocks and stones—none of the dull grays and tans of this world as I had seen it up to that point.

At first I didn't recognize it for what it was. It was so far in the distance that as the base of the far off mountain came into view, the change in scenery was vague—a darkness, almost black, began to dominate the view as it continued to rise from above the ridge. The blackness continued to spread from west to east, farther and farther with each approaching step.

It wasn't until I was within a hundred yards that I realized that it wasn't black at all—but green—the dark, lush green of a forest. The sight was as surprising as it was welcomed, having been so long since I had seen any kind of vegetation. It was what I was hoping for, yet my brain failed to recognize and believe it until I was close enough to remove all doubt.

I was approaching the end of the long slope, and I kept expecting more land to come into view beyond the ridge. But it didn't happen. I approached the end cautiously, the feeling of great height, a huge drop to the valley below, becoming apparent. I still could not see what was beyond the ridge or what was at the bottom. What I *could* see was still a mile or more out, the vastness of the forest growing, the detail of the trees coming into view. I did the last few yards on my hands and knees, crawling slowly to the edge, afraid that a gust of wind, or crumbling rock would send me over the ridge, falling how far and into what I didn't yet know.

I kept my eyes down, watching the rock's fine powder stir and float into the air as I passed over it. I reached the end, grabbing the lip with both hands, breathing heavily, feeling the fine dust tickle my nostrils, sting my eyes. Ignoring the pain in my chest, the dryness of my throat, I used my arms to drag my body forward, my head extending beyond the edge of the ridge, my eyes closed.

I stayed that way for several minutes, anxious to open them, to see what lay below and at the same time scared shitless to find out. What if the ledge dropped into a deep chasm with no way out? What if it was a thousand feet to the bottom, with no way down? What if there was nothing down there but thousands of acres of forest, with no dinosaurs?

What if this had all been for nothing?

I gripped the lip so hard that my arms trembled. The sweat dripped down the bridge of my nose, falling—who knows where. I pulled my chin into my neck as I opened my eyes. I looked upon a smooth, flat, granite surface just inches below where I lay. It was on a perpendicular from the long rise that I had struggled up during the last several hours. I began to lower my line of sight, slowly at first, inch by inch, and then more quickly, taking in feet, then yards at a time. The wall ran flat and smooth, the black dotted, and brown streaked, tan surface running straight down beneath me.

My gaze traveled down the rock two hundred feet before seeing the clear blue-green water. I paused there, watching the water run past the base of the cliff, slowly, much more slowly than it had millions of years before, when the rushing water had cut through the rock above. It was a river, much like the Colorado River that created the Grand Canyons, perhaps the above ground part of river that had carried me out of the cave more than a month before. Once upon a time, it was more than just a river. Perhaps it was part of the great Western Interior Sea. As it carved out the cliffs to the east, it receded gradually, leaving behind the rich fertile ground that grew the forests to the west.

I found the opposite edge of the river, not far away, perhaps a hundred feet, perhaps a hundred and fifty. At its western shore lay brown sandy soil that grew darker, richer, as it extended out from the water. The ground looked fertile, yet nothing seemed to be growing on it. Beyond that was a meadow, a half-mile deep, filled with dazzling color—reds, pinks, yellows, and violets—acres of wildflowers. Beyond that was the forest, a jungle really, so dense and dark that it would rival any in the Amazon Rain Forest.

They came from the north. I hadn't seen them because my line of sight had traveled straight down and then directly across from the spot below me. I hadn't seen anything to either side for more that a few hundred feet. But as I swung my vision to the right, they came into focus.

Triceratops, a dozen of them, eight adults and four adolescents, strolled on the path alongside the river. If I had had any water in the last twelve hours, I would have pissed my pants.

Tears of joy clouded my vision, turned the twelve animals into a dozen indiscriminate shapes, surrounded by blue halos.

It worked. It actually worked.

Dermot's experiment worked. There was no longer any doubt in my mind. I was living in the Cretaceous period, among the dinosaurs. They were right there, two hundred feet below.

Wiping my eyes, I swung around and sat up, letting my legs dangle over the edge of the cliff—yet another stupid thing to do, but I wasn't exactly thinking clearly. I was euphoric, senseless, beside myself with joy and relief. The pain in my chest was forgotten, as were any lingering thoughts about what the hell I was doing here.

I watched the group as they sauntered along the river's edge, occasionally stopping for a drink, the adults playfully nudging the smaller ones forward. It was a communal group, impossible to tell which were of one family unit and which ones were not. They all seemed to intermix randomly, one trading places with another, dealing with the smaller ones depending on which was closer. Of the eight adults, there were four males and four females, but I couldn't tell which group was which. Four were considerably larger, had longer horns, and had more distinctive frills. But that group could have been either the males or the females. From this height and this angle I couldn't find any differences in their anatomy. With the adolescents, it was even harder to tell, their differences not having yet manifested themselves.

They were brown, not dark, but nearly tan, a dusty sort of color, almost identical to that of the sand that they trod upon. The color was uniform, no stripes, spots, or wild variations, just a dull tan—all over. They blended in beautifully with the color of the path—a place where they would be most vulnerable. The carnivores would have trouble picking them out from the surrounding cliffs and mountains. The perfect camouflage—all except the three magnificent horns. They were white—pure white—each of the three horns, the bony structure of its chin, and the knobs along the top of its frill stood in stark contrast to the rest of it. They *would* have been noticed in the dense underbrush. But, perhaps, that was the point.

I watched as they paraded by, understanding now why the wide stretch of land before the meadow was barren. This was a game trail. It stretched on as far as I could see it, both to the north and to the south, curving out of sight in both directions.

The ground along the river had been trampled flat, scoured clean of all vegetation, barren and laid to waste by herds of herbivores traveling on it over thousands of years. Perhaps it was migration, animals moving southward when the cool winds of autumn set in. Or, perhaps, it was just the peculiar habits of a species that man knew very little about—maybe they just wandered the trail year around because that's what their ancestors did years before. Either way, millions of dinosaurs had taken this path over the years.

It took the group an hour, frolicking along the path, taking an occasional drink from the river, a lot of playful nudging and poking, before the *Triceratops* wound their way around the bend, out of sight. I looked back to the north, feeling that something else was about to emerge from the right, another batch of *Triceratops*, or maybe another species altogether. I thought that a small group of *Tyrannosaurs* might be coming up the path, stalking them from a distance, ready to attack as they cleared the expanse of the meadow.

But there was nothing more.

I waited, watching the path closely, especially in the areas where it disappeared into the forest, hoping for something else to enter the scene. I used the time to check out the rest of the valley. To that point, I really hadn't raised my eyes beyond the edge of the meadow. I did it then, and marveled at the sight that lay before me.

The most dominant feature was the volcano, smoldering fifty miles to the west, sending out black clouds high above the jungle. Below it, miles of dense woods, thick enough that from this distance, it appeared as one solid, tangled mass. The scene looked incredibly familiar, but I wasn't sure why, until I saw the pair of *Pteranodons* fly toward me from the direction of the mountain. Then it struck me—hard—like a bolt of lightning. It was Susan's window—exactly. It was the scene in the beautiful stained-glass window on the third floor of Susan's home. The mountain, the jungle below, the dashes of color that dominated the bottom edge of the panels, even the pair of *Pteranodons*, was the same—as far as I could remember—exactly the same.

It was exactly the same as the picture I had drawn.

I continued to watch. For an hour, there was little more other than an occasional flock of birds passing overhead, too far to see with detail. I began to think that it was all a dream, perhaps an image conjured up from a lack of water, the missing hours of sleep, or perhaps just an intense desire. And yet, the valley was still there, the meadow as colorful as when I first saw it, the beaten down path along the river hadn't changed in any way. Looking closely, I could still see the footprints of the beasts, the tracks in the earth where they twisted and turned trying to reign in their kids, muddy areas where they stepped back from the edge of the shore dripping water onto the hard dirt.

No, it wasn't an illusion. I had really seen it, and I was sure that there was more to come. While I waited, I concentrated on my predicament. I was sitting on the cusp of a two-hundred-foot cliff—a plateau actually. It extended to the north and south as far as the eye could see. I didn't see any way out. The walls were steep and straight, dropping vertically into the river below. There was no way to simply climb down, not from where I sat, and not from anyplace that I could see.

There was but one way to enter the valley, at least from this side, and that was straight down. Back at the time machine, I had enough rope to descend to the bottom. But just then I wasn't quite sure how to get the supplies down and across the river, nor did I relish the thought of having to scale the cliff at some later date using just a rope. I guess I'd just have to figure something out back at the cave. I knew one thing—I wasn't going to be exploring the valley on that day.

But I stayed there until the daylight passed beyond the fiery mountain, the descending darkness permitting the coal-like glow from its tip to cast a dull pink shadow down upon the darkening valley. The crimson of the mountain merged with a sky of the same color as the sun fell behind the mountains, making it hard to distinguish one from the other.

Other than the *Triceratops*, *Pteranodons*, and a few birds of indistinguishable character, I hadn't seen anything more, but as dark descended, the sounds of the night began to creep forward.

It was the sounds of the jungle … but it wasn't. There were the familiar songs of the birds, bidding a final goodnight to their flock as they settled in for the night across the treetops of the valley. The low-lament of the frog blended in, their low groans audible above the monotonous buzz of a billion insects. And above it all were the sounds of animals that no human had ever heard. They were mostly mournful songs, as if they knew that their time was almost over.

An ear-piercing shriek, ending in a burst of short, staccato trills entered the cacophony, muting the other sounds by comparison. The sound came from the north end of the jungle, carrying with the breeze across the valley. Within seconds, the time that it took the sound to travel to the receiver, it was answered—four short bleats, matching in timbre the final notes of the caller. Two animals were trying to find one another, or perhaps two that were saying goodnight to each other, unknown circumstances separating them for the night. A single bleat followed from the north, recognition of the reply, a final goodnight.

A few minutes later, moments before the sun disappeared altogether behind the uncapped pinnacle, a low, moaning sound came from the center of the forest, echoing off the rise below me, louder and more haunting than any that came before it. It was the sound of loneliness, or perhaps of pain, the sound of something that had lost its mate, or was perhaps dying itself. It had a bovine quality to it, but louder, much louder, and longer, the monotonous tone of it trailing off in nearly a whimper.

It went on for several minutes, starting, stopping, and starting up again, each time lasting for a briefer period, the volume just a bit less from one to the next, as if running out of gas. The brief pauses between each sorrowful note seemed to hold for a period as if waiting for a response that never came. It ended with a final, frail tone, which just seemed to fade into the complete silence that now dominated the valley.

I continued to hear the sound long after it was gone, wondering what had made it, and why. It was a lonely, haunting sound, a finality to it that I could only associate with death. I wondered if it had died alone, killed by a predator, or some disease that no one had ever heard of before, a strain of virus that had died out with the dinosaur. Did anything mourn its passing? Would it be missed?

Sitting in darkness, I wondered if *I'd* be missed. There was but a handful of people that knew I was gone, fewer that would care. Former co-workers, students, old classmates, perhaps even a neighbor or two, would someday wonder, "Whatever happened to David Williams? I haven't seen him in years. Probably off on one of his digs somewhere." And that would pretty much be the end of it.

Dermot would care, but he wouldn't miss me. On the contrary, the longer I was gone, the more data I would provide, the more proof he would have that his precious experiment was a success. No, Dermot would never see me again. Even the chance of finding the smallest fragment of what was once me was astronomic. Seeing me *alive* was the very last thing in the world that Dermot wanted. He needn't worry about that, but, of course, he couldn't know that for sure.

Jakes would miss me, but not for very long. He had a family to love and care for. In no time at all, they would help fill whatever small space my absence created. And for just the briefest of moments, I thought that the money would help to fill that void, as well, but that was unfair, and I knew untrue. Jakes wouldn't give a damn about the money. He wasn't the kind of guy whose friendship could be bought. On the contrary, years from now when he was retired early, or paying for his kid's college tuition, he would remember fondly where the money came from ... and he *would* care.

Then there was Susan. Susan would care, *and* she would miss me—if she could. But she probably wouldn't know I was gone, probably didn't know anything beyond that terrible day on the rock pile. But I still clung to the hope that she did. That somehow, she not only knew that I had taken the trip to the past, but somehow, in some kind of magical, mystical way, she was with me now, seeing what I was seeing, feeling what I was feeling. I kept thinking back to the scene in the window and how closely it matched the real thing, thinking that Susan actually saw this valley, and not just because of my drawing. Maybe it was a sixth sense that we shared—an ability to look beyond the three dimensions, to sneak a peak under the curtain of time to see what was actually there. Perhaps there was a connection between us that went beyond the metaphysical, a psychic link of some sort. I couldn't feel it, but that didn't mean it wasn't there. I prayed that it existed, because without it, I was really alone.

The dark, unseen black clouds coming from the mountaintop blotted out the stars. Rising above the mountains behind me, the full moon was visible only in fragmented streaks as the tendrils of smoke drifted between the earth and the heavens, sending dim, intermittent shadows across the plain to the east.

I had to pull myself away, despite the overwhelming desire to stay. The thirst and hunger of the past day had been forgotten during the amazing afternoon sitting on the ledge. But as I thought about it, my stomach began to growl, my throat tightened up from the lack of water. I had a long trek back, several hours before I reached the small remainder of my supplies. If I didn't get moving right then I wasn't going to make it back.

In the dark, I arose, turned towards the east and began the long, slow descent across the plain.

*****

I hadn't brought pen or paper on the first trip into the valley of the dinosaurs, so I had to type it into the computer as best that I could remember it. But it wasn't a problem—it was an afternoon that I wasn't likely to forget.

The final leg of that first trip, back to the cave, had been uneventful, although exhausting and frightening. Nearly starved and half out of my mind from thirst, I had made it back to the odd-shaped obelisk hours before the sun began to rise. To that point, the walk was relatively free of obstacles, and all downhill. Despite the darkness, I made that part of the trip faster than I had on the way up, my footing sure and steady.

I couldn't go back through the tunnel because the bottom had been blocked by the falling rock, so I had to take the long way around. The way was far from being without its hazards—steep and rocky—a hundred possibilities for an accident. Despite my raging thirst, I didn't dare attempt the crossing in the dark. Instead, I found the least painful rock to prop my weary body against and instantly fell asleep while the dawn approached.

*****

It was a hundred aches and pains, rather than the sunlight, that awoke me from my too short nap—the deep pain in my chest that exploded with each movement and every breath was the worst of the bunch.

Coming fully awake, my vision was blurred, my head hammered with a migraine caused by too little sleep, not enough food and water. The long, slender shadow was once again upon me. I turned to see the stony needle, its tip pointing to the west, forcing me back to reality, telling me loud and clear that I was in trouble and needed to get moving.

It took more than an hour to stumble my way down and around the short distance to the bottom of the tunnel. Like a drunken man, I staggered from side to side, bumping up against one bolder after another like a pinball machine, falling into one slot, jumping out only to slip into the next. It's a mystery how I didn't kill myself, or at least break an ankle. Of course, a broken ankle would have killed me off just as well—it just would have taken longer to die.

I found my backpack, and fought the desire to rip it open and drink down the entire bottle in one satisfying gulp. Instead, I carefully unwrapped the plastic seal with trembling fingers. Pulling out the little blue spout, I brought it to my lips and took but the smallest sip, swishing it around inside of my mouth, feeling each cell absorb the precious fluid like a sponge.

I took one more small sip, swallowing it this time, before it could be absorbed elsewhere, feeling it trickle down my throat, giving me a chill that literally shook me down to my toes, raised gooseflesh up and down my arms. It was miraculous how one small sip of water could revive me so, could give me a whole new outlook.

I sat down upon the nearest rock, slowly sipping on the water, staring across the short valley that led to the long gravel rise to the ridge, formulating a plan. Once gaining the ridge it would be a straight shot home, downhill, flat, an easy stroll. But getting to the ridge was a problem. It was steep and slippery. I remembered half running, half sliding down it, gravity propelling me down it much faster than I wanted to go.

I decided that I would need all my strength for the gravel-climb, so I would shoot my wad at the bottom of the rise. It looked to be no more than a few miles away, a distance I could cross long before the sun hit mid-way across the sky, a relatively flat space that would not sap what was left of my strength. I looked at the water bottle, a quarter of it gone. Fighting the urge to take one more, big swallow, I pushed the top in and tossed it into my pack. I headed toward the incline, pulling on the backpack as I stepped out onto firm ground.

It was farther than I thought, taking more strength than I had reckoned, but I got to the leading edge of the gravel in one piece. I started across it, my paces shortened and slowed by the soft and slippery footing. The sun had indeed made it to the center of the sky, perhaps a few degrees beyond, so I decided to move on just a bit farther before emptying my rations.

The climb was hard, as hard as I imagined. I pushed upward, forgetting about my meal, thinking only of pushing on—one small step at a time. Like the descent, I slid a half step for every one that I took, but this time my direction was continuously reversed, having to take two full steps to traverse the distance of one.

I refused to look up to gauge my progress. Instead, I just kept my head pointed forward, staring onto yard after yard of pulverized stone, sliding down beyond my vision as gravity sent them forward to fill the void created by each footstep. It became a challenge to me, not only to make it to the top, but to do it without breaking into my pack. The water would taste all the sweeter from the top. The long journey back to the cave would be that much easier.

It wasn't one of the smarter things that I had ever done, but I made it. The palms of my hands were raw, bleeding from the rough texture of the tiny stones. Every one of my fingers were blistered from digging handholds into the coarse pebbles. My pants were shredded, my knees bloodied and torn from halting the never-ending half-step slide. Physically, I was on my last legs, not able to go one more step, but I was on an incredible high. I had made it to the top, and my pack was still unopened.

I didn't stop to enjoy the high. Instead, I ripped the pack from my back and drank half the remaining water in one long swig. Following that, I tore into the can of beans, inhaling it rather than just eating it, using my bare hands, uncaring of the sharp inner edge left from the can opener, caring even less about my grubby fingers. I had the last of the jerky for desert. I thought about saving the last of the water for the trip down. But then I thought to hell with it, and drank that, too.

The sun was setting in the west, perhaps an hour left of daylight. It was not nearly enough time to make it all the way down the long, winding ridge, and I longed for a good night's sleep, but the thought of sleeping in my own bed, in my own home, was just too much to withstand. I slung the lightened pack across my shoulders and started out.

For once, luck was with me. The full moon was not nearly as hidden by the volcanic smoke as it was on the previous night. It shined brightly through the blackness, lighting my way. The sea to my right reflected the starlight, further aiding my every step. I was fed and watered—only the pain in my chest and the ache in my legs kept me from running all the way home.

CHAPTER 16

The first winter of my new life had been warm compared to the sub-zero temperatures of Chicago. The days were shorter and the nights colder as the season changed from autumn. But cold is a relative thing, as is any reference to the changing seasons.

In Chicago, the change is a physical presence, a hard thing that you can feel in your heart and soul, as well as in your fingers and toes. It's a change so profound, that it's like living in two distinctly different worlds, switching back and forth between them twice a year. It changed the landscape, and changed the people, as well. Each year as the leaves fell from the trees, leaving the limbs bare like blackened skeletons, and the grass turned to the sickly yellow brown of death, the people began to change. They hid behind the closed doors of their offices and homes as their once rosy complexions faded to the ghostly gray of inactivity. Faces that so easily split into huge grins during the warmth of the summer became as short and as rare as a sunny day in the winter. And people that were friends and neighbors during the hot months, seemed distant and remote, infrequently seen, as they disappeared into their hideaways when the cold winds bit and the snow flew.

In my new world, the change was subtle—little things that only mattered when checking things closely—comparing. My breath was visible first thing in the morning, seeing just a bit of color among the few leaf-bearing trees hidden away within the lush green of the conifers and palms, having to wrap myself in blankets in the middle of the night when I awoke shivering—I was always surprised by it.

The changes were small, imperceptible from one day to the next, barely noticeable when comparing one week to the next. The temperature varied pretty much as it did between daytime hours and nighttime hours in my former world. And it varied little from day to day, from one week to the next, much less than Chicago during the seasonal changes.

It was probably mid-December in my new world before I even noticed the change.

That's why, in my second winter it was such a surprise when I saw the first few snowflakes fall. The sun was down, had been for more than an hour. I was wrapped in a warm blanket, enjoying the last few chapters of one of Susan's novels. I was leaning in close to my reading torch, which is probably why I hadn't noticed it sooner.

I felt wetness on the side of my face, brushing the first of it away thinking it was nothing more than a light rain shower. The second time, I noticed that it felt cold to the touch, too cold for just rain. When I pulled my fingers away, I could see the ice particles sparkle in the firelight.

I sprung from my warm cocoon, letting the blanket fall from my shoulders in a heap on the wet deck. I peered over the handrail, down between the trees, fifty feet to the ground below. Even in the darkness, I could see a shiny coating of white reflecting the moon's glow. Peering upward, I could see the same frosted coating on the trees, the ice particles shimmering as the breeze stirred the branches. The same breeze struck my face, numbing my cheeks, sending a tiny chill through the rest of me. Like a kid, I stuck out my tongue, catching the snow, feeling it melt instantly, swallowing it, delighted in the feel of water that was actually cold. I scooped up what had accumulated on the rail in front of me, sucking at it greedily, loving the feel of it as it trickled down my throat.

I dashed into my shelter, rummaged through my belongings, easily finding the makeshift calendar. For more than a year, I had been charting the days, carefully noting the exact time of each sunrise and sunset, always measured from the same spot. Always timed from the point that the sun first appeared over the eastern cliff until it passed behind the smoldering volcano to the west. The longest day was just over fifteen hours. I noted the day as June 22, the summer solstice.

I had been recording the length of day, yet not really noticing *what* day it was. Without civilization, one day's pretty much like the next. But as I looked upon the calendar I realized that this day was not like any other. A smile spread across my face as my finger stopped on my most recent record—December 24—Christmas Eve.

I had failed to follow through on my promise to observe the holidays. I had been so busy, so caught up in discovery, so tied up in just trying to stay alive from one day to the next, that each day passed without being aware of what day it was, or even what month it was.

I renewed my commitment to celebrate the holidays, my birthday, the days that I met Jakes and Dermot, the day that I went back in time, and anything else that I could think of worth celebrating. And I began that night.

I broke open my supply of scotch, not the whole barrel, which was still back in the machine, but one of the two water bottles that I had filled with the precious fluid. I grabbed a fresh, warm blanket and hunkered down next to the torch to finish my book.

It was just about perfect. I was warm, comfortable, finishing off the last of a novel, and prepared to get a little buzz on. It wasn't a great novel, at least by my standards, but it was Susan's so it was damn special to me. I had no deadlines to make, no bills to pay, no asses to kiss. Instead of digging in the hard-packed earth of the mid-west, looking for little bits of fossilized bone so that I could make impossible guesses about a creature that lived seventy million years ago, I was living among them, studying them first-hand.

Life was good.

I finished the book, feeling mellow and content, with still a couple of fingers left of fine old scotch. I kept the blanket wrapped around my shoulders as I rose and walked the short distance over to the railing. I looked out across the shimmering jungle, watching as the light snow continued to drift down in a swirling pattern caught by the valley's circular breeze. I was so mesmerized by the surprise squall that I failed to notice the eerie stillness that permeated the jungle. It was so quiet that I could hear the tiny particles of snow hit the floorboards of my treetop home.

It was eerie and unnatural. The forest was always alive with sound, even in the dead of night, even in the worst of the rains.

Not all of the creatures slept at night or hid during the rains. Many were nocturnal, even the mating calls of some of the dinosaurs could be heard late into the night, beyond the darkness and the storms—but not on that night. On that night, with the snow, came the silence, and it frightened me.

Listening carefully, I could hear the breeze whistling through the branches of the trees, a low moaning sound, one of loneliness, one of impending doom. I had been here through an entire winter, plus the beginnings of another, without seeing snow. And I didn't think that it had been anywhere near cold enough to snow the previous year.

It really didn't feel cold enough to snow then. Yet, there it was. I knew that the ideal time to snow was when the air temperature was just above freezing. It didn't take the bone chilling, sub-zero temperatures of Chicago in February to produce it.

The snow, combined with the unusual silence, made me worry about the animals. The changing seasons of the late Cretaceous period was one of the theories regarding the extinction of the dinosaurs.

For most of the Mesozoic period, the climate was mild, meaning—hot, and humid—a tropical environment. As the K-T boundary neared—the end of the Cretaceous period, the ice caps at the poles began to form, changing the weather, creating seasonal variations. Some felt that the colder environment spelled the end of the dinosaurs—that they couldn't cope with the drastic change in the weather. And perhaps they were right. The snow of that night had caused a dramatic change. All was quiet. Perhaps this was the first time that any of the animals had ever experienced snow and the cold that accompanied it. The dinosaurs went under cover, or they simply didn't know how to deal with the change in the weather. Perhaps they just sat there, not sure what to do, some of them perhaps dying in the cold.

Was this the beginning of the end?

The first snow made me realize that it had been too long since I had left my summer home on the beach—too long since I had put my story into the computer. If something happened to me now, Dermot wouldn't have much of the tale. The computer only held the report of my first sighting of a dinosaur, the group of *Triceratops*, viewed from a distance atop the plateau. So much more had happened since the last time that I saw the time machine. With the cold coming, it was definitely time to return to it.

*****

It took only a day to prepare for the return trip. There really wasn't much that I had to do, or much that I had to take. I still had a good supply of food supplements back in the machine: books, blankets, clothing, the odd assortment of tools, medical supplies, a stove, weapons, cooking utensils, and of course the computer. I also had my easy chair and an actual bed, replete with an honest to God mattress and pillow. Just the thought of a soft, comfortable bed made me anxious to get back.

So, I packed only what I needed for the trip—food and water for four days, a small medical kit just in case something happened on the way, a blanket, a knife, and my handgun—and, oh yeah, firewood—lots of it. I had almost none back at the cave, and if the snow of the night before were any indication, I would need plenty.

I left early the next morning, at first light, knowing that the first part of the journey would be the most difficult and dangerous. I had close to a half cord of wood piled high on the cart that I had built with the help of the Dermot-supplied wheels, the wood strapped down tight. It was heavy, but Dermot had supplied good wheels, the kind with precision ball bearings, not just an iron axle through the holes of the wheels. It rolled easily over the rough ground the hundred yards through the jungle to the edge of the meadow.

It rolled equally well over the meadow, although a bit more slowly, the ground soft from the thawed snow of the night before. I made faster progress over the hard-packed dirt of the game trail. I just had to worry about a band of dinosaurs interrupting my progress. But it was early, and a year of watching the trail told me that the animals rarely traveled it before noon.

The thick nylon ropes were just as I left them, strung on a diagonal from the top of the plateau, across the river, anchored to the opposite shore. At the top of the ridge, attached to a double piton, was one of two pulleys Dermot had packed. Each gave me a ratio of ten to one—I could hoist ten times the weight that I could, using my strength alone. It had been enough to allow me to safely lower my supplies down to the river on that first trip down into the valley. I prayed that it would be enough to get my pallet of wood back up again.

I attached the rope to the top bindings on the woodpile and slowly rolled it into the water. The wide flat base of the cart made for an excellent raft, but I had to keep enough tension on the other rope so that the base of the raft just skimmed over the surface of the water. Too much force and I would lift the raft completely out of the water causing it to swing in an arc, crashing into the wall more than a hundred feet away. Too little, and the mild current would take the raft quickly downstream, pulling me up the face of the cliff without it. It was more difficult to control the wide, heavy load than it was to lift it, and my strength was sapped by the time it bumped harmlessly against the edge of the plateau.

I rested there for a few minutes, keeping enough tension on the rope to keep the load from drifting downstream. I tied it off to the piton in which I had first anchored the ropes some fifteen months ago.

The lift was tiring, but then came the difficult, dangerous part—I had to scale the wall. I had another rope, one that was knotted every twelve inches, which I untied from the piton and, holding on tight, began wading across the river.

Back on the other side, I began to climb, using the knots as footholds, pulling hand over hand, one knot to the next. I was in the best shape of my life, so the climb wasn't all that strenuous, but it scared the shit out of me. I wasn't terribly fond of heights, and I wasn't at all sure that I had driven the pitons far enough into the granite two hundred feet above.

The most difficult part of the climb was contending with the face of the rock. The rope was draped directly against it, forcing me to have to push myself away from the rough surface as I ascended. It tore at my knuckles, banged hard against my shoulders and knees, and made the climb more difficult the higher I went.

And I hadn't done a very good job of engineering my pulley setup. There wasn't enough space between the two sets of ropes. The one I was climbing pushed hard against the side of the wood-laden cart, causing it to tip. I was less concerned with it spilling its load than I was of the extra strain on the rope holding it. It became even more precarious as I reached the top and I had to literally climb aboard the cart in order to pass over it.

It did, however, offer the advantage of being able to step from the top of the cart directly onto the crest of the plateau, like stepping out of an elevator. I fought off a moment of panic as the load of wood swayed backwards as I stepped off, seeing in my mind a snapshot of me plunging down between the rock and the cart, falling two hundred feet into the shallow waters of the river below.

I paused and looked out over the valley of the dinosaurs. The view looked different than it did the first time that I had taken it in from this altitude, but I couldn't quite put a reason to it. Perhaps it was because it was still early in the morning, the sun still in the eastern part of its arc, casting the long shadow of the plateau across the jungle foliage. Perhaps, it actually had changed in the time since I had last stood on the ledge. Well over a year had passed, and it was later in the year than the last time—the snow indicated that things were indeed changing. Or perhaps it was only that I was looking at it differently. The first time, I had no idea what lay ahead, what the jungle looked like up close, what adventures and hardships lie ahead. Now, I couldn't help but look at it differently.

The cart full of wood caught my eye and I realized that I had made another engineering blunder. Even with the advantage the pulley system gave me, there was no way in hell that I was going to be able to pull the weight over the lip of the cliff.

I had really only one option, and that was to remove the wood from the cart, one piece at a time. I wasn't on a suicide mission, so first, I pulled up the knotted rope, gave myself ten foot of length from the piton, and tied it tightly around my waist. I had to climb back atop the wood and ease myself down along its side to remove a couple of the binding straps.

Back on top, on my hands and knees on the edge of the plateau, I pulled up the strapping and began digging into the firewood. It wasn't pretty. I felt goddamn uncomfortable hanging out over the rim, so I just began pitching wood behind me ... as fast as I could. My arms flailing away at a speed that would have been but a blur to an observer, I emptied the cart in less than half an hour. Thankful that I was wearing gloves, I fell back against the hard rock as the last of the wood hit the ground behind me.

Regaining my strength, I thought about how I was going to get the cart over the edge.

At that point, the pulley was of no help whatsoever. It was all muscle, adrenaline, and sheer willpower. The cart flipped over onto its top as it caught the lip of the crest, landing an inch from where I was kneeling.

It landed without a scratch—I had built a solid cart. I flipped it over, and more slowly than I had unpacked it, began to load it up once again. I took my time, no real need to hurry, but by the time I had it all back, lashed down again, I was bushed, sweating and panting even though the weather was cool.

I praised Dermot for the two pulley systems, and cursed him for not giving me three. When I got to the long gravel slope leading to the ridge overlooking the sea, I was going to need both pulleys. No way was I going to be able to pull the cart up the sliding slope by myself, and the pulley I had left at the top of it hadn't enough rope to make it to the bottom. I was going to have to go back down the side of the plateau, cross the river, and free the other rope. I was a little pissed at myself, as well. I had another long length of rope back at the machine. Why I didn't take it was a mystery. I guess that I didn't want to put all my eggs in one basket.

By the time I had returned, the day was pretty much shot. I was content to call it quits for the night. I had a long way to go—at least one more really difficult part—but I was satisfied, even proud, of what I had accomplished so far. It was time for a rest, and a reward.

I had been sipping on water throughout the day, and sweating it out faster than I was putting it in. I finished off the opened bottle and started in on another. Water was plentiful in the valley. The river I had just crossed—three times—was fresh, not salt water, meaning it was not once part of the intercontinental sea, nor was it a part of the underground river that had taken me from the cave. It tasted a little strange at first—Lord knows what was in it—but I had gotten used to it pretty quickly. I drank it in huge quantities, remembering all too well what it was like to be thirsty.

With the water, I had a couple of strips of dried meat—not beef—but something a little more exotic. But that's a story for another time.

*****

It took two more days to cross the plain leading to the base of the gravel slope of the ridge that led back to my beach. The trek was long, but mostly downhill and free of any major obstacles. It was much longer than my original trip in the other direction. With the cart, I had to stay on the clearest path, having to travel many miles to the north in order to find the route between the two mountains. Pulling the cart hadn't been that big a problem, the rock was hard, kept swept clean by the easterly winds.

Yet, by the time I reached the base of the gravel, I was worn out. I still had an hour or so of daylight, and I really wanted to get the pulley system hooked up, but the thought of climbing half the slope to reach the loose end of the rope was just more than I could take. Instead, I wrapped myself in a blanket, settled in against the side of the cart, popped open another bottle of water, and watched the sunset, thinking that tomorrow at this time, if all went right, I'd be sitting in my overstuffed chair in my winter home.

*****

I slept longer than I had intended. I guess I was as tired as I felt. The sun had already passed beyond the ridge, the sun bright in my eyes as I stared at the daunting task ahead of me. I remembered the grueling ordeal the year before, climbing and sliding up the steep rise. It had worn me out, yet I wasn't trying to pull a cart laden with several hundred pounds of wood along with me.

I climbed to the halfway point in less time than I had expected. I guess that I was in better shape than the last time—certainly better nourished. I couldn't stake the pulley in the loose gravel. There was no place to drive in the piton. Instead, I connected the system to the end of the dangling rope, hoping that the piton anchored at the top of the ridge would hold the combined weight.

The bearings of the wheels were top-notch, but the wheels were not meant to travel through gravel that was several meters deep. Pulling it upward was much harder than hoisting it up from the river, despite the slope, which normally would reduce friction considerably. I found that the easiest thing to do was to walk back down the slope, pulling on the rope as I went, raising the cart at an equal speed, but opposite direction. It worked reasonably well, although I was going to have to walk back up a second time just to get to where I started.

I had to repeat the entire process in order to get up the second half of the mountain.

By the time I got there it was near dark, and I was wasted. As much as I longed for the safety, warmth, and comfort of the machine, I just couldn't do it.

As tired as I was on that night, I didn't sleep very well. I was exhausted, and I ached from head to toe, every muscle screaming in protest for what I had put them through. But my mind raced.

Mostly, I thought of Susan.

In a year there had been no change in her condition. But that had been nearly two years ago. What had happened to her in that time? I had to believe that something had occurred since I had last seen her—either she had come out of her coma … or not. I hated to think of the or not part. I knew that people in comas, did not normally survive for any extended period. It was surprising to her doctors that she had hung on for as long as she had. And that was a long time ago.

I felt guilty, terribly guilty. If she had come out of it, then I should have been there for her. She had no one else, and she would have been terribly disoriented, alone, devastated by my abandonment. She had no one else to turn to. In the time that had passed, her few friends and colleagues would have forgotten her, gone on to other things. Other than Jakes, who I knew would honor my request, no one was visiting her. Probably no one thought much about her … other than some vague, but fond memory.

And if the worst had happened, who would mourn her? Her obituary would be expansive, would tell of her many great accomplishments in the field of paleontology, would relate her compassion and her love of life, her unquenchable thirst for knowledge. I knew ... I had written it. And many would read it. Little old men and little old ladies would read it, looking for the name of a friend or acquaintance, silently happy in the fact that they had outlasted yet another one. But how many would read it and be touched by what she was—who she was?

It was a cruel world. People just didn't give a damn. By now, they would have forgotten her. If she had come out of it, who would be there for her? Could she make it on her own? Before the accident, she was as tough as nails, could handle any situation by herself. But God only knew what kind of physical and emotional state she'd be in after all that time unconscious. And, on top of everything, she'd find me gone.

I was of mixed emotions. I didn't want Susan to be alone, yet, at the same time, I hoped that she had come out of it. It was important to me that she discovered the truth about what had happened to me—even more important that she learned the truth about how I felt about her.

I dreamt of Susan. I dreamt that she was with me, that, side-by-side we had made the journey through time, and that together we discovered all the things that we had fantasized about most of our lives. In the dream, we had built a home together high above the jungle, like Tarzan and Jane, but instead of lions and tigers, there were animals much larger, and much more fascinating.

I awoke at sunrise, the dream still fresh in my mind, and for just a moment, I thought that it was real, that Susan really was with me … and I looked for her. But like all dreams, the images drifted away like so much smoke, leaving me in despair—a loneliness such that I hadn't felt since those first few days of the experiment.

I made the last, and easiest, leg of the journey in a fog. Although the details of the dream faded, the loneliness left behind refused to follow. I could barely remember the trip, my thoughts so consumed with Susan. Before I knew it, I was stepping down onto the rocks that made up the last fifty feet to the beach. Not really thinking about it, I had dumped the contents of the cart off the side, letting the wood bounce down below to scatter across the sand. Leaving the cart on top seemed to make sense. I would certainly never be able to get it back up again loaded. I was saving myself some work next time out.

The first week back I didn't accomplish very much. I was too busy beating myself up over deserting Susan. The first couple of days I refused to get out of bed for more than an hour at a time. I convinced myself that it was because I was so tired from my trip, and the soft bed felt so damn good. It took until the third day to realize that I was only feeling sorry for myself—missing Susan—tired of being alone.

I had to force myself to do something useful, even if my heart wasn't in it. The first order of business was to get the wood out of the weather, into the cave before the rains came and soaked it.

It took most of a day to move it, piling it up neatly against the back of the time machine. It felt good having accomplished something useful, but I still felt that I was moving in slow motion, my past still dragging behind me like a lead weight.

Each morning I foraged for food along the shore, the shellfish a welcome change to a diet that had become almost exclusively meat. Each morning I walked across the white sand toward the water, the sun reflecting brightly off the waves, making it difficult to look straight ahead. I returned to the cave each morning with my catch of the day, my head hanging down, not wanting to face either the day or the machine that had brought me to this lonely spot.

The beach was a refuge, a safe haven where I didn't have to worry about becoming something's lunch every day. But it was a terribly lonely place—a place that, other than an occasional glimpse of a *Pteranodon* flying high above or an *Elasmosaurus* swimming below, was devoid of life. It was a constant reminder that I was truly alone.

I could survive on the beach. I had everything that I really needed—food, water, shelter—I could survive, but was it really living? Other than measuring the length of each day, noting the climatic changes, there wasn't a hell of a lot to do. I had the computer, a lot of catching up to do, but my heart just wasn't in it. I needed a distraction.

I found it in a most unusual way. It wasn't until the beginning of the second week back that I noticed something remarkable. I had gone down to the beach like I did to begin each new day. Only on this morning I decided to stay for a while instead of marching directly back to the cave with my breakfast. I stood at the water's edge, watching the waves slide up to within a couple of inches of my boots. The air had a chill to it, my breath coming out in little white puffs like a cartoon character.

I stared out to sea, watching an early rising pelican skim the choppy surface, its legs dipping into the tips of the white caps, flying away with a prize that I couldn't quite see. Everything looked as it should, the same as it had every morning that I had spent on the beach.

Turning to the south, I strolled down the shoreline, kicking at a shell, shuffling along aimlessly. Time and distance had no meaning. I thought about Susan, and Jakes, and Dermot, never lifting my eyes from the sand. I just kept walking along the beach until there was no more beach to walk along, halting beside the rock cliff as it disappeared into the sea.

I shifted my eyes upward, scanning the rocky slope to the top.

It was all wrong.

I knew every inch of the beach, every rocky surface, each view—from every angle. Where the rock met the water never looked like this. The rise towered above me, higher than it had before … much higher.

I turned and looked to the north. Something was wrong. I trotted—then ran—back to the center of the shore, directly opposite the entrance to the cave. It was a view that I had seen a hundred times, the image firmly imprinted upon my brain ... it was not the same.

For one crazy moment, I wondered how the hell the mountains moved backwards from the shore. A crazy notion, but for just an instant, it was the only thing that popped into my head. For a moment I was stymied until it struck me. I looked both to the north and to the south. The beach had changed in a fundamental way—it had grown.

The entrance to the cave, the front end of the time machine protruding forward, looked noticeably farther away. I knew this view. I had taken it in every morning that I was here. It was no optical illusion … it *was* farther away. The sea had receded.

I knew that the snow of the week before was no fluke. It was a reminder that the world was changing—the climate, too. The globe was changing from one of subtropical to one of seasonal variation, especially in the Northern Hemisphere. And along with the environmental changes, there was a drastic change in sea level—one that would result in the demise of the sea that separated eastern North America from its western counterpart.

I wasn't sure just how much the sea had pulled back. It never occurred to me before that it was happening. I hadn't thought to check. But now I knew. It gave me yet another thing to track. Something to keep me occupied during the long winter in the machine.

And yet, it wasn't something that was going to keep me busy for much of the time. The sea was receding, but not something that I was going to be able to measure from day to day. More likely, I was going to have to track it on a monthly basis, probably by the year.

I wandered back over to the northern edge of the shore, where the rock met the water. I looked upon the surface of the rock, looking at the striations, trying to make some sense of the changes rising up the slope. There were hundreds of subtle changes, slight variations of color and texture, minor changes in the rippling of the stone. I wished that Brian Huntsville were with me. He would have read the rock, would've known what each variation meant. He could have told me exactly where and when the sea had formed and exactly how fast it was receding.

But Brian wasn't here, nor was anyone else for that matter. I would just have to do with exploring on my own and setting up my own little experiments.

I began with marking the perimeter. I used the iron bars from the destroyed gate that once blocked the entrance to the cave. It was hard work trying to separate, straighten, and cut them to a usable length, but by the end of the day I had five usable markers. Of course, in due time the iron would rust, more quickly if exposed directly to the salty water. So I backed each marker off the water line by twenty-five feet, the length of the longest, accurate measuring devise that I had—a metal tape measure.

Using a sledgehammer, I drove them several feet into the sandy shore, an equal length exposed, easily visible from a hundred yards. I placed the first two along the edges of the slope where they entered the water, the other three equally spaced across the shore.

The next morning, I paced off the distance between the two end markers, and the distance between the cave's entrance and the center marker, which roughly bisected the shore into two equal halves. I walked off the steps twice and averaged the two. The beach was two hundred and twelve paces across and one hundred and eighty paces from the cave to the shore—perhaps eight hundred feet by seven hundred. It wasn't very accurate, but I figured precise measurements were pretty damn unimportant. I just wanted to measure the relative change over time.

I wasn't sure how much the beach had changed while I was gone, perhaps a hundred feet in depth, twice that in width. Where the earlier shoreline existed, it created a neat half-circle of beach. Fifteen months later, with the water pulling back, the symmetry was gone, as the southern rise of the cliff curved away quickly, expanding the width of the beach exponentially. The slope rose quickly as it made a right turn to the south.

I measured the distance a second time with the tape measure, from the markers to the water's edge, noting the time and day so that I could factor in the tides.

Looking back at the cave's entrance, the view hadn't changed much, except it looked smaller. The elevation didn't really seem any different. I could still see the base of the time machine, meaning that the slope of the newly exposed beach was very gradual.

I had my notepad and a pencil, jotting down data as I went along. I made little drawings as well—the general shape of the beach as I found it on that day, as if from above, noting the dimensions and location of the markers, as a draftsman would do—the approximate height of the cliffs from a point directly above the point where they met the water—the shape and color of the stone. I tried as best I could to approximate the same data from the year before, noting that these were only estimates, having not thought to do it during my first stay on the beach.

By the end of a very long day, I had filled two-dozen pages of my little spiral notebooks. I had charts and graphs, dimensions and data, little notes in all the margins, and several pages of theories and hypotheses. I had pages of ramblings, illegible scribbling that even I would probably not be able to decipher. But I would try.

It was time to pull out the computer.

I was anxious to get started. I was up half an hour before the sun woke me, motivated again for the first time in weeks. The door of the machine stood open, bidding me exit to my home, entrance to a new day filled with new adventures, a chance to record the events of the past.

I ate a meager breakfast of some reconstituted orange juice and some dried oatmeal, made palatable with hot water instead of milk. It was nourishing but tasteless, like munching on soggy cardboard flakes. But it was filling, and I was grateful. Too often I had awoke with nothing to eat, too many times I had gone a whole day with nothing.

I exited the time machine just as the full circle of the sun cleared the great sea. I brought out the computer, facing the solar panels recessed within the lid to the east to catch the brilliant rays, as I marched out to the shoreline to see what I could find.

This time I paid attention. It was a longer walk than I had made the year before—not a long distance, but more than before. I wasted some time plodding along the shore, giving the batteries time to recharge, afraid as always that they would fail to do so.

It was strange. Somehow, I took pride in the expanding width and depth of the beach. Like a homeowner, who just added an addition to his already large home, or added the half-acre of land when his neighbor went into receivership, I was excited by the growing dimensions of the beach—my home. And it *was* my home, and there was no mortgage company to take it away from me.

I strutted back and forth along the beach, feeling like the lord of the manor surveying his domain. I had no family, no servants, no orchards or livestock, yet as the only human being alive, I felt like a king—ruler of all the lands that I could cross, all that I could see. And there was no army to conquer my lands, no one to trespass on them, no lawyer to swindle them away. No one was going to outwit me or take advantage of me, or foreclose on a mortgage. I had a world full of fantastic animals to rule over. I was their master—I was smarter than them all. Of course, it was always a very real possibility that one of my loyal subjects might simply eat me as a light snack.

I was even more excited with the change itself. The pulling back of the waters of the Western Interior Sea meant that the epoch was coming to an end. Although I was only going to experience the most infinitesimal portion of it, I was excited to witness it, to be a part of it. Maybe I could answer a few of the thousands of questions that scientists had puzzled over for more than a hundred years. Perhaps I could unravel some of the mystery of it. Even untying a knot or two would be something!

I found nothing significant during my wandering, probably because I was preoccupied by my own sense of grandeur. And, I was just killing time, letting the batteries charge, anxious to get back to the cave, to my computer.

I was delighted to see that the solar cells were fully charged, the program already booted up. The year plus in storage apparently left the laptop none the worse for wear. I pulled up the program that I needed and began to type.

It was only mid-day, lunchtime, but I was on a roll. My stomach growled, and I had plenty of food in the machine, even more, fresher stuff in the sea. But I had half a dozen books full of notes from fifteen months in the valley of the dinosaurs. It was time to get it all down.

CHAPTER 17

I swung back and forth, gripping the rope with all my strength, my feet cramping from how tightly I had them squeezed together on top of the knot. The few feet of rope beneath me dangled into the water, swaying from right to left, all the while, being pulled downstream by the current.

I thought back to that ominous day of Liz's burial—the growing pool of rainwater inching toward my feet—wondering what would happen when it came in contact with my shoe. My wild imagination conjured up the most bizarre consequences, none of them pleasant. I felt the same way then. I was afraid to drop down into the river at the base of the plateau. The unknown was terrifying.

It looked like water, like any other river that I had seen over my entire life, no ... better than that. It was the transparent, silver-blue of all clean rivers—rivers not yet polluted by man's lack of diligence, rivers that were pure and free of those things that were not meant to be a part of them. It looked like a river that you could bathe in, or drink from without fear of a terrifying bout of Montezuma's revenge, or something worse.

And I had seen this one some weeks before. At the time, it looked fascinating, not frightening, the beginning of a journey that I had been daydreaming about all of my life. And here I was about to enter a world that I had studied, had wished that I could enter for as long as I could remember. But, hovering just inches above its surface, I had second thoughts ... even thirds.

On the day of Liz's burial, I had been lost in sorrow, devastated by the loss of the one that I cared most about. My mind had shut down, unwilling to accept the reality of the situation. But this fear was real, not imaginary.

What was water like seventy million years ago? My thoughts returned to the scene at the cemetery, fantasizing about the acidity of the pool. It wasn't so far fetched now. Acid could indeed be an ingredient of this ancient body of water. Perhaps it was laden with sulfuric acid, washed down from the volcanic activity of the western mountains. If it was, and I stepped down into it, how fast would the acid work? Would I be able to climb back up to the top, and what would happen to me when I got there?

If it wasn't acid, perhaps it was poisonous. Not harmful to the touch, but what if I ingested it? I had no idea how deep the water was. If I stepped down into it, what if I sank straight down, like plunging into the deep underground tunnel when I fell from the cliff? Would I panic, sucking in another lungful of water as I did then? Were there poisons that would eat me up from the inside out? Or, perhaps there were bacteria of some kind, taking its toll in the same manner?

Maybe it wasn't acidic, or poisonous, or full of germs. Maybe instead, the river was filled with piranha, or a dozen other kinds of carnivorous fish. Maybe that was worse than acid, or poison, or bacteria. Perhaps just being a few inches above the surface was enough to alert a swarm of man-eaters, and they were now just below the surface, ready to strip the flesh from my bones the instant I touched the water.

I waited, swinging back and forth, picturing fish with huge, sharp teeth circling beneath me, ready to strike when my big toe caused concentric circles to form in the water above their heads. Were they smart enough to circle below, silently, not stirring up the water, alerting me to their presence? Probably not ... but I wasn't at all sure.

My imagination was getting the better of me ... once again, so I closed my eyes and dunked my foot in, all the way to the ankle. I kept them shut for five seconds ... ten seconds, and the tension was too much, and I pulled my foot out again.

But nothing happened. My flesh didn't burn or rot away. Nothing bit me, or jumped out of the water as I pulled my foot out. But my relief was only temporary. I still didn't relish the thought of dropping down into the water, letting go of the rope, and possibly going under.

But I knew that I was going to do this—had to do this. I took a big gulp of air and let go of the rope. I dropped down into the cool water, my feet touching bottom at the same instant that my chin smacked the surface, popping back up quickly. After all, I hadn't dropped very far. I grabbed hold of the rope, but didn't pull myself up. I waited, cautiously, holding my breath, emerged in the water up to my armpits, my feet just above the bottom, churning, discouraging anything from nipping at my toes.

I waited, paralyzed with fear for several minutes, my panic gradually subsiding as nothing happened. I released the rope, settling down in the water, the tops of my shoulders just clearing the surface. I bent my knees, sinking down in the mild current until it just reached my lips, exhaling bubbles into the water, inhaling through my nose, while I gazed across to the far shore.

All was quiet. It was still very early in the morning, the cliff casting a shadow that stretched clear across the long meadow, into the trees. Only the tip of the forest was lit up, the contrast making the tops of the trees look like a thousand shades of emerald-greens and golden-yellows. There was a haze settling in across the valley, the lower portion of the forest, beneath the shadow, cloaked in a ghostly white, nearly invisible.

The brilliant colors of the flowers in the foreground were muted by the deep shade and early-morning fog, but still visible. From my view at ground level, I could see that they were tall plants, several feet high, growing taller closer to the forest, disappearing into the mist. I wondered what lurked beneath the groundcover.

Even before I navigated the river, I was worried what lay beyond. It was my nature to worry, to consider what was around the bend, what the future had in store, to consider the worst possible scenario. I couldn't help but see a pack of meat-eaters coming around the bend of the game trail just as I was climbing on to the shore, or some mysterious, voracious animals lurking among the wildflowers, attacking me in pack.

I continued to wait, paddling my feet, treading water with my arms, more for pushing away whatever was swimming nearby, rather than an attempt to just stay afloat. After all, I could have stood up, my head above the water. I scanned to the right and then to the left, making sure that the coast was clear before pushing off from the base of the cliff.

It was a foolhardy thing to do. Other than a pair of shorts, a baseball cap, and my hiking boots, I was naked—no shirt, no food, no water … and no weapon. My intent was to go only as far as the water, to make sure it was safe, possible to cross.

Everything I had brought was still up top, waiting to be lowered down to the surface, if I thought it was possible. I didn't want to lower it to the water only to find out that I couldn't cross it—for whatever reason. I wasn't at all sure that I'd be able to haul it back up again. It was a heavy load, much heavier than the load of wood that I would haul up some fifteen months later.

On that day it was filled, mostly with tools, heavy steel tools to be precise. I took as many of them as I thought the cart would accommodate. Handsaws, axes, hatchets, planes, files, rasps, braces and bits, wood chisels, hammers, mallets—at least one of everything. I would have taken it all if I could. They were of no use back at the cave.

Packed in between the tools were clothing and blankets, half of my medical supplies, a very modest supply of food and water, and a handful of books. I didn't pack as much clothing as I should of, thinking that at the first sign of cold weather, I'd hightail it back to the machine. At least that's what I was thinking on that day. And I didn't take much food, sure that food would be much more plentiful in the lush valley than it was on the deserted beach.

I looked one more time from right to left and started toward the shore. It was a stupid thing to do—cross to the other side without a weapon—having no idea what lay beyond the meadow. I knew that it was stupid, but I did it anyway. The temptation to cross the river, to see what was on the other side, was just too much to ignore.

I went across slowly, cautiously, half swimming, and half walking along the sandy bottom. The water was so clear that I could see my knees as I lifted each one to take another step—the image distorted only by the ripples in the water that the current had created. There were fish, hundreds of them, in every conceivable size, shape and color. They swam past me, circled me, and darted between my legs, not the least bit afraid. But so far, none of them had taken a bite of me.

The depth of the water decreased smoothly as I progressed across. By the time I was half the way across, the water reached only my waist and the schools of fish began to diminish as I found it easier to move forward, the current less forceful.

I stepped out of the water and onto the short patch of sand. It was only ten yards or so before it gave way to hard-packed, dark soil, trampled flat by thousands of footprints. I walked forward, stopping after just a few paces, turning back to look down upon the ground. Alongside of the huge three- and four-toed prints were the faint impressions of my own. I smiled, thinking what a surprise this would be in another seventy million years, if someone should find them. Let's see them explain this one. For a second, I wondered if I should erase them on my way back. And then I thought, the hell with it. Let them have some fun with it.

I walked across the dirt trail, heading toward the meadow, alert, trying to distinguish any threatening sounds. The flowering shrubs that reached only to my knees at the edge of the meadow gave way to stunted trees covered with sweet smelling white and pink petals before I had gone more than fifty yards. The meadow was thick, but not nearly as dense as it had appeared from atop the cliff. I could see butterflies and dragonflies flitting nearly everywhere between the limbs.

The dwarf, flowering trees gave way to giant ferns, oaks and elms, and many bushes and trees that I had never seen before. They were of unusual shape, their trunks and limbs twisting about one another like they were locked in passionate embrace. Some had leaves nearly as big as I, brilliant green, their tips pointed, dripping with the morning dew. I peered to the west, as dark as night, the sunlight almost entirely blocked by the dense canopy overhead.

Without even realizing it, I had entered the jungle.

I wasn't willing to go into it very far. It was dark and threatening, and I wasn't prepared. Not more than a few yards into it, I heard the low moan of something waking up—something very loud, and, no doubt, very large. An instant later, I heard footsteps, equally as loud, crashing through the foliage, coming in my direction.

Whatever curiosity that may have gotten me that far deserted me, and I stopped and turned, nearly slipping on the rotting vegetation beneath my feet, and began sprinting back to the river.

I could hear the footsteps getting closer, the snorts of an angered animal not far behind as I exited the forest. I sprinted across the meadow, dodging the low-lying branches, many of them whipping my arms and legs as I sped past. Across the meadow, the footsteps and sounds of the attacker began to diminish, as if it were afraid of coming out of the jungle, into the sunlight. But I didn't look back, and didn't slow down until I hit the river, diving forward after just a few strides into the shallow water.

I didn't look back until I reached the rope dangling down from the cliff into the river. When I turned, I could see nothing that wasn't there before. The animal, whatever it was, did not cross the meadow. Perhaps it wasn't even after me. Perhaps it didn't even know that I had invaded its territory. Perhaps, but I wasn't quite ready to go back and check it out.

I rested there in the cool water, holding onto the rope, paddling my feet back and forth slowly to keep me higher in the water. I was no longer afraid of the fish, but my heart was pounding all the same. I stayed there for several minutes pondering. Was I afraid because of the close encounter with what I assumed was a predatory dinosaur, chasing me for an early breakfast? Or, was I excited *because* a predatory dinosaur was chasing me for an early breakfast? I realized at that point that my life was to consist of moments of absolute terror, followed by periods of curiosity and thoughtful reflection.

There was no one else to talk to, so I'd just have to figure it out for myself. I'd have to figure out a lot for myself from now on.

*****

For the second time, I approached the forest from the edge of the meadow. It was an hour before daylight, and it was pouring rain. I was drenched, the rain falling from the brim of my cap in a solid sheet, making the morning mist even more opaque, obscuring my vision, unable to see more than a couple of feet in any direction.

Only one day had passed since I was here before, and, with the exception of a camouflage, short-sleeved shirt, I was wearing the same clothes as the last time. It had been foolhardy to shinny down the rope in the dark and rain, but I needed to check things out more closely while the jungle was asleep, before the creatures were on the prowl. And this time I came better prepared.

I had my Glock, a hunting knife and the other shotgun. Across my shoulder, like a bandito, I had a bandoleer, filled with shells for both weapons. Even though it was dark, and, hopefully safe, I was taking no chances. This time I was not going to run in fear at the slightest noise. I couldn't live the rest of my life that way.

In the dark and drizzle, I passed into the jungle. The lack of light was even more pronounced than the time before. It wasn't quite absolute, but close enough. It was a struggle to find the same landmarks that I had seen less than twenty-four hours before. In a matter of minutes though I had found the spot where I had turned and fled. Off to my right was the same jumble of huge green leaves, not just dripping now, but pouring rain from their cupped surfaces.

I continued on, feeling my way as much as seeing it, wishing I still had the flashlight that had been smashed to pieces on the day that I had entered the cave.

I hadn't gone more than a hundred yards into the dense overhang when the first sign of filtered gray daylight appeared. I pushed on ahead, finding a small clearing, a circular area, flattened and dark, as if a small fire had been set to clear away an area leading to the entrance of interior of the jungle. Surely not set, but dark as if charred by fire, perhaps a lightning strike that flared up for a brief moment, extending out a mere fifty feet in all directions before a torrential rain snuffed in out.

On the left edge of the clearing was a most unusual tree. It was huge—as wide as it was tall—its massive roots extending out of the ground a full six feet. They lifted the ancient tree high above the ground, the space beneath, large enough for a full-grown man to walk in a crouch beneath. The roots were gnarled and twisted, some as thick as the width of my body, strong enough to hold erect a trunk the width of a compact car, and branches that extended more than eighty feet from side to side, eighty feet to its peak.

The canopy of the tree was even more impressive—not tapered, ending in a point the way that most trees do, but rather spread out like a huge umbrella, a gigantic half sphere that was nearly perfect in its symmetry. The umbrella impression was intensified by its foliage—thousands of tiny, red-brown leaves clumped in small bunches, but only growing around the outermost tips of the branches, giving the tree a hollow appearance from below—like looking at an open umbrella from underneath.

The umbrella was an apt comparison on that morning. The rain was noticeably lighter as I stepped beneath the tree's massive branches. It was just drizzle, droplets running steadily down from a hundred random spots like a leaky old roof. But there were dry spots, as well. I sought one out as I gazed up into the tree's magnificent boughs.

Even from below, I knew that the tree dwarfed those around it, its highest branches perhaps the perfect place to view the valley below. If I could get up there I would be able to see the river to the east as well as the mountains to the west. More importantly, I could see danger before it was on top of me.

Although the main branches extended outward some thirty feet above the ground, it looked possible to climb, at least to the first level. Like the exposed roots, the massive trunk was twisted and deeply grooved, as if several trees had wrapped around each other until they had grown together as one.

Despite the rain, which made the rough bark rather slick, I used the deep seams, wedging the rubber soles of my boots into them, while grabbing the cord-like protrusions that spiraled around the trunk. Hand over hand, and foot over foot, making more than a full revolution around the base of the tree, I made it to the first fork. It wasn't a climb that I'd want to make if I was in a hurry, but it got me there.

I paused there, in the pool formed at the fork of the branches, waiting for the sun to make an appearance over the cliff. There was just the slightest hint of gray to the blackened sky in the east, gloomy daylight just twenty minutes away. To the west I could see pink from the volcano through the tops of the trees.

The tree forked out from where I sat in four directions, each limb striking out on the horizontal before arching gradually upward fifteen feet away. From the position at their center, I waited patiently for the rain to subside, content, feeling safe, above any threats.

As the sun brightened the day, I could see more clearly the four branches as they extended upward. It was a very special tree, unique in both size and shape. I took it as a good omen that it was one of the first things that I had seen since entering the valley and the jungle within. A million pinpoints of light filtered through the web of leaves from above like the stars at night.

I lost track of time. It was as peaceful and safe as I had felt in a long time. Only the largest of the predators could reach me up here—if they could see me. Perhaps their sense of smell would find me out, but I was well armed, not afraid. If they were big enough to reach me thirty feet above the ground, then they were big enough to make a lot of noise as they came crashing through the forest. Long before they arrived, I would be up one of the branches to the next level.

It was the sounds of the jungle coming alive, well after the rain had ceased and the sun had passed over the eastern plateau that brought me back to reality. The birds were the first to awaken, their young ones shouting for their breakfast, the sounds carrying across the valley on warm, moist air. I heard distant thrashing about in the jungle minutes later. Something large was awake and on the move, but I couldn't see it.

I looked out at the cliff, just able to see the thin line formed by the knotted rope pulled taut across a diagonal, the current forcing the dangling end downstream. The end of the rope and the river passing below the cliff were just fragmented images, glimmers passing in and out of the spaces between the intermittent colors of the meadow. The rope had a hypnotizing effect, as I watched it sway in the wind, pulled to the north by the river's current, yet, all the while, glad that it was still there—a way to escape if the need arose.

I withdrew the rifle from my shoulder and left it in the crook of the tree while I climbed the broadest of the four branches. It ran fifteen feet out, gradually arching upward another twenty feet, before branching on yet again outward and upward. The grooves were cut less deep into the bark at this height, but the limb was thinner, thin enough to wrap my arms around. I climbed it like an island boy retrieving a coconut for a tipping tourist.

The view from this height was breathtaking. It wasn't the tallest tree in the valley, but close enough. To the east, the game trail was clearly visible, its light brown surface hugging the strip of water that ran the length of the cliff from north to south, disappearing into the jungle at either end. It was a panoramic shot—the way the path curved inward at both ends made it appear as if it was taken with a fisheye lens.

Nothing blocked my view in this direction. I could see the farthest portion of the meadow before losing it to the smaller trees below. I would be able to see clearly anything that approached the forest from the east. More importantly, my escape route was in plain sight and obstacle free. I could get there in a hurry.

To the west, the scenery was even more dramatic. I was able to look out over most of the vegetation, here and there the taller trees popping up, most of them exotic and tropical in appearance. In the foreground, there were snatches of clearings, areas where the jungle seemed much less dense than it had first appeared. Farther to the west, miles away, everything tended to blend together into a continuous blanket of deep green. It ended abruptly at the base of the mountain.

Even at fifty miles away, the mountains were incredible. Due west was the central peak, towering thousands of feet into the air, wispy tendrils of black smoke rising into the air above it, dissipating quickly in the cool light of the morning. It was surrounded on either side by a chain of mountains, smaller, yet still impressive. The details were obscured by distance, yet it was clear that each was sharply angled, as if created yesterday by colossal forces colliding, sending piles of huge, broken stone a mile into the air.

The colors of the mountains ranged from brilliant gold to jet-black, each radiantly reflecting the sun coming over the plateau on the opposing side of the valley. The colors were earth tones—hard, cold, inanimate—not those of living things. Nothing lived on the mountainsides ... at least, not yet. They were too new, the growth below not yet having sufficient time to push roots up their ledges, sufficient soil having not yet accumulated in the nooks and crannies of the slopes. They were just as I had pictured them two years ago with Brian Huntsville at my side—just as I had drawn them ten years before that—just as in Susan's window.

To the north and south there was nothing but an endless sea of lush, green jungle, for as far as I could see. There was a whole world to explore here, and I would make this tree my base for that exploration.

This tree would become my home.

*****

A couple of smashed thumbs and an assortment of cuts, bruises and gouges hadn't deterred me from becoming a pretty good rough carpenter. I had just finished laying the final log into place on the upper deck, fifty feet high in the tree. I jumped up and down on it, checking its stability, as I gazed twenty feet down to its larger mate. Like the one below, it was sturdy—rough hewn and uneven—but built to last.

The lower deck was where I planned to do most of my living. It was twelve feet square, centered within the four main branches, each log six inches in diameter, hacked out of the forest, cut and shaped with my own two hands. The twenty-four logs were notched at the ends, set into a framework of larger, stronger beams using nothing but wooden pegs. The framework was built such that it incorporated each of the four branches in its structure, making it as strong and stable as the old tree itself. No hardware was used in its construction—no nails, screws, or brackets—no metal of any kind. There was no mysterious evidence to leave behind, nothing that could damage the tree.

Just off-center on the platform was a hatch, two feet square that opened, swinging upward, on a wooden pivot. At the other end was a heavy latch made up of an oversized peg that was inserted through the side of the hatch and into a log header built into the deck. I wanted to be able to block the entry because I wasn't yet convinced that the valley had no animals that could climb the ladder, which extended thirty feet from the ground to the underside of the hatch.

A second homemade ladder extended at a thirty-degree angle from the edge of the lower deck to the one above. The upper deck was a smaller twin to the one below, just eight by eight, but identical in every other respect—except, I didn't see the need to provide a latch for the hatch. Instead, the hatch was flush to the floor, not raised above it. This is where I planned to sleep, and I didn't need any obstruction getting in the way. It was also where I planned to hide when I had to. Thirty feet wasn't high enough for me—not if the big carnivores came hunting. That is, if I ever found one ... if they existed.

Fifty feet, on the other hand, would raise me above all but the biggest dinosaurs—and those were herbivores—no threat to me, or, so I hoped. And, fifty feet made for a great lookout. I could see across the entire valley, the cliff to the east, the mountains to the west, and everything in between. If the volcano acted up, I would see it. If a lightning strike started a fire somewhere in the forest, I would know about it. And if the bigger creatures were stirring, I would be alerted while I still had time to do something about it.

I smiled with satisfaction at what I had built, even more so because I knew that on that night, I would sleep in the valley of the dinosaurs for the first time.

It took me well over a month to construct the modest platforms. During all of that time, I had been coming down the rope at daybreak, and climbing back up again at sunset. Each morning I brought down only the tools and supplies that I thought I would need for that day's work—just what I could fit in my backpack, or drape around my neck. Each night, I would return empty-handed, except for an empty pack and my sidearm, worn out from that day's labor.

What was left of my supplies were still at the top of the plateau, and I had vowed not to move them until I had a suitable place to store them—a suitable place to live. The top of the cliff, as uncomfortable a place as it may have been, represented safety and security. I could sleep at night soundly, without fear of some meat-eater sneaking up on me for a midnight snack.

For five weeks I had lived off what the river below had provided. I ate only one substantial meal a day—fish—every evening. The river was full of them, and I was amazed at how easy they were to catch with nothing but a sharpened stick. If I arrived at the shore just before the sun was down, it rarely took more than a couple of attempts to spear one. Despite my lifelong aversion to eating fish, they tasted pretty damn good cooked over an open fire after a long day of physical labor.

In between, it was nothing more than the nuts and berries that grew wild in the forest, and all the fresh water I could drink. It was sustaining, and healthy as hell to boot, but I had gotten pretty tired of eating healthy after five weeks. I was ready for a change.

My home was not nearly finished. I had yet to build the railings around both decks, and neither one had a roof. I had no place to cook food and no place for storage. All my tools lay in a corner of the lower deck, covered by a green canvas tarp. But, I intended to sleep there that night, and for all the nights that followed until I was ready to head back to the cave.

I had another hour until sunset and I hadn't eaten anything substantial since the night before. I had plenty of time for a trip to the river and back, but instead I picked up my rifle and headed out into the jungle.

There was a clearing about two hundred yards to the southwest. I had seen it from the upper deck on that first day that I had found the tree, and I explored it a couple of weeks later. It was the farthest that I had ventured out to this point.

It really wasn't a clearing though, but rather an area, perhaps a hundred feet across, where there were no trees. Instead there was thick ground cover, mostly ferns and a few low-lying flowering shrubs, some covered with strange, oblong, purple berries, the likes of which I had never seen or tasted, but they were good, sweet like a grape, but with a bit of a nutty flavor.

The clearing was one of only two places that I had explored since I first entered the valley. The other was along the far northern edge of the meadow, where the forest, river, and meadow came together. I had been there on the first day. I went that way because I thought that if I encountered any trouble, the river was the best option. If something came out of the woods after me, it was a short run into the water. It was unquestionably a totally unreasonable assumption being that the river was no more than five or six feet deep. I only hoped that whatever was after me didn't know that ... and couldn't swim.

That first venture turned out to be an important one, perhaps one of the most important discoveries that I would ever make. No, it wasn't dinosaurs, or any kind of animal. And, no, I didn't find gold, silver, or any other precious metal. A hell of a lot of good that would have done me, although, I guess that I could have loaded up the time machine with it—perhaps funding Dermot's next project.

No, what I found on that day was nothing more than a copse of trees—poplar to be specific. About an acre of them, two or three hundred trees, each exactly like its modern-day counterpart—straight trunks, thin branches that curved upward paralleling the growth of the tree, small heart-shaped leaves. It was a light tree that was nearly all trunk—an ideal tree for producing logs to build with.

At the base of the path they were short, not more than four or five feet—new growth—not more than a few years old. As they extended westward, they got taller, fifty or sixty feet, their trunks, twelve inches at the base. Beyond that, they were dying out, their leaves yellow, the ground below littered with their spindly branches.

I cleared the area of the dead and dying ones, using a pruning saw to remove the thin branches, a good, old fashioned adze-like tool to quickly remove the thin bark. Cutting them into twelve and eight foot lengths, I had more than a hundred logs to build from. The ones from the middle of the trees, those that were approximately six inches in diameter, I had used for the two decks. The ones from the tops of the trees, smaller in diameter, I cut up into firewood. The larger logs, from the lowest portion of the trees, I left intact. They would come in useful later on.

Cutting the trees down, and tuning them into useable logs was a simple task, even for someone like me who wasn't much of a craftsman. It took only a few days, a couple more to drag them back to the tree that was to become my home, and stack them up on the burned out patch beside it.

It was then that I had longed for the computer. The job of building my home would have been so much easier with it. There was a CAD program that I had had a few quick lessons on. It would have been so much easier to design the decks with it. But of course I wasn't nearly ready to make another trip back to the cave so quickly, and I didn't dare take the risk of moving it so far from the time machine.

Instead, I did most of the planning in my head, drawing rough sketches in the charred soil alongside the pile of logs. It was aggravating as hell. I'd sketch an idea in the ground, and then go take a set of measurements in the tree, constantly climbing up, and back down again, making light scratches in the bark that I would have to cross out and remake the next time up because something wasn't quite right.

Almost every day, I was stopped by the lack of a needed tool, and have to wait till the next day to retrieve it. A week into it, I started making double trips up and down the cliff, bringing down twice as many tools. It shortened my day and tired me out before I was even half the way into my daily routine, but my progress was accelerated.

I also made the first of the two ladders following that first week, cutting down two more trees, using nearly their full length, notching the log every twelve inches for the rungs. I cut a couple of the thinner logs into twenty four-inch lengths, notching each of these as well, not on the ends, but six inches in. Matching up the notches, inserting them into the logs from the front made a sturdy ladder.

Having the tools I needed and a quick way into the tree made the job go much faster. The frame was the hardest part. It was a double-X configuration, each open end of the design capturing one of the four main branches. I had to continuously hack out the depth of the notches of each log until, at long last, the frame settled into a level position. From that point, it was just a matter of cutting and notching the deck logs.

Knowing what I was doing, the second ladder and deck went up quickly. At the end of five weeks it was complete. I had pushed myself harder and harder each day, each afternoon heading back to the river later than the day before. Some nights, I did without dinner, content to pull my way back up the cliff and collapse into my sleeping bag. I was hungry all the time, and losing weight, perhaps dangerously so, but I was driven by a need to finish the decks, to be done with climbing up the goddamn rope every night.

During those last few days, I longed for food. Not fish, and sure as hell not nuts and berries, but meat. I fantasized about hamburgers, pork chops, hams, and chickens. And especially steaks—big ones—two inches thick, cooked over an open fire. The little bits of ground meat in the cans of chili and beef stew just weren't cutting it. I needed fresh meat, *big* meat, and where in the world could one find bigger meat than in a world full of dinosaurs?

The last time that I had entered the clearing to the southwest, I had spooked something. Critters of some sort scampered away as I cleared the taller brush on the edge of the low ground cover. I could hear their squeals, see the parting of the ferns as they ran away, even if I couldn't actually see them.

I guessed that they were some kind of small mammals, which were in abundance at the end of the Cretaceous period. They were among the original mammals, predecessors of the opossum, the groundhog, and the raccoon. They were to be among the few species that survived the purge at the K-T boundary.

Nobody was really sure why they, and a handful of others, survived, when all the dinosaurs did not. How did tiny mice survive, when the biggest mammals did not? The *Pterosaurs* were gone, as were the *Plesiosaurs*. So many of those that lived both in the air and in the seas did not survive. Three quarters of all the species in the world became extinct, but few of the mammals did.

Some said that the survival and expansion of one caused the death and extinction of the other. That the mammals were egg-eaters—that the proliferation, and subsequent huge population growth, of the smaller, omnivorous animals indirectly caused the extinction of the larger animals—animals that lay eggs.

Dinosaurs were a fragile population. A significant percentage of the eggs they laid needed to hatch and grow to maturity in order to propagate the species. As the number of egg-eating mammals increased, the fewer eggs survived, making it likely that there would not be enough left to mate sufficiently to hold the population stable.

On the other hand, many mammals were small, living close to the ground, many burrowing into the earth for protection. When the comet struck, *if* it was the cause of the extinction, the smaller animals were best equipped to hide from the devastating aftermath. They could hide beneath the foliage and in the ground, somewhat protected from the poisonous gases formed by the fallout of iridium. And food for the smallest mammals: bugs, worms, and other things that crawled in the earth, would still be plentiful.

The same was true for the months of winter that followed the impact. The millions of tons of debris blasted into the atmosphere would have blotted out the sun—globally. The lack of sun would have brought about freezing temperatures, not gradually so that the animals might have adjusted, but suddenly, within days and weeks. As each one died from exposure, there would be less food for the carnivores. And as the plant life gradually wilted away from the lack of sunlight, there would be less food for the herbivores.

But dinosaurs were not all huge. Some were the size of large birds and mammals. What happened to them? Why did they die out at the same time as the large ones? Perhaps it was because they were egg layers, perhaps because they were not burrowing animals—perhaps a hundred other things. There were a thousand theories. But, they were exactly that: theories. Nobody knew for sure.

Whatever the reason, I was hungry—for meat—and I was going after some. Just thinking about it made me smile as I approached the clearing. A couple of years ago I never would have considered hunting for my dinner, let alone hunting something akin to an opossum—maybe a deer or rabbit, but not an opossum. I thought of Granny Clampett and her 'possum stew, and I smiled all the more. Well, if it was good enough for the folks down south, it was good enough for me.

A few yards before entering the clearing, I began hearing strange noises and seeing shadows moving between the thick branches of the trees. I stepped forward, gun at the ready, holding it out in front of me, using it to part the branches. I peered in through the leaves of a giant fern, fear and awe freezing me to the spot.

If I had come for small mammals, I was too late. Something had gotten there before me. Clogging the small clearing, each bobbing their heads in and out of the greenery, ignorant of my intrusion, was a flock of *Gallimimus ballatus*—a dozen of them. I was too startled to even breathe. Frozen to the spot, I stared at the sight before me.

Even as they stretched their long bodies forward, they towered over the ferns and small plants, as tall as I was, and at least twelve feet from the tip of their tails to their small pointed beaks, perhaps two fifty, three hundred pounds. They had long, thin necks, thin tails as well. Their legs were spindly below the knees, yet massive above, covered with thick slabs of muscle, capable of propelling them forward at forty to fifty miles per hour. They had plump bodies, covered in a brilliant, almost iridescent green, with a fine, scaly finish. They had darker underbellies, almost black, running up the inside of their upper legs, across their bellies, up through their necks and lower jaws. Despite their obvious speed, they had adapted themselves to the lush jungle, taking on its colors, like chameleons.

Their arms were much smaller than I remembered from their skeletal remains. They were more like those of a *T-rex*, proportionally too short for their bodies—useless, unnecessary. The *Gallimimus* held them at their sides, bent at the elbow, close to the body, seemingly frozen in place. Seeing them, it was easy to believe that some species of dinosaurs evolved into birds. This was certainly one of them. Their arms were transforming. In another hundred thousand, perhaps a million years, they would be wings. And maybe in another million, they would be functional wings, capable of flight.

But the animals didn't quite appear as I had imagined them. Besides the shorter arms, they were generally smaller and lighter than I had pictured in my mind, smaller than the fossils had suggested. It was then that I remembered that the fossil remains of this bird-like animal were found only in Mongolia—none had been found in North America.

This was not a *Gallimimus ballatus*. This was a cousin of what had been found in central Asia. Separated by thousands of miles of geography and a couple of million years of evolution, this animal had changes in subtle, yet dramatic ways. It was smaller and more aerodynamic, its arms lighter, less useful for pushing, pulling, and grabbing—ready for change—ready *to* change into something else. It was a species that had not been discovered in North America. Perhaps no one ever would. But I had found it, and as the discoverer I had the right to name the new species. I named it *Gallimimus williams*, not for me, but for Elizabeth. I kind of hoped that no one ever found fossil evidence of this species. I didn't want someone else to name it.

I continued to stare at the strange animals. Although they were lizard-hipped, they resembled and moved like ostriches, pecking away at what was below the foliage. Four of the animals were at the center of the clearing, taking turns dipping their heads into the shrubs, coming back up with their beaks dripping the bright yellow of egg yolk. In turn, each one straightened its neck, lifting its head high into the air. With its beak pointing straight up, it nodded its head from front to back, letting the slimy yolk run down its throat.

The remaining *Gallimimus* searched the far side of the clearing, lifting each long leg up high, bent at the knee, its thin splayed toes pointed toward the ground. Its steps were slow and exaggerated, as if it was afraid of stepping on something. They moved from the opposite side of the perimeter, in either direction, moving steadily toward my hidden position.

They were no more than a half dozen yards from me, on both sides, when they were alerted to something strange in the air. As one, they stopped in their tracks and raised their heads high in the air as if smelling danger.

I brought the rifle to my shoulder as slowly and silently as humanly possible. I sighted in on the closest animal, my shoulders trembling in fear and anticipation, hoping that they would return to the forest without seeing me.

I had no idea how aggressive these animals were. If they spotted me, would they attack? They had no teeth, but their sharp beaks were more than capable of tearing me to shreds. And there were twelve of them. My mind flashed back to the feeding frenzy of the sharks as they attacked and devoured the *Elasmosaurus* the year before. But this time *I* was the *Elasmosaurus*.

The searing pain in my lungs reminded me that I had been holding my breath ever since I had first laid eyes on the creatures. Probably two full minutes had passed. As quietly as I could, I exhaled ... but it wasn't quiet enough. The lead animal heard the slight hiss of air as it slid through my lips, turning its head instantly in my direction.

They all followed the leader, eleven other heads turning towards me at once. My finger began to put pressure on the trigger, the gun aimed in the general direction of the lead dinosaur, but my eyes were firmly fixed on the shining black orbs of the one closest to me. They were so deep, dark, and glossy that they looked like glass. For the moment, not more than a few seconds, I was lost to those eyes, forgetting everything else—where I was—the danger I was in.

Unconsciously, I sucked air in through my nose as I continued to squeeze the trigger. Sweat was running into my eyes and my gun swayed from side to side, as my shaking intensified. The acute sense of hearing of the *Gallimimus* picked it out. The leader threw back its head and let out a high-pitched squawk, short but startlingly loud, echoing through the valley.

It caused a panic among its followers, as each of them, almost at once, let out an immediate response. The cacophony of sound blasted my eardrums and sent me sprawling backwards, my rifle discharging as I landed on my ass among the brush.

I spun, turning to face the ground, and rolled into a defensive ball. I cowered in terror, waiting for the first pain as the piercing and tearing began.

I was breathing again, panting actually, saliva dripping down my chin onto the ground, my heart racing uncontrollably. But the pain didn't commence, and, as my senses returned, I could hear nothing but the far off thunder of several thousand pounds of animals disappearing into the forest.

I remained motionless for several seconds before I began crawling back toward the clearing. All was silent. Even the normal sounds of the forests—the chirping of the birds, the buzzing of the insects—had disappeared. I paused at the edge, trying to look beyond the branches of the perimeter trees, looking for more surprises. Perhaps there was still one animal left, a sentry, waiting for my return, ready to signal the return of the rest.

But I could see nothing there. Much of the clearing, the ferns and other greenery, were trampled flat, but there were no signs of the animals. They were long gone.

Cautiously, I crept into the clearing, on all fours, like an animal, looking for … I didn't know what. In the middle of the clearing I found what the *Gallimimus* were after. There was a nest settled into a shallow spot, clearly dug out from the earth by something with sharp claws. The ground was scraped clean: long, ragged furrows carved deeply into the rich soil. Nestled in the middle were a half dozen eggs, four of them broken open, their tops gone, a ragged edge surrounding a rich yellow center, surrounded by a clear fluid. They looked like every other egg I had ever seen—just twenty or thirty times bigger.

Despite my nervous condition, my stomach growled, thinking of scrambled eggs, eggs over easy, huge omelets, eggs benedict. I had to pull myself away, afraid that I might just attack what was left of the broken eggs—raw—no telling what germs or bacteria the *Gallimimus* had left behind.

I walked the edge of the clearing in a clockwise direction from a point opposite of where I had entered. About a quarter of the way around, at the point where the frightened animals crashed through the heavy brush, I found blood—a lot of it. The soft green leaves of the ferns were painted with it—thick, sticky—dripping from the tips in stringy globs.

I followed the blood trail into the denser part of the forest. Even without the blood, the trail was easy to follow. The lower foliage was trampled flat, and the branches of the taller trees were broken and bent, forming a corridor through the forest that a blind man could have followed.

From the few short minutes that I watched the *Gallimimus* in the clearing, I knew that it was a graceful species, cautiously stepping over the low vegetation, moving with a slow, deliberate step—quiet, wary. But they had fled the clearing in abject terror, crashing through the forest, blindly, panicked. And not from the gunshot that had occurred a half second later, a half second after spotting me hidden behind the trees. For just that instant, I could see the terror in the eyes of their leader. *Gallimimus* were not hunters. There were timid creatures that traveled in flocks for protection, and moved cautiously through the thicker parts of the forest—hiding—always a heartbeat away from being afraid.

I traveled through the corridor, in and out of spotty sunlight, ducking under low branches, dodging the broken ones. I kept one eye on the blood that seemed to be everywhere. An animal that size would have a lot of it, but there seemed to be more than even the largest animal could lose without dropping to the ground.

I had traveled a quarter of a mile through the dense forest when I heard the strange squawking sound again—this time, lower in pitch and drawn out, a quiver ending in a breathless rasp.

The sound was close, no more than twenty yards away. I looked between the branches in all directions, not able to see anything moving about as I slowly moved toward the sound. It started up again, this time more faint, even though I was getting closer. I was within twenty feet when I saw the brush move, the creature's head rise up from a prone position, blood dribbling from its mouth. I approached the beast, no longer afraid. It was down, blood running from its abdomen, slowly now, its pressure dropping rapidly—bled out. I looked into its eyes, eyes that minutes ago were so beautifully shiny and black. Now there was a dullness to them, more gray than black, the life draining from them.

It let out one more, short gasp as its head eased back down into the soft bed of ferns. Its pain and fear were obvious, enveloping me with a devastating feeling of guilt and an overwhelming sense of loss. I knelt down beside it, touching the upper part of its chest, above the wound. It didn't move, but stared at me with those big, sad eyes.

Its chest was still rising and falling, slowly, a rattle coming from deep down. It was in pain and I knew that I had to end it. I pulled the Glock from its holster, aimed it between the suffering creature's eyes and squeezed the trigger.

*****

The fire was nice and high, too high. I had to let it die down a bit. I had plenty of firewood, and it was dry, compliments of the dying poplars that I had cut down a couple of weeks before. But I had piled on a few too many, anxious to get my dinner going. The dry wood was popping and crackling, sending a shower of sparks into the air.

While I waited, I sipped a cup of hot coffee while I thought about the grisly scene in the woods. I felt bad about shooting the *Gallimimus*, even though it was an accident. I felt even worse about putting it out of its misery, although it was the humane thing to do. But I also knew that I'd have to get over that. If I were to survive, I'd be killing many more animals, and, no doubt, many of them would be dinosaurs.

The shot had been a clean one, right between those sad, distant eyes. Its head had simply dropped into the brush without a sound, other than the echo of the gunshot. The blood that had been flowing from the chest of the *Gallimimus* stopped within seconds, its heart beating its last, the little bit of blood left settling into the lower portions of the beast.

I walked over to the animal's head, my legs barely keeping me upright, shaking from the events of the last few minutes. The animal's heart may have stopped, but mine was making up for it—it was about to bust through my chest. I looked the animal over from nose to tail, a shiver rising from my tailbone, up through my shoulders, and into the nape of my neck, spreading out into my skull like I could only imagine a stroke felt.

As I kneeled at its head, my mind flashed back to the day that I had walked away from that asshole Fairbanks and into the wastelands of central Utah—to a rise that only I knew contained something special. I passed my hand over the dinosaur's long neck, just as I had passed it over the wind-swept earth on that day nearly twenty year before.

That had been my first experience with a dinosaur—dried old bones from an animal that had been dead for seventy million years. It was a thrill that I never quite got over. Every time that I found a new fossil, each time that I saw a dinosaur assembled in some dusty old museum, I got that same chill—that same ice cream freeze of the brain that started off as a snow cone in my shorts.

I didn't think that the feeling could be more intense, but here I was, kneeling over the real thing, a dinosaur, that only minutes before had been a living, breathing animal. My eyes misted up, and my throat tightened, as my stomach clinched. I turned away from the beautiful creature and vomited the few nuts and berries that I had eaten for my day's only meal.

I sat down in the soft pile of the forest's underbrush, my head between my knees, trying desperately to clear the confusion from my brain. As I sat there, a noxious drizzle dropping from my hanging lower lip, I became aware of the sounds starting up again in the surrounding woods.

The gunshots had quieted things down. Although I was oblivious to it at the time, I knew that the creatures of the forest had gone still, like a dog hiding from its master's condemnations after it had soiled the carpet. But like a dog, whose memory was as short as that of an adoring parent, the sounds of woodland life began to return.

The animals would smell the blood, would know that there was a recent death nearby. Some of them were carnivores, and many of *those* were scavengers. They would be heading toward this position, possibly in packs, looking for an easy meal.

Within minutes, maybe only seconds, other animals would enter the kill zone, more animals than I could hope to fend off with my tiny arsenal. But this was an animal that I had killed, and I had a right to my share.

I took out my hunting knife from the sheath on my belt and began to slice into the thick meat at the joint between the *Gallimimus'* hip and thigh. The meat separated easily with my razor-sharp knife, cutting through muscle and tendons alike, as if they were butter. Only the hard bone stopped the steady progress of my blade. I cut around it, neatly carving full circle to the point where I started.

Grabbing the lower end of the leg, I pulled upward, twisting as I walked the leg up at an unnatural angle to the beast's body. Using the dinosaur's own weight against it, I bent the leg back, hearing the hollow bones splinter, falling forward onto the beast as the leg came away.

I hauled the leg up onto my shoulder, all seventy or eighty pounds of it, just as I heard the leaves of the jungle begin to rustle. Whatever it was—was close, maybe twenty yards out. I looked up, seeing the lower branches of the trees and the ferns below swaying, parting as if by magic. I didn't wait for a better look. I hauled ass back toward the safety of my tree house.

I went back the way I came, dodging branches and hopping over plants and a maze of exposed roots as fast as my legs and heavy load would allow, the sounds of approaching animals quickly fading into the distance. On the way, I passed through the clearing where I first sighted the flock of *Gallimimus*. I screeched to a halt as I spotted the remains of the dinosaur nest.

I paused, trying to suppress the noise coming from my heaving lungs, listening carefully, making sure that I wasn't being pursued. Convinced that I was alone, and safe for the moment, I set my load down and pulled off my backpack. On one knee alongside the ruined nest, I looked around, full circle, feeling like a thief in the night, and slid one of the eggs into the pack.

I made it back to the tree, moving more slowly, afraid of breaking the egg. During the short walk my mind was traveling a lot faster than my feet, trying to justify removing the egg from its nest. If the dinosaurs became extinct because of the mass destruction of their eggs, then how could I justify taking one and hastening the process? On the other hand, if I hadn't shown up when I did, wouldn't the *Gallimimus* have eaten them all? In taking only one, didn't I save the other?

I wrestled with the puzzle all the way back to my home high into the tree, and still hadn't solved it. As I climbed the ladder, the increased load weighing me down, I came to a conclusion. I was one man, and unless I introduced some new disease that the animals were incapable of combating, or I started a fire that wiped out the entire valley, I wasn't going to make one bit of difference to their environment. The animals in the jungle had a hell of a lot more to fear than me.

*****

With the fire down to a manageable level, I set up the homemade spit, a pretty simple contraption really. With four sections of log, each notched a little off center, I constructed two X-shaped frames, each one planted a foot into the ground about four feet apart, one on either side of the fire pit. Inserted into either end of the hollow bones of the upper leg was a small pry bar. The opposite ends of the bars rested into the intersection of the frames. The pry bars even had an angled handle—easy for turning.

It was a giant slab of meat, would take all night to cook all the way through. But I didn't intend to wait all night. As the outer portion cooked, I would slice off thin strips and gobble them down. To pass the time I had a nice big glass of scotch to sip on. After all, this was a celebration of sorts. This was to be my first two meals that were home grown—well, discounting the nuts and berries of course—leg of *Gallimimus* tonight—scrambled dinosaur egg tomorrow morning.

I stood by the side of the fire, sipping scotch, turning my leg of dinosaur, tired as hell, but feeling pretty damn good. I had survived a month in the valley, several months in another time, where things were unbelievably different, different than any human being had ever experienced. And I was alone—not yet lonely—but alone. I had no one to talk to, no one to do things with, no one to say, "Hey, you wouldn't believe what the hell I saw today." But I was still feeling good, still amazed at everything that was happening to me, still too wrapped up in adventure to feel anything but amazement and the most astounding sense of awe.

I had been rotating the meat on the spit, pretty much oblivious to everything, when the smell started getting to me. It was the smell of food cooking, the smell that one experiences at a barbecue, or at a really good restaurant that grills rather than fries or bakes. It reminded me of the summer cookouts that Liz and I used to have—a couple of really good porterhouse steaks on the grill, Liz in the kitchen, fixing a killer salad, the ballgame on the radio. Everything being so perfect, the smell coming off the grill such that you could hardly stand to wait until it was cooked just right.

I snapped back to the present, looking down at the rotating hunk of meat. It sizzled, the outer coating turning a nice golden-brown—little wisps of smoke bubbling up in random patches from the better-cooked parts. I turned the handle, searching for the darker portions, bringing them to the top. I put the blade to its side, slicing off an inch-thick fillet, ten inches long.

I turned it a quarter turn, and sliced off another piece, placing it on the plate along side the first. I did it one more time, my plate piled high with the steaming meat. Its aroma was incredible, my mouth watering, ready to dig in, make a complete pig of myself.

I walked the twenty feet back to the tree, the plate held jut below my nose, the enticing aroma and anticipation of biting into the first real piece of meat in months, forcing my feet into a little skip. I backed up against the ladder and slid my ass down its length, plopping onto the ground, never taking my eyes from my heaping plate.

That first bite was even better than I imagined. It was moist and tender and hot enough to burn the roof of my mouth, making me toss it back and forth between the inside of my cheeks, while I desperately sucked in air to cool it off.

I'd like to say that it tasted like chicken … but it didn't. I'm not sure just what it *did* taste like—nothing I had ever tasted before, but good, *damn* good. Perhaps a little like lamb, but more exotic, a bit more gamy.

By the second bite, my stomach was growling, little spasms that rolled from side to side and from back to front. Not painful, more like a question, "*What the hell are you sending down here*?" It may have been because it was something it had never seen before, or maybe it was just because it had been empty for too long and was simply saying, "*It's about damn time*!" At any rate, it didn't hurt, and it didn't feel that it was going to toss it back up again. I continued on, faster and faster, as the meat began to cool.

By the end of the first piece I had juices all over my face and dripping down my chin. My hands were soaked with it. I could feel it running down both arms beneath my shirtsleeves (I hadn't bothered with utensils). Not caring a wit about manners or cleanliness, I simply wiped my hands on my pants, my face with my shirtfront and dug into the second hunk.

I was halfway through it when it happened.

They came out from the heavy woods that surrounded the clearing, attracted by the smell of the roasting meat. I saw their eyes first, red, sparkling, like rubies in the reflection of the fire. As they came out of the shadows, into the firelight, their features became distinct. Long rows of dagger-like teeth reflected back the light, mouths agape, dark tongues flicking out, pulling back in.

Hissing noises came from each of them, almost in turn, as if communicating in some unrecognizable language. An occasional growl, almost a loud purr, came from deep down in the throat, like an exclamation point, punctuating the important parts of the conversation. They moved cautiously, but aggressively, nudging one another, taking little nips at the heads and necks of whichever one was closest.

As they moved closer, the light from the fire revealed their terrifying detail. They were small, no more than three, three and a half feet high, six feet from the nose to the tail. They were slender, but sinewy, thick muscles in the thighs and neck—strong and fast. Their jaws were huge for their size, as were their heads—disproportionately large brain pans—indicative of their intelligence. They wore feathers—tiny, closely woven ones along their sides—longer, more sparse across their backs—a regal plumage atop their heads. Their coloring was startling—mustard yellow across the breast and abdomen, darkening toward the back and head—a fist full of long curled red feathers atop their heads. They were colored in stark contrast to their surroundings. They were vicious predators. They didn't need the advantage of camouflage. They were only seventy or eighty pounds, but they were deadly, either in pack or alone.

They continued to move closer, their eyes aimed toward the flames—unsure steps—wary of the heat. They hadn't yet spotted me. The overpowering aroma of the cooking *Gallimimus* disguised whatever smell was emanating from me—the intense light of the fire diverted their vision. They approached within five feet of the fire, ducking their heads against the threatening flames. As they strode forward, their feet came out of the shadows, placing them in plain view. On the middle toe of each, protruded a huge sickle-like claw, six or seven inches long, curved into a murderous point, capable of disemboweling a much larger animal … or a man.

The claw was the dead giveaway. These were not the animals of *Jurassic Park*. They were half the size, a quarter of the weight of the movie monsters. Their skin was not roughly pebbled, and was not green or dark gray like the average cinematic creature. And they looked nothing like smaller versions of *T-rex* ... except for their killer jaws and teeth, which were designed to destroy, to bite through flesh and bone, to annihilate. The feathers had fooled me, disguised their looks completely. But I knew what they were. They were pint-sized, feathered killing machines. They were *Velociraptors*.

If I was afraid when they first emerged from the darkness, I was now terrified. *Velociraptors* were vicious pack hunters, capable of killing the largest, most ferocious beasts of the Cretaceous. Unlike the *T-rex*, they had strong arms, capable of holding their prey while they slashed at the soft belly with that murderous claw. They were thought to be incredible jumpers and were smart, perhaps the smartest of any dinosaur that ever lived.

Like the *Gallimimus*, they were dinosaurs whose remains had only been found in Asia—dated more than ten million years before the very end of the Cretaceous. One of the world's most famous finds occurred in Mongolia in 1971—a *Velociraptor* and a *Protoceratops* locked in mortal combat. The raptor, with a stove-in chest had just ripped into the belly of the *Protoceratops*. They had died that way, in Mongolia, seventy five million years ago. But, like the *Gallimimus*, the *Velociraptor* was here ... now.

They were still mesmerized by the fire, tantalized by the smell of the cooking meat. They circled it, letting out little mewing noises, occasionally raising their snouts into the air and sniffing. Every time one got too close to the fire, it reared back, letting out a loud snort. In anger from the heat, from the fiery moat that kept their prize captured, it would nip at the one closest. It wasn't playful in the least. These were aggressive, dangerous animals that would have killed anything that got between them and food. Anything ... including each other.

I was sheathed in darkness, the light of the fire blinding the dinosaurs from anything behind them. I was still holding the piece of meat to my lips, my other hand still grasping the plate with the remaining piece. I put the piece back on the plate, and slowly lowered it to the ground. I grasped the sides of the ladder in each hand, straightening my legs as I pushed with my arms, sliding my backside against the rungs. One by one they bumped into my tailbone as I was straightened into nearly a vertical position.

They still hadn't spotted me, and apparently hadn't heard me either. I let out a long silent breath through my nose. I turned my head and shoulders nearly a hundred and eighty degrees, my feet anchored to the spot at the base of the ladder, and saw my rifle standing up against the tree, right were I left it, ten feet away.

I pressed the palms of my hands against the rails of the ladder, taking my weight off the rungs, so that I could straighten up completely. As I did, the top of the ladder rubbed against the inside of the wooden hatch, making a creaking noise that sounded like it had been amplified a hundred times. The *Velociraptor* closest to me turned its head in my direction with astonishing speed. I could see its eyes, black in the shadows, but its body was perfectly outlined by the glow from the fire. It looked like a picture from hell.

The animal's head was tilted upward toward the origin of the sound. It seemed to sniff at the air, searching for something. I held my breath, rooted to the spot, like the tree behind me. The *raptor* turned its head, a few degrees to the left, a few degrees to the right. It raised it, then lowered it until it was looking right at me. My hair stood on end, my breath caught in my throat like a plugged up pipe. I could feel my knees shake, terrified that my pants were sending out an audible vibration that could be heard by the little monster not twenty feet away.

It was looking directly into my eyes, when suddenly, a loud thump came from the area of the fire, followed by a shower of sparks, the fire jumping into the sky. Somehow, the remaining three *raptors* had managed to dislodge one side of the spit frame, causing the massive leg of meat to crash down onto the fire. In surprise and anger, the one who had been staring at me turned and attacked the others, knowing that it had just been deprived of a meal.

I stepped sideways, needing to clear the left post of the ladder, silently thankful for the savagery of the predators. It was a surreal scene that played out behind the dancing flames of my campfire. Flashes of red-feathered heads with those sparkling eyes of the same color dipped in and out of the flames, jaws agape and teeth snapping, here one second, there the next. The sizzling of the juices and the popping of the pockets of fat as the meat settled into the red-hot poplar could still be heard below the grunting and snarling of the combatants.

I used the noise as a cover to make my move. The burned out ground helped to muffle my footsteps as I backed toward the base of the tree, reaching blindly behind me for the rifle. I picked it up, my movements protected by the intense light between them and me. I raised it to my shoulder, sighting in on the fire and the frenzy of activity behind it.

They were too fast to pick off all four. As soon as I fired, even if I was a good enough shot to take one of them down, the other three would be on me before I could draw a bead on the next. My only chance was to get up the ladder to the deck with the hatch closed and bolted behind me.

I stood there for several minutes, mesmerized by the action around the fire, but also because I was too terrorized to move. As well as intelligent, these animals were believed to have incredible senses: sight, hearing, and smell—all thought to be among the best of the dinosaurs. The longer I stood there the more I was convinced that the slightest move I made, they would see me ... or hear me ... or smell me. After all, wasn't I covered in the aromatic juices of the *Gallimimus*?

But the gun was getting heavy, held out such as it was. I could feel my right shoulder begin to burn, the barrel start to drop, swaying from right to left. Trying to freeze my upper body into a statue, I slid my left foot forward six inches, slowly centering my body to keep my balance.

All was well. They were still too busy to pay any attention to what was going on beneath the tree. I brought my right foot next to the left, lifting it, not sliding it, deathly afraid to make any kind of a scraping sound. So far ... so good. I repeated the process until I was posed in front of the ladder, the heel of one boot settled into the first rung, holding the rifle up with just one arm, my shoulder screaming in protest.

I eased my weight onto it slowly, afraid of starting the creaking noise again. I used but one arm to help pull myself up the rungs, holding the gun in the other, but no longer aiming it, just holding it out there, waving from one side to another. I had made it to the eighth rung, as many feet off the ground, when my heel kicked the rung out of its notched position on one side. Starting to slide down the ladder, I let go of the rifle, reaching out with both hands to grab the sides.

That's what finally got their attention. A startled cry reached out from all four in unison, and their battle ceased in an instant. The leader, the same one that had scoped in on my deck, nudged the others aside and took two steps forward. I don't know why I felt he was the leader, unsure if he was actually the same one that had approached my position before. But somehow, I just knew it. Perhaps it was just because there seemed to be one that was first to respond, someone that stepped up, like any leader would. This was the one.

I had a reverse grip on either side of the rail, when the leader sprung forward. It took it no more than three strides and it leapt upon me. But I was ready for it. I swung my hips forward, brought my knees up to my chest, and kicked out with everything that I had. I caught it flush in the jaw, but its talons had caught my left arm, rendering it useless, forcing me to release the grip on that side of the ladder. I hung onto it with one hand, watching through the rungs of the ladder as the *Velociraptor* bounced and rolled toward the flames.

The three others were unsure what to do as their leader tried to right itself, letting out a bellow as it touched the outer edges of the fire. With no time to waste, I swung by my one good arm around to the front of the ladder, and started the rest of the way up. The *raptor* leaped toward me, falling just a rung short, even through I was half the way to the top. I climbed the rest of the way, stopping with my hand on the hatch, feeling that I was beyond immediate danger.

CHAPTER 18

It was cold—midwinter in the late Cretaceous: snow squalls, bitter winds, but nothing that settled down onto the earth, no blanket of white, just little sprays of snow that came and went depending on the direction of the wind. If you looked close, you could see it accumulating in the cracks and crevasses of the rocks that made up the cliffs, little flecks of sparkling white in the shade of the cave behind me, but no accumulation like I had seen that one time a year before.

The sky was dull, heavy, a gray that seemed almost palpable, the sun nothing more than a haze above the Western Interior Sea ... but cold. I knew that it was cold without really feeling it. Even ignoring the patches of snow, the bitter leaden sky, I could see it in my breath, frosty with each exhale, feeling it each morning when I crawled from my warm comfortable bed. But I didn't feel all that uncomfortable sitting there outside the cave. It was nice to be back home—one of my two homes now—the one that lacked excitement, but was comfortable, safe, a place that I could relax without fear of making a mistake that would cost me my life.

The waters were choppy, waves coming onto the shore every few seconds, white caps sending foam across my beach a few inches farther with each crest. I could hear them, the quiet lapping onto the salt-laden sands each time, like the sounds of a heartbeat. Pa-lump, pa-lump, they resounded, having a hypnotic effect that added to the overall calm that was with me on that day.

The sounds were clear, yet made fainter by distance. There had been no mistake—the waters were receding—faster than I would have thought possible. The markers I had posted the year before were now fifty feet inland, and dry, the tide hadn't reached them for many months. To the south, where the cliff continued to curve away in that direction, there was another hundred yards or more of exposed beach. My seaside property was expanding, but its value was still pretty much only in the fact that it was all mine.

I wore an army field jacket, camouflaged, and I wore it for no other reason than it was warm. I wore long-handles underneath, had been wearing them every day since my return. On my head, I wore the world's most ugly hat—fatigue green, insulated, with earflaps that would button beneath my chin if I so chose to fasten the little snaps dangling at their ends. And I had on thin leather gloves, cut off at the fingers so that I had some sense of touch, so that I could feel the keys beneath my fingers.

As I sat in front of the computer, I couldn't get over how many stupid things I had done during those first few years in the valley, more amazed that I had lived through them. And yet, here I was all those months later, in relatively good shape physically (although suffering from some incredible lapses in judgment that could be attributed to a certain mental instability), and (I hope) a hell of a lot smarter.

That first year had been the most incredible, at least in terms of a propensity to survive a series of really dumb things: wandering into the woods on that first day, naïve, too stupid to think that something could actually happen on day number one, stepping into the dark woods, too inexperienced to go in armed, sitting out there in the middle of nowhere, my gun just setting out there, out of reach, no sidearm strapped to my waste, cooking meat in a valley full of meat-eaters. Dumb, no?

I reached for my left arm, feeling the wide, ragged, healed-over scar through the material of my jacket. Even through the thick cloth, I could feel the raised surface, and as I rubbed a finger lightly across it, it sent a little tickle all the way down to my fingertips, despite the passage of more than a year. I thought back to the night that I had got the scar.

*****

I had made it safely to the lower deck, closed and latched the hatch. On my ass I scooted over to the supply pile, half leaning and half lying against the tarp. I sucked hungrily for air, holding my wounded arm. The numbness that I had felt moments before had started to disappear, replaced by the first painful stirrings of a serious wound. Squeezing my upper arm beneath it, as if it might somehow slow the impending agony, I could feel the warmth spread over my right hand. Bringing my sticky fingers to my face where I could catch the faint moonlight, I could see that my hand was covered with an ominous blackness that stretched across my fingers like some hideous web as I spread them.

My concern over my injury faded into the background as I heard the commotion from below. Growls that turned into gargle-like shrieks shattered the night and I could feel the massive tree shudder as they attacked the ladder. Forgetting my arm for the moment, I crawled over to the edge, like a three-legged dog, leaving a wide trail of blood in my wake.

The *raptors* were good jumpers, but they were not good enough to make it thirty feet to the deck. But that didn't stop them from trying. I peered down at them, and I shit you not, they *were* trying. It was almost comical how they jumped and snarled, one after the other, leaping high into the air, bouncing onto the ladder, rolling and falling back to the ground, only to pop up and try again. But they weren't even close—not by twenty feet. Looking back at it, I think that maybe they weren't really trying to reach the deck—they were smarter than that. I think that they were just hopping mad (if you'll excuse the pun).

The jumping and snarling lasted for the better part of an hour, their anger, stamina, and ability to withstand pain amazing. When they finally wore themselves down, they still refused to leave. They wandered about the tree, going over to sniff at the remnants of the meat, the fire reduced to smoldering embers and a few random flames that popped up every few seconds. They rejected the food, obviously a bit too well done to suit their taste. But they still stuck close to the tree, knowing that I was there. Like I said, they were smart. They knew that if I went up, eventually I'd have to come down.

They had my rifle, or at least had separated me from it. I had the feeling that they knew what the strange tubular object was laying there on the ground, and as long as I didn't have it in my hands, they were safe. What they didn't know was that I had my Glock tucked away under the tarp.

They worried me, even if they couldn't reach me. I crawled over to the supply pile and dug through my belongings, tossing tools and clothing aside, finding the pistol, snatching it from its nylon holster.

It couldn't have been more than two minutes, three at the most, when I approached the hatch and threw it open. I don't know how the *raptor* did it. Perhaps it had been scheming and calculating all that time that it had been down at the foot of the ladder, thinking about the wooden obstacle that separated us. In time it had figured out its meaning—had solved the puzzle of it. It was still a mystery to me how it did it, but it had figured out how to climb. I said that they were smart, but even I hadn't understood just how smart they really were.

I had removed the latch, pulling the peg from its hidey space in the header, and had just began to lift the hatch, when, suddenly, it sprung open with such a force as to throw me backwards into the pile of supplies. Scrambling to my feet, I saw the *raptor* emerge from the hole. Its strength was matched by its anger. It came through the hatch with mouth agape, saliva dripping from its angry yellow lips, teeth that reflected back the moonlight, looking even longer and even sharper up close, shrieking a god-awful howl that sounded like squealing tires on wet blacktop.

It looked from side to side, fixing those dangerous eyes onto mine, pausing for just a moment, one last step to climb. It was sizing things up, smart enough to know that it had arrived at an entirely new situation—it had an enemy that it was unfamiliar with. It took the last step, crouched on those muscular thighs, about to launch itself at me.

The pause was its mistake. I swung the pistol around and fired. It was no more than three feet away. Even as inexperienced as I was, I couldn't have missed it, yet, I kept firing until the entire clip was gone—kept firing until the *raptor* had fallen back through the hatch, and bounced from the ladder to the ground.

When the aerated body plopped onto the earth, leaking red from a dozen spots, the three surviving *raptors* stopped in their tracks, glanced up at me through the hole in the deck, then down at their fallen pack mate. Up, then down they looked, and then again, and then over and over again, as if trying hard to understand what the hell just happened.

They were confused. I had to believe that I was right in my original assessment—what lay before them was their leader. It was dead, and for just a minute or so they didn't know what to do. They wavered, undecided, back and forth—the thing up in the tree that killed it, or the thing lying at their feet ... smelling like so much dead meat.

They knew that they had no chance at me ... so they took the second option. With one short glance at one another, a silent agreement among comrades, they attacked the fallen *raptor*, leaping high into the air, coming down seemingly face first, jaws open wide, into the animal.

It was a nightmare scene, surpassed only by the terrifying sound of the attack. It was dark, made more so by the shadows of the tree obscuring the moonlight. The dying embers of the campfire provided the only light. It reflected off the wicked teeth of the three attackers in bits and snatches as each maneuvered in closer to get its share. The darkness masked the horrible vision that was taking place thirty feet below, but it did nothing to mute the sounds of the carnage.

The ear-piercing screams and nerve-wracking shrieks stopped as their comrade hit the ground, only to be replaced with the horrible sounds of carnivores at work. I could hear the teeth gnashing against one another, and banging and scraping against the bones of the newly dead animal. And the crunching was the worst—the snapping and shattering of the hollow bones like a garbage disposal that was chewing on something that was not meant to be there. And across it all was an unholy slobbering, smacking of lips, and slurping, gulping sounds, intermixed with heavy, sloppy breathing as the three cannibals devoured one of their own.

When they were done, there was nothing left but broken bones, feathers, and a pool of blood, hardly recognizable for what it once was—another killer. Even in the darkness, I could see that they had cleaned their plates, taken everything edible, and they didn't seem the least bit ashamed. But I thought, why should they? They weren't subject to the tenants of man—there were no rules and regulations of fair play in the jungle. They were just animals. They were only creatures trying to survive from one day to the next—just like me.

But the terrifying brutality of it still left me shaken. I lay at the edge of the deck, trembling, as much from the awful experience, as from the loss of blood, which I knew was draining down my arm and in between the boards of the wooden platform in large quantities. Inside my head weird things were happening—little demons poked at my brain, twisting and turning their little pitchforks, sending little sparks through the back of my eyes, a staticky little buzz that came and went in my inner ears.

As my vision dimmed, I watched as the deadly trio disappeared into the dense growth of the jungle.

The pain in my arm, which was exquisite just moments ago, began to fade, but I knew that the deep cut wasn't getting better—I was just getting closer to losing consciousness—the pain just taking a temporary backseat to things of a more critical nature.

I had to stop the bleeding within the next few minutes or it would simply run out of me uncontested. Using the last of my strength, I staggered over to the hatchway and like a man hopped up on drugs, stumbled and slid down the ladder, ending up in a pile at the bottom.

I had to get to the fire, to reach the last of the dying coals of the poplar. If you had asked me right then why, I would have had no idea. I only knew that the fire was my only chance. I crawled over to it, using both arms, unmindful now of the pain, ignoring the growing loss of feeling. I went down twice, face first, as the left arm gave out, scratching my chin and cheek on the burned out stubble poking out of the blackened ground.

I arrived at the edge of the fire pit, grabbing on to the one remaining upright wooden frame piece and pulled myself to my feet. I gazed down on the few bits of flame that had managed to stay alive, the light painful to my eyes, causing the little devils to jab faster into the part of my brain that controlled eyesight, causing indescribable pain to shoot throughout my mind, if not actually my brain. The flames seemed hypnotic, causing me to loose precious time as I gawked deep into the heart of them. The tiny flames burst across my retinas, forming pictures of the raptor crawling through the hatch, the bullets ripping into its feathered skin, it being blown back through the hole from which it came. Images, that, had they not already been burned into my brain, were sure as hell there now.

I shook it off, and stared down into the fire, finally understanding what I had to do, terrified at the thought of actually doing it. But what I needed was all the way across the other side of the pit. I thought about just taking the shorter route, directly across the hot coals ... then thought better of it. Instead, I lurched around its perimeter, staggering, nearly falling into the hot pit, waving my one good arm in front of me in a lame attempt to keep my balance.

Somehow making it around to the other side, I stopped, glaring down at the red-hot pry-bar that poked out from the little pile of burning wood that still remained. The forked-end with the little turn in it stuck out into the cooler air, blackened, probably still hot as hell, but not hot enough for what I needed. The opposite end of the bar was still protruding through the hollowed bones sticking out of the end of the cremated hunk of meat. But the center of the bar, that's what I was after. It glowed, red-hot, like a smithy's rod, ready for forming.

With my one good arm, I tore the shirt from my back, the left sleeve sloppy with sticky wetness that adhered to my skin as I peeled it off. Wrapping it around the palm of my right hand, I reached for the bar, twisting and jerking it free from the remnants of my last meal.

In the light of the shrinking fire I could see the gaping wound, slicing deep into both the biceps and triceps muscles, halfway between my elbow and shoulder. Blood, black as the night itself, bubbled and flowed in waves from the inch-wide gash, soaking everything below. The sight of it, and knowing what I had to do, made the darkness grow yet dimmer, and I had to fight to keep the lights from going out altogether.

I shoved the wedge-shaped end into the burned earth with all my remaining strength, pulling it toward me so that it formed a forty-five degree angle with the ground ... then I pushed it in deeper yet. I lay down next to it, on my back, my left arm positioned within inches of the sizzling iron rod. I scooted in close, lining up the cut with the length of the rod—close enough where I could feel the heat begin to burn the hairs on my arm and start the blood to boiling. Once again I grabbed the bent end with my shirt-wrapped hand, steadying it as I crept in even closer, the pain sending shock waves into my brain, tears filling my eyes.

Before I had a chance to change my mind, knowing that it was now or never, I pulled on the bar with all my might, pressing the red-hot iron into the gash. My muscles instantly locked in shock, but there was nowhere to go, stuck as I was between the ground and the bar. My right arm was paralyzed, pulling on the bar with all my might, the bar pressing into the skin and muscle, causing the fluids to sizzle, a horrible stench filling my nostrils, unable to let up. The pain was like nothing I had ever felt before. It only began in my arm. Within milliseconds, it had conquered my entire body, filling it with a torment that I had nothing to compare to. Perhaps being struck by lightning was the only thing that flashed into my mind, a kind of white-hot, super-sudden uncontrollable shock that made all other sensations, all other bodily functions halt all at once. My entire body clenched into one gigantic fist, screaming for release, the sound following the lead of my inner voice, trailing off as I slipped into unconsciousness.

*****

I opened just one eye, the other pressed painfully into the stubble of the clearing. I had passed out, but I hadn't been out for long. It was still dark, and the embers of the fire pit continued to glow. The pain in my left arm had woken me, less than an hour had passed since I had pressed the metal to the flesh, maybe just a matter of minutes. And yet, as I came to, it took several moments before I was aware of where I was and what had happened. My head throbbed and my entire body ached, but it was nothing compared to the agonizing pain in my arm, as if it had been ripped from the rest of my body, leaving but a bloody stump hanging uselessly from my shoulder.

I looked to see that it was still there, but it was a useless lump, no feeling below the agony of the scalded wound. The bar was still there, as well, pressed up against the skin, painfully so, but the heat was gone, replaced by pressure that ground deep into the bone. I released the grip of my right hand, pushing the bar away, feeling dead tissue pull away, welded to the rough surface of the makeshift spit, the brutal pain sent to even greater heights.

I was nauseous and so weak that I felt that it would be preferable to just lie there and let the pain take me away. The mere thought of moving was too much to bear. But within minutes the basic instinct for survival kicked in and I was terrified to find that I had just been lying out there in the open, completely vulnerable.

At least several minutes had passed, perhaps longer, and during that time I was totally at the mercy of whatever happened to come wandering by, whatever happened to smell the charred remains of the *Gallimimus* meat, the remains of the *raptor*, or the fresh blood pouring from my own body. What if the other three *raptors* returned? My weapon, wherever I had dropped it, was useless, spent. I couldn't have fended off one of them, let alone three.

I stood up … and immediately went back down again, the dark, fuzzy world around me spinning faster and faster. My vision failed and everything went black.

As my eyesight began to return I was left with little wavy, horizontal lines that made distorted images out of the hot coals. It made me feel like I had drunk a quart of cheap rotgut whiskey. My head throbbed with the pain of something trying to get out—without a doubt the little devils with their pitchforks. As I tried to gather some sense of reality, the image of that night in the bar with Dermot jumped into my mind as I tossed up the no longer savory chunks of dinosaur meat.

Lying in a pool of my own vomit, I forced myself to my feet a second time, reeling and swaying, but somehow staying upright. With difficulty, I spotted the ladder, the image coming and going, fading out of sight one moment, sliding back in the next. I stumbled toward it, passing through the middle of my barbecue, sending out a shower of sparks from the last of the dying embers as I trod through, tripping on a burned out chunk of poplar, sprawling yet again against the coarse stubble of the clearing.

Climbing the ladder was a blur and interminable at the same time. I passed in and out of semi-consciousness, barely remembering making the climb at all, yet what I did remember was like trying to climb an infinite series of steps out of hell. Climbing a ladder with two good legs and one good arm is not such a difficult task. I had done it a hundred times, carrying a bucket of paint to put another coat on the peak of the house, to hang the flower pots on the soffit, or to haul the hose up to the roof to flush out the gutters. But this was nothing like that. Climbing up the thirty rungs with a head full of cotton, my sight as well as my consciousness fading in and out, my body mostly numb from pain and weariness, was just about as difficult as anyone could imagine. I'm not sure how many times I attempted that first rung, how many times I slid down one for every two that I climbed, no idea how long it actually took. I only vaguely remember making it to the first level and collapsing, half in and half out of the hatch.

*****

The sky had the easy gray of daylight that was just minutes away. I awoke to the first sounds of the birds, still too early for the larger creatures to announce their presence. My first sensation was not that of the pain in my left arm, but that of my stomach and hips, which were painfully folded over atop of the header on the back edge of the hatch. Moments later I took note of the numbness in my legs, the blood flow being cut off for too long a stretch. Only after that did the memory of what happened the night before come flooding back—and with it, the pain and horror of my injury.

I was still exposed, my lower half sticking out the bottom of the hatch, my feet planted three rungs below. The raptors could climb—I learned that the hard way the night before. Lying there all night was another dumb thing in a quickly growing list of dumb things that I had done—albeit unintentional—this time.

I was shivering from the morning chill, my naked upper body covered with a thin sheen of dew, my chest bruised from lying atop the rough-hewn logs of the deck. The real pain struck as I tried to haul the rest of me up through the hatch, my left arm buckling under, my feet sliding out from the rung, nearly sending me back down the ladder. Only the header saved me as

I reached out in a moment of panic, latching on to it with my one useful hand, the rest of me spread-eagled across the sloping ladder.

My feet scrambled for purchase on the ladder, slipping repeatedly on the morning-moist wooden rungs. My body twisted helplessly as I began to lose my grip on the header. At the last instant, my rubber-soled boots locked onto the rung and I sagged against the inside of the hatchway, shaken and breathless. Looking back at it, it was probably a hilarious sight—but it was damn unfunny at the time.

More carefully, this time conscious of the uselessness of my left arm, I climbed through the hatch and crumpled onto the deck. I didn't pass out, although that probably would have been preferable. The pain that had started in mid-upper arm had spread through the elbow and across the shoulder and into the left side of my neck. I reached across with my right had to assess the damage. It felt as bad as I expected, a slick, sticky trench across the entire width of my arm, hard, ragged surfaces at the outer edges, my fingers causing new waves of pain as they traced the mutilation.

I turned toward the east, bringing my arm up toward the emerging light to see if it looked as bad as it felt ... it was worse. My entire arm was coated in blood, smeared in purple-black streaks over its entire length, bits of dirt and grass ground into the congealing mess. The blood was thickening, giving each finger an extra quarter inch of length, congealing as it dripped. The massive flow of blood had slowed to a trickle, weeping from a half dozen places. Around the swollen edges was black, crusted, dead skin coated with the charred remnants of the pry-bar. In the center there was a disturbing patch of white—bone, tendon—I wasn't sure what, but I knew that I couldn't look at it, and I didn't much want to think about it either. The slightest glance at it made me nauseous, little sparks of light danced before my eyes.

I had a first aid kit, one of those little tin boxes, painted in red, white, and blue that every home has, and every cub-scout leader carries on overnight camping trips. I found it easily, the contents of my supplies having been strewn over half of the deck in the search for my pistol the night before. I popped opened the lid using one hand, digging out a tube of antiseptic salve and a role of gauze that were among the standard issue.

I smeared on the soothing cream in liberal amounts, stuffing it into the crevice, smearing it around the stiff, hilly outlying surfaces of the gash. The coolness felt good on the fevered skin, giving me just the smallest reprieve from the pain, but at the same time, the slightest touch of my fingers started it up again. I applied it gently, mounding the goo everywhere within six inches of the wound, caring not at all if I used the entire tube—I knew that there was plenty more where that came from. When I had covered it sufficiently, I wrapped the gauze around it, layering it loosely from my armpit to the elbow, the salve quickly seeping through the porous surface of the gauze.

With that done, I leaned back into the scattered remains of my stores, thinking that I was just in need of a short rest.

*****

Intermittent flashes of light beyond the closed lids of my eyes woke me. The sun low in the horizon slipped in between the gently swaying leaves forming the edges of the tree's canopy. The better part of a day had passed, the sun just beginning to set over the mountain range, it hot on my face and chest, its rays blinding as I struggled to open my eyes fully. I was stiff from lying for so long in such an uncomfortable position, hard corners and edges of the supplies beneath the tarp poking at my back and shoulders. The pain in my arm had subsided to a dull throbbing ache, little prickles of pain deep in the center of the wound, regular as my heartbeat.

I had a monster headache, the little devils obviously not quite done with their work. The bright sun was hard on my eyes, harder yet on my head. Turning away from it only hurt more—moving in any way hurt more.

My stomach rumbled from hunger. The only thing that I had eaten in two days was the *Gallimimus* meat, most of which I tossed back up. And I could smell it … not the meat, but the other. The smell was all over me, as was dried blood, sweat, and the leftover stench of unadulterated fear. I was rank!

I wanted food, but I didn't think that I could stomach eating something over my own smell. My own odor would infiltrate anything that I attempted to cook. The mere thought of passing a spoonful of food through the vapor surrounding me would cause the gag reflex that would keep it from going down. No, what I needed right then was a bath—food later—a bath now.

But first things first. Peering down through the open hatch, I could see my rifle lying by the foot of the ladder, just a yard away from what was left of the *raptor*. The gun was loaded, but it was thirty feet away, and I had learned my lesson. I replaced the empty clip in the Glock with a fresh one, shoved it into the waistband of my pants and backed down the ladder.

I was just halfway down when the sight of the dead *raptor* made me stop suddenly, my breath caught in my throat, the little hairs on the back of my neck standing at attention. The thing that I had shot full of holes, had then been devoured by the other three predators … the thing that just last night had been nothing but a bloody pile of broken bones and plucked feathers … had moved.

I was squeezing the side of the ladder so hard with my one good hand that the muscles of my arm began to cramp. I eased up my grip and let go, reaching through the rungs to wipe away the sweat from my eyes that had to be causing an optical illusion. But when the image failed to change, I took a precautionary step back up the ladder.

The damn thing *was* moving. And it had somehow grown a new skin, the broken pieces reforming themselves beneath into a solid body once more.

I stepped down two rungs, then two more, slowly, gun in hand, not taking my eyes off the hideous thing. As I got in closer, I could see that it wasn't the thing itself that was moving ... it was the skin that was moving ... *it* was alive. A solid black mass rolled in waves over the remains of the *raptor*, continuously changing its shape in subtle, yet frightening ways. A slight turn of the head, a tiny shift of the legs, its body rolling a few degrees to one side, and the illusion of its chest rising and falling—like breathing.

I continued down the ladder, just five rungs to go, when I understood what I was seeing. Some kind of beetle, thousands upon thousands of them, rolling as one over the remains of the *raptor*, picking its bones clean, finishing the job that had begun the night before. They weren't quite black, but a dark plum color, their tiny hard shells reflecting the light of the dying sun, a hundred thousand points of fire that shifted continuously, one way, then another.

As I stepped down from the last two rungs I became aware of the sound, a low drone, barely audible, but undulating, a slight change in both pitch and volume, matching the speed of the perceived heartbeat. Standing alongside, I saw them up close—large hooked pincers, smaller barbed legs—tiny, but threatening, flying carnivores. As I stepped over them to retrieve my rifle, a few of them lifted into the air, their shells splitting and opening, their tiny little wings beating with a frequency that was just a blur. One of them landed on my right shoulder, taking a bite, ripping a tiny chunk of flesh away before I could swat it into a red and black blob. As I wiped it from my skin I looked back at the feeding frenzy, seeing another dozen rise into the air.

For the second time in twenty-four hours, I unloaded the Glock, blowing away what was left of the *raptor*, sending the buzzing horde into the sky as one contiguous black mass.

They came my way, but they weren't interested in me. I ducked as they shot past my head, no doubt terrified by the blasts of the gunshots, their sounds amplified by the rapid beating of thousands of pairs of wings. As I dodged, I swung my one arm high over my head, fighting them off, or, I hoped, at least scaring them away.

In seconds, they were gone, heading as one for the site of their next meal. On one knee, breathless once again, I looked over to check their work. The bones were still there, as were the feathers, but nothing else—not a shred of meat, muscle, or tissue, just the broken, disjointed bones of the animal, now picked clean, gleaming whiteness that stood in sharp contrast to the burned earth beneath.

My sidearm was empty, useless once again, and I tossed it at the base of the ladder, not afraid that it would disappear while I was gone. Firing my weapon until it was dry was yet another stupid thing to do. How many of the beetles did I think I could hit? A couple of dozen at most—a couple of thousand remaining. The sound of the gun had scared them away—one shot would have probably done it—the rest were due to my own fears.

I picked up my rifle and headed out toward the river. After all that had happened I should have expected something more—another attack from one direction or another. But the simple fact of the matter was that I was just too damn tired to care. I walked through the little patch of jungle and through the meadow, my rifle dragging behind me, my left arm on fire, and smelling to high heaven, with a chip on my shoulder … just daring for something to fuck with me.

But nothing did. I staggered onto the shore, removing my boots and stripping off my pants, wading into the cool water, leaving the rifle on the bank, numb to everything other than the refreshing water. I didn't think about the wound on my left arm, strolling out to the center of the river where I could submerge myself and let the currents take the dirt and grime from my body.

It was the first bit of relief that I had felt in the last twenty-four hours. The water was cool, but not cold—just the right temperature to revive me, yet not dull my senses. Some feeling returned to my hand, the pain in the upper portion of my arm still terrible, but no longer overwhelming. I paddled over to the cliff, pressing my back up against it, and just kicked my legs enough to keep me afloat, while I stared out over the meadow as the light faded into night.

*****

It was three days later when I first realized that something was wrong … really wrong, and I wasn't too sure what to do about it.

On the first day following the trip to the river, I felt good. My arm was stiff, sore, and throbbed like so many other injuries that I had survived over my lifetime—nothing terribly out of the ordinary—nothing to be really concerned about. When I had returned to the tree, I had changed the soggy dressing on my wound and immediately fell into a deep, untroubled sleep. When I awoke, I felt refreshed, alert, just a dull pain in my arm that was little more than a distraction. I appeased my angry stomach with a huge meal of scrambled dinosaur egg, cooked on an open fire that I had dragged fifteen feet closer to the tree, a loaded gun strapped to my waist while I cooked. It was delicious and I managed to keep it down for a change.

The rest of the day was uneventful—discarding the remains of the *raptor* at the foot of the ladder, rearranging the mess I had made of my supplies, a light supper of canned food, a little light reading as the sun went down, a couple of sips of scotch for medicinal purposes. I hardly left the safety of the tree, sleeping on the second deck, the safest of all possible places.

On the next day, I stuck pretty close to the tree as well. I felt lethargic, not in the mood to do much of anything. I ate out of the can again, not caring that my supplies were getting dangerously low. My arm hurt a little more than it did the day before, and when I went to change the dressing I noticed that the pink color that had oozed through the gauze was mixed with a sickly yellow. As I unwound the last of the wrap, an unhealthy smell became all too apparent, the skin around the gash swollen and angry-red. I pushed the spongy mass lightly with my fingertips, pain running down the length of my arm, awful yellow-green pus trickling out from the edges.

My arm had become infected. It may have been from dirt that had been ground into the open sore when I approached the fire, or from whatever was on the pry-bar that I had used to cauterize it. Or perhaps it was from the water that I had bathed in afterward. But what I really thought was that the claw of the *raptor* that had caused the wound in the first place was the carrier of some exotic bacteria that was working its way into my bloodstream. Whatever it was, I had to stop it, and I couldn't just drop into the nearest emergency room.

I pulled off the deadened skin around the wound and picked away the beginnings of the scab, gritting my teeth against the pain. Opening one of the gauze pads from the first-aid kit, I soaked it in scotch and pressed it into the freshly opened sore. A quick intake of breath turned into a scream that faded as I began to swoon. I didn't quite go down, but everything got all kind of squirrelly-like, and the light dimmed for a few seconds. The pain passed nearly as quickly as it started, leaving my upper arm with more of a numb feeling than actual pain. I soaked a fresh pad in scotch and placed it over the injury, wrapping it with another gauze bandage.

I slept fitfully that night—my head throbbed nearly as much as my arm. I alternated between freezing cold and feverish sweats, huddling into a ball under my blanket one minute, throwing it off the next. And in those brief, infrequent periods of sleep, I had nightmares that rotated between the scene on the mountain slope when Susan went down nearly four years ago, and the attack of the *raptor* as many days ago. At some point they got all sort of tangled up, until, finally, it was Susan being attacked by the *raptor*, and me sitting up on the second deck, powerless to do a goddamn thing about it.

I really didn't awaken with the coming of the sun, more like I had just had enough of lying there awake, waiting for the new day. The chills had passed but I was still feverish, my body hot, yet somehow dry as dust, several day's growth of beard dirty and smelly like a pile of cut grass that had been left out too long. My left arm hurt like hell and was pretty much useless as I staggered down the ladder to the first deck.

I reached to unwrap the bandage, wincing at the slightest touch. I sucked in my breath and pulled the wrapping off, wincing yet again as I saw the mangled flesh of my upper arm, some of it pulling away in sticky pink and yellow strands, stuck to the gauze. The area around the tear had gone beyond red, now a horrifying black and purple that only tended toward red as the coloration reached my elbow. It extended that way upward as well, disappearing across the top of my shoulder, beyond the width of my peripheral vision. It was even more swollen than it had been the day before, like a sausage in a hot pan, ready to burst.

Treating it was beyond anything that I had in my little tin box. I needed serious medicine. I only hoped I had what I needed in what was left of my supplies at the top of the cliff, above the river. With trembling fingers, I refilled one of the empty clips, dropping as many bullets as I actually snapped into place, before slapping it into the Glock. Gun in hand, I threw the empty backpack over my good shoulder and started toward the river.

It was mid-day of what was surely the end of a long, hot summer when I stepped out from the meadow onto the dirt path. The temperature was easily in the upper nineties, the sun making the throbbing in my head that much worse, my skin made even hotter than the fever that was growing by the hour. It was a short walk to the river, and I had run into no opposition, yet my heart was beating rapidly in my chest and my breath was labored. I had to stop at the edge of the water, my hands on my knees to catch my breath. I had to calm down. It felt like I was hyperventilating, and there was no paper bag to breathe into. I was dizzy and I had to sit down on the hot sand, my head hanging below my knees. I wasn't a doctor, at least not that kind of doctor, but I knew that I was going into shock.

The nausea only added to the dizziness. It hit me in waves, my stomach clenching, but sending little up but a foul gas that choked and burned and made the sweat pour from my face. When it passed I crawled on all fours into the cool water, too weak to even stand.

The water refreshed me to some extent, but did nothing for the disorientation that was quickly becoming a problem. During the short swim to the face of the cliff I had to stop continuously, unsure of where I was heading, at times even unaware of where I was. Each time, it was the knotted rope gently swaying to the currents that reminded me of my mission. A bit confused about why, I knew that I had to climb the rope to the top. There was something up there that I needed, and it had something to do with the useless length of flesh hanging from my left shoulder.

Knowing that I had to climb it, and actually doing it, were two different things. The rope didn't dangle down into the water enough to get a grip on it with my feet, and I didn't have the strength in my right arm to pull myself out of the water enough to catch the last knot. After trying unsuccessfully for five minutes, I took a deep breath and let myself drop down below the surface of the water, placing one hand along the wall as my legs bent to my chest, my feet touching bottom.

Focusing the last of my strength into my legs, I sprung upward, my head clearing the water by three feet, reaching up as far a I could, grabbing the rope, my hand sliding down six inches until it met the next lowest knot. I hung there for a moment, barely holding on while my feet searched for the bottom of the rope.

I twisted and turned, banging repeatedly against the rock, a death grip on the rope, afraid to let go, knowing that I didn't have the strength to do it again. At last catching the bottom of the rope between my feet, I wasted no time in moving upward. The climb was difficult using only one arm, the hardest part keeping my balance while I reached for the next knot, having to let go from the one below.

Time was a damn funny thing. The climb seemed to take forever, every foot more difficult then the next. Several times, I had to reach out quickly between pulls as I forgot what I was doing, grabbing the rope in a panic, the instantaneous pull of gravity forcing me back to reality. More than once I lost my footing, dangling there, hanging by one arm, seconds away from dropping into the river below. And yet, when I reached the top, grabbing the spike driven into the rock, it was all a blur. The climb to the top had been little more than a dream. Only the incredible tiredness that I felt was a reminder of the huge ordeal.

As I swung my leg over the edge and rolled onto the flat plateau, I wanted nothing more than to just lie down and sleep, but that damn annoying little voice in my head told me to keep on going. Walking the few steps to the cart was like walking through quicksand, my brain fuzzy with the same infection that was traveling in both directions through my left arm.

My supplies had dwindled down to medicine and a few tools. The food was gone, as were the blankets and extra clothing, most of which had been hauled down during the previous month. It was pretty dumb that I hadn't even covered it with a tarp. Thankfully, it hadn't rained in the past several days.

There were a dozen or so white cardboard boxes, each carrying hospital supplies that Dermot had packed. I had no idea what they contained, but I tried to grab a sampling of each from the machine on my last trip back to the cave. If I hadn't grabbed the right one, I feared that I wouldn't survive to the next day, would never live to see my dream fulfilled—to see a *Tyrannosaurus rex*.

Each of the boxes was filled with an assortment of odd-shaped bottles and different colored pills, powders, and liquids. Each one contained a label pasted to the outside, in Dermot's handwriting, stating, in laymen's terms, what the medicine was for and how to administer it. Scanning down the sides of the boxes I spotted one with a label reading, *cefazolin (antibiotic)*. Opening the box and seeing the twenty-four tiny bottles and two-dozen cellophane wrapped disposable hypodermic needles, I recalled what Dermot told me about the drug.

I had asked him about penicillin, the wonder drug of the twentieth century, and why I couldn't find it among the list of medical supplies. He responded with a question of his own, "How did you think you were going to keep it refrigerated?" I had no answer to his question, and as I looked at him with a puzzled expression on my face he pointed down the list to the word cefazolin, which, of course, I had never heard of before.

Cefazolin is a powerful antibiotic that medics carry in the field and in remote sites where refrigeration and electricity are rare or nonexistent. It is mixed with distilled water and injected directly into the muscle. The label on the box stated that the dosage was three cubic centimeters, three times, once every twelve hours. What a coincidence, both the bottles and the syringes were three CCs.

I held one of the little bottles up to my face, in a line with the westbound sun. The tiny white crystals took on a rainbow of colors as I tilted it from one side to another, the glass envelope acting as a prism, separating the natural hues of the sunlight. I twirled the bottle in my fingertips, sending the colors spinning across my retinas in a hypnotizing effect.

I was back in the cave again, the sharp slivers of ice coming through the opening on the diagonal, huge rainbow halos surrounding the spotlights. It was just the beginning of the storm, before the snow hit, before we were all buried under it. Only I knew what was yet to happen.

I could just barely make out Christine on the opposite side of the cave, still standing, talking to her two dig partners—still alive. I thought that they were all smiling—it was still just a big adventure to them. They were pushing one another out toward the center of the cave, daring one another to step into the driving, painful ice. Somehow, the two boys got hold of each of Christine's arms and began to drag her out into the storm. I could see the look of pure joy on her face turn to one of horror ... and then to pain as her heart began to pound painfully in her chest.

I looked over to my right, seeing the other two kids standing like statues, a smirk plastered on each face, mocking me, telling me that it was too late—I couldn't do shit!

The noise of the storm was deafening, but I could see Christine's tormented face clearly through the ice as she screamed, frozen tears running down her face. Her tormentors laughed hysterically as they held her at arm's length, her body torn by the needles of ice. I couldn't hear her but I could see her mouth the words, "Help me, please help me," over and over again.

I tried to move, but my feet wouldn't budge. I looked down to see that they were encased in ice up to my waist, a solid block that held me as firmly as iron. I tried to yell across the raging storm to Christine, to tell her I was sorry, but my voice was drowned out by the roar of the howling wind. I turned at the sound of the two boys closest to me. They still wore the smirks of someone that knew a secret. They were both stroking one index finger against the other in the old universal shame, shame symbol, saying in unison, "You should have known better Doctor Williams, you sure as hell should have known better..."

The sounds of my own screams brought me back. The swirling colors of the mercury vapor lights blurred into the tiny sparkles of the white powder. But the cold remained. I sat there cross-legged on the sun-warmed rocks of the plateau, the temperature hovering at the century mark, shivering like I was still back in the cave on that fateful, early-winter night of the storm.

It took all my concentration to figure out what I was holding, what the little bottle full of white powder was for. As reality took a short, but halting step forward, everything became clear, and in that moment I realized that I had no water. I had taken the last of it down below on my last trip. I had no choice but to go back, right away, while I was still able to.

I filled the backpack with the white box of antibiotics, tossed in a couple of boxes of other medical supplies, for no other reason than there was room, and holding onto the piton, I dropped back over the ledge.

Going down the rope was easier than going up. It took less strength, which was just now in short supply, but it was still damn hard. The muscles in my right arm and shoulder shook as I tried to ease my weight down from one knot to the next, sweat flowing from every pore, making my grip even less sure. I didn't bother with searching for the knots to place my feet, instead I just wrapped my legs around the rope, the knots chaffing the inside of my thighs, tearing into my shins, with each foot that I descended. At times I had no idea where I was or what I was doing other than the knowledge that I had to continue the climb down, content to let gravity do its thing.

I wasn't much more than half the way down the rope, sliding my one good hand down, trying to keep my grip loose enough to keep from burning yet another layer of skin from my palm, tight enough to not miss the next lower knot … when I felt the rope slip. Just an inch, maybe two, but it nearly jarred me from the rope. I increased my speed, nearly sliding down the rope rather than rappelling down it. I had gone another ten feet, still thirty feet above the surface of the water, when my speed got the better of me. I missed the next knot and flipped over, my legs still wrapped around the rope … and then I was falling. Somehow I managed to summersault, hitting the water feet first, touching the bottom a second later, too fast, turning an ankle.

I sprung back upward, my one arm flailing, sucking in water, panic setting in even though the water was only shoulder high. As my head cleared the surface, I spun from one side to the other, trying to figure out what had just happened, where I was. I turned in the water, spotting the knotted rope, one piece of the puzzle settling into place, but there were still too many pieces missing. I looked away, down stream, seeing a battered green hunk of material floating with the currents, thirty feet away … then forty.

It looked like something important, but as I stood there on one good leg, treading water with one good arm, I couldn't quite grasp the significance of it. As I continued to stare at the object getting farther and farther away, shadows fell over the water that separated us. I looked up to see the pair of *Pteranodons* weaving in and out of the sun's rays. And as I marveled at the strange looking animals, all the pieces fell back into place.

My pack!

The green object that was quickly floating out of sight held the medicine that meant the difference between life and death. I stretched out in the water and started pulling across the surface with my right arm. I ignored the pain in my ankle, kicking with both legs as hard as I could.

The pack was moving faster than I was. I lost sight of it within the first few minutes, but I continued to paddle and kick—turning back was not an option. The pack had to be somewhere up ahead. There was no place else for it to go.

After twenty minutes I had passed the stand of poplars, the farthest north along the river that I had ever been. Fifteen minutes after that I still hadn't spotted the pack, but the landscape had begun to change. The river narrowed and became more shallow, water only up to my waist. The bottom was no longer hard and sandy, but soft and muddy, my footsteps sending out inky-dark clouds in the water. The path that had run alongside the river for the entire part of its length that I had known had angled off into the trees a hundred yards back. Replacing it was jungle, right up to the water's edge. Giant ferns and trees with great leaves and hanging boughs leaned out over the water, casting shadows nearly up to the walls of the cliff. As I moved closer to shore, and into the darkness, I could feel plant growth whipping at my legs.

I continued on for another quarter mile, in and out of random patches of sunlight that somehow managed to penetrate the dense growth of the foliage. The sweats and shaking had begun again, and my head took up the steady pounding that I knew would only get worse. In the soft muck of the river bottom, I felt like I was moving in slow motion, my brain moving at about the same pace. I was beginning to lose touch with reality again, brief periods where I couldn't remember what I was doing in a swamp, periods that were occurring more frequently where I couldn't quite remember what I was searching for.

I was in the middle of one of those little fugues, standing in the center of the narrowed river, looking around for I didn't know what, when I spotted it. The straps had hung up on some reeds growing through the muddy river bottom. The pack was just floating there, a few feet from the edge of the water, bobbing up and down like a cork to the currents of the river. I waded toward it, the water now only up to my knees, so dark that I couldn't see my legs moving through it. As I reached for the life-saving pack, something caught my eye off to the right. Twenty feet away was the largest snake that I had ever seen. It was dropping into the water from a tree branch that was hanging just a few feet above. It was hidden in the shadows of the tree, but looked dark, mostly browns and greens, and was as big around as the upper part of my arm.

With the pack clutched tightly to my chest I stepped backward through the water, in the direction that I had come. The snake was totally in the water, its full length disguised as it wriggled against the current, coming right for me. Its head was a foot out of the water, staring at me with unblinking yellow eyes. I was too far from shore to make my escape in that direction, and heading into the unknown darkness of the underbrush was the last place I wanted to go. The snake could move onto the ground as easily as it had dropped from the tree into the water. I continued to step backward, slowly, never taking my eyes from the gliding serpent, but I was losing ground quickly.

The snake was within a couple of yards from when me I turned sideways, my bad arm toward it, my right hand clutching the straps of the pack, my arm extended up and out. The snake seemed to take no notice of my motion, just kept coming. When it had halved the distance, I twisted my upper body away from it and swung the laden pack with all my might, striking the snake's head squarely.

I doubt that I had inflicted any permanent damage, but the snake came several feet out of the water, thrown back in the opposite direction and quickly swam away. It crossed the river at an angle away from me, disappearing into the dense jungle.

I felt more lucid than I had all day. I knew exactly where I was, where I had to go, and what I had to do, but I knew that that was a temporary reprieve due to the adrenaline rush caused by terror. It was a rush that would wear off when I could least afford it. I had to get back to the tree.

I continued to walk backward, angling toward the safety of the cliff, one eye on the shoreline, the other on the dark part of the river. I followed the cliff for an interminable distance, all the while my strength fading, my arm and ankle throbbing more intensely with every step. My mind was starting to drift in and out of again, remembering only that I had to follow the cliff. And I was cold, freezing, my teeth chattering uncontrollably, my skin a mass of gooseflesh.

The sun was low in the sky when I spotted the rope dangling down into the water. I thought it odd that a rope would just be hanging there for no apparent reason. It seemed so out of place. I hadn't seen another one like it, even though I'd been moving forward in the water, hugging the wall for—well, forever. I was a hundred feet beyond it when a spark of recognition brought me back. I knew that it was *my* rope, although everything else was kind of all jumbled up, bouncing around in my brain, but not falling into any kind of recognizable pattern.

Not fully understanding why, I paddled away from the cliff and, staggering across the dirt path, entered the meadow.

The walk through the jungle didn't even register, nor did climbing up the ladder into my tree. The next thing I remembered was sitting on the lower deck, my pack resting on my lap, staring into the jungle. The chills had passed, I don't know when, only to be replaced by burning fever, and an incredible thirst. My heart was doing double time against my breastbone like I had just run a marathon, and I was having trouble catching my breath.

I turned and reached into my supplies, pulling out a bottle of water. I drank half of it before I ran out of air, water splashing down my chin as I gasped for breath. I sat there breathing slowly and evenly, trying to gain some sense of normalcy, staring down at the water bottle resting atop the backpack. The proximity of the two must have triggered some connection buried deep with my tormented brain. I dug into the box, finding three white, crumpled, waterlogged boxes. Inside the third one were two-dozen little glass vials filled with the white powder and the paper-wrapped syringes.

With only marginal understanding of what I was doing, I latched onto another water bottle and tore off the plastic seal and unscrewed the blue plastic top. While I still could, I fumbled with the paper sealing the syringe, ripping it open after several failed attempts. With hands that shook nearly uncontrollably, I filled the hypo with water and found the little soft seal in the bottle, plunging the needle in. I unloaded the syringe, and, without even removing it, I shook up the bottle and drew the solution back into it.

Not bothering to clean the area, I plunged the syringe into the back of my thigh, just below the edge of my shorts, eight inches above the knee-joint. If I had expected some kind of instant relief, some magical transformation to the person that I was the week before, I was sorely disappointed.

Other than a tender little lump in the back of my leg, I felt nothing. My heart continued to race, by body alternating between waves of unbearable heat and mind-numbing cold. My brain was as foggy as a spring morning on Lake Michigan. Grabbing a single blanket, I limped up the ladder to the second deck.

I was shivering, cold beyond human endurance. Making myself as tiny as possible, I rolled into a tight little ball so that I would fit within the folds of the thin blanket. The rough surface of the hand-cut logs dug into my hips and shoulders on my right side—painful, but unquestionably, the better alternative. Indescribable pain in my arm and leg jumped up to greet me every time that I rolled onto the other side. I had no idea why that was—I only knew that it was best not to do it.

I lay there and prayed for daylight, hoping that with the new dawn would come the warmth—with the light, a clearer understanding of what was happening to me. But the night seemed to last forever, time standing still as I went from little bits of reality to longer periods of fantasy. I saw snakes and raptors coming at me, sometimes singularly, sometimes in tag-teams. Each time, I popped back into real life just moments before their hungry jaws clamped down on my throat.

At times I understood that I was in the tree, the second deck, fifty feet above the ground, high above anything that could harm me. But in my temporarily deranged mind, I couldn't help but to worry what might come from above—aggressive, carnivorous birds pecking at my eyes, while I did nothing about it—Pteranodons nibbling at my flesh after I was dead, my corpse nothing but a feeding trough for the last of the flying mammals.

Other times, I thought that I was back home, just another bout of the flu, back in Chicago, Liz administering to my needs, just waiting for it to pass so that I could go back to work. She would feed me chicken soup and crackers, shoving the thermometer into my mouth every couple of hours, giving me aspirin, wiping the sweat from my forehead, caring for me, worrying about me.

But I always seemed to come back to the here and the now, shivering from the cold, and on fire from the fever at the same time.

When I thought that I could get no more miserable, that I had pretty much reached my limit, the corner of the blanket lifted, letting in another lung-sucking blast of cold air, sending me into an uncharted realm of pain and misery. But I was too weak to do anything about it, too cold to emerge from my tight little ball with my hands tucked into my stomach, my knees pulled up into my chest.

The sudden warmth came unexpectedly, welcomed, but more than the thin blanket could provide. It was a warmth borne of soft substance, an object that radiated a heat to match my own. The source of the heat pushed against my knees and chest, forcing me to open up, to accept the gift across the entire length of my body.

She crawled in alongside of me, her back to me, her body molded against mine like two spoons in the silverware drawer. She was as naked as I, and her skin was soft and warm against my own. I could feel the twin globes of her bottom pressed tightly against my groin, feeling stirring down there despite my weakness. She wore no perfume, but I could smell soap and shampoo as I nuzzled her neck. And there was another scent, as well—a musty, bedroom kind of a smell—the smell of lovemaking. It was an odor that I hadn't experienced in a long, long time—not since before Liz was killed.

But the scent wasn't Liz's. It was different—wonderful, but not the same. Perhaps it was as simple as a new kind of soap or hair conditioner, although I knew that it was the other smell that was a little different. It was a womanly smell, but not the one that I was so familiar with—not that of Elizabeth. And there were other differences. Liz always wore her hair short, this hair was long, my face buried in it. I could feel it draped across my chest and shoulders. The body was different, too—slim like Liz, but longer, much closer to my own length than Liz was. I slid my left arm across hers, surprised that the pain was gone, and cupped her breast. They were different as well, larger, yet with smaller nipples that rose sharply as I pinched one between thumb and forefinger. As the stirring in my groin became more acute, a familiar voice whispered, "I found you, thank God I found you."

CHAPTER 19

Even a year later, the dream had felt real.

In the days afterward, I had refused to believe that it was a dream, or more accurately, a hallucination resulting from the raging fever of septic shock. It was so much more than a dream. I could still smell the scent of her hair, still feel the heat emanating from her soft body. The feeling of intense intimacy and sexual excitement floats in and out of my mind as any real memory does. It refused to fade the way that dreams do, instead finding a corner of my mind in which to dwell, a tiny spot, but a permanent one.

I had recovered quickly after that night, my brain attributing my miraculous recovery to the regiment of drugs that I managed to complete during the next day, my heart knowing that it was something else, something much more precious.

I had been without human contact for too long, without the love of another human being for even longer. But I had had it on that night. And it was something so much more than just physical contact on that night—there was love. It was real, in a sense that's hard to explain. The experience left a sense of awe, of happiness, a feeling of completeness that I had hung on to for days afterward, was still hanging on to a year later. I just couldn't believe that the closeness that I had shared on that night was anything but real, and it had been what healed me. Susan's love had done it.

There was a connection there that went beyond the physical. I had felt it before. All those days talking to Susan as she lay there in that hospital bed, I felt something special, like she could hear me despite what the doctors said. Sometimes I almost felt like she was talking back to me. Not in a physical sense, but more like her thoughts just kind of drifted into my head. On that last day, I knew that she heard me, and I knew that she was telling me that it was okay to go. And the day when I first came over the ridge, spotting the valley of the dinosaurs that first time, I experienced some kind of spiritual connection with her. There had been something magical that had connected us, not just at that moment, but over a long period of time, going back years, many years, maybe back to the first day that we met.

Of course it was Elizabeth that had lit the spark within me, some months after I had first met Susan, and that spark had turned into a fire, one so hot and bright that it pushed Susan into the darkness. But Susan's own fire had begun, and perhaps something much more than just a spark had caused it. She saw something in me that was more than just physical desire, more than simple love. It was a kinship, a joining of the minds if not the body. But I was only just getting it.

Looking back, maybe I got a glimpse of it that first time at Susan's house and it had everything to do with the stained-glass window. I remember thinking that it was more than just beautiful—it was real. Somehow, God only knows how, she knew that what I had drawn was not just a picture from out of my imagination—even if I didn't realize it. It's what I *did* see as I came across the plateau on that day. The view before me was exactly as that of the window. It wasn't a coincidence, although I can't explain how something like that was possible, I only know that it was.

And the house itself was a clue. There was a surreal quality about the place, especially the top floor, a quality that I should have recognized as something extraordinary. There was a haunting, but not haunted, quality about it. I think now that the feeling was one of being watched—watched by Susan. Somehow, even in her comatose state, she knew that I was there. I think that in some way she had led me on that night, had directed me through the search, showed me where to find the will, as though it was all part of some master plan to help me in the decision that I had yet to make.

And she was still here for me. What had happened in the dream was both magical and enduring. The thoughts of Susan and what she did for me on that night were never far away. I felt special knowing that someone loved me, even though she was beyond my grasp. Yet at the same time the experience had left me with a longing that drilled deep into my soul. It had left me with a loneliness that I could only compare to that which I felt immediately after Liz's death.

When Liz had died I was caught between anger and sadness—anger at those responsible for her murder—sadness for the loss of the most important thing in my life. For months afterward, it made it hard to concentrate on my job, ignoring my friends and coworkers. I existed, but not much else. I didn't care much about anything or anybody else, even less for myself.

I stayed that way pretty much until the expedition when we found the four dinosaurs—and Susan was there by my side—at least at the beginning. Maybe after all, it was Susan and not the discovery that had begun to bring me back to my old self. Some of the old excitement had returned. I began to look forward to each new day, and whether or not I was willing to admit it at the time, I had begun to feel something special for Susan, something beyond the well-established friendship, something more than just buddies.

But Susan's accident plunged me right back into the deepest depression. Only my daily visits with her kept me going from one day to the next. That, and knowing she would expect me to, kept me going. And every time that I tried to get back on my feet, something knocked me back down again—Christine's death, Green's escape, and finally having my dinosaurs taken away from me. Each time, the depression got deeper, and I began tuning everything out.

This was the same kind of feeling. I had trouble focusing on anything, my thoughts constantly on Susan. Even a year later, I couldn't shake the dream, couldn't rid myself of the loneliness and longing that it caused. Almost every day I found myself in a situation where I was lost in thoughts of Susan, forgetting completely what I had been doing, or where I was. On those occasions, I had no idea how much time had passed—usually only minutes—but I feared that they were frequently much longer. And those times didn't just occur in the safety of my home. They occurred in the clearing in front of the tree, on the banks of the river, and even while I was exploring the jungle. It was yet another miracle that nothing befell me while I was in such a state.

Even as I sit in front of the computer, I have to pull my thoughts back to the present, although at least here I don't have to worry about some disaster befalling me while I'm in one of my little tune-outs. Things were calm and safe here. Aside from wandering too far into the sea, I didn't have a hell of a lot to worry about.

I give a great sigh accompanied by a little smile as I marvel at the fact that I'm still here despite my obvious attempts at the contrary. Sometimes I think that Susan not only sees what I see, feels what I feel, but somehow controls the events that are separated by hundreds of miles and millions of years, at least those events as they apply to my actions—or lack of action.

How else can I explain the events of the last few years—surviving all the dumb moves that I've made, lived to write about them despite my best attempts to the contrary? I kind of liked the thought of having a guardian angel, especially when mine was Susan. It embarrassed me to think how badly I had abused the privilege in the months that followed the dream.

In the days and months following my recovery from the *raptor* attack, I went way beyond just doing dumb things, more than just being forgetful of where I was, more than simply not being aware of the dangers surrounding me. I had begun taking chances.

I had already been near death on several occasions, been faced with any number of impossible situations. I should've been wary, on my most defensive behavior ... all the time. Instead, I took to wandering into uncharted territory, dangerous situations, with just minimal protection. It wasn't a conscious thing, but maybe, just maybe, the loneliness forced me to do things that I wouldn't normally do. Perhaps I felt that Susan was already dead, and I wanted nothing but to join her.

I think that the real problem was that I just didn't give a damn ... one way or the other. Because I didn't, I took to taking chances—daring the unknown to do its worst to me, taking ridiculous risks, just asking for trouble. It was stupid, and it was wrong, and it was six months after the dream, in the middle of what this time took for mid-winter, when I knew that I had gone too far.

*****

Autumn in the late Cretaceous meant rain—day after day of it. Not snow, at least not yet, just rain that seemed to have no end. The temperatures, as best I could tell, ranged from the low forties to the mid sixties, not quite cold enough for the white stuff, but cold enough so that it soaked everything, driving the cold right through to the bone. Staying warm and dry had become my primary preoccupation.

In the months preceding, I had made major advancements on my home, putting up the railings, hanging a roof over each deck made from woven palm fronds, smoothing out the rough floors by doubling up on the boards with overturned split logs. More important than mere comfort, I fortified my little compound, making it nearly impregnable from outside intruders.

Over the months, I had dug a trench around the perimeter of the clearing, encompassing the tree at one edge. Four foot deep, V-shaped, I tossed the dirt to the inside of the ring, needing it again when I finished. Into the trench I laid, side by side, the twelve-foot poplar trunks that I had cut from the stand by the river. Each pointed up and outward from the center of the clearing, their tips shaped to wicked points, charred by fire to seal them against the weather. They were bound together, both top and bottom with tough vines from the jungle, bound from one to the next except for a three-foot section opposite the tree. This section looked like all the rest, but with one difference, obvious only to me. This section ended at ground level, not below, and was tied to either side mid-way to the top with strong nylon rope. The section was well balanced so that it easily swung upward from the bottom, pivoting effortlessly at the center ties. A simple rope that could be tied from either the inside or the outside secured the section in place. Nothing was getting into the clearing—at least not from ground level.

My tree was truly becoming my home—safe, secure and comfortable, at least comparatively so. But I wasn't exactly enjoying it. I didn't even take much pride or satisfaction in my accomplishments. I just went through the motions, day after day and week after week, doing what I knew that I had to do for no other reason than just the basic instinct for survival. I was lonely and miserable, but while I worked on my fortress, at least I wasn't bored.

When the rains came, all that changed. Day after day it came down—gentle showers, only to be followed by torrential downpours. Brief respites that were far short of the required drying time. Days went by without seeing a hint of the sun, dark enough for long periods that it was hard to tell the difference between night and day.. And the nights were the worst, eight or ten degrees above freezing, almost impossible to stay warm. My newly installed roofs helped, but staying dry in such conditions was like putting screen doors in a submarine—you just weren't going to keep the water out. I found the spot on the second deck that was most free of drips and tended to just stay there.

I lived mostly on the birds that frequented my tree. I didn't dare use precious ammunition on a single small bird that would serve as only as one meal, a snack at best. Instead, I configured a trap from some netting Dermot had supplied as protection against whatever insects dwelled in prehistoric times. From the nuts and berries, plentiful in the valley, I made a bait pile, easily luring the birds into the trap, unfamiliar as they were to such deception. I even managed to catch a few squirrels, or something that resembled what I guessed to be a squirrel's earliest ancestors.

I took to cooking in the tree as well, my concerns over burning down my home dissipating as the rains continued, soaking the tree long beyond any chance of a stray spark igniting it. I had one good-sized pot, a supply of firewood that I kept dry under the tarp stretched across half the width of deck number one, and a good sharp knife. Together, they made for a good makeshift barbecue. It wasn't gourmet cooking, but it kept me alive. Some of it was actually pretty good, if not consistently all-that filling.

The rains left grudgingly, the storms and pounding rain slowly lessening so that I almost didn't notice the change. Several days of relentless drizzle—no let up, but no deluges either. I had become so accustomed to hiding from the raindrops under the canopy of palm leaves that I hardly noticed. I was used to being soaked through, the degree of wetness a relative thing that passed unnoticed.

And then one morning, almost magically, I awoke to bright sunshine. It was still bitter cold, so I didn't fully recognize it for what it was until I had had a chance to come out from under my blanket, mostly dry for the first time in weeks. The sky was blue, the sun unbelievably bright on the eastern edge of it, balancing on the flat top of the plateau. The birds were in full-voice, despite the lack of warmth, obviously up long before me. Their songs had been absent for so long I had forgotten just how beautiful they were.

Their melodies surrounded me, even though I couldn't see them, and I realized that they had missed the sunshine as much as I had.

During the long weeks stuck in the tree, waiting out the rain, I thought about what I would do should the sun ever return. The obvious answer was to explore. After all, wasn't that why I was here in the first place?

But where?

The valley was huge, and I had seen no more than a few square miles of it. Other than the accidental trip down the river, most of which I couldn't remember, I hadn't ventured more than a few hundred yards in any direction from the tree.

What I did remember about the river was the path that ran alongside it and how it angled off into the jungle a mile or so north of the meadow. It had piqued my curiosity—wondering what lay down that path. The dinosaurs were using it. I had seen any number of them passing by the meadow that lay between the tree and the cliff. Where were they coming from? It hadn't really occurred to me that they were also heading *to* someplace. I only thought about where they were coming *from*, as if it were some mythical place, a place where the dinosaurs were born. I guess it was because of the path. I thought that it was damn strange the way it left the banks of the river after running alongside it for so long.

I remembered the snake, as well—vaguely—in a hazy kind of way, like the fading images of a long ago, nearly forgotten nightmare. Perhaps had I remembered the terror in more vivid detail, I would have made a different choice. But the fear was as translucent as the memory itself and fear was something that I didn't much give a damn about at that point.

I had a giant chip on my shoulder. Had I been back in Chicago I would have been spoiling for a fistfight with the first person that looked at me crosswise. I say that even though I had never been a troublemaker or an aggressive person. I was a turn-the-other-cheek kind of guy. But at that point I was lonely, angry, screwed up, and just plain pissed off.

So in my slightly unbalanced state, I picked the path heading northward. As I said, I was spoiling for a fight, and I figured that I just might find it at the bend in the road.

I left the next morning, after reloading my guns and spare clips. I took the Glock, which hadn't been more than two feet from my side in months, and the shotgun. I packed one of the small first-aid kits. Added to it were three ampoules of antibiotic, my knife, some small cooking utensils, a lightweight sleeping bag, and a roll of mosquito netting. And six water bottles—empty—I would fill them at the river on the way out. I took nothing else, no change of clothing, no other weapons or tools, and no food. I would catch my meals on the way, either in the river, or on the land. I tried to reason it all out, to justify my lack of supplies, but I think that it was just a matter of attitude, and mine was none too good. I was daring something to fuck with me.

As I passed the stand of poplars, I was surprised at how naked it looked, how many I had cut down. It looked like a team of lumberjacks had passed through, taking all but the youngest, most immature trees. I felt guilty at first for taking a large part of a rare stand of leaf-bearing trees, and then I remembered that this was *their* time. Nothing that I could do would prevent the emergence of the forest and the demise of the jungle. It was a time of change, a time of seasonal distinctions, a time for cold weather to change the landscape. As I hiked passed them, I could see brown and dying leaves among the bare branches.

I stayed toward the outer edge of the path, one short step away from good hiding spots among the brush. This was a well-traveled path and I was a stranger heading in the wrong direction on it. It was still early in the morning, the shadow of the cliff stretched across the river and into the jungle, too early for the path to see any traffic. But it would come. Animals in groups both large and small would begin their trek southward when the sun was high in the sky.

I had been watching them from my tree for a year. It was always the same—never too early in the morning—never too late in the afternoon. It was as if they were on some very strict time schedule—they had to leave someplace at a specific time in order to be somewhere else before it was too late. Perhaps they did it because, in the daylight, their vision was more acute, their enemies more easily spotted. The animals that wandered the path were herbivores—gentle animals that traveled in packs. Not just for protection, but because they were social creatures with a highly developed sense of family. They were stronger in numbers, more able to fend off their carnivorous enemies, more able to keep their families safe, so they traveled in herds, different species intermixing freely.

I had first seen it with the pack of *Triceratops* when I peered over the edge of the cliff for the first time. Since then, I had seen plenty. It wasn't a constant parade of dinosaurs continuously clogging the path, never a steady stream, but hardly a day passed when the sun was high in the sky that they failed to pass by. Sometimes in small groups of two and three, other times more than a dozen. One day, I counted a pack of thirty-seven dinosaurs of at least five different species. They acted as one, wandering in and out of the pack, the little ones nuzzling against whatever big one was close by. They related to one another the way that humans were still trying to do in the dawn of the twenty-first century.

Twenty minutes after I passed the stand of poplars I came upon the change in the river. The clear, sparkling blue began to dull and thicken, the life of the river taking on a new and ominous personality. The massive granite wall of the cliff moved closer to the path as the river began to narrow, the sound of the muddy water lapping against the stone now clear.

The high-pitched constant chatter of the birds had faded into the background, overtaken by a more reserved, lower-toned drone that sent a chill down my spine. It was the sound of creepy, crawly, slithering things—of things that lurked below the surface of the water, crawled low to the ground beneath the brush. I could hear the rustle of the leaves as a light wind blew, the sound of a billion insects at work, the low lament of the frogs, an occasional sound like a door on rusted hinges that sent the chalk-on-blackboard icy fingers through my chest.

The smell had changed as well. Actually, a smell became apparent, where none had existed before. In this time, a time free of pollution, waste dumps, and chemical fires—a time when there were no septic tanks, sewers, or artificial fertilizers, the air was sweet and pure. It was easy to become accustomed to the purity of the air, the lack of noxious odors and disgusting stenches. Within days, I became used to it, had taken the lack of smells for granted.

But here it assaulted me. It was a rich, loamy smell—a smell of wetness and decay—one of mold and rot. It was the smell of creepy, crawly, slithering things ... and the smell of death.

A hundred yards ahead, I could see the path begin its turn to the west, small plants and weird stunted trees beginning to form at the edge of the water in an ever widening area between it and the path. Shadows began to creep their way across the river, adding further to the dark murkiness of the churning waters. I was happy to follow it, to steer away from the troubling change in attitude of the river.

The path widened as it turned, at least a hundred yards across, the side farthest from the river beaten flat and foliage-free, a jumble of footprints, both large and small. There was a distinctive difference to the look of the jungle from one side to the other. It might have been the way the sunlight filtered through the trees, but it was high noon, the sun directly overhead. Even so, to my left, the sun seemed to penetrate the dense jungle, to give it an airiness—a lightness that created a gentle, almost friendly quality. To the right, it was gloom and doom. The sun refused to penetrate the space, the jungle so dense as to rebuke the light. It was an omen, a warning to stay the hell out.

The path took a gradual turn, continuing on for a mile before bending back to the north. Again it struck me as strange. The path was created, or at least maintained, from a plain that had probably existed for thousands of years, and it made sense that it followed the river. It appeared to be the only source of water for miles, water that the animals needed to survive. Yet for some strange reason the path moved inland some half-mile or so.

It was as if the animals were deliberately avoiding this section of the river.

I avoided it, as well. I kept to the left side of the path, willing to jump into that side of the jungle if necessary.

Another mile down the path I had to do just that.

I heard them before I saw them. There was a mild vibration under my feet that I thought was the early warning of an earthquake. I stopped walking and looked down at the earth between my feet, seeing the dust and small pebbles dancing to the tune of the tremor.

I stared northward up the path. It looked as if it ran straight and clear, as far as I could see, yet several hundred yards in the distance, they emerged from a clump of trees that jutted out on the left. *Triceratops*—three of them—lumbered toward me—two adults with an adolescent in between. I ducked into the growth at the edge of the path as they continued coming. They were like any other young family, out for a leisurely Sunday stroll. The fact that the stubby legs of the youngest one had to churn with twice the speed of the parents in an attempt to keep up didn't stop it from playfully bumping and nudging each of the others in turn. It looked like a game as each of the adults, with a simple, gentle flick of its massive head bounced the tyke back to the other side, like a giant game of pinball. I could hear the sounds of their snorts and chuffing, little plumes of dust coming from the ground in front of them as they continued to come closer.

At a hundred and fifty yards, they were still too far away to see clearly, but they began to look different than the three or four groups I had already seen. Their coloring was not the same. The *Triceratops* had been a dusty tan color, the uniformity of it broken only by the whiteness of their horns and tips of their frill. These animals, on the other hand, were more of a drab greenish coloring, but not uniform, patterned with various shades of greens, browns, and even streaks of black. I grinned as they came closer, staring down at my own camouflaged jacket and pants, nearly a perfect match.

At fifty yards, I could see them clearly, the rough texture of their skin, the patches of bristly hairs sprouting from the gaps between the wide, irregularly shaped segments. It was their frills that gave them away. They were huge, extending back along the backbone nearly half the animal's length. They were like massive twin scoops, covered entirely with the same coloration as its body, but with a tighter pattern of smaller shapes, the patches of hair less evident, if at all. They were *Torosaurs*.

A larger, longer-frilled version of the *Triceratops*, the *Torosaurus* was nonetheless a relative of the latter. Unlike its cousin, the *Torosaurus'* much larger and elongated frill laid close to the body, rather than extending upward, suggesting a natural evolution that allowed for better protection of the soft, vulnerable area of the neck and shoulders. The twin horns above its eyes were longer, the nose horn shorter than that of the *T-tops*, and its snout was both longer and thinner. As it passed by me, I could see that the head alone was more than eight feet long.

The fossilized skull of the *Torosaurus* was the only portion ever found. It was surmised that the rest of it was like that of the smaller *Triceratops*—and that wasn't far from the truth. It did look like a *Triceratops*, but considerably larger, and I suspect slower. As they passed me, the adult animals did it with an unsure gait, their legs seeming to tremble in support of their massive weight. They were no more than ten feet away and I could hear their labored breathing.

The one closest seemed to sense my presence and stopped directly in front of me. It turned and with its huge horns brushed aside the leaves that separated us, looking me right in the eye. It paused for a second, realizing that I was no threat to it, and with a sharp snort, lurched back on to the path and took its position alongside the infant.

My heart was racing as I watched them shrink into the distance.

It was a slow day on the path. The *Torosaur* trio was the only thing that passed by. As the sun began to sink into the west, I knew that there would be no more on that day.

I had no company on the second day. I traveled the road alone, mile after mile, accompanied by nothing other than the eerie silence. As I walked, my breath was visible in the air—little bursts of white vapor that told me that it was only a few degrees above freezing. I was sure that the near-freezing temperatures were keeping the dinosaurs off the path—keeping them at home—wherever that was. I wondered how they were coping with it—*if* they were coping with it.

Into the third day I was still traveling to the north. Every now and then, when the sun was just right and the breeze parted the trees in just such a way, I could see flashes of the cliff beyond the jungle, far off to the east, several miles out. The sky was clear, the unencumbered sun warming the valley to more moderate temperatures—sounds returning to the jungle.

By mid-day, the path began to take a slow, but steady turn to the east. At first I thought that the path was rejoining the river, but after an hour, I found myself traveling due east with no sign of it. I could still see snatches of the cliff above the dense foliage, but it was at least a mile in the distance.

The path was clearly still following the direction of the cliff, but a mile from the river. Curious!

In the distance a group of animals came into view—two adults and two infants. They were too far away to see clearly, but they traveled on four legs, rising up on the hind two to reach the taller branches of the trees. I did a double take when I realized that they were feeding on trees along the south side of the path—the scary side of the path. Within fifteen minutes the unique shape of their heads revealed their identities. They were a species of hadrosaurs. They were large, forty-feet in length, with unusually long duck-like bills and long, wide tails—*Edmontosaurs*.

It made sense that they were on the river side of the path. Hadrosaurs were amphibious animals, living in and around the waters where the edible plants were generally softer and easier to chew.

As they approached the spot directly across the path from me, I walked out into the clearing, and just stood there. They didn't seem to notice me. I moved closer, my moves deliberately animated to attract their attention. Still nothing. They were too focused on plucking their meal from the treetops.

Wanting to get their attention but afraid of scaring them off, I began a very soft moaning sound, gradually increasing in intensity until one of the adults turned and looked directly at me. It had to have seen me—I was waving my arms back and forth. But there was no reaction. It just turned back toward the trees. I walked slowly toward them, no longer afraid, but still wanting not to spook them. I was within forty feet when both adults turned toward me, emitted a little squawking noise, looked at one another, and went back to feeding. Clearly, I had made a huge impression on them.

I took one more step toward them when all hell broke loose.

Snarls, shrieks, and screams, blood flying everywhere as jaws clamped down, severed flesh and bone. One of the adults and one of the babies taken in the wink of an eye, their gory remains dragged back into the swamp in a matter of seconds. It happened so quickly, it was if the damned swamp just reached out and grabbed them. I froze in position, my brain not comprehending what was happening. The remaining two *Edmontosaurs* backed away from the jungle, as surprised as I was. When they were twenty feet away, two more crawled out from the edge of the swamp.

Cretaceous crocodiles, gigantic—fifty feet in length—came out of the brush with amazing speed, propelled by massive legs that moved faster than I could see.

The *Deinosuchus*. I had read about them, had seen the pictures of the massive six foot skull recovered from the banks of the Rio Grande in Texas. I believed the skull was the real thing, but thought that it was nothing but an anomaly, a freak of nature that didn't represent any kind of normal creature … in any time.

I had seen crocodiles, had seen them in a frenzy of feeding—lightning quick, huge jaws with dagger-like teeth. I had seen film of them taking small animals in a single gulp—saw the massive scars and amputations of humans who had gotten too close. It was hard to picture anything more terrifying. I had refused to accept a killing machine even bigger than the ones I had seen in my own time. Thinking of them in terms of three and four times the size was just too much to imagine.

But here they were and both of them ran towards the remaining adult, which refused to protect itself. Instead it pushed the infant toward the center of the path, sacrificing itself for its child. In an instant the adult was down, the first crocodile severing the dinosaur's massive leg in a single bite, the second tearing into its flank as it fell. Blood soaked the heads and backs of both crocodiles, turning their knobby, coarse skin instantly from green to red.

As the two crocodiles fought over the remains of the already dead animal, the infant stood on its hind legs and emitted a bellow, the sound of its small lungs amplified by an air-filled sack on its head just behind its eyes. It was backing away with unsure steps when one of the crocodiles raised its head from the gore that had moments ago been a beautiful, live animal. The crock had a hunk of red meat hanging from its jaws, its white teeth smeared with blood, bones breaking as it clamped its jaws down again and again, the meat sliding down its throat. It eyed the tiny dinosaur and started towards it.

Without thinking, I charged toward the infant *Edmontosaurus*, raising my shotgun to my waist. The crock was faster than I was, but I was closer. Its jaws were wide opened, the deadly toothed-gap wider than the small dinosaur was tall, just mere feet away. The tiny *Edmontosaurus* stood in my way. I dove to the right and fired from the hip, catching the giant *Deinosuchus* between the head and front leg, spraying blood over the last live dinosaur. I hit the ground, rolled and fired a second time at the other crocodile that had already begun its attack. This time it was I that got soaked in the gore as the shot ripped into the crock's head, its jaws slamming shut as they hit the ground a foot from where I stood.

I swung back toward the infant *Edmontosaurus*, seeing the first crock still moving. Its left foreleg was hanging by mere tendons, useless, but it continued forward, flopping forward on three legs, its jaws snapping repeatedly.

My two shotgun shells were spent. I pulled the Glock from its holster and began firing at the huge crock's head, hearing the bullets strike bone and teeth, blood spraying the air, soaking the ground. Chunks were torn from the jaws of the crocodile, but it kept on coming in a lopsided gait. I jumped onto its huge back just behind the forelegs, jammed the pistol to the back of its head and pressed the trigger.

Its jaws stopped snapping by the second shot, but I kept firing until long after the bullets were gone, nothing but empty clicking noises coming from the gun. Even after my brain registered the death of the crock, I was still screaming, "Die motherfucker, die!"

The little guy was still standing on its hind legs bellowing with everything it had left. It was shaking and covered with droplets of blood, sparkling in the sunlight like ruby rhinestones against a background of light green-gray. The inflated half-balloon atop its head looked as if it were about to pop.

I approached it slowly. It didn't move, but kept sucking in air and blowing it back out again in a long high-pitched moan. I reached out and touched it. It didn't move away, but I could feel it trembling beneath my gentle fingers. I looked down at its forelegs, its four fingers sheathed with skin that looked like mittens, webbing that stretched across each digit.

I sat down before it and pulled off my pack. I removed one of the bottles and poured water into my cupped palm. It was warm, having been in the pack pressed up against my back all day. I placed my hand against the chest of the little guy, letting the water run down its abdomen, little pink trails dribbling down into the dirt.

It seemed to calm it, its breathing returning to normal, the membrane on its head growing smaller with each breath, the shaking subsiding. I squirted water from the bottle across the front of it, rubbing constantly with the palm of my hand until the water ran clear, the remnants of the crock washed away. I looked up to see the bubble on its head deflated, nothing to it but a few folds of orange flesh lying back against its skull. It sagged against my shoulder, spent, accepting me as a friend ... or, at least not as an enemy.

I had no idea what to do with this little creature, no way that I could replace its loss. I only knew that I couldn't just leave it. I picked it up, cradling it in my arms. It wanted no part of being carried. It squirmed and kicked its young, yet powerful legs until I had to drop to my knees and let it go. I thought that it would flee, but instead, it just stood there by my side, cocking its head, staring into my eyes.

I turned and started off into the east. Glancing back over my shoulder, I saw that it was right behind me. Like it or not, I had found a new friend.

I wasn't about to desert it.

We stayed to the safe part of the trail, seeing no other animals that day. By nightfall, the temperature had dropped again to near freezing and the diminutive dinosaur was shaking and letting out little mewing sounds. I built a small fire on the smooth dirt at the edge of the jungle. As the flames grew, the little creature's eyes grew huge and it stepped backward several feet into the brush. Ignoring it, I climbed into my sleeping bag, and pretended to sleep. Within minutes I could hear a light rustling of the brush behind me as it crept slowly back. With one eye opened, I watched it settle in alongside me, pulling its legs in underneath. I draped my jacket across it and we both slept through the night.

*****

The next morning I awoke alone, the jacket lying empty in a heap beside me. In a moment of panic, I sprung from my sleeping bag and spun around to face the jungle. It was there, just a few feet away, up on two legs, its head stretched out, sniffing at the tips of a giant fern. It had to be hungry, yet it didn't seem to be eating any of the leaves, just smelling them.

I walked into the jungle finding an assortment of edible plants and flowers, not very appealing to me, but the kinds of vegetation that I had seen other dinosaurs feed on. I brought them back to the path, holding them in the palm of my hands, offering them to the little one. But it only sniffed and turned its head. Sitting down cross-legged in front of it, wondering what I could do, what food it would eat, I thought that perhaps it was still being fed by its parents, maybe it didn't really know how to feed itself—perhaps if I showed it.

I stuffed a mouthful of leaves into my mouth and began chewing—a big stupid smile plastered on my face like it was the best thing I ever tasted. I had never been a parent, but I figured that this was how they went about getting their kids to eat mashed cauliflower or beets for the first time.

I kept up with the charade even though it was awful, a terrible bitter taste that brought tears to my eyes. I mashed it to a pulp, its juices collecting in my mouth until it was drizzling down my chin. I refused to swallow the vile stuff, figuring I'd just throw it back up again. What kind of example of fine cuisine would that prove to be? When I could stand it no more, I spit it out. My new little buddy wandered over to the masticated mess, bent over and sniffed at it. It then stuck out a thin, pointed, pink tongue and licked it. It glanced in my direction, and put its tongue back into the mess, pulling it into its bill.

I tried it again, chewing up another mouthful, this time not bothering to hide my disgust. Taking it from my mouth, I held it to the dinosaur's bill. It gobbled it up as if it were starving, which it probably was.

It worked, but although it was undoubtedly saving his life ... it was killing me! I had to find a better way.

It took some searching, but eventually I found a good-sized flat rock. The dinosaur stayed with me every step of the way in anticipation of a continuation of its morning meal. I filled my backpack with assorted leaves and sat down before the rock, the *Edmontosaurus* watching my every move. Using my knife, I chopped the greenery into fine pieces, like making a salad, tossing out the fibrous stems and woody parts as I went along. I soaked them with water from my supply and began to mash up the whole mess with the butt of my pistol.

My newfound buddy kept pushing its bill into the *salad* and I kept pushing it away. I was afraid of what might happen if it was too coarse or too dry. Maybe it would get it caught in its throat and choke on it. I knew how to administer the Heimlich maneuver ... but not on a dinosaur.

But nothing like that happened. I mashed and watered until it was a disgusting green paste, the consistency of stewed seaweed, before I let it have it. It gobbled it down and begged for more. At least I think that it was begging. It just sort of sat there with this pleading look in those huge liquid eyes.

Progress was slow that day. We'd walk for an hour, and I would prepare its next meal. It seemed to always want more, and I wasn't at all sure how much I should feed it. It was an infant, but an infant dinosaur that would grow to two tons. It would probably spend most of its adult life seeking out food. But this was little more than a baby that probably didn't know when enough was enough. I kept worrying that I would keep feeding it, and it would keep eating it, until it just exploded. Of course that didn't happen, and I kept right on feeding it, and it kept right on eating it.

We traveled for another day together. Only a couple of times did other dinosaurs pass by heading the opposite way along the path. Each time I stepped into the jungle to hide, leaving the little one to decide for itself what it wanted to do. All the animals on the path were herbivores, not a threat to the little hadrosaur. But each time the little guy followed me, mimicking my actions, hiding among the brush.

On the second day, the path began to widen. We had traveled for two days to the east, and the right side of the path kept right on going in that direction, when unexpectedly, the left edge turned north, the path turning into a vast plain. We rounded the bend, and I stopped short, not believing my eyes.

Before me lie hundreds of acres of gently rolling hills, small stands of winter-bare hardwoods scattered here and there, random patches of evergreen shrubs and trees that gave a splash of color to an already beautiful setting.

To the east, the tall cliffs glowed golden in the sun, the river beneath it catching its reflection, a shimmering ribbon of gold and silver. They ran northward together for a mile or more before gently turning again toward the east, and disappearing into the distance.

The jungle formed the other natural boundary, retreating northward as far as the eye could see—the dark, thick tangle of growth, a sharp contrast to the fertile plain stretching off into the distance. It was a valley within a valley, a Garden of Eden.

It was beautiful, but what made it incredible was something else. There were dinosaurs here, hundreds of them, thousands of them. They roamed in small groups and in large herds. They drank together at the river, different species mingling freely.

The sun was bright on that day, the temperature warmer than it had been in weeks. It's what brought them out. I thought back to those first warm spring days in Chicago, how the people flocked to the parks and the shore, young women in short skirts, families with picnic baskets and strollers, bicycles and skateboards whizzing by, people worshipping the sun. It was like that in the valley on that day—sans the picnic baskets, strollers, bicycles, and skateboards—I don't remember seeing a lot of short skirts either.

It was peaceful and quiet in the valley on that day … and warm. But I knew that it had not been warm in recent weeks, and would get cold again. Unlike the people in Chicago who had warm homes to go to when the weather turned cold, the dinosaurs had nothing. They were at the mercy of the elements, and the elements had been none too friendly of late—and were going to get worse. What would happen to the animals when the temperatures dropped below the freezing point? Where would they go?

It was at that moment that I realized the significance of the path. Every dinosaur that I had seen on it since the very first day was heading in the same direction. They traveled from north to south, and never the opposite way. They were aware of the changing weather, not necessarily the seasonal variations, but that it had grown gradually colder from year to year. The change was slow, taking thousands of years, hundreds of generations, but it was there, and the animals were aware of it. Call it instinct or animal intuition, whatever, but they knew it was going to get worse and south was the direction to head.

*****

It was a new year on the beach. Who knew for sure what year it was, but according to my definition of the calendar, it was the first of January. More than a year had passed since I had traveled to the valley in the valley, a month since I had returned to my machine.

Like nearly every morning since my return, I awoke in the dark, shivering, my teeth rattling violently against one another, my exposed cheeks and ears tingling with near numbness. Like every other night, the modest fire had burned out long before the night came to a close, the temperature in the machine dropping rapidly as the metallic skin cooled in the cold winter winds.

It had only been a month, but I was already rationing the firewood, saving it mainly for the nighttime when the temperatures dropped consistently below the freezing point. I wasn't sure whether the winter temperatures varied dramatically from the valley to the beach, or if the substantial drop was real from last year to this. But, it was the coldest I had been since entering this time. If it stayed this cold, the firewood would never make it till spring.

With a heavy wool blanket draped across my shoulders, I stepped from the machine onto the cold, hard ground. As I turned left toward the mouth of the cave I was met by a blinding, dazzling sight—so bright that I had to turn my head toward the shadows of the cave's interior.

Even from ten feet inside the cave and my back turned away from the entrance, I could see little white flakes circling the interior as the cold winds whipped at my legs. There was a loud, mournful moan like a kid blowing across the mouth of a pop bottle as the winds blew across the opening of the cave, sending a chill up my spine beyond what just the frigid temperatures did alone.

I turned to the blinding whiteness, the ground half hidden by the blowing snow, the sea, now three hundred yards out was completely obliterated by the squall. I stared out into the nearly colorless haze, wondering if the snow was falling in the valley, if it was as cold there as it was here.

My first thoughts were of the little hadrosaur that I had rescued from the giant crocks. Almost immediately it had been taken in by a herd of like dinosaurs. In fear, or excitement, or perhaps in recognition, the little guy had let out a high-pitched bellow as soon as we entered the valley, seeing the hundreds of animals before us. The bag-like membrane on its head stretched taught, its little face nearly turning color from the exertion.

For myself, it was pure and simple terror. Every dinosaur within the sound of its voice turned its heads in our direction. I was so terrified I nearly pissed my pants. Almost, but not quite. Instead, squeezing my legs together, I waddled off into a clump of evergreens to hide as a dozen adult hadrosaurs began walking toward us, trumpeting a response in a similar but much more resonant tone.

I needn't have worried. The dinosaurs took no note of me, instead circling the little one and playfully nuzzling it as if it were one of their own. With the small one in tow, they marched down into the valley toward the river, around the bend, and out of sight.

The image stuck in my mind like it had happened yesterday. It seemed an idyllic setting: warm, sunny, peaceful. Things were perfect, just the way I had always pictured the valley of the dinosaurs. But that was more than a year ago, and a lot had changed in that year.

The memory of the littlest dinosaur walking off into the distance left me with an empty feeling as I watched the snow come down, a blanket of white creeping its way onto the floor of the cave. Would the tiny hadrosaur survive the cold and the snow? Could it survive? Could any of them?

I wondered how many of them had managed to make their way south, how many were left in the valley. And I worried. They had become more than just brutish animals to me, more than just creatures to be studied and analyzed. They were beautiful and fascinating, many of them so much smarter than any of us had believed, and I felt a closeness to them that was unexpected. I wanted to protect them, but knew that it was hopeless.

Hell, I had trouble enough trying to protect myself. What had happened in the valley was proof enough of that.

CHAPTER 20

I stayed in the valley within the valley for nearly a month, fascinated with the daily lives of the dinosaurs. So many mysteries were resolved in those four weeks, things that I had questioned, theorized about, and puzzled over, all my dreams realized.

The first few days I kept to the grove of evergreens at the edge of the valley, hidden, not yet comfortable in my new surroundings. I wasn't convinced that all the natives were friendly, nor was I sure that the valley was without predators. So I hid like a coward.

And yet I was not really hidden from them at all, so many had seen me enter the valley with the little hadrosaur. Some were curious and approached the tiny stand of trees where I cowered. But, as if they could sense my fear, they never entered my space, instead satisfied to peer at me through the limbs and needles of the trees, occasionally emitting a brief grunt or snort as their eyes met mine.

Each morning I took the short walk across the clearing into the jungle to forage for food, filling my backpack with nuts and berries and a few edible flowers and ferns that I had learned to stomach.

Some of the animals began to watch my daily routine, and more each day began to anticipate it, leisurely, almost politely, waiting around the clump of greenery for me to emerge. A few took to following me, keeping their distance, as I disappeared each day into the thick overhang of the jungle. But they always stopped at the edge, refusing to enter the darkness, as if there was something threatening inside.

By the third day, they were coming in large numbers, waiting for me, even as I awoke. News of me was spreading across the valley. I had become something of a celebrity ... or at least a curiosity. They huddled in small groups nudging one another, taking short, subtle glances in my direction. I couldn't get over the thought that they were talking about me, perhaps even gossiping about me in their dino-speak. But they always gave me plenty of room, like they were afraid they'd scare me off.

It didn't take long for my own fears to dissipate, blown into the wind, like so much smoke. Curiosity, and even a sense of camaraderie, replaced it. They weren't humans. They couldn't talk to me. Certainly, they didn't understand me, even if they did hear me. But that didn't stop *me* from talking to *them*.

The first time I did it I had already crossed the clearing and was standing at the edge of the jungle. I turned and said in a loud and boisterous voice, "Good morning," and then jumped into the brush, afraid that the sound of my voice might frighten them away, or worse, piss them off. Instead, they just looked at me in the same questioning way, a few of them cocking their heads as if to say, "*The hell you say*?"

From that point on, I talked to them like they could understand everything that I said, like we were pals. And they responded. Not they had any idea what I was saying, but they knew that I was no threat. I was just one more kind of animal in the valley. A tiny, skinny, funny looking animal that talked weird.

I became one of them, following them around, and sometimes them following me around. Either way, I was pretty much free to go throughout the valley with little to fear, and plenty of company. And being accepted as one of them, and with the fear and nervousness behind us all, I began to observe ... and to learn.

I saw them feed ... almost continuously. They were all plant-eaters, but each species seemed to have their favorite dining spots, particular leaves or stalks that they preferred. At the same time they were not possessive of their territory, many different kinds of animals feeding in the same area. It was normal to see some of the smaller ones feeding on the ground cover, standing between the legs of the larger ones as the giants reached for the tallest branches. And they all drank from the same river, congregating there in large groups, the youngest ones splashing about like children tend to do, under the watchful eyes of the adults.

They slept in groups as well, but in smaller, more segregated units—family groups—and extended family groups made up of like species. They had little shelter, yet they tended to stay within the valley, avoiding the perimeter of the jungle, instead seeking out the scattered stands of trees and bushes to hunker into or upon. Within a few days I could tell how each dinosaur rested. It was based on their body structure. The smaller and thinner animals like the hadrosaurs tended to lie down on their sides, their arms and legs curled up into their bodies. The large, squat animals like the neoceratopsians and ankylosaurids just sort of dropped straight down, their legs folded in underneath them, looking much like a herd of quadruple amputees. The giants of the valley, the titanosaurs, just stood there like huge sentinels, their massive tails stretched out on the ground, their tiny heads lowered, their eyes closed. And they all slept at night. During the days they were active, even more so on the warm, sunny days. They didn't lie in the sun to soak up the warmth—they were warm-blooded.

And it seemed that I had encroached upon their rutting season. There was mating going on everywhere—no hiding in the bushes, no monogamy, no shame in what they were doing—just non abashed, get down and dirty ... animal screwing—everywhere, and all the time.

If there was any problem in determining an animal's sex from the poor, partial remains found in the twentieth century, it was no problem here seventy million years before the common era. Upon first look it was nearly impossible to tell their gender, especially before I understood the subtle differences in coloration, and crest and frill size and shape, but when the time was right it was pretty simple. One animal approached the other from behind, kind of secretive, on the sly, or so it seemed. It would lower its head toward the hindquarters of the other, take a sniff, and voila. From the folds between its legs, like magic, the huge member slid forward, slick and red, ready for action. The females never seemed to shy away, no matter how many times that day they had been approached in the same manner. Instead, they lowered their upper bodies toward the ground and actually backed into the male, accepting willingly what they were offered. And let me assure you, the human species had nothing on the mating sounds of dinosaurs locked in passion. There were grunts, shrieks, moans, and bellows that rivaled the most verbose of the sexually gratified man or woman.

And, oh yes, I nearly forgot one little detail. Although the valley was probably the most beautiful sight these eyes had ever beheld, it was sometimes hard to focus on the beauty through the tears in my eyes. For the valley was as odiferous as it was beautiful. There were no designated areas for defecation, no communal rest areas, no porta-potties or commodes that flushed. To put it as delicately as possible ... this place was full of shit. There were piles of it everywhere, little piles, huge piles, and everything in between—greens and browns, and a lot of colors I couldn't even describe, and they all smelled, well, like shit. And there was no shame or embarrassment in the valley. They shit wherever and whenever. Some of them squatted, but most just let it plop onto the ground as they lumbered along, leaving a disgusting, lumpy trail in their wake. The valley was filled with the sounds of their farts and the smell of methane. It's a good thing I didn't smoke. One small spark and the whole valley would go up in one giant fireball.

I was amazed at the variety of animals in the valley. There were thousands of them and dozens of species. I had no idea what half of them were, although in most cases I at least knew what family they belonged to.

They were all plant-eaters, the largest number of them belonging to two distinct families of dinosaurs.

The largest number and variety were of the hadrosaur family—duck-billed, aquatic dinosaurs—varying in size and especially in head décor—but similar in shape and coloration.

There was the *Maiasaura:* 30 feet long, eight-feet tall, weighing at least four tons. One of the larger hadrosaurs, it ate constantly, standing on its two hind legs to pluck the nuts and berries from the higher reaches of the trees, eating what must have been hundreds of pounds of food each day. Like the other hadrosaurs, they were intelligent, alert and responsive to the sounds and activity of the valley. And they were quick, rising up on two legs when they wanted to, breaking into a long-striding run that left me breathless.

Even though the word dinosaur meant terrible lizard, there were little of these animals that reminded me of lizards—except perhaps the skin of the hadrosaurs. Each of them was one shade or another of green and was covered with small, bumpy, tightly packed scales. Most had markings and patterns of browns and blacks, yellows and reds. The *Maiasaura* was mustard yellow across its breast, which turned to fading magenta stripes as it approached its backbone.

The *Corythosaurus*, on the other hand, was a very dark dinosaur. Slightly smaller and lighter than the *Maiasaur*, it had an olive green underbody that faded into a dull, dark gray, nearly black. It had a pure black bill-like snout and a matching crest upon its head, shaped like the plumage of a Roman soldier's helmet. Its nostrils went up through the crest, which resulted in a loud blast of noise like an amplified trumpet when they vocalized. Both male and female had the distinctive frill, but the adult male's were considerable larger and much lower in pitch. During the rutting season, their calls could be heard all over the valley.

The *Parasaurolophus*, another crested hadrosaur, had a long, backward pointing crest that itself was longer than the rest of its head. Its crest was so long that there was a notch in the back of its neck where the crest fit when it reared its head back. It was one of the larger hadrosaurs, a brighter green than the rest, with a brown and orange splotchy arrangement on its back. The magnificent crest was a brilliant orange with streaks of red, and its tone was higher, but loudest of all. It was a regal beast, and it had quickly become my favorite.

There were other hadrosaurs as well, each with the familiar duck-shaped bill, each with four-fingered, webbed hands, each a distinctive green. Each had a toothless beak, but hundreds of cheek teeth to grind up its food. They were fast and they were smart. Like so many herbivores they had eyes on the sides of their head so that they could see two directions at once. Their tails were relatively inflexible and were used to keep their balance when walking on just their hind legs.

The ceratopsians were frilled dinosaurs with pointed beaks like parrots and facial horns like that of the *Triceratops*. The color and size of the ceratopsians varied more than that of the hadrosaurs, but there was no mistaking those frills.

The *Eucentrosaurus* had a similar frill and was a much smaller animal than the *Triceratops*—eight or nine feet in length. It had a forward curving eighteen-inch nasal horn and a pair of small horns above its eyes, and was dark brown with small black spots spread across its pentagonal shaped scales.

The *Montanoceratops* was smaller yet, five to six feet in length at adulthood. Its frill was more scoop-shaped than the *Triceratops*, more like that of the Mongolian *Protoceratops*, but it lacked the prominent nose horn. It had very short, stubby legs, and moved in a slow, awkward gait. It had the tan coloring of the *Triceratops*, but with a distinctive plum hue around its beak and frill. Every time that I saw them I felt like they were all dressed up for the Easter parade.

The *Chasmosaurus*, much like the *Torosaurus* that I had encountered on my trip into the valley, had a huge, square-shaped frill that was much longer than the skull itself. The frill was replete with several small, sharply pointed bones at the corners, which must have provided a wicked defense when it flicked its head. It was nearly twenty feet in length and had a short nose horn and long, pointed eyebrow horns. It was a tan color with darker brown streaks starting at its head and back and working down its sides.

The *Styracosaurus* had a six-spiked frill, each long and curved at odd angles and irregularly spaced. I tended to think of them as the snaggle-toothed dinosaur. To make them even more bizarre looking, they had a two-foot, upward pointing horn on their nose, and two small horns above their eyes. It was as frightening as it was strange looking. The *Styracosaurus* was probably a considerable foe when provoked, but here in the valley it was just another friendly animal.

The hadrosaurs and ceratopsians were the most plentiful and diverse families in the valley, but there were plenty of other dinosaurs as well.

The *Titanosaurus* were by far the largest creatures in the valley and among the largest creatures to ever walk the face of the earth. One of the few remaining sauropods of the late cretaceous period, the *Titanosaurus* was a huge herbivore that had oval-shaped armor plating across their sides and backs, light gray, nearly silver, reflecting the sunlight like stars in the heavens. They were surrounded by tiny bony protrusions, also mirroring the sun, a million dazzling sparkles glittering among the stars. They lay in a field of dark gray that turned abruptly to gleaming white on their chests and bellies and inside of their massive tree trunk-like legs. They had long tapering tails, and even longer, thicker necks that held up relatively small heads. They were not intelligent animals … but they were spectacular!

As beautiful and magnificent as these animals were, there was something very disturbing about them. Sauropod dinosaurs flourished in the Jurassic period, but only a few survived into the Cretaceous, mostly in South America and India. The experts theorized that they were just too large, too big a target, to survive long-term. They laid relatively few eggs, the chance of them hatching and growing to adolescence becoming more remote as the number of omnivores continued to grow. It was really pretty amazing that they survived for the entire Mesozoic era. What I saw in the valley lent credence to that theory. Although there were hundreds of animals from every other species … there were only three *Titanosaurs:* a family unit—one adult male, one adult female, and one adolescent.

Among the most fascinating animals in the valley were the *Ankylosaurs:* huge armor plated dinosaurs, measuring more than thirty-five feet in length. The tail was the most fascinating part. At its tip was a massive club that resembled a medieval mace. Beneath the thick, leathery skin was solid bone, twin orbs fused together to make a hundred pound wrecking ball. They stood upon short, thick legs, the animal's height a mere four feet, but weighing in at well over five tons. Its top side was heavily covered with thick, oval plates fused into its leathery skin and it had two rows of spikes along its body. It was huge around the midsection, its belly nearly dragging on the ground. It was a timid animal and not very intelligent. At the slightest noise or sudden movement close by, it would drop down upon its massive gut, pull its legs in underneath, and just lie there bellowing continuously with a loud, deep resonant tone. It was fortunate indeed that nature had provided it the nearly perfect defense.

Among the other strange looking dinosaurs were those with the domed heads—the slow, dim-witted *Pachycephalosaurus*, and its smaller, quicker cousin, the *Stegoceras*. Both had huge domed-heads with incredibly thick skulls. The larger of the two had a multitude of bony bumps around the edge of its dome, the skin below a brilliant crimson that spread across its head, shoulders and arms, before fading into a burnt-orange color. It was one of the few herbivores that were covered in brilliant colors, a dinosaur that wasn't meant to blend into nature.

The smaller relative, the *Stegoceras*, was barely ten feet long, less than half the size of the *Pachy*. It was similar in color, but not as vibrant, as if faded by the sun. It was as if nature said, "You can take care of yourself, but maybe not as well as your larger relative. So I'll make you faster and smarter and easier to hide."

Both of them used their heads. After all, it was the mating season. But they didn't butt heads as most of the experts thought. No, their skulls may have been ten inches thick, but they were not solid bone. They were actually rather fragile, filled with air sacks and blood vessels. A head-to-head collision between the two would have most probably resulted in death ... to both of them. Nevertheless, they did use their bony heads as offensive weapons.

They *Pachycephalosaurus* were among the very few of the dinosaurs that tended to be monogamous, although that didn't mean there was a lack of rival suitors. Any time one got a little too amorous, a bit too close to the hind quarters of a female that was already spoken for, it could expect a powerful blow to the ribs.

The female's mate would lower its head, its neck vertebrae locking into one another to form a rigid battering ram, and run full speed at the flank of its foe. The *Pachycephalosaurus* was not a fast animal, but at several tons, it made a hell of an impact. More often than not the misguided suitor was knocked off his feet, the enraged mate backing up ready to make a second charge that was most often unnecessary. Usually they struggled to their feet and limped away, battered and bruised, but not beaten.

There had only been a single time that I witnessed when the damage was severe, when the animal wasn't so quick to rise. What happened afterward was nearly the end of me.

*****

It was at the end of four weeks in the valley, nearly at the end of my stay, but of course, I didn't know that at the time. By *that* time I had been half-starved and food was becoming an increasing problem. Nuts were still plentiful, as were a number of edible leaves, but the berries and flowers that I found palatable had disappeared as the winter came full force. I was healthy, but my ribs showed through in an alarming way, and I was constantly hungry.

There was meat in the valley, thousands, millions of tons of it, but I just couldn't find it in myself to use my gun. Certainly not on the dinosaurs, but not even at the birds and mammals, which were plentiful there. Firing a weapon at anything just didn't seem appropriate. It was peaceful and quiet, the thought of killing anything here, in the presence of such harmony, was just out of the question.

Instead, I lived off the few things that remained in the middle of winter, those things that I could keep down—just like the animals did.

It was on a clear, cold morning that I arose shivering in the meager covering of palm fronds. Emerging from the center of the tiny copse of evergreens, I was surprised to see only a handful of animals there to greet me. They stood motionless—little plumes of frost billowing from their nostrils a couple of times a minute. It was the only thing that told me they were alive.

They stood there like the Queen's Guards, frozen in place, their eyes open, but unmoving. There was an eerie silence in the valley as I walked among the animals. They stood like giant statues as I walked from one to another, touching each one, feeling the warmth of the skin beneath the cold coating of morning dew.

I forgot about my morning forage, just like I forgot about my backpack and shotgun. Instead, armed only with the Glock, I headed out towards the center of the valley.

It was if I was walking through a dream. A cold mist was coming off the ground, the brush and trees hovering above it, glistening in the morning frost. There were animals here and there, some half hidden by flora and fog, some rising above them like apparitions taking form from a bubbling cauldron. They were so still that it appeared that time had just stopped, freezing them into position, just waiting for someone to hit the resume button, sending everything, all at once, back into motion again.

The only sound was of my feet crunching the frozen ground, the slight hiss of air sliding in and out between my clenched teeth as I walked across the valley. The constant monotonous hum of the insects was gone, the songs of the birds were silenced, and the trumpets of the hadrosaurs and grunts of animals in heat were absent. There was absolutely nothing but the sounds of my own making. When I stopped, the silence was absolute ... like a tomb.

As the sun warmed the valley, life returned, but slowly, as if someone hit the resume and slow motion buttons at the same time. The smaller animals came around first, walking tentatively and awkwardly as if drugged, turning their heads back and forth to clear out the cobs.

The larger they were, the more slowly they returned, the tiny family of *Titanosaurs* coming around last, huddled together like they were unsure of what to do, terrified at what had just happened. Not smart enough to understand it, but plenty smart enough to fear it.

By mid day it was if nothing had happened. Life went on much as it had every other day that I had been there. In no time at all the sounds returned, first the insects, then the birds, and last but not least, the passionate sounds of the dinosaurs. The rutting season had recommenced at the same feverish pitch in which it had left off.

It was getting late in the day, perhaps another two hours of light, when I stopped by a grove of trees to gather a few nuts that had fallen and the animals hadn't yet gotten. I had covered perhaps ten or twelve miles, mostly northward, down the center of the valley. It was the farthest that I had ventured. I had crossed several small streams that had branched out from the river along the cliff, and had passed through a small forest of hardwoods.

As I came out of the forest I marveled at the size of the valley. I couldn't see an end to it even after having walked a brisk pace for nearly the entire day. To the east, in the far off distance, I could still make out the cliffs, a few mountain peaks cropping up even farther away.

To the west, several miles in the distance, lay the blackness of the jungle, like an impenetrable wall that went on for miles before ending abruptly at the base of a chain of mountains that seemed to reach for miles into the sky.

I watched as a small group of *Pachycephalosaurs* drank from the tiny stream that bordered the northern edge of the forest. One from the group waded across the stream and walked thirty yards out, sniffing at the bare branches of the trees, searching for the familiar scent of food. It was a male—I could tell from its size and the more brilliant crimson hue and more pronounced bony lumps surrounding its thick skull. It continued to move downstream as it found little left from the winter-stripping of the leaves. It buried its head into the decomposing pile of leaves on the ground, hoping to find a bit of green that had survived the frost. It snorted in disgust at not finding anything palatable.

I glanced back downstream to what remained of the small herd, and saw the opening moves of the mating ritual. Another male, the largest of the small group, was checking out the rear end of what was obviously one of the adult females. Monogamy seemed to be more of the makeup of the male, because the female immediately lowered her head and positioned herself to allow penetration.

As it began, the male grunted in satisfaction, a loud noise that was easily heard for a hundred yards, well within range of the other male downstream. This one raised its head from the pile of leaves, a few still plastered across its snout, and cocked its head, sniffing at the air

It waded back across the stream, and there the problem started. In getting to the other side, it was in direct line of the scene that was taking place some two hundred feet away.

It began moving slowly upstream, making little grunts as it went, as if the simple act of walking was painful, but more likely the sounds originating from anger. The other male was in the throws of ecstasy and failed to hear the other's approach. When it had closed the distance by half, a hundred feet away, it lowered its head, and lifted its tail, aligning its spine until it formed a perfect line parallel to the ground.

It then began to run.

The female was standing half in and half out of the stream. The male was on dry ground, perpendicular to the edge of the water, its head turned the other way, its flank fully exposed.

The charging *Pachy* hit it at full speed, easily twenty-five miles an hour. There was a resounding thud and the crunching sound of several ribs being stove in. Both the male and female that only an instant before had been locked in passion were thrown in two directions. The female went headfirst into the drink, while the male was lifted right off his feet and thrown sideways more than twenty feet. It rolled over twice before staggering to its feet, hobbling just a few steps away from the stream before crashing to the earth, blood bubbling from its mouth.

I watched in silent fascination as the female rose from the water on shaky legs. Her snout was covered in mud, which she shook off with a violent twist of the head. She walked onto dry land, her head hung low, refusing to meet the eyes of her mate.

But the mate didn't see any of this. The mighty collision had knocked him off his feet as well. For a minute I thought that both of the males had been killed in the terrible blast, but the mate eventually got to its feet. It cocked its head in her direction, a gesture of contempt, if such a thing was possible, and walked over to the injured dinosaur.

The female joined her mate, staying a few paces back, and they both looked over the prostrate body of the injured animal. The male, giving just the briefest of snorts, walked into the distance, the remainder of the small group hurrying to catch up.

Squatting there on the edge of the little copse of trees, my heart was racing, my hands tightly gripping my knees to keep them from shaking. What I had just witnessed had frightened me, but not nearly as much as what I was about to do. The amorous *Pachycephalosaurus* was lying on its side—unmoving. Even from fifty feet, I could see a pool of blood forming around its still head. I don't know what I was more afraid of—it being dead, or it only being wounded. Dead would be sad. Wounded could be worse. Wounded animals were dangerous.

I approached it tentatively, on feathered steps, afraid of alerting it, more afraid that I wouldn't. As I got in closer I could see that it was still alive. Its chest was moving rhythmically, but the breath that came out of its mouth was ragged and frothy with pink foam. I touched its side, which was already beginning to swell and discolor. It winced and turned its head toward me, its huge eyes, once clear and sparkling, were dull and opaque, as if the life were draining out of them. It took little interest in me. I wasn't even sure that it saw me. It just laid its head back down on the ground and let out a long, slow, gurgling breath.

It had begun to grow dark, but I couldn't just leave the suffering creature. Instead I stepped across the stream and gathered an armload of dead branches and twigs. I built a fire ten feet from the *Pachy*, pulled the hood of my jacket over my head, shoved my hands into my pockets and scooted up against the warm skin of the dying beast to wait out the night. Lying there against the warm body, despite the circumstances, I slept better than I had in weeks. I didn't stir throughout the night—no dreams, no waking up shivering from the cold—just sweet, uninterrupted sleep.

It was after the sun came up when I was tossed sideways into the cold pile of wood ash, that I awoke.

I rolled past the spent wood and looked upon the injured animal. It staggered to get to its feet, twice failing and falling back onto its side. On the third attempt, it rose shakily to its feet, its muzzle coated with sticky crimson, the congealing mass dripping down from its pointed beak. Its head was lowered—a beaten animal. It stared at me with that faraway look in its eyes and, in a pronounced limp, favoring its left side, began to stagger in a northern direction.

I could do nothing less than follow. I had no idea where it was heading, but I had to follow ... I simply had no choice.

Following it was heart wrenching. Sometimes the *Pachy* went several hundred yards before having to stop, walking in an unsure gait, tiny spots of blood dotting the ground and plants as it passed. Other times it struggled to make it more than twenty. I followed behind, keeping my distance, unsure what to expect from a wounded animal that was three times my size, ten times my weight. And yet, my heart poured out for it. It had done nothing wrong—not really. It was just being what it was—an animal, with animal passions and animal instincts. It was just trying to make its way and it just happened to be the mating season. And it had paid the price for indiscretion. It had set its sights on someone else's mate. Among the other dinosaurs, it would have been overlooked. But the *Pachycephalosaurus* was a step up on the evolutionary ladder. It was a species that didn't take kindly to infidelity, and it was punished for it. Whether it deserved it or not, I was sure of one thing. It was dying, and this was its death march.

We walked northward through the valley the entire day, starting and stopping, but still covering a lot of ground. I stayed twenty yards behind, afraid that it would take exception to the intrusion on its privacy, but it never looked back, just kept heading north as if being pulled by some irresistible but invisible force. More and more frequently, it would stop to rest, never lying down, just standing there with its dome hanging low, its breathing irregular and bubbly.

As dark approached, it continued on, not interested in sleep. I was amazed at its stamina, its determination. I was wearing down. My legs ached and my feet were like dead stumps. I had sweat running down my sides despite the dropping temperature, and I hadn't eaten anything in a full day. But then the *Pachy* hadn't eaten either. Not once did it stop to so much as sniff at the leaves of a plant as it passed by, and unlike me, it was injured, mortally, so I feared. It had a destination and was determined to get there. I was determined to stay with it to the end—whatever happened.

We marched across the valley through the long, cold night. The lack of the moon and the stars made the night that much darker and feel that much longer. I was constantly tripping over rocks and brush, stubbing my toe, bumping my shins, ending up on my ass more than once. The dinosaur seemed to have no such problem. Perhaps its night vision was far more acute than my own, but I think that it was some kind of built in guidance system, like a kind of radar, that kept it safe and pointed in the right direction.

The night was so black that my eyes refused to adjust. I could barely see the dinosaur in front of me, but I could hear it. Its labored breathing made a wet sloppy sound that was backed by a continuous high-pitched hissing like air escaping from a wounded balloon. Periodically, the ghastly sounds were punctuated by deep, barking noises that might have been coughs—perhaps choking. These periods grew closer together and longer in duration as the night progressed. Each time they occurred, I stopped and waited a few steps behind, thinking that it was the end. But each time, it kept on going, and I continued to follow, staying a few paces behind the sound.

The night was long, as long and miserable as any I could remember. But as all nights do, it eventually came to an end. As the sun began to rise over my right shoulder, I could see that the valley had changed in the night. The river was now no more than a few hundred yards to my right, the jungle not much farther to my left. And the valley was coming to an end.

The jungle was no longer just on my left, it was in front of me as well, perhaps a mile in the distance. The wall of green curved toward the east, running right to the edge of the river, as thick and foreboding as it appeared from miles out.

In the light of day, I could see that the *Pachycephalosaurus* had just about had it. It was on all four legs now, crawling, its head nearly dragging on the ground, still bleeding from its mouth, a permanent red ribbon attached to the ground. Its breath was short and labored, its legs trembling with each halting step. It headed toward the center of the arc formed by the perimeter of the jungle.

It seemed to take forever to cover that last mile. The *Pachy* spent longer and longer periods resting, trying to summon the strength for just a few more steps, its life draining away with each cough, each pint of blood that flowed to the ground. In increasingly shorter, more difficult steps, it continued to head toward the central edge of the jungle.

I thought that it was hallucinating, or perhaps delusional from the loss of blood. Or maybe it had gone blind, because I could see nothing in the direction it was heading but jungle, thick and black and unforgiving. It followed a beacon of some kind, the source of which was invisible to me.

As the light grew brighter, my eyesight wasn't the only thing that seemed to improve. I became aware of an aroma, a stench actually. It was a bittersweet, cloying smell that made the little bit left in my stomach start to toss and turn. Saliva filled my mouth, my stomach rumbling as I tried to breathe through my mouth to keep the smell from entering my nostrils. I turned my back to the jungle, thinking that the smell would be less powerful coming from the opposite direction.

I was wrong. The smell permeated the air, and there was no escaping it. I had a handkerchief in my back pocket, which I pulled out and held over my nose, thinking that it would help. And it did, but probably only because it kept me from breathing through my nose.

And this was not the smell of methane that so permeated the southern part of the valley. It was not the healthy stink of manure, or the sulfur-like smell of the noxious gas that propelled it. Matter of fact, as I looked behind me at the miles of valley spreading out in three directions, there wasn't an animal to be seen, not a single dinosaur in a hundred square miles. This place was not a place were animals lived. It was something else altogether.

The air was filled with the smell of sickness and disease, of death and decay. It was the stench of putrefaction and rotting meat, and we were getting closer to the source with every step. I watched in growing horror as the dying animal staggered towards the heart of it.

And yet, even with the sun high enough in the sky to chase the shadows away, I still couldn't tell where the *Pachycephalosaurus* was heading. We were within a hundred yards and the jungle looked as impenetrable as it did from a mile away. Even light had trouble forcing its way through—only blackness stared out from the thick tangle of ferns and palms, the snarled, tangled web of the jungle.

I closed the gap with the *Pachy* to just a couple of feet, stepping cautiously just beyond the tip of its tail, knowing that it was now too weak to do anything about my presence, even if it wanted to. Its tail dragged on the ground, which was not how a healthy animal carried it. And it was now dragging its left leg as well, its body curled toward that side in an attempt to lessen the pain that was there. Wherever it was going, it better get there quickly because it was fading fast.

It was crawling and dragging itself toward the edge of the jungle, throwing its drooping head and shoulders to the right with each step, as if giving its dead side the momentum to carry on. It made a grunting sound each time, what little blood was left flew from one side to the other, and I was sure that it would topple over on the next step.

But it didn't. Rather, it walked head on into the dense covering of jungle, parting the branches without even noticing they were there, disappearing into the darkness, almost as if by magic. I followed, swatting at the branches as they snapped back from the passing dinosaur.

Looking down at my feet, I could see that there was indeed a path … of sorts. Stray, dug up patches of earth where nothing would grow, broken limbs and branches, with old, weathered wounds, twisted and deformed plants that pointed away from the trail, and away from the valley, told me that something had passed this way before. But it was a path not heavily traveled, and not very recently. And, judging by the way the jungle was pushed aside, whatever followed the path in this direction, never made the return trip.

The *Pachy* no longer stopped to rest, instead plowing through the brush as if it could sense that its final destination was within reach. I stayed close, picking up my own pace to match that of the injured animal, being poked and slapped by the branches left in its wake.

The dense jungle and the earthy, lush smells of it, failed to mask the stench that was growing stronger and more repulsive with each step. The cloth held to my nose became worthless as the awful odor drenched everything, entering every pore of my body, filling my mouth with a disgusting taste that I couldn't hide from. I choked and gagged as I tried to keep up with the *Pachycephalosaurus*.

Within minutes we popped out of the jungle into the bright sunlight. It was a clearing, circular shaped, several hundred yards across. It was completely surrounded by the same thick jungle that we had just passed through. The smell here was even worse, indescribable and unimaginable, like the wall of foliage was holding the worst of the smell in. And it held in the sound as well. A cacophony of birdcalls filled the space—loud, angry, greedy birdcalls.

Filling the back two thirds of the clearing was the cause of the sound, and the source of the smell—the remains of thousands of dinosaurs. Bones and rotting carcasses rose thirty feet into the air in places, skeletons piled three and four deep—millions of bones, millions of *year's* worth of bones.

It was the dinosaur's graveyard.

Along the front edge of the pile were the most recent additions. Forty or fifty animals in varying degrees of decomposition littered on the ground in front of the rising pile, thousands of birds picking at the remains. The huge corpse of a *Titanosaurus* dominated the scene. Stretched out on the ground for nearly a hundred feet, giant holes carved out of its sides, grisly pieces of fat and muscle hanging from their edges, glints of white bone showing through. I took two more steps toward it and tossed up the tiny fragments of nuts that still resided in my belly.

It was the beasts in the front that were causing the incredible stink. These were the animals that had only been dead for weeks, perhaps months, and the flesh was still putrefying in the moist air of the surrounding jungle. It's where the smell was the worst, and where the dying *Pachycepholasaurus* headed.

The once beautiful animal that I had spent the last thirty-six hours with was moments away from its own death. It was walking straight into it, and it scared me like few things ever had. I knew what this place was, and I knew that in another minute the dinosaur would just lie down next to the rotting remains of the others without really understanding why. It was instinctual, a behavior that was born to it, but it was not intelligent enough to really understand it ... not really. And yet, still, I wanted to warn it, as if anything that I could say or do could change the inevitable. I needed it to understand what it was about to do even if it didn't change a thing.

In my head, I shouted, *wait, don't go there*, as I drew my pistol and fired into the air. The only thing I accomplished with the irrational act was to startle the birds, scattering them to the four winds in a huge black, screaming mass.

The *Pachy* didn't appear to have even heard the shot. It never broke stride, never even flinched. In what must have been a Herculean effort, it raised its head, lifting its tail from the ground, and marched like the regal beast that it was the final few steps to where the giant *Titanosaurus* lay.

That last majestic act took from the animal everything that was left. With one final step it crashed to the ground, making the earth at my feet tremble. Without having to check, I knew that the *Pachycepholasaurus* was dead before it hit the ground.

And yet, I walked over to it, kneeling alongside its massive domed head. It was an act of respect, and of gratitude. The animal should have died back by the side of the stream. But it refused to. Instead, it survived into the second day after the attack, walking across half the valley, probably twenty miles, because it knew that's the way it was meant to be. And it had allowed me to tag along. As terrifying as this graveyard was, as sad and as smelly as it was … I wouldn't have missed it for the world.

I left the *Pachy*, mumbling a final goodbye, and set out to explore the bone pile. I had to walk a hundred yards along the leading edge of the heap, past the most recent of the dead, those that were still decomposing, hurrying my pace to get past the grotesque image and the worst of the horrid smell.

There was a beaten-down path than ran around the edge of the pile, between it and the jungle, not wide, perhaps ten feet or so, three and four-toed footprints lightly etched into the hard-packed soil.

The path and the footprints continued around the bone pile as I slowly made my way to the halfway point. I found this curious. Either these prints were really, really old, which I doubted because something had been keeping the path clear of the encroaching jungle. Or, dinosaurs had been wandering the perimeter of the pile continuously and often over all the years. Why would a dying animal do that? Wouldn't they just march directly to the closest point after entering the clearing—just as the *Pachycephalosaurus* did?

One more riddle, but this one didn't take long to solve.

I had made it a little beyond halfway around the circle, and to that point it had been a fascinating trip. If one could amass all the dinosaur bones ever found, on every dig, in every corner of the globe, they wouldn't equal the sheer number of bones in this one concentrated area. But more importantly, these were complete skeletons. There was no digging necessary, no scraping and brushing the matrix away, no tiny remnants of incomplete skeletons, no plaster casts, no guessing about what went where, which piece fit to what other. It was all here.

The most dominant features of the pile were the vertebrae and rib cages of thousands of animals. They seemed mostly intact, filling up the most space with an airiness from animals that were huge across the middle, animals that when fully fleshed out weighed several tons, more than a hundred tons in some cases.

Other bones were there as well. The bones that made up the arms and legs were there—somewhere—but they tended to lie in massive piles, scattered beneath and around the central structure, as if falling off during the decaying process … or perhaps, torn off, and cast aside.

The same was true for the skulls. They were there, but scattered about, mixed in with so many other bones—few were still attached to the neck vertebrae, but they stuck out from the others. They were so large and so distinctive.

Like in the southern valley, the bone pile was made up predominately of various species of hadrosaurs and ceratopsians, replete with distinctive crests and frills, each gleaming white, every bit of flesh and sinew picked clean by the carnivorous insects and birds over the millennia. Hundreds of them had been separated from their bodies and had rolled down the pile to take up residence at the base. It looked like a bone garden, skulls all lined up in a neat row bordering the curving path. Looking closely, I could see that there were skulls hidden within the thick folds of the forest too, just beyond the edge of the path. But none were on the path. Again, how curious!

There was one skull in particular that caught my attention. Some forty or fifty feet into the pile, perhaps fifteen feet above the ground, was a skull that was very familiar to me. Yet I was shocked when I saw it. It was much more massive than the ones of the hadrosaurs and ceratopsians. It had huge jaws filled with six-inch long, backward-pointing, serrated teeth. Unlike all the others, it was not a herbivore—it was a carnivore—it was a *Tyrannosaurus rex*.

Other than the small pack of *Veloceraptors* that nearly killed me beneath the tree, this was the first real evidence of meat-eating dinosaurs in the valley. I knew that they had to be here. It was all part of the natural order of things, part of the food chain. There had to be both predators and prey. It's what kept the animal population in balance. A law of the jungle, one in which the Cretaceous fossil evidence supported, was that the ratio of herbivore to carnivore was about ten to one. Based on what I had seen thus far, the ratio was much greater.

Now I knew that there were meat eaters in the valley, and the king of them all was here, or at least what was left of him. This was the first real proof, although there was no telling how old this skeleton was, how many years since it had died. It proved that *Tyrannosaurs* were here once upon a time. But were they still?

I had to have a closer look. I began to scale the hill of bones, treading a maze of long white cylindrical shafts, still slippery from the morning dew. It was a dangerous climb, the bones shifting underfoot, broken ends sticking up through the pile at odd angles, waiting to impale me with the slightest misstep, the constant fear of the tenuous pile coming down on top of me, burying me. I couldn't shake the image of my own bones all mixed up with the others. How out of place, yet ironic would that be? What a puzzle that would be if my bones were discovered among all of these, some seventy million years from now. I wondered what kind of name they'd put on me.

The skull was resting on a mound of indiscriminate bones of every size and shape, which were, in turn, piled up against the backside of the huge ribcage of what must surely have been one of the *Titanosaurs*. It was large enough to drive a car through—a large car. I grabbed a rib in either hand and tried to shake the structure, hoping to dislodge the skull, but it was as sturdy as if it were anchored in concrete. Instead, I climbed to the top, pulling first at one rib, then the next, until I was staring right into the frozen smile of the *rex*.

It was an incredible moment. There was no mistaking that it was a *Tyrannosaurus rex*, and yet it was so different than looking upon something that was incomplete, damaged, and discolored. This skull was wider, more three-dimensional, having not been ravaged by time, gravity, and the compression that the seventy million years and tons of rock caused. The eyeholes were set farther apart, on either side, proving that this particular dinosaur did indeed have stereoscopic vision. As if it really needed it, the enhanced vision would make it an even greater threat—a better hunter. The theory that it was a scavenger had been dealt yet another blow.

The teeth, oh, the teeth were something special. They were the teeth of a *Tyrannosaur*—huge, six-inches, at least—angled back toward its throat so that the chunks of flesh of the prey ripped away easily, not slipping out of the predator's grasp. But they were something else when they weren't pulled out of the earth millions of years afterward—cracked, chipped, dark and worn. New, they were even more terrifying. They were more real somehow, gleaming white and razor sharp. The back edges were serrated, not just a hint of sharp scalloped edges like the hundreds of teeth that I had studied in my former life, but sharp and distinct, like those of a steak knife. There wasn't a single one missing—thirty on the top, thirty on the bottom. Together, with a complete jaw, it was hard to imagine anything more horrifying. Some claim they were scavengers—what bullshit!

These were animals that did anything that they wanted. They were truly the kings of the dinosaurs. All before them would tremble in their presence. I was trembling now, even though it was nothing but a skinless, eyeless skull from a long-dead animal.

I stood balanced on the top of the ribcage, my feet awkwardly planted on the irregular surface of its vertebrae. I *had* to know how heavy this thing was, so I reached down, got a grip along its jaw, on either side, and lifted. Nothing. I bent at the knees as best I could in order to gain some leverage, all the while struggling to keep my balance on the animal's skeleton and tried it again.

Just as it started to rise, there was a thunderous roar from my right. I looked over to see two small *tyrannosaurs* coming out of the jungle right for me. In the same instant the spine of the *Titanosaur* gave way and I crashed a dozen feet onto the pile of bones.

I landed with a thud, and scrambled to my feet, frightened but unhurt. Mouth agape, I stared out between the skeleton's ribs as if from a jail cell. The pair of flesh-eaters stood at the edge of the pile, snarling and emitting a low growling sound that came from deep within their throats. Their jaws opened and closed, teeth gnashing, saliva dripping from their mouths. They stepped tentatively out onto the pile, pulling back as the bones rolled and shifted, cracking under the massive weight of the carnivores.

Watching in fearful fascination, I saw differences between this pair and the skull balanced above my head. Besides their size, which was not much larger than half of that of the *Tyrannosaurus rex*, their snouts were shorter and slightly thinner, the eyes smaller and pointed forward, both on the front of its face, rather than on the sides. Their teeth were but three, maybe four inches in length, but every bit as sharp and deadly. Overall, they were smaller than a *Tyrannosaurus*, perhaps thirty feet long—probably the size of adolescent tyrannosaurs, but these were no adolescents.

These were *Albertosaurs*, the smaller cousin of the giant *Tyrannosaurus rex*.

Their arms were short, but proportionately larger than those of its bigger relative. They were heavily muscled in their thick legs and stout necks and their jaws looked like they could sever a good size tree trunk in a single bite. They were brightly colored, green that began as brilliant chartreuse on their bellies and between their legs, growing into more of an olive drab on their upper bodies, but punctuated with bright red diamond shaped patterns. Their skin was heavily lined like an elephant's, thick and tough.

They were mad as hell, or perhaps just damn hungry. Or it was just their nature—an instinctive reaction to live prey. Whichever way, I was the object of their attention and they were trying to climb the pile to get at me.

It didn't take them long to get the hang of the shifting mound of bones. Methodically, they began pawing at the bones with their hands, pushing aside those that fell to the ground around them with their feet, propelling them with tremendous force into the brush on the other side of the path. They worked side by side, as a team, creating a clearing at the base of the pile, deepening and widening it, slowly but surely moving towards me.

They tore into the pile, the clicking of their claws on the dried, hollow bones sounding like a band of battling skeletons, rhythmic, but macabre and terrifying.

As they continued to make progress toward my position, the mound of bones beneath me began to shift and I could feel the cage of ribs around me begin to pitch forward. For just the blink of an eye, I visualized the ribcage rolling down the pile, me pinned inside, holding on for dear life like a cheap carnival ride, shattering at the bottom, flinging me into the waiting jaws of the hungry dinosaurs.

I turned and squeezed through the backside of the ribs, snapping one off in the process. I helped the progress of the forward-moving ribs as I passed though, pulling on them, shoving them forward, giving them the initial velocity necessary to break the bonds of whatever held them in place.

A thousand pounds of rib bones began rolling to the bottom, bouncing and pitching from one side to the other as they glanced off hundreds of other bones. I scrambled backwards, higher and deeper into the pile as the turning cylinder of bones found its mark.

The *Albertosaurs* were not fast animals. They saw, but failed to react to the accelerating bony remains of the *Titanosaur*. It crashed into them, sending the two meat-eaters flying in opposite directions like so many bowling pins, the ribs shattering and coming apart as if a bomb had gone off.

They were dazed, but little more. If anything, all that had been accomplished was to further piss them off. They arose, stared momentarily at one another as if sharing the same thought, and with dual deafening roars, attacked the pile with a renewed vengeance. Bones flew everywhere, the *Albertosaur's* arms and legs a blur of frenzied activity. Their breathing was labored, their mouths hung open, and saliva dripped to the ground in massive quantities.

Like the village idiot, I stood there staring at the scene before me, amazed and terrified all at the same time. The pair continued to approach, and I did nothing but stare at them like a rube ... until they were close enough to smell. It was a horrid smell, rancid, like the taste that we sometimes get in our mouths after eating rare beef ... but worse, a hundred times worse. It was the smell of macaroni salad that had sat in the refrigerator for six months, the smell of a toilet that hadn't been flushed in three days. It was the smell of rot, of decaying flesh and regurgitated beef. It was the fetid smell of a carnivore.

It was then that I came to my senses. I tried scrambling up the pile, falling face forward as the bones shifted underfoot. I lay there looking up at the daunting pile before me, soaring high above my head, twenty feet of disastrous missteps, a fluid heap that would shift beneath me with every move. I saw myself taking just one wrong step, sinking down into the pile, hopelessly trapped, unable to extricate myself, all the while the two dinosaurs coming closer, anxious to make me their next meal.

I shifted my position, siting on the edge of the pile, facing the two dinosaurs. I pulled the Glock from my shoulder holster and raised it, taking a two-handed shooters grip. I aimed at the closest *Albertosaur*, the one making the most progress up the pile, and began to slowly squeeze the trigger as I exhaled through my nose. At that very moment, the pile below me began to drop away, and I plunged forward, sliding and rolling toward the snarling beasts. Panicked, the gun flew from my hand and was instantly swallowed up by the shifting, sliding pile of bones.

I slid to a halt not twenty feet from the lead animal. Sprawled out on the pile, spread-eagled, nearly upside down, I watched in horror as the *Albertosaurus* raised its head and gave out a long roar of anger and frustration, attacking the pile once more with a manic fury.

I spun around again so that I was facing it and furiously tried to push my way back up the pile, pushing more bones down the slope only to be thrown across the path by the powerful legs of the enraged meat-eater. I was making their job more difficult by throwing more obstacles in their path, but as the bones kept giving way beneath me I made little progress up the mound. My legs worked like pistons, but the huge jaws of my enemy were still no more than twenty feet away.

Instead of moving up into the pile, I began making my way in a circular fashion, continuing the round trip that I had started an hour before. I stayed twenty feet from the path, moving to my right, slipping and sliding with every step, my feet sinking down into the pile continuously. But, by moving away from the path created by the *Albertosaurs* I didn't have to work as hard to keep from sliding to the bottom. Instead, I started moving up the pile.

For the first few seconds, the *Albertosaurs* were so preoccupied that they failed to notice my movement, and I managed to increase the distance between us to forty feet. Then they wised up. The smaller one shifted its head in my direction and gave a short snort, which alerted the other. Working as a team the lead dinosaur altered its direction and started pawing its way toward my new position while the other backed away from the pile and came around the path directly below me. Rather than beginning to dig its own, shorter, path to get to me, it stood there at the perimeter of the path and just sniffed the air.

As I moved farther up the pile, I continued to make my way around the circumference. The smaller of the two *Albertosaurs* followed my progress, not entering the bone pile, but staying on the path directly beneath me. It continued raising its head high into the air, its snout pointed forward, sniffing the air and letting out a continuous stream of grunts and snarls, as if communicating with the digger, giving it directions, telling it where I was. Perhaps I was giving them more credit than they deserved. But I didn't think so. They knew that as long as they kept me on the pile I was trapped. In time I would either have to come down, or I would perish there atop the bones.

Either way, they'd have me.

As I continued to work my way around the pile, the distance between the larger of the two *Albertosaurs* and myself increased, but the small one kept pace, progressing slowly around the path at the edge of the pile. I found it strange that the one closest seldom seemed to look in my direction. I wondered if it could actually see me, or if it was just following the racket I was making. There was some thought that a tyrannosaur's vision was based on motion. Perhaps if I kept still, they wouldn't know I was there.

Far enough away from the larger dinosaur to eliminate the immediate threat, I found a comfortable position among the bones and stopped moving. I held my breath for twenty seconds, thirty seconds … nothing happened at all. The larger one kept attacking the pile, angling slowly but surely toward me, and the other remained below, looking not at me, but down the path in the direction that I had been heading.

I picked up a loose bone from the pile, a jawbone from a small hadrosaur, and threw it a good fifty feet off to my left. It landed with a loud, hard sound that could be heard above that of the dinosaur's noisy digging. The one guarding me heard it, swiveling its head and taking a single step in that direction down the path. It sniffed once at the air and came just the one step back and looked again in my direction, but its eyes seemed focused on a point well above my head. I remained motionless—terrified. I knew that with the *Albertosaur's* powerful legs it could reach me if it chose to take one giant leap into the pile. Its sheer mass would cause the pile before me to collapse, sending me sliding right to it.

But it remained frozen in place—waiting—listening.

Sitting still, trying to keep the loose bones beneath me from moving and making a noise, I raised my arms above my head and slowly waved them back and forth. The dinosaur lowered its head and seemed to stare directly into my eyes. It then raised its head, but instead of letting out with another enraged roar as I thought it would, it just sniffed the air once again.

The dinosaur couldn't see me.

But it could hear me, and could probably detect motion if I moved from my position.

I couldn't just sit there. Somehow I had to distract them for long enough to make my getaway.

Slowly and cautiously I reached for another bone, tossing it again to my left I far as I could. This time the *Albertosaurus* stayed where it was, simply lifting its head and sniffing repeatedly at the air above its head. Still, it looked in my direction, but not right at me. It was then that I realized that I wasn't going to trick it by using sound. It could smell me.

I nearly panicked at the thought. How could I possibly escape the small tyrannosaur's powerful sense of smell? I couldn't just wipe it off. It was a part of me, as distinctive as my fingerprints or my dental work.

I was filthy. I hadn't had anything resembling a bath in days and I became acutely aware of my own stench. But I knew that even had I scrubbed myself raw, the animals would still detect my aroma. It was *me* they could smell—not what had accumulated *on* me.

An idea popped into my brain and I began to work frantically once again to complete the circumnavigation of the bone pile, back to a spot adjacent to where I entered the clearing, back to where the rotting flesh of the recently dead lay. I couldn't wipe off my smell, but I just might be able to mask it.

Where I first began my journey around the bone pile there was a smell that was much more pungent than my own. Surely the smell of thousands of pounds of rotting meat would hide my own stink. If tyrannosaurs were scavengers as some paleontologists thought, the smell of all that decaying flesh would certainly be more appealing than a tiny, live creature such as myself.

I had no concept of time as I continued to make my way around the rest of the bone pile, but it seemed to take forever. One wrong step and I could break an ankle or fall and be impaled on a piece of broken bone protruding at an odd angle from the pile. Or worse, I could start a bone slide that would take me into the hungry, drooling jaws of the *Albertosaurus*. So I moved in patient steps, ever wary of my predicament. For every two steps that I took sideways, I had to take one step up in order to maintain my distance from the edge of the path. No matter how careful I tried to be, the loose pile continued to shift below my feet. I felt like I was walking on a bed of marbles.

Even before I could see the bodies of the new additions to the pile, the smell told me that I was getting damn close. It was so overwhelming that it was hard to believe that the dinosaur could still discern my own unique, but unquestionably less powerful, aroma. And yet, there it was, forty feet away, directly beneath me on the path, its head stuck in the air, sniffing away for all it was worth.

There was one thing that had changed however. I could no longer hear the sounds of the other dinosaur digging its way through the pile. In fact, I couldn't remember hearing the distinctive sound of claws on bone for quite a while.

I wondered where it was.

Five minutes later I had my answer. As I entered the area above the rotting carcasses, the other dinosaur, the larger and apparently more aggressive of the two, came into view on the other side of the dead animals. Unlike its smaller mate, who remained passively below me on the near side of the pile, this one was animated and decisively angry. I didn't know when it had decided to cease its digging and circle around the other way, but I knew that some form of communication between the two was at play.

There was an *Albertosaurus* on either side of the pile of rotting meat, about sixty yards apart, each standing in an area where the smell was the worst, where the oldest of the ripening cadavers rested. I was still ten feet above them, forty feet from the smaller of the two. I continued moving around the pile until I was centered between them. I sat down and grew still.

They alternated their attention between me on the rise of the bone heap and the pile of stinking meat at their feet. They seemed confused, one minute pawing a dead carcass with a wickedly pointed, clawed foot, the next turning their attention to me, and sniffing at the air—trying to find me.

The stalemate dragged on as the two meat-eaters pawed the ground and sniffed the air. They didn't seem the least bit interested in the spoiled meat all around them. They may have been scavengers, but they could still tell when good meat had gone bad. They lost interest in it, instead, began to paw gently at the dried bones at the base of the pile, while inhaling repeatedly through their noses, trying to separate my smell from the other.

I remained motionless, spread across the bone pile, too frightened to move, but also exhausted, consciousness drifting in and out from the lack of food and sleep. I asked God for just a little help, but as the minutes went by with nothing happening, I took it that He wasn't tuned in on that day. If I was going to get out of this I was going to have to do it myself.

As I lay there, I thought about the *Pachycephalosaurus* at the foot of the pile. It had only been dead for a matter of hours, not nearly enough time for the flesh to begin to rot and smell. If I could somehow draw the two dinosaur's attention to the *Pachy*, maybe they would be willing to forget about me in favor of a much more substantial meal. I hoped that they had short memories because now they were damn mad, as well as hungry—and I hoped that they were more the latter than the former. I prayed that they didn't prize me as a first-course appetizer or some exotic dish that they just had to have despite my diminutive size.

I started down the bone pile, my legs shaking from fear and weariness. Both heads, heads with massive jaws filled with razor-teeth, turned in my direction the moment that I arose from the pile. The bigger one began emitting a low, sustained growl, while the other remained nearly quiet. The growl turned to an ear-piercing roar of outrage as I continued to move closer. It tore at the earth with those gigantic claws and nipped at the air, the sound of its sharp teeth, like huge steak knives clanging against one another. They didn't try to climb the pile, and for some reason they refused to enter the mound of rotting flesh.

I was on all fours, gagging and choking as I climbed the slimy flank of some gigantic beast that had long since lost any identifying characteristics. It was headless, its neck terminating in grisly shreds of muscle and a large mangled flap of skin that was covered with crawling insects. A single white vertebra protruded through the end like a gnawed chicken bone. Its skin, where there was skin, was a mottled gray with sickly yellow pockets of puss that ruptured and ran under my touch. The monster's ribs showed through in random patches like the framework of a derelict wooden schooner, areas where I could see through them to its hollowed-out remains. I shut my eyes to the horror, but I couldn't hold out the smell, and now it was a part of me that I feared I would never rid myself of.

On top of the smelly beast, my cheek pressed into its sticky, putrefying flesh, I looked across to see the *Albertosaurus*. As I had hoped, it was still following me as I made my way closer to the *Pachycephalosaurus*. It was still clawing at the earth and crying out in a constant roar that was intensifying right along with its outrage. But it still hadn't spotted or smelled the *Pachy*, which was now no more than a hundred feet away. I turned my head to the other side, smearing my face in the vile, yellow ooze, getting a taste of it that instantly set my stomach into racking spasms that threatened to tear it from its moorings. The other dinosaur was there, as well, agitated, but silent, holding its massive head high in the air, emitting a series of soft chuffing sounds.

Neither had seen the *Pachy*. They were still too intent on finding *me*, and I wasn't yet lost enough in the smell of the foul cadavers. And, although my movements were minimal, lying low, keeping close to the bodies of the dead dinosaurs, I was still high on the pile, high enough where they could see my movements against the dark background of the jungle some hundred yards to my right. They could smell me, but they were unsure. My movements were slight and my smell was beginning to be confused with those of the others—some horrific—some tantalizing. My chance was now, now that they were just the tiniest bit unsure.

Beneath me was an opening, my one chance to completely confound my stalkers. There was a gaping hole in the side of whatever this huge creature once was. I looked down between its ribs, to a natural cavern that was to be my hiding spot. I took the risk of showing myself, standing on my knees so that I could spread the ribs. I slid easily between them, dropping down into a gelatinous mass that I knew to be the fermenting remains of the animal's internal organs. I didn't dare look down, horrified at the thought of what I would see. The smell told me that I shouldn't look. Instead, I focused on the sun shining through the gap above me, tuning my ears to the sounds outside.

Even with the sound muffled by the walls of my morbid cocoon, I could tell that the roar of the beast had intensified, and was echoed by the second one, which had started up the moment that I had dropped out of sight. I was gone to them. In a wink, they had lost track of me, both in sight and smell, and it confused them further. And it enraged them further yet.

I stood motionless in the belly of the beast, staring up through the hole that was nearly ten feet above my head. I clenched my teeth to control my panic, trying desperately to slow my breathing so that it couldn't be heard from the outside. One sound and I could forget the idea of them moving on.

Standing there looking straight up into the bright sunlight caused me to lose my balance and I had to reach out, steadying myself against what was left of the damp, slick abdominal muscles of the dead dinosaur. My head began to throb and things began to go gray, the light above my head spinning wildly in circles, faster and faster until I was forced to drop onto one knee into the ooze.

Momentarily forgetting where I was, forgetting just about everything else as well, I eased down into a sitting position, my back pressed up against the inner curvature of the animal's ribcage. The slime instantly penetrated the seat of my pants, gently caressed the cheeks of my ass with a soft, warm touch. Exhausted, I pulled my legs in close to my body, rested my head atop of my crossed arms, and fell asleep to the sound of the angry *Albertosaurs*.

*****

I awoke to silence and darkness.

I awoke confused and disoriented.

I lifted my head, my sticky cheek pulling away from the fabric of my coat sleeve with a sound like tearing paper. I looked up to see a patch of stars twinkling in a black velvet sky. Leaning back to stretch my sore neck and shoulders, the dank, sharp smell of rot and putrefaction quickly brought me back to reality. I sat in silence, surrounded by the darkness and the dampness, listening for the sounds of the two predators.

It was an eerie quiet, the only noise that of my own breathing, the sound amplified as it rattled around the inside of the barrel-shaped chest of the huge animal. How ironic it was to hear my own breathing from the chest of this long dead creature. How beautiful it was that it was the *only* sound that I could hear.

I waited, listening intently, but all was still. I waited not only to listen. I waited because I was too afraid to move, too terrified to stick my head up through the hole. What if they knew where I was? What if they were smart enough to plan? What if they were up there waiting for me to show myself? Perhaps raising my head through the hole would be the last thing that I did in this life.

Fatigue was robbing me of the ability to think clearly. I had to focus on the situation—what I knew about the *Albertosaurs*—what I *thought* I knew about them. They were not highly intelligent animals, not even among the dinosaurs—their brain pans were too small as compared to their overall size. They were not smart enough to plan an attack, at least not one that involved stealth and deception. They were not nocturnal. They slept at night, not hunted. And they tended to sleep together in family groups. At least all of them that I had seen to that point had—all except the raptors, of course. Unfortunately, they were the only other meat-eaters that I had met. I was betting my life that the pair of *Albertosaurs* had returned to whatever group they belonged to.

On unsteady legs, I rose from the goo, the silence disturbed by the loud, sucking noise made when my ass popped free. I was dizzy and had to reach out to steady myself against the ribs of the animal. Looking up, the hole looked like a hundred feet away. I tried to jump to grab onto the exposed ribs above my head, but I didn't have the strength to overcome gravity and the suction of the viscous slime at my feet. I tried again, the attempt feebler than the first. On my third try, I ended up sprawled on my back, hardly having gotten off the ground at all. Now I was covered front to back, and head to toe in the disgusting muck, and I was still stuck inside.

In the dim light offered by the star's brilliance, I examined my surroundings. I did it more by feel than by sight, pushing my hands against the hard ribs and soft, rotting tissue between them, searching for another opening. What was left of the skin and muscle of the beast was soft and spongy and wet with decay, but I hadn't the strength to punch through. An image of my hunting knife nestled comfortably in my pack back in the copse of evergreens back in the valley flashed through my mind and I cursed myself for being so careless.

But the dinosaur was literally coming apart. It didn't take long to find another opening through the ribs. My hand pushed through at a spot just above eye level, a long strip of rotted flesh tearing away as I brought my hand back through the hole. In minutes I had torn away the flesh between the ribs large enough to squeeze through.

The flank of another cadaver that was piled up against the first abruptly halted my progress. Using the last of my strength, I twisted by body through the makeshift escape hatch, pushing my back up against the slick hide of the second beast and grabbed a rib on either side. Pulling with my arms, and pushing with my knees, squirming and wiggling, I pushed my way up through the bodies of the two dinosaurs. Even dead and gutted, half their weight taken by rot and scavenging, their mass pressed upon me from either side like a giant vice that continued to tighten for every inch that I moved. My chest was compressed, my lungs starved for oxygen, my face was contorted by the two opposing masses. The greasy pustules that burst and ran down my face were largely ignored, the terror rising within me as my air began to run out.

As the panic was about to overcome me, my head popped free from between the two beasts. My chest was still constricted and I was still gasping for breath, but the clean, cold air gave me a burst of strength, and I forced my way from captivity.

I sat on the back of the second beast with my feet propped up upon the first and sucked my lungs full of the clean, sweet air. Momentarily forgotten were the two meat-eaters. I looked around the clearing—all was absolutely still. The sky was brilliant with stars, not a cloud to block the view, the moon a silver crescent in a backdrop that was so black that the contrast was startling. The air was cold, a harsh wind blowing from the west that stung my ears and dried the slime on my face into a pasty, skin-stretching crust. Looking around the perimeter of the bone pile I saw that the *Albertosaurs* were gone—gone to wherever predators went for the night.

CHAPTER 21

The snow and wind were pouring into the entrance of the cave. I had to grab the laptop and duck into the shelter of the machine. It was just as well. I had been at it all day and what there was of good light was fading fast in the shortened days of mid-winter. And I was hungry, having eaten nothing on that day, too consumed with getting the facts set down before I forgot them, or something happened to *keep* me from getting them down.

Not that anything ever happened on my beach. Life here was as different as night was to day. Where there was discovery, excitement, and danger in the valley, here there was boredom, repetition, and a blandness that caused each day to run into the next, nearly unnoticed. It was strange. In the valley, life was a precarious thing. There was danger around every corner, death lurking behind every rock and tree. Here on the beach was just about the safest place in the world. There were no dinosaurs, no poisonous snakes, no carnivorous beetles. I didn't have to worry about loading my pistol, keeping my rifle in sight, sharpening my knife, or hiding in the tree. I didn't have to concern myself with watching my step, looking over my shoulder, looking up, looking down, or just plain looking out. No, it was a safe as could be, but every day that I spent here I could feel myself growing older, one day closer to death. Not that I missed the danger, but in the valley I felt alive. Here, I felt next to nothing.

Beyond the beach, there was a sea to explore, but the winter-chilled water prohibited much in the way of exploration. Besides, there wasn't a hell of a lot to explore with my raft gone. And there were only so many measurements I could take of the expanding beach—once every month or so was plenty.

The sea was pulling away quickly, more quickly than I would have thought possible. But I knew every inch of the shoreline, every nook and cranny of the face of the cliffs surrounding the cave's entrance, and every loose rock and shell scattered on the sand. I had trod every foot of beach and could walk the area of the cave blindfolded and never run into a wall.

I spent the daylight hours entering data into the computer and walking the beach. It had become one of my few distractions, and my only form of exercise. One hour before twilight I took to running the beach, back and forth, from one edge of the cliff to the other, a cloud in my wake as my boots kicked up the white sand. I ran to exhaustion. Not for the exercise, but just to have something to do, something to wear me out so that I could sleep at night.

It was the loneliness that got to me, that kept me awake at night. With so little to occupy my mind, I had time to think—too much time. I thought of Liz—the wonderful ten years that we spent together, all that we had shared, how much in love we were. And I missed her, but like one of those computer morph programs, my thoughts always shifted into those of Susan. I wondered why that was, and all that I could come up was that she was still alive while Liz was not. Or at least she was alive when I left. Something deep inside told me that she still was. I loved Susan and I knew that she loved me, but it was too late to do anything about it, even if she had survived. And that's what hurt the most—being in love and not able to do anything about it. It was the most frustrating kind of love because we hadn't been separated by any of those things that usually kept two people apart. Distance hadn't separated us, and Susan's injury hadn't kept us apart. It was time—sixty five million years of it to be exact—and time wasn't something that I could do a damn thing about.

So, we were in love, but a love that was never shared in a physical sense. And perhaps *that* was the worst—unfulfilled love was the epitome of loneliness.

And it was at night that the regret slipped in. I had left so many things unfinished and unsaid. I had stole away like a thief in the night. Until I was gone, no one outside of Dermot's team knew what I was up to. Not that I had that many friends, but there was Jakes—Jakes and his family. They had become like my own, but I didn't even have the courage to tell them what was going on. I simply disappeared and left them with nothing but a letter—the letter … and the money.

They had it now—my money—but it did little to lessen my guilt, and I knew that it was unimportant to them, as unimportant as it was to me. I owed them so much more than money. They took me in as one of their own, and asked for nothing in return but my friendship. I betrayed that friendship when I left. I should have trusted Jakes to understand. Whether he supported me or not was immaterial. He would have understood.

I wish I could talk to him now. There were so many things that I would like to say to him. Not saying them when I had the chance was my biggest regret.

It was because of this that I grew to hate the beach, detested the infernal machine that brought me to it. When I first came to this place I thought of it as my home.

But no more.

It was a cold, hard, unfriendly place that was as devoid of life as a cemetery. More and more I thought of it in that way, a place where there was only death. And why not, it's where Dermot expected to find what was left of me when the time machine suddenly popped back into his time. It would be a cemetery for one, a huge metal coffin that would house my remains for a million lifetimes.

I hated the place!

Day after day, and night after night, I tried to concentrate on the positive. The time machine did offer the slightest bit of comfort. There was a real bed, complete with mattress and pillows. I had my big, old chair, the comfort of which couldn't be matched by anything in my tree. Here, I had a real stove, which made cooking a lot easier than over an open fire, although in all honesty, I couldn't say tasted as good. And I had a secure home. I had but to shut the door and nothing could get at me—nothing could get past the solid titanium skin. Even the weather was kept somewhat at bay. The cold still penetrated, but unlike the tree, whose roofs leaked despite my best attempts to weave them tight, the rain and snow could not get past the seamless metal skin. And with a good fire going in the stove, there was just enough warmth to get me through the first few hours of the night. The problem was, I had run out of firewood a week ago, and there was another month of cold nights to get through.

The nights were the worst, nearly as cold as those in Chicago. The titanium skin of the time machine soaked up the cold like a sponge, transmitting it through the vast interior as if the whole thing was one big meat locker, and I was nothing but a side of beef. It was only made tolerable by the half-dozen blankets that I wrapped myself in each night.

But as cold as I was, I had been colder—much colder.

*****

Maybe it was as simple as being sheltered from the harsh winds that kept me from feeling the cold, or perhaps it really was warmer deep in the belly of the beast, the fermentation of the internal organs still generating heat after all those weeks and months. Or perhaps it was sheer panic that numbed me to other sensations. The two *Albertosaurs* had filled me with terror, the kind that pretty much swallows up everything else, the kind which blocks out rational thought and action. It was one of the few things that I remembered—the fear.

When I had awoken, the fear was still there, as well as the disorientation of waking to strange surroundings, the smell accosting me long before any sense of cold had crept in. The smell never faded, but the disorientation did quickly as I realized where I was, what had happened the day before, the fear doubling, and bubbling back close to the surface.

But sitting there atop the dead body of the giant dinosaur, the fear of the two meat-eaters gone and the night still and quiet—the cold began to set in. My legs, up through my hips, were soaked clear through from lying in the pool of liquefied viscera. It was on my coat, coming through in stray patches here and there, little stinging swatches that stuck to my skin like a tongue on an icy metal post. The goo on my face stiffened in the cold breeze, pulling painfully on my cheeks, stretching my lips into a death's rictus. The wind stung my eyes, causing tears to run down my face, adding to my misery. It was time to move.

Sliding down the side of the huge animal, I landed on a small patch of hard bare ground, encompassed on three sides by the prone body of a *Triceratops*. Even in the dark, I could see that it was a more recent addition to the bone pile. Its flesh was nearly intact, the color just beginning to mottle, a glistening sheen coating it, the first signs of decomposition. It looked almost as if it was sleeping, lying on its side, its legs pulled in tight to its body. It *almost* looked that way, but I knew better. I knew that the *Triceratops* slept on its belly, with its legs folded up underneath, not on its side. And its head rested at an unnatural angle, the large diameter of the frill holding the head off the ground, turned sideways—too far sideways. It looked like its neck was broken, but how it got that way was pure conjecture. It sure hadn't hiked all the way from the valley like that.

I crawled over the animal where the journey was the shortest—just behind its frill. Grabbing the edge of the circular crest with my left hand I hoisted myself to the top. The normally smooth knobby bones of the frill tore at the palm of my hand, splitting it open, causing me to let go, sitting down suddenly onto the side of the animal. Momentarily forgetting the pain, convinced that it was nothing serious, I reached up with my right hand feeling the irregular surfaces of the frill. Several of the bones were splintered and the frill itself was split, a large portion of it hanging loose like a large hinged flap.

The mystery deepened until I slid down to the other side. There I found the gigantic *Titanosaur* that I had first seen when I entered the clearing the morning before. It was perhaps this huge creature that, in its final death dance, took one last stumbling step onto the already dead *Triceratops*, crushing its frill and breaking its neck.

Neither of the dinosaurs were aware that it happened.

There was plenty of bare ground underfoot by then, the pile having not yet settled into the empty space at the back of the dead *Titanosaur*. It was a strange sensation—walking on ground that didn't move under my feet, but even with sure footing, it was a long hike around the back end of this stupendous animal.

As I stepped over the last few feet of its tail I was struck by the fierce wind that whipped around the clearing, blowing hard in a circular path directly into my face. I turned my back to it, and with my head down, began walking backward toward the trees.

My eyesight was still blurred by tears as I took the first dozen steps. Through my fuzzy vision something sparkled back the starlight off to my right. In a moment of terror, I turned and began to run, tripping after just two steps, falling onto the hard path. Lying flat on my stomach, my feet pointed toward the ring of jungle, I threw my hands over my head in a useless defensive posture and waited for the end, sure that the *Albertosaurs* had tricked me.

Minutes passed and nothing happened. The ground was cold, pressed hard against my left cheek, and fear-sweat trickled down my hairline and down my sides. I lay there, trying to muster the courage to jump up and make a break for it. It was only twenty yards to the trees. If I could get there, I had a chance. On the other hand, if the pair of meat-eaters were close by, they would be on me before I could even rise.

Moving no other muscles than that of a single lid, I opened my right eye. Blinking away the tears, the source of the sparkle crystallized. It was blood, lots of it, still wet, shimmering like liquid fire under the radiant shine of a million stars. It covered the scattered remains of the once beautiful *Pachycephalosaurus*, dripping from its shattered bones and torn flesh.

I crawled over to it, rising as I came abreast of what was left of the bony skull. The head was the only recognizable part of the animal. It was relatively intact, hanging by a few strands of tendon and muscle, the spine severed just below the skull. Its eyes were still open, but they never saw what had occurred after it had hit the ground the day before.

The *Albertosaurs* had found it after all. I had been sound asleep, exhausted past the point of mere noise waking me. I could only imagine what sounds had occurred after I had drifted off. The signs revealed nothing less than a furious attack on the still-warm body of the *Pachy*. It was literally torn to shreds—bones broken and thrown thirty feet in every direction, only scattered morsels of flesh remaining for the smaller carnivorous animals and flesh-eating insects. It made me weak in the knees to think what sounds were made during the frenzy. I had heard them when they were mad. By the time they found the *Pachy*, they were mad *and* hungry. And these were among the most awesome predators that ever walked the face of the earth. The sounds of their attack must have been extraordinary.

I was thankful to not have heard them.

For the second time in twenty-four hours I gave my thanks to the *Pachy*. It would never understand what it had done. Even given the intelligence, it wouldn't have known because it had long since passed on. But it had saved me. The hungry *Albertosaurs* had turned their attention to the smell of fresh meat, forgetting me in their haste to appease their appetite. Their hunger satisfied for the moment, they wandered back with full stomachs to wherever they had come from, their small brains forgetting everything about me. So, for the second time, I said farewell to the *Pachy*, turned away and headed into the trees.

Entering the slim patch of jungle from inside the clearing was easier than entering from the other side. The path that the *Pachy* had taken was still clear, the branches and brush still bent and crushed, showing the way.

I staggered through them, anxious to get away from the horrible pile of bones, moving like a drunken man, half starved, frozen, and worn out despite several hours of awkward, troubled sleep in the past few hours. I didn't feel, and could barely see, the branches as they slapped at my legs and torso as my feet raced forward, one after another in a kind of clumsy dance.

It was warmer in among the trees, the wind blocked by the thick foliage. I wanted nothing but to lie down in the soft ferns and sleep until daylight, but I dared not. I had been too long without food, too long exposed to the elements, too long in a state of terror. I needed to keep moving. I needed to get back to the valley of the dinosaurs. I needed to get back to my tree.

Coming out of the jungle, I began retracing the steps that led me here the day before—due south hopefully. I had no compass, and with the sun still hours from rising, I only hoped that I was heading in the right direction. I could barely see the outline of the cliff to my left, and as the space between it and the jungle increased, I lost sight of it all together. I was afraid that by daybreak I would be wandering in circles.

The stiff wind pressed hard against my right side, drying and stiffening the wet, sticky mess that soaked my clothing. I could feel the stiff fabric rubbing against the tops and insides of my thighs with every step, a raw, burning sensation that increased with every mile. I fought the urge to head east to the river. I was desperate to wash the filth from my body and clothes, to rid myself of the reminders of what I had been through. I fought off the urge knowing that a dunk in the water would surely mean death from the harsh winds long before I reached the safety of the tree.

I was disgustingly filthy, but I didn't stop to wash. I was agonizingly hungry, but I didn't stop to eat. Most of all, I was incredibly cold, and I would only get colder if I stopped. Or worse. I knew about hypothermia, about how if I got cold enough I would forget about the pain, forget about the cold altogether, and just sort of fade out, falling asleep until my heart just gave up. So, I didn't dare stop. I plunged forward, the hood pulled up over my head, my hands stuffed deep into my pockets.

My eyes and nose ran continuously, mixing together, running across my lips, dripping from my chin. I could barely see through the tears, but I refused to take my hands from my pockets to wipe them. Instead, I just kept blinking at a maddening rate, keeping my failing eyesight aimed at a spot a few feet in front of me.

I continued on, one foot in front of the other, sometimes staggering, sometimes stumbling, sometimes tripping over my own big feet. I walked on for hours, the sweat dripping down my temples, cooling instantly in the cold, my body temperature the only thing keeping it from freezing. The cold had worked its way through my wet boots—my feet like useless blocks of ice. Like walking on those ridiculous, huge platform shoes of the '70s, my feet didn't seem to touch the ground.

Mile after mile, I staggered on, until the first golden hue of a new day showed itself above the rise of the cliffs. The thought of the sun, and all of its life-giving warmth coming over the mountains in the east, spurred me on. In an hour it would show itself, and I imagined the radiant heat coming from it chasing the cold away like magic. I increased my pace.

But it didn't happen.

The sun rose into the sky as only a hazy bright spot against a backdrop of dingy gray, its rays filtered and stunted, doing next to nothing to heat the earth below. It was a cold, nearly dead thing that gave up only enough light to make the valley an ominous, lifeless place.

In the dim light, the valley looked bigger somehow, the cliffs off to the east much farther away than they should have been. In all other directions, the valley seemed to go on endlessly, nothing but gently rolling hills and scattered, lonely stands of trees. But the cliffs were still over my left shoulder, meaning that I hadn't been wandering aimlessly in circles, even though I had traveled several miles too far to the west. I altered my course and kept going, determined to get back home, too afraid to stop.

The misdirection had cost me an extra hour or two of traveling, time that my weary body could not afford. At some point I forgot about the cold. Not that it had warmed up much, but everything—the cold, the hunger, the pain—everything, had just sort of disappeared. Or, more realistically, they kind of all blended together into an overwhelming sense of misery. No, that wasn't quite right either, because by then I didn't feel miserable. In fact, I felt nothing, at least nothing that I could really remember later on. I was like a zombie, walking along mindlessly, aware of nothing other than the need to remain upright, placing one foot in front of the other.

And that's how it was until an hour or two before sunset. The light was growing dimmer, even though I was unaware of the passage of time. I couldn't even say for sure that it was still the same day, as disoriented as I was. Only thinking about it later, realizing that during the original journey it had taken only a single day, did I fully understand that I was still working on the same day.

There were no shadows, yet the light was growing ever dimmer from the setting sun when I stumbled over the exposed root of a straggly, half-dead tree. I didn't quite go down, but made a few comical gyrations until I ended up on one knee, painfully, jarring myself into full consciousness.

I tried to rise, but my strength had deserted me. My legs gave out from under me and I landed hard on my ass. I sat there for the longest time thinking about the pain in my backside, my legs trembling, my breathing labored, my eyes trying hard to focus.

I couldn't get my eyes to settle on anything, and yet my ears still seemed to work okay. In the near distance I could hear water running. I rubbed my eyes until I could get them focused again. There, directly in front of me, not twenty yards away, was a stream, the clear, shallow water rushing along in a convoluted path, bouncing off rocks and branches, making delightful little gurgling noises.

Along its far bank was the edge of a forest, hardwoods mostly, their branches bare, a few evergreens poking their still-green color through an otherwise monotonous picture of blacks and browns. I knew this forest, as I knew this stream before it. It was where the amorous *Pachy* was dealt his deathblow. And I knew that across the narrow strip of forest, some two hundred yards away, was the valley of the dinosaurs.

*****

It took another full day to cross the valley, the trip made possible with a meager meal of pine nuts and a decent night's sleep tucked away under a huge mound of fragrant leaves in the middle of the forest. But it was not a pleasant journey, nor was it completed without concern that increased the closer that I got to the other side.

The day had begun crisp and clear, cold, but with a bright ball of sun in a robin's egg blue sky that raised the temperature a good ten degrees above the freezing mark before mid-day. And yet, I was still freezing, the cold of the past twenty-four hours having settled in me like a cancer. I shook, sometimes uncontrollably, my joints stiff, arthritic-like, my fingertips swollen and unfeeling despite the protection of my pockets. Some feeling had returned to my feet during my walk in the sunshine, but the scalding pain that replaced it made walking even more difficult than when I couldn't feel them at all.

And I was hungry—starving actually. I had eaten nothing in the last several days except a few handfuls of nuts, and some of those hadn't stayed down for very long. The hollow feeling in the pit of my stomach that I had had been carrying around with me for weeks had turned to severe cramps, hitting me when I didn't expect it, doubling me over, making me suck in a breath through clenched teeth. Finding food should have been a higher priority, but I was just too damn cold to think about eating.

To go along with the cramps, I had picked up a racking cough. A cough that left me starved for oxygen, a cough that made me feel as if I were dying. Each time it started, it was harder to stop, the harsh bark coming from deeper and deeper in my chest, threatening to turn my lungs inside out, leaving me gagging and sweating, tears flowing from my eyes. My lungs felt as if a giant hand was squeezing them, but every time that I tried to draw a breath big enough to fill them, the cold air kicked off another fit of hacking.

I had tuned out the world. If there were sounds, I didn't hear them. I saw nothing but the ground in front of me, the tip of each scuffed, dirty boot coming into view, alternating left then right, right then left, one each second, a monotonous shuffle that carried me through the valley as the sun traveled in its day-long arc. Had I been more alert, I would have realized sooner that something was different on this day. Something was terribly wrong in the valley of the dinosaurs.

There were no dinosaurs.

I don't know what had changed, what had diverted me from my constant marching forward, what had made me aware of anything beyond the shivers, the hunger, the cramps, and the dullness of leaning forward into my pace—ever forward, one foot in front of the other. Whatever made me do it, several hours had passed, the yellow globe high in the sky, when at last I raised my head from the path in front of me.

What I saw was nothing.

Well, not exactly nothing. I could still see the distant cliffs off to my left. They were as I remembered them from two days before. The horizon to my right was broken by the newborn mountains of the Rockies, a thick dark, hazy line below that was dark jungle that would circle to the south some eighty miles before my tree. That hadn't changed either. I remembered passing the same streams, saw the same familiar landmarks, everything looked the same. Everything was as I had left them ... except for the dinosaurs.

They were gone.

When I had entered the valley a month before, they were everywhere. I couldn't look in any direction without seeing several different species, dozens of individual animals. Even at night, they were there—everywhere. Now they were gone.

During the past four or five hours I hadn't looked for them, hadn't even given them a thought, lost in my own misery as I was. But I was looking then. I was in the center of the valley, equal distance between the bone pile and where the path along the river began. I had a spectacular view of the entire valley, but I saw not a single living thing.

It occupied my mind through what was left of the day. Trying to solve the mystery of the lost dinosaurs filled my thoughts while I completed the journey through the valley. It was a blessing of sorts. I forgot about the hunger and the cold. Even the constant cough seemed to be but a mild irritation as I covered the last ten miles back to the edge of the valley.

I was no longer staring into the dirt beneath my feet as I marched forward. Now I was looking. My head swiveled from horizon to horizon, my eyes scanning over every tree and rock, searching for any trace of them. But there was no sign. Even as I approached the far end of the valley there was no sign of them.

It was nearly dark when I found my little stand of trees, my pack and rifle tucked in under a giant fern, just as I had left them. I'm still not sure if it was just plain weariness, or a need to sit down and try to figure things out, but I stopped for the night. Whatever it was, it probably saved my life. I was thirsty, hungry, sick, and just plain worn out. I needed to rest. The tree was still five day's journey ahead. I needed time to eat, to drink, and to sleep.

I had lived here among the small group of trees and brush for nearly a month, so I had made it as comfortable as possible. A huge pile of soft ferns had made a decent place to sleep, a heap of small branches and twigs made for a nice fire at night, and an assortment of nuts and roots had kept me from starving.

I ate, and I warmed myself in front of a small fire. My head throbbed, and my face was burning, not from the tiny flames of the campfire, but from the fever that had gripped me during the past few hours. I took aspirin from the small first-aid kit, but it was like trying to treat a gunshot with a band-aid.

Through the night the fever raged and my breathing was shallow and constricted, like trying to suck air through a straw. I coughed continuously, my chest ached, my throat raw and raspy.

I snuggled down deep inside the pile of ferns, yet I slept fitfully, if at all. I wondered, and I worried about the dinosaurs. How in the hell could they just disappear, completely, in a period of less than three days? My fevered brain conjured up the most bizarre reasons.

Maybe this had all just been a dream. I wasn't really back in time, and there really were no dinosaurs—at least not here, and not now. Perhaps I was just out on some remote dig, and I had been separated from my team. I had fallen ill, the fever playing games with my brain, disconnecting and reconnecting neurons into a weird pattern of fantastic images and false memories.

I scraped a fingernail against the hardened crud on my jacket sleeve and brought it to my nose. The terrible smell was as real as the substance that caused it. Where it had come from was real. Two nights before, I had been sleeping in the decaying remains of a dinosaur. Just as sure as I was lying there on that night in a pile of giant prehistoric ferns.

So, it wasn't a hallucination brought about by the fever. I was really here, and so were the dinosaurs—or, they *had* been here—just three days ago.

As the night went on, my fever got worse, and my imagination got even more bizarre. What if the dinosaurs were still there? They were just invisible. Or what if some super-intelligent, super-advanced civilization just sort of beamed them up.

Well, it could happen.

Well, couldn't it?

After all, wasn't the fact that I was sent seventy million years into the past pretty far fetched? Were invisible dinosaurs more unrealistic than me sleeping in the belly of one? Was the thought of visitors from outer space more fantastic than that of a man of the twentieth century visiting the valley of the dinosaurs?

I think not!

Like I said, by then my brain was anything but normal. Somewhere deep down inside, in that small part of my mind that was still functioning on some nearly normal level, I knew that the dinosaurs weren't invisible, that they didn't just *beam up*, and that they really were here just a few short days ago. And, about an hour before dawn, I knew where they had gone.

I didn't wait for the sun. Knowing there would be no sound sleep for me until I found them, no rest until I was back in the tree, I threw the pack over my shoulder, grabbed my rifle, and left the valley.

I headed south. Back the way I had come, back toward the tree.

I hadn't slept, not really, but the rest had done me good. My feet were killing me, each step like walking barefooted on glass—especially the right one. The outer toes felt like they were on fire, each step sending fresh waves of pain through my foot, up into my leg, causing me to rock onto the balls of my feet. My cough had gotten no better, now a rumbling, gurgling kind of sound that came accompanied by a disgusting yellow, god-awful tasting phlegm that I had to spit out every few paces. The gut wrenching cramps had departed, leaving my stomach with a constant rumble as it digested the inadequate morsels of food from the night before.

Despite it all, I was more alert than I had been in days, a new sense of purpose filling my being. I was hot on the trail of the lost dinosaurs.

When daylight chased away the shadows from the path, I knew that I was right. Stamped indelibly into the hard-packed earth were thousands of footprints—trackways as paleontologists would call them millions of years later. They were of every size and shape, print upon print, extending across the entire width of the path. And they were all pointing south.

I had never seen so many tracks in one place at one time, not from any kind of animal, in any time. And there was something very uniform and very orderly about them. Not only were they all pointing in the same direction, but, as strange as it sounds, they looked *calm*. They were orderly. Even stacked one upon another, I could pick out the tracks of individual animals. Each print was distinct and clear, not twisted or distorted, as it would be if the animals were running or panicked or confused. The length of the stride seemed nominal—a casual walking pace, and the direction was straight and true, their course unaltered. These animals were heading south. Not in a panic, but as if it were just a natural thing to do—traveling south when the weather turned frigid.

The path was no longer truly flat. It had taken on a three-dimensional profile now. Random patterns of piles rose from the path like a lunar landscape, some big, some small, some brown, and some green, but all fairly disgusting. That many dinosaurs travelling together left a hell of a mess as they passed.

I examined one of the piles, picking up a handful, bringing it to my face. It was cold, nearly dry, crumbling between my fingers, the smell just barely discernable for what it was. I was no expert, but it had to be at least a couple of days old.

*****

For two days I traveled the path alone, dodging the piles, checking one every few hours. Even without touching them, without bringing my nose down to them I knew that I was getting closer. There was an unmistakable scent in the air that continued to grow more powerful during the second day. I no longer thought of the odor as unpleasant. In comparison to the smells of the bone pile, it wasn't. I guess that one can get used to anything.

I wasn't sleeping at night, at least not *through* the night. Instead, I would continue to walk long after sunset, stopping when the moon was high in the sky, and build a fire from the twigs and branches scattered along the edge of the path. Sitting cross-legged in front of the fire, my head hanging down, the warmth taking just the slightest edge from a chill that had drilled right down to the bone, I would fall asleep. For an hour, perhaps two, if I were lucky, and I'd be off again long before first light.

It was just an hour after the sun rose on the third day that I found them. As I rounded a slight turn in the path I could see them a mile ahead. The small family of *Titanosaurs* had taken the rear position of the herd. It was like a huge army on the march, the giant *Titanosaurs* protecting their rear. Their size alone would make them a formidable foe.

Then again, maybe they were just the slowest of the dinosaurs. They were at the back simply because they couldn't keep up. They moved slowly, almost in a daze, the little one tight against the side of its mother. I caught up to them easily. Even with their huge size and long stride, it wasn't hard to overtake them and pass them by. One of them twisted its long neck to watch me as I approached, but otherwise the small group paid no heed of me.

Several hundred yards ahead, the rest of the herd was hidden in a cloud of dust. I limped forward on bad feet, my breathing labored, my cough no better than the night before.

In a couple of hours I seemed to make no progress, the cloud of dust still several hundred yards ahead. Yet turning around to look, I saw that I had moved ahead of the three stragglers by an equal distance. It would probably be after the sun went down, when the animals stopped for the night that I would catch up. A couple of hours later, the *Titanosaurs* would catch up, as well.

It had to be taking its toll on the giant herbivores. At a hundred tons, movement over any great distance, over a sustained period of time, had to be extremely difficult. They weren't built for speed or continuous motion. The extra time that it took to catch up to the herd each day—the shorter rest periods—had to cost them, especially the two adults. Their heads hung low and their tails dragged the ground. Their eyes were nothing more than tiny slits as they lumbered clumsily along the path blindly.

I was having my own trouble keeping up. The pain in my toes had caused me to walk on the inside edges of my feet, kind of knock-kneed, new pain shooting up the inside of my shins with each step. Like the dinosaurs behind me, my head hung low, and even though I had no tail, it felt as if my ass were dragging, too. My breath was ragged in my chest, the cold air biting into the scarred linings of my lungs, my teeth chattering as I staggered on mile after mile.

As the shadows grew long and the temperature began to drop, the herd began to slow. As I approached them, I could see that the back part of the herd was mostly ceratopsians and anklasaurids, big, heavy, short-legged animals. Faster than the titanosaurs, but much slower that the hadrosaurs and the pachycephalosaurs, they traveled together for protection.

Over a brief period of an hour or so each one came to a halt, slowly, like mechanical creatures whose spring mechanisms had wound down. I wandered among them, unafraid, accustomed to being around them. They paid no attention to me, content to flop down the short distance to their massive underbellies, lower their heads to the ground, and, like flipping a switch, wink out.

They seemed to fall asleep instantly, effortlessly. Liz had been like that. No matter how bad her day had been, what was troubling her mind, she somehow had that uncanny ability to just set it aside, her breathing already slow and steady even before her head nestled into the pillow. She could get a good eight-hours of sleep the night before, and yet go to bed early the next night if there was nothing to do, and sleep again for another eight … or ten.

I envied her for it. And I envied the dinosaurs for that same ability. I needed sleep desperately, having averaged no more than a few hours a night for more than a week. I thought back to the last time that I had had more. It was the night with the mortally wounded *Pachy*. I had slept well on that night, situated between the small bonfire and the warm body of the animal. Thinking about it, it was the last time that I was really warm, too. I was tired, but I was also cold.

And the cold won out. It kept me from sleeping. It was much too cold to stand still, too cold to lie out in the open, even too cold to think about building a bed of ferns along the edge of the jungle. It was too cold to think about much of anything except getting warm.

More than anything, I was afraid to sleep—afraid that I wouldn't wake up again—afraid that my already stiff joints would freeze as solidly as the fossils that I dug up in my former life. That my blood, too, would stop flowing in my veins, thickening into the consistency of maple syrup on a cold New England mid-winter's night. I wondered at what point the brain ceased to function, when it was so cold that the synapses stopped firing. Was there an absolute temperature when that happened or a definitive period of time in sub-freezing temperatures that finally shut it down, completely and irrevocably? I couldn't help but feel that I was very near that point.

I continued to walk amongst them, my hands jammed into my pockets so hard that I feared I'd burst the stitching, my arms pressed into my body so tightly that my sides ached. I limped badly, favoring my right side to the point that I was surprised not to be wandering in an endless clockwise circle. My lips were pressed tightly shut, breathing shallowly through my nose—anything to limit the cold air that stabbed like daggers in my lungs.

The cough—yes, it was still there. But now it was a pathetic little, single-syllabic bark that was constant with nearly every breath that I took. It punctuated the end of each inhale, like a badly running machine that was about to seize up from lack of oil. Like an old-time auto that relied on frequent, if not constant, tuning, to keep the plugs firing every time, the carburetor sucking gas at the command of the right pedal. That's just how it felt—like I was running out of gas. If I didn't get some sleep, some substantial food, some medical attention, I would soon just peter out like the little mechanical monkey with the cymbals whose clanging grew farther and farther apart until they wound down. They would stop just a sixteenth of an inch before one last resounding clang, frozen in time just the tiniest space before touching one last time.

My own cymbals were slowing down, as well. They were days, perhaps only hours, from stopping altogether. And there was no one around to rewind my mechanism.

I envied the dinosaurs. They were all fast asleep. Hundreds of them, scattered in groups of twos and threes across the entire width of the path, extending along it for more than two hundred yards, looking in the dark like so many piles of boulders, perhaps the aftermath of a landslide. They could have been mistaken for dead if not for the little plumes of white fog lifting off from the head of each in nice rhythmic patterns. It reminded me of a movie I saw once on the American Revolution. Hundreds of tents set up on the frigid ground of Valley Forge, small campfires before each sending white trails of smoke into a clear, cold night. I remembered from the movie that the soldiers were freezing, poorly clothed and near starving from eating nothing but small bits of rancid, salted beef and spoiled potatoes. I remembered how miserable their existence was, how heroic they were for surviving it.

I was every bit as miserable as those soldiers on that night, but I found nothing even remotely heroic in my selfish will to survive. I wasn't here to be a hero. I was here because I was a coward. I was here because I was too afraid to cope with the pile of shit that life had handed me, too afraid of facing a future without a job, without justice, without love.

I was a two time loser, unwilling to become a three time one. Elizabeth was dead. Susan was comatose, and probably dead. Having stuck around in the twenty first century, where there were real people, especially those of the other persuasion, I would have ended up in love a third time. I liked being married—being loved. I liked being the most important person in someone else's life. I was miserable by myself. How in the hell did I think I could survive in a time where there was no chance of love, no chance of even encountering another human being?

I must have been out of my mind.

I was cold and alone. I thought about just ending it all. I knew that surviving was a matter of will, and if I wanted, I could just find a nice open patch of ground, one where the wind swept briskly across the path, and lie down and let the cold take me away. I would die before the next new day. Hypothermia would be the cause—apathy would be the reason.

Or, I could simply take the shotgun, position it under my chin, and pull the trigger. It would be over in a microsecond, finished before I even knew that it had started, a done deal before my body hit the ground.

But, I wasn't a suicidal kind of guy, not one to kick my own bucket. And I wasn't the kind of person to give up without a hell of a fight—never had been—never would be. I was determined to make it back to health and some measure of contentment, if not happiness. I was determined to get back to my tree and resume the bizarre life that I had built for myself.

In the middle of the herd, I spotted a family of *Triceratops*—two adults and two adolescents. They were huddled together for warmth, the two youngsters squeezed in tightly between the massive torsos of the two adults. The heads of the larger pair rested flat on the ground, the regal frills rising high in the air, huge knobby semicircles that touched the ground on either side, the two just barely touching in the center. The two small *Triceratops* had their heads tilted upward and angled away from one another, their pointed chins nestled in the soft recess behind the frills of their parents. Their own, smaller frills fanned out at odd angles, forming a lopsided triangle-shaped pattern with the larger pair. Seeing them from the front, the tight little group looked like a two-headed, four-frilled, no-legged monster.

Asleep or awake, I had nothing to fear from them. They were gentle creatures, and they were familiar of my scent. They knew me, and understood that I was no threat. The *Triceratops* had always been a favorite of mine, so I had spent a lot of time with them during my month-long stay. I guess that you could say that we had formed a special bond of sorts. The two adults trusted me with their children.

*****

I had sought them out immediately on that first day, approaching them tentatively, mindful of those huge twin horns above the eyes. The horns were easily six feet long and wickedly pointed. With a flick of their heads, they could easily penetrate the thickest hides of the biggest dinosaurs. With a puny human, the horn would have passed right through. They were herbivores, plant eaters, but their sharp, pointed beaks were capable of severing the stalks of huge, woody plants, trunks of trees that were seven or eight inches in diameter, capable of cutting a human being in half.

As I approached them that first time, the largest of the four lowered its head and backed up three or four paces. The second adult used its horns to gently push the two tykes off to the side. Sensing their alarm, I moved away from the group of three and walked slowly toward the largest of the animals, the one with lowered head—a defensive position I thought, or perhaps an about-to-attack position. It remained absolutely still as I approached. Only the huge, dark pupils of its eyes shifted upward as I came closer, peering directly into my own. I could sense no hate or anger in those eyes—only an unease that I should have recognized instantly, as I must have had the same look in mine. Its breathing was slow and even, but loud, a shuttering, stuttering sound accompanying each long inhalation. I reached out slowly with an open hand, outstretched fingers, showing the magnificent beast that I held no weapon, meant it no harm. I gently touched one of the bony protrusions of its frill, running the tips of my fingers down the short length of bone, onto the ridge of dusty, tan skin that held it all together. It was dry and warm, covered with a pebble-like finish that was irregular in both size and shape. I could feel the huge animal tremble under my touch, its pupils nearly disappearing behind its upper lids as it tried to fix them on the hand that was tracing the curve of its frill down toward the horns that began just above its eyes. I brought my hand down the length of its snout, holding it out so that it could smell me. It seemed to understand because I could see its nostrils flare and there was a sound of air whistling by. Its eyes were back on mine as it raised its head acknowledging that I was not its enemy. It emitted two short grunts of surprisingly high pitch for such a big animal, and the rest of its family lumbered over.

They gathered in close and I was caught in a moment of panic as four pairs of horns bobbed and weaved within inches of my fragile human form. Like eight rapiers, they seemed to thrust and parry, coming from all directions, threatening to skewer me at any moment. But they seemed to sense my vulnerability, never getting too close with the tips of the horns, never moving so quickly that I couldn't avoid them.

I stepped around the two giants and patted the dust-covered flank of one of the adolescents. It seemed to enjoy the attention, nuzzling in close against me, nearly knocking me off my feet. They were probably little more than a year or two old, but already weighed more than the family car. Their skin was already tough and thick, but without the heavy creases of the adults, without the little sprouts of fine hair across the body. The pebbly finish was much less course, kind of like that of a football, but not nearly as uniform. Like the adult animals, the coloring was tan, but up close I could see that it was a few shades darker than the adults, as if the sun would fade them as they aged.

One of them had an unusual, hand-shaped mark on its flank, a thumb and three fingers, not four. Like a cartoon character had dipped its hand in maroon paint and gave the little dinosaur a pat on the side. It was probably a birthmark. Hell, if humans can have them why not dinosaurs? It made the little one distinctive, special.

After that first encounter, the fear had left their eyes, and they no longer trembled beneath my touch. They no longer backed away as I approached. Rather, they came toward me when they saw me coming. Although the adults watched me closely during those first few days, they learned to relax in my presence, even wandering off for short periods, leaving the small ones in my care. I felt almost like a babysitter, which was fine by me. I *wanted* to protect them.

But a month later, it was they who would protect me.

*****

This time it was me who was shaking as I slid in between the two little dinosaurs, the roughness of their hide making scraping noises against the encrusted material of my jacket. The heat coming off the two bodies warmed me within minutes. I could hear their hearts beating, slowly, twenty, twenty-five beats per minute. Their breathing was slow and steady—they were sleeping.

I fell asleep as well, quickly, feeling like an unborn baby, safe and warm—protected in the womb of its mother. But I had fallen asleep too quickly, hadn't really thought about the predicament that I had put myself into.

I awoke when I couldn't breathe.

I was nearly petrified with fear. If there's anything more terrifying than not being able to breathe, I couldn't think of it. It has a panic all of its own. It gets into your head quickly, like a dream, but unlike a dream, it's not so quick to leave, feeding upon itself, getting stronger, more terrifying with each successive attempt at a breath.

I opened my mouth wide, as if that would do any good. It felt like steel bands were wrapped tightly around my chest, locking the muscles, keeping them from expanding, keeping the bellows from working. All I could think about was the weight pressing against my chest, my next breath. I tried to calm the panic, to take tiny, shallow breaths, if that was all that I could muster.

It had been the warmth that I was after when I snuggled down between the two infants. And it was warmth that I found, but I had found something else, as well.

I remembered hearing the twin heartbeats, my body rocking gently to the rhythm of their breathing. Like a tiny ship on the sea, my body rolled gently to and fro to the caress of the waves. It was soothing, comforting. I had drifted off that way, settling deeper between the two small dinosaurs as I sunk ever deeper into a mindless sleep.

During the night one, or both, of the infants moved, found new, more comfortable positions, separating themselves just far enough for me to slip through the space between them. It must have happened gradually because I didn't feel it, didn't wake up when I hit the ground. The pair shifted once more and I was pinned beneath. The warmth, the gentle swaying kept me content and peaceful until I had nearly suffocated.

I was still alive, but in serious trouble and no idea how to get out. I forced myself to concentrate on the problem at hand.

The ground was at my back. I could feel it pressed hard against my shoulder blades and tailbone—solid, unyielding. The front of my shoulders were pinned by the dual masses of the *Triceratops*, not nearly so solid, but every bit as unyielding. The weight forced my arms painfully to my sides, my hands prickly from sleep, my feet the same. My knees ached from being squeezed together, as if in a vise. I could feel the rough skin of one of the two against my cheek, pressing the stubble of my beard into the filthy skin beneath. It tore at me like sandpaper as I forced my jaws apart, desperate to get some air.

I yelled, but my compressed lungs only allowed for a pitiful wheeze, which turned quickly to a strangled cough, dispelling little bursts of air that I could ill-afford to lose. They made a hollow sound that was quickly gobbled up by the compact space of my tiny hide-covered prison.

I tried rolling my shoulders, successful in moving perhaps an inch—no more. My arms fared no better, but I could move my hands, clenching and unclenching my fists to get the blood moving. I slid one hand along the curve of my thigh, not looking for anything in particular, just trying to establish the perimeters of my confinement.

As my hands roamed aimlessly, I strained to raise my head, successful only in tuning it a few degrees. But it was enough to see a small crescent of black sky above, a handful of stars twinkling in what must have been a clear night. The tiny passageway meant that there was air, and plenty of it—a never-ending supply of it—a whole world of it that hadn't yet been used up by six billion oxygen-sucking people—air that was fresh and clean and sweet. And yet it did me little good with a few tons of animal setting on my chest, paralyzing the muscles necessary to pull it in. The panic began to resurface as I thought again about the little boy stuck in the drainpipe. My worst fear realized not once, but twice.

I feared that I was about to die—not from a lack of oxygen, but from pure, unadulterated terror—when my roving hand struck something hard. It was the haft of my hunting knife. I had forgotten that I had it. It was strapped to my waist, just where I had put it when I had returned to my tidy little stash three days before.

Last night I was freezing. Now, I was sweating—partly from the heat generated by the huge foursome—mostly from fear. Sweat stung my eyes, and my hands shook as I fumbled with the snap that held the knife handle close to the sheath. From shoulder to elbow, my arm was useless, pinned so tightly against the side of the dinosaur that I was surprised that there was any life left at all in my hand. But there was, and with tingling, clumsy fingers, I eventually popped the snap and managed to slide the knife from its scabbard.

I had no intention of harming the young dinosaurs. My only objective was to get their attention, to get one of them to move, to free me from my confinement. I had almost no room to maneuver. It took several minutes, all my concentration, to get an overhand grip on the knife.

The blade was ten inches long and wickedly sharp, its edge finely honed from hour after hour of polishing against a whetstone. But I had no leverage, no strength to push even the tip past the thick, tough skin of the *Triceratops*. Rather than trying to push the knife in, I wedged the end of the handle into my thigh and twisted my wrist back and forth the few degrees that I could move, hoping to make a shallow incision. I continued to work at the small cut until it became aggravating enough for the slumbering dinosaur to notice. If nothing else, perhaps I could tickle it until it moved.

I worked away for several minutes—sweat pouring from every pore, my breath a strangled little wheeze that felt like I was sucking air the consistency of heavyweight motor oil.

At some point the tip of the knife must have penetrated at least the outer layer of skin because I felt a warm, slick substance run between my fingers, threatening my grip on the knife. But the little dinosaur was either impervious to pain, or it was so deep in slumber, that it was going to take a hell of a lot more than my puny knife and faltering strength to wake it.

More minutes passed and I was running out of whatever little bit of steam was left. It was all that I could do to just hold on to the knife, no longer twisting the blade, but just pushing and releasing, pushing and releasing, anything to work deeper into the sore that I had started.

Stars began to sparkle in front of my eyes. Not the ones in the sky, but the ones in my mind, the ones caused by lack of oxygen, spurred on by pain and terror. When I was about to succumb to it, the small *Triceratops* let out a grunt, and for one second, maybe two, I felt the weight that was pressing against one side suddenly gone. I felt a wonderful rush of cold air hit me, and I had time for a single deep breath, before the weight came crashing back down on top of me.

It knocked from me the one good breath that I had taken in for what seemed like an eternity, and the mass of the beast seemed to double, aided by the velocity of its fall. The weight numbed me as it rolled over my left side, the stars now exploding into a super nova.

At the same instant the dinosaur let out a roar, and all hell broke loose.

The scream of the animal had awakened the other three and no doubt every other living thing within earshot. The second twin rolled away from me, freeing my right arm and leg, and at the same time, the first one, the one that I had been whittling away on, tried to rise, only to roll back over on me, sending a new wave of pain and panic. Both of the infants were now wailing, and beyond the noise I could hear the grunts and snorts of the two adults as they rose from the pile.

The twin rolled over my left side repeatedly as it struggled to rise. A harder object of even a tenth the weight would have pulverized the frail bones of my body as it continued to roll on top of me in its unsuccessful attempt to get to its feet. But this was an animal, and despite its size and mass, was covered with hundreds of pounds of fat and muscle—tissue that was elastic, resilient. It hurt and it numbed, but it didn't kill.

Their feet, on the other hand, would. I could feel the ground tremble as the three dinosaurs stomped around in an impossibly small area surrounding me, could taste the dust being stirred up as they stumbled about in half-asleep fear and confusion.

The three were afraid, but they didn't know why. They were simply reacting to the frightened howling of the fourth, startled by having been wakened from a sound sleep, confused and afraid.

One wrong step, from any of them, even junior, and I'd be crushed to dust, with the ease and equanimity of which I would mash an ant underfoot while taking a casual stroll around the neighborhood. I rolled into the dinosaur that had me pinned, dodging the huge, hard feet of the others, feeling them brush against my backside, bump into my legs.

The dinosaur's next attempt to rise released me momentarily, and I rolled away from it and tucked myself into a tight little ball, trying to make myself as small as possible. With my eyes squeezed shut, I waited for the giants to step on me or at least kick me. I imagined myself bouncing and rolling across the path, bumping into one dinosaur after the next, like a game of dinosaur soccer. But nothing happened. I opened my eyes seeing the dust just begin to settle, the three upright dinosaurs forming a little circle around the small one that was still struggling to right itself, while continuing to bleat out a mournful howl.

I got to my knees, taking in huge gulps of the cold air, setting off another round of painful coughing. My left arm and leg began to throb and ache as the blood flow returned. I began to shiver as the cold air cooled my sweat soaked body. My head was pounding and the pain in my right foot started up again, as I struggled to stand.

I limped over to the group. The two adults had begun to nudge the prostrate animal, confused and fearful over its inability to rise. The other youngster, the one with the port wine handprint, began its own howl in sympathy with its twin. I placed my hand on the belly of the one still down, feeling it shudder with each breath, breath that was much too rapid. It was still dark, so I got back down on the ground alongside it to get a better look. I spotted the problem immediately. The handle of the knife was protruding from the abdomen of the dinosaur. The blade was buried right up to its hilt—all ten inches of it. Blood was tricking down the animal's side and forming a small pool beneath it.

I didn't know if the wound was mortal. To a human, the ten-inch long, two-inch wide blade would have killed no matter where it had penetrated. To an animal the size of one of the *adult Triceratops*, the knife, unless it had severed an artery, would have probably been little more than a flesh wound, felt hardly worse than a pinprick. But this animal was little more than a baby.

The other three dinosaurs didn't know what was wrong with the little one, didn't have any idea what the knife was or how it was related to the current situation, even if they had seen it. And they sure as hell didn't know how it had gotten there.

I had done it.

Not on purpose of course, but I had caused it nonetheless. I had apparently aggravated the little wound to the point where the dinosaur had felt something and had shifted its position—not tried to rise, but just to find a more comfortable place to sleep. As it settled back in, it settled into the knife. The knife slid in easily, and would have gone in more than a mere ten inches had the haft not prevented it. The dinosaur's considerable weight had done easily what my lack of position and strength could accomplish on its own.

The two parent dinosaurs came over to me, sniffed at the knife, not recognizing it at all, but familiar with the scent of the blood leaking from the wound in their baby. I thought that perhaps they would attack me, somehow associating me with the knife, blaming me. But they only looked at me with those big black eyes, a look of fear and confusion in them.

I didn't know what to do. I was afraid to pull the knife out, more afraid to just leave it, knowing that the sharp edge and point would continue to do more damage whenever the animal moved.

Forgetting about the cold, I pulled off my jacket and my shirt. The two larger *Triceratops* tilted their heads with an inquisitive look as if I had just peeled off a layer of my own skin, which I would have gladly done if I could get their little one patched up and moving again. I ripped one of the sleeves from the shirt, the stitches parting easily, from rot and filth. I had bathed neither myself nor my shirt in well over a month. I was surprised that the sleeve didn't just fall off of its own accord.

I folded the sleeve into a thick pad and pressed it up against the wound as I slid the knife out of its thick flesh. Blood followed the blade. It gushed out in frightening quantities, instantly soaking the hand that now held the knife. I slid it back into its sheath, hiding its business end, its lethal side, from the eyes of the others—getting rid of the incriminating evidence. At the same time I pressed the pad hard against the weeping puncture in the side of the tiny *Triceratops*. Within seconds, the pad was soaked through, the blood running freely down my bare arm. It was warm—hot actually, against the cool skin of my own flesh, and the copper smell of blood was mixed with another odor, one that was as pungent as it was terrifying.

I had struck something vital—its stomach or liver—perhaps its intestines. With my fingers, I examined the wound. It was longer than the two-inch width of my blade, wider by twice at least. The blade must have slashed through the tough skin when the handle hit the ground, forcing it sideways, cutting a wide path through the softer muscles and organs, veins and blood vessels.

The animal had resigned itself to its fate. It no longer tried to rise to its feet. Instead, it simply rested its pointed jaw against the ground and closed its eyes. Its breathing was shallower with every breath. Its heartbeat grew more faint and more widely spaced, each one sending fresh rivulets of blood through the hole. My feeble bandage couldn't hold it back. I could do nothing but sit there, useless, and watch as the life drained from the baby animal.

The other three watched in stunned silence until I got to my feet and took several steps away. The smaller of the two adults, what I assumed to be the female—the mother of the twins, walked cautiously over to her baby and nudged its small frill with the tip of its nasal horn. The baby responded with a single shuddered breath and was still.

I watched the blood flowing from the hole become a trickle as the rising and falling of its abdomen slowed to a halt.

CHAPTER 22

If I had had any doubts about dinosaurs being loving, nurturing parents, about how they had evolved to at least the same level of many modern day species, I lost them on that morning.

With the death of the young *Triceratops*, mourning and anguish began. The mother wailed in long sustained howls that vibrated across the path, waking the few dinosaurs that had not already been alerted to the tragedy. She raised her head high into the air, her crest splayed hard across her back, and emitted a sound such that I had never heard before … or since. It was a sound that had no comparison in the modern world. It was the most frightening sound that I had ever heard. It was the sound of pain and sorrow—the sound of a mother that had lost a child.

It went on long after the sun had risen over the top edge of the cliffs, long after the other dinosaurs had recommenced their southern trek along the path, long after the last drop of blood had dripped from the dead baby's belly. It went on for hours, the sound filling the valley until the mother's voice was only a raspy groan, and then little more than a stuttering hiss.

The other two: the adult and the other infant, made not a sound during that whole time. They stood motionless, perhaps knowing that there was nothing that they could add to change what had happened or to ease the anguish of the female. Or perhaps they were just dumb animals that hadn't a clue as to what had happened, or understood the reason for the female's cries. Perhaps. But I didn't think so then, I don't think that way now, more than three years later. A mother had lost a child. Was there anything in the world more painful, more sorrowful?

No, no way!

These were not dumb, unfeeling animals—at least not the ones here in the valley—the gentle herbivores. These were animals that had survived, prospered, and had grown intellectually over the millions of years of their existence. I really believed that their intelligence was superior to any kind of animal, short of Homo sapiens, that existed in what had become the twenty-first century in my old life. *None* of the animals were quite what I had expected.

During the long, drawn out mourning period of the immediate family, the other dinosaurs paraded by. None of them were indifferent. Many of them actually stopped, pausing momentarily before the body of the dead infant, not praying the way the humans tended to, but bending their heads low, sniffing at the cadaver. They were probably just curious, smelling a dead body, seeing what kind of unique aroma it emitted, filing it away for future reference. But I thought that it was more a sign of respect, even if they didn't fully understand it.

None of them passed by without taking note. Some walked on without breaking stride, unwilling to stop, perhaps afraid of having the same them happening to them, terrified of tempting fate. But each of them turned to look at the body, to stare at the little family holding vigil. Some just looked on with sadness in their eyes, while others seem to nod their heads, imperceptibly if you didn't look closely, undeniably if you did.

The whole scene was just way too human. It reminded me of Elizabeth's funeral. The day-long parade of mourners passing by her casket, some stopping to pray over her lifeless body, others passing by with only the requisite glance, moving on quickly so as not to catch anything fatal. All the while, I stood about feeling utterly alone despite being surrounded by hundreds of my fellow human beings—alone, lonely, and confused. I didn't understand Elizabeth's death any more than these three understood the death of one of their own.

It was just about the time that the last of them passed by when the mother *Triceratops* ceased her crying, having lost her voice, if not her grief. She simply turned and began walking southward along the path. The remaining two followed her, staying just a few paces behind. Instinctively, they knew that she needed time to grieve ... alone.

I stood there alone as well, my head hanging down, staring down but not seeing the dirt at my feet. When I looked up I half expected to see Elizabeth's silver casket in front of me instead of the body of the small dinosaur. Other than the lack of rain, I felt just as I had on the day that I buried her. Once again I felt that I was to blame. This time I actually *was* to blame.

I wished that I could take back what I had done. If I had just left the goddamn knife in its sheath, the young *Triceratops* would still be alive, playfully bounding down the path alongside its twin and its parents. But then again, would *I*? I thought hard about what I could have done differently, but came up with nothing short of just staying put, waiting until they awoke on their own and moved from atop me. But had I done that, it would be me lying dead on the path and not the young animal.

With my head hanging low, I took up my spot at the back of the herd and headed toward home.

I hadn't been walking for more than an hour, feeling pretty sorry for myself, even more so for the little family walking morosely just fifty yards in front of me, when I detected an unpleasant odor in the air.

Being at the back of the herd meant that I was walking in their wake … and their waste. I had to constantly dodge their piles, sidestep their puddles. It was everywhere, but I had pretty much become oblivious to the smell. It was no longer objectionable, or even noticeable by that time.

But it was another smell that I was detecting, something that was strong enough, bad enough, to overwhelm that of rivers of urine and mountains of feces. It was an odor that I had smelled before.

The overpowering smell of rotting vegetation sent a cold chill from the back of my neck clear down to my toes, causing an icy-cold shiver to rattle my chest. I kicked myself in the ass for forgetting.

During the trip north, I had been alerted to a change when the path left the riverbank. I wondered at the change in the path's direction, about why it had suddenly veered off away from the water. At the time it hadn't made sense. I knew that dinosaurs had traveled the path even before I had discovered the valley within the valley. I had seen them from the top of the cliff on that first day, and had seen them dozens of times from my perch atop the tree. I knew that the dinosaurs, being warm-blooded, needed to drink in order to keep their systems operable, like a car needed coolant, both from overheating and from freezing up. The path was created from millions of animals making their way from north to south for millions of years. Why should they veer from the side of the path where water was plentiful? Why they did it had become painfully apparent damn quickly on that trip northward. It was the smell that first told me that something wasn't right. And it was only minutes later that the giant crocks climbed from the swamp and attacked the little family of hadrosaurs.

But I had forgotten that the path ran alongside the river, just around the bend, and that just this side of that bend was the swamp where the crocks lived. Moving southward, mile after mile, jungle on either side, I wasn't attuned to any change. And in the misery of the morning's events and the numbness that had overwhelmed my body and my soul, I wasn't looking for trouble. I wasn't looking for anything.

Despite my battered and bruised body, and forgetting the pain in my feet, I broke into a lopsided run, my eyes shifting back and forth between the edge of the jungle on my left and the herd growing larger directly in front of me. They were moving slowly, spread out for more than a mile along the path, but I could see that the smell had gotten their attention as well. They seemed nervous: their heads bobbing with little stuttering moves from left to right and then back again, their nostrils flaring as they sniffed at the air.

I had made it into the herd, deep into the middle of the pack, when the giant crocodiles attacked. I couldn't see them, but there was no mistaking the surprise and terror in the voices of a thousand dinosaurs. The massacre began at the front of the herd and in a matter of seconds, the panic spread all the way to the rear, causing the animals to stampede directly into the waiting carnivores.

It was chaos as hundreds of animals, some the size of dump trucks, ran past me, around me, and over me, in a blind frenzy. These were the larger but slower animals, and yet it was all I could do to stay out from in front or underneath them. Within seconds the dust and dirt of the path rose high into the air, suspended by the air currents as the huge beasts raced by. I was blinded by it, nearly suffocated by it. I could do nothing other than go with the flow. With one hand covering my mouth and my eyes narrowed to mere slits, I ran into the retreating herd.

I was no match for them. Even the slowest of the dinosaurs when they were running for their lives ran considerably faster than I did. I could feel them thundering by, feel the wind pass over me from back to front. But I ran on, blindly for several minutes, the roar of the dinosaurs' terror growing louder, more panicked with each second, when some unknown behemoth grazed my side, sending me sprawling into the dirt.

I lay there unmoving as the last of the dinosaurs passed by leaving me somehow, miraculously, untouched. I struggled to my feet, watching the cloud of dust solidify in a widespread area a quarter of a mile ahead. Holding my shotgun out in front, I marched toward it.

The thundering sound of the fleeing herd grew more faint as the lucky ones raced ahead of the killing ground, and was replaced by the sounds of massive carnage. It was the sound of what great battles must have been like before the advent of guns and powder. When men fought with knives and swords, and battleaxes … and with their bare hands: the sounds of pain and suffering, of fear and anger, overriding the noise of the weapons that caused them. But this was worse. The noise was borne of sheer terror and agony, as the battle was decisively one-sided. The gentle dinosaurs, even the horned and armored ones, were no match for the huge, aggressive predators.

As the dust began to settle, I could see that there were at least ten crocks and more than that number of dinosaurs, some dead, the others dying. Most were hadrosaurs, having been the faster animals thus at the head of the herd when the surprise attack commenced. They were fast but not fast enough to avoid the quick reactions of the crocks coming out of the dense jungle.

Blood soaked the ground and sprayed high into the air as the crocodiles lunged and ripped at the flesh and muscle of the dinosaurs. Within seconds, the last of them were down, their cries snuffed out as their limbs were ripped from their bodies. The only sounds left were those of the crocodiles—the wet, sloppy noise of meat-eaters at work.

But it was something else that had caught my eye, stopped me in my tracks. Standing between the massacre and me, cut off from the rest of the herd, was the little family of *Triceratops*. It seemed impossible, but they appeared to be oblivious to what was going on right in front of them. They continued their slow, shuffling stroll, heads down, right into the fray. I couldn't believe that they didn't see what was going on not two hundred yards in front of them, even harder to believe that they failed to hear the awful shrieks of the other animals as they were attacked, the sickening sounds of their fellow creatures being consumed. The mother seemed to be leading what was left of her family to a sure death.

Running toward them just as fast as I could, I fired the shotgun into the air. The two at the rear halted, their heads still lowered, surprised, but confused. The mother marched on, now a mere hundred yards away from the giant crocodiles. I ran on, easily catching up to her slow gait. I ran in front of her, veering off to the right, sure that she would follow me. I was wrong. She just kept plodding along, now no more than fifty yards from the ten killers. I heard renewed aggression from the pack of crocodiles and looked in their direction. Two of the giants were fighting over the remains of one of the *Pachycephalosaurs*, as vicious with one another as they were with their prey. With near lightning speed, it was over, the one receiving a painful but not fatal bite to a rear leg. The vanquished one moved away from the pack, turning in our direction, spotting us instantly and starting for us, quickly but with a noticeable limp. I ran toward it until I was equal distance between it and the *Triceratops* and went down on one knee. I raised the shotgun and waited. I could hear the heavy footsteps approach from behind, knowing it wouldn't stop, as I watched the angered and wounded crocodile race toward me. I saw clearly what I had to do, but I didn't know if I could get it done before being crushed by the huge, catatonic *Triceratops*. I waited until the last possible second, when the crock was just a few feet away and it had opened its jaws wide to take me. I fired into its gaping maw, a portion of its head disintegrating in a cloud of red. The *Triceratops* stopped in its tracks, inches from me. I could feel its hot breath on the back of my neck.

I didn't know if it was the shotgun blast that stopped it. I doubted it. I think that in that one moment, that one split-second, before the crock took me out, the mother *Triceratops* realized that the other twin, the last of her babies, was in jeopardy.

She seemed confused, tuning her head from side to side in a quick motion, as if just waking up, trying to shake away the last of a bad dream. I went to her, grabbing on to her nasal horn, stopping the side-to-side motion. She could have easily sent me flying, but she didn't. Instead, she lowered her head once more and I looked deep into those sad eyes. I stroked the area above her nasal horn, talking to her in soft, soothing tones, like one would when comforting a child. It seemed to calm her.

I hadn't forgotten the scene that was still being played out just fifty yards up the path. The giant crocodiles were single-minded in their pursuit of filling their bellies, their attention totally on the bloody flesh before them. But I didn't expect them to simply crawl back into the swamp when they were done. Full stomachs or not, if they saw us they would be on us. They were the predators and we were the prey. They wouldn't pass up the opportunity. Its what they lived for.

I walked away from the dinosaur toward the jungle on the opposite side of the path. Now that I had her attention, I thought that she would follow me as she had on countless occasions in the valley. Although I knew that the spell was broken and she was back with us, she still wasn't following. She just stood there, alternating a look between the crocks and me, unsure of what to do. At five tons, I knew that she wasn't going anyplace that she didn't want to go, but I had to get them out of there. Hell, I had to get *me* out of there.

By then the two other *Triceratops* had rejoined us, both of them waiting for the female to retake the lead. Seeing that she couldn't decide what to do, I took the initiative, one that could have gotten me killed if the momma didn't comprehend my intentions. I still wasn't all that sure that she didn't understand my role in the death of the infant.

I went over to the little one, grabbed the side of its frill, and pulled with all my might until I forced it to turn ninety-degrees, facing the far side of the path. Before it could turn back, I raced around behind it and, as hard as I could, slapped it across the rump. My open palm against its young, but tough hide made a resounding crack, but it hurt my hand a hell of a lot more than it did the backside of the animal.

The little one began to move, tentatively at first, but definitely heading in the direction that I had intended. I ran out in front, giving it a target to follow, leading it away from the feeding crocodiles. The male followed closely. The female was still undecided, swinging her massive head in a wide arc between the scene of the bloody massacre and her retreating baby. It bothered me that she seemed to fear me as much as the ten meat-eating giants at the edge of the swamp. Did she really see me as an equal risk, as big a danger?

She understood the knife. That had to be it. She knew that it was mine, and somehow, although surely not fully understanding it, knew that I was to blame for the death of her child.

Not that it made me feel any better, but her fear worked to my advantage. I had made it across the path, close to the edge of the jungle, the baby close on my heels, when she began moving toward us—first, in slow, cautious steps, picking up speed as the remaining three of us turned southward following the western edge of the path. By the time the female had halved the distance from us she was in a full run: rapid, short little steps on stubby legs that would have almost looked comical if they weren't propelling an enraged ten thousand pound mother intent on crushing me underneath.

When I realized that she wasn't running just to catch up, but rather was coming after me, settling the score, so to speak, I dove into the bushes, and scurried away like some giant rodent. On all fours, I crawled a hundred feet into the dense underbrush. Peering from behind the trunk of a giant conifer, I could see the female *Triceratops* halted at the edge of the brush, looking through the dark foliage, trying to find me. She was breathing hard, snorting her anger and contempt for me loudly through her nostrils, but she refused to step into the dark, foreboding place. Her hearing and sense of smell was acute, but I knew that she couldn't see worth a damn. No way could she see me hidden away in the shadows from that distance.

I think that at some level she knew that there was still danger lurking close by, not from me, but from the crocks that could still be faintly heard feasting on their dinosaur dinners. Giving up on me quickly, probably figuring that I was long gone, she turned with a final snort, and headed up the path.

If I was smart, I *should* have been long gone, but I had to see this thing through, make sure that the small family that I had made smaller by one, made it back to the relative safety of the herd. Besides, with my severe lack of any sense of direction, I knew that I'd be lost within ten minutes of deviating from the path.

I counted to a hundred and then retraced my steps back to the edge of the path to see the three dinosaurs rounding a curve a couple of hundred yards ahead. It seemed longer, but it had only been a few short minutes since we had left the scene of the carnage. The crocodiles were still there, their actions slowed by sated stomachs, yet still dangerous and all too close. I left the camouflage of the jungle, it being too dense to traverse quickly and safely, and stepped out onto the path. Staying close to the edge of the jungle, stooped down in a low crouch, moving silently, I followed the retreating herd.

Throughout the day I stayed behind them, not too far, just far enough so I could leap into the protection of the jungle on short notice. They knew that I was there. Every hour or so they would halt and turn to glare at me—especially the female who continued to lead the small group. But she made no move to come after me, satisfied that I was staying far enough away to pose no threat.

We made the trip around the bend, to the point where the path rejoined the river, without further incident. There the dinosaurs' journey slowed, as their immediate need for water overshadowed the longer-term need to travel farther south. I was thirsty too, having drained the last of my water bottles earlier that morning. But I didn't stop, didn't dare approach the two adult *Triceratops* that guarded the path while the youngster drank from the river. Besides, I had but a few hours more to travel before I was home.

I slunk my way past the *Triceratops*, past the entire herd, staying close to the edge of the forest. The sun was just beginning to set beyond the western mountains. Its reflection turned the face of the cliffs across the river a bright golden hue, chasing away the shadows along the nearly flat face. Swaying gently against its surface, pulled at a slight angle by the gentle current of the river, was the rope.

I had made it home.

*****

The shadows were long, just as they were on that day three and a half years ago. But these shadows were comforting—necessary even. They sheltered me from the broiling sun and they signaled the end of another unbelievably hot day in what I hoped was the tail end of a long string of equally hot days.

All the experts said that the climate of the Cretaceous was moderate. It had been five years, and I was still waiting for moderate. I froze in the winter and baked in the summer. I saw snow, torrential rains, windstorms, sandstorms, and even hail. I was wondering what moderate meant. Moderate, as compared to what? I guess that it was moderate when compared to Chicago—Chicago, where people had central air-conditioning in the summer, forced-air heating in the winter. Chicago, where houses didn't tend to leak when the rains came, where roofs kept the hail from making little bumps on the noggin. I guess that it was moderate compared to that. But not to much else.

My fingers were stiff from pounding the keys all day. It had been too long and they weren't accustomed to working the computer hour after hour, from sunrise to sunset. I flexed them as I let the shade cool the sweat dripping from my forehead and from down beneath my armpits. I rose from the one and only chair that I had, one of those aluminum, folding jobs with the green and white webbing stretched across the back and the seat. Two of the webs had broken, green plaid ribbons dangling uselessly to the ground, swaying in the breeze. One more gone and I'd be sitting on the ground, the chair useless, as useless as the dust covered time machine behind me.

I turned to look at it. It sure as hell wasn't a time machine anymore. It wasn't going anywhere any more than I was. It wasn't even a machine any longer, even though I tended to still think of it in that way. It no longer qualified as one. It didn't do anything but sit there. And it wasn't much of a home anymore either, nor was it much of a storage container. It was just a nearly empty metallic, strangely shaped, porcupine looking husk. It held nothing but the fold-down bed and the nearly empty storage racks. There was food still. A couple of half-empty boxes of bland canned beef and pasta, a few bottles of spring water. A single book that I hadn't yet read, a half used first aid kit, and a couple of lonely pieces of firewood were all that was left. Everything else had been gone for years. This was the first time that I had been back.

I returned my gaze to the east. The sea was now so far away that I could hardly discern it from the horizon—a mile away, maybe more. I had taken the walk that morning, when it was still cool enough to take a long stroll. I hiked out to the water's edge, walked along a shore littered with small stones, worn smooth by millions of years of sea currents, thousands of fish remnants, and empty shells that once held the fleshy bodies of marine crustaceans that had long dried out from the summer sun.

I had walked into the south until my lungs began to burn from the exertion. It was no longer a barren, sandy beach. Bits of green growth popped up from dark soil in stray patches close to the edge of the cliff. The farther that I traveled, the more the vegetation covered the ground. I turned back when my breath came up short in my chest, when the foliage had become thick enough so it was difficult to traverse.

It seemed strange to see green where once there had only been dull shades of browns and yellows, things growing from an area that was completely under water a few short years ago. I wondered where the plants came from, how they got their start. Perhaps the currents of the inland sea had carried the seed here, although I wondered if seed could survive the salty brine. Then again, I could no longer see far enough south to where the water came right up to the edge of the cliffs. Perhaps it didn't. Perhaps, there was now a direct connection to another forest around the bend, on the other side of the cliffs.

Looking closely, I could see that there were more than just low-lying foliage—ferns, junipers, and the like. There were tiny leaf-bearing trees—elms, oaks, and maples. And there were the beginnings of sparse, long-stemmed grasses, something that I hadn't seen in the valley before then. This would one day be a forest—not a jungle. The world was changing—evolving.

I looked out from the entrance to the cave wondering what I was doing back here again after all this time. Of course I knew. I knew—it's just that I didn't want to be here. This was no longer my home. My home was in the valley, in the tree, year round. There was nothing for me here on the beach. The scenery was monotonous. Measuring the change in the shoreline no longer held any interest for me. The emptiness and darkness of the cave only depressed me. I was tired—literally—of making the arduous, yet boring trip back and forth—from the tree to the cave—from the cave to the tree—every trip the same. There was little danger, or even excitement to it. I knew what was over every hill, around every ridge, behind every rock. Every trip was faster, made so by familiarity, yet seemed longer. Each trip all I could think about was how many more times I would have to do it before it was done.

And I had made a lot of them leading up to the last time that I was here—an entire summer full of them. Two days to make the trip up the cliff, around the mountains, and down the ridge to the machine—another day to load up supplies, eat, and rest—three more days to make the return trip to the tree. Hours of setting and resetting the pulley system, using every muscle to pull the fully-laden cart up the long ridge, using them again to ease it down the mountain of gravel.

I lost track of the days, of how many times I made the back and forth trek. One day blurred into the next as the sun toasted me to the color of fine walnut. Half the time I had to check whether the cart was empty or full in order to figure out if I was coming or going. There were times when I cursed Dermot for packing so much, times when I thought that I would just give up, satisfied to just leave the rest, to make do with whatever the valley could provide.

Three or four days back in the tree was usually enough to change my mind. Rested and well fed, I would think about all the things that the supplies provided, much of which was still back in the machine. If the hunting went poorly on that day, I didn't go hungry. The supplies provided that. If I was sick or sore from too much physical activity, or had a terribly upset stomach from eating something a little too strange and exotic, I had medicine. The supplies provided *that*. And at the end of a long day and I wanted to relax in the comfort of the tree, I had books and even a deck of cards. The supplies provided for that, *too*.

But no matter how many supplies I transferred across the mountains, down the cliff, and across the river, they were exhaustible. At some point, they would run out. So, as long as there was more in the machine, I would go back. If I wanted to stay away from the cave in the future, I had to get it all.

But ... there *was* the computer. It was back in the machine, where it would have to stay. It's the one thing that had to stay, even though I was sick of it. I was tired of dredging up the past when all I wanted to do was live in the present, to see what the future held.

I wasn't only tired of it. I had become somewhat possessive of my story, as well, and bitter about recording it. Not so much the physical act of writing it, or the time I spent in doing it, but rather the fact that I should share with others what I had given my life for. I *had* given up everything—even the chance of anything. I would see no old friends, or make new ones. I would never eat ice cream or a hot dog, never watch a ballgame or listen to the symphony. I would never again walk down to the corner pub for a draft, would never taste the dry, bitter taste of a fine old scotch (mine was long since gone), would never again wake to the smell of fresh brewed coffee in the morning. And I would never again feel the touch of a woman, smell the perfume in the nape of a feminine neck, or make love in the morning as the first rays of sun peeked through the half-open blinds on a Sunday morning.

I would never again do any of these things ... or a million others. And yet here I was spending precious moments, time that I knew was becoming all too short, writing for some reason that I could no longer understand, or barely remember. I sure as hell wasn't doing it for me. I didn't need to write about it, or read about it. I was living it.

Oh, the reason that I began this story was simple enough, and it made sense at the time. I was a paleontologist. Digging around old riverbeds and carving out the sides of old cliffs was just part of my job. Writing about them was the other.

I was a scientist, and being a scientist meant dealing with empirical evidence. But less than half of what I had written as a scientist was fact. The rest was speculation, theorizing, proposing, postulating, idealizing, romanticizing, and just plain guessing. Taking a SWAG, as we liked to call it—a Scientific Wild Ass Guess. Facts were boring, even when dealing with the remains of animals that had been extinct for millions of years. Even when digging up a partial skeleton of a species of a dinosaur that had never been seen before. Facts were only interesting to other paleontologists and a few eggheads who liked to wear their calculators on their belts and keep their colored pens and screwdrivers in little plastic pocket protectors.

For those who were strictly field men, paleontologists who did little but dig, facts were okay, facts were good, it's what distinguished a good scientist from a bad one. And it's how they got their next project funded. It's how they made their livings.

For those of us who ran a museum, or a piece of one, those of us who relied on the excitement (thus funding of the public) were, however, under a different set of rules and expectations. Facts were not nearly as important as speculation. The public liked a good story, a bit of fantasy, a little embellishment, and some terror thrown in for good measure. The public liked a good scare. It's why horror books were so popular, why authors like Stephen King, Dean Koontz, and Clive Barker were millionaires many times over.

The public didn't want to see a few chipped and broken bones stuck on a plaque on the wall with a couple of paragraphs about where they were found, how old they were, and what species they belonged to. They wanted to see whole, fully assembled, sixty-foot monsters with rows of dagger-like teeth, posed ready to pounce—killers. This is what they were after. It's why they paid their ten dollars a head to enter the museum. It's what funded the next dig.

And it's why I proposed theories, assembled full skeletons from little bits of bones, and speculated about what the dinosaurs looked like, their habits, their life and their death. It's why I made SWAGs, and it's why I wrote.

The past five years, I lived in the late Cretaceous, among the dinosaurs. I saw things, both good and bad, comical and horrifying, painfully sad and wonderfully joyous. All of it went way beyond anything that I could have imagined. And they were all real. I didn't have to speculate or embellish. I didn't have to make SWAGs. I could rely one hundred percent on observations—on facts.

At first it was exciting to write the truth. It was even more exciting than the best of fiction writers could conjure up. I couldn't wait to get it all down on paper, knowing that someone, somewhere, sometime, would read it and know that it was the truth. The truth would answer so many questions, solve so many riddles, and complete so many puzzles. More than just the dinosaurs, I would tell them about the weather conditions, the flora and fauna, the topography, the marine life, the Intercontinental Sea, the butterflies and the beetles—everything. I was happy to do it ... at first.

Over time, the writing became a chore, not a joy. It was one more hardship in a life that had already become too hard. The computer was in the machine, and the machine was in the cave, and the cave was on the beach. And I couldn't move any of them. I laughed at the notion that it was a *portable* computer. It was as firmly tied to the machine and thus to the beach as if it had grown iron roots. If I moved it from the machine, I might as well have not used it at all—not have written a damn thing. The machine was the only thing that would be identifiable in Dermot's time. It's the only place where they could look.

But with each trip, with each chapter that I wrote, I felt as if I were giving up a little piece of myself, like little bits of me were jumping from my fingertips, entering through the keyboard, and onto the page with each letter that I typed. The computer was taking my soul, piece by piece, and bit by bit, leaving me a bitter, empty shell of a man.

I was fine in the valley, but here on the shore it got to me. My computer was a constant reminder of what I had left behind in the twenty-first century, a nagging memory of all that was gone. The story itself was worse. I was wrong to make a story of it. I would have been much better off sticking with data, perhaps a nice big spreadsheet full of facts and figures.

Making the trip to the cave, writing my story, served me no purpose. I had no doubt that someone else would find it useful. Someone else would profit from my story, but it sure as hell wouldn't be me.

If the computer was found seventy million years from now, and *if* my tale was still retrievable, and *if* someone actually believed it, it would be the biggest story of the century. Hell, not just the century, it would be the biggest story of the millennia. Not just this one, but the last one as well, perhaps the biggest story of all time. Someone would write a bestseller, someone else would offer the movie rights, and all over the world, in every museum, in every classroom, in the heads of every paleontologist, geologist, and historian, the real story would be told. The real story, according to Doctor David Williams.

I doubted that I would get the credit, but even if I did, what good would it do me. I was stuck here, and would never even know what had happened, what my work had accomplished. Someone else would reap the rewards—win the acclaim of others. Some would get rich. Others would get world recognition. Perhaps it would be Dermot. Surely, he would want his share, his research required funding, and even though he was a wealthy man, riches had their limits.

I would get nothing. Not that I longed for recognition, or riches, but it really got me that someone who didn't earn it would.

And as much as it pissed me off that someone else would benefit from my sacrifice, I was also getting pretty damn tired of making the trip. It was taking its toll. Every trip that I made to the cave cost me a week of my life. A life that I feared would be much too short, much more brief than it would have been in my own time.

Just trying to stay alive in this ancient land was using me up, accelerating my aging, shortening my life span. I paused to take stock of the physical changes that had occurred over the past five years. My body had made the most amazing metamorphosis. I had no scale, no way to weigh myself, yet I knew that I was a good fifty pounds lighter than when I first stepped into the machine. The huge slabs of muscle that I had worked so hard over the years to build were gone. Not that I wasn't still strong, still athletic, but now I looked like a runner, or an aerobics instructor, nothing like a world-class weight lifter. My body fat was even lower than it was during my years of training, every muscle standing out in stark contrast, dangerously low levels of fat covering them. My diet was healthy, but not fattening, eating mostly fresh fruits and vegetables ever since my first garden started producing.

It was something that Dermot hadn't considered, nor had I—my clothes. My calves and thighs had shrunk considerably, but my waist was still the same size, so my pants still fit pretty well, albeit a bit baggy. However, the thickness of my chest and width of my back and shoulders had decreased to the point that my shirts and jackets looked as if they were hanging from a scarecrow.

In the winter my emaciated condition proved to be an advantage. The extra room allowed me to dress in layers, comfortably, without binding me up like a mummy. And the summers were okay as well, being that I rarely dressed in anything but shorts, boots, and socks. When I really noted the change was when the weather turned from hot to cold, or vise versa. In the spring and in the fall, when I took to wearing a moderate level of clothing, I felt the difference. I was swimming in my clothing.

I didn't have anything as convenient as a full-length mirror, but every once in a while, when the winds were calm, and the river at the base of the cliff was still, I could see my reflection, and was surprised, if not shocked, by it.

Even the ripples that caused a distorted image in the water couldn't disguise the nasty scar on my left arm. It was a trough actually, long and wide and deep enough to fit my index finger into. At times it made me squeamish just to look at it. Squeamish, and always surprised that it had healed as well as it had. Probably it was the thought of how it had happened, rather than the ghastly scar itself that caused me to tremble and my stomach to tighten every time that I touched it.

It wasn't as good as new, would never be as strong as the other arm. It still throbbed on cold days, ached and burned when I used it a little too much. But all in all it still worked, remarkable considering the damage that the *raptor* had done, the added harm inflicted by the infection. Even after more than four years, the fingers of my left had tingled when I brushed against the scar.

But the arm was whole, even though a bit weaker and a tad deformed. I couldn't say the same for my right foot. It was short two toes.

I had paid a price for the trip to the bone pile. I had escaped with my life, amazing in itself considering what I had been through. But, the cold and the soggy conditions of my hiding spot on the night of the *Albertosaurs* had cost me.

By the time I had made it back to the safety of the tree, it had been days since I had removed my soggy, nearly frozen boots. The socks had to be peeled painfully from my feet, fungus and half healed-over blisters and torn calluses having melded with the fabric. The toes on the right foot were white, nearly translucent, and were numb to the touch. In the hours to follow, they began to turn black at the tips, and began to burn and throb with every movement, every heartbeat. They were frostbitten and gangrene had begun to set in. They had to be removed.

The book said that the gangrene would spread quickly if not halted. The only way to halt it was to excise it, remove the infected tissue, every cell of it. Dermot had the tools to do it. The book provided the knowledge. I just had to have the guts.

I knew that I shouldn't be drunk when I did it, but I also knew that I couldn't do it stone cold sober. One drink—one really big drink—just enough to steady my nerves, give me the courage.

I poured a big cup of scotch from the shrinking supply, while I boiled the instruments and read up on the procedure. It all came together at the same time. The water was bubbling and the scotch was gone as I closed the book, a little tipsy, more than a little scared, but ready to proceed.

I used way too much Zylocaine, anesthetizing most of my right foot, instead of just the two toes, and proceeded to carve out a patch of skin extending across the top of the little toe up to the first joint. From there, I extended the knife around the base of the knuckle across the underside, cutting deep, to the bone. Exchanging the scalpel for my hunting knife, I pressed down hard, severing the bone, separating both joints of the little toe.

I couldn't actually feel the pain, but my brain knew that it was there. The thought of it, and the blood, which poured from the severed appendage, made me swoon, the stars once again dancing before my eyes. I had to force myself back to full consciousness, couldn't just pass out and bleed to death. I stanched the blood with cotton gauze that I hoped was sufficiently sterilized with the steam of the boiling water. Taking a metal instrument from the fire, I touched its tip to the severed end of the veins from which the blood was flowing. As the blood slowed to a trickle, I pulled the flap of skin over the wound, and began to sew.

I repeated the process with the second toe. It was less severely damaged by the encroaching infection, but I took no chance. I removed it right up to the knuckle, just as I had the little toe. It was more difficult than the first. My hands shook, my vision was blurred by little jumping dots, and my stomach was clenching and unclenching, way past mere nervousness. But I got it done. The job was not neat, the stitching erratic. It was a job that would definitely not be the envy of even a third-rate surgeon.

I was proud that I didn't pass out from the loss of blood, even more so that I didn't keel over from pure fright. But I did pass out. An hour later, the last of my scotch was gone. With my foot covered with antiseptic, heavily bandaged, and the rest of me covered in blankets to fend off the massive chills that racked my body, I threw up rather violently, my head began to spin uncontrollably, and I went out like a light.

But now it was summer on the beach, hot enough to hardly believe I had once been so cold. I wore nothing but a thin pair of gym shorts. My feet were bare. I gazed down at them, wincing at the sight of my misshapen foot. It had healed well—no infections—no complications. But it still startled me when I looked at it, especially when it was lined up against the other one, which was still whole, unmarred. I was still getting used to walking with it. The pain was gone, as was most of the limp, but the loss of those two tiny, little toes sure threw the hell off my balance.

The toes weren't the only things that I had sacrificed during my trip to the valley within the valley. I had developed a frightening case of double pneumonia, as well. Back at the tree, a week of heavy antibiotic injections cleared it up, but it had left me with scarred lungs. I could feel it during heavy exertion, running short of breath long before I should have. It made the trips back and forth to the beach that much more difficult, having to stop so much more often to catch my breath. Things that I used to take for granted: chopping wood, long five-mile hikes along the river, climbing the rope ladder up the side of the cliff, even ascending the two flights to the upper deck in the tree—were so much harder now.

I may have looked like an athlete, like a marathon runner, but I sure as hell wasn't one—not any more.

The winter was the worst. The cold, damp air made my chest ache with the slightest effort. It had gotten a little better from the first winter to the next, and a little less better from the second to the third. Now they were about as good as they were going to get, which wasn't that good at all.

I had taken on a hermit-like existence—especially in the winter. I went for days at a time never leaving the little compound enclosed by the ring of pointed logs. I ate sparingly from my stores of preserved vegetables, an occasional bird or squirrel that found its way to my tree, always afraid of running out of food before spring. I spent most of my time sitting on the top deck in my recliner, bundled up in blankets against the cold, staring out across the meadow to the cliffs, wishing for the warmth of summer.

Even during the previous three summers, other than the trips to the shore, I rarely traveled more than a few hundred yards beyond the compound. And only then to gather nuts and berries and to hunt for small mammals to supplement my meager diet. I could say that I stayed close to home because my wounds were still mending, but I would be less than honest. The plain truth was that I had become terrified to wander very far.

I had only encountered two carnivorous species of dinosaurs, and on both occasions, they damn near killed me. And then there were the *Elasmosaurus*, the *Mantillis* and the giant crocodiles—almost dead—almost dead *again*—almost dead *yet* again. Even the herbivores damn near took me out. The *Triceratops* almost killed me—accidentally—and they were just about the gentlest creatures there ever were.

Even if you took the animals out of the equation, I was in nearly continuous trouble, never more than one wrong turn, just a few feet, one direction or another, from disaster. I had been trapped by a cave-in, nearly drowned, almost suffocated, half starved, and more or less frozen. I had taken more spills, falls, and tumbles than I could count—more bumps, bruises, cuts and scrapes than I cared to think about. I had been lost on so many occasions that I had become afraid of leaving the path along the river, scared of moving beyond the view of the second deck perched high in the tree.

I was afraid for myself, tired of being too close to death too often. But more than that, I was afraid for my story. I was terrified of not finishing what I started—afraid to leave it only half done. I had given up almost everything for it.

And all for what—so that I could validate Dermot's experiment—so that I could make someone else rich and famous for my story?

Well, nuts to that!

I was not going to dedicate what was left of my life to the advantage of someone else. I would not go making countless journeys to the beach, sacrificing my health and what was left of my life so that Dermot could fund his next grand adventure.

And I was tired of living my life in fear. I was the only human being in this entire world. I was smarter than all of them, if not bigger and fiercer, if not the product of this time. I was not natural to this place. I was an intruder. I didn't belong, wasn't someone who was meant to be here. But here I was, and here I was king—my intellect proclaimed it. It was time that

I started using it. It was time to quite being afraid. And it was time to stop worrying about my story.

If this is all there is, than it's enough. It's all the proof that Dermot needs to confirm that his infernal contraption works, all the evidence he needs that time travel is indeed possible. He'll never find my body, or what's left of it. It won't be in the machine. It will be somewhere miles away—perhaps in the tree, perhaps not. Either way, it will be no place that he will ever find it. And chances are, there will be nothing left to find.
But the computer will be here, tucked safely away in its sealed titanium case, behind the closed doors of its titanium cupboard, within the titanium skin of the machine. I had no doubt that it would still be here in another seventy million years. Titanium was durable, a hell of a lot more durable than flesh and blood.

As for all the scientists, well, there's enough here to write a thousand papers, fill in hundreds of blank spaces, answer infinite questions. There's enough here to begin all new theories, start a few more controversies and create endless discussion. Some will think it but a hoax. Dermot will convince a few that I actually went through time—that I actually arrived in the time of the dinosaurs. But that didn't mean that they would believe my story. Some would think it to be pure fabrication, playing a cruel joke on my fellow paleontologists, perhaps as a way to get back at those bureaucrats that had cost me my job.

If they believe me or not, that's just fine with me. And if the story is incomplete, only half-finished, that's okay with me, too. What is life without a little mystery? Besides, there were still more mysteries for me to solve, even if I chose not to share them with the world. There was still a lot that I hadn't seen, still a lot of ground undiscovered. And there was still the *Tyrannosaur*. It had been five years, and I still hadn't found a *live* one.

CHAPTER 23

Reading this so quickly following my complaints about the loneliness of the beach and the desire to end my story, the reader (should there ever be one) might tend to believe that I had changed my mind. That perhaps the beach wasn't so bad after all, or perhaps I had second thoughts about taking my story through to its completion. Maybe having thought about it, I realized that life in the valley of the dinosaurs, with danger ever present, was no picnic. That living out in the open, in the tree, exposed to the elements was no bed of roses. Or perhaps I only opted to lengthen my stay at the machine a few days before beginning the tiring trip back to the cliff, adding a bit more to my story before I left.

It would be easy to think that, what with one page following so quickly after the last, just a few short inches on the screen of the computer monitor, less than a hundredth of an inch in thickness from one page of paper to the next.

One might question, how could anything significant have happened within such a small space? One might think that not enough time has passed for anything meaningful to occur to make me change my mind and once again put pen to paper, or in this case, fingers to keyboard. And from the context of some reader seventy million years from now, one would be right. After all, it takes but a second to flip the page or to hit the down-arrow enough times to scroll down the screen from the end of one chapter to the beginning of the next.

But things are not always what they seem. Distance can not always be measured with a scale, any more than time can always be measured with a pocket watch. Dermot proved that to me unequivocally. The journey between two points, with respect to both distance and time, is not always a straight line. The journey is filled with twists and turns, pitfalls and roadblocks. And I had had my share of them since last I opened the laptop.

I sit on the ground, my back propped against a large rock, probably one of the many that had sealed me in the cave all that time ago. Not a very comfortable position, but my options are limited. The cheap aluminum chair lies against an interior wall of the cave, a worthless heap of rotting webbing and rusting rivets.

While I ponder how to begin what surely will be the end of my story, I gaze out to the east to where the sun tries valiantly to shine through the dirty gray haze. The sea is gone, or at least has retreated far enough off into the distance that I can't see it from the entrance to the cave. It is several miles out now, maybe as many as ten, but I haven't attempted to measure the distance. I really don't care one way or the other. It no longer holds any fascination for me.

It is curious however. I would have thought that to move an entire sea even a few feet would have taken years, probably hundreds of years. This one has moved several miles and has taken but a small fraction of a century. The seasons are changing, the winters becoming colder and longer. The ice caps are undoubtedly forming, shrinking the ocean levels, and draining the seas. But this one has shrunk much too quickly for that explanation to hold water—so to speak.

There are other forces at work here!

The sea isn't the only thing changing. The young forest is encroaching ever farther northward along the edge of the cliff, blocking half the view of the horizon. Seated as I am on the ground, the growth looks taller than it was, yet I know that traveling to the south I will find new saplings as tall as I—taller.

The beach is no longer barren, and it is not only plant life here—there are other kinds of life, as well. Birds and butterflies flit and fly from one tiny branch to another. Several species of crawling insects have taken up residence here as well. And I have seen several small mammals scurrying through the brush—shrews, I think, or some related species. As hard as I try, I can't remember ever having seen any kind of animal, even insects, on the beach, other than what had come from the sea or the sky in all the trips that I had made here. Things have indeed changed.

I haven't yet taken the long walk to the new shoreline. Nor have I ventured southward along the face of the cliff, through the newly emerging forest—at least not far enough to see where it ends—or starts. It is a curious thing to think—kind of like a corollary to the old, "is the glass half empty or half full," question. I see the southern route along the cliff as coming to an end of at some point, the cliffs turning eastward to once again meet the sea, trapping me between the two insurmountable barriers. I know that to the plants that are pushing their way onto the beach, and to the animals that had made it as far north as the cave, whatever lie to the south is a beginning for them. Deep down I know that to be true, but I can't stop thinking of it as the end. And perhaps it is much more significant than just the end of the young forest. Because if whatever lie to the south is not truly a beginning, it is most certainly the end ... at least the end for me. I have no place else to go.

I am tired, a weariness that seems to drill right down to the bone. So tired that in the week that I've been back, I've hardly done a thing other than sit in front of the cave and stare out to the eastern horizon. Each morning I gaze out to the east, watching the sun rise higher and higher in the sky until it disappears overhead. Nine years ago it was one of the most beautiful sights I had ever seen. A clear, still sea, its glassy surface occasionally broken by a leaping fish or the head and long graceful neck of a *Plesiosaur*. A yellow-crested *Pteranodon* might just swoop down, effortlessly, from a brilliant blue sky to capture its dinner from the skin of the water. The sun was a huge ball in the sky, bigger and brighter than any that I had ever seen.

All that has changed. The sea is no longer visible, but I know that even if I were standing at its shore, I would see little activity, either on, or above its surface. The skies are dark, even though it is mid-day, the beautiful blue has been replaced by a disturbing gray. The sun is only a bright spot in the sky, nearly blotted out by the black, soot-filled clouds rolling in from the west. Even from a distance of fifty yards, I can see that the green leaves of the foliage have picked up the dusty color of fallen ash. I can feel its gritty texture on my bare arms and legs.

The end of the time machine protrudes through the right side of the cave's entrance, just as it had nine years before. It no longer has a silky black finish, but wears a coat of gray, made from nearly a decade of dust, and ten day's accumulation of ash.

I adjust the makeshift facemask covering my mouth and nose, protecting my damaged lungs from further injury from the tiny airborne particles that seemed to have no end. In the machine, packed neatly within the metal shelves, is what was left of my supplies. They occupy a very small section of one rack, a tiny fraction of what I had brought originally, and all that is left… anywhere. There are no supplies left in the tree, and no tree for that matter. That and every other living thing in the valley is gone.

*****

The long hot summers of the late Cretaceous were ideal for growing things, and the natural boundaries of the mountains seemed to trap the moisture like a greenhouse. The jungle flourished in the warm, damp environment, as did my garden.

I sat in the tree, my bare legs dangling from the rough sawn logs of the lower deck, my arms hanging over the lower railing. I looked down upon the thousands of plants bearing fruit that would be ready to harvest in just a few short weeks. I smiled inwardly thinking that maybe Liz could somehow see me.

During our marriage I had had the most *ungreen* thumb in all of Chicago. Liz used to joke that she dared not bring a plant into the house for fear that my presence alone was enough to kill it. And it was true. Either I under watered them, over watered them, gave them too much sunlight, or not enough. I added too much fertilizer, too little, or used the wrong kind. According to Liz, I didn't *love* them enough.

The truth was I really didn't care much about them one way or the other. They were just decorations, and decorations that required that much work just weren't worth the effort.

The plants below me were hardly for decoration though. The fruit that they bore is what kept me alive, long after the twentieth century provisions were gone, long after my desire to be the *great white hunter* had passed. I ate them not just out of necessity. I ate them because they were good—damn good.

I was a city boy, raised on store-bought food. Everything that I ate had come from the supermarket or from a restaurant. If it could be unwrapped, unfrozen, taken out of a box, can, or bottle, if it could be fried, baked, broiled or thrown in a microwave, it would find its way to my stomach. I never took the time to really taste the food—I just ate it. I had no idea what fresh food really tasted like.

Looking down from the deck I could see the bright crimson of the tomatoes, the sun reflecting off their skins still wet with the morning dew. There were more than a hundred plants, forming several curved rows following the inside perimeter of the compound's fence. They were on the western part of the garden where they would get most of the morning light and not cast shadows over the lower-lying crops. The tomatoes were the most plentiful and colorful in my garden, but there were so many others. Carrots, lettuce, eggplant, onions, cauliflower, several kinds of peppers and squash, and at least a dozen others, all in circular rows that got smaller and smaller as they approached the center.

I used no pesticides—Dermot had forbidden it—and I agreed. We had no idea what they would do to the animals in an age when there was no built-up immunity against them. And still, there was no problem with insects. It was as if they didn't quite understand what I had here, which was probably just how it was. None of these vegetables were indigenous to the Cretaceous period. Nothing had yet developed a craving for them.

I used rocks from the riverbed to form two bisecting lanes through the center of the garden. It made it easy to get the cart in closer to the plants, to unload the fertilizer, to bring in the tools, to harvest the fruit, but it also looked damn good from the height of the deck. A combination vegetable and rock garden—Liz would be so proud.

It hadn't been easy. It had taken nearly all of that first summer to ready the ground for planting. The topsoil had been damaged by whatever fire had caused the large circular burned out area that I had noted on that first brief trip down the cliff, into the valley. Nothing except for the tree, which was situated on its southern edge, would grow there. But beneath the crusty covering, the soil was black and rich with nutrients. When I broke the surface and mixed it with Dermot's minerals, plowed in the natural fertilizer so plentiful along the path, it was incredibly good dirt to grow in.

It was difficult work—a month of making countless trips back and forth to the path, laying the dried dinosaur manure down, mixing the minerals in, tilling over a quarter acre of dirt with nothing but a shovel. Even with work gloves on, my hands were a mass of blisters, calluses by the second week—calluses that were torn off by the third—only to blister once again and turn to calluses once more.

It was hard, but making sure that there was sufficient sunlight for the crops to thrive was harder. I was fortunate that my tree was on the southern edge of the clearing and didn't interfere with the sun coming over the cliffs in the east. I didn't want to mess with that. I didn't want to even trim any of the outer branches and leaves—it made a natural umbrella against the rain and the worst of the winds.

But there were other trees standing in the way. They had to come down. I didn't just trim the branches back. The next year I would have to come back and do it again, and the next year, and the year after that. I took them all they way down, some of them three feet across the trunk. I had no power tools, no chain saw. I did it all with my trusty ax. When I had it done, I had a year's supply of firewood, and a brand new appreciation for lumberjacks.

The fence took another month. The long logs pointed away from the center, but they still rose high into the air, high enough where I feared they would put too much of the garden in shadow, for too many of the daylight hours. I was no gardener—I had no idea how much sun the plants actually needed, but with all the moisture in the valley, I figured they could use all that they could get. I had books—Dermot had packed several. But the books didn't exactly address the situation that I was in. They said nothing about how things grew during the later part of the Mesozoic age.

Log by log, I dismantled the eastern portion of the barrier, cutting them in half, reburying them, retying them to the ones before. I worried about compromising the perimeter of my compound, but other than the *Raptors*, nothing had threatened my little fortress, no other carnivores had shown themselves in the valley. I knew that the *raptors* were smart, and that they could jump. The incident on the ladder pointed that out in a most painful manner. I knew that they could clear the height of the barrier, but I thought that the angle and the sharp points would solve that problem. If their leaps weren't exactly timed they would impale themselves on the top. Besides, I no longer went anywhere without firepower—my last shotgun and last pistol—both.

It proved to be a needless worry. I hadn't seen another *raptor* since that first time, and had seen no other predator since I'd left the giant crocks at the swamp more than four years before.

Spring came early in the Cretaceous. By my estimate it was mid March when the last threat of frost was over and I was ready to plant. Dermot had provided not packets of seeds, but bags of them, hundreds of kinds that I was still experimenting with into the second and third year. Through trial and error, I learned the best pace to plant, what plants used what fertilizer, and which ones required more water than what nature so amply provided. I learned the best way to stake the plants, which ones needed thinning, how to rotate the crops, when was the best time to pick—I experimented with just about everything. I had to—this was all new to me.

By the end of the third summer, my garden was flourishing. Now, in its eighth year, the ninth year of residency here in the valley, it was a remarkable sight. It was a garden that would have made the most professional gardener green with envy. They say that pride is a sin, but I think that only applies if pride manifests itself in boastful relations with others. Being that there were no others, I didn't see pride as a fault. Which was a damn good thing, because I was proud as hell of my garden.

I was just sitting there admiring my handy work, a big shit-eating grin plastered on my face, when I smelled sulfur. I had smelled it many times before, when the winds were just right, and the volcano was smoking a bit more than normal.

I looked off to the west, seeing the small clouds of black smoke drift lazily from the spout of the mountain. It was a mountain that did not exist in the twentieth century. I knew that because it was massive, dominating the scenery for hundreds of miles in any direction. And I knew this area, not just as it looked now, but how it would look seventy million years from now. I had worked the site east of here for two years, the site where the machine now rested, the site where we found the buried cave, the dinosaurs unearthed within. And yet I knew about the mountain even before my trip through time. It existed in my drawing and in Susan's stained glass window. It was why I had named it Susan's Picture Mountain—Susan's Mountain for short.

Susan's Mountain was active that day, as it had been on and off for all the years that I had been here. It was never quite at rest. On any given day, if I watched closely enough, I would see slim tendrils of white smoke that dispersed almost immediately into the easterly breeze. On days like that one, however, the smoke was black and thick, heavy enough so that the currents of air could do little but form it into dark, ominous clouds that drifted over the valley, leaving its sooty residue as it passed.

On days like that, the earth trembled, the ground succumbing to tremendous, unseen forces deep below. I tended to think of the mountain as the source of that unimaginable power, even though I knew that it wasn't. Hundreds of miles away, the massive tectonic plates that supported the continents were shifting, one against the other, deep underground. The opposing forces caused the earth to tremble, the mountains to shake. When the forces became more than the earth above could bear, the land would be ripped apart, cliffs would crumble, mountains disappear, earthquakes born. In modern times, Californians knew all too well the destructiveness of earthquakes, but in prehistoric times, no place on earth was immune to them. It's what changed the landscape throughout the millennia.

On days like those the mountain seemed to be alive. It wasn't the source of the power, but was certainly the recipient of it. Disturbances in the ground caused fissures in the rock from which magma—molten rock—worked its way up through the funnel into the mountain's core, creating the black, smoky clouds in the day, a fiery red glow in the night sky.

The tremors were much more pronounced in the tree, the roots picking up the tiny vibrations from below the surface, transmitting them and amplifying them through the trunk, across each branch. The leaves danced, as if to the sounds of a frantic jitterbug, and the decks would groan as they resettled themselves into a slightly different position.

I had attached human qualities to the mountain. No, more like superhuman qualities. It ruled over the valley like a god. When it was at peace, it stood like a colossal guard, protecting the valley and all its creatures from intruders from the west. It served as a majestic landmark, guiding the path for all the inhabitants of the valley. When it was angry it shook with rage and threatened to rain fire down on those that worshipped before it. It seemed as if there were times when it was only moments away from losing its temper altogether and blowing its stack. Those times seemed to grow in frequency and duration as the years went by.

And it was angry on that day. The tree shook more than normal and the deck pitched noticeably, forcing me to grab tightly onto the rail. With a jolt, the deck dropped an inch on one side, stopping so suddenly that it jarred my teeth. Some of my supplies fell from the tall piles, scattering across the deck, some rolling over the edge to be swallowed up by the thick garden. A scattering of tiny leaves filled the air, littering the wooden timbers.

As things settled down, I stared out at the mountain, wondering at its intentions. My thoughts were filled with a strange combination of terror and delight, an equal measure of anxiety and astonishment. I had long been in awe of the mountain. I would sit on the deck for hours on end staring out at it. Winter and summer, day and night, more so when it was active. It was both beautiful and frightening at the same time. I knew that it was the source of unspeakable power, of cataclysmic potential, yet I was drawn to it like a moth to a flame.

I was drawn to it in an emotional sense, perhaps even in a spiritual sense—but not in a physical sense. I had been no closer to it than the day when I found the group of hadrosaurs feasting on the giant eggs—the day that I had killed one of them with the errant rifle shot—the day of the *Raptor* attack. I had been no closer than perhaps two miles nearer than I was at that very moment. I stayed away very deliberately. The truth was, I was scared to death of the mountain.

The mountain was due west from the tree, forty or fifty miles through the densest, darkest part of the jungle. I knew from the sounds at night that there was a lot of life out there—strange sounds, loud and sometimes, angry sounds. It was a jungle, and only natural that there would be an abundance of creatures there. But, what kind of creatures inhabited *this* jungle?

There were no lions or tigers, no cheetahs or panthers, no wild boars or bears. They wouldn't be around for a few million years, and some of them would never inhabit North America. But there were poisonous snakes and carnivorous insects, giant crocodiles and sharp-toothed mammals that were strange and dangerous. And there were dinosaurs, most friendly, some not so much. I would never know if the *Raptors* from nine years ago had come from the jungle or from the path, but not knowing was just as frightening. And there were things that I had no idea about—things that were perhaps more dangerous than anything that I had encountered to that point. That scared me—perhaps more than the mountain did. Perhaps it wasn't the mountain at all that frightened me. Perhaps it was just the journey that would get me to it.

I had made a vow four years earlier. On a particularly lonely day on the beach, when the boredom, and the frustration, and the shame got the better of me, I promised that I would no longer cower in the compound, no longer hide from the habitat surrounding my tree.

I hadn't done a very good job of keeping that promise. I had gone to the river to bathe and fetch water, ventured along the path a mile or two in both directions, spent a lot of time just outside the perimeter of the tree. But I had never traveled very far. I told myself that there was nothing beyond the river, the path, and the immediate vicinity of the compound that I really needed. I convinced myself of it, but it was all a lie. I was hiding … and not entirely sure what I was hiding from.

It was just about then that I realized that I had really very little to be afraid of because I had so very little to lose. I was but forty-five years old, but forty-five in this time was old. Earliest man was considered absolutely ancient at the age of forty. Even a mere thousand years before the twenty-first century, fifty was an age that very few attained. And here I was when life expectancy beyond the age of forty could be measured, not in years, but in months. I had already beaten the odds—the odds, and my own expectations.

I had no family to worry about, no friends to mourn for me, no job to leave unfinished. No one would miss me. It would be as if I had never even been here. I didn't yearn for death, but to be done with it all, to see what lie ahead, was not such a terrible thought.

I came to this time for a reason. I came here to see for myself what the real truth was about life seventy million years before the common era. And even though I had seen a lot, there was still so much more to learn, so much more to experience. I sure as hell wouldn't find it from the safety of the tree.

Looking down at the garden, now dark in the shadows from the heavy black clouds overhead, I knew that there was nothing important that I had to do here. I had a good two weeks until the first of the harvesting began. I would do nothing during that time other than to walk through the paths checking the plants for brown spots or disease, retying the loose stalk to the stake, brushing off the white ash from the leaves. It would all be just to have something to do. There was no disease in the valley. I had never found a single brown spotted leave, and with nothing to disturb them, hardly ever anything that I needed to restake. I knew the white ash wouldn't harm the plants, in fact, the potassium that it contained was good for them.

I had absolutely no good reason to stay.

Although I was ambivalent about death, I prepared against it, unwilling to go without a fight. I had the knife, the pistol, *and* the shotgun. I refilled a dozen clips for the Glock and wore the bandoleer, filled to capacity with shells. I wouldn't kill for pleasure, not even very often for food. But I would protect myself with my entire arsenal if I had to.

I filled only a few water bottles, and packed no food, knowing that it would be plentiful in the jungle, especially that time of year. I brought the lightweight tent and a single change of clothes. I didn't care a thing about cleanliness, but I did want to stay dry. I had one of the little first aid kits, replenished with an assortment of bandages and medicines. Two lengths of nylon rope were coiled across my chest, crisscrossed against the bandoleer. The pack was full and weighty after I stuffed it with a half dozen pitons and a hammer.

I had this absurd idea to scale the mountain. I had no idea why back then. Even today, I have no idea why, except that I was drawn to it. I saw the mountain as some kind of magical place, where all the mysteries of the valley would be revealed to me, where whatever questions remained would be answered. I felt the kind of awe and humility that Moses must have felt when he stared up at the glowing summit of Mount Sinai. I was seeking no burning bush, but I was after enlightenment, perhaps even salvation. I was looking for a reason to keep on living.

*****

The jungle was thick and dark, but not as much as it appeared from a distance and from the height of the tree's decks. The canopy of green was thick, letting through the sunlight in just infrequent, stray patches. Traveling in and out of it kept me in a permanent state of semi blindness, my pupils shrinking and expanding with the constant change. The ground cover was not uniformly thick—no doubt the covering overhead had stunted the growth below. So I made good progress on that first day out.

As night approached, the darkness became absolute. In the blackness, I put up the tent and snuggled in for the night. It had been a relatively uneventful day. I had seen few animals, which surprised me. But I knew that they were all around me. I could hear them scurry away as I approached. They were more afraid of me than I was of them. At least that's what *they* thought. I was content to let them think that way. With that knowledge, I made no attempt to travel in silence.

I was surprised that the ground was as dry as it was, this being a jungle and all. I guess that the overhead umbrella of thick leaves kept it that way. I had crossed over two streams that day, neither one was deep or wide. Neither had that stench of rot and decay like the swampy area along the path. There were no giant crocodiles here.

And there appeared to be no *Raptors*, at least on that day. Unlike the other creatures, the *Raptors* would not have fled in fear. I knew at least that much about them. They were aggressive, dangerous creatures that hunted in packs. They were fast and they were smart. They would have surely ripped me to pieces before I even knew that they were there. It's why I had carried the twelve-shot pistol out in front of me—the safety off—my finger on the trigger.

I saw not a single dinosaur either, other than the birds, which were their closest relatives. I saw any number of *them*, as well as snakes, frogs, lizards, and the ass-ends of what I was pretty sure were small mammals. It's probably why I saw no *Raptors*—they were after bigger game—the small animals of the jungle provided them no challenge. That was okay by me. If I could make it to the mountain without any extra adventures, that would be just fine. I was sure that what I was seeking was on the mountain, not in the jungle.

By the end of the second day I had become comfortable in my surroundings, confident as I journeyed farther west, following the clearest route, staying away from the dark tangle of bush. I spent the day stepping over huge, log-sized roots, ducking beneath others. I stopped often, my rapidly growing-old body not accustomed to the long hours of continuous exercise. I ate right from the bush, easily finding nuts and berries that I had become familiar with.

The trees in this section of the jungle were taller, undoubtedly much older. The jungle must have begun at the foot of the mountain some thousands of years earlier. As it aged, it spread itself out, heading toward the river and the cliffs beyond.

The trees here were more diverse in both size and kind, and broke the monotony of the canopy, creating more frequent openings to the sky. From time to time I could see huge chunks of blue from above, and an occasional glimpse of the mountain, reaching higher into the sky as I got closer.

Traveling on, I saw fewer animals. It was if they were steering clear of it, like they were afraid of the mountain. Even the birds became more scarce, the bugs and amphibians likewise. By mid-day they were gone, leaving an unearthly silence that was both strange and spooky.

As night approached, the sun dropped beneath the towering peak, sending the valley into deep shadows, but lighting up the edges of the mountain like they were outlined in luminescent paint. The mountain now seemed directly overhead. Looking up at it, it seemed powerful, but ominous, even more alive than ever. For the first time I thought that perhaps I had made a mistake in coming here, like maybe my presence was an intrusion, like it was angry with me. Perhaps the animals knew what I *should* have.

And the mountain was indeed angry that night—as angry as I had ever seen it. The tip glowed red like the end of a giant cigar, the sulfur smell more pronounced, more objectionable than it had ever been from the distance of the tree. The sky had disappeared behind a cloak of darkness, but I knew that there were angry dark clouds of ash spewing from the funnel. And the ground rumbled throughout the entire night.

I slept fitfully, anticipating a catastrophe that failed to materialize. I lay there in the tent like a clenched fist, squeezing every muscle to the point of pain with each groan from the mountain, from each little vibration that came from beneath me. The night sounds of the jungle were absent. Other than the intermittent sounds of the earth grinding and groaning from down below, it was as quiet a night as I could ever remember.

I lay awake, staring up at the blackness of the tent, waiting anxiously for the first rays of sunlight to penetrate the thin skin of the nylon. I had never been afraid of the dark—even as a kid, but on that night I was terrified—terrified of the darkness—terrified that the day would never come.

But of course it did. Somehow, some time, I had fallen asleep, waking to not only the gray light filtered through the finely woven nylon, but to an unusual sound as well. In the distance, very faintly, I could hear running water. I found it strange that I hadn't heard it during the night. Absurdly, it sounded like a faucet that had been left on. It could only be a river of course, one much larger than anything that I had passed in the last two days. Those had been nearly silent until I was right on top of them.

Whatever it was, it was more than just a river. As I continued my march through the jungle the sound intensified with each step that I took. It sounded not like a faucet, but like a thousand faucets, all turned on full blast, the water falling a considerable distance before crashing into some huge, but unseen basin. The noise filled the jungle, replacing those of the animals that had faded away the day before.

I had become numb to the potential dangers of the jungle. The journey had been uneventful, and I had lost all caution into the third day. I had been anxious to reach the base of the mountain, more so by the increasing intensity of the sound of what surely must have been a raging river. I was moving too quickly through the thick brush, unmindful of my steps.

I knew that I was close. The water was a roar in my ears as I squeezed between two giant ferns...

...and stepped out into space.

In total mind-freezing panic, letting go of the Glock, I reached out, catching hold of the tough, thick leaves of the fern. It stopped my fall, slamming me to the ground, one leg dangling over the precipice. With my heart dancing to the marimba, the leaf tore free, and with my free hand, I grabbed onto the woody stalk of the plant and hoisted myself back over the edge.

I had only inches to scoot into the brush, the edge of the cliff running close up against the jungle. Sucking oxygen into lungs that had too little capacity to adequately calm my nerves, I felt along the ledge searching for ground that wasn't there.

I finally opened my eyes, which I had instinctively slammed shut when I felt myself about to drop off the edge. What lay before me was an amazing sight. Across the river, two hundred yards away, was a huge waterfall, as wide as a football field, thousands of gallons of water per second slamming into the river a hundred feet below. It struck with a force that caused the water beneath to boil and churn, sending up a cloud of vapor that extended nearly to the ridge on which I held fast.

I had come out of the jungle about a mile north of the central portion of the volcano. I had to crane my neck to see its peak towering above and to the left. The mountain was really pissed. Black clouds didn't just drift lazily from its peak—they shot from its tip with incredible velocity, as if propelled by some huge bellows deep within the mountain's core. The ground beneath me shook, the roar of the rushing water absorbing whatever agonizing sounds were made as the earth was being torn apart from somewhere deep down below.

I was at a level lower than that of the top of the waterfall, an equal distance between it and the river below. Water poured from a ragged rift in the southern slope of Mount Susan—an ugly, jagged maw of a hole that looked like the terrible smile of some half-toothed ghoul. Giant rocks protruded from the gaping hole, like badly made false teeth, rocks that had been pushed outward—pushed outward by a fit of rage from deep within the mountain.

As the ground continued to shift, bits of earth falling away beneath me into the haze below, I tried again to push myself away from the edge, farther into the thick roots of the brush. I scraped against the loose soil with the tips of my boots, trying desperately to move the bigger part of my body away from danger. My feet did nothing but tear up the ground, sending more of it over the edge. With both hands I took a strangle hold on the base of the giant fern, pulling my hips forward, bits of the ledge still crumbling from beneath me. Using just my knees, I tried to twist my hips away from the ledge. The shift in my weight caused the earth to drop way. I felt myself falling over the lip and I grasped even tighter to the plant.

But it was growing from shallow soil. It gave way, pulled free at the roots, and I tumbled over the edge. My arms and legs flailed away at nothing as I plunged through the heavy fog of the boiling water, hitting the river fully across my back. The wind was knocked from me and I could feel myself sinking as the churning waters tossed me from side to side like a piece of dried out driftwood.

The pack! The pack was pulling me to the bottom.

In that one instant I had given up the idea of scaling the mountain as I struggled to remove the heavy pack laden with the hammer and pitons. As I tore at the straps, I realized that I was also giving up the ammunition, but I had lost the Glock at the top of the ridge, and the rifle on the way down. The ammunition was worthless.

In a mad struggle, I tore the pack off, followed quickly by the rope and the bandoleer. I was lighter by forty pounds, but completely disoriented. I tumbled in all directions, buffeted by the churning water of the falls. I didn't hit bottom, couldn't tell up from down, right from left.

As my breath began to run out, I let myself relax, knowing with a surprising clarity, that panic was going to get me killed. I focused on the bubbles. They traveled at amazing speed from right to left. Not fully comprehending the connection, I kicked to the left, following their path. I broke the surface seconds later, trying to suck in the air—air made impossibly thick by the salty spray and rolling surface of the water.

Blindly, I bobbed in the water, coughing and choking, trying to snatch a breath away from the tumultuous spray. It seemed to come from every direction at once, and I had to be content with cupping my hands around my mouth and nose and take tiny, soggy breaths.

I let the crashing waves slam into me, pushing me away from the source. My legs kicked madly, a desperate attempt to stay above the churning water. I thought that I was holding my own, when, a minute latter, I was slammed against the granite wall of the cliff. My right shoulder and the back of my head struck the hard, unyielding surface with enough force to make everything go black.

The force of the water held me against the rock as black quickly turned to gray, than back to dazzling, shimmering white and silver, as I tried in vain to blink away the pain and the tears. The worst of the spray and surf was in my face, making it impossible to see anything but a bright haze, impossible to breathe through my mouth.

I fought hard against the push of the water, clumsily turning in the river until I was facing the cliff. The water splashed off the rock directly into my face, pelting me with the same ferocity as it did face on. Still nearly blind, I reached along the slick, hard wall, searching desperately for something to grab hold of. But there was nothing. The rock had been worn smooth from years of scouring by water and bottom sand, by tiny water impurities and volcanic pumice. It was as slick as glass, and my hands flailed against it with the effectiveness of silk on ice.

As the water pummeled me, I could feel my hands slide along the slick surface, pushing me to the left, farther southward. The direction that I traveled meant nothing to me, so I went with the flow.

I tried to lean into the push, to let my body recline in the churning water, to relax and let the currents do their thing. But the chop was too rough, the water splashing down on my face, filling my mouth, pressing hard on my body, forcing me back upright again. I pushed with both legs and arms to get away from the turmoil as fast as I could.

It was the wrong way.

About the time I felt the strong currents from the waterfall begin to back off, the natural currents of the river took over. They were going in opposing directions.

I treaded water, spinning first in one direction, then the other, as the two pressed equally hard against me. Which way to go was an easy decision. I had not the slightest desire to go back into the meat grinder of the waterfall. I turned and began to stroke south against the current.

I made slow but steady progress, strength returning to my muscles as my breathing returned to normal. I turned onto my back, using a leisurely reverse stroke to propel me against the steady, but not powerful current. I kept my breathing shallow and steady, my arms and legs reaching out, then pulling in tight, propelling me another couple of feet with each stroke.

The water pushed gently against my head and shoulders, but I made steady progress, watching the different colors of the rock drift by me on either side. It was like being in a tunnel, fifty feet of slick, solid rock on either side, above me thick clouds of heavy, black smoke. The sides of the rocks grew darker toward the top, merging with the black, ash-laden skies. It was mid-day, but it was like twilight. It was hard to tell where the edges of the cliffs stopped and where the beginning of the sky began.

As the sound of the waterfall receded, other sounds took over. I had been pushing water before me for thirty minutes at least, and I had nearly reached the base of the mountain, which appeared over my left shoulder. The thundering roar of the falls had begun to slowly fade into the background when the sounds of the earthquake took over.

The earth rumbled in a long, sustained growl. Rocks began to fall from both sides of the cliff, dropping into the river below. I swam away from the eastern cliffs, toward safety in the center of the river. My eyes lost focus as the rocks of the cliff blurred, tremors making the landscape vibrate at a dangerous frequency.

The black clouds of ash obscured the sun and the sky, but I could still see the glowing tip of the mountain. As I watched, the southern portion of the mountain's top seemed to dissolve and a wide stream of steaming orange and red began to flow down its side. Lava—hundreds of tons of molten rock, thousands of degrees hot—began to flow down the mountain. It seemed to pick up speed, as well as volume, as it absorbed everything in its path, making it part of itself—growing—alive. It branched out in an ever-reaching web of tentacles, each finding a new route down the steep slope, separating, then reconnecting, over and over again as it headed toward the bottom and the river. And I was heading right for it.

It was still a couple of miles away, more than two thousand yards above the river, but the distance was rapidly shrinking. I turned in the water and began kicking furiously in the other direction. The current was now helping me, pushing me away from the mountain—back into the falls.

Behind me, at the foot of the mountain, rocks began falling into the river with greater frequency. Granite sheets, thirty and forty foot wide sections of it, broke away and slid into the water. The destruction was spreading along the river, moving quickly right for me.

Within minutes I had entered the first of the ripples sent out by the falls. Moments later I was battling the worst of the raging waters. It kept pushing me toward the eastern cliff where the rocks were falling with frightening regularity, thousand pound slabs of stone that could crush me in an instant and drive me to the bottom of the river.

Taking a huge breath, I dove into the depths of the water, searching for a less turbulent path through the falls. If there was a bottom to the river, I didn't find it. Thirty feet down was as deep as I could go before the pressure threatened to burst my eardrums, like an old-fashioned pair of ice tongs had a hold of me, the pointed ends driving deep into my ears. The turbulence was still there, but less severe. I could see—the water was crystal clear. But I couldn't see far. Even at thirty feet, the water churned and bubbled, a kaleidoscope of blues, and whites, and silvers.

I didn't stop to enjoy the show, as fascinating as it might have been. I began kicking and stroking, angling toward the surface as I ran out of air.

It took a half dozen more dips into the depths before I crossed the worst of the falls. When I got to the other side, I surfaced to a scene from hell. The cliffs on either side of the river continued to crumble, cascading down with a crash that could be heard above that of the waterfall and the continuing thunder of the quake. And the edges of the river were no longer the only source of the falling rock. Burning debris, chunks of molten lava, shot through the dark skies, hundreds of them dropping into the river all around me, sending up little tendrils of steam as each one hit the cold water.

One more time I gathered a deep breath and plunged below the surface. I swam ahead, deep in the water, waiting any second for a random hot rock to come crashing down to the surface, driving through the water to strike me. Every second seemed like the last as I continued forward. My lungs ached from the exertion, my arms and legs equally tired.

I did it over and over again, each time cringing as I came to the surface, amazed that I had been able to avoid the blazing stones hurled at such a distance and with such velocity. I saw them enter the river, some no more than a few feet from where I tread water. They hit with a resounding splash and a hiss, sending up a cloud of steam and an acrid smell.

No matter how many times that I came up for air, the scenery was the same—sheer, steep cliffs on either side—cliffs that were insurmountable—cliffs that offered no way out. They rose high above me, the once sheer surfaces crumbling as I watched, helpless to do anything about it.

I thought that it was the end. The quake caught up with me and rocks were falling from both sides of the cliff, others, ignited, falling from the sky. It seemed as if they struck everywhere, constant along the edges of the river, randomly, but nearly everywhere across its broad surface. It continued to grow darker. Nighttime was falling, or perhaps the smoldering mountain's emissions had just made it seem so. The fire that shot from the top of the mountain seemed to be the only source of light. That and the lava that burned for a second as it struck the water, an infinite number of tiny flames reflecting off the nearly still waters.

I could see no way out. It was just a matter of time when the odds caught up with me, when one of the blazing rocks would find their target. Or a heart attack, or maybe a stroke would mercifully take me out first.

I was frantic. Crazy thoughts filled my head, and I knew that as slim as the odds were I needed to get a grip if I was to have any chance at all.

As I headed for the surface again, I rolled over onto my back, defying the flaming missiles to strike me, defying all odds. What I saw behind me caused me to pause. For the moment, I forgot all about the crumbling cliffs, about the raining, burning rocks, as I watched the lava pour from the base of the mountain into the river two miles upstream. Huge clouds of steam where the hot lava met the cold water obliterated the scene.

I had only minutes before the growing flow of lava would raise the temperature of the water to the boiling point, less time before the heat would send my body temperature high enough to kill me.

I looked along the western side of the river, seeing new streams of lava inching their way to the cliff only fifty feet away.

I didn't have minutes, but only seconds, as I swam toward the opposite cliff, ignoring the rocks falling from that side. Through the gloom and burning meteors that burned momentary white-hot patches into my retinas, I spied an opening in the rock.

It was a long irregular shaped fissure, fifty feet wide, perhaps fifteen feet high, and it was four feet above the top of the water … four feet above my head. It was nearly flat across the bottom, with no sides to speak of. The ceiling curved downward from the center until it met the floor, tapering to a thin, ragged slit at the ends.

I swam toward the cliff, letting the river's current push me toward the cave's entrance. I kept thinking that I would be struck at any second by one of the tiny flaming comets. The fear was ever so much more real with my back turned to the source, as if I could do anything if I faced them head on.

Just knowing that I wouldn't see it coming, even if it wasn't so much a conscious understanding of what was about to happen, was ever so much more frightening.

Passing by the entrance I reached up, barely grabbing the ledge with my fingertips. My body was light, the salt-filled water supporting most of my weight. It was easy to pull myself out of the water, the lip of the cave's floor nuzzled against the pit of my arms. I waited but a heartbeat before swinging my leg up and over the edge, the other leg following quickly. I scrambled several yards into the interior of the cave as the burning projectiles struck the cliff with a dramatic show of sparks, others hitting the floor in front of me, bouncing and rolling past my dodging feet.

The floor of the cave was sandy, salty, covered in patches by brown and yellow dried out plankton and seaweed. There were a few clamshells and skeletal remains of fish, and the space had the overpowering aroma of the seaside. It was a familiar smell—it was the smell of the beach that stretched out before the machine. The same smell, but more potent, a smell that wasn't subject to the winds of open spaces, a smell that was confined. It was the smell of seawater. This had been a river somewhere in the recent past. A river that had disappeared as the one below began to shrink, much like the sea before the machine.

I stepped into the darkening interior of the cave, the dim twilight of the night illuminated only by the continuous bursts of fire from the volcano. It was like watching the Forth of July fireworks, the sky alternating between total darkness and bright bursts of sparklers from above.

I moved far enough into the darkness of the cave, squatted down close to the right side until I was safe from the volcano's spitting lava, just close enough where I could still see the tip of the mountain beyond the left edge of the opening.

I had no idea what my next move was. I was just content to be in the cave, in a position of relative safety, out of the water, and out of the line of fire from the spitting volcano. I stretched out across the floor, resting on an elbow and just watched the magnificent light show.

It was only an hour, perhaps a little more, perhaps a little less, when the show came to its grand finale.

The roar of the earthquake became deafening and sustained like an unending tympani crescendo. The walls of the cave shook, the smaller rocks falling to the floor. The sand at my feet danced—frenzied, tiny little steps that rolled like waves toward the cave's entrance. The inside of the cave was lit by an unearthly red glow like the caverns of hell.

Fire shot from the top of the volcano—flame and sparks hundreds of feet wide, thousands of feet up into the night sky. As I watched, fear replaced by awe and fascination, the entire top of the mountain exploded, blowing outward from some unseen, unimaginable pressure from within. The night became as day as the sky was lit up by the white-hot explosion. I turned from the blinding light and began to run into the interior of the cave, knowing that the accompanying shock wave was imminent.

I didn't make it ten steps before the blast hit me full across the back, sending me flying forward another thirty feet. I bounced once on the hard floor before my forward momentum was halted abruptly by a large rock that caught me across the shoulder and the side of my head. I was stunned, but not seriously injured. The cliff had absorbed most of the blast, its power dissipated quickly once inside the cave. It's why I was only battered and bruised, and not dead. As the initial shock began to wear off, I began to rise, suddenly realizing that someone had turned out the lights.

The face of the cliff had indeed taken the full measure of the blast, sheering off several feet of it, filling the entrance of the cave with tons of rock. As I approached it in the dark, I could feel the heat radiating from it like a furnace. I moved in slowly, my arm outstretched before me, reaching out to touch the source of the heat. I pulled my hand away, even before I had actually touched it, the heat sending searing pain into my fingertips. I reached out with the tip of my foot, contacting the rock—hard, solid. I kicked out at it—once, then again, and again, harder each time. Nothing. It was like kicking a building—solid and immovable. The heat of the blast had fused the rock together into one huge mass. It had forever sealed the cave's entrance—with me inside.

*****

I had been walking blind for what must have been hours, but in truth I had absolutely no sense of time. I was sure that I had traveled miles, but also, I had no sense of distance. If it wasn't for the all too real smell of decaying fish and the coarse, rough surface of the cave walls that brushed and bumped painfully against me, I might well have been dreaming.

I had absolutely no idea where I was going. The sealed entrance of the cave had left me only one alternative, which was to move deep into its interior to see if there was another way out.

I stayed close to one side of the cave, constantly brushing my hand against the worn surface, not because I was afraid of taking a wrong turn somewhere. Hell, one way was as good as the next. Even if there were an entire maze of underground passages, what difference did it make? If there was a way out, I didn't know it. It would be completely accidental if I found it, whichever way I chose to go.

No, what I worried about was that I would lose my bearings and end up back where I started, and in the dark I wouldn't even know it. Coming to a sudden and impenetrable roadblock, I would think that it was the end of the trail. It would have been easy to accidentally double back because the cave opened up into an immense space. The sound made by my shuffling feet against the sandy floor sounded like wood against sandpaper and created a soft echo against the hard walls of the cave. And my breathing came in raspy little bursts caused by the damp air and exertion. Both sounds changed as the space expanded around me.

Every now and then I reached down and found an object in the darkness, sometimes a small rock, sometimes a clamshell, other times something unknown and probably unwanted. Each time I pitched them across the width of the cave, listening to the sound as the object struck the hard surface of the opposite wall, gauging the distance. On the third throw, there was no hard, solid sound, but rather a dull sound as it struck the sand covered floor. I flung a second object across the space, flinging it just as hard as I could with the same results, except the sound was even fainter. The cavern was huge, both wide and tall.

Despite all that had happened, I was in good shape—thirsty, but otherwise pretty damn okay. I should have been terrified. The last time that I was in such darkness, such a life-threatening situation, I was out of my head with fear. Now, it seemed just one more inconvenience. Maybe I just didn't give a damn any more. Perhaps I felt that dying in the cave was just as well as being buried under the volcanic ash of the mountain, better than being swallowed up by some giant predator, no worse than drowning in some ancient sea. Somehow though, I felt that deep inside I was going to extricate myself from this mess, that one way or another I was going to get out of there, see the daylight, breathe fresh air at least one more time.

And so I plunged ahead. Hour after hour and mile after mile I continued on. The cave narrowed and widened again, turned one way then the other, long stretches of downward slopes followed by even longer stretches of uphill ones. There were obstacles to climb over, trenches to climb down into. There were rocks and outcroppings to walk around, and stalactites hanging down to duck under. And everywhere there were the remnants of dead animals, their dried bones crunched under my boots, their fishy smell still heavy in the air. Some were too large to merely step on, or even step over. Some were my size—twice my size.

The river that had once existed here was gone, but it had not been gone for long. Its remains were still evident. What had once been an amazing underground river filled with marine life of every kind was now a dead, dried-up place.

I had been walking downhill for a very long time, hours perhaps. The slope varied from hardly noticeable, to having-to-scoot-down-on-my-butt steep, with very few stretches where there was an incline, or even a level path. It surprised me when the monotonous sound of my boots suddenly made a different kind of noise. Instead of the scratching sound that had accompanied every footstep, there was a squishy, sucking kind of noise, followed quickly by the sounds of water splashing.

I tried to walk around it, following the edge of the water clear to the other side of the cave, several hundred feet. I ran into the other wall before finding a way around it. It was the first time that I had been on the other side of the cave since I had first found myself trapped inside. It gave me another option. I could follow it back in the other direction, perhaps finding another tunnel that led the way out. Of course I didn't know what path I *had* been following. Perhaps I wasn't in the main tunnel at all—I had just been following the left edge of the cave. I might have been wandering through any number of tributaries and auxiliary tunnels, hopelessly lost inside the mountain. But I *felt* like I was in the main tunnel, even if I had no real reason to feel that way. Continuing on in the direction that I had been headed just *seemed* the right thing to do.

I stepped into the water, moving cautiously, the water quickly covering the tops of my boots, moving up my legs. It was cold, cold from not having seen the warmth of the sun, cold from having been years since warmer currents had passed through here. When the water reached my waist, I had to clench my jaws to keep from yelling out. I nearly turned back, but by the time the water reached my chin I had become accustomed to the cold. But I knew that I couldn't stay there long.

I may have started the walk through the tunnel in good shape, but my strength was fading quickly. I had been without food or water for far too long and my stamina wasn't what it once was. What little I had left was being taken quickly in the cold waters of the cave. I had to risk swimming hard, even if it meant using up the last of my strength. I had to get out of the cold water soon—and I had no idea how far I would have to go.

I began to swim.

It didn't take long to lose the fear of the water. When I had begun, I wasn't sure what problems I might encounter, what animals might lurk in the dark. But there was nothing. The underground lake was completely devoid of life, which really shouldn't have surprised me. There was no sunshine here, meaning that there were no ultraviolet rays to keep the plankton alive. If there was no plankton, there was no small marine life to feed off of it. And if there was no small marine life, there was no large marine life—no large fishes and no aquatic mammals either. There was also no connection to either side. Nothing had passed this way in years.

Whatever was here when the plug was pulled, was still here—long dead—long since decayed and sunk to the bottom.

For some reason the salt here seemed even more concentrated than in the river before the volcano. It made swimming easy, but stung my many cuts and scratches, burned my eyes and dried my lips. It made me incredible thirsty. It made me think about how long it had been since I had had a drink, and made me worry about how much farther I might have to go.

I turned over onto my back to keep the salty water off my face. My breathing had become raspy, audible enough where I could hear it echo against the walls of the cave on either side.

There was something very familiar about the whole thing—lying there in the viscous water, the total absence of light, listening to the sound of my own breathing. I had the feeling that I had been here before. All else was absolutely still as I backstroked through the cold water. I could feel the heart beating in my chest—much too fast—getting faster with every stroke. I had the feeling of impending doom, a feeling that I was all too familiar with.

My mind wandered, shapes formed in the darkness of the cave. I began to hear strange sounds, strange in that I thought that there was nothing here to make them. The sounds came from behind me—something large, something dangerous. I changed direction, turning to my right, heading toward the edge of the lake, to the safety of the ledge. I swam with everything that I had left in me, hearing the creature rise high above me. Water cascaded down upon my head and shoulders, the beast's breath loud in my ears, smelling powerfully of fish, as I reached for solid ground, ready to throw my body up and over the lip and roll into the tiny alcove that I knew was there.

I heard the strange yet familiar clicking sound from up high as I reached out toward the safety of the wall. The sound increased in volume and frequency the closer I got. From the sound, I could tell its position and its movement. I could tell when its head began its descent, when its toothy jaws had opened wide to strike. It happened in less than a second. It happened just as my fingertips brushed the cold, hard surface of the rock. The high-pitched clicking sound had turned to a continuous ear-piercing shriek as my shoulder slammed against the wall of the cave. I pressed my cheek hard against the stone, my face wet with sweat despite the cold.

There was no ledge, just the nearly flat, worn surface of the cave's wall. My fingers clawed at the scum-covered surface of the granite, trying desperately to find the ledge.

It wasn't there.

I panicked as the noise from above descended to meet me, a wall of water pouring down on me. I raised my arms over my head in a feeble attempt to protect myself against the hungry mouth of the *Elasmosaurus*. I screamed as the rows of tiny, razor sharp teeth were poised on either side of my head, about to snap shut. I let go of the wall and pulled my knees up, wrapped my arms around them, dropping below the surface of the water as the giant reptile struck.

Nothing!

Nothing at all happened except that I continued to sink downward in the underground lake, my lungs not keeping me buoyant because I hadn't bothered to take a breath as I coiled up in fear from the certain attack.

There was no attack. There was no *Elasmosaurus*.

It had all been a figment of my imagination—my overly tired, distinctly light-deprived, exceedingly imaginative brain, had conjured up a paranoid delusion. No, more than a delusion—a memory. It was all too real because it had happened before. Nine years before, it had happened. The day after my journey began—the day that I had squeezed my way though the narrow tunnel leading from the cave. On that day I had popped through the tiny opening at the end of the tunnel, fallen down the gravelly slope, and plopped into the underground river—this river—or what used to be this river. Now, it was but a remnant of the river—a long-dead lake, but it was the same. It was the spot of the *Elasmosaurus* attack nearly a decade earlier.

The ledge wasn't where it was then, at least not relative to the surface of the water. But it was there. It was there—somewhere out of reach. Perhaps just inches beyond my outstretched fingers, perhaps fifty feet above my head. Somewhere a few miles behind me, and high above the surface of the water was the exit to the tunnel, the tunnel that led back to the safety of the cave and the time machine. I couldn't find it in the dark, and even if I could, it was well out of reach. But if it was there, somewhere behind me, and if the ledge with its tiny little alcove was somewhere above me, then I knew that there was a way out. And it was only a few hours away.

I stayed close to the right-hand wall of the cave as I continued swimming through the black water. I knew that a few thousand yards out, the space would narrow, and beyond that there would be a tunnel that led directly to the great prehistoric sea that divided what was to become the North American continent from east and west.

An hour later, as it did on that day so long ago, light entered the cave, barely noticeable at first, nothing more than the faint impression of ripples in the water, of shadowy images on the walls of the cave. As I righted myself in the water to have a look about, my boots touched bottom. I stood up, the surface of the water at chest-level. The lake was coming to an end.

The cave's air was cool on my body. My shirt stuck to my skin like an icy shroud, the chill moving downward as the level of the water continued to recede. The slope rose quickly, leading me out of the water in less than a hundred yards. The light continued to improve and for the first time since the volcano erupted, sealing the cave, I could hear sounds that weren't of my own making.

It was a long, low moaning kind of a sound, like the bawling of a badly wounded animal. The sound had a haunting quality like that of a ghost in a graveyard and sent shivers up my wet back, added height to the already goose-like flesh of my arms. It was an inhuman kind of a sound.

The sound grew louder, closer, as I continued to walk on. Cautiously now, I moved between an ever growing number of obstacles as I made my way toward the source of the terrible noise. With the increased volume came the stirring of air. I could feel it on my face, cooling the fear-induced sweat, hastening the process of drying my clothes.

The channel turned to the right and, as the river had before me, I followed it. As I proceeded around the bend, fierce winds and the overpowering aroma of the sea assaulted me. The light was still very dim, but better, like being in a darkened basement at midnight on a cloudy, moonless night, with only a single tiny window set up high, just above ground level.

And the window *was* there. Fifty feet above the floor of the cave, dim, gray light filtered in from an odd shaped hole, irregular in shape but worn smooth by millions of gallons of water flowing through it for millions of years. The wind howled through the opening, promising a way out, even though it seemed beyond my reach.

Piled up against the wall below the opening were thousands of rocks, packed tightly together by sand, seaweed, and millions of shells and fish skeletons, all fused into one solid mass by the immense pressures of the water pounding against it for untold years. It was a sound pile, a firm climb, to the top, but it looked to end far short of the bottom edge of the hole.

But I had come too far to turn back now. Besides where would I go? No way was I climbing back into the cold sea. I wasn't at all sure that I could survive the return trip.

Water hadn't been this way in years. The rocks were dry, not covered in the thick, slippery slime that coated the walls surrounding the underground lake. It made climbing possible—possible—but not easy. As I stood back, eyeing the pile, looking for the easiest route to the top, the lighting continued to improve, filtered sunlight emerged from the hole. It must have been dawn on the other side of the stone wall.

I wondered what day it was—surely not the morning following the volcanic explosion. More than a mere nine or ten hours had passed, surely I had been walking and swimming longer than that. The fact that I was still alive told me that it hadn't been three days. Thirty-six hours I had been lost inside the mountain—thirty-six hours and counting.

Minutes later, bright rays of sunlight shot through the hole, filling the interior of the cavern with a warm glow, the entrance on the other side of the wall unquestionably on a direct line with the rising sun. It warmed the space noticeably, made the wind less objectionable. It gave me hope that I might still make it out of there.

I wasted no more time. I began to pick my way up the pile while the light was at its best. Moving from rock to rock, zigzagging from left to right and back again like I was drunk, I looked for the most stable route, always upward, but never in a straight line. It was not a terribly difficult climb. Not for a strong, healthy, young man. For me it was murderous.

I was sweating, my muscles aching and quivering by the time I reached the summit. I stood on the highest rock, my face and body pressed up hard against the flat wall beneath the hole that was to be my escape route. I traced the texture of the stone with the palm of my hand, reaching slowly upward to the gaping hole that I knew was well out of reach, hoping that by some miracle it would be there, that my arm would magically grow to the required length. I squeezed my eyes shut, went up on tiptoes, willing myself to be taller, and stretched out, tracing the rock with the very tips of my fingers. My hand scrubbed the wall in an arc from right to left, as far as I could reach, feeling nothing but the smoothness of the rock.

I backed away, just a step, just enough to raise my head a few inches, enough to see my probing fingers. I was short. Not by inches, but by feet—five at least.

I stepped from the rock onto another, larger boulder, and sat down, my face to the wall. I let out a little sigh, followed by a slight chuckle, then an honest-to-God laugh. To have gone through all this and found myself just five feet short was just too much. To have survived the waterfall, the fiery missiles of the volcano, the explosion of the mountain, rivers of lava, and being trapped by a cave-in with no food or water, to end up a mere sixty inches from salvation was just more than I could take. I shook with laughter until tears sprung my eyes, until the laughter turned to sobs, until the tears were ones of anger and frustration, of fear and self-pity.

I was losing it.

I rose on shaky legs, steadying myself against the wall, the lower edge of the hole now eight feet beyond my reach, its right most edge directly above me. Surprisingly, the wall felt warm to the touch, nearly hot.

Through the tears, I could see bright sunlight settle on the rock before me, my own shadow showing a striking demarcation between light and dark. Forgetting my own misery, I spun around searching for the new source of light.

There, on a nearly flat surface of wall, a hundred feet opposite the hole, the sun's rays were reflected back as from a mirror's surface. I had to shield my eyes the light was so intense. Looking away from the brilliance, I could see the detail of the rock. It sparkled like diamonds—patches of mica or quartz sending back the light in all directions.

I turned back to the hole, seeing it for the first time in all its detail. From the topmost rock, the wall beneath it was as smooth and even as it had felt. But from the rock below, the one from which I was standing, there was a long fracture in the stone than ran from the lower right portion of the hole down to where it disappeared beneath me. Where I lost it behind the rock, it was little more than a hairline fracture, no more than a quarter of an inch. But the crack widened as it rose, perhaps three or four inches across where it met the edge of the hole. At eye level I could stick my fingers into it all the way up to the last knuckles. I tried wedging both hands into the tiny crevasse and lifting my body off the rock. There was no real leverage and nothing for my hands to really grip. I accomplished nothing other than jamming my fingers down lower into the crack, nearly breaking them.

The crack in and of itself was not going to get me out of there, but I knew that there must be a way that I could use it. I cursed myself for letting the pack with the climbing equipment go. With that I wouldn't even need the crack in the rock. I could just drive a couple of pitons into the wall and climb my way out from the top boulder. With the crack, I wouldn't even need the hammer. I could just wedge three or four pitons into it and climb them like a ladder. Hell, I could even use a rock to pound them in deep enough to easily support my weight.

And then it struck me. The crack *was* there, even though I didn't have the pitons. There had to be something that I could wedge into the fracture, pound it in with a rock.

I climbed back down the pile. It was easier going down than it was up. Normal I guess, but I had a renewed sense of energy, a new sense of purpose. I'd say a light at the end of the tunnel, but at the time I wasn't in the mood for making sappy puns.

Back on the floor of the cave, I scoured the area searching for something that I could use. It had to be long and thin, but strong—strong enough to accept my weight. I was lighter then, but still heavy enough to make useless anything that I could construct with seaweed and fish bones. Even the larger bones, the ones big enough, and long enough to wedge deeply into the crack, would not support my weight. They were dry and snapped easily in my hands with the slightest pressure.

That left the rocks. There were plenty of those, rocks of every size. Some were no larger than peas—others were bigger than an automobile. They had one thing in common however, they were all smooth and nearly as wide as they were long, the currents having rolled and tumbled them, end over end, until they were nearly spherical. Thousands were big enough to take the width of my foot, large enough to support my weight, but I would never be able to wedge one into the crack—they were just too damn wide.

I spent precious minutes trying to find one that was longer than it was wide, something wedge shaped, but with no luck. I would have to make my own.

I found one long enough to do the trick—oval shaped, but wider than I needed by half. It had a crystalline laminate that ran down the long dimension of its shape, one that I thought I could split in half. I placed it on top of a larger stone, picked up a third, one of perhaps twenty-five pounds, and took careful aim. I didn't ease into the blow. I didn't experiment to see how it would go. I gave it everything that I had, knowing that time was running out. I was about to lose the light, not to mention what little strength and courage I had left.

My blow struck cleanly, the rock falling into two nearly equal pieces. In the fading light, I found several more stones of similar shape, but of different size—some smaller than the first—others larger.

I wasn't quite as lucky with the others as I was with the first. Some failed to split cleanly, fractured in a useless place, or shattered altogether. Others took repeated hits, sometimes fracturing the hammer stone instead.

It was tiring work. My right shoulder ached from the exertion, and my hands were stiff, the fingers bruised, from handling the stones. I could barely see from the sweat pouring into my eyes. But as the bright reflection of the sun left, returning the cavern to the dim basement gray, I was ready.

I had five stones, ranging in thickness from about one to three inches. I figured that I would only need three. I just wasn't sure which three. I piled them into my shirt, hoping that the old, worn threads that held the buttons on wouldn't fail me now. I carried the hammer stone cradled in one arm, knowing that the old fabric of the shirt, let alone the button threads, wouldn't survive another twenty-five pounds. I started back up the pile, heavier now by sixty pounds.

I tried each one in a spot in the crack as high as I could reach, a spot that would be my second step. I'd need one at that height in order to pull myself up to the first. One fit quite nicely. It was the mid-largest of the five. Two inches stuck out from the face of the granite—not as much as I'd hoped, but it would have to do. I placed the smaller of the two remaining about half way between it and the boulder on which I worked. I threw the mid-sized one down to the floor, and pounded the stone into the crevasse.

Grabbing the upper stone, I hoisted myself up onto the lower. The first step was the easiest. I knew that it would get harder from that point on. I was no longer standing flatfooted on the wide, stable rock. Now I was standing on a tiny one inch by two inch stone peg, on one leg, holding tightly on to the stub of the second peg, my body pressed hard against the wall to keep from falling backward. I knew that if I fell from this height, a mere three feet, I would likely fall on to the boulder from which I had just stepped. A twisted ankle would probably be the worst that would happen to me. But as I scaled the wall, the results of a fall would be much worse—catastrophic. I wouldn't get a second chance.

Pounding in the next stone, four feet above the second, was much more difficult. Pulling the stone from out of my shirt caused me to nearly fall. Pounding it into the crack was worse. The change in my center of gravity as I positioned the hammer stone a foot and a half away from the wall in order to strike the wedge, made the fingers of my left hand cramp up from the squeeze that I had to put on the peg below. I nearly fell and almost dropped the hammer stone.

But I didn't, and I managed to get the last peg hammered into position. Hoisting myself up to the one below it, I was now standing twelve feet above the top of the rock pile, the edge of the hole, less than eight feet away, above and to my left.

Holding on to the highest peg with my right hand, I stretched as far as I could go to the left. Reaching up, my fingertips brushed the edge of the hole, but that was it.

I had used the last of my stone wedges. I had thrown away the fifth and final one, having been too narrow to do me any good. I could have gone down and made one more. One more would have put me within easy reach of the hole.

Even now, I'm not sure why I didn't. Perhaps I couldn't stand the thought of another trip down and back up the pile of rocks. Maybe it was thirst that drove me to do it. I'm not sure now, and I didn't even think about it then.

I leaped from the peg.

I leaped with all the strength that my one leg could manage, as far as I could go to the left, as close as I could get to the flattest section of the hole's edge. My knees banged into the stone, my body slid painfully along the rock of the wall as the palm of both hands slammed hard against the rock, my hands instinctively curling to catch the edge. They both hit their mark, but the left found nothing but a slick rounded edge, slipping off nearly as fast as it came in contact. The right hand held, my fingers locked into a claw around a small rough lip formed just on the inside edge of the hole. I hung by one arm, fifteen feet over the huge mound of rocks and boulders, fifty feet from the bottom of the pile. My right hand had a death-grip on the rock, as my left searched frantically for a second handhold.

There was nothing there that I could trust. Instead I grabbed my right wrist with my left hand. Like the one-armed pull-ups that I used to do in the gym, I pulled with both arms while pushing against the wall. I was considerably weaker than I was in my gym days, but also considerably lighter. I pulled my head above the level of the ledge.

The wind assaulted me, whipping my long hair across my face, stinging my eyes, bringing fresh tears. Blurry eyes scanned the floor of the opening, which had been swept clean and smooth by the winds and the waters. With nothing to latch on to, I risked letting go with my left arm, throwing it across the floor of the opening, the edge of the hole caught painfully in my armpit. I flexed the fingers of my right hand as I let my other arm take the weight of my body. My legs hung uselessly against the stone wall beneath the hole, but I knew that I had made it. Pausing for only a moment, I swung them up and over the lip, into the hole.

I rolled into the space, afraid that the fierce winds would push me back out through the opening. I lay there for the longest time, not really believing that I had made it, that soon I would be back on the beach, back to the machine. Euphoria is what I should have felt. Exhausted and tired of being alone was all that I could think of.

Eventually, with my face pressed hard against the scrubbed floor of the granite, I opened one eye, seeing the bright blue skies that hovered over the Intercontinental Sea. It was the first time that I had seen blue skies in days. Little did I know that it would be the last time that I would see them for more than a week, perhaps it was the last time that I would see them … ever.

*****

Sitting there in the time machine, looking out through the eastern porthole, I saw no blue skies, hadn't seen them in ten days. In their place were heavy, impenetrable black clouds of smoke and ash. If I had known it at the time, perhaps I would have stayed in the tunnel a bit longer just to appreciate them. But of course, at the time, I was in a hurry to get the hell out of there.

The skies weren't all blue on that day—only the lower horizon to the east was clear and sunny—only that thin strip of sky that I could see from deep within the tunnel. When I reached the end of it, I could see the huge dark clouds high above, working their way from the west.

I came out of the tunnel thirty feet above the sea. I stood at the edge looking out over waters that had to have dropped fifty or sixty feet since I had last been there. I breathed deeply of the fresh air, expecting to be assaulted by the stench of sulfur that I was sure permeated the black skies overhead. But it was not sulfur. It was something altogether different, and much more disconcerting. It was the unmistakable smell of wood burning.

Knowing that I was only a few hours away from my beach, I didn't hesitate even a second—I dove head first into the water, not giving a thought to how tired and thirsty I was, or what might be laying in wait below the surface of the water. The way my luck had been running, there was probably a school of *Mantillis* waiting for me. Or another *Elasmosaurus*, a real one this time, maybe just passing by. For all I knew the water might only have been a couple of feet deep. I could have broken my neck.

It was yet another stupid thing to do, in a long—getting longer—list of stupid things. But the water was deep—deep and without predators.

As I stroked through the waters on my back, I marveled at the cliffs rising high above me on the left side. They were so much taller than they had been nine years ago, meaning that the level of the water was so much lower than it was then. The rumbling of the ground that I had heard so frequently over the years, and had reached such a dramatic climax over the last few days, had something to do with that. It wasn't just the formation of the polar ice caps that had shrunk the sea. Something had drained it as well, like pulling the stopper from a tub of water. Not letting all of it out, but just a portion of it, maybe half, before shoving the stopper back into its well. Or perhaps the stopper was still out, the seas continuing to drain. There was little doubt in my mind that a seismic event, perhaps a whole series of such events, had opened up the floor of the Intercontinental Sea and swallowed up a huge part of it. Not being a geology student, I would never know for sure. But in my wild imagination I saw the earthquakes opening up huge deep canyons in the sea floor, millions of cubic feet of water rushing in to fill them, lowering the level of the sea by a hundred feet, pulling it back by miles from its earlier shores. I saw the birth of the Grand Canyons, opening not all at once, but separating a few miles at a time, growing wider and deeper with each successive quake. I had only experienced the early part of the birth. It would be thousands of years before it was complete.

Of course there may have been another explanation, probably was in fact. But it was a nice daydream. I had seen the canyons on several occasions, both from high above in an airplane, and up close, standing at the very edge, looking down onto the Colorado River thousands of feet below. It was one of the most spectacular sights that I had ever seen, and now, even though it may have only been a figment of my imagination, I kind of liked the thought that I was there to see the beginning.

And on that day I was mighty thankful for it, because I had only been in the water for an hour or so when the cliffs began to bend off to the west and the beach magically appeared before me, miles sooner than when they had the last time.

I had only to follow the cliffs as they made the turn, walking on flat sandy beach, skirting the shells and skeletal remains of fish, mounds of sea kelp and plankton turned brown by the sun.

I had nothing to fear from the beach. It was home. I knew exactly where I was going. I knew that in twenty or thirty minutes I would see the entrance to the cave, the end of the machine sticking out from it. There was water inside, not salt water, but fresh water, not much of it, and not much of anything else, but water was exactly what I needed just then.

*****

I didn't spend much time in the machine when it showed itself—just one night—just enough time to drink, to eat a simple meal of dried granola, and to sleep. It wasn't a great sleep. The night was haunted by explosions, by giant aquatic, prehistoric beasts, and by climbing. I climbed upward, hand over hand, and foot over foot, climbing to somewhere, never sure exactly where. I climbed to get way from something, but no idea what.

The next morning, the dreams troubling, but beginning to fade, I was off, carrying nothing but two bottles of water and a granola bar, not in a backpack, but stuck into the oversized pockets of my fatigue pants. I had to get back to the tree, to my home.

The trip was nothing. It was little more than going to the neighborhood store, just down the block and around the corner. I had made the trip so many times before that I could have done it blindfolded. And on that trip, I had nothing to carry, nothing to lug behind, nothing to drag up the long incline, and pulley down the gravel slope. I went just as fast as my tired legs would carry me, as quickly as my healed lungs would allow.

I had to get to the tree. I didn't stop for the night, just kept on going as the sun sank in the west. I had nothing to fear in the night. I knew every rock and every obstacle. Even in the dark, I knew every landmark and every turn.

As the night drew long, I became witness to a most extraordinary event—the sunset—or so I thought.

I was getting close, the edge of the plateau no more than five or six miles farther. In the distance, coming from beyond the cliff was the emerging light. It got brighter the closer that I got.

The sun was rising in the west.

I knew that I hadn't mistakenly doubled back in the night, and I wasn't delusional. As if by magic, the sun was coming up from the wrong end of the world. It wasn't until I was just yards from the edge that the magic trick was revealed to me.

The entire valley was ablaze.

CHAPTER 24

Goddamn computer!

It had taken to dying on me from time to time—more often lately. I was forced to punch the save button after nearly every sentence that I wrote, having been burned several times by the damn thing cutting out in the middle of a lengthy thought. More often than not I forgot exactly what I had written since the last time that I had saved it, having to recreate the words over again, knowing that I had lost at least a part of what I was trying to say. I never felt that I said it exactly right the second time—that a part of what I was thinking just a few short minutes earlier left my brain as soon as I had typed it. When the computer was bad it pissed me off, and I responded in kind, punching at the keys with such force as to sometimes send the plastic caps flying.

Like me, the computer was getting old. I couldn't even imagine how many hardware and software upgrades there had been since this one was built. It was old and I had treated it badly—punching at the keys, slamming the monitor down, tossing it haphazardly onto the bed or the desk. Its case was grimy and scratched—a crack ran across the corner of the keyboard, growing longer from one day to the next. The screen was so hazy that if I didn't set it at exactly the right angle, I couldn't see a thing. Several of the keys stuck—several others I had to hit repeatedly to get a response. It made impossible to decipher sentences if I didn't pay attention. It was old and sick, and I was making it worse. A good shrink might suggest that I was doing it on purpose. I'm not at all sure that I would have argued.

It wasn't a new problem. It had begun more than a year ago when I had trouble getting it to power up. The problems started back during the time when the sun was blotted out from the sky for days at a time. A time when I took the laptop out of the machine and out of the tunnel to try to gather as much of the daylight as possible to keep the solar cells charged up. It was during the time when black and gray ash fell from the skies, covering everything in a fine coating of soot—including the computer. I wondered if the lack of sunshine kept it from powering up, or whether the gritty ash had clogged up something important, something that kept it from coming alive.

During that time, there were but a handful of occasions when I got it to boot up. And on those rare, infrequent times, I chose not to chronicle my adventure. It wasn't that I had nothing significant to add to my story—on the contrary—I had plenty—more than plenty. But after losing my home and damn near everything else that I had, about the last thing in the world that I wanted to do was write about it. To do as much would have started up the bad dreams again. Instead, I took to playing the assortment of computer games that Dermot had installed. Even then, I really didn't pay much attention, the computer beating me every time. There was no doubt that it was smarter than I was, but I really never gave myself much of a chance.

I spent most of my time, most of my conscious time, thinking about the old times, the times when I was but one of six billion souls packing an ever shrinking planet. I was of such insignificant importance back then, just one of thousands of scientists, all trying to make a mark, but failing miserably in the greater scheme of things. I was of no more importance that just about any other human being on the planet. I had some reputation among my small group of peers, but to the rest of the world, the other ninety-nine–point–nine–nine–nine-percent, I was as unknown as the horse who finished tenth in last year's Kentucky Derby.

But I had been significant to some back then, although most were gone even before I was. My parents had died years before I left, their memories fading with each day that passed. At times I had to struggle to remember very much about them, about how they looked, how they talked.

My wife had gone before me, as well—gone much too soon. In some ways it seemed like it was only yesterday that Jakes had called to tell me of Elizabeth's death. The shock and sadness still crept in when I thought about that phone call, the anger bubbling quickly to the surface when I thought about *how* she died.

In other ways it seemed like a lifetime ago. I guess that in some ways it really was a lifetime ago—at least a *different* life. It had been twelve years since that phone call—enough time to heal—more than enough time to get on with my life. And I thought that's why I was here—to get on with it—to build a new life for myself. For nine years I thought that I was doing exactly that—building a new life.

I had created a home. High in the tree, beneath the cliffs in the valley of the dinosaurs, I had built my house. It had no electricity, no plumbing, no heating and air conditioning. There were no windows, or doors, no thick-pile carpeting, or plastered walls. I had no refrigerator, microwave, electric can opener, or food processor. There was no attached garage with two cars sitting in the driveway, no manicured lawns, and no neighbors. There were none of the things that once defined a home for me, but the tree was as much a home to me as any that I had ever lived in.

The tree was my sanctuary. It's where I escaped to when dangerous animals were on the prowl. It's where I went to get out of the rain and the cold, and even the heat. It's where I ate and where I slept. It's where I read, and played solitaire, and entertained myself in a hundred other ways. It's where I planned and where I dreamed.

And they were mostly good dreams. The nightmares about horrible, meat-eating dinosaurs, and about being trapped in caves and drowning in dark rivers became less and less frequent, fading from memory before I even climbed from my warm bed. Even the others, the ones about Elizabeth, became rare and less troubling. Over time, they were replaced by good dreams.

The good dreams were mostly about Susan. I dreamt about how this was *our* home—not just mine.

Everything that I did around the house, everything that I made, or changed, or thought about, I first asked myself—would Susan like this? This was my home, and I cared about it, but Susan's opinion was most important.

Susan wasn't one who put a lot of stock in possessions, wasn't a person that gave a damn about what other people thought about her or how she lived. But she was someone who was passionate, who cared deeply about her own likes and dislikes, who wanted to live life on her own terms.

Susan would have loved the tree—everything about it.

She would have loved living out in the open, high above the ground, waking to a panoramic view of the valley every morning. Tending the garden, eating fruit right off the vine would have been so much better to her than having to shop at the market. Bathing in the stream beneath the cliff would have been preferred over a bathtub. She wouldn't have minded a bit that there were no means of transportation other than what her own two feet provided. The fact that there were no other people wouldn't have bothered her either. She had always been a loner, never afraid to be on her own. Other people only got in her way—kept her from doing what she really wanted to do, which, most of the time, was to dig.

Of course, in the valley, Susan wouldn't have had to dig to find dinosaurs. If she chose, she could just sit in the tree and watch them parade by along the path by the river. She wouldn't do that however. She'd want to be right in there among them—to study them in their natural habitat, up close and personal—and alive. She wouldn't have to guess about how the broken old bones fit together, how the muscles attached, what the texture and color of their skin was like. With live dinosaurs to study, she would have nearly everything that she had ever wanted.

And she could still dig. There were hundreds, thousands, of species that had died off long before the Cretaceous period. Massive extinctions took place at the end of the Triassic and Jurassic periods, causing the mysterious demise of animals such as the *Stegosaurs* and the *Brachiosaurs*. In this time, they hadn't been dead and buried for a hundred and fifty million years, but only half that time. The chances of finding something of them, something significant, was much greater here. I knew Susan. She wouldn't have stopped digging. She would have spent her time equally between studying live dinosaurs and digging for the old.

And she would have been happy.

The tree served as a bond between us. Other than my memories, which were fading like all the rest, it was perhaps the final bond. I felt that there was a part of her in the tree, like her spirit was there with me. Like somehow she knew all about the tree. I could feel her presence, only as a fleeting image at first, more powerful and consistent as the years went by. Sometimes I could almost see her— walking through the garden, climbing up the ladder to the second deck, standing against the railing, staring out over the meadow. At times it seemed so real that I called out to her. She never answered, but the feeling persisted.

It was my most special bond. But it was a bond that had been broken for more than a year, a bond that had gone up in smoke and flames, along with the tree and nearly everything that I possessed.

It had been like a scene from hell as I came over the ridge on that early morning. The sky above was lit up by millions of acres of jungle in flames. Even separated by the width of the river and the hundred feet of cliff, the heat was so intense that I could barely take it for more than a few seconds at a time. I had to lay atop the ridge with just the top half of my head peering over the edge. What I saw was as amazing as it was horrible.

Plants and trees that were normally so wet with the summer rains that I thought impossible to ignite were throwing flames hundreds of feet in the air. The meadow too was aflame, tiny brush and shrubs sending out heat and fire way beyond what their meager energy provided. Sparks and flaming debris from the mountain had unquestionably started the fires. Lava coming up through the cracks in the valley floor really got it going. Looking closely, I could see tiny streams of the molten rock dribbling into the river below, sending up huge clouds of steam.

As sweat poured from my brow, the upper part of my face scalded lobster-red, I watched the fire eat my beautiful jungle. The flames extended as far as I could see to the north and the south. To the west, I could barely see what was left of the decapitated mountain, its ruined shell still sending out waves of black clouds into the morning sky that was to get no brighter than it was right then. The cliff on which I cowered was a natural firebreak, halting both the flames and the spread of the lava from moving eastward.

Nothing in the valley was spared. Directly in front of me, just beyond the flaming meadow, was my tree, a huge ball of fire standing out from all the rest. Hotter, bigger, more colorful with reds, yellows, and blues, that seemed to pale the rest of the inferno. Bursts of sparks jumped out from within, the flooring, rails, and woven roofs of my house adding fuel to the intense fire. Through the blaze I could see a perfect ring of fire as the perimeter logs of my compound burned. Like Roman candles, the dried wood of the poplars shot flames up and out from their pointed tips. Small explosions could be heard above the roar of the fire as my munitions discharged under the incredible, smothering heat.

I knew that within the next few hours, there would be nothing left of the valley but the black, skeletal remains of a few misshapen trees sticking grotesquely from the charred earth, and streams of smoky lava, hardening in ugly, rough patches across the valley floor. There would be nothing left of the tree, nothing left of my worldly possessions except unrecognizable lumps of steel and iron. Of this I was sure.

I couldn't bear the thought of seeing what the fire had reduced my home to. I turned and fled from the horrible sight.

*****

The fire had left me with next to nothing: no tools to rebuild my home, no seeds to replant my garden, almost nothing in the way of clothing, books, cooking utensils, packaged food, or bottled water. And except for my hunting knife, I had no weapons, no way to protect myself. What I hadn't lost in the Intercontinental Sea, the bone pile, and the river that ran before the mountain, I had lost in the fire. Pistols, rifles, and ammo were all gone. Even the machetes and garden implements that could have been fashioned into weapons had been lost to the flames.

For weeks afterward I hid in the machine, cowering in the dimly lit interior of the metal box, reading the last of the books, eating what remained of the food, shivering in the dark as the earth continued to shake beneath me. The volcano may have been gone, reduced to a massive, smoldering pile of rubble, but the quakes continued on, nearly every day. Sometimes they were barely perceptible, just the tiniest of shimmers, feeling only like I had had a bit too much coffee to drink. Other times the machine shook beneath me like a freight train on bad rails, cascading small rocks down the slope of the cliff above, pummeling the titanium skin of my new/old home.

The one, the only thing that I had managed to replenish, was my water supply. I was continuously bordering on the edge, just a few sips away from running out, but somehow I always managed to keep the supply from reaching bottom, usually down to the last plastic bottle. I always nursed them, afraid that it would run out before I had a chance to refill it.

Summer ran into fall—the rainy season. Fresh water was plentiful, if I could just find a way to capture it. Ten years ago I had used my rain gear to deflect the rain into an assortment of pots and pans, transferring the water into the bottles. Now I had no rain gear, no pots and pans, and but a handful of bottles.

But I had learned how to improvise over the past ten years. Using my knife as a screwdriver, I managed to disassemble one of the shelves. Using rocks as hammers (I had plenty of rocks) I fashioned one of the metal shelves into a crude funnel. When the rains came, it took only minutes to fill the half-dozen bottles, after first putting the end of the funnel to my lips and drinking till I could hold no more, taking it in as fast as I could swallow it. Not having to ration it was such an overwhelming sensation of joy that I tended to forget what it was like to be thirsty. Reality always set in within a few days.

With reality came the realization that my funnel was but a short-term solution. When mid-winter hit, rainy days would be a rarity. Mid-summer would be worse. Sooner or later I would have to decide what I was going to do for the rest of my life—and where I was going to do it.

There was always the river to the west, the one below the cliff, the one just a few hundred yards from what used to be my tree. But I would use up half the water that I collected just in making the trip. My life would consist of little more than hiking back and forth to the river. What kind of life was that? Besides, I had serious doubts that the river still existed, the flow of lava having probably consumed it. And anyway, I really didn't want to go back. There were just too many memories there.

Staying in the time machine wasn't much of an option either. Besides the lack of water, which would continue to be a source of struggle, perhaps an insurmountable one, there was the problem with food. It was available, ten miles out, where the new shoreline now existed. I had already been forced to use it, having run out of the few canned stores that I had left behind in the machine. It was a long hike—there and back—and I had tired of it quickly after just a few days.

I had but one other option.

The new forest that was quickly emerging from the south continued to develop. The so-called moderate climate of this period seemed to accelerate the growth. Perhaps the ash that fell from the sky in huge quantities during the past year quickened its normal pace even more. I had read somewhere, in one of Dermot's gardening books, that wood ash from the fireplace was excellent for a garden. I had used piles of it from my fire pit in the compound in the garden. It sure as hell seemed to work there. The ash was working its magic on the new growth popping up outside the cave, as well. Making the trip southward, to see where the new forest led, seemed like the only thing left to do.

And as the wet fall gave way to the dryer winter, with my water stores getting stretched further every day, I decided that it was time. Putting on nearly every bit of clothing that I had, tying my knife onto a long piece of rail from the shelving unit to make a serviceable spear, and stuffing four nearly empty water bottles into the extra-large pockets of my camouflaged pants, I headed out.

I hadn't been this way for more than a year. It surprised me how much it had changed. The birds, insects, and rodents seemed to have multiplied ten-fold. They were everywhere. There were times when the hunger pains were at their worst that I actually tried to skewer one of the little varmints. But they were just too quick, and my heart wasn't really in it. Nevertheless, my stomach growled in anticipation when I tried, and for just a few seconds afterward it was angry with me when I missed the target.

The hunger didn't prove to be a huge problem, as the growth became denser, and more diverse. Those things from the valley that I recognized as edible began to appear the farther south that I traveled. I was in a perpetual state of hunger, but I had enough to survive. Water, on the other hand, became an increasing problem. By the third day out, the bottles were empty—empty, and no sign of precipitation. The dew on the early morning foliage became my only source of moisture for the next two days.

And then the skies opened up. It started off as snow, early, before the sun was up fully over the eastern horizon. With it hiding behind a stale-looking sky, the snow changed to sleet, light at first, growing heavier as the temperatures struggled to climb just a few degrees. By noon it had given way to rain—torrential rain. It came straight down, not in drops, but in sheets, boring into my head and shoulders with a force that stunned me. Within seconds it had penetrated my jacket and pants, the inner layer of clothing soaking up the water until it was saturated. And it was cold—freezing cold.

My teeth chattered and my body shook as I looked in vain for someplace to hide from the punishing rain. I could hardly see ten yards in front of my face, but I knew that that didn't matter. The trees were not tall, nor full enough to offer much protection, not from this kind of downpour. Squatting under the lower lying shrubbery was out as well. The rain was coming down so fast that I was standing in several inches of it, despite the relative flatness of the ground.

I headed directly west, toward the cliff that was only a few hundred yards away, hoping to find an overhang, a cave, or just a crack in the rock wide enough to squeeze into—anything at all to get out of the rain.

I found the cliff easily enough. It rose high above me, blurring and breaking up by the waves of water, disappearing into the opaque sky. Water poured down its flat surface, pooling quickly at its base, icy water covering my feet and ankles.

With my head bowed against the pouring rain, my right hand tracing the surface of the cold granite, I continued my journey south. I walked for hours, the rain never letting up for even a second. It pounded down on top of me, my strength flowing from me as my body temperature began to drop. The sounds of the birds and scurrying animals were gone, drowned out by the roar of the water striking the cliff, the ground, and me. I couldn't distinguish one from another. It just all blended into one continuous roar, like a radio tuned off-station, its volume control twisted to full on.

My mind was beginning to shut down, to go as numb as my body had before it, when my fingers lost track of the wall. I looked up for the first time in perhaps an hour, trying to see through the temporary wall of water to the permanent wall of stone.

The continuous rock face had come to an end—or, at least a break in the wall. There stood a massive opening in the rock, just in front of me. I dove into it, even though I still couldn't see it clearly through the rain that was a heavy sheet across its opening.

The change as I passed through the portal was instantaneous. Like floating through the air, my body seemed to lose half its weight as the rain abruptly stopped pounding down on me from above. I staggered a few dozen paces into the interior of the space like a man strung out on drugs, slamming against one rough-hewn wall, sliding down it into a sitting position.

I passed out, or simply fell immediately to sleep, my body as well as my mind more than willing to shut down and drift of into a slumber that was dry, if not warm.

I dreamt poorly. The cold invaded my sleep. I dreamt of the cave, a dozen years ago. I dreamt of Christine. It wasn't the first time that I had dreamt the dream, but it was still as frustrating, as horrifying, as it was the first time that I dreamt it—as terrifying as when it had happened in real life.

Only this time I hadn't actually seen Christine. Unlike the previous dreams where she scolded me for bringing her into the cave, yelled at me for letting her die there, me all the while powerless to do anything—in this one I couldn't see her at all. I couldn't see her, and yet I knew that she was there, somewhere beyond the mountain of snow, across the other side of the cave.

I couldn't see anything at all, except what the entombing block of ice allowed me to see. My arms and my legs, all of me was paralyzed by the unyielding ice. I knew that it was a block of ice, an imperfect cube of frozen water, yet I could see perfectly, like it was finely cut glass. My eyes were frozen in place, focused entirely on the blue skies, on the sunlight coming through the tiny opening between the top of the cave's entrance and the mound of snow below. I watched in horror as the head of a *Tyrannosaur* entered the space. Entombed in ice as I was, I could still hear perfectly well. The huge beast snorted in anticipation, its breath forming matching jets of white vapor from its nostrils. It stared at me for long seconds, not put off in any way by the block of ice, but rather ambivalent. It didn't give a damn about me. It was after one thing. It was after Christine, somehow knowing that she was buried in ten feet of snow on the opposite side of the cave.

I continued to watch, absolutely unable to do a damn thing about it, as the *rex* began pushing the snow aside with its snout. It was moving inward and to its right, throwing snow in my direction, although it never seemed to obscure my vision. Instead, it was just kind of absorbed into the perfection of my frozen prison.

The *Tyrannosaur* continued moving toward the interior of the cave toward the opposite side. My eyes were unable to move from the cave's tiny opening, which was now nearly obliterated by the mass of the killer dinosaur. Its head was nothing but a watery blur on the edge of my peripheral vision as I began to hear Christine's screams.

The level of the snow began to drop rapidly as the massive hind legs of the *rex* sent it flying through the growing entrance to the cave. Flashes of brightly sunlit skies jumped into my limited range of vision as the meat eater frantically pawed at the snow. I could tell by Christine's intensified screams that she could now see the hungry animal. I could tell by the roar of the beast that it had spotted her, as well. In my mind I screamed out for her to run, to take cover, to bury herself in the snow if she had to. But even without seeing her, I knew that she hadn't heard me.

I awoke as both cries were at their peak, just an instant before they halted in one brief moment of terror and satisfaction. I awoke shaken, but not from the cold. I awoke soaking wet, but not from the rain. I awoke so that I didn't die from pure unadulterated terror.

The dream was still fresh in my mind as I tried to reason it out. It was the ghost of a memory, something that was based in terrifying reality with just a touch of mystery and a twist of the bizarre. Or it was prognostication, an insight of things to come. It was only afterward that I discovered that the latter was more the truth.

I awoke to the noise of the rain that hadn't abated even a decibel. If anything, it was louder than before, coming at me from both directions. The feeling that it was booming static coming from a radio poorly set between stations seemed even more appropriate now as I seemed to be situated between the stereo system's two massive speakers. The short, wide tunnel that I had found myself in only seemed to amplify the sound. It assaulted my ears with a continuous, thunderous roar.

The floor was wet with the runoff from the storm, but it was flat, perhaps thirty feet across. The walls were smooth and straight, no sign of wear. They rose toward one another at an angle, meeting some fifty feet overhead. A river or stream running through hadn't carved the space. I knew what *that* looked like, and this was nothing like that. Some force had split the cliff at a natural fault line, cleaving it and separating it at its base, opening a path to the other side. The tunnel was no more than two hundred feet in length at its peak, opening up from a single point, widening out as it extended well beyond what I could see through the pouring rain. The rain poured through the opening, creating a solid wall of water that was shaped like the point of an arrow—pointed right at me.

I was still wet and cold as I found a dry patch of ground to spread out on, but at least I had solved my immediate water shortage. It took no more than a few seconds to fill each of the bottles from the wall of water. I drank it greedily, even though it did nothing to stop the shivers that had recommenced as soon as I awoke.

I sat huddled against a large rock situated midway between the two ends of the tunnel, my arms wrapped tight around me to conserve my body heat. I watched the rain fall until once again I fell asleep, for the second time in as many hours.

This time there were no dreams, no waking to fear-induced sweats, no horrific noise jarring me to my senses. I awoke to the birds singing and brilliant rays of sunshine peaking into the tunnel from the eastern opening. It had warmed considerably, even in the shade of the cavern. My clothes had dried and I wondered just how long I had been asleep. The gnawing pains in my belly told me that I had been here for the better part of a full day.

I walked over to the western side of the tunnel, seeing it clearly for the first time. The roof above me opened gradually from a point midway in the center of the peaked roof. I walked on, like being in a half tube, the ground flat and sure beneath me, the walls angling up above, their length growing shorter as I proceeded forward. More daylight entered the space before me as I continued on, the opening above widening for every step that I took, letting in even more of the encroaching daylight.

I emerged from the tunnel onto a flat rocky ledge that overlooked a narrow canyon. On either side were cliffs that soared hundreds of feet into the sky, their surfaces layered with eons of erosion, row after row of horizontal ripples that, following the rough contour of the rock, separated it into alternating colors of reds, browns, and yellows. There were countless rock formations that took on bizarre, even comical shapes—rocks impossibly balanced on top of other rocks, tall spires that twisted and turned at odd angles, hundred ton boulders that looked more like they had been shaped by man rather than the forces of nature. The cliffs were pockmarked with irregular shaped ledges and cave-like openings. Deep shadows shrouded the slope making it impossible to judge the depth or destination of any of them.

Directly across a chasm that stretched a quarter of a mile, was a mirror image of where I stood. The sun reflected brightly off the western wall, the colors vibrant and startling in their diversity, like the cliff was dressed in brightly colored Christmas ribbons. They stretched far into the distance in both directions, curving out of sight, one end heading east, the other west. The steep slopes were covered with the same strange rock formations, the same caves and ledges.

Below, four hundred feet at least, was a river, not very wide, with rocks protruding above its surface, white foam surrounding each as the water slammed into them. Even from this height, I could see that it wasn't deep, but it was fast, the water rushing from the right to the left at frightening speed, twisting and turning as the rocks dictated its course. From that height I was only guessing, but the river looked to be no more than a hundred feet across, varying in width to perhaps twice that. There were patches of dry land that appeared randomly on either side. Scraggly stands of spindly trees and copses of stunted brush popped up wherever they could find enough stable soil and sunlight to exist.

I sat at the very edge of the ledge, my legs dangling over the side, marveling at the amazing sight. Again, I couldn't help but think of the Grand Canyon. The sheer forces of nature that created this natural wonder, the absolute power of it, was nothing short of staggering. Although it was neither as deep nor as wide as what I had seen when I was a younger man—in a different time—it was so much more spectacular. Maybe it was the lighting, which was now just creeping high enough to reflect in the water far below—hundreds of tiny rainbows birthed by the watery haze that burst forth around every rock, the cliffs across the chasm lit up in spectacular fashion. Maybe it was because no one else had ever seen it—no human at least. Millions had seen the Grand Canyon and the scores of canyons on this continent and others. But no one had ever seen this one, not this way, and not in this time. It made it pretty damn special.

But then again, maybe it was so special because it gave me hope.

I didn't know what was down there, where the canyon led to beyond the curve in the river, what dangers lurked there. But I saw it as an opportunity, a chance to follow the bend in the river, to wherever it led, and maybe, just maybe, find a new start. Or, at least, I saw a chance to live out my few remaining years with a sense of purpose.

The easy route would have been to just turn around, march back through the tunnel, and head back to the machine. I could survive there—maybe—if I could keep my small supply of water from running out. I was inventive. I could fashion some large containers from the remaining shelves of the storage racks. I could use them to store the spring rains, but how would I keep it fresh? Stagnant water was no good. It would make me sick. The things that grew in it would first give me the shits, and it would only get worse from there. I had to have a regular supply of fresh water, and I couldn't count on that from the vicinity of the machine. And I knew that if I stayed there I'd die, more sooner than later. I'd die from lack of adventure, from the lack of purpose. I'd die from sheer boredom.

Or I could take the more difficult route. I could enter the canyon below, follow the river to the south, not knowing where it would lead me, but following it to wherever it went, knowing that there would be discovery and adventure—danger and adversity.

My decision would be irreversible. It would be difficult enough to get down the steep slope, impossible to climb back up without the proper equipment. I didn't have so much as a length of rope. The face of the cliff was nearly vertical, but its surface was rough and layered, like badly worn steps tilted at a nearly impossible angle. There were enough outcroppings, formations, ledges, and seams that I thought that I could kind of slide on my backside from one to the next.

But once I stepped off from the ledge, there would be no turning back.

I stepped off the ledge.

I stepped off from the right side, targeting in on a tall, twisted formation about thirty feet below, ten feet off to the side. In my right hand I held the spear with all my might, knife end up, terrified of losing my one and only weapon, and pressed my back up against the rough stone.

I started down faster than I had anticipated, my legs churning, digging my rubber heels in to slow my descent. I jabbed at the rock with the square end of my spear, trying to push myself over to the right. I saw the spire as a blur as I began to accelerate. I reached my arm out, catching it at the last possible instant in the crook of my arm. Pain shot up through my shoulder as my arm was nearly yanked from its socket, but I held on.

I swung from it, my feet kicking desperately to grasp a hold on one of the ruffles in the rock. With my spear, I managed to dig the sharp corner into the stone, pushing my body sideways just enough to tuck the outcropping of rock under my armpit, to stop my legs from swinging from one side to the other.

The rock was even rougher than I thought. Like a cheese grater, it easily shredded the back of my jacket, the ass end of my pants. My elbows and back of my head were already bruised and screaming at me for the decision that I had made. And I had barely started my descent.

Directly beneath me, another fifty feet, was a ledge, fifteen feet wide, a mere three of four feet sticking out from the wall. There was nothing else to try for. It was the ledge or nothing, and it was too late to turn back.

It looked impossible. I thought for just an instant about just letting go, pushing out with my legs, and doing an impressive swan drive all the way to the bottom. What a magnificent sight it would make—me crashing down onto the rocks below—my bloody body dashed from one rock to another as it sped down the rapids. Too bad there was no one here to see it.

I didn't dive, but I did let go of the strange twisted spire. I spread my body across the wall, pushing every inch of my backside into the stone, garnering every possible bit of friction to slow me down. My elbows and tailbone took the most abuse, banging painfully across every ridge, the end of the spear clanging out a frantic rhythm as I sped toward the tiny ledge. I used my spread arms and legs as rudders, pushing here, letting up there, in an attempt to remain upright.

I had to hit the ledge feet first. Any other way and I'd be seriously injured, or worse, I'd likely bounce and roll right over the edge, turning head over heels all the way to the bottom. There was a recess above the ledge that I hadn't noticed from above. I passed over the lip of it and dropped the last ten or twelve feet straight down.

I landed feet first, but hard, the shock instantly transmitted up from my feet, through my legs and into my back. I pitched forward, going down on all fours, skidding to a stop as my hands gripped the very edge of the ledge. I peered over it to the sparkling river below—more than three hundred feet below.

As if the fall hadn't frightened me enough, there was a sudden cry from behind me, and a pair of *Pteranodons* rose into the air above, their long wings nearly knocking me from my perch. I watched them fly away, catching the canyon's breeze under their wings as I crouched there trying to catch my breath. I sagged down onto my belly, shaken and sore, feeling my age, or some other person's age … if that person was ninety.

So far it wasn't going exactly according to plan, but it got a little better from there. The slope of the cliff changed a bit as I made my way down its side, the angle becoming just a little less steep, slowing my acceleration to something more acceptable. I was able to scoot down it, one ridge at a time, digging my heels into one ridge, bumping my rear end up and over the one above. My ass was on fire, my hands raw and bloodied from the roughness of the rock, but I had made it to within fifty feet of the river.

The ridge lay on one of the more pronounced steps of the cliff. It was nearly a shelf that ran sixty feet above the river, navigating the curves and uneven surface for as far as I could see. I sat on it, pressing the palms of my hands hard against the slim horizontal portion of the rock to take just a little pressure from my bruised and bloodied butt. It was nearly impossible to see what remained of the cliff—the last of it dropped suddenly, as vertical as the wall of a building constructed to the truest of specifications.

Using my arms, I lifted off of the slim ledge onto the surface of the even slimmer ruffle. Carefully, I scooted to my left, digging with my heels, pushing off with both arms, searching for another point of descent. I worked my way slowly to the south, perhaps a hundred yards or more with no change in the angle of the rock for as far as I could see.

If this had been the sea, or even a really good-sized river, one that was deep, I would have considered jumping. But what lay below me was anything but deep. Below me were shallow waters and hundreds of rocks, either of which would result in sure death. Jumping into the river from this height would be only an involuntary option that would happen when I lost consciousness and fell from the cliff.

I wasn't at that point yet, and was determined to find a way down—an easier way down. I continued to lift and scoot across the narrow ridge, another hundred yards … two hundred.

It seemed like I had traveled for hours when I reached an impasse. A fissure in the rock blocked any farther southern movement. At my level, it was perhaps two feet wide, extending upward a hundred feet, narrowing as it went. What it did below my level I had no idea. I couldn't peer over the ridge without risking falling and I couldn't tell what was directly beneath me.

The fracture in the rock wasn't so wide that I couldn't slide across it. If I was careful, I could place one hand and one foot on the other side, shift my weight from right to left, and simply cross over. Not a huge challenge, but where would I go from there? The cliff turned gradually to the west, meaning that I could see it clearly for more than half a mile. In all that distance there seemed to be no better alternative. And if I kept sliding sideways along the slim edge, sooner or later I was going to make a small misstep, a tiny miscalculation about where to place my foot, my hand, where to position my weight. And the rock wasn't all that stable. The rough surface kept eroding beneath me, pieces continuously rubbing off, falling down into the river below. Sooner or later, more than just a small piece would break away and I'd go down with it.

I removed one of my boot's laces, tying one end to my makeshift spear, the other to my belt so that it dangled three feet below me, freeing both hands. I twisted on the rock, sliding my left foot into the crevasse, the right foot following. I snaked into it, pushing my body tight against the rightmost edge, working myself into the tight space.

I was completely into the fissure, my feet and back pressed hard against opposite sides. Looking down from between my bent knees I could see the water below, churning and splashing, white foam gurgling as the waves rolled into the interior of the crevasse, but I couldn't actually see the edges of the rock as it disappeared into the water. Pressing hard with the back of my arms, I took the weight from my back and let my bottom scrape along the rock, creeping downward six inches. I repositioned my feet, one at a time, matching the six-inch drop of my body.

I continued on this way for twenty minutes. I had cut the distance by more than half, now no more than twenty feet above the roar of the water pounding the rock below. But the descent had become increasingly more difficult, the crack in the wall widening the farther I climbed. Ten feet above, my back had lost contact with the rock. With some difficulty I had managed to turn my body over so that now I was facing the water, my right shoulder jammed against the cold, hard stone, my neck bent painfully to one side. In another few feet, the pressure was off my shoulder, as only my hands and feet stayed in contact.

My arms and shoulders were screaming, my wrists bent back painfully, as I *walked* a few tentative steps down the fracture. At fifteen feet, I could feel the spray, a cold mist that rose up to greet me. By then I was nearly fully stretched out, my hands beginning to slip on the wet, slick, rock. My spine felt as if it were about to snap, gravity pushing down relentlessly, as I stretched every muscle across the widening span of the fissure.

The water sprayed hard and cold into my face, blinding me. I had gone as far as I could go and I could feel my hands begin to slide one last time. Without being able to see what was below, I pushed off from the rock, first with my feet, then with my hands, turning my body in a clockwise rotation so that I dropped feet first.

By some miracle, I wasn't impaled on my own spear as I spilled into the water, but I hit hard, the water only a few feet deep. Stunned, the water slammed me into the hard rock at the back of the shallow cave. I stood, the pain in both ankles and both knees attesting to the speed at which I hit the water and the hard riverbed that was much too close to the surface. The pain dissipated quickly as my legs grew numb in the freezing water. It was up to my chin, but the way that it swirled and swept into the small cavern, the way that it crashed into the walls made it impossible to see, nearly impossible to breathe.

In a moment of panic I reached down below the surf to the rope attached to my belt. Surprisingly, the spear was still there, the knife firmly attached. Holding tightly onto it, I backed away from the wall into the rapids that tried desperately to push me back. I had to lean into the onrushing water, the force great enough to push me back in if I didn't. Every time that I lifted one leg, the force overtook me, sending me back into the little cave, pounding me into the rock. I tried three times, each time thrown back in with greater force that the time before.

The force pounded me from above, not so much from below. In fact, the tumultuous waves from the top tended to push me backwards while the currents from below pulled my feet out from under me. Each time I toppled over backward, in a crude half somersault, crashing headfirst into the rocks in the rear of the cave.

I stayed there, a mere twenty feet from the opening, studying the waves as they came crashing in. There was symmetry to them, a pulsing heartbeat kind of timing to them. I watched for a couple of minutes until I thought I understood their pattern. At the moment the wave came crashing in, I dropped below the surface, and with my legs, I pushed against the rock with all that I had.

I stayed on the bottom, grazing its hard-packed surface, and let the current do the rest. I flew through the water like I was shot from a cannon, until I passed though the entrance to the cave, out into the river. It was like hitting a brick wall as the main rapids of the river slammed into me, tossing me like a rag doll, end over end.

I flew down the river, my legs and arms reaching frantically for anything to grab hold of, bouncing painfully, uselessly, off a hundred rocks that were of no help. I gasped for breath as the rapids tossed me from side to side, end over end, scraping bottom one moment, thrown high into the air the next. The blue sky appeared in snatches from above, and the cliffs raced passed me at frightening speed. I tried to catch a shallow breath each time that I felt the water pitch me above the boiling surface, only to sink below the waves before I had time to fill my lungs. I alternated between choking to death and briefer feelings of flying high above the river, my mind torn by contrasting terror and euphoria, when I felt the rock come in contact with my skull. It was a nearly instantaneous thing, no pain, but just the swift release from the torment as blackness enveloped me.

*****

I came to, half in and half out of the water, lying on a wide flat rock that came out of the river at a slight angle. Not sure how long I had been out or how far I had gone along the river, I looked up to see that the rapids had diminished considerably in intensity. It was still choppy, thousands of rocks breaking up the river into as many bursts of sparkling spray, the water swirling around in hundreds of tiny pools, as the current began to slow.

The sun was bright in the sky, bright enough to hurt my eyes, bright enough to send a throbbing pain through my brain. I reached up to touch the back of my head, my hand coming away bright and sticky with blood. It stung as I traced the wound, which was three inches long, the skin around it already starting to swell.

I had a handkerchief in my pocket, one of the few things that I had left. I soaked it in the icy stream and pressed it into the gash, hoping that the cold water would help to slow the bleeding. It came backed soaked, dripping pink, diluted by the cold water. The cut needed to be stitched up. If I had a needle and thread, and a mirror I might have attempted to do the job. But I had none of those things. Instead, I took off my fatigue coat, followed by the outer of the last two shirts that I owned. I then wrung out the handkerchief, soaked it in the cold water again, and tied it to the back of my head with the shirt. The long sleeves of it hung down on either side of my head like droopy ears, making me look—and feel—like a whipped hound dog.

I hadn't yet lost too much blood, but I felt woozy from the blow to the head. I had been knocked cold—a concussion surely—a fractured skull perhaps. My vision was blurry and I felt sick to my stomach.

I still hadn't gotten to my feet. When I did, I was dizzier than ever, everything kind of swimming, my vision going from fuzzy to a watery gray, the bright sun flashing kaleidoscope colors alternating between brief periods of dimming light. I sank back to my knees and crawled away from the river to a bright sunny spot along the western wall of the canyon, where I passed out again.

I awoke just minutes later—the position of the sun told me that that was so. My pants were still wet, but drying fast in the bright sunshine. It wasn't warm, even though it felt so—the temperature probably in the low fifties. I reached up to the still damp head dressing, still wet with river water, but with just a tinge of pink showing up on my fingertips. My head throbbed, my eyesight still shaky, as I finally looked around to check out my surroundings.

The canyon had grown wider, as had the river. But the water was noticeably shallower, the current running with less force—less speed. On the eastern side, the water ran right up to the cliff's wall, just as it had upstream. But on the opposite side, the side where I sat, there was land. Not much of it, but a patch that was growing wider as I gazed to the west. Thick green brush prospered along the base of the cliff, growing thicker as the river traveled farther southwest. There were trees, short ones, none more than ten or fifteen feet, but I knew that as the water receded, they would become taller, older.

And the cliffs were shorter here. I had no way to measure them, no way to adequately gauge their height, but I knew that they were not as tall as they were a few miles farther north. I knew because I had climbed down from them.

I spent the next several hours just resting against the hard rock of the western cliff, moving just once to drink from the fresh, cool stream. I checked out the cliff on the far side of the river as I sat there resting, better able to see the detail of the cave-like openings that dotted its face. A few of them were at ground level, and looked much like the one in which my time machine resided. One or two of them appeared to have some depth to them, as well, the bright sunlight failing to penetrate far enough into the interior to see exactly where they ended.

There were caves on this side, as well, but there were none nearby, none that I felt the need to explore right at the moment. But I would shortly, as I didn't relish the idea of sleeping out in the open come nightfall.

And as I sat there, I observed something else. There were fish in the river—lots of them. I could see them leaping in the water as they battled the currents, their silver, pink and blue scales sparkling iridescent in the sun as its rays reflected from their backs. They looked like salmon (not that I really knew what the hell salmon looked like). I convinced myself that they were because I knew that salmon were good eating.

I watched them until the pain in my stomach overcame the one in my head, until the hunger overrode the nausea. I still had the spear, although the metal shaft was bent and the knife-edge badly chipped. I carried it over to one of the tiny pools where the water was barely a foot deep. As I looked down into it, I finally understood the phrase "shooting fish in a barrel". Every minute or so, one would swim in, just sort of rest there for a few seconds before heading out again. They were beautiful. I had never thought of fish quite that way before. Or perhaps I had never been quite this hungry before. Whichever, it only took a couple of tries before I had one wriggling on the end of my knife.

I crawled back to the warmth and security of the cliff's face. I remembered the day that I washed up on the shore of my beach, the day that I had crawled through the tunnel and made my way through the underground river, the day after my journey had begun. I had eaten fish on that day right from the sea—not even cooked, despite my lifelong aversion to seafood.

I had it a little better now. At least I had a knife to scale the fish. Cutting off the tail and the head, peeling back the skin, I sliced in along the backbone, carving out what I assumed were the fillets from either side. The fish was easily eighteen inches long, the meat plump and juicy—no bones, which would have made me gag. It was incredibly good, making me forget for the moment about my headache.

But the headache came back as the hunger diminished, although not quite as severe as before. Now it was a dull ache that began at the back of my skull and seemed to travel through my brain, making my eyes hurt whenever I shifted my vision from right to left, from up to down. Despite the cool temperature, the sun, which was about to drop over the rim of the western cliff, made beads of sweat pop up along my brow, made my hair itchy.

With the light just beginning to grow dim, I knew that it was time to head out. I swayed on my feet as I stood, my full stomach protesting the motion. I used the spear, square end down, as a staff, and began to walk to the south.

It didn't take long, less than an hour. Only the upper portion of the east-side cliff glowed from the setting sun when I came upon a cave at ground level. Inside was dark with shadows. I approached it tentatively, peering in from around the outside edge of the opening. It was fifteen feet across, twenty-five feet high—plenty big enough for me to enter—more than big enough for a lot of things to enter. I held the spear out in front of me as I slid around the corner, entering the cave.

It had a powerfully gamy, unhealthy smell that reminded me of the zoo or the inside of a barn. But worse—like a zoo or barn full of diseased, dying animals—like some had been left there to rot. Something terrible had lived here—or died here. Something had been here recently—or a rotting corpse of some huge beast was still here. I backed against the interior wall, just inside the entrance, holding my spear at the ready, while my eyes adjusted to the thin light. My nostrils flared, taking in the pungent stench, as if I could pinpoint the source with my nose, even if I couldn't see it in the half-light.

As my pupils dilated to take in the low-level of light, I could see that there was nothing alive, or dead, in the main part of the cave, and I could see that this was nothing like the cave back on the beach. This one was huge, extending upward and outward well beyond my limited range of vision. And it wasn't just a single space like that of the one that housed the machine. This one appeared to be a whole series of separate, but interconnected vaults—a maze of corridors and tunnels. Stalagmites and stalactites grew everywhere from the uneven floors and ceilings, some of them coming together to form unusually shaped pillars, as if they were structural supports, holding the whole thing together—and perhaps they were.

Taking advantage of what was left of the light, I decided to do some exploring. The floor of the central portion of the cave was as hard and flat as those of a building foundation, like a professional cement man had laid it. It was a semicircular area that extended fifty feet to the left and right, a hundred feet straight ahead. It was broken up by nothing more than a few loose rocks and stray cracks that wandered here and there like any well-used driveway.

But beyond the outer perimeter of the half circle, everything changed. If the open part had been laid down by a professional, the rest had been done by someone deranged, someone who took pleasure in tortuous shapes, impossible angles, and bizarre, dangerous outcroppings—a cavern of horrors.

To the right of the midpoint, the floor dropped away, leading into a row of tunnels that descended even farther. The light was too poor to see just where they led, but it was down into blackness, some big enough to allow a moderate sized dinosaur to enter, some small enough to hold back all but the smallest of rodents.

I got down on one knee at the entrance to one of the mid-sized caves to try to get a better look. I could hear water dripping in the distance, the rocks surrounding the porthole slick with moisture. I reached up to one of the oddly shaped stalactites growing down across the entrance. It was cold and smooth. My hand came away wet. I ducked down underneath it, squeezed my body between it and a similar one growing up from the bottom edge, and stepped down into the cave. The light dimmed almost immediately, and the smell changed from the barnyard-like odor to one of dampness, mold, and decay. It felt ten degrees colder—the humidity near a hundred percent. The sound of dripping water intensified and originated from many different sources.

There was a lot of water somewhere below, perhaps another underground river or sea. I thought that it might even be the southern portion of the one that ran beneath the now dead volcano, the one that passed below my machine.

I had already visited that particular river—not once, but twice. I had no desire to try for a third. Besides, it was growing much too dark to travel farther down into the unknown regions of this slippery, foreboding place.

I squeezed back through the opening where the light was better, but the smell was so much worse. I had to swallow repeatedly to keep the half-digested fish from coming back up. It was like crawling up the butt of some monstrous carnivore that had just had a really big lunch of spoiled meat.

Reflexively, I reached into the back pocket of my pants for the handkerchief to cover my nose. But of course it wasn't there. Remembering where it was, I thought about tearing it from my head, the smell was so bad. But I didn't. Instead, I put my hand over my nose and mouth, accomplishing exactly nothing, and headed to the other side of the cave while there was still just a little bit of daylight.

Stepping past a tiered ledge, weaving through a couple of slick, stone columns, I stepped up into one of the tunnels. This one was apparently dry—no sound of dripping water—no wetness to the touch. It angled up sharply, turning to the left as it went up at nearly a forty-five degree angle. My thighs quivered as I hauled myself up the steep slope. There were numerous handholds, countless things to grasp to pull myself upward. I did it all by feel, the light having left me within a few feet from the entrance. I climbed blindly, the stone turning coarse and rough, painful to the touch as I climbed the ragged shaft upward.

I had come to hate the darkness. It terrified me the way that very few things did. And in the dark, I couldn't be sure that I was taking a singular route, or perhaps just one of several blind choices. How could I be sure that I would take the same route down as I did up? I had decided that I had had enough, and turned to face the entrance, satisfied that I could revisit the dark tunnel the next day when the sun would show itself bright from the east.

I should have gone all the way back—back to the main part of the cave, where the floor was level and the river was just outside the entrance. But instead, I stopped short. I was just a few feet above the floor, a couple of steps into the tunnel when I stopped. I eased myself down onto the uncomfortable rocks, sitting down, wiggling my ass into the less painful of the uneven surfaces, and watched the faintest of light fade from the entrance from which I came.

Even now I'm not sure why I hesitated. Perhaps it was because I was afraid—afraid of the approaching darkness. Perhaps I just wanted to sit calmly and soak up the last of the dim light that filtered into the cave. And my head was still throbbing, still bleeding. It hurt every step that I took, every time that I turned my head, each time that I tried too hard to think about what to do next. Perhaps I had only paused to catch my breath, paused to see if the hammer would stop pounding from the inside of my head, even if I was just mere feet from being able to stretch out on the flat floor of the cave.

Maybe it was the stench. From where I sat I could still smell it, but I knew that it would get infinitely worse when I stepped down into the main vault. They say that one can get used to pretty much anything, but I'm not so sure that they were talking about a smell so bad that it could chase a swarm of horseflies from a pile of shit.

I'm not sure that I was thinking about any of that stuff at the time, but for some reason I hesitated, halted for just a moment before I took that last step.

The hesitation saved my life.

My eyes were fixed on the half oval shape of the cave's entrance. It was at that point where day was about to turn into night, that fine line where the sun had long before dropped below the western horizon but you weren't quite sure if its far off rays were adding to that which the moon provided. It was that point where you weren't quite sure if this was as dark as it was going to get on that particular night. There was either a trace of daylight left, or it was a full moon, cloudless kind of nighttime. The cave's opening was still clearly visible. The sharp, rough edges of its sides separated the blackness of the cave from the grayness of the outside.

Except for the dripping of water that could just barely be heard off to the right, it was as quiet as could be. So quiet that I heard it a full thirty seconds before I saw it.

It started as a low growl, barely audible, but growing louder as it moved closer. At first I thought that it was another earthquake just beginning to rev up. Not at all surprising or alarming considering that they had rarely stopped in recent days. They had been so regular that I had become oblivious to all but the worst of them. They started just like this, and within a few seconds I would feel the slight tremors underfoot—just like this.

It was just seconds before I saw it that I realized that it wasn't just another earthquake. The tremors were too regular, like a heartbeat, and beneath the growl there was something else—the sound of raspy breathing, slow and labored, like that made by a huge, tired, hungry animal.

I saw it only as a giant black shadow as it dipped its head to clear the top of the entrance. I could tell nothing more than that it walked on two legs, and was gigantic, having to lower its head more than just a few feet to pass beneath the top of the opening.

It blotted out nearly the entire space from which the meager light emitted, but the noise coming from it told me that it was coming for me. I stumbled back and up a step, clutching at the rough rock to keep me from falling back down onto the floor of the cave as the terrible smell hit me like a blow from a baseball bat. I didn't think the smell could get any worse … but I was wrong.

The source of the terrible smell came closer, approached my position in just a few strides, as if it knew where I was hiding. And somehow, it did know. The low growl of tiredness and frustration that I had heard earlier turned to a roar of anger and anticipation as it came within a few feet of my hiding spot.

Its breath was hot and smelled foul, like the cave itself, but even more so. A moment ago I would have thought that impossible, that nothing could have been worse.

This *was* worse.

The smell was even more intense and had a quality that even now I can't quite explain except to say that it had a *live* smell. It was if I could see the bloody, gristly pieces of torn flesh hanging between its teeth, the half-digested remains of some equally smelly animal fermenting in the digestive track of this huge carnivore. In my mind I could see maggots crawling through the rancid, half-eaten meat, flies buzzing above it. It was worse than the bone pile. This smell was coming from something that was *alive*, and that seemed so much worse than dead … and so much more terrifying.

Instinctively, I backed farther into the tunnel, my feet climbing another few feet up the uneven slope until I had passed above the upper edge of the tunnel's opening. I was out of its range of sight, but then, it was out of mine as well. All that I could see were faint shadows moving about on the rocks beneath my feet—everything else was blackness.

I was sure that it couldn't see me, but I knew from past experience that it could still smell me. It knew exactly where I was and it continued to roar its anger and frustration at the rock separating us. The roar from the beast was as loud as anything that I had ever heard, painful and all consuming in the relatively small confines of the narrow tunnel. Like combining a hungry lion's roar and the scream of metal on metal when a locomotive slams on its brakes, the sound seemed to get right inside of me, making my hair stand on end, my insides turn to Jell-O.

The warmth flowing down my leg startled me. I had pissed myself and the animal seemed to know it before I did, increasing the intensity of its roar, sensing my sign of weakness, identifying an easy meal. My simple act of cowardice had enraged it further.

I would be embarrassed later. Just then I was but a few feet of rock away from being eaten by the most terrifying creature that I had ever seen—that had ever lived.

The howl of rage bounced off the rocks of the tunnel as the creature lowered its head below the height of the opening. The walls shook and little chunks of stone fell from above as it stuck its snout into the tiny cave. I could see nothing but tiny flecks of light bouncing off its teeth—a larger, brighter spot that I could only assume was an eye. I could hear its teeth gnashing together as it snapped at something that was just beyond its reach.

It was only yards away and I could do nothing but back up farther into the tunnel.

I was defenseless. The spear was somewhere else, propped against one of the cavern walls. It seemed like such a puny weapon to use against such an enraged monster, but it was all that I had. In the closeness of the tight space, it may have done me some good. A hard stab to the snout might back it off. A direct hit in the eyeball might prove fatal, at least send it on its way.

But I had nothing but my wits, and I was running out of them pretty damn quickly.

I continued to back away from the beast, moving upward, still facing it, afraid to turn my back on it. As it took brief time outs to catch its breath, silent moments between the ear-shattering roars, I could hear the destruction of the cave. Stone columns were being torn down, stalagmites and stalactites alike were being uprooted and torn from the ceiling as the creature tried to bore into the tiny opening to get at me.

Small chunks of rock below my feet shook loose, rattling down the slope before me, plunking down on the dinosaur's snout, pissing it off further yet. Rocks tore loose from the ceiling as well, pelting me about the head and shoulders. The air was filled with dust, making it hard to breathe. The walls of the narrow, crooked tunnel shook, either from the rampaging monster below, or from something else.

The thought of another major quake, thinking about being buried alive once more, made me move my ass. I turned my back on the animal and began to climb. The fear of the dark vanished. No longer concerned that I'd take a wrong turn somewhere, unable to find my way back, I raced up the tunnel, the desire to return to the main part of the cave gone in an instant.

Climbing in the darkness, I heard a loud crash from behind, a whoosh of air and an invisible cloud of dust pushed against my back. And as the initial sound of the cave-in faded to faint echoes that died a slow death in the length of a dozen tunnels, the sound of the dinosaur disappeared.

I had but a momentary sense of relief to have been reprieved from impending death, a moment to catch my breath and calm my nerves before I realized that I was still in serious trouble. The killer animal was no longer a concern, hopefully killed in the cave-in. A good thing, but I was in total darkness, my only known route of egress gone—no water, no food, no weapon, and no idea where this tunnel led.

I had no choice but to continue to climb the tunnel—to wherever it led.

It seemed to run straight, so I felt that I was staying close to the edge of the cliff. To head in any other direction would have been a much bigger problem. Leading into the western mountain in a path that might have gone on for miles, or back in the direction that I had already come, and had no desire to return. If I kept heading in the direction of the cliff's edge, I had a chance of popping back out again at some point.

If only it hadn't been in darkness.

I kept contact with the wall to my left, fear and panic beginning to slowly erode whatever relief I had felt when the tunnel had sealed itself, the man-eater on the other side of thousands of pounds of stone. I had no idea where I was going. The darkness was absolute, the feeling of being blind slowly taking hold of whatever rational thought I was clinging to. My climbing slowed down to a snail's pace as I began to imagine that the air was growing thinner, running out, terrified that at any moment I was going to run into an impassable barrier.

But I hadn't been climbing for very long, even though it felt like forever, when I was surprised at being able to see the rough texture of the rock before me. There was light—dim and dusty—like being in a room filled with black smoke—a brighter area coming from a small spot above and to the left.

I reached it quickly, a small hole in the rock, maybe fifteen inches across, about the size of the old-fashioned milk chute on the side of some older people's house, the one that the milkman used to fill with milk and butter, back in the days when there *were* milkmen.

The light was somewhat better on the other side, the cliff on the opposite side of the river vaguely visible across the moonlit canyon. The opening was only ten or twelve feet long and opened into what looked like another cave. But the opening was small, the stone rough and uneven. I thought I could crawl into it—not at all sure that I would be able to make it all the way through to the other end—or even back out again. Then again, where else could I go?

I climbed the slope until the hole was level with my waist, and slipped into it sideways. I could only fit into it that way, and only with my arms outstretched in front of me, forcing my shoulders together to compact my girth. With my upper body into the tiny space I stepped away from the floor ... and then thought, okay what the hell do I do now? I was wedged in tight, most of my legs sticking out from the side of the rock wall like a weird modern artistic impression of some kind. I was stuck—able to move muscles but no major body parts.

My feet kicked like a swimmer's, but swatted only air, nothing to push off from. All that I could do was roll my shoulders and hips, creeping forward a few millimeters at a time.

I tried to hold the panic at bay as I thought about the last time that I was pinned in such a tight, small space. Ten years ago, minutes before I fell from the cliff into the underground river. It was the same—sealed in by a cave-in—my only route of escape through a tiny, ragged tunnel, unsure of what awaited me at the other end. If I wasn't so scared shitless, I would have laughed at how one man could get himself into such deep shit. Not just once, but over and over again.

But what did I expect? One man, alone, in a time and place that he had no business occupying, sharing a foreign world with animals not meant to coexist with humans, in a land where volcanoes and earthquakes were as natural and regular as day turning into night. It was goddamn amazing that I was around ten years later to think about such things. And pretty damn ironic that I was thinking about it here … stuck in a hole again … in yet another tight spot.

Wriggling and squirming, rolling my hips back and forth until the exquisite pain in them turned to the relief of numbness, I inched forward. After what seemed like hours I could feel the toes of my boots pass over the lip of the hole. Fully into the tunnel now, I knew that I had reached the point of no return. I would either make it to the end, or I would die there, stuck like a cork in a bottle.

It got just a little easier with something for my toes to push against. If I rolled my hips an inch in one direction, taking some of the weight from one side of my body, I could push off from the opposite foot, moving forward a quarter of an inch. Damn slow progress, but by rolling from hip to hip, pushing out with the toes of each foot, one after the other in perfect synchronization, I had established a kind of tiny, rapid rhythm that moved me through the narrow passage.

I had built up a kind of momentum, afraid that if I stopped, I wouldn't get it back again. And I so much wanted to stop and rest. My knees, elbows, hips, and the back of my shoulders were rubbed raw, the rough stone shredding my clothes and skin alike. I was afraid that if I didn't get through pretty damn quick, I'd be worn to a nub.

The stone had been cold to the touch when I first entered the tunnel. As I finished my journey of but a dozen feet, it felt warm. The stone was heated by my hot, sweaty body, and by my warm, moist exhale of air that was more panting than breathing.

As my head popped through to the other side, the air felt suddenly cool, as the breeze from the canyon swept through the cave. The sweat that poured from my face turned cold and evaporated in only minutes

My arms hung limply down from the edge of the hole while I caught my breath, and then, using my arms for the first time in hours, I pulled the rest of my body from the hole.

I dropped eight feet onto the hard floor, not quite flipping far enough to land right side up, but rather in a clumsy four-point landing—both feet and both cheeks of my ass. I grunted as the wind was knocked out of me, the shock spreading all the way up my spine. I knew that tomorrow I'd hurt all over, but right at that moment all I felt was joy to be out of the hole. I rolled over to where the floor met the wall and was instantly asleep.

*****

The sun woke me, its bright rays entering the floor of the cave. I was still deep in shadow, fifty feet from the cave's entrance, resting tight against the back wall, eight feet below the hole that I had spent half the night crawling through.

The memory of the night before was fresh in my mind despite a dreamless sleep. The terrible smell and the roar of the beast even now sent a shiver up my spine. As I rose to a sitting position, my tortured muscles and the dozens of patches of abraded skin were further reminders of the agony of the tunnel.

Pain rocketed through my skull as I sat up. I reached for the back of my head, the makeshift dressing gone, blood still weeping from the nasty gash. I looked on the floor for the blood-soaked shirt and handkerchief, but they were nowhere to be found. I must have lost them somewhere in the tunnel although I didn't remember quite when—not surprising considering the narrowness of the space, the long, floppy sleeve-ears of the shirt. Not going back in after them was an easy decision to make.

As I awoke, it wasn't the sun, nor the frightening memories of the long night before, not even the pain and soreness that wracked my body, that first caught my attention. It was something else that crept into my consciousness, even though at the start it was barely audible.

It was that same low growl, that same intermittent tremor in the rock, that I had heard the night before, and like the night before, what made them was getting closer, the sound getting louder, quickly.

I rose all the way to my feet, shaky and sick to my stomach, and staggered over to the opening of the cave. The light was nearly blinding as I stepped from out of the shadow into the bright sunshine, looking down, shielding my eyes, as the pain in my head intensified.

As I made it to the edge, I focused on the river below me, trying hard to stop the little black floaties from drifting back and forth across my eyeballs. They were a sign of impending blackout, and they made me, for the moment, forget about everything else. I stared at the rippling waters, blocking out everything else, twenty-five feet below where I stood.

The tremendous roar from the monster brought me back to reality in a way that nearly knocked me off my feet. I had but a brief instant to look to my left, the sight so startling and terrifying that I fell backward, away from the edge of the cliff, and started backpedaling on all fours, trying to get away from sure death as quickly as I possibly could.

The night before, I knew what it was. I was just too afraid to admit it to myself, understanding that it was the ultimate nightmare, the perfect killing machine, the Tyrant King. Or perhaps I was just so overjoyed to see my lifelong dream finally realized that I refused to believe what I thought that I saw, blocking it out because it was just too damn impossible.

I backed into the shadows, slamming against the far wall of the cave, amazed, surprised, overjoyed, but mostly just plain scared shitless, as it pushed its massive head into the cave.

The all too familiar stench filled the space of the cave as the *Tyrannosaurus rex* opened its huge jaws and let out a roar of recognition—recognition, and anger for what had happened the night before.

I froze, my back pressed hard up against the back wall of the cave. Its massive head was level with the cave's entrance, even though it was more than twenty feet above the ground. It stuck its snout inside, the sound of heavy breathing coming from between two rows of huge, sharp teeth, a low growl starting from somewhere deep inside its throat.

I remembered the bone pile. I remembered the *Albertosaurs*. They had an acute sense of smell and hearing, but lousy eyesight. They had trouble seeing me when I was still, even though they could hear me and smell me.

I was still deep in shadow—the *rex* was in bright sunshine. It would have trouble seeing me even if I did move. I was sure that it would have no trouble picking up my scent, but if I remained frozen in place, not moving a muscle, not making a sound, perhaps it would lose interest and move on.

I was in no immediate danger, fifty feet away from the predator's hungry jaws. But I couldn't stay there forever—the thought of traveling back through the tiny passageway not at all inviting, even if I could reach it, even if there was some way out of the maze of tunnels once I struggled through. I knew that I would wait out the animal, no matter how long it took.

My heartbeat settled into a more regular rhythm as the fear left me. I sat there in complete fascination as the *rex* searched for me. It had stereo vision, its small eyes set on either side of a bony ridge that ran up the length of its snout. It had difficulty seeing anything directly in front of it, so it swept its head back and forth in a short arc across the width of the entrance, looking first with one eye, then the other. The eyes were completely black, as was the skin surrounding them, like a bandit's mask. The blackness continued down its long snout, wrapping around both nostrils, which were large and long, teardrop shaped. They flared, and even at fifty feet I could hear the air being sucked into them, trying to sniff me out. The black surrounded its mouth as well, like a witch's lipstick. And with black gums, the white teeth stood out in startling contrast, making them look even longer, sharper, and somehow even more dangerous … if that were possible. The *rex's* long, black, pointed tongue slid out from those razor teeth, searching the ground five feet beyond its black lips. It didn't come anywhere close to me, yet the sight of it was terrifying. It was long enough to wrap itself around me and pull me into its thresher of a mouth—*If* it could get that close.

As it swiveled its head, the light caught the colors than ran from the blackness surrounding its features, disappearing down its neck, and out of sight below the edge of the hole. They were brilliant reds and purples, thinner streaks of a mustard yellow that seemed to outline and separate them, making the more effulgent colors stand out all the more. The colors were amazingly bright, but there was nothing pleasant or festive about them. They stood out as a warning—a warning that the most terrible killing machine to ever walk the earth was on the prowl. And at the moment it was prowling for me.

I held my ground, not moving so much as a muscle, taking tiny, shallow breaths so that my chest didn't rise and fall too much. The only things that moved were my eyes as I watched the huge head swivel back and forth … back and forth … trying to find me.

It was a good five minutes, or maybe fifty, when the *rex* stopped moving its head from side to side, and faced directly towards me, like it was looking straight into my eyes, even if its own were focused elsewhere. If such things were possible, I'd swear that it smiled at me, turning those hideous black lips back into a sort of grin, like it was saying, "*Just stay there. I'll be back.*" Or perhaps, "*I don't care a damn about you, you're not worth the effort, you little shit.*"

I gave it far too much credit. It probably wasn't thinking much of anything. It was just pissed off because it had lost a chance for an easy breakfast, and as huge as it was, it was probably hungry as hell. Whatever it was, I was thankful because, seconds later, the head pulled back and disappeared from the cave's entrance.

I waited until I was sure that the diminishing sound of its footsteps meant that it had actually left before I scrambled across the floor of the cave to the edge of the opening. Sticking my head out, I saw that it had already traveled a hundred yards to the south.

It stood upright, straighter than I would have thought, almost a regal gait to it, its tail longer than I imagined, its tip not quite dragging the ground, but flitting from side to side, slashing the ground like the end of a long, leather whip. Its back was as brilliantly colored with reds, purples, and yellows as the sides of its head, like a kid gone mad with a box of crayons. Its legs were as black as night. It walked at a leisurely pace, but one that traveled twenty feet with every step. Within minutes it had followed the western turn of the cliff's edge, out of sight. It was magnificent, and absolutely huge, much larger than the one that I had unearthed all those years ago.

I peered over the edge, seeing a ledge ten feet below. I scurried over the lip, holding on to the edge with my fingers, letting go, dropping onto the slim ledge.

Repeating the process, I dropped to the ground, fifteen feet below, tucking and rolling away from the cliff, ending up in a tangle of low brush growing at the river's edge.

I jumped to my feet, afraid that the *rex* might have heard me when I hit the ground. I was still shaking from the close encounter, yet at the same time, I was fascinated and euphoric. I was only yards away from my dream. I had seen something that I had longed for all of my life—something that no human being had ever witnessed. But I had become smarter over the past ten years. Instead of chasing after the *rex*, I headed north—north to find the cave from where this little adventure first began.

I ran in that direction, following the steep rocky wall on my left, not very far, not more than three or four minutes, when I came upon it.

Entering, I found that the damage was much less than I feared. The cave-in had been limited to the confines of the left side of the cave, the upward slopes of the dozen or so tunnels blocked off forever. The rest of the cave was untouched except for the few hundred rocks that had spilled out onto the floor from above.

There in the brilliant light that streamed into the cave from above the eastern cliff was my spear, almost where I had left it. The handle was even more crooked than before, the *rex* unquestionably having stepped on the metal shaft. It was bent at nearly a right angle, the strong steel twisted by a tremendous force that was nothing more than a misstep to the giant dinosaur.

Positioning a rather large stone the right distance from the wall of the cave, wedging the blunt end of the shaft beneath a heavy brow of rock that ran just above the floor, I forced the strong metal back into a semblance of straightness.

I then I proved that I was still not as smart as I thought I was—not nearly as smart as I should have been, given all my mistakes and foolishness. I grabbed the spear and headed out on the southern trail, after the *Tyrannosaur*.

I ran after it, knowing that my puny walking pace would never catch up with the dinosaur's huge stride.

I didn't catch it, but within a mile, I had it in sight once again. It was a mile that left me panting and wheezing—every bruise, scrape, and cut screaming out to me to just stop and rest. But I couldn't do that. I had come too far to just let the *Tyrannosaur* walk away. After all, it was really what I had come here for.

The cliff continued its slow curve to the west, and I kept close to the edge of it, the tail end of the *rex* just barely in view as it stayed just a step out of sight around the bend. It had stopped twice to look behind, checking out the noise that I tried to suppress. Each time I froze against the cliff, invisible to the dinosaur, or so I hoped. Each time it stared for a few seconds, snorted once, and turned and walked away, back in the direction it had been heading.

We traveled that way for hours, me just a hundred yards behind, always looking for a way to hide just in case it decided to double back. Most of the time there was no route to safety. All of the caves that we passed were high into the cliff, much too high to serve any purpose for me, and the trees were much too small for me to escape the reach of the three-story tall beast.

When it happened, it happened so quickly that it surprised the hell out of me.

I was having trouble keeping up and had lost sight of the *rex* for several minutes when I heard its all too familiar roar. A moment later, I saw it back up, its profile coming into full view not a hundred and fifty yards away. Pushing it away from the edge of the cliff was a second, even larger *Tyrannosaur*. Its pattern of color was the same, but they were more subdued, as if it had been rolling around in the dust. It was bigger and it was also the aggressor, barking at the smaller one, holding its huge jaws spread wide, showing off its giant teeth, making like it was ready to bite.

The smaller of the two responded with another roar of its own, but was obviously intimidated, lowering its head, staring at the ground. The aggressor approached from the side, lowering its head as well, nudging the other along the belly, just inside the thigh.

I thought for sure that I was about to witness a titanic battle between two rival carnivores. Instead, the larger one positioned itself in front of the other, facing the same direction, and lowered its massive head nearly to the ground, lifting its long tail up, curled around its own neck.

What I knew now to be the male turned slightly, for just a second, revealing its massive penis to me, and approached the female. At the moment of penetration, the male grabbed the back of the thighs of the female with those tiny little arms, and penetrated the thick hide with the two long pointed claws.

The female let out the shortest of snorts, whether from the entry or from the four wounds to her meaty thighs, I had no idea. She tried to take a single step forward, the male holding on tight, the claws digging in like grappling hooks, and followed the step with one of its own.

The female emitted a continuous, low growl, while the male seemed to shift its weight from one leg to the other, its hips undulating in the process. The male's head lolled to one side, buckets of drool pouring from its dagger-lined jaws, its tongue hanging out from the side.

In a manner of minutes it was over. The smaller, more colorful male raised its head, letting out a sustained, earsplitting roar, pulling its four claws from the female, taking a quick step backward. But it wasn't quite fast enough. The female turned, and almost quicker than my eyes could catch, sunk its teeth into the short, thick neck of the male.

It wasn't a mortal wound, but it had injured the animal. Blood spilled from more than a dozen punctures, mingling with the brilliant colors of its skin, and dribbled to the ground. The female then let out a roar of her own, even louder and longer than the one coming from her partner just seconds before.

The male *Tyrannosaur* had been summarily dismissed. It turned and resumed its march to the south, angling toward the river, staying as far away from the female as it could. The larger *rex* simply disappeared from view around the bend in the cliff.

I stood there at the base of the cliff trembling, tears running down both cheeks. But not from fear—I wasn't even frightened when I thought they were about to wage war on one another. Fear simply hadn't entered the picture. In fact, I hadn't been less afraid since the day that Dermot had laid out his crazy plan to me.

Astounded was one word that I could come up with, although it didn't come close to the feeling that I had on that morning. Rapture was a better word. It was a forty-year-long dream that had just played itself out, in real life, and while I was awake.

The arms—those tiny little arms with the two seemingly meaningless, pointy claws—those minuscule, mysterious little forelegs actually had a function, a damn important purpose. And I was the only human in the entire history of the world that knew what their purpose was.

CHAPTER 25

This is my last trip to the beach, the last night that I sleep in the machine that brought me here, the last time that I sit before the computer entering a story that likely no one will ever find, let alone read.

So much has happened the past year that I hardly know where to begin. The encounter with the *Tyrannosaurs* was just the dramatic start to what happened over the next twelve months. Not all of it had been exciting, only modest discoveries—minor mishaps and adventures—not really much worth writing about. There were few things that I thought important enough to chronicle, even less that would interest the other paleontologists, scientists, or even Dermot. About the only thing that Dermot would care about is whether I was alive or dead, and he'd learn that soon enough.

But the things that did happen were damn important to me, dictated the course of things to come, and said a lot about whether I would live or die. Oh, we all die. Even if we're lucky enough to die warm in our beds at the age of ninety-five, we all die. Even if we eat healthy, exercise every day, don't drink, don't smoke, drink our milk, go to church, be good to our kids, love our neighbor, and live by the golden rule, we all die.

It's just that some die sooner than others and some more violently. And there are but a very few of us who can predict the end with a little bit more accuracy than most. People who live their lives on the edge, face risk and uncertainty every day, do silly and dangerous things on a routine basis, are like that. Firemen and policemen, and soldiers are like that. Poor people in third world countries and minorities living in the ghetto are like that, as well. And kids prowling the streets at night in gangs are like that, too. Their life expectancy can sometimes be measured in weeks and days, their deaths not from old age and natural causes, but borne of violence and dangerous circumstance. It was like that for me in the days following the *Tyrannosaur* mating ritual.

I came back one last time to write one last chapter to my story, to describe the events of the last year, to let someone know where I was and what had happened to me. I didn't do it for my fellow scientists, or for Dermot, or even for myself. I did it for just one person. I did it for Susan.

I still held out hope that Susan was alive. I had always felt some small connection, a lifeline of sorts with her. It was the same feeling I had when I was hovering over her in the hospital—that somehow my words were getting through to her, despite all evidence to the contrary. All the time that I'd been gone I never lost that feeling. That connection was helping to keep her alive just as sure that it was helping me do the same thing, even though we were separated, not only by the eleven years that I'd been gone, but by the seventy million years between her time and mine. Although only a mere thread, that connection was still there. When it went, I would feel the sudden disconnection just as sure as I would feel the loss of an eye, or an arm … or the little toes on my right foot.

If I still felt the connection, then I knew that Susan was still alive, maybe in the coma, maybe not. And if not, I wanted her to know everything. It was important to me that she knew that I had made it beyond the fire that destroyed my home—our home—that I had found yet another life beyond the valley of the dinosaurs. It was a meager kind of existence, filled with emptiness and longing, with loneliness and deprivation. But it was my life and I was intent on hanging on to it for as long as I could. I wanted to tell her that, so I went back to the machine, to the computer, one last time.

I had been back on the beach for a nearly a week, on the laptop every chance that I could, every chance that the cranky old computer would allow. It had become as cantankerous as an old dog with the mange. Sometimes it worked, sometimes it didn't. Sometimes it powered up, sometimes it refused to until I had coaxed it for whatever time it felt it required at the time. Other times it came on the first try, only to simply freeze up on me when I least expected it. It was always during a time when, despite my best intentions, I had forgotten to save regularly. I rant and rave, shout and swear, and mistreat it just a bit more—begging for it to shut down altogether. But it always seems to come back for more abuse—sooner or later. I needed just one more day out of it—one more day to finish my story so that I could leave this place forever.

*****

When the male dinosaur had fled the scene, having been both rebuked and injured, I still had a problem. The female, the bigger and more dangerous of the two—as if that were possible—was still somewhere up ahead, around the bend. I had no idea what a female *Tyrannosaur* was like after sex. Perhaps it was satisfied, mellowed out, wanting only to find a nice warm spot and go to sleep. That was a pretty funny notion, even a year later. More likely, she was hungry, even more so than usual—as if that were possible—and had disappeared quickly in search of her next meal. Unfortunately, it was the latter of the two that was the reality of the situation—as if the other *could* have been possible.

I had nowhere else to go and nothing else to do, so I followed. It was as if nothing had changed in the past half-hour. I ran along the western bank of the canyon, sticking close to the wall, until I caught up to her some thirty minutes later. I followed her, just like the male before her, keeping her tail in sight, praying that the wind didn't suddenly shift, sending my unique aroma her way.

The path kept turning gradually to the west, the distance between the river and the cliff growing with each mile. Two hours into my surveillance, the cliffs to my right abruptly ended. Before me was another valley, not a jungle, but a forest, sparsely populated by leafless, deciduous trees, scattered patches of evergreens and brush … and dinosaurs.

A herd of *Titanosaurs* were the first ones that I saw. Not just a small family of three, like in the northern valley, but perhaps thirty of the huge plant eaters. They were more than a mile out, to the west, feeding on a small stand of spruces.

I was sure that I wasn't the only one that was aware of the group. The wind was blowing from the west, bringing their scent right to the *Tyrannosaur*, while sending the *rex's* own terrible smell away from the herbivores. The *rex* knew that they were there and headed straight for them. It raised its tail and lowered its head. From the tip of its nose to the tip of its tail it formed a straight line, parallel to the ground. It increased its pace, quieter that I would have thought possible for such a huge animal. It was in stealth mode … and it was hunting.

What the *rex* smelled was live prey, not the decomposing stench of a dead animal.

This was not a scavenger. The *Tyrannosaur* did not have to rely on something else to do its killing for it. It was more than capable of doing it itself. Just seeing it live and in the flesh, as they say, was enough to convince almost anyone. Seeing it in action would convince even the truest non-believer.

Yet another common-held theory blown all to hell, but it was not the only one.

The *Tyrannosaurs* lived in the caves in the cliffs, at least these did. Just like the one that I had found after Susan's accident. They were big enough, strong enough, and terrifying enough to live just about anywhere they wanted. Why not a cave, where they were protected from the torrential spring rains and the harsh winter winds? What would evict them? What *could* evict them? And they were intelligent, much more so than my contemporaries or I believed. I didn't for one-minute think that it was just coincidence that they picked a spot downwind to set up house, even though in this particular incident, it seemed convenient. They selected this spot because they knew that they could sneak up on their prey from this direction. During the next year, I saw dozens of caves that would have served their need for protection from the elements. In the central and southern parts of the cliff that traveled far to the west before returning to a southerly route, there were plenty of good homes for the *Tyrannosaurs*, but they were all empty. They were too smart to live upwind from their next meal.

I was at a complete loss as to what to do next. I wanted to warn the group of *Titanosaurs* that trouble was heading their way. But if I raised my voice, the *rex* would turn on me, taking the shorter of two routes to its breakfast. I really wanted to take the coward's way out—to do nothing but stick close to the edge of the cliff, just short of where it did an abrupt turn to the west.

I compromised. I took out after the *rex*, but quietly, running a few yards at a time, hiding in the patches of brush that dotted the area between us. Spear or no spear, I had no intention of getting in the *rex's* way, but I had to see this, as horrible as I knew that it was going to be.

The *Titanosaurs* were preoccupied, or their eyesight was as bad as that of the *Tyrannosaur*, because the *rex* had managed to get within a hundred yards of them before they knew anything was wrong. I watched from behind a bush as one of the giants turned its head toward the *rex*, looking as if it was staring right at the predator. But it just stood there for nearly a full minute, frozen in place, as if it didn't know what it was, like it didn't understand the danger there. It stretched its amazingly long gray neck out almost horizontal to the ground, pointed at the *rex*, like it was trying to get a better look at it, or catch a whiff of its scent. All the while the *rex* was closing the distance.

I watched from my position in the bushes, two hundred yards out. I couldn't see anything but their shapes, but I'd swear that I saw sudden recognition on the face of the *Titanosaur*. It suddenly raised its head nearly straight up, a quick jerking motion that seemed to alert the others because they all turned to face the same direction.

The *Tyrannosaur* is not a particularly fast animal—quick yes—fast no. The *Titannosaur* is slower—much slower. As one, the gigantic plant eaters turned to the west and started moving. As they separated from the small grouping of trees, I could see that there were nearly a dozen adolescent dinosaurs, ranging from ten to thirty feet in length. The smallest ones couldn't be more than a year old. And they moved slower than the adults, which surprised me. I thought that the younger dinosaurs would be quicker, despite being of a size and shape that was definitely not meant for speed. There was a pair of adult *Titanosaurs* that lagged behind, as well. At first I thought that they held back to protect the young, but I could tell by the way they moved that they were old, probably ill, and lagged behind only because they couldn't keep up.

It bothered me that the adults didn't remain behind to protect their young. They weren't like the *Triceratops* and the hadrosaurs that would gladly sacrifice themselves for their offspring. These were animals whose sheer size and stupidity had selected them for extinction no matter what really happened at the K-T boundary. They were just plain dumb and didn't know enough to protect one of their own. But it still pissed me off.

The *Tyrannosaur* increased its speed. It didn't run, it wasn't built that way, but the increased length of its stride, pushed it forward much faster than the shorter, heavier legs of its prey. Within seconds it had overtaken one of the little ones. The *rex's* huge head moved downward with lightening speed, catching the little one mid-way along its neck, severing its head and three feet of neck. Even at three hundred yards, I could see the crimson spray arcing high into the air as the two parts were separated. I thought that it would pause to swallow the little dinosaur. It could have easily tossed it into the air, catching it on the way down and swallowed it in a single gulp. Instead, it just let it lay there and went after another one. This time it went for one of the adults. This one was twice the size and four times the weight of the *Tyrannosaur*, but still it was no match.

The *rex* opened its jaws to their fullest, releasing the double hinge at the back to separate them even farther, and bit into the back end of the *Titanosaur*, just at the base of its thick tail. The huge dinosaur then did something that I would have thought impossible, even had it been younger and healthier. It reared up on its hind legs like a wild mustang, its massive feet clawing at the air, its long neck curving backward. It looked at the *Tyrannosaur*, letting out a low-pitched wail that echoed throughout the valley. The *rex* only clamped down harder severing the spine where the tail joined the back. As a huge chunk at the rear of the *Titanosaur* tore free, the *rex* finally released its grip. But it was too late for the herbivore. Its rear legs gave out from beneath it and it came crashing down to the earth, shaking the ground like yet another quake.

The downed animal was still moving, its head rising off the ground, its long neck circling back on itself, staring into the eyes of its enemy, as the *rex* began to feed. It worked on the huge meaty thighs of the dying animal, ripping out huge slabs of raw meat. The winds brought the horrible sounds of the carnage to me. They were wet, sloppy noises, an occasional sharp cracking of bones breaking, and the almost metallic sound of teeth gnashing.

Hundred pound chunks of meat were torn free, the *rex* tossing its massive head back, swallowing as it bobbed up and down. Even from a distance and against the blackness of its mouth, I could see that its muzzle was stained bright red, pieces of similarly colored meat falling from its strong jaws as it bit down.

I wept for the gentle *Titanosaur* when I saw that it was still alive. It raised its head, just a foot or two off the ground, and slid its one massive foreleg across the dirt. It looked again at the feasting victor as the *rex* changed its position, attacking the soft belly of its prey. The *Titanosaur's* head slammed to the ground as the *rex* tore into it.

Its suffering was over, and the *Tyrannosaur* recognized the fact. As it swallowed a big part of the giant's internal organs, it let out a tremendous roar of satisfaction—a roar of victory over a much larger, but less able adversary.

It was over in a matter of minutes. The *Tyrannosaur* had filled its belly, carved out hundreds of pounds of meat from the *Titanosaur*, and was done for the day. Only half of the gigantic plant eater was gone, the remaining part left for the scavengers of the valley. The tiny, dead, adolescent dinosaur left two hundred feet behind was neglected by the *rex*, as it ambled off to the east, perhaps seeking out the cool water of the river, or perhaps searching for the male for another go round.

The *Tyrannosaurus rex* was not only *not* a scavenger, it was a vicious killer. It didn't need to kill both dinosaurs. The small one would have been enough, the big one way too much. But it killed them both anyway. It killed them because it could. It killed them because it liked it.

*****

It took me a week to get to where I ended up.

I headed farther south into the heart of the valley, staying close to the river where food and water were plentiful.

I moved cautiously at first, wary of another *Tyrannosaur* encounter. I traveled in short little bursts from one wooded shelter to the next, running, keeping my head low.

By nightfall of that first day, I had gained confidence, having seen no other predators on the way. I made my way on a diagonal, heading mostly south, but east toward the river, as well. Hiding had become easier. In either direction, the trees and brush grew thicker and taller, the patches of bare ground in between shorter, and less frequent.

And although there were no other *Tyrannosaur* sightings, or other predators that I needed to fear, there was life in this valley. I ran into the herd of *Titanosaurs* milling about a tall stand of trees, feeding and just lounging around, acting like they hadn't a care in the world, as if two of their troop hadn't been savagely attacked and killed, one of them eaten just a few days before.

It was just another day in the late Cretaceous.

They paid me no mind as I walked past them. One of the adults turned its head to watch me go, letting out a short honking kind of a sound, perhaps showing contempt for such a small creature as myself. Perhaps it was saying, "*Don't worry, this one's got no teeth.*" But they were pretty stupid. I had probably just surprised it, and the little grunt was its way of vocalizing it.

I felt guilty for thinking it, but I was glad to put them behind me, between the cliffs and myself—a nice big distraction for any *rex* heading my way. I wouldn't have made much of a meal for the tyrant king, at least not in comparison to the huge herbivores. I felt guilty, but not too guilty. There were a couple dozen *Titanosaurs*. There was only one of me. If I could have just been sure that all the predators were behind me instead of in front of me, I would have slept a lot better at night.

During the next few days I encountered few animals. It was wintertime—many were hibernating—others were farther south in the warmer climes. There were almost no insects that I could see and damn few birds.

As I searched the skies overhead, a pair of *Pteranodons* circled, gliding down to skim the surface of the river, picking up a fish so effortlessly that they barely broke the skin of the water. I wondered if they were the same two I had seen during that first week on the beach, one of them perhaps the very one I had scared the hell out of on that first morning on the shore. Probably not. There were hundreds, maybe thousands, of the beautiful flying mammals. And yet I felt that these were the same ones—that they had been watching over me since the beginning, kind of my own personal guardian angels. I wondered why, with their wonderful gift of flight, they hadn't headed south like the birds.

Six days I traveled south along the water. Six nights I found shelter in the caves that dotted the far side of the river, or in the thick brush along the shore.

On the morning of the seventh day, I headed into the forest, on a path due west. The forest had become dense, like the north woods of New England, like the woods to the west of Susan's magical, Maryland house. At midday, with the majority of the trees dressed down for the winter, the floor of the forest came. to life as light and shadow moved across it in constantly changing patterns as the gentle winds swayed the huge canopy of branches high above. I didn't fear getting lost being that I didn't know where I was or where I was going. Besides, the sun still traveled from east to west, and as long as it continued to do so, I would always find my way back to the river.

This forest was much older that the one of the northern valley. Oaks that were hundreds of years old dominated it, their twisted trunks fifteen feet across, their limbs several feet thick spread out fifty feet in any direction.

It was just such a tree that I found on the edge of a clearing, two miles west of the river. It was a huge tree—a perfect tree. Its main branches began ten feet up the trunk, fanning out in four directions, symmetrical and nearly horizontal, before curving gracefully upward. Thirty feet above that, the trunk ended abruptly—replaced by three thick branches that angled outward and upward another forty feet. Between the three was a wide, cup shaped depression.

It was the kind of tree that a photographer would just have to shoot if he wandered by, the kind of tree that a kid would just have to climb if he spotted it. And that's exactly what I did on that day—I climbed it—right up to where the one trunk separated into three.

As I settled into the large hollow I found a sense of contentment and security that I hadn't felt in months. The huge arms of the tree just sort of wrapped themselves around me, shielding me, protecting me. The depression was deep enough and the three branches thick enough to block out the chilly wind, trap my own body heat like a blanket. It was such a welcome change that I spent the night there—that night, and every one after.

The new tree would never be the same as the old tree. I hadn't the tools to make it into the kind of home that I had in the northern valley—no seeds to plant a garden, no weapons to protect it from aggressors—well, except for the spear that is. But over the months, I made due.

I passed the winter in lonely isolation, busying myself with making my new home more comfortable. I had found another stand of poplar trees growing not too far from the river, not unlike the one upstream from the cliffs that surrounded the valley. This one was much larger—the trees more mature, more plentiful, much older. I didn't have a saw or an axe to fell them, but their smooth bark proved to be useful.

Using my knife, I cut long, inch-wide strips from the trees, weaving them into mats. Even in the winter, the bark was soft and pliable, easy to work with. Weaving them tight, they were strong, nearly waterproof. The first of them I strung high in the tree, between the three main branches, ten feet above where they came together. It made a serviceable roof, keeping the worst of the spring rains off my head. The second mat hung down from the edge of the first, on the western side of the tree, blocking the harsh winds that came out of the valley.

As the months passed, I continued to cut and weave the bark until a whole section of the stand of trees stood naked from a few inches above the ground to the height to which I could reach. The stand of trees looked like a brigade of soldiers standing at attention—all with their pants down around their ankles.

I continued to depants the troop until my little shelter high in the tree had four walls.

I fashioned rope from the long, thin leaves of the willows. They were plentiful in the valley, although on their own, they were not very strong. But by tying and weaving them in thick bundles I made sturdy ropes. It made getting into the tree so much easier. And from them I made a pretty comfortable hammock—stretched just above the crotch of the tree—I wasn't so confident in the strength of the thin willows that I would risk falling out of the tree.

It solved the short-term problem of how to sleep—I couldn't keep doing it sitting in the hollow of the tree where the branches came together—my back had gotten damn stiff after a few weeks of that. In the longer-term I would have to build a deck, I just wasn't at all sure how the hell to do it.

When I wasn't weaving mats or ropes, I spent my time down at the river fishing. I had grown accustomed to eating fish, but I would have killed for a good steak, even a mediocre hamburger.

I fished from the river, and drank from it, as well. And I searched its shores for hours on end, always looking for flint. It was the one thing that I missed the most—fire. I was tired of eating the fish raw, tired of being cold at night. It even seemed lonelier without it, the nights so much longer. In years past, a fire in the evening was almost like having someone else there—someone to talk to. It never answered, but the warmth that it gave made it seem like someone else was there. But I had lost my flint and steel kit—all my matches, as well, in the fire. I had steel, in the shaft of my spear. Now, if I could just find the missing ingredient.

I never did find the flint, but as the winter turned to spring it seemed so much less important. And with the warmth of spring, life returned to the valley. There were not nearly as many dinosaurs as I had thought there would be, not nearly as many as what I had found in the valley within the valley, or that paraded past the tree at the base of the cliff. Most had probably continued their journey south, knowing that winters were going to continue to get worse for the next few thousand years or so. Or perhaps they had simply found a nicer place to live—one with more food, and fewer predators.

The *Titanosaurs* returned—no doubt because they traveled so much slower and hadn't made it very far south. Or perhaps because they weren't smart enough to sense the changing seasons. But I thought that it was the slowness that brought them back. I thought so because none of the smaller and faster dinosaurs returned. The ceratopsians came back, as did the ankylosaurs, but not the hadrosaurs, nor the dome-headed dinosaurs. They were slim and light, comparatively so, and they were long gone. Perhaps, later in the season I would see them return from the northern route, followed, I was sure, by the *Tyrannosaurs*.

The insects, mammals, and birds returned, as well. They were even more plentiful than I saw in the northern valley. Nothing was quite as I remembered from the twentieth century—they were all just a tad different. I saw skunks, opossums, beavers, and gophers, but they were larger, smaller, taller or shorter than what I remembered. Some had colors that were not as they would become. Some had traits that would change over time. The skunks, for example, were not nocturnal, they traveled and hunted by daylight, and the gophers didn't dig. They traveled above ground and fed off the insects that dwelled there.

Insects were there by the millions, the only ones recognizable to me were the mosquitoes—they were as plentiful and as big a pain in the ass as I remembered from evenings in Chicago, by the lake. If anything they were bigger and more ferocious. More nights than not I lay awake in the tree, scratching and clawing at the huge welts up and down my arms.

But the butterflies were the things that I couldn't quite get out of my mind. They were everywhere. And they were huge, some with wingspans exceeding nine or ten inches. And the colors were magnificent—every color of the rainbow and some that defied the normal spectrum—colors that no one had ever seen before, or dreamt of.

But the thing that really surprised me, turned me upside down and inside out in wonder, was the little family of *Triceratops* that showed up in the late spring. There were three of them—two adults that I could only assume were the mom and pop, and one baby. Not more than a few months old, the little one could barely walk. It wasn't surprising that they were *Triceratops*—many of their species had showed up in the past few months. No, what surprised me—astounded me actually—was the smaller of the two adults. Its coloring and size told me that it was the female—the mother—yet it was just barely an adult, certainly not more than four or five years old, probably in just her first year of procreation ability. I knew that beyond a shadow of a doubt.

I knew it because of the deep red, Mickey Mouse handprint on her left flank.

I had been walking the edge of the river under the guise of looking for flint. In reality, I was just relaxing, wasting time, taking a break from my weaving duties, when they came into sight. I crossed the river, pressing up against the edge of the cliff so that I wouldn't spook them. They saw me, but didn't seem to care, content to drink from the stream and let the little one frolic in the shallow waters. As they passed me, only her right flank was exposed and there was nothing recognizable about her, nothing reminiscent of the little dinosaur whose twin I had killed three years before.

They stopped right in front of me, separated by nothing more than the fifty feet of shallow water. I was content to just squat down on my haunches and watch them—a little family out for a stroll on a warm, spring day. The two adults just stood by silently, facing directly toward me, keeping on eye on the tiny dinosaur walking clumsily through the few inches of water along the shore.

As the little one began to wander a bit too far to the south, the other way from where the group was heading, the smaller adult turned to nudge it back in the right direction. When she did, her left side was suddenly exposed.

I was so startled that I fell over backward into the cold water.

My sudden movement startled them as well, and they all turned to look in my direction. For a moment I wasn't sure if they were going to attack or not. They were gentle creatures, but I had surprised them, and their baby was between themselves and me, much too close to an unknown, potential threat. The male stopped dead in its tracks, while the female herded in her young. When she had him in tow, she did a surprising thing—she marched across the water, right for me.

To this day I will never know for sure if she recognized me, or was just curious. I had a moment of terror as I was convinced that the former was true. I had been responsible for the death of her sibling, directly accountable for the sadness of her mother. It didn't matter that I had helped to save the other three from the giant crocodiles on the southern path—she wouldn't remember that. And of course she didn't remember the other part either.

Sometimes I tended to credit the dinosaurs with more than they were capable of. Some were smarter than what was generally thought—some were not. The ceratopsians in general were not all that intelligent, and the *Triceratops* a bit less so. They were friendly, timid animals with a strong commitment to family, with a real love for their offspring—but bright they were not. I seriously doubted that she remembered *me*, let alone remembered what I had *done*.

And yet there was recognition in her eyes as she came in close, bowing her head before me, looking deeply into my own eyes. I knew that it was my smell. I *was* the only human, with an aroma unlike any other living creature in the land. In some tiny area in her very small brain, my scent set off a reaction that was familiar, even though confusing.

It obviously wasn't a memory of fear or intimidation, as she gently nudged my knee, the one that protruded from the top of the water.

Standing in the shallow river, I took hold of the horn above her left eye, not tugging, but letting her know that I was there, and I wasn't going to do anything stupid. As I released the horn, she came in closer, pushing me flat up against the wall of the cliff. I looked into her eyes, no longer afraid. Her pointy beak was just barely touching my own chin, and she let out a long shuddering breath.

From that point on, she rarely let me out of her sight. If the little family had intended on moving farther to the north, she put a damn quick stop to it. They camped out in the clearing beneath the tree, the maroon-marked female escorting me right up to the trunk every evening. They followed me everywhere that I went in the daytime, the female always taking the lead. I could have been offended, thinking that my privacy had been invaded, but I wasn't. I was just a little bit flattered, and hugely relieved that I wasn't blamed for what happened three years before. And it was damn nice to have some friendly company for a change.

*****

It was a month after our meeting that I thought it about time to do a little exploring. And the best place to do it was to head south along the cliff, close to where there was plenty of fresh water and fish.

Summer had hit full force, the temperatures well into the nineties. The sun beating down on my head, the sweat streaming from my pours, felt marvelous after the long winter living out of doors. I vowed never again to complain about the heat.

More and more animals took to the path along the river—all heading north. We passed group after group of them during the first few days until it seemed to be one long, non-stop parade of them—all going in the opposite direction. The dinosaurs paid little attention to me, but they seemed confused by the trio of *Triceratops* heading the wrong way down the path. Their heads would turn as we passed by, sometimes accompanied by a snort or low growl, their eyes questioning in a way that seemed to say, "*Hey, where you guys going—that's not the right way. Don't you know its summertime, and in the summertime, we're supposed to be going this way?*" The *Triceratops* didn't seem to notice at all. They just kept heading south—like me.

We continued to walk along the river, which ran along the edge of the cliff, mile after mile. All the while the face of the rock was slowly shrinking in height. By the fifth day, it was nothing but a sharp escarpment, no more than forty feet high.

By day six, it was gone altogether, opening to the east in a wide flat plane. Following a hunch, I left the relative safety and security of the river and began hiking towards the east.

The walk was easy, the ground hard and flat, only a few stands of young trees and bushes to skirt around. The four of us covered a lot of ground on that day and I worried about the animals, and the lack of water. Three of my water bottles had survived and I knew from long experience how to ration, so I would be okay for a while. But I worried about the tiny one. I poured a bit of the water into the palm of my hand and let the baby drink from it. It lapped it up greedily, its rough tongue nearly taking the skin from my hand. It was obvious that it wanted more, and needed more—more than my meager supply could provide. And with the dry season upon us it would be days before we saw any rain. And I had no idea where we were headed.

I couldn't risk the animals. In the morning, if daylight revealed no new travel options, I would lead the trio back to the river, and back to the tree.

As the sun began to set we found a grove of small evergreens to bed down in. The animals fed on the soft needles of the pines, extracting what little moisture there was there, while I snacked on the pocketful of dried nuts and berries that I never left home without.

*****

The next morning, as the sun rose over the eastern horizon, I suddenly, magically, knew exactly where I was, as if someone had just spread out a map before me with a great big old X marking the spot.

The rising sun was split in half by the horizon, as straight and as clean as with a surgeon's scalpel. The horizon was perfectly straight for as far as I could see, not the slightest irregularity—no trees, hills, or mountains. I understood what I was seeing because I had awoken to it every morning that I was at the machine. A horizon like that meant just one thing. I was looking across a body of water, a really big body of water.

I was looking across the Intercontinental Sea.

It was miles in the distance, but looking at it closely I could see the slim demarcation between land and sea, the thick, nearly black line, brilliant yellow across the center section as the water threw back the rays of the sun.

I knew exactly where I was. If I walked due north, keeping the rising cliffs to my left, I would be back on my beach, back at the machine.

I needed to go back there one more time—I just didn't think I'd ever have the opportunity. I knew that I'd never be able to climb back up the steep cliffs to get to the tunnel that led through them. I would never be able to find the right hole in the rock. But I needed to go back. I had two things to get, and one thing to do.

There were still two empty water bottles back there, and the three that I still had were about my most valuable possessions. They were the only things that I could store and carry water in, and with the dog days of summer setting in, I would need them all more than ever. And I needed metal—metal like from the storage racks. There were a hundred things that I could do with them—a ladder for the tree, the framework for a deck, weapons, and tools—there was a nearly inexhaustible list of things that I could make with them. And there was a ton of them in the machine.

It would be a difficult trip for me, more than a week's journey, probably two. It would be an impossible trip for the little family of *Triceratops* unless there were frequent sources of fresh water. As this whole area was once the sea—*a salt-laden sea*—I really doubted that there would be any. I had to find a way to keep the dinosaurs from following.

I began walking back the way we had come, not far, just far enough to put the idea in their heads that we were going home. When the female took the lead, as I knew she would, I slowed my pace, the distance between us growing rapidly. The distance increased, but not for very long. The female sensed my absence and turned to find me. Before she had a chance to turn the others, I raced ahead, and grabbing hold of both eyebrow horns, forced her back the other way.

I had to repeat the process a half dozen times, swatting her hard across the rump to get a slow, awkward trot out of her, before the idea sunk in. She stopped one last time, turning to face me before regaining her western trek, walking slowly now with her head hanging low, her pointed chin dragging the ground.

I felt like such a heel, even though I knew that within a month I'd be back at the tree, back with the three of them ... if they were still there.

Somehow, I felt that they would be.

*****

In ten days I hadn't made it to the beach, but I knew that I was getting close. Two days before, I had passed the entrance to the tunnel that led to the canyon and the river on the other side of the cliff. At least I think that it was the same one. I had passed some other pretty important things as well—two bodies of water. They were too small to be considered lakes, hardly more than pools, but the water was fresh, runoff from an opening high in the rock, probably from a rain-catching basin atop the cliff. They provided plenty of water for me, but they were several days journey apart. I wasn't at all sure that the animals would have survived the distance.

I hurried my pace, feeling that I could cut three days of hiking to two if I increased my speed. After another day, things really began to look familiar, and I knew that I was close. I traveled long after the sun had set, before exhaustion forced me to quit for the night. Finding a soft patch of shrubbery to lie in, I was out like a light.

I slept late, long after the sun was up, and even before I felt the gentle nudging, I could tell by the all too familiar barnyard-like smell that things weren't as they should be. But it wasn't fear—just the opposite. A huge smile spread across my face as I realized that somehow, some way, they had managed to follow me.

I rolled over to see the mother *Triceratops* right in my face. I knew better, but I'd swear that she was smiling, and I couldn't help but laugh out loud. She rolled me over with a gentle push, and I hammed it up, rolling over the shrubs and twenty feet beyond until my laughter was just too much to take and I had to sit up and grab my sides, wipe the tears of surprise and joy from my face.

These animals were smarter than I gave them credit for. There wasn't a doubt in my mind that they had faked me out of my boots. They must have marched away, toward the tree, just far enough to convince me that they were gone ... and then did an about face ... tracking me.

It seemed impossible that they had been following me for all these days and I didn't have a clue. They were large animals, not capable of traveling quietly, and yet they had managed to sneak up on me, to hide it for almost two weeks. Again, I was probably giving them too much credit, but this time I didn't think so. Whatever! I was damn happy to have them back.

We regained our march, now a family of four—happy, chatting nonsensically about anything and everything. It didn't matter that they couldn't understand me. I was just so damn happy to have them with me, to know that they were together, safe and sound, that talking to them seemed to be just about the most natural thing in the world.

It was late when we rounded the bend in the cliff that surrounded my beach. It was twilight, perhaps another thirty minutes before in was fully dark. It was raining, not the gentle kind of sprinkle that would refresh after a long, hot day on the road, but a torrential summer storm, replete with frightening bursts of lightning and long, ear-splitting rolls of thunder. I could barely see the end of the machine protruding through the cave's entrance behind the pouring rain.

We were all bone-tired, the breaths from the animals now lagging behind, audible even through the pounding rain. The rain was a constant thunder in my ears as it pounded the ground, the dirt beneath my feet a quagmire, rivers of mud flowing to the east.

I picked up the pace, knowing that shelter for all of us was just yards ahead. The rain poured from my face, plastering my eyelashes together, so that I could hardly see. I wasn't looking at the ground, or even paying attention to it, blindly trying to make my way the last short distance to the safety of the cave. Perhaps had I been paying attention, had I been able to see the earth before me, I would have seen that something was terribly wrong.

We were just feet from the cave when the animal behind me let out a low rumbling growl that I could hear beyond the sound of the rain. We were within inches of the cave's entrance when the smell became recognizable, even to me. I spun around to see the look on the face of the *Triceratops*. Its eyes went wide with terror, as it tried to reverse its direction and head away from the cave—away from the source of the terrible smell, but only managing to slide across the slick mud.

It emerged from the cave. Like a rag doll, I was tossed to the side by a nudge from its massive head as the *Triceratops* was caught in mid-turn, just short of the entrance. The *Tyrannosaur* struck quickly, the dagger-like teeth sinking deeply into the back of its prey, just below the base of its thick tail. The *Triceratops* let out a roar of fear and pain as it turned to face the *rex*, a huge slab of meat ripping away from its hindquarters as the *Tyrannosaur* lost its grip. Even in the downpour I could see blood pouring from the torn backside of the bloodied *Triceratops*, spraying into the nose and eyes of the attacker, enraging it further.

I stood helpless in the rain, not inches from the back of the time machine. The other adult and child animal stood on the other side of the clearing, frozen with fear. The *rex* raised its head and released a bloodcurdling roar that breached the sound of the thundering rain, as the *Triceratops* lowered its head, and prepared to defend itself.

The *Triceratops* began to back away from the larger, quicker predator, trying to draw it away from its family, its head low to the ground in a submissive gesture. The *Tyrannosaur* approached slowly, mindful of the dangerous horns of the *Triceratops*, and lowered its head to peer into the eyes of its foe. Blood and saliva ran from the mouth of the *rex*, washing down into the mud, and the *Tyrannosaur* snorted its contempt for the cowering dinosaur. It took two huge strides alongside the *Triceratops*, casually, as if it were moving away, when then, with astounding speed, turned and sunk its teeth into the animal's neck, just behind its bony frill. But the *Triceratops* had been in a defensive posture, not a submissive one, and it knew the tactics of the ferocious killer. As the *Tyrannosaur* moved to the side, the *Triceratops* pivoted towards the attacker, keeping its head low, its pointed chin dragging through the mud. Instinctively, it raised its head just as the *Tyrannosaur* attacked, burying one of its three-foot long horns into the soft belly of the *rex*. At the same instant the *Tyrannosaur's* powerful jaws clamped down on the neck of the *Triceratops*, blood spraying and pouring from both wounds.

Each animal was injured—mortally—but each refused to back off. Blood was pouring down their sides, disappearing into the dark mud. The *Tyrannosaur* refused to let go. Instead it began throwing its head from side to side to inflict more damage to the dying animal. But with each twist of its head, the horn of the *Triceratops* tore deeper and wider into the belly of the *Tyrannosaur*.

The *Triceratops* was dead—its neck broken in the mighty jaws of the fierce *Tyrannosaur*. But the *Tyrannosaur* still refused to release its grip, instead using the last of its strength to drag its prize the few yards into the cave to feed. In the exhilaration of victory, and in the anticipation of the well-deserved reward, the painful wound was momentarily forgotten by the *rex*. But the blood continued to flow from the animal in huge and life-threatening quantities, and as it dragged its meal into the cave, the horn continued to dig deeper into its stomach.

The three of us stood outside the cave in the pouring rain watching in stunned horror and disbelief. The littlest dinosaur stood beneath the huge head of the adult, trembling in fear and sadness. The adult stood frozen in place, facing the cave, angled slightly away from me so that his left flank was exposed. Even in the darkness, even through the heavy downpour, I could see that its side was of one color, uniformly light brown throughout. There was no dark, four-fingered shape there.

Inside the cave, safe from the torrential rains, the *Tyrannosaur* finally released the *Triceratops* from its jaws. As the dead animal crashed to the ground, the horn slid from the belly of the *Tyrannosaur*, releasing a huge stream of dark blood. The *Tyrannosaur* knew that it too was about to die, and raised its head, making one last earth shattering roar before staggering and falling to the ground alongside the *Triceratops*, their blood mingling one last time as it soaked into the ground.

*****

The dim glow from my computer screen is all the light there is. It surprised me that it had come on, having tried it a hundred times in the last few hours. I sat and stared at it for several minutes, amazed to again be able to see my hands on the keyboard, my legs, deep in shadow beneath the little metal table. I could make out the skeletons of what were left of the storage racks in the darkness, the metal interior skin of the machine reflecting back the white square of light in a dozen spots. I wept for joy at the light, even if I knew that it wouldn't last very long—a few hours at best—just a few hours with no sunlight to recharge it.

There would be no more sunlight, and when the batteries died, there would be no more light of any kind—ever. And this is the last that I would write—the end of my story.

I shouldn't have come back. Even if there was that one in a million chance that Susan had recovered her health and might at some point actually read my story, I shouldn't have come back. I should have just stayed in the tree, content with how things were, despite the hardships. It had been difficult, nearly impossible at times, yet I had survived it, even had some brief periods of joy. But I still had one thing to do.

It's not at all how I pictured it ending—with a whimper instead of a bang. For a long time I knew that I wouldn't die of old age, my heart giving up at ninety simply because it was too tired of beating. I would never be bound up by osteoarthritis, wouldn't suffer from cataracts, dementia, or loss of hearing. I'd never experience angina, or hypertension, prostate problems, hair loss, or the embarrassment of incontinence. I would never be afflicted with the things that we associate with the later stages of life. I would be dead long before the onset of any of those things.

I had already shattered whatever odds Dermot had placed on the length of my survival, exceeded my own expectations by a long way, too. Hell, I should have died on that first day when the machine tore loose from its moorings—then—and a hundred times since then. But I kept beating the odds ... until now.

I didn't long for death. I was perfectly content to push it as far into the future as I possibly could. But I always thought that it was just around the corner and that when it came, it would come quickly, and violently. Being eaten by a predator, caught in the middle of a volcanic eruption, take a header into a crevasse during an earthquake, tumble out of the tree or from the edge of the cliff, were but a handful of things that I thought about. They were all very real, highly probable possibilities, considering my circumstances.

I always believed that it would happen outdoors, breathing fresh air right up to the end, basking in the bright sunshine. Or at least under a full moon, the sky lit up by a billion, brilliant stars. Even when I was lost in the underground sea all those years ago, even more recently when I was trapped by the small cave-in where the *rex* lived, I didn't really think that it would end there.

My odyssey began in the machine, and other than the day that it carried me here, I never thought that it would end here, as well. And it *would* end here, and soon. I could already feel the air getting thinner, having to force a breath instead of the natural, don't-even-think-about-it rhythm. I was so thirsty, and hungry, too, but the lack of oxygen would get me long before the other two had a chance at me. I hoped fervently that the computer stayed alive for a while longer, that there would still be light left when the end came.

It had begun several hours ago, maybe as few as twelve, perhaps as many as twenty-four. Time was meaningless in the absolute darkness and you're trying to count the minutes until the end. It had begun when I stepped into the machine to pick up another couple of metal rails from the storage racks. I had the middle row completely disassembled and was hauling them out to the pile outside the cave. I had already constructed a crude travois to haul several dozen pieces back to the tree, getting ready to head out the next morning at first light.

It had been almost dark, just shadows formed by the dim light coming from behind the western cliff. It was darker yet in the cave, almost too dark to work in the interior of the machine. But knowing that I had just one more trip, I had no problem scrambling around in the dark, one last time.

I was careless, which I knew better than to be.

The mountains had been active, even more so than usual, the ground shaking noticeably, sometimes violently, small rocks falling from the sides of the cliff, dust clogging the cave, settling down onto the two dead animals, onto the two live ones as well. They refused to budge from inside the cave since it happened.

I had stepped past the bodies, the father and child *Triceratops* eyeing me closely as I stepped up into the machine, its titanium gull-wing door propped open by my spear. I had but to grab the final two metal rails and I would have been out of there for good. I shuffled my feet toward the center of the machine, feeling my way in the near darkness, when a tremendous crash came from the roof, followed by the sound of the door slamming shut.

In the next few seconds it was like Armageddon. A thousand rocks hammered the titanium skin of the machine. It was so sudden and so loud that my heart jumped in my chest, an ice-cold thread ran through every vein. I went down to the floor, my legs dropping from beneath me, without even realizing it. The noise was like nothing I had ever heard before, the echoes rattling through the interior of the metal coffin, like sticking your head in the exhaust of a turbine engine. I grabbed for my ears as I slid underneath the far metal rack, coiled up in a tight little ball, my insides turning all liquid as I was in an instant terrified out of my mind.

Even before I hit the cold, hard floor, what little was left of the light winked out. The small, round glow from the eastern portholes disappeared, the tiny, supposedly unbreakable Plexiglas windows fracturing under the tremendous weight of the rocks pouring down. The machine quivered and jumped, threatening to come apart at the joints as I, myself, trembled under the steel supports of the rack that offered no real protection whatsoever.

I could taste the dust in my mouth as the stainless steel rivets began to fail, the weight on the machine threatening to crush it like a tin can.

It was over in seconds. I was left in total darkness, the sudden silence as ominous as the terrible noise before it was frightening. As the vibrations through the titanium hull faded away, the only sounds were those of the metal machine groaning under the strain, and my own shallow, rapid breathing.

I spent the next half hour trying to find a way out. The door was as unmovable as if it had been welded shut. I pushed and kicked at it, fear and frustration forcing me to hammer at the door like a lunatic in an iron cell, until my hands were bleeding and my shoulders bruised and battered. Fear and the lack of air made the sweat start to pour, and I knew that panic was imminent.

I had to force myself to calm down, to think my way out of this predicament, like I had to do so many times in the past. There were two ways out of the machine. The door was no longer an option, but there was another way. It was how I managed to get back into the machine after that first rockslide, the one caused by the machine slamming into the wall of the cave all those years ago. It was the small square access hatch in the ceiling.

Somewhere deep inside, I knew that it was a silly notion, that I shouldn't pin my hopes there, but I did, and as I found the hatch, what I knew deep down came quickly and painfully to the surface. The tons of rock that had come down on top of the machine had completely blocked the hatch.

The edge of a particularly big boulder protruded three or four inches through the opening. I stretched my body out, pushing outward against the rock with everything that I had, until the sweat ran down my sides in streams, until my arms shook from the effort, and pain pulsed in my temples. The rock didn't so much as wiggle.

I tried using one of the steel rails from the disassembled rack, pushing it through the corner of the hatch, poking, pushing, and prying. I accomplished nothing but to bend the rail into a piece of twisted junk. I wasn't even able to push the rail though the opening more than a foot.

*****

As my breathing became more forced, the air thinner, a strange calm came over me. There was nothing more that I could do—nothing more that I *had* to do. As I slid down against the slick surface of the machine, sitting cross-legged on the hard floor, I resigned myself to my fate.

It was the machine that had brought me here, had been my home for a time, and would be my home again—my final home. I thought about all that had occurred, and as I did, whatever fear I had felt when I first realized I was trapped here, slowly washed away as the memories of the past eleven years flooded in.

The sadness too, disappeared as I thought about Susan. In another few hours, I would leave this life—this time—and as I did, the machine holding my remains would suddenly reappear in Dermot's time, perhaps right before his very eyes. I guess that when it did appear, so would all the rocks burying it.

I no longer worried about him not finding the computer, not being able to get to my story. It was as hermetically sealed beneath the rock as the four dinosaurs in the cave. Nothing would ever get at it. Nothing until Dermot, that is.

*****

My breathing was becoming labored, not much air left, but there was no pain or discomfort, no terror, or even sadness. Instead, I was overcome by a feeling of lightness, as if I was just floating inside the machine—weightless—no other physical sensation whatsoever. There was a constant buzzing in my head, a pleasant kind of numbing sound. I listened intently to it, words forming beneath the sound, lightly spoken, indistinguishable—just random, whispered syllables that formed no coherent words. They were spoken in a soft voice—a woman's voice.

Gray shapes formed in the darkness, forms that floated through the machine like ghosts, forms that had no real shape or meaning. Like weightless tendrils of smoke they drifted before my eyes, putting a smile on my lips, knowing that I was hallucinating or just plain dreaming. It wasn't a bad way to go.

I looked over at the computer screen, seeing the glow from it begin to fade, or maybe it was just me, my eyes failing as the light within began to dim. The smile stayed on my face as I looked at the laptop one last time knowing that Susan would indeed read my story and know that the last thing that I was thinking of was her.

CHAPTER 26

In the dream, the image persisted. Like an apparition, the figure floated down from above, weaving back and forth across the machine. It was cloaked in a thick, smoky fog that refused to lift so that I could see it for what it really was. It was ghostly, but not frightening or threatening in any way. I felt completely detached from it, as if I was watching an old eight-millimeter, black and white movie on a well-worn screen, in an old-fashioned, smoke filled theater.

I could detect no source of it, but there was light, dim and hazy, dark—like a foggy midnight in London. I couldn't seem to make my eyes move within their sockets, yet I had a limited field of vision directly in front of me. My eyes looked where they could, scanning the spot before me where the laptop was just moments ago, unable to see the little patch of light from the screen—unable to see much of anything, anywhere that was brighter than anything else—everything just a dark, mysterious blur. Perhaps the light was coming from above. I just couldn't force my eyes upward to check. Perhaps it was *the* light, and in another few moments I would drift into it, taken away to wherever it is that we all go when we're gone.

Every muscle felt relaxed, like wet cloth. I don't think I could have moved if I tried, and I didn't feel much like trying. I was no longer struggling to breathe yet I wasn't at all sure that I *was* breathing. I had no conscious thought of doing it—couldn't feel my chest going up and down—there was no sensation of air filling my lungs, passing through my lips. It was like a dream, but I couldn't quite convince myself that I was dreaming.

The buzzing continued. Not the sound of a power saw or an angry swarm of bees, but the kind of gentle, hypnotic hum that can lull you to sleep. Above it, the spirit-voice continued, still softly, the sounds indistinct, and I could make no sense of them. Now and then I thought I heard my name called out, but garbled and muffled, as if spoken across a long distance, like listening to someone speak from across a room with a mouthful of peanut butter.

I listened intently to try and make out the words, but instead of picking up on them, they began to fade, until there was only the buzz, and then the buzz too began to fade away, slowly, as if the source of the sound was moving away from me. Perfectly timed with the diminishing sound, the modest light began to fade, total darkness returning. Just one precious moment before my world went silent and black, I had the realization that I had heard and saw nothing—that it was all in my mind. And at that instant, all was gone.

*****

It was like waking from a deep sleep—coming to slowly—my senses coming back on-line gradually, one at a time. Or I wasn't awake, but just beginning another dream, or perhaps the start of the next life—the afterlife if you will. Either way, I liked it just fine so far.

The first thing that entered my consciousness was the cool, softness of whatever it was that I was stretched out on. I was in that confused state, that just-having-awakened-from-a-dream state, yet I knew that what I was feeling was wrong, totally out of place. I wasn't sure where I was, or what had happened to me. It took a few minutes to remember just where I had left off—sitting on the floor of the machine, propped up against the wall. It confused the hell out of me that I had somehow, magically been transported from the floor of the machine to this wonderfully comfortable … thing.

I was in no hurry to test out my other senses, content as I was to just luxuriate in the marvelous sense of touch. I was also somewhat fearful of opening my eyes, afraid that it would force me to wake up, finding that I was still on the hard floor of the machine, in the darkness, with no air to breathe. I squeezed my eyelids tighter, trying to make things black, to hide what I knew was light before them.

I squeezed them tighter yet, until a few more cobs were swept free from my brain, and I realized that sooner or later, I would have to open them.

When I did, I saw daylight. Not like I was outside in the open air, but bright light nonetheless. It streamed in from several points, bright rays of light shining through like tiny spotlights, scouring the wall and floors of the machine. Billions of tiny particles swam within the light, like sunshine filtering in from the tall windows of a dust factory.

I focused on the beam coming from my left, a perfectly round circle of light, so bright that it hurt my eyes, made me squint. I settled on it until my eyes were accustomed to the brightness. As things came into focus, I saw that it was a tiny window, the eastern most portal of the machine. It was incredibly bright, as if a miniature sun was shining through. I couldn't see clearly beyond it, the glass no longer clear, a spider's web of fractures running through it.

It felt so real, but how could it be? How could sunlight be penetrating through the hundreds of tons of rocks that buried the machine? How could I awake in a sealed vault that hours ago held no air?

Had the rockslide been just a bad dream brought about by thirst and hunger and exhaustion? Had I entered the machine last night to pick up the last of the rails, only to decide to go to sleep and finish up in the morning? Was I but waking from a good night's sleep in the machine?

The dream theory fell apart as I passed my hand over the soft, smooth material beneath me—springy under my touch—an air mattress. How in the hell did I get an air mattress? I was sure that mine had gone up in the fire, along with everything else.

I flexed my hand—stiffness and soreness making me wince. I looked at it, seeing the discoloration, patches of blood on the knuckles that were already beginning to scab over. I damn sure didn't get bruised and bloodied knuckles from a dream—I got them from beating on the door, trying to get it open after the rocks came down.

I realized that I was lying on the metal fold-down bed. Not so mysterious if you discounted the mattress and clean white sheet on it, which of course I couldn't account for. Still groggy and more confused than ever, I swung my legs off the bed, knocking something over, hearing it roll across the floor, bumping into the wall underneath the narrow bed. I leaned forward, reaching far underneath the cot, my fingers immediately recognizing what they grasped. It was one of my water bottles. Being more precious than gold I pulled it toward me, surprised that it felt full. Now, just when had I filled it, and how did it get in the machine?

I had yet another surprise when I extracted it from under the bed and turned it over in my hand. It looked like one of my bottles ... but it didn't. The few that I had left, that had survived ten years, looked like they had been through a war. The plastic that had once been as clear as the water within was so scratched that it was opaque, impossible to see what was inside. *This* bottle hadn't a mark on it. It looked like the day it came off the shelf.

I had to rethink the notion that I was still dreaming when I saw the little cellophane wrapper around the nozzle still intact.

If it weren't for the fact that I hadn't had a drink of alcohol in more than eight years, I'd swear that I was drunk. Not a damn thing made a lick of sense. But if I wasn't drunk, and I wasn't dreaming—what the hell was left? Damn, maybe I actually *was* dead and this was God's waiting room.

It's just that I didn't *feel* dead.

To prove that I wasn't, I finally decided to get to my feet. As I did, I noticed two things pretty damn quickly. First was that I got up too fast, and had to sit right back down again, my head swimming, the room spinning. I had a moment of nausea, and I had to lean back against the wall, taking deep breaths.

It wasn't till then that I realized that I *was* breathing—*must* have been right along. It had just been so effortless, so natural, that I hadn't given it a thought. I was breathing as you're supposed to, unconsciously, without effort. I looked over to the door. It was still closed. Several of the glass portals were frosted over from cracks, but they were still whole—no air was coming through there. Where the hell was it coming from?

The question was answered quickly as, for the first time, I looked toward the roof of the machine. There, right smack in the middle, was the hatch. The boulder that I was sure was there, was gone, nothing but blue skies above.

I forgot about everything else, knowing that I had a way of escaping the machine that only hours before, was my tomb. I didn't even think about the magic that had cleared the tons of debris from the roof, about whether or not it was just another dream or a cruel prank by the Man upstairs—setting me up for yet another disappointment.

I didn't think about any of those things as I reached up to grab the outer edges of the hatch. It was buckled inward, confirming the fact that there had been a hell of a lot of weight on it. It might have just expanded the opening by just a few millimeters, not that that really mattered. I was a lot lighter, a lot thinner then I was on that day eleven years ago.

I pulled myself up through the opening until my head and shoulders were through, my elbows supporting my weight.

What I saw so stunned me that I nearly fell back through the hatch.

At first I thought that it was an optical illusion, or a giant mirror held upright less than two hundred feet away. I thought again that I was dreaming because a dream was about the only plausible explanation. Perhaps it *was* the Man Upstairs, continuing on with His practical joke, teasing me shamelessly.

I shook my head violently until it ached, and it the image didn't change—it was no dream and it was no practical joke. I had to blink my eyes repeatedly just to make sure that my vision wasn't playing another trick on me. But the image was still there.

Before my eyes, settled six inches into the mud, a hundred and fifty feet in front of me, was another time machine.

I hung from the top of my own machine, feet just kind of dangling there in free space, startled like I had never, ever, been in my life. I looked at it, the sun reflecting off the black metallic roof. It was exactly like mine, except newer. There were no years of accumulated dirt and grime, no dents, bends, or scuffs. Even the series of little rods, with black balls on the ends, were intact. It rested in the one area that it could—the open patch of ground where just the day before, the *Tyrannosaur* and the *Triceratops* battled to the death.

I just hung there, amazed beyond speech, beyond rational thought. If my elbows hurt from the pressure put upon them, I didn't feel it. If my shoulders screamed from the force of gravity trying to pull my body back through he hole, I was unaware. I thought that I could be no more astounded had Jesus himself walked from the door of the other machine.

I was wrong!

The door on the other machine was already raised, an open invitation for something to go in… or something to come out. In what might have been a few seconds, or several minutes, something did.

A slim figure clad in shorts and a plain, white tee shirt stepped down from the machine. It was a woman, or a girl—her tall, slim figure that of an athlete or a dancer. Her long hair was tied in a ponytail. It whipped across her shoulders as she stepped onto the ground, turning in my direction.

She strode purposefully toward me, unmindful of the thick mud beneath her feet, her head held high, as if she were on a mission, or extremely satisfied in a mission just completed.

As she approached my machine, I could see that she was no girl, even though her body and the way she walked said otherwise. The sun that reflected off the silver streaks in her hair told me differently.

When she was a hundred feet away, I saw the smile on her face, and I realized that she was looking directly at me. Fifty feet closer and the first signs of recognition began entering my own mind, and in another ten feet I could see the detail of her face, the thin, white scar that arched across her brow, just above her left eye.

I pulled myself the rest of the way through the hatch, blinking back the tears, my breath caught in my throat, my whole body shaking. I scrambled across the top of the machine at the same instant that she arrived at the bottom.

On my hands and knees, peering over the edge, Susan said the most beautiful words that I had ever heard—"It's about time you got your lazy ass outta bed."

*****

Through that day and long into the night we held each other, afraid to let go, as if losing touch with one another would end the dream—that if we lost sight of one another, even for an instant, we would lose sight of one another forever. I would return to the cave, with time running out—or already out.

Susan would return to wherever she had come from—back to the coma or back to the grave—back to her own time at any rate.

When we weren't hugging, we were sitting next to each other, holding hands, weeping unashamedly one minute, laughing like school children the next. And she cared for me like she would have a small child, feeding me, bathing me, shaving me, until I had begun to feel whole again—whole in every way that a person can be whole. And I was convinced that I wasn't dreaming, and this was really happening.

In between it all she answered the hundreds of questions that had jumped into my mind the second that I saw the second machine, the instant that I realized who it was walking toward my own machine.

Susan had come out of her coma two years after I had left. Not suddenly—one minute gone, the next minute back—like you see on TV, but slowly over weeks and months. That she came out of it at all astounded the doctors—they began calling her their miracle girl. But her recovery was slow and discouraging. She had to learn practically everything over again—talking, walking, even the simplest things like tying her shoes, feeding herself.

Her career was gone, her coworkers, her few friends, gone, as well. All that remained of her studies, her years of fieldwork, was reduced to fragmented thoughts and bits of random facts that would take years to reassemble … if ever. It would take years to become a functioning paleontologist again—*if* anyone ever wanted her in that role again.

Although she remembered almost nothing when she first regained consciousness, she did remember something. The first word that she spoke in nearly three years was my name. Somehow, she knew of the days that I had sat by her side, understood what I was telling her even if she couldn't quit remember the details. That's why the letter that Jakes eventually gave her was no surprise at all.

Jakes himself was fine—retired, the children grown, out on their own. He had made good decisions about the money that I had left him—all the kids completing college—invested wisely so that he was comfortable even with his meager retirement pay. But he never quite got over police work—being in the middle of things, investigating crimes, solving mysteries. That's why it took only a modest amount of cajoling for Susan to get him to go along with her plan.

It took years for the plan to develop, for Susan to be in a position to carry it out, even though from the day that she read my letter, she knew what she had to do. She was going to find me, and in order to do that, she first had to find Dermot, which is where Jakes came in. Not that finding Dermot would be much of a problem. Susan knew that someone from Dermot's team would be at the cave in Utah around the clock. All Jakes had to do was a bit of investigating to find out where Dermot was. It was a piece of cake for someone like Jakes.

The hard part was convincing Dermot to do what Susan wanted—to send *her* back in time.

Dermot was not someone to look a gift horse in the mouth. Volunteers for this kind of experiment didn't exactly grow on trees. But he had already done the trip to the Cretaceous bit, and he was still waiting to evaluate the results of that one. He wasn't about to sink millions of dollars in an experiment that had already been done.

What finally convinced Dermot was a little friendly persuasion from Jakes—just a little discussion about the whereabouts of one Doctor David Williams—and perhaps Dermot knew more than a little something about his disappearance. Of course Dermot had committed no crime, but the last thing he needed was a bunch of cops digging around in his business, fouling up the works at the cave.

It didn't hurt that Susan was willing to fund the entire project. It had everything to do with how quickly Dermot acquiesced. Dermot saved face by stating that Susan's follow-up visit was good insurance—just in case something that he hadn't thought of had happened to David.

Susan was a millionaire, several times over. While she was in the coma, her books continued to sell well—even more *because* of her coma. And when she was well enough, she wrote two more—both best sellers. Her miraculous recovery from nearly impossible odds made Lacy Wanderlust an even bigger celebrity. Her public couldn't wait for her next book. It made Susan wealthier than she already was, which was considerable.

The sale of her home brought her even more wealth.

I thought, how hard it must have been for her to sell her house, to give up on her plans for the incredible third-floor that she had worked so hard on. At that, all she did was smile and tell me that it was the best trade that she had ever made. At first I thought that she was referring to being here in the Cretaceous, being able to study the animals that had been her passion for most of her life. But like I had been for most of my life when it came to matters of the heart, I had it dead wrong.

It made her start to cry again as she told me how she didn't need the house anymore, how Jakes and his family had taken her in the day she got out of the hospital. They had treated her as one of the family with no strings attached, just as they had me thirteen years before. She told me that the house was so unimportant as compared to what she really wanted—what she had always wanted.

She was in love with me—always had been, always would be—that no matter where I was, or *when* I was, she would find me. She would have followed me to the ends of the earth.

And that's when my own tears began again.

Jakes knew about Susan, but didn't *know* Susan—he had done this for me. Just thinking about him, his family, the unconditional love that they gave an almost total stranger caused the tears to continue to fall down my cheeks. Telling me that she loved me, when I thought that I would never have that feeling again had made them fall faster yet.

When we had recovered enough to continue, she told me the rest.

Even with the money paid up front, Dermot committed to the project, it still took two years before the attempt. Dermot was in the middle of another experiment, one that he refused to discuss with Susan, and it took well over two more years to build an exact replica of my machine, to reassemble the exact same crew and to ready the provisions. Everything had to be exact—just exactly the same as they were for *my* trip—every nut and bolt, every wire and titanium panel had to be to the exact same specifications. The dimensions and the weight of the machine and all of its supplies had to be correct to within the ounce. Dermot even had to account for the difference between Susan's weight and my own. She would have no chance if there were the slightest of variations in any of the parameters.

It was one of the fundamental mysteries that confounded me almost as soon as I had gotten over the shock of seeing Susan walk out of the second machine. If there was one thing that Dermot drilled into my head was that time travel was not yet an exact science. Oh, he was confident that he could send me back, and equally confident that he could send me back where I wanted to go—the late Cretaceous, but the late Cretaceous was a pretty damn big stretch of time. He estimated a tolerance of plus or minus one percent. When dealing with a span of time seventy million years, we're talking about an error of the better part of a million years.

How in the hell did Dermot manage to send Susan back with such accuracy?

The answer was relatively simple. It was as simple to him as it was confounding to me—do everything exactly the same as he had before, not one bit different—same computer software, same personnel, same supplies, same machine. It's why I had been here eleven years, and not ten years, or twelve. Eleven years, almost exactly, before the second machine appeared. Susan had left her own time exactly eleven years after I did, eleven years almost to the day. And in that eleven years, eleven years had passed in my own time.

The only thing not exactly the same—besides Susan—was the location. They couldn't very well send the machine from exactly the same spot as the one before. Two objects cannot occupy the same space at the same time. They could place it there, in their own time—there was nothing to prevent it—but when it appeared in my time, my own machine would still be here, or so they supposed. They didn't know about my own machine ripping loose from its foundation and was now displaced by several yards. And, according to Dermot, they didn't want to put it in the cave, or anywhere close by. They feared that I had probably taken up residence in the cave and they didn't want to put the machine on top of me.

At the same time, they had to put it somewhere where they knew was relatively unchanged in the last seventy million years. That left the area a hundred and fifty feet in front of the cave, the place where the two dinosaurs had their epic battle, the place where I had first discovered the trackways that started me on this adventure, the place where Susan magically appeared before me.

There were still so many questions to be asked, and answered—what happened to Green—had he been captured—was he still alive? How about my dinosaurs—what museum did they end up in—how did they look? Eventually I would know the answers to them all, but right then they were all so unimportant. The only thing that mattered was that Susan had found me, despite the almost incalculable odds. She had found me and nothing would ever separate us again.

As the first light of day ended our first night together, we made love for the first time. It was as tender and gentle a moment as I had ever experienced. What began as timid exploring, and gentle caresses, softly spoken words of love and affection whispered into each other's ear, ended in passion and ecstasy, each holding out to match the finish of the other. As so many things had concluded in the past thirty-six hours, this too ended in tears—tears of joy.

We fell asleep wrapped in each other's arms, as I vowed to do every night for the rest of our lives. But just before drifting off, I asked myself why this wonderful woman was willing to give it all up, to travel seventy million years into the past, not even sure if I was alive or dead.

I was sure that I had said it to myself—that no sounds had passed my lips—but as I drifted off to sleep, I heard her say in a soft, sweet voice, "Because *I* did know … I always knew."

EPILOGUE

My dear Doctor Dermot,

It's the middle of the night, and David is sound asleep. He's been sleeping better that he ever has in his life ... and so have I. I write this in secrecy because I don't want David to think that I would renege on a promise.

We sleep better because we are where we're supposed to be, and with whom we are supposed to be with. I have you to thank for that. For that reason, I owe you this last communication.

This is the last chance that I'll have to do this, as tomorrow we leave this place forever. Tomorrow we take what's left of the supplies and haul them the ten days journey south to get to our home. It's our third time back, once a year, and there's not too much left to take. It was just a vacation of sorts, one last time to say good-bye to the things that brought us here, the means that brought us together. It was just a lark, but it was fortuitous that we came here when we did. We would not have survived if we hadn't.

I write in longhand because David's computer has long since died, leaving me with the acid-free paper that you had left for him in case of other things going wrong. I find it improbable that it will last the time necessary to get into your hands, but I make the attempt ... because I can.

I write because I owe you this. You reprogrammed the time machine to send me back to David. You reran the software just as you had eleven years before so that I would end up in a time that David was still alive. And it worked. I found him, just in time to save him—to save us both.

But you also failed. You failed in your estimates about how your technology worked, about where exactly you had sent us. The technology is incredible, but it's not perfect. You didn't send us back seventy million years ...

... but only sixty-five.

It's been more than three weeks since we were both awakened from a sound sleep by the shaking of our bed, the few supplies remaining on the shelves rattling and tumbling onto the floor. David, who is much more accustomed to these tremors than I said, "It's nothing but another quake. Go back to sleep." He was right. I was not as used to them as he, but in three years, this one felt different. I'm not sure how, or why, but it was not the same as the hundreds that I had felt before. I went back to sleep, not at all convinced that things were as they should be.

The next morning was nothing but the bluest of skies, the sun brilliant as it traveled to the west. We prepared to depart, but, as the morning waned, huge black clouds began rolling in from the southeast—faster than any storm cloud. Within an hour, black, gritty soot began falling from the sky. And a few hours later, flaming hail began raining down on top of us, pounding the steel hull of the machine.

The sun was blotted out from the sky for a full three weeks, the plants shriveled up and died, the birds fell from the sky. It's been more than a week since we've seen an animal, or even an insect, of any kind.

I can't help but feel that this is the beginning of the end, hopefully not for us, but for the dinosaurs, and about seventy percent of all life on the planet. Life that David and I have become accustomed to—life that we looked on as neighbors—even friends.

If there is still controversy in your world about how life in the Cretaceous ended, I hope that this will put it to rest. The blackness, the fire falling from the sky, is surely the result of a cataclysmic event—not an earthquake, or a volcano—although those have certainly accelerated in recent weeks. This had the destructive power of worlds colliding, of one celestial body striking another. This was the devastation caused by a comet—a huge one—several miles in diameter. And from the direction of the blackness and the fallout, it is obvious to me that the theories claiming that Chicxulub, in the Yucatan peninsula being the point of impact, were right.

We traveled back to the machine for no other reason than to pick up the last of our belongings and to see how things had changed since the last time that we were here. Instead we found a safe haven from the greatest calamity that the world had ever faced.

The bodies of the four dinosaurs in the cave are buried beneath tons of rock and dirt, nothing more than bones now, not all that different than what David would dig up millions of years from now. We could hardly find the entrance to the cave though, the cave-in of three years ago was but the first of several, burying everything inside, including David's time machine. You'll have quite a time excavating it.

But we're content to stay here—now. We have no idea what lay before us, but we know that we'll face it together. David and I love each other, a love that defied incredible odds and impossible distance. Few could probably understand it—fewer could experience it.

We'll spend the rest of our lives together, and we'll die here together. If we're as lucky as I know we are, we'll die at the same time, probably from something completely unexpected, something that could only happen here, and at this time. Nothing will ever separate us again.

A million lifetimes were enough… More than enough!

S. L. A.

ACKNOWLEDGEMENTS

As I've discovered, writing a novel is hard work. It takes a tremendous amount of research, concentration, determination, and even sacrifice to see it through to the end. Finishing a novel, a *good* novel, takes the support and encouragement of a lot of others—I suspect that it is rarely done otherwise. In my case, I have had the benefit of a supporting cast of friends and family that not only provided solid ideas and suggestions, but just the right kick in the pants to keep me on the right track when things got tough. My heartfelt thanks to: Howard Heyl, Barbara Lebeck, Lynn Lebeck, Debra Luesse, Steve Murphy, Alex Simonov, and Art Wagner. I couldn't have done it without you.

Also, special thanks to Alex Simonov for his help with the cover artwork, and to Don Alley for his photographic work.

I hope that you have enjoyed reading it as much as I enjoyed writing it.

Douglas Lebeck
May, 2002

Printed in the United States
727800001B

9 781403 342256